THE ENCHANTED FOREST CHRONICLES

Dealing With Dragons
Searching For Dragons
Calling On Dragons
Talking To Dragons

Patricia C. Wrede

GuildAmerica Books®

Portions of chapters 1 and 2 were previously published in a slightly altered form as "The Improper Princess," a short story in the collection *Spaceships and Spells,* Harper & Row, Publishers, 1987.

This Book Club Edition published by arrangement with
Jane Yolen Books
Harcourt Brace & Company
525 B Street, Suite 1900
San Diego, CA 92101-4495

ISBN 1-56865-173-2

PRINTED IN THE UNITED STATES OF AMERICA

Contents

DEALING WITH DRAGONS

For ALAN CARL *and* ANNIE BUJOLD,

because they liked

the other one a lot

Contents

1

In Which Cimorene Refuses to Be Proper and Has a Conversation with a Frog

Linderwall was a large kingdom, just east of the Mountains of Morning, where philosophers were highly respected and the number five was fashionable. The climate was unremarkable. The knights kept their armor brightly polished mainly for show–it had been centuries since a dragon had come east. There were the usual periodic problems with royal children and uninvited fairy godmothers, but they were always the sort of thing that could be cleared up by finding the proper prince or princess to marry the unfortunate child a few years later. All in all, Linderwall was a very prosperous and pleasant place.

Cimorene hated it.

Cimorene was the youngest daughter of the King of Linderwall, and her parents found her rather trying. Their first six daughters were perfectly normal princesses, with long, golden hair and sweet dispositions, each more beautiful than the last. Cimorene was lovely enough, but her hair was jet black, and she wore it in braids instead of curled and pinned like her sisters.

And she wouldn't stop growing. Her parents were quite sure that no prince would want to marry a girl who could look him in the eye instead of gazing up at him becomingly through her lashes. As for the girl's disposition–well, when people were being polite, they said she was strong-minded. When they were angry or annoyed with her, they said she was as stubborn as a pig.

The King and Queen did the best they could. They hired the most superior tutors and governesses to teach Cimorene all the things a princess ought to know–dancing, embroidery, drawing, and etiquette. There was a great deal of etiquette, from the proper way to curtsy before a visiting prince to how loudly it was permissible to scream when being carried off by a giant. (Linderwall still had an occasional problem with giants.)

Cimorene found it all very dull, but she pressed her lips together and learned it anyway. When she couldn't stand it any longer, she would go down to the castle armory and bully the armsmaster into giving her a fencing lesson. As she got older, she found her regular lessons more and more boring. Consequently, the fencing lessons became more and more frequent.

When she was twelve, her father found out.

"Fencing is not proper behavior for a princess," he told her in the gentle-but-firm tone recommended by the court philosopher.

Cimorene tilted her head to one side. "Why not?"

"It's . . . well, it's simply not done."

Cimorene considered. "Aren't I a princess?"

"Yes, of course you are, my dear," said her father with relief. He had been bracing himself for a storm of tears, which was the way his other daughters reacted to reprimands.

"Well, I fence," Cimorene said with the air of one delivering an unshakable argument. "So it is *too* done by a princess."

"That doesn't make it proper, dear," put in her mother gently.

"Why not?"

"It simply doesn't," the Queen said firmly, and that was the end of Cimorene's fencing lessons.

When she was fourteen, her father discovered that she was making the court magician teach her magic.

"How long has this been going on?" he asked wearily when she arrived in response to his summons.

"Since you stopped my fencing lessons," Cimorene said. "I suppose you're going to tell me it isn't proper behavior for a princess."

"Well, yes. I mean, it isn't proper."

"Nothing interesting seems to be proper," Cimorene said.

"You might find things more interesting if you applied yourself a little more, dear," Cimorene's mother said.

"I doubt it," Cimorene muttered, but she knew better than to argue when her mother used that tone of voice. And that was the end of the magic lessons.

The same thing happened over the Latin lessons from the court philosopher, the cooking lessons from the castle chef, the economics lessons from the court treasurer, and the juggling lessons from the court minstrel. Cimorene began to grow rather tired of the whole business.

When she was sixteen, Cimorene summoned her fairy godmother.

"Cimorene, my dear, this sort of thing really isn't done," the fairy said, fanning away the scented blue smoke that had accompanied her appearance.

"People keep telling me that," Cimorene said.

"You should pay attention to them, then," her godmother said irritably. "I'm not used to being hauled away from my tea without warning. And you aren't supposed to call me unless it is a matter of utmost importance to your life and future happiness."

"It *is* of utmost importance to my life and future happiness," Cimorene said.

"Oh, very well. You're a bit young to have fallen in love already; still, you always have been a precocious child. Tell me about him."

Cimorene sighed. "It isn't a him."

"Enchanted, is he?" the fairy said with a spark of interest. "A frog, perhaps? That used to be quite popular, but it seems to have gone out of fashion lately. Nowadays, all the princes are talking birds, or dogs, or hedgehogs."

"No, no, I'm not in love with anyone!"

"Then what, exactly, is your problem?" the fairy said in exasperation.

"This!" Cimorene gestured at the castle around her. "Embroidery lessons, and dancing, and–and being a princess!"

"My dear Cimorene!" the fairy said, shocked. "It's your heritage!"

"It's boring."

"Boring?" The fairy did not appear to believe what she was hearing.

"Boring. I want to do things, not sit around all day and listen to the court minstrel make up songs about how brave Daddy is and how lovely his wife and daughters are."

"Nonsense, my dear. This is just a stage you're going through. You'll outgrow it soon, and you'll be very glad you didn't do anything rash."

Cimorene looked at her godmother suspiciously. "You've been talking to my parents, haven't you?"

"Well, they do try to keep me up to date on what my godchildren are doing."

"I thought so," said Cimorene, and bade her fairy godmother a polite good-bye.

A few weeks later, Cimorene's parents took her to a tourney in Sathem-by-the-Mountains, the next kingdom over. Cimorene was quite sure that they were only taking her because her fairy godmother had told them that something had better be done about her, and soon. She kept this opinion to herself. Anything was better than the endless rounds of dancing and embroidery lessons at home.

Cimorene realized her mistake almost as soon as they reached their destination, for the King of Sathem-by-the-Mountains had a son. He was a golden-haired, blue-eyed, and exceedingly handsome prince, whose duties appeared to consist entirely of dancing attendance on Cimorene.

"Isn't he handsome!" Cimorene's lady-in-waiting sighed.

"Yes," Cimorene said without enthusiasm. "Unfortunately, he isn't anything else."

"Whatever do you mean?" the lady-in-waiting said in astonishment.

"He has no sense of humor, he isn't intelligent, he can't talk about anything except tourneys, and half of what he does say he gets wrong. I'm glad we're only staying three weeks. I don't think I could stand to be polite to him for much longer than that."

"But what about your engagement?" the lady-in-waiting cried, horrified.

"What engagement?" Cimorene said sharply.

The lady-in-waiting tried to mutter something about a mistake, but Cimorene put up her chin in her best princess fashion and insisted on an explanation. Finally, the lady-in-waiting broke down.

"I . . . I overheard Their Majesties discussing it yesterday." She sniffled into her handkerchief. "The stipulations and covenants and contracts and settlements have all been drawn up, and they're going to sign them the day after tomorrow and announce it on Th-Thursday."

"I see," said Cimorene. "Thank you for telling me. You may go."

The lady-in-waiting left, and Cimorene went to see her parents. They were annoyed and a little embarrassed to find that Cimorene had discovered their plans, but they were still very firm about it. "We were going to tell you tomorrow, when we signed the papers," her father said.

"We knew you'd be pleased, dear," her mother said, nodding. "He's *such* a good-looking boy."

"But I don't want to marry Prince Therandil," Cimorene said.

"Well, it's not exactly a brilliant match," Cimorene's father said, frowning. "But I didn't think you'd care how big his kingdom is."

"It's the prince I don't care for," Cimorene said.

"That's a great pity, dear, but it can't be helped," Cimorene's mother said placidly. "I'm afraid it isn't likely that you'll get another offer."

"Then I won't get married at all."

Both her parents looked slightly shocked. "My dear Cimorene!" said her father. "That's out of the question. You're a princess; it simply isn't *done.*"

"I'm too young to get married!"

"Your Great-Aunt Rose was married at sixteen," her mother pointed out. "One really can't count all those years she spent asleep under that dreadful fairy's curse."

"I won't marry the prince of Sathem-by-the-Mountains!" Cimorene said desperately. "It isn't proper!"

"What?" said both her parents together.

"He hasn't rescued me from a giant or an ogre or freed me from a magic spell," Cimorene said.

Both her parents looked uncomfortable. "Well, no," said Cimorene's father. "It's a bit late to start arranging it, but we might be able to manage something."

"I don't think it's necessary," Cimorene's mother said. She looked reprovingly at Cimorene. "You've never paid attention to what was or wasn't suitable before, dear; you can't start now. Proper or not, you will marry Prince Therandil three weeks from Thursday."

"But, Mother–"

"I'll send the wardrobe mistress to your room to start fitting your bride clothes," Cimorene's mother said firmly, and that was the end of the conversation.

Cimorene decided to try a more direct approach. She went to see Prince Therandil. He was in the castle armory, looking at swords. "Good morning, Princess," he said when he finally noticed Cimorene. "Don't you think this is a lovely sword?"

Cimorene picked it up. "The balance is off."

"I believe you're right," said Therandil after a moment's study. "Pity; now I'll have to find another. Is there something I can do for you?"

"Yes," said Cimorene. "You can *not* marry me."

"What?" Therandil looked confused.

"You don't really want to marry me, do you?" Cimorene said coaxingly.

"Well, not exactly," Therandil replied. "I mean, in a way. That is–"

"Oh, good," Cimorene said, correctly interpreting this muddled reply as *No, not at all.* "Then you'll tell your father you don't want to marry me?"

"I couldn't do that!" Therandil said, shocked. "It wouldn't be right."

"Why not?" Cimorene demanded crossly.

"Because–because–well, because princes just don't do that!"

"Then how are you going to keep from marrying me?"

"I guess I won't be able to," Therandil said after thinking hard for a moment. "How do you like that sword over there? The one with the silver hilt?"

Cimorene left in disgust and went out to the castle garden. She was very discouraged. It looked as if she were going to marry the prince of Sathem-by-the-Mountains whether she wanted to or not.

"I'd rather be eaten by a dragon," she muttered.

"That can be arranged," said a voice from beside her left slipper.

Cimorene looked down and saw a small green frog looking up at her. "I beg your pardon. Did you speak?" she asked.

"You don't see anyone else around, do you?" said the frog.

"Oh!" said Cimorene. She had never met a talking frog before. "Are you an enchanted prince?" she asked a little doubtfully.

"No, but I've met a couple of them, and after a while you pick up a few things," said the frog. "Now, why is it that you want to be eaten by a dragon?"

"My parents want me to marry Prince Therandil," Cimorene explained.

"And you don't want to? Sensible of you," said the frog. "I don't like Therandil. He used to skip rocks across the top of my pond. They always sank into my living room."

"I'm sorry," Cimorene said politely.

"Well," said the frog, "what are you going to do about it?"

"Marrying Therandil? I don't know. I've tried talking to my parents, but they won't listen, and neither will Therandil."

"I didn't ask what you'd *said* about it," the frog snapped. "I asked what you're going to do. Nine times out of ten, talking is a way of avoiding doing things."

"What kinds of things would you suggest?" Cimorene said, stung.

"You could challenge the prince to a duel," the frog suggested.

"He'd win," Cimorene said. "It's been four years since I've been allowed to do any fencing."

"You could turn him into a toad."

"I never got past invisibility in my magic lessons," Cimorene said. "Transformations are advanced study."

The frog looked at her disapprovingly. "Can't you do anything?"

"I can curtsy," Cimorene said disgustedly. "I know seventeen different country dances, nine ways to agree with an ambassador from Cathay without actually promising him anything, and one hundred and forty-three embroidery stitches. And I can make cherries jubilee."

"Cherries jubilee?" asked the frog, and snapped at a passing fly.

"The castle chef taught me, before Father made him stop," Cimorene explained.

The frog munched briefly, then swallowed and said, "I suppose there's no help for it. You'll have to run away."

"Run away?" Cimorene said. "I don't like that idea. Too many things could go wrong."

"You don't like the idea of marrying Prince Therandil, either," the frog pointed out.

"Maybe I can think of some other way out of getting married."

The frog snorted. "Such as?" Cimorene didn't answer, and after a moment the frog said, "I thought so. Do you want my advice or not?"

"Yes, please," said Cimorene. After all, she didn't have to follow it.

"Go to the main road outside the city and follow it away from the mountains," said the frog. "After a while, you will come to a small pavilion made of gold, surrounded by trees made of silver with emerald leaves. Go straight past it without stopping, and don't answer if anyone calls out to you from the pavilion. Keep on until you reach a hovel. Walk straight up to the door and knock three times, then snap your fingers and go inside. You'll find some people there who can help you out of your difficulties if you're polite about asking and they're in the right mood. And that's all."

The frog turned abruptly and dove into the pool. "Thank you very much," Cimorene called after it, thinking that the frog's advice sounded very odd indeed. She rose and went back into the castle.

She spent the rest of the day being fitted and fussed over by her ladies-in-waiting until she was ready to scream. By the end of the formal banquet, at which she had to sit next to Prince Therandil and listen to endless stories of his prowess in battle, Cimorene was more than ready to take the frog's advice.

Late that night, when most of the castle was asleep, Cimorene bundled up five clean handkerchiefs and her best crown. Then she dug out the notes she had taken during her magic lessons and carefully cast a spell of invisibility. It seemed to work, but she was still very watchful as she sneaked out of the castle. After all, it had been a long time since she had practiced.

By morning, Cimorene was well outside the city and visible again, walking down the main road that led away from the mountains. It was hot and dusty, and she began to wish she had brought a bottle of water instead of the handkerchiefs.

Just before noon, she spied a small grove of trees next to the road ahead of her. It looked like a cool, pleasant place to rest for a few minutes, and she hurried forward. When she reached the grove, however, she saw that the trees were made of the finest silver, and their shining green leaves were huge emeralds. In the center of the grove stood a charming pavilion made of gold and hung with gold curtains.

Cimorene slowed down and looked longingly at the cool green shade beneath the trees. Just then a woman's voice called out from the pavilion,

"My dear, you look so tired and thirsty! Come and sit with me and share my luncheon."

The voice was so kind and coaxing that Cimorene took two steps toward the edge of the road before she remembered the frog's advice. *Oh, no,* she thought to herself, *I'm not going to be caught this easily!* She turned without saying anything and hurried on down the road.

A little farther on she came to a tiny, wretched-looking hovel made of cracked and weathered gray boards. The door hung slantwise on a broken hinge, and the whole building looked as though it were going to topple over at any moment. Cimorene stopped and stared doubtfully at it, but she had followed the frog's advice this far, and she thought it would be silly to stop now. So she shook the dust from her skirts and put on her crown (so as to make a good impression). She marched up to the door, knocked three times, and snapped her fingers just as the frog had told her. Then she pushed the door open and went in.

2

In Which Cimorene Discovers the Value of a Classical Education and Has Some Unwelcome Visitors

Inside, the hovel was dark and cool and damp. Cimorene found it a pleasant relief after the hot, dusty road, but she wondered why no sunlight seemed to be coming through the cracks in the boards. She was still standing just inside the door, waiting for her eyes to adjust to the dark, when someone said crossly, "Is this that princess we've been waiting for?"

"Why don't you ask her?" said a deep, rumbly voice.

"I'm Princess Cimorene of Linderwall," Cimorene answered politely. "I was told you could help me."

"Help her?" said the first voice, and Cimorene heard a snort. "I think we should just eat her and be done with it."

Cimorene began to feel frightened. She wondered whether the voices belonged to ogres or trolls and whether she could slip out of the hovel before they made up their minds about eating her. She felt behind her for the door and started in surprise when her fingers touched damp stone instead of dry wood. Then a third voice said, "Not so fast, Woraug. Let's hear her story first."

So Cimorene took a deep breath and began to explain about the fencing lessons and the magic lessons, and the Latin and the juggling, and all the other things that weren't considered proper behavior for a princess, and she told the voices that she had run away from Sathem-by-the-Mountains to keep from having to marry Prince Therandil.

"And what do you expect us to do about it?" one of the voices asked curiously.

"I don't know," Cimorene said. "Except, of course, that I *would* rather not be eaten. I can't see who you are in this dark, you know."

"That can be fixed," said the voice. A moment later, a small ball of light appeared in the air above Cimorene's head. Cimorene stepped backward very quickly and ran into the wall.

The voices belonged to dragons.

Five of them lay on or sprawled over or curled around the various rocks and columns that filled the huge cave where Cimorene stood. Each of the males (there were three) had two short, stubby, sharp-looking horns on either side of their heads; the female dragon had three, one on each side and one in the center of her forehead. The last dragon was apparently still too young to have made up its mind which sex it wanted to be; it didn't have any horns at all.

Cimorene felt very frightened. The smallest of the dragons was easily three times as tall as she was, and they gave an overwhelming impression of shining green scales and sharp silver teeth. They were much scarier in person than in the pictures she remembered from her natural history books. She swallowed very hard, wondering whether she really *would* rather be eaten by a dragon than marry Therandil.

"Well?" said the three-horned dragon just in front of her. "Just what are you asking us to do for you?"

"I–" Cimorene stopped short as an idea occurred to her. Cautiously, she asked, "Dragons are . . . are fond of princesses, aren't they?"

"Very," said the dragon, and smiled. The smile showed all her teeth, which Cimorene did not find reassuring.

"That is, I've heard of dragons who have captive princesses to cook for them and–and so on," said Cimorene, who had very little idea what captive princesses did all day.

The dragon in front of Cimorene nodded. One of the others, a yellowish green in color, shifted restlessly and said, "Oh, let's just go ahead and eat her. It will save trouble."

Before any of the other dragons could answer, there was a loud, booming noise, and a sixth dragon slithered into the cave. His scales were more gray than green, and the dragons by the door made way for him respectfully.

"Kazul!" said the newcomer in a loud voice. *"Achoo!* Sorry I'm late, but a terrible thing happened on the way here, *achoo!"*

"What was it?" said the dragon to whom Cimorene had been talking.

"Ran into a wizard. *Achoo!* Had to eat him; no help for it. *Achoo, achoo.* And now look at me!" Every time the gray-green dragon sneezed, he emitted a small ball of fire that scorched the wall of the cave.

"Calm down, Roxim," said Kazul. "You're only making it worse."

"Achoo! Calm down? When I'm having an allergy attack? *Achoo,* oh, bother, *achoo!"* said the gray-green dragon. "Somebody give me a handkerchief. *Achoo!"*

"Here," said Cimorene, holding out one of the ones she had brought with her. "Use this." She was beginning to feel much less frightened, for the gray-green dragon reminded her of her great-uncle, who was old and rather hard of hearing and of whom she was rather fond.

"What's that?" said Roxim. *"Achoo!* Oh, hurry up and give it here."

Kazul took the handkerchief from Cimorene, using two claws very delicately, and passed it to Roxim. The gray-green dragon mopped his streaming eyes and blew his nose. "That's better, I think. *Achoo!* Oh, drat!"

The ball of fire that accompanied the dragon's sneeze had reduced the handkerchief to a charred scrap. Cimorene hastily dug out another one and handed it to Kazul, feeling very glad that she had brought several spares.

Roxim went through two more handkerchiefs before his sneezing spasms finally stopped. "Much better," he said. "Now then, who's this that lent me the handkerchiefs? Somebody's new princess, eh?"

"We were just discussing that when you came in," Kazul said, and turned back to Cimorene. "You were saying? About cooking and so on."

"Couldn't I do that for one of you for a while?" Cimorene said.

The dragon smiled again, and Cimorene swallowed hard. "Possibly. Why would you want to do that?"

"Because then I wouldn't have to go home and marry Therandil," Cimorene said. "Being a dragon's princess is a perfectly respectable thing to do, so my parents couldn't complain. And it would be much more interesting than embroidery and dancing lessons."

Several of the dragons made snorting or choking noises. Cimorene jumped, then decided that they were laughing.

"This is ridiculous," said a large, bright green dragon on Cimorene's left.

"Why?" asked Kazul.

"A princess volunteering? Out of the question!"

"That's easy for you to say," one of the other dragons grumbled. "You already have a princess. What about the rest of us?"

"Yes, don't be stuffy, Woraug," said another. "Besides, what else can we do with her?"

"Eat her," suggested the yellowish green dragon in a bored tone.

"No proper princess would come out looking for dragons," Woraug objected.

"Well, I'm not a proper princess, then," Cimorene snapped. "I make cherries jubilee, and I volunteer for dragons, and I conjugate Latin verbs–or at least I would if anyone would let me. So there!"

"Hear, hear," said the gray-green dragon.

"You see?" Woraug said. "Who would want an improper princess?"

"I would," said Kazul.

"You can't be serious, Kazul," Woraug said irritably. "Why?"

"I like cherries jubilee," Kazul replied, still watching Cimorene. "And I like the look of her. Besides, the Latin scrolls in my library need cataloguing, and if I can't find someone who knows a little of the language, I'll have to do it myself."

"Give her a trial run first," a purplish green dragon advised.

Woraug snorted. "Latin and cherries jubilee! And for that you'd take on a black-haired, snippy little–"

"I'll thank you to be polite when you're discussing *my* princess," Kazul said, and smiled fiercely.

"Nice little gal," Roxim said, nodding approvingly and waving Cimorene's next-to-last handkerchief. "Got sense. Be good for you, Kazul."

"If that's settled, I'm going to go find a snack," said the yellowish green dragon.

Woraug looked around, but the other dragons seemed to agree with Roxim. "Oh, very well," Woraug said grumpily. "It's your choice, after all, Kazul."

"It certainly is. Now, Princess, if you'll come this way, I'll get you settled in."

Cimorene followed Kazul across the cave and down a tunnel. To her relief, the ball of light came with her. She had the uncomfortable feeling that if she had tried to walk behind Kazul in the dark, she would have stepped on her tail, which would not have been a good beginning.

Kazul led Cimorene through a long maze of tunnels and finally stopped in another cave. "Here we are," the dragon said. "You can use the small room over on the right. I believe my last princess left most of the furnishings behind when she ran off with the knight."

"Thank you," Cimorene said. "When do I start my duties? And what are they, please?"

"You start right away," said Kazul. "I'll want dinner at seven. In the meantime, you can begin sorting the treasure." The dragon nodded toward a dark opening on the left. "I'm sure some of it needs repairing. There's at least one suit of armor with the leg off, and some of the cheaper magic swords are probably getting rusty. The rest of it really ought to be rearranged sensibly. I can never find anything when I want it."

"What about the library you mentioned?" Cimorene asked.

"We'll see how well you do on the treasure room first," Kazul said. "The rest of your job I'll explain as we go along. You don't object to learning a little magic, do you?"

"Not at all," said Cimorene.

"Good. It'll make things much easier. Go and wash up, and I'll let you into the treasure room so you can get started."

Cimorene nodded and went to the room Kazul had told her to use. As she washed her face and hands, she felt happier than she had in a long time. She was not going to have to marry Therandil, and sorting a dragon's treasure sounded far more interesting than dancing or embroidery. She was even going to learn some magic! And her parents wouldn't worry about her, once they found out where she was. For the first time in her life, Cimorene was glad she was a princess. She dried her hands and turned to go back into the main cave, wondering how best to persuade Kazul to help her brush up on her Latin. She didn't want the dragon to be disappointed in her skill.

"Draco, draconem, dracone," she muttered, and her lips curved into a smile. She had always been rather good at declining nouns. Still smiling, she started forward to begin her new duties.

Cimorene settled in very quickly. She got along well with Kazul and learned her way around the caves with a minimum of mishaps. Actually, the caves were more like an intricate web of tunnels, connecting caverns of various shapes and sizes that belonged to individual dragons. It reminded Cimorene of an underground city with tunnels instead of streets. She had no idea how far the tunnels extended, though she rather suspected that some of them had been magicked, so that when you walked down them you went a lot farther than you thought you were going.

Kazul's section of the caves was fairly large. In addition to the kitchen—which was in a large cave near the exit, so that there wouldn't be a problem with the smoke from the fire—she had a sleeping cavern, three enormous treasure rooms at the far end of an intricate maze of twisty little passages, two even more enormous storage rooms for less valuable items, a library, a large, bare cave for eating and visiting with other dragons, and the set of rooms assigned to Cimorene. All the caves smelled of dragon, a somewhat musty, smoky, cinnamony smell. Cimorene's first job was to air them out.

Cimorene's rooms consisted of three small connecting caves, just off Kazul's living cavern. They were furnished very comfortably in a mixture of styles and periods, and looked just like the guest rooms in most of the castles Cimorene had visited, only without windows. They were much too small for a dragon to get inside. When asked, Kazul said that the dwarves had made them in return for a favor, and the dragon's tone prevented Cimorene from inquiring too closely into just what sort of favor it had been.

By the end of the first week, Cimorene was sure enough of her position to give Kazul a list of things that she needed in the kitchen. The previous princess–of whom Cimorene was beginning to have a very poor opinion–had apparently made do with a large skillet with three dents and a wobbly handle, a wooden mixing bowl with a crack in it, a badly tarnished copper teakettle, and an assortment of mismatched plates, cups, and silverware, most of them chipped or bent.

Kazul seemed pleased by the request, and the following day Cimorene had everything she had asked for, except for a few of the more exotic pans and dishes. This made the cooking considerably easier and gave Cimorene more time to spend studying Latin and sorting treasure. The treasure was just as disorganized as Kazul had told her, and putting it in order was a major task. It was sometimes hard to tell whether a ring was enchanted, and Cimorene knew better than to put it on and see. It might be the sort of useful magic ring that turned you invisible, but it might also be the sort of ring that turned you into a frog. Cimorene did the best she could and kept a pile in the corner for things she was not sure about.

There was a great deal of treasure to be sorted. Most of it was stacked in one of the innermost caves in a large, untidy heap of crowns, rings, jewels, swords, and coins, but Cimorene kept finding things in other places as well, some of them quite unlikely. There was a small helmet under her bed (along with a great deal of dust), a silver bracelet set with opals on the reading table in the library, and two daggers and a jeweled ink pot behind the kitchen stove. Cimorene collected them all, along with the other things that were simply lying around in the halls, and put them back in the storerooms where they belonged, thinking to herself that dragons were clearly not very tidy creatures.

The first of the knights arrived at the end of the second week.

Cimorene was busy cleaning swords. Kazul had been right about their condition; not only were some of them rusty, but nearly all of them needed sharpening. She was polishing the last flakes of rust from an enormous broadsword when she heard someone calling from the mouth of the cave. Feeling somewhat irritated by the interruption, she rose and, carrying the sword, went to see who it was.

As she came nearer to the entrance, she was able to make out the words that whoever-it-was was shouting: "Dragon! Come out and fight! Fight for the Princess Cimorene of Linderwall!"

"Oh, honestly," Cimorene muttered, and quickened her step. "Here, you," she said as she came out into the sunlight. Then she had to duck as a spear flashed through the air over her head. "Stop that!" she cried. "I'm Princess Cimorene."

"You are?" said a doubtful voice. "Are you sure? I mean–"

Cimorene raised her head cautiously and squinted. It was still fairly early in the morning, and the sun was in back of the person standing outside the cave, so that it was difficult to see anything but the outline of his figure against the brightness. "Of course I'm sure," Cimorene said. "What did you expect, letters of reference? Come around here where I can see who you are, please."

The figure moved sideways, and Cimorene saw that it was a knight in shiny new armor, except for the legs, where the armor was dusty from walking. Cimorene wondered briefly why he hadn't ridden, but decided not to ask. The knight's visor was raised, and a few wisps of sandy hair showed above his handsome face. He was studying her with an expression of worried puzzlement.

"What can I do for you?" Cimorene said after several moments had gone by and the knight still hadn't said anything.

"Well, um, if you *are* the Princess Cimorene, I've come to rescue you from the dragon," the knight said.

Cimorene set the point of the broadsword on the ground and leaned on it as if it were a walking cane. "I thought that might be it," she said. "But I'd rather not be rescued, thank you just the same."

"Not be rescued?" The knight's puzzled look deepened. "But princesses *always–*"

"No, they don't," Cimorene said firmly, recognizing the beginning of a familiar argument. "And even if I wanted to be rescued, you're going at it all wrong."

"What?" said the knight, thoroughly taken aback.

"Shouting, 'Come out and fight,' the way you did. No self-respecting dragon is going to answer to a challenge like that. It sounds like a child's dare. Dragons are very conscious of their dignity, at least all the ones I've met so far are."

"Oh," said the knight, sounding very crestfallen. "What should I have said?"

" 'Stand forth and do battle' is the usual challenge," Cimorene said with authority, remembering her princess lessons. She had always been more interested in what the knights and dragons were supposed to say than in memorizing the places where she was supposed to scream. "But the wording doesn't have to be exact as long as it's suitably formal. You're new at this, aren't you?"

"Rescuing you was going to be my first big quest," the knight said gloomily. "You're *sure* you don't want to be rescued?"

"Quite sure," Cimorene said. "I like living with Kazul."

"You *like–"* The knight stared at her for a moment. Then his expression cleared and he said, "Of course! The dragon's enchanted you. I should have thought of that before."

"Kazul has *not* enchanted me, and I do *not* want to be rescued by *anybody,"* Cimorene said, alarmed by the knight's sudden enthusiasm. "This place suits me very well. I *like* polishing swords and cooking cherries jubilee and reading Latin scrolls. If you don't believe me, ask anyone in Linderwall. They've been complaining about my un-princesslike behavior for years."

"I did hear something about fencing lessons," the knight said doubtfully, "but knights aren't supposed to pay attention to that kind of thing. We're supposed to be above rumors and gossip."

"The fencing lessons were just the beginning," Cimorene assured him. "So you see why I'm perfectly happy being a dragon's princess."

"Um, yes," said the knight, but he did not look convinced. "Speaking of dragons, where's yours?"

"Kazul's not *my* dragon," Cimorene said sharply. "I'm *her* princess. You'll never have any luck dealing with dragons if you don't get these things straight. She's gone to the Enchanted Forest on the other side of the mountains to borrow a crepe pan from a witch she knows."

"She's *what?"* said the knight.

"She's gone to borrow a crepe pan," Cimorene repeated in a louder voice. "Perhaps you'd better have your helmet checked when you get back. They're not supposed to interfere with your hearing, but sometimes–"

"Oh, I heard you," the knight said. "But what does a dragon want with a crepe pan?"

"She doesn't want it; I do. I found a recipe in the library that I want to try, and the kitchen just isn't equipped to handle anything but the most ordinary cooking. Kazul will fix that eventually, but for the time being we have to borrow things like crepe pans and souffle dishes."

"You really *do* like it here," the knight said wonderingly.

Cimorene refrained from replying that this was what she had been trying to tell him all along and instead said, "How did you know where I was?"

"Things get around." The knight waved a hand in a vague manner. "In fact, I had to hurry to make sure I was the first. Half of the Kingdom of Linderwall and a princess's hand in marriage is a reward rich enough to tempt a lot of people who wouldn't normally bother with this sort of thing."

"Father's offered half the kingdom to whoever rescues me?" Cimorene said incredulously. "That's more than all my sisters' dowries put together!"

"It's the usual thing in cases like this," the knight said mildly.

"It would be," Cimorene said in tones of deep disgust. "Well, at least you can go back and tell them I don't want to be rescued. Maybe that will keep anyone else from coming up here."

"I can't do that!" the knight said. "It's–"

"–just not done," Cimorene finished. "I understand perfectly." She gave him a polite farewell, more because she had been well brought up than because she felt like being polite, and sent him on his way. Then she went back into the cave and polished the broadsword until it was mirror-bright, which relieved her feelings a little.

There were two knights the following day, and four more the day after that. On the fourth day there was only one, but he was exceptionally stubborn, and it took Cimorene nearly two hours to get rid of him. By then she was thoroughly disgusted and even considered letting Kazul handle the knights from then on. She could not quite bring herself to do it. The knights would certainly attack Kazul as soon as they saw her, since that was what they were coming for, and sooner or later someone would get hurt. Cimorene did not like to think that someone might be hurt trying to rescue her, particularly since she did not want to be rescued, so with a sigh she decided that she would continue to handle the knights as long as Kazul would let her.

Prince Therandil showed up at the end of the third week. He was limping a little, as if his metal boots pinched his toes, and the feathers attached to the top of his helmet sagged badly. He stopped and carefully struck an impressive pose before issuing the usual challenge.

Cimorene was not in a mood to be impressed. Besides, she could see that his helmet was a different style from his gold armor and that the armor had gaps at the knees and elbows where it didn't fit together quite right.

"Aren't you a little slow?" she asked irritably. "There've been eight knights here before you."

"Eight?" the prince said, frowning. "I thought by now there'd have been at least twelve. Perhaps I'd better come back later."

Cimorene stared at him in surprise. "Why?"

"Well, it would look better," Therandil explained seriously. "There's not much glory in defeating a dragon that hasn't already beaten ten or fifteen people at least. Sir Gorolax of Mirstwold won't even consider going after a dragon whose score is less than forty-five. I don't think I want to risk waiting that long, but eight just doesn't seem like enough."

"You're going to go away and wait until Kazul has defeated fifteen knights before you come back to rescue me?" Cimorene said. She found

Therandil's smug confidence very annoying, but she didn't like to say so straight out.

"Not if you'd rather be rescued now, of course," Therandil said hastily. "Though you ought to consider the advantages, and I expect it won't be so very long . . ." His voice trailed off, and he looked at her hopefully.

"I'm afraid it will be a very long time," Cimorene said with satisfaction. "You see, Kazul hasn't defeated any knights at all yet."

"B-b-but I thought you said there'd been eight," Therandil spluttered.

"I said eight of them had come by; I didn't say they'd fought anybody. I sent them away."

"You *sent them away?*" Therandil repeated, plainly horrified. "But that's—that's—"

"—not done, I know." Cimorene smiled sweetly. "But I've done it. And I intend to go on doing it, so you might as well go home and warn your friends. They'd feel so foolish, you know, if they came all this way into the mountains to rescue me and then had to turn around and go back home without doing anything."

"They certainly would!" Therandil said indignantly. "What do you mean by playing these kinds of tricks? Don't you want to be rescued?"

"No," said Cimorene, losing her patience at last, "I don't. And I'm tired of having my work constantly interrupted. So please go away, and don't come back."

"You can't possibly mean that," Therandil said. "Besides, everyone expects me to rescue you."

"That's your problem," Cimorene told him. "I'm going to go fix dinner. Good-bye." Before he could say anything else, she turned and ducked back into the cave, hoping the prince wouldn't follow.

3

In Which Cimorene Meets a Witch and Has Doubts about a Wizard

Therandil left, but he came back again the next day, and the day after that. It got so that Cimorene could not even step outside the cave without running into him. She might have been flattered if it hadn't been so obvious that Therandil was only worried about how foolish he'd look if he went home without fighting the dragon. On his fifth visit Cimorene was very sharp with him, and when he had not returned by midafternoon of the next day, she began to hope that he had finally left for good.

Cimorene was in the kitchen taking the pits out of cherries when she heard someone knocking at the mouth of the cave.

"Go *away,*" she shouted in complete exasperation. "I've told you and told you, I don't want to be rescued, and I'm not going to argue with you any more!"

"I didn't come here to argue," said a no-nonsense female voice from outside. "I came to meet the person who keeps borrowing my crepe pan. It's not something there's normally much call for."

"Oh, dear," said Cimorene. She wiped her hands hastily on a corner of her apron and hurried out to greet her visitor. "I'm sorry," she said, coming around the gray rock at the cave mouth. "But I've been having a problem with knights lately, and I thought–" She stopped short as she got a good look at her caller for the first time.

The woman standing outside the cave was considerably shorter than

Cimorene. Her ginger hair was piled in waves on top of her head. She had on a loose black robe with long sleeves, which she wore unbelted. A small pair of glasses with rectangular lenses sat firmly on her nose, and she carried an extremely twiggy broom in her left hand. Despite her unusual appearance, she projected an air of great self-assurance.

"I quite understand," she said, studying Cimorene shrewdly. "You must be Kazul's new princess."

"Yes, I'm Cimorene. And you are . . . ?"

"Morwen," said the black-robed woman, leaning the broom against the rock. "Kazul and I have been friends for a long time, ever since I moved to the Enchanted Forest, so I thought I'd come have a look at her new princess."

"You're the person Kazul's been borrowing dishes from, aren't you?" Cimorene said, and blinked. "But then you must be–"

"A witch," Morwen finished. "I don't see why you find it surprising. It's not exactly an unusual profession in these parts."

"It's just that I haven't met one before," Cimorene said, not mentioning the fact that in Linderwall witches were considered dangerous and probably evil and were therefore avoided if at all possible. But then, people in Linderwall didn't like dragons much, either. "Won't you come in and have some tea?"

"I certainly will," said the witch, and she did. She prowled around like a nervous cat while Cimorene put the kettle on the stove and got out the tea things.

"Well," Morwen said approvingly as Cimorene filled the teapot, "you're the first princess I've ever met who has the sense to keep up with the kitchen."

Cimorene decided that she liked Morwen's down-to-earth manner. She soon found herself telling Morwen everything, from the fencing and philosophy and Latin lessons to the seemingly endless stream of knights. The story lasted through two cups of tea and finished with Therandil's stubborn insistence on rescuing her.

"That is absurd," Morwen said decidedly when Cimorene finished. "If this continues, you'll never get anything done."

"I know," Cimorene said. "I keep telling them I don't want to be rescued, but they're all so honorable that none of them will tell anyone when they go back because they think it would be gossiping."

"More likely they don't want to look foolish."

"Maybe, but even if they did tell people, I'm not sure anyone would believe it. I have a hard enough time convincing the knights when they show up in person."

"It's just as well that your visitors *have* been honorable," Morwen said, looking thoughtful. "Linderwall's a prosperous kingdom. Sooner or later the chance of getting hold of half of it is going to tempt someone to try rescuing you whether you want to be rescued or not."

"That hadn't occurred to me," Cimorene said with a worried frown. "What can I do about it?"

"I'm not sure," Morwen replied. "The situation's not at all usual, you know. I've never heard of a princess *volunteering* for a dragon before. Which rather surprises me, now that I think of it. A dragon's princess is practically guaranteed a good marriage, so you'd think princesses from the smaller kingdoms would be clamoring for the job."

"They're probably worried about being eaten," Cimorene said. "Do you think it would help if I sent my parents a letter?"

"Probably not," Morwen said after a moment's consideration. "But it can't hurt to try. I'll check my spell books when I get home. It may give me an idea. I suggest that you hunt through Kazul's library. She's been collecting scrolls for centuries; you ought to be able to find *something* useful. Meanwhile, we'll put up a sign."

"A sign?" Cimorene stared at Morwen for a moment, then began to smile. " 'Road washed out,' " she said. " 'Use alternate route.' Is that the kind of sign you were thinking of?"

"Exactly," Morwen said with approval. "It won't stop anyone who's really determined, but it will certainly slow them down. That should give us time to come up with something better."

The two women set to work at once and in a short time produced a large, official-looking sign. Morwen offered to set it up on her way back to the Enchanted Forest, but Cimorene thought it would be too awkward for her to carry while riding the broom. So, once Morwen had gone, Cimorene tucked the sign under her arm and started down the path.

Cimorene had not had a chance to do any real exploring before, though she had looked out at the mountains every day and wondered. She was happy to have an excuse to see more of the outside of her new home.

It was a lovely day, warm and sunny, and at first the path was level and easy. Cimorene was just beginning to wonder whether anyone would believe her sign, once she got it put up, when the path swung left around a boulder and narrowed to a tiny ledge that sloped steeply upward.

Cimorene stopped. Now she knew why none of the knights had ridden up to the cave. The ledge was barely wide enough for a person on foot to edge along sideways; the best rider in the world couldn't have gotten a horse down it. Cimorene rolled her sign up into a firm, tight cylinder and stuck it through her belt, so she would have her hands free while she climbed. Then she stepped out onto the ledge.

Sidling up the slope took a long time, for Cimorene was careful to make sure that each part of the ledge would hold before she trusted her weight to it. She was also careful not to look down. Heights had never bothered her before, but there was a big difference between standing solidly on top of a tower in Linderwall Castle behind a four-foot parapet and inching along a ledge barely six inches wide with nothing between her and a long fall.

She had almost reached the top of the slope, where the path widened again, when a portion of the ledge disappeared just ahead of her. Cimorene pulled her foot back and tried to figure out what had happened. She hadn't seen or heard the rock crumble and fall away; there was simply a two-foot gap in the ledge that hadn't been there before. She studied it for a moment, trying to think of a way of getting past. Nothing occurred to her. She felt a twinge of annoyance at the thought of all her wasted efforts, but cheered up at once when she realized that this would solve the problem of the visiting knights. If she couldn't get around or over the gap, an armored knight wouldn't be able to get by, either. Cimorene smiled and turned her head to creep back to safety.

There was another two-foot gap in the ledge on her other side. Cimorene frowned. Something very odd was going on, and she didn't like it.

"You look as if you are in need of assistance," said a deep voice from above her. "May I be of help?"

Cimorene turned her head and saw a man standing four feet away, on the path at the top of the ledge. He was tall and sharp-featured, and his eyes were a hard, bright black. Though he had a gray beard that reached nearly to his waist, his face did not look old. He wore loose robes made of blue and gray silk, and in one hand he held a staff as tall as himself made of dark, polished wood.

"Possibly," Cimorene answered. She was certain that the man was a wizard, though she had never met one before, and she did not want to agree to anything until she was sure of what she was agreeing to. The court philosopher had always claimed that wizards were very tricky. "May I know to whom I am speaking?"

"I am the wizard Zemenar," the man said. "And you must be Kazul's new princess. I hope you're not trying to run away. It's–"

"Not done," Cimorene said, feeling particularly annoyed because for once she was *not* doing anything improper. "Yes, I'm Cimorene."

"I was going to say that it isn't *wise* to run away from your dragon," the wizard corrected mildly. "I believe it's *done* all the time."

"I'm sorry," Cimorene said, but she didn't try to explain. "And I'm not running away. How did you know who I was?"

"It seemed unlikely that I would find any other charming young lady walking so casually through the Pass of Silver Ice," Zemenar answered. He smiled. "As you see, it is easy to find oneself in difficulties if one is not properly . . . prepared."

Cimorene decided that she didn't like him. He reminded her of one of her father's courtiers, a humorless, sneaky little man who had paid her compliments only when he was after something and who couldn't resist giving advice even when nobody wanted it. "The ledge was all here when I started," she said. An idea crossed her mind, and she looked hard at Zemenar. "I don't suppose *you* know what happened to the two missing bits?"

A flash of startled annoyance crossed the wizard's face; then his expression smoothed back into pleasant politeness. He shrugged. "The Pass of Silver Ice is a strange place. Odd things frequently occur."

"Not like this," Cimorene muttered. She was sure, now, that the wizard had made the ledge vanish so that he could pretend to rescue her, but she had no idea why he would want her to think she owed him a favor. Actually, it surprised her that he had destroyed the ledge. She didn't think the dragons would be too happy when they found out. Unless he hadn't really destroyed it.

"What did you say?" Zemenar said, frowning uncertainly.

Cimorene ignored him. Without looking down, she slid her right foot along the ledge. The rock felt firm and solid. Slowly she transferred her weight and brought her left foot up beside her right. She shifted again, still careful not to look down, and slid her right foot forward once again.

"What are you doing?" Zemenar demanded.

"Getting off this ledge," Cimorene replied. "I should think that was obvious." One more step would bring her to the path, but Zemenar was squarely in her way. "Would you mind moving back a little so I'll have somewhere to stand?"

Zemenar's eyes narrowed, but he backed up several paces, and Cimorene stepped onto the path. She wanted to heave a sigh of relief, but she did not. She wasn't going to let Zemenar have the satisfaction of knowing she had been worried. Instead, she gave him her best royal smile and said with polite insincerity, "Thank you for offering to help, but as you see, it wasn't needed. Do stop by and visit some time."

"I will," Zemenar said as if he meant it. "And a very good day to you, Princess Cimorene."

With that he vanished. There was no smoke or fire or whirlwind. There wasn't even a shimmer in the air as he disappeared. He was simply and suddenly gone.

Cimorene stared at the place where the wizard had been and felt a shiver run down her spine. It took a very powerful wizard indeed to vanish so quietly. And she still didn't know what he wanted.

She shook herself and started down the path. She would worry about the wizard later; right now she had to find a place to put up her sign so she could get back to the cave. She didn't feel much like exploring any more.

She hadn't taken more than two or three steps when a dark shadow passed over her. Looking up, startled, she saw a flash of yellow-green scales. An instant later a dragon landed on the path in front of her, blocking the way completely. His tail hung over the edge, and he had to keep his wings partly unfurled in order to stay in balance. Cimorene recognized him at once. It was the yellow-green dragon who had wanted to eat her the day she arrived so unexpectedly in the dragons' cave.

"I saw the whole thing," the dragon said with nasty, triumphant glee. "Running away–and talking to a wizard! Just wait until Kazul hears. She'll be sorry she didn't just let us eat you and be done with it."

"I offer you greetings and good fortune on your travels," Cimorene said, figuring that it was best to be polite to anyone as large and toothy as a dragon, even if he wasn't being at all polite to her. "I'm not running away."

"Then what are you doing? Kazul doesn't have any business that would bring you down this side of the pass."

"I came out to put up a sign to keep the knights away," Cimorene said.

"That's ridiculous." The dragon sniffed. "I've been on patrol in this part of the mountains for the past week, and I haven't seen or smelled even a hint of a knight."

"You haven't been by Kazul's cave, then," Cimorene said. "At least nine of them have shown up there in the past week. Though for the past couple of days it's been mostly a prince."

"Princes don't smell any different from knights, and I'd have noticed if any of them were hanging around," the dragon said flatly. "And what about that wizard you were talking to?"

"Chaaarrge!" shouted a familiar voice from the other side of the dragon.

"Therandil!" Cimorene shouted. "I told you to go *away!*"

The yellow-green dragon twisted his long neck and glanced back over his shoulder. He seemed to bunch together like a cat crouching. Then he sprang straight up into the air, and Cimorene was blinded by the cloud of dust raised by the flapping of his enormous wings. She had the presence of mind to flatten herself back against the rocks by the side of the path, and a moment later she heard someone blundering by. She stuck out a foot.

"Ow!" she said as Therandil fell over with a clatter. She'd forgotten that he'd be wearing iron boots along with the rest of his armor.

"Cimorene? Is that you?" Therandil said.

"Of course it's me," Cimorene replied, rubbing her ankle. "Open your eyes; the dust's settled." She looked up as she spoke and saw the dragon soar out of sight behind a cliff.

"I'm sorry," Therandil said, and then in an anxious tone he added, "I hope I didn't hurt you, stumbling into you like that."

Cimorene started to say that it was nothing and that it had been her fault anyway, when she suddenly got a much better idea. "I think you've sprained my ankle," she declared.

"Oh, no," Therandil said. He sounded truly dismayed, though Cimorene couldn't see his face because he was wearing his helmet with the visor down.

"I probably won't be able to walk for at least a month," she declared. "And there's certainly no way I can climb down this mountain."

"But if you can't walk–" Therandil said, and paused. Then he squared his shoulders and went on, "–then I suppose I'll have to carry you." He didn't sound as if he liked the idea.

"I don't think that would work very well," Cimorene said quickly. "How will you fight when all the dragons come back if you're carrying me? No, you'll have to leave me here and go back alone."

"You can't stay here!" Therandil protested, though Cimorene's talk of *when all the dragons come back* had plainly made him nervous.

"I have to," Cimorene said, trying to sound noble and long-suffering. "The dragons will make sure I get safely back to Kazul's cave, and a month isn't too long a wait, after all."

"I don't understand," Therandil said, and he did look thoroughly puzzled.

"There's no point in you or anyone else coming up here to rescue me for at least a month, not till my ankle's better," Cimorene explained patiently.

"Oh, I see," Therandil said. He tilted his head back and scanned the empty sky. "You're quite sure you'll be all right? Then I'll just be going before those dragons return." He turned and started down the path as quickly as he could manage in full armor.

4

In Which Kazul Has a Dinner Party, and Cimorene Makes Dessert

Cimorene watched Therandil go with feelings of great relief. Now she had at least a month to find a permanent way of discouraging the knights, for she was quite certain that Therandil would spread the news of her "injury." She decided to put up her sign anyway, just in case, and after a little looking she found a scrubby tree beside the path and hung the sign on it.

On her way back to Kazul's cave, she noticed that the two pieces of the ledge were still invisible, and she was very careful about crossing them. She looked down once, out of curiosity, and was immediately sorry. She was not comfortable with the sight of her own feet firmly planted on nothing at all, with the sharp, spiky tops of spruce trees in full view some fifty feet below.

Kazul arrived only a few minutes after Cimorene herself. Cimorene was looking for some thread to mend her skirts (which had gotten torn and stained while she was climbing along the ledge) when she heard the unmistakable sounds of a dragon sliding into the main cave.

"Cimorene?" Kazul's voice called.

"Coming," Cimorene called back, abandoning her search. She picked up her lamp and hurried out to greet Kazul.

"I'm glad to see you're still here," Kazul said mildly as Cimorene came into the large cave. "Moranz was quite sure you'd run off with a knight or a wizard. I couldn't make out for certain which."

"Is Moranz the yellow-green dragon who wanted to eat me?" Cimorene asked. "Because if he is, he's just trying to make trouble."

"I'm well aware of that," Kazul said with a sigh that sent a burnt-bread smell halfway across the cave. "But things would be easier for me if you didn't provide him with any material to make trouble with. Exactly what happened?"

"Well, Morwen came to visit this afternoon," Cimorene began. "We were talking about all the . . . interruptions I've been having, and she suggested putting up a sign. . . ." She explained why she had gone to put up the sign herself and told Kazul in detail about her meetings with the wizard, the dragon, and the prince.

"So Morwen was here," Kazul said. She sat back, and the scales on her tail rattled comfortably against the floor. "That simplifies matters. Did you bring the sign back with you?"

"No, I found a tree and hung it by the path," Cimorene said, wondering what this was all about. "In case Therandil doesn't tell everyone about my ankle after all."

"Better still," Kazul said, and smiled fiercely, showing all her teeth. "Moranz is going to regret meddling."

"Meddling in what?"

"My business."

"I'd like a little more of an explanation than that, if you don't mind giving one," Cimorene said with a touch of exasperation.

Kazul looked startled, then thoughtful. Then she nodded. "I keep forgetting that you're not as empty-headed as most princesses," she said. "Sit down and make yourself comfortable. This may take a while."

Cimorene found a rock and sat on it. Kazul settled into a more restful position, folded her wings neatly along her back, and began. "It has to do with status. Dragons aren't required to have princesses, you see. Most of us don't. There are never enough to go around, and some of us prefer not to have to deal with the annoyances that come with them."

"Knights," Cimorene guessed.

"Among other things," Kazul said, nodding. "So having a princess in residence has become a minor mark of high status among dragons."

"A *minor* mark?"

Kazul smiled. "I'm afraid so. It's the equivalent of, oh, serving expensive imported fruit at dinner. It's a nice way of showing everyone how rich you are, but you could make just as big an impression by having some of those fancy pastries with the smooth glazed icing and spun-sugar roses."

"I see." Cimorene did see, though she found herself wishing that Kazul had found something else to compare it to. The talk of dinner reminded her too much of Moranz's repeated desire to eat her.

"Moranz is young and not very bright, I'm afraid," Kazul said, almost as if she had read Cimorene's mind. "He seems to have the mistaken impression that if a princess behaves badly, it reflects on the dragon who captured her. Possibly it comes from his inability to keep any of his own princesses for more than a week. Some of the lesser dragons were very snide about it when he lost his third one in a row. I believe she sneaked out while he was napping."

"I don't see how he can blame his princesses," Cimorene objected. "I mean, if most princesses are unwilling, it must be fairly usual for them to try to get away."

"Of course, but Moranz doesn't see it that way. He's been trying to catch someone else's princess in a similar foolishness for years, and he's quite sure he's finally done so. He's undoubtedly spreading the story of your escape far and wide at this very minute."

"Oh, dear," said Cimorene.

Kazul smiled again, and her teeth glittered silver in the lamplight. "He'll look extremely foolish when it becomes obvious that you're still here. Which is one reason I've asked a few of my friends to dinner tonight."

"You've *what?*" Cimorene said. All her worries about Moranz were instantly replaced by worries about fixing dinner on short notice for an unknown number of dragons. "How many? What time will they be here? Where are we going to *put* them all?"

"Six. Around eight-thirty. In the banquet cave. And you won't be doing anything but dessert. I've already arranged for the rest of the meal."

"Arranged? With whom?"

"Ballimore the giantess. She's loaned me the Cauldron of Plenty that she uses when her twelve-headed son-in-law drops in for dinner unannounced. It'll handle most things, but all it can produce in the way of dessert is burned mint custard and sour-cream-and-onion ice cream."

"Ugh!" said Cimorene. "I see your problem."

"Exactly. Can you manage?"

"Not if you want cherries jubilee," Cimorene said, frowning. "I haven't got a pot large enough to make seven dragons' worth of cherries jubilee. Would chocolate mousse do? I can make two or three batches, and there should be time for all of them to chill if you're not starting until eight-thirty."

"Chocolate mousse will be fine," Kazul assured her. "Come along and I'll show you where to bring it."

Cimorene picked up a lamp and followed Kazul into the public tunnels that surrounded Kazul's private caves. She was a little surprised, but when she saw the size of the banquet cave, she understood. It was enormous. Fifty or sixty dragons, perhaps even a hundred of them, would fit into it quite comfortably. Obviously it had to be a public room; there simply wasn't enough space under the Mountains of Morning for every dragon to have a cave this size.

Kazul made sure Cimorene could find her way to the banquet cave without help and then left her in the kitchen to melt slabs of chocolate and whip gallons of cream for the mousse. By the time she finished, she was hot and tired, and all she really wanted to do was to take a nap. But Kazul was expecting her to serve the mousse, and Cimorene wasn't about to appear before all those dragons in her old clothes with sweaty straggles of hair sticking to her neck and a smear of chocolate across her nose, so instead of napping, she pumped a cauldron of water, heated it on the kitchen fire, and took a bath.

Once she was clean she felt much better. She checked to make sure the mousse was setting properly, then went into her own rooms to decide what she should wear. Unfortunately, she was afraid she didn't have much choice. The wardrobe in her bedroom was full of neat, serviceable dresses suitable for cooking in or rummaging through treasure, but the only dressy clothes she had were the ones she had arrived in. She got them out of the back of the wardrobe and found to her dismay that the hem of the gown was badly stained with mud from her long walk. There was no time to clean it; she would have to wear one of the everyday dresses.

With a sigh Cimorene turned back to the wardrobe and opened it once more to look for the nicest of the ordinary clothes. She gasped in surprise. The hangers were now full of the most beautiful gowns she had ever seen. Some were silk, and some were velvet; some were heavy brocade, and some were layers of feather-light gauze; some were embroidered with gold or silver, and some were sewn with jewels.

"Well, of course," Cimorene said aloud after a stunned moment. "Why would a dragon have an ordinary wardrobe? Of *course* it's magic. What's in it depends on what I'm looking for."

One of the wardrobe doors waggled slightly, and its hinges creaked in smug agreement. Cimorene blinked at it, then shook herself and began looking through the gowns.

She chose one of red velvet, heavily embroidered with gold, and found matching slippers in the bottom of the obliging wardrobe. She let her black hair hang in loose waves nearly to her feet and even dug her crown out of the back of the drawer where she'd stuffed it on her first night. She finished getting ready a few minutes early. Feeling very cheerful, she went to the kitchen to fetch the mousse.

* * *

It took Cimorene four trips to get the mousse down to the serving area just off the banquet cave. A dragon-sized serving was a little over a bucketful, and she could barely manage to carry two at a time. When everything was ready, she stood in the serving area and waited nervously for Kazul to ring for dessert. She could hear the muffled booming of the dragons' voices through the heavy oak door, but she could not make out what any of them were saying.

The bell rang at last, summoning Cimorene to serve dessert. She carried the mousse into the banquet cavern, two servings at a time, and set it in front of Kazul and her guests. The dragons were crouched around a shoulder-high slab of white stone. Cimorene had to be very careful about lifting the mousse up onto it. Fortunately, she didn't have to wonder which dragon to serve first. She could tell which dragons were most important from their places at the table, and she made a silent apology to her protocol teacher, who had insisted that she learn about seating arrangements. (Protocol had been one of the princess lessons Cimorene had hated most.)

As she set the last serving in front of Kazul, one of the other dragons said in a disgruntled and vaguely familiar voice, "I see the rumors are wrong again, Kazul. Or did you have to go after her and haul her back the way the rest of us do?"

Cimorene turned angrily, but before she could say anything, a large gray-green dragon on the other side of the stone slab said, "Nonsense, Woraug! Girl's got more sense than that. You shouldn't listen to gossip. Next thing you know, you'll be chasing after that imaginary wizard Gaurim's been on about." Cimorene recognized the speaker at once. He was Roxim, the elderly dragon she had given four of her handkerchiefs to.

"I suppose it was that idiot Moranz again, trying to cause trouble," a purple-green dragon said with bored distaste. "Someone should do something about him."

"Kazul still hasn't answered my question," Woraug said, and his tail lashed once like the tail of an angry cat. "And I'd like her to do so if the rest of you will stop sidetracking the conversation."

"Here, now!" Roxim said indignantly. "That's a bit strong, Woraug! Too strong, if you ask me."

"I didn't," Woraug said. "I asked Kazul. And I'm still waiting."

"I'm very pleased with my princess," Kazul said mildly. "And no, I didn't have to haul her back, as you would realize if you'd given the matter a little thought. Or does your princess normally leave seven servings of chocolate mousse in the kitchen when she runs away?"

"Hear, hear!" Roxim said.

Cimorene noted with interest that Woraug's scales had turned an even brighter shade of green than normal and that he was starting to smell faintly of brimstone.

"One of these days you'll go too far, Kazul," he said.

"You started it," Kazul pointed out. She turned to the gray dragon. "What's this about Gaurim and a wizard, Roxim?"

"You haven't heard?" Roxim said, sounding surprised. "Gaurim's been raving about it for weeks. Somebody snuck into her cave and stole a book from her library. No traces, but for some reason she's positive it was a wizard. *Achoo!"* Roxim sneezed, emitting a ball of flame that just missed hitting his bowl of mousse. "Gives me an allergy attack just thinking about it."

"If it wasn't a wizard, who was it?" the dragon at the far end of the table asked.

"Could have been anybody–an elf, a dwarf, even a human," Roxim responded. "No reason to think it was a wizard just because Gaurim didn't catch him in the act. Not with the amount of time she spends away from home."

"Which book did she lose?" said the thin, brownish-green dragon next to Kazul.

"What does it matter?" the purple-green dragon muttered.

"Some history or other. And that's another thing–what would a wizard want with a history book? No, no, Gaurim's making a lot of fuss over a common thief. That's what I say."

"It could have been a wizard," said the dragon at the far end. "Who knows why they want the things they want?"

"Ridiculous!" Roxim replied with vigor. "A wizard wouldn't dare come through this part of the mountains. They know what we'd do to 'em, by George! Beg pardon," he added to the silver-green dragon next to him, who appeared to have been rather shocked by his language.

"I'm afraid you're wrong there," Kazul said. "Cimorene met one today, less than a two-minute flight from my cave."

"What? What?" Roxim said. "You're sure?"

"That's done it." The purple-green dragon rolled his head in an irritated gesture, so that his scales made a scratching noise as they rubbed together. "You'll never get him to quit talking about it now."

"Quite sure," Cimorene assured Roxim, after glancing at Kazul to make sure she was expected to answer Roxim's question for herself. "He made two bits of the ledge I was standing on turn invisible so I would think it wasn't safe to keep going."

"Certainly sounds like a wizard to me," the dragon at the far end commented.

"What did he look like?" asked the silver-green dragon.

Cimorene described the wizard as well as she could, then added, "He said his name was Zemenar."

"Zemenar? That's ridiculous!" Woraug snorted. "Zemenar was elected head of the Society of Wizards last year. He wouldn't waste his time playing games with somebody's princess."

"Not unless he had a great deal to gain by it," the thin dragon said in a thoughtful tone. She turned her head and looked speculatively at Cimorene.

"Such as?" Woraug said. He waited a moment, but no one answered. "No, I can't believe it was Zemenar. The girl's made a mistake; that's all."

"Perhaps it wasn't him," Cimorene said, holding on to her temper as hard as she could. "I've never met Zemenar, so I wouldn't know. But that's who he said he was."

"And wouldn't it be amusing if she were right?" the purple-green dragon said, showing some interest in the proceedings for the first time.

"I don't see that it matters," the silver-green dragon said. "The important thing is that he was a wizard, poking around smack in the middle of our mountains. What are we going to do about it?"

"Tell King Tokoz," Roxim said. "His job to handle this sort of thing, isn't it?"

"What can Tokoz do about it?" Woraug said, and there was a faint undercurrent of contempt in his tone.

"He could use the King's Crystal to find out what the wizards are really doing," the thin dragon said in a prim tone.

"He won't use the crystal for anything less than a full-fledged war," Woraug said. "And why should he? What could Tokoz do even if he did find out some wizard was preying on poor defenseless dragons like Gaurim?"

"Lodge a formal protest with the Society of Wizards," Roxim answered promptly, ignoring Woraug's sarcasm. "Proper thing to do, no question. Then the next time anyone sees a wizard . . ." His voice trailed off, and he snapped his teeth together suggestively.

"He'd probably just set up a committee," the purple-green dragon said. "Can't anyone think of something else?"

"I don't think we should do anything until we have some idea what Zemenar was after," said the thin dragon. "It could be important."

"We have to do something!" the silver-green dragon said. Her claws clashed against the stone table. "We can't have wizards wandering in and out whenever they please! Why, we'd lose half our magic in no time."

"Not to mention everyone sneezing themselves silly every time one of those dratted staffs gets too close," added the dragon at the far end.

The dragons began arguing among themselves about what to do and how best to do it. It reminded Cimorene of the way her father's ministers argued. Everyone seemed to agree that something ought to be done about the wizards, but they each had a different idea about what was appropriate. Roxim insisted huffily that the only thing to do was to inform the King, who would then make a formal protest. The thin dragon wanted to find out what the wizards were up to (she didn't say how this was to be done) before anyone tried to chase them off. The silver-green dragon wanted patrols sent out immediately to eat any wizard who ventured into the Mountains of Morning. The dragon at the far end of the table wanted to attack the headquarters of the Society of Wizards the following morning, and the purple-green dragon thought it would be most entertaining to wait and see what the wizards did next. Woraug was the only one of the guests who did not have a proposal, though he made occasional comments, usually sarcastic ones, about everyone else's suggestions.

Kazul did not say anything at all. Cimorene was at first surprised and then puzzled by her silence, since Kazul was the one who had set the whole discussion going to begin with. As the argument grew more heated, however, Cimorene began to be glad that there was at least one dragon present who was not involved in it. The dragon at the far end of the table was starting to breathe little tongues of fire at the purple-green dragon, and Roxim was threatening loudly to have another allergy attack, but Cimorene was fairly sure that Kazul would stop the discussion before things got completely out of hand.

She was right. A moment later, while the dragon at the far end was taking a deep breath to continue arguing and the thin dragon was winding up a long, involved train of logical reasons why her proposal was the best, Kazul said, "Thank you all for your advice. I'll certainly think about it before I decide what to do."

"What do you mean by that?" the thin dragon asked suspiciously.

"It was my princess who met the wizard," Kazul pointed out. "Therefore, it is my decision whether to report the matter to the King, or to take some action on my own, or to ask for cooperation from some of you."

None of the other dragons appeared to like hearing this, but to Cimorene's surprise none of them gave Kazul any argument about it. The dragon at the far end of the table made a few half-hearted grumbles, but that was all, and the conversation turned to the intricacies of several draconian romances that were currently in progress. As soon as her guests appeared to have calmed down, Kazul gave the signal for the empty mousse dishes to be taken away, so Cimorene only heard a few incomprehensible snatches of the new conversation. She did not really mind. She had plenty to think about already.

5

In Which Cimorene Receives a Formal Call from Her Companions in Dire Captivity

Kazul slept late the following morning, and Cimorene was afraid that she would leave before Cimorene had a chance to ask about the dragons' after-dinner conversation. To her relief, Kazul called her in as soon as she was thoroughly awake and asked Cimorene to bring in the brushes for cleaning her scales.

"What was that crystal your friend mentioned last night?" Cimorene asked as she laid out the brushes. "The one she thought King Tokoz could use somehow to find out what the wizards are doing?"

"The King's Crystal?" Kazul said. "It's one of the magical objects that belongs to the King of the Dragons."

"But what does it *do?* And why did Woraug think that King Tokoz wouldn't want to use it?"

"Using the crystal is difficult and tiring, and Tokoz is getting old," Kazul replied. "Zareth was right to say that the crystal ought to be used, but it will take more evidence than we have right now to persuade the King of that. As to what it does, the crystal shows things that are happening in other times and places. It's useful, but it can be very difficult to interpret correctly."

"Oh, a crystal ball," Cimorene said, nodding. She tapped Kazul's side, and the dragon bent her elbow so that the scales were easier to reach. "The court wizard at Linderwall had one, but I had to stop my magic lessons before he got a chance to show me how to work it."

"The King's Crystal is more like a plate, but the principle is the same," Kazul said.

"A crystal plate?" Cimorene blinked. "No wonder nobody talks about it much. It just doesn't sound right."

Kazul shrugged. "The King's Crystal is much more accurate than an ordinary crystal ball, and if 'crystal plate' sounds odd to most people, it means that fewer of them will try to steal it."

"Was that what the silver-green dragon meant when he said that if the wizards started wandering through the mountains you'd lose half your magic in no time? I never heard that wizards stole magic rings and swords and things."

"Not magic things," Kazul said. *"Magic.* Wizards steal magic. That's where their power comes from."

"How can a wizard steal magic?" Cimorene said skeptically. She climbed on a stool and began working at the ribs of Kazul's wings.

"Wizards' staffs absorb magic from whatever happens to be nearby," Kazul said, stretching out her left wing so Cimorene could get at the base. "That's why they're always hanging around places like the Mountains of Morning and the Enchanted Forest. The more magic there is in the area, the more their staffs can soak up."

"What would happen if someone stole a wizard's staff? Would the wizard still be able to use it?"

"The wizard wouldn't be able to work any magic until he got it back," Kazul said. "Most of them have a great many anti-theft spells on their staffs for exactly that reason. Of course, it happens anyway, now and then. And as long as the wizard and the staff are separated, the staff doesn't absorb magic."

"It doesn't sound like a very good arrangement to me," Cimorene said. "I can think of half a dozen ways a staff could be lost or forgotten or stolen or something. It doesn't seem sensible for a wizard to depend so much on anything that's so easy to mislay."

Kazul shrugged. "They seem to like it."

"I can see why you don't want them in your part of the mountains."

"Can you? Do you have any idea how unpleasant it is to have part of your essence sucked out of you without so much as a by-your-leave? Not to mention the side effects."

"Side effects?" Cimorene said, puzzled. "There! Turn around, and I'll do your other side."

"Roxim isn't the only dragon who's allergic to wizards," Kazul said dryly as she shifted her position. "Or rather, to their staffs. We all are.

Roxim's just a little more sensitive than most. That's why we made the agreement with them in the first place."

"The dragons have an agreement with the wizards?"

Kazul nodded. "To be precise, the King of the Dragons has an agreement with the head of the Society of Wizards: the wizards stay out of our portions of the Mountains of Morning, and we allow them partial access to the Caves of Fire and Night. At least, that's the way it's supposed to work. King Tokoz is getting old and forgetful, and lately wizards have been turning up in all sorts of places they aren't supposed to be."

"Like that wizard Zemenar I met on the path," Cimorene said. "Do you think he really *was* the same Zemenar that's the head of the Society of Wizards?"

"I doubt that anyone, even another wizard, would dare impersonate him," Kazul said. "He has a nasty reputation."

Cimorene remembered the hard black eyes and sharp features of the wizard she had met. He had certainly looked nasty enough, even when he was pretending to be nice. He was sneaky, too, or he wouldn't have tried to trick her. And he had been very annoyed when Cimorene got off the ledge without his help. Cimorene frowned.

"I wonder what he wanted, really," she mused. "Do you suppose he'll stop by the way he said he would?"

"I almost wish he would try," Kazul said. There was an angry glint in her eye, and her claws made a scratching sound against the stone floor of the cave as she flexed them.

"Don't wiggle," Cimorene said. "If Zemenar is as tricky as everyone says, he won't come while you're here. He'll wait until you've gone somewhere and I'm alone."

"True." Kazul frowned. Then she looked at Cimorene, and her eyes took on a speculative gleam. "He probably thinks you're as silly as most princesses, so he'll be hoping to trick you into giving him whatever it is he's after. And if he does–"

"Then maybe I can fool him instead," Cimorene finished. "And once we know what he's after, we can decide what to do about it."

Kazul and Cimorene discussed this idea while Cimorene finished brushing the dragon's scales. There was very little they could do to prepare since they did not know when Zemenar might show up at the cave or what he might do when he arrived. Then Kazul went off to inspect the ledge where Cimorene had met the wizard, to see whether bits of it were still invisible.

When Kazul had gone, Cimorene went into the library to hunt through all the books and scrolls of spells. The behavior of the dragons at dinner the previous evening had made a considerable impression on her, and she wanted to see whether she could find a spell to fireproof herself. Until then she hadn't realized that when a dragon lost his temper, he started breathing fire. Not that she was planning to do anything to irritate Kazul–or any other dragon, for that matter–but the dragons at dinner had been too annoyed to be careful, and she didn't want to get burned by accident, no matter how sorry the dragon might be afterward.

At first Cimorene didn't have much luck. She hadn't had time to do much organizing in the library, and most of the books and scrolls were lying in haphazard, dust-covered piles. Some had even fallen onto the floor, and there were spiders everywhere. Cimorene realized that if she wanted to find anything, she was going to have to do some more cleaning first. With a sigh she went to get a bucket of water, some cloths for washing and dusting, and a handkerchief to tie over her hair.

She worked for several hours, dusting books and manuscripts, wiping off the dirty bookshelves, and putting the books back in neat rows when the shelves were dry. She found two books and five old scrolls that looked as if they might be interesting. These she set on one of the tables to look at later. She had just pulled a stained and yellowed stack of papers out of the back of the second-to-last bookshelf when she heard someone hallooing outside.

"Now what?" she muttered crossly. She set the papers on the table with the rest of the books she was planning to look at later and went out to see who was there.

To her surprise, the noise was coming from the back entrance, not from the mouth of the cave. She hurried into the passage, rounded the corner, and found herself facing three beautiful, elegantly dressed princesses. They were all blonde and blue-eyed and slender, and several inches shorter than Cimorene. The first one wore a gold crown set with diamonds, and her hair was the color of sun-ripened wheat. The second wore a silver crown set with sapphires, and her hair was the color of crystallized honey. The last wore a pearl-covered circlet, and her hair was the color of ripe apricots. They looked rather taken aback by the sight of Cimorene in her dust-covered dress and kerchief.

"Oh, bother," Cimorene said under her breath. Then she smiled her best smile and said, "Welcome to the caves of the dragon Kazul. May I help you with anything?"

"We have made the perilous journey through the tunnels to see the Princess Cimorene, newly come to these caverns, to comfort her and together bemoan our sad and sorry fates," the first princess said haughtily. "Tell her we are here."

"I'm Cimorene," Cimorene said. "I don't need comforting, and I'm not particularly sad or sorry to be here, but if you'd like to come in and have some tea, you're welcome to."

The first two princesses looked as if they would have liked to be startled and appalled by this announcement but were much too well bred to show what they were feeling. The princess with the pearl circlet looked surprised and rather intrigued, and she glanced hopefully at her companions. They ignored her, but after a moment the first princess said grandly, "Very well, we will join you, then," and swept past Cimorene into the cave.

The other princesses followed, the one with the pearl circlet giving Cimorene a shy smile as she passed. Cimorene, wondering what she had gotten herself into, brought up the rear. The princesses stopped when they reached the main cave, and the ones in the gold and silver crowns looked a bit disgruntled. The one in the pearl circlet stared in unabashed amazement. "My goodness," she said, "you certainly do have a lot of space."

"Alianora!" the gold-crowned princess said sharply, and the princess with the pearl circlet flushed and subsided, looking unhappy.

"This way," Cimorene said hastily, and led the three princesses into the kitchen. "Do sit down," she said, waving at the bench beside the kitchen table.

The gold-crowned princess looked at the bench with distaste, but after a moment she sat down. The other two followed her example. There was a brief silence while Cimorene filled the copper teakettle and hung it over the fire, and then the gold-crowned princess said, "I am remiss in my duties, for I have not yet told you who we are. I am the Princess Keredwel of the Kingdom of Raxwel, now captive of the dread dragon Gornul. This"–she nodded toward the princess in the silver crown–"is the Princess Hallanna of the Kingdom of Poranbuth, now captive of the dread dragon Zareth. And this"–she waved at the girl in the pearl circlet–"is the Princess Alianora of the Duchy of Toure-on-Marsh, now prisoner of the dread dragon Woraug."

"Pleased to meet you," Cimorene said. "I am Princess Cimorene of the Kingdom of Linderwall, now princess of the dragon Kazul. What sort of tea would you like? I have blackberry, ginger, chamomile, and gunpowder green. I'm afraid I used the last of the lapsang souchong this morning."

"Blackberry, please," Keredwel said. She gave Cimorene a considering look. "You seem to be most philosophic about your fate."

"Would that I had so valiant a spirit," Hallanna said in failing accents. "But my sensibility is too great, I fear, for me to follow your example."

"If you don't like being a dragon's princess, why don't you escape?" Cimorene asked, remembering that Kazul had said that three princesses in a row had run away from the yellow-green dragon, Moranz.

Keredwel and Hallanna looked shocked. "Without being rescued?"

Hallanna faltered. "Walk all that way, with dragons and trolls and goodness knows what else hiding in the rocks, ready to eat me? Oh, I *couldn't!*"

"It isn't done," Keredwel said coldly. "And I notice that *you* haven't tried it."

"But I'm enjoying being Kazul's princess," Cimorene said cheerfully. "I suppose I might have been upset if I'd been carried off the way you were, but I can hardly complain as it is, can I?"

Alianora leaned forward. "Then you really *did* volunteer to be Kazul's princess?"

Keredwel and Hallanna turned and stared at their companion. *"Where* did you get *that* ridiculous idea, Alianora?" Hallanna said.

"W-Woraug said–" Alianora faltered.

"You must have misunderstood," Keredwel said severely. *"No one* volunteers to be a dragon's princess. It isn't *done."*

"Actually, Alianora's quite right," Cimorene said as she set the teacups in front of her visitors. "I did volunteer." She smiled sweetly at the thunderstruck expressions on the faces of the first two princesses. "I got tired of embroidery and etiquette."

Keredwel and Hallanna seemed unsure of how to take this announcement, so they made polite conversation about the tea and asked Cimorene questions about the current fashions. Alianora didn't say very much, and the few times she tried either Keredwel or Hallanna jumped on her. Cimorene felt rather sorry for Alianora.

The princesses swept off at last, still somewhat puzzled by Cimorene's attitude. Cimorene gave a sigh of relief and set about cleaning up the kitchen. She was just rinsing the last of the cups when she heard someone hesitantly clearing her throat behind her. Cimorene turned and saw Alianora standing timidly in the doorway.

"Hello again," Cimorene said. "Did you forget something?"

"Not exactly," Alianora said. "I mean, I told Keredwel I did, but actually I just wanted to get away from them for a while. I hope you don't mind."

"I don't mind at all as long as you don't expect more hospitality," Cimorene assured her. "I have to get back to work on the library."

"What are you doing?" Alianora asked. She seemed really interested, so Cimorene explained about the fireproofing spell.

"It sounds like a wonderful idea," Alianora said when Cimorene finished. "The dragons are careful around us, but it would be nice not to have to depend on them not to lose their tempers." She hesitated. "May I help?"

"I don't think Kazul would mind," Cimorene said. "But you'd better change clothes first. The library isn't very clean, I'm afraid."

Alianora looked down at her silk gown, which was embroidered heavily with silver and pearls, and giggled. Cimorene took her into the bedroom and found a plain, serviceable cleaning dress in the magic wardrobe. It took two tries before the wardrobe figured out that she wanted a dress for someone else, but once it caught on, it provided a splendid selection in Alianora's size. Then they went to the library and got to work.

Cleaning was much more enjoyable with Alianora for company. By the time they finished dusting and straightening the last bookcases, the two girls were fast friends, and Alianora was comfortable enough to ask Cimorene straight out how it was that she had come to volunteer for a dragon.

"It's a long story," Cimorene said, but Alianora insisted on hearing it. So Cimorene told her and then asked how Alianora had happened to be carried off by Woraug.

To her surprise, Alianora flushed. "I think it was the only thing left that they could think of," she said, not very clearly. "My family, I mean."

"I don't understand," Cimorene said.

"It's because I'm not a very satisfactory princess," Alianora said. "I *tried,* I really did, but. . . . It started when the wicked fairy came to my christening."

"She put a curse on you?"

"No. She ate cake and ice cream until she nearly burst and danced with my Uncle Arthur until two in the morning and had a *wonderful* time. So she went home without cursing me, and Aunt Ermintrude says that that's where the whole problem started."

"Lots of princesses don't have christening curses," said Cimorene.

"Not if a wicked fairy comes to the christening," Alianora said positively. "And that was only the beginning. When I turned sixteen, Aunt Ermintrude sent me a gold spinning wheel for my birthday, and I sat down and spun. I didn't prick my finger or *anything."*

Cimorene was beginning to see what Alianora was getting at. "Well, if you didn't have a christening curse . . ."

"So Aunt Ermintrude told Mama to put me and a spinning wheel in a room full of straw and have me spin it into gold," Alianora went on. "And I tried! But all I could manage was linen thread, and whoever heard of a princess who can spin straw into linen thread?"

"It's a little unusual, certainly."

"Then they gave me a loaf of bread and told me to walk through the forest and give some to anyone who asked. I did *exactly* what they told me, and the second beggar-woman was a fairy in disguise, but instead of saying that whenever I spoke, diamonds and roses would drop from my mouth, she said that since I was so kind, I would never have any problems with my teeth."

"Really? Did it work?"

"Well, I haven't had a toothache since I met her."

"I'd much rather have good teeth than have diamonds and roses drop out of my mouth whenever I said something," Cimorene said. "Think how uncomfortable it would be if you accidentally talked in your sleep! You'd wake up rolling around on thorns and rocks."

"That never occurred to me," Alianora said, much struck.

"Was that everything?" Cimorene asked.

"No," Alianora said. "Aunt Ermintrude persuaded one of her fairy friends to give me a gown and a pair of glass slippers to go to a ball in the next kingdom over. And I *broke* one before I even got out of the castle!"

"That's not so surprising," Cimorene said. "Glass slippers are for deserving merchants' daughters, not for princesses."

"Try telling Aunt Ermintrude that," Alianora said. "I think she was the one who found out that Woraug was going to ravage a village just over the border and arranged for me to go and visit on the right day so I could be carried off. She didn't even warn me. I suppose she thought that if I knew, I'd mess it up somehow."

"I don't think I would get along very well with your Aunt Ermintrude," Cimorene commented thoughtfully.

"Oh, it wasn't so bad, at least at first," Alianora said. "Woraug ignored me most of the time, especially after he found out I can't cook, and it was a real relief not to have Aunt Ermintrude around any more. Only then Gornul brought Keredwel and Zareth brought Hallanna, and . . ."

"And they've been making life miserable for you ever since," Cimorene finished. "Why don't you stand up to them?"

"I tried, but you don't know what they're like," Alianora said, sighing. "Keredwel goes on and on about correct behavior, and Hallanna dissolves in tears as soon as it looks like she's losing an argument. And they've both had *dozens* of knights and princes try to rescue them. I've only had two."

"How do you do it?" Cimorene asked. "I've had nine already, and they're a dreadful nuisance." Alianora stared at Cimorene, then began to giggle. "What's so funny?" Cimorene demanded.

"Keredwel bragged for a week because two knights and a prince tried to rescue her the first month she was here," Alianora explained between giggles. "She said it was some kind of record. You've barely been with Kazul for four weeks, and you've had *nine,* and you didn't even mention it when Keredwel was here. She's going to be furious when she finds out."

"If she wants them, she can have them," Cimorene said. Her expression grew thoughtful. "Maybe they'd be easier to get rid of if I sent them along to another princess, instead of just trying to get them to go home."

"Oh!" said Alianora, and went off into gales of laughter again.

Cimorene gave her a questioning look. "It's the idea of Keredwel being–oh, my–being rescued by a secondhand knight," Alianora gasped. "Oh, dear!"

Cimorene's eyes began to dance. "I could take a good look at them first, to make sure they're worthy of her before I sent them on," she suggested.

This was too much for either of them, and they both collapsed in laughter. "You wouldn't, really, would you?" Alianora said when she began to recover.

"Send the knights to rescue someone else? I certainly would," Cimorene said emphatically. "I meant it when I said they were a nuisance. I wouldn't want to upset Keredwel, though. I'll have to think about the best way of handling it. It's a good thing there probably won't be any more of them for a few weeks. I should have plenty of time to figure something out."

"How do you know that?" Alianora asked. Cimorene explained about the sign and Therandil and her "sprained ankle." Alianora was impressed and promised to help if she could. "I'll tell Hallanna that you've twisted your ankle. I *know* she'll tell the next knight who comes to rescue her, and then it won't matter if your Prince Therandil doesn't tell anybody."

This settled, the two girls sat down and began looking through the books and scrolls Cimorene had piled on the table. Alianora, having been brought up as a proper princess despite the tiny size of her country, did not read Latin, so Cimorene had to examine those scrolls herself. There was a sizable stack of books left, however, and Alianora waded into them with a will. It was Cimorene, however, who finally found the spell they were searching for.

"I think this is it!" she said, looking up from an ancient, crumpled scroll. " 'Being a Spell for the Resisting of Heat and Flames of All Kinds, in Particular Those Which Are the Product of Magical Beasts,' " she read. "Yes, there's a list and it includes dragons."

"I would think dragons would be at the top," Alianora said. "Is it difficult?"

"It doesn't look hard," Cimorene said, studying the page. "Some of the ingredients are pretty rare, but it says you only need them for the initial casting. After that, you can reactivate the spell just by throwing a pinch of dried feverfew in the air and reciting a couplet."

"That's not bad," Alianora said. She came around the table and peered over Cimorene's shoulder at the faded ink. "Is it Latin?"

"No, it's just an ornate style of writing," Cimorene assured her. "It's not hard to read, once you get the hang of it. See, there's the couplet.

"Power of water, wind and earth,
Turn the fire back to its birth."

"It's a variation on a dragon spell," Cimorene added thoughtfully.

"How do you know that?" Alianora asked.

"The court wizard at home mentioned it when he was teaching me magic," Cimorene replied, studying the directions.

"Then maybe it really *will* work on dragon fire. Can we get all the ingredients for the initial casting?"

"I think so, but it'll take a while," Cimorene said. "I don't have any wolfsbane, and I'm not at all sure about unicorn water. Come on, let's check and see what we need to get."

They took the scroll into the kitchen and began hunting through the shelves and supplies. They found more of the ingredients than Cimorene had expected, and she began to wonder whether one of Kazul's previous princesses might have studied magic. They did not, however, find any wolfsbane or unicorn water, nor were they able to locate any white eagle feathers. Alianora discovered a very cobwebby jar labeled "POWDERED HENS' TEETH," but it was quite empty.

Cimorene made a list of the ingredients they still needed, while Alianora changed back into her pearl-embroidered dress. Alianora took a copy of the list and went back to her quarters, much excited, to see whether she happened to have anything useful in the dusty, disused corners of her dragon's kitchen. Cimorene doubted that she would find anything, but there was no harm in letting her look.

As soon as Alianora left, Cimorene tidied up the kitchen and put all but two of the books back on the shelves in the library. One was the scroll of spells in which she had found the fireproofing spell, because she wanted to take a more careful look at some of the other charms and enchantments it described. The other book was a fat volume bound in worn leather, with the words *Historia Dracorum* in cracked and flaking gold leaf on the cover. Cimorene had decided it was time she really got to work on her Latin.

6

In Which the Wizards Do Some Snooping, and Cimorene Snoops Back

For the next three weeks, Cimorene spent most of her free time studying the fireproofing spell and collecting the ingredients she would need to cast it. A few, like the wolfsbane and feverfew, she could gather herself from the herbs that grew on the slopes of the mountains. Alianora found a little jar of hippopotamus oil among the cosmetics left by her predecessor. The unicorn water Cimorene got from Morwen, after promising her a copy of the spell if it worked. She went to Kazul about the white eagle feathers, though she was a little afraid to explain what she wanted them for. She didn't want Kazul to think that she was worried about Kazul losing her temper and accidentally roasting her. Fortunately, the dragon found the whole idea very interesting.

"It could be very useful," Kazul said reflectively. "There are enough hot-tempered youngsters around that it would be well worth fireproofing the princesses who have to deal with them."

"I'm not sure I'll be able to fireproof anyone at all," Cimorene said. "I still need the white eagle feathers and the powdered hens' teeth, and nobody seems to have any."

"I'll see what I can do," Kazul said, and a few days later she dropped a bundle of white feathers at the door of the kitchen. Half a feather was stuck to one of her right claws, and another was caught between two of her teeth, and she looked very pleased with herself. Cimorene decided not to ask any awkward questions. Even Kazul, however, could not find any hens' teeth, so Cimorene had to keep putting off trying out the spell.

When she wasn't working on collecting the ingredients for the fire-proofing spell, Cimorene read the *Historia Dracorum.* It was very difficult at first. After all, it had been a *long* time since her last Latin lesson. She kept working at it until she started to remember the right endings for the declensions and conjugations and cases. Shortly after that she realized that she was not having to look up quite as many words as she had at the beginning.

From then on, her progress was rapid. It helped that she found the book fascinating. Dragon history was not a subject commonly taught to princesses in Linderwall. But as she was now a dragon's princess, she had personal reasons to be interested. Besides, the history of the dragons was very exciting. Every page was full of descriptions of dragons ravaging villages, carrying off princesses, defeating knights and princes (and occasionally being defeated by them), and fighting with wizards, giants, and each other. When the book wasn't describing battles, it was describing famous dragons' hoards and peculiar draconian customs.

Cimorene was in the library with the *Historia Dracorum* in front of her and her Latin dictionary on the table beside her left hand when she heard someone calling from the front of the cave. She had hoped it would be at least a little longer before the knights started coming back, so she couldn't help sighing as she stuck a leather bookmark in the book and closed it. Then she went out to argue with whoever it was until they went away.

Two wizards were standing just outside the mouth of the cave. Cimorene saw their wooden staffs first, before she was close enough to see their faces. As she came nearer, she recognized the one on the left as Zemenar. The one on the right was taller and younger; his brown hair and beard showed no trace of gray. His blue and brown robes were identical to the older wizard's, except for the colors. His eyes were the same bright black as his companion's, and he looked at Cimorene in a way that made her feel uneasy.

"Good morning to you, Princess Cimorene," Zemenar said. "I thought I would take you up on your kind invitation to visit. I hope we haven't come at an inconvenient time?"

"Not at all," Cimorene said, thinking hard. She had promised Kazul that she would try to find out what Zemenar was after if he showed up, and here he was. Maybe if she convinced him that she was as silly as her sisters, he would be careless enough to let something slip.

"I thought perhaps we might have since it took you so long to come out," Zemenar said mildly, but Cimorene thought there was a hint of suspicion in his eyes.

"I must not have heard you right away," Cimorene said, batting her eyes innocently, the way her next youngest sister did whenever she had done something particularly foolish. "Kazul has quite a large set of caves, and I was in one of the ones at the back. I'm *so* sorry."

"Ah." Zemenar stroked his beard with his left hand. "That would make it difficult for you. Perhaps we could set up a spell for you, one that would let you know whenever anyone comes to visit. It would be more pleasant for visitors, too, if they didn't have to shout. What do you think, Antorell?"

"Like the one at the headquarters of the society," the second wizard said, nodding. "We could do it in two or three minutes, right from here. It'd be easy."

Zemenar shot a dark look at his companion. Cimorene was sure that he'd wanted to pretend he was inventing a difficult new spell, so that he would have an excuse to wander around Kazul's caves. "Quite so," said Zemenar. "Well, Princess?"

"Oh, dear, I don't know," Cimorene said, doing her best to imitate the way her eldest sister behaved whenever anyone wanted her to decide anything. "It sounds very nice, but Kazul is so *picky* about where things go and how things are done. . . . No, I couldn't, I simply *couldn't* let you do anything like that without asking Kazul first."

"What a pity," Zemenar said. His companion coughed and shuffled his feet. "Ah, yes. Allow me to present my son, Antorell. I hope you don't mind my bringing him along?"

"Of course not," Cimorene said politely.

"I am pleased to make the acquaintance of such a lovely princess," Antorell said, bowing.

Cimorene blinked. This wasn't getting anywhere. Maybe if she brought them inside they'd relax a little. "Thank you," she said to Antorell. "Won't you come in and have some tea?"

"We would be delighted," Zemenar said quickly. "If you'll lead the way, Princess?"

"This way," Cimorene said. She stopped just inside the mouth of the cave and gave the wizards her sweetest and most innocent smile. "You can leave your staffs right here. Just lean them up against the wall."

Antorell looked considerably startled, and Zemenar frowned. "Is this, too, something your dragon requires?" he said.

"I don't know," Cimorene said, wrinkling up her forehead the way her third-from-eldest sister did whenever she was puzzled (which was often). "But they'll be so awkward in the kitchen. Don't you think so? There's not very much room."

"We'll manage," Zemenar said.

Cimorene hadn't really expected to get the wizards to let go of their staffs, but it had been worth a try. She shrugged and smiled and led them on into the kitchen, where she made a point of bumping into the staffs or tripping over them every time she went by. Finally Antorell turned his sideways and stuck it under the table. Zemenar hung onto his with a kind of grim, suspicious stubbornness that made Cimorene wonder whether she was fooling him at all with her pretended silliness.

The wizards made uncomfortable conversation about the weather and the size of the kitchen for several minutes while Cimorene fixed the tea and poured it. "Are the rest of Kazul's caves this large?" Zemenar asked as Cimorene handed him his teacup. She had given him the one with the broken handle, even though he was a guest, because she didn't trust him.

"Oh, yes," Cimorene said. She was beginning to think she was never going to find out anything. The two wizards seemed perfectly happy to sit at the kitchen table and talk about nothing whatever for hours.

"Remarkable," said Antorell in an admiring tone. "You know, we wizards don't often get to see the inside of a dragon's cave."

I'll bet you don't, thought Cimorene as she gave him a puzzled smile. "That's too bad," she said aloud.

"Yes, it is," Zemenar said. "Perhaps you'd be willing to show us around?"

Cimorene thought very rapidly. It was obvious that she wasn't going to learn anything if the wizards just sat at the kitchen table and drank tea, so she decided to take a chance. "Well," she said in a doubtful tone, "I suppose it would be all right as long as I don't take you into the treasure rooms."

"That's fine," Antorell said, a little too quickly.

"You won't touch anything, will you?" Cimorene said as they stood up. "Kazul is *so* particular about where things are kept . . ."

"Of course not," Zemenar said, smiling insincerely.

Cimorene smiled back and led the way out into the hall. She watched the wizards carefully as she took them through the large main cave, the general storage caverns, and the big cavern where Kazul visited with other dragons. Zemenar made polite noises about the size and comfort of everything, but neither he nor Antorell seemed very interested. "And this is the library," Cimorene said, throwing the door open.

"I am impressed," Zemenar said, and Cimorene could tell that this time he meant it. She stepped sideways, so that she could keep an eye on both of the wizards at the same time.

"A remarkable collection," Antorell commented. He began walking around the room, admiring the bookshelves and scanning the titles of the books.

"What's this?" Zemenar said, bending over the table. "The *Historia*

Dracorum? A surprising choice for light reading, Princess." His eyes met Cimorene's, and they were hard and bright and suspicious.

"Oh, I'm not *reading* it," Cimorene said hastily, opening her eyes very wide. "I just thought it would make the library look nicer to have a book or two sitting out on the table. More–more lived-in."

Zemenar nodded, looking relieved and faintly contemptuous. "I think it works very well, Princess," he said. "Very well indeed." Then he looked over at the other side of the room and said sharply, "Antorell! What are you doing?"

Cimorene turned her head in time to see Antorell put out a hand and deliberately tip several books off one of the shelves. "Stop that!" she said, forgetting to sound silly.

"I'm very sorry, Princess," Antorell said. "Will you help me put them back where they belong?"

Cimorene had no choice but to go over and help him. It took several minutes to get everything back in place because Antorell kept dropping things. Cimorene got quite annoyed with him and finally did it all herself. As she started to turn back to the center of the room, she caught a glimpse of Zemenar hastily closing the *Historia Dracorum.* Cimorene pretended not to notice, but she made a mental note that he had been looking at something near the middle of the book.

"That was dreadfully careless of you," Cimorene said, frowning at Antorell.

"Very clumsy," Zemenar agreed.

"I don't know what Kazul will say when she finds out about it," Cimorene went on. "Really, it is *too* bad of you. I did ask you not to touch anything, you know."

"Yes, you did," Zemenar said. "And I wouldn't like to think that we had gotten you in trouble. Perhaps it would be best if you didn't mention to Kazul that we were here at all."

"I suppose I could do that," Cimorene said in a doubtful tone.

"Of course you can," Antorell said encouragingly. "And I'll come back in a few days, to make sure everything's all right."

"I think it's time we were on our way," Zemenar said, giving his son a dark look. "Thank you for showing us around, Princess."

Cimorene escorted them out of the cave and made sure they had left, then hurried back to the library. She spent the next several hours poring over the middle parts of the *Historia Dracorum,* trying to figure out what Zemenar had been looking at. She was still there when Kazul arrived home and called for her.

"That wizard Zemenar finally came, and he brought his son along with him," Cimorene said as she came out of the library.

"I know," said Kazul. Her voice sounded a little thick, as if she had a cold. "I could smell them the minute I came in."

"Is that why you sound so odd?" Cimorene asked. "You're not going to sneeze, are you?"

"I don't think so," Kazul replied. "Don't worry about it. I'll have plenty of time to turn my head away."

"I *wish* I could get hold of some hens' teeth," Cimorene said, frowning. "That fireproofing spell–"

"Have you looked in the treasure rooms?" Kazul asked.

"No," Cimorene replied, startled. She remembered seeing a number of jars and bottles of various shapes and sizes when she had been organizing the treasure, and none of them had been labeled. "I didn't think of it, and besides, it's your treasure."

"You're my princess, at least until someone rescues you or I decide otherwise," Kazul pointed out. "Go ahead and look, and if you find any hens' teeth, use them. Be careful when you're checking the jars, though. There are one or two with lead stoppers that shouldn't be opened."

"Lead stoppers," Cimorene said. "I'll remember."

"Good. Now, what did those wizards want?"

"I'm not sure." Cimorene explained everything that had happened, including how she had seen Zemenar closing the history book as she turned and how the two wizards had been perfectly willing to leave right after that. "But just before they disappeared, Antorell said he might come back another time," Cimorene concluded. "So I don't know whether they found what they were looking for or not."

"Do you know which part of the *Historia Dracorum* Zemenar was reading?" Kazul asked.

"Somewhere in the middle, a little past my bookmark," Cimorene replied. "I was just looking at it when you came in. It's the part about how the dragons came to the Mountains of Morning and settled into the caves and chose a king."

"That's the section where the *Historia* describes the Caves of Fire and Night, isn't it?" Kazul said.

Cimorene nodded. "There was a whole page about somebody finding a stone in the caves so that the dragons could pick a king. It didn't make much sense to me."

"Colin's Stone," Kazul said, nodding. "We've used it to choose our king ever since the first time. When a king dies, all the dragons go to the Ford of Whispering Snakes in the Enchanted Forest and take turns trying to move Colin's Stone from there to the Vanishing Mountain. The one that succeeds is the next king."

"What if there are *two* dragons strong enough to move it?" Cimorene asked curiously.

"It's not a matter of strength," Kazul said. "Colin's Stone isn't much larger than you are. Even a small dragon could carry that much weight twice around the Enchanted Forest without any trouble at all. But Colin's Stone has an aura, a kind of vibration. When you carry it, you can feel it humming through your claws, and the humming gets stronger the farther you go until your bones are shaking. Most dragons have to drop it or be shaken to pieces, but there's always one who is . . . suited to the stone. For that dragon, the stone's humming is just a pleasant buzz, so of course it's easy to get it to the Vanishing Mountain."

"You sound as if you've had experience," Cimorene said.

"Of course," Kazul responded matter-of-factly. "I was old enough to participate in the tests when the last king died." She smiled reminiscently. "I got farther than anyone expected me to, though I wasn't one of the top ten by any means."

Cimorene tilted her head to one side, considering. "I think I'm glad you didn't win."

"Oh? Why is that?" Kazul sounded amused.

"Because you wouldn't have had any use for a princess if you were the Queen of the Dragons, and if you hadn't decided to take me on, that yellow-green dragon Moranz would probably have eaten me," Cimorene explained.

"You mean, if I were the King of the Dragons," Kazul corrected her. "Queen of the Dragons is a dull job."

"But you're a female!" Cimorene said. "If you'd carried Colin's Stone from the Ford of Whispering Snakes to the Vanishing Mountain, you'd have had to be a queen, wouldn't you?"

"No, of course not," Kazul said. "Queen of the Dragons is a totally different job from King, and it's not one I'm particularly interested in. Most people aren't. I think the position's been vacant since Oraun tore his wing and had to retire."

"But King Tokoz is a male dragon!" Cimorene said, then frowned. "Isn't he?"

"Yes, yes, but that has nothing to do with it," Kazul said a little testily. " 'King' is the name of the job. It doesn't matter who holds it."

Cimorene stopped and thought for a moment. "You mean that dragons don't care whether their king is male or female; the title is the same no matter who the ruler is."

"That's right. We like to keep things simple."

"Oh." Cimorene decided to return to the original topic of conversation before the dragon's "simple" ideas confused her any further. "Why would the wizards be interested in Colin's Stone if it's only used for picking out the kings of the dragons?"

"I doubt that they are," Kazul replied. "However, Colin's Stone was found in the Caves of Fire and Night, and wizards have always been interested in the caves. But the dragons control most of them, and all the easy entrances are ours, so the wizards have never been able to find out as much as they would like. The *Historia Dracorum* is one of the few books that talks about the caves at all, and there aren't many copies. I'll wager Zemenar would have stolen it outright if he'd thought he could get away with it."

"I thought the dragons let wizards into the Caves of Fire and Night," Cimorene objected. "Why would Zemenar be poking through history books looking for information if he can just go and look at them whenever he wants to?"

"We don't let wizards visit the caves whenever they want," Kazul said. "If we did, they'd be running in and out all the time, and nobody would be able to breathe without sneezing. No, they're limited to certain days and times, and if they want to visit the Caves of Fire and Night otherwise, they have to use one of the entrances we don't control. Few of them try. The other ways of getting into the caves are very dangerous, even for wizards."

"Maybe they're looking for an easier way in."

"Mmm." Kazul did not seem to be paying much attention. She thought for a moment, then turned toward the cave mouth. "I'm going to go see Gaurim. Roxim said a book had been stolen from her library, and I want to know which one. I'll be back in a few hours."

"I think I'll go look at the *Historia Dracorum* again while you're gone," Cimorene said thoughtfully. "If there *is* something useful in it about the Caves of Fire and Night, maybe I can find it, now that I know what I'm looking for."

Cimorene spent the rest of the afternoon carefully translating the chapter that talked about the caves. She was disappointed to find that there was very little about the caves themselves, though what was there was interesting. The book told how the dragons had discovered the back way into the caves and described some of the things they had found in them–caverns full of blue and green fire, pools of black liquid that would cast a cloud of darkness for twenty miles around if you poured three drops on the ground, walls made of crystal that multiplied every sound a thousandfold, rocks that spurted fire when they were broken. Most of the rest of the chapter was about Colin's Stone, and how it was taken out of the caves by the first King of the Dragons.

Kazul returned just before dinner, and she and Cimorene compared notes. Cimorene told Kazul what she had learned from the chapter on the Caves of Fire and Night, and then Kazul explained what she had learned from Gaurim.

"The stolen book was *The Kings of the Dragons,* and the entire first section was about Colin's Stone and the Caves of Fire and Night," Kazul said. "And only a wizard could have gotten past the spells and safeguards Gaurim puts on her library. I think that settles it. The wizards are definitely collecting information about the Caves of Fire and Night."

"Then why do they keep looking at books of dragon history?" Cimorene asked. "It seems like a roundabout way of finding out whatever it is that they want to know."

"There isn't any other way to do it," Kazul said. "Nobody but dragons has ever had much to do with the caves, and no one has written much about them except in dragon histories. Even the wizards weren't particularly interested in them until a few years ago, except as a reliable route into the Enchanted Forest."

"But from what I've been reading in the *Historia Dracorum,* the caves sound fascinating," Cimorene said. "You mean to say that *no one* has ever written anything about the Caves of Fire and Night except dragons?"

"That's–" Kazul stopped suddenly, and her eyes narrowed. "No, that's *not* right. There was a rather rumpled scholar who talked his way into the caves a century or so back, and after he left he wrote an extremely dry book about what he found there. I'd forgotten about him."

"Do you have a copy?" Cimorene asked hopefully.

"No," Kazul said. "But I don't think the Society of Wizards does, either. There weren't very many of them printed, and a lot of those were lost in a flood a few years later. Some hero or other shoved a giant into a lake to drown him. The silly clunch didn't realize that if he put something that big into a lake, the water would have to go *somewhere.*"

"Well, that doesn't do us much good," Cimorene said. "It's nice that the Society of Wizards doesn't have a copy of that book, but if we can't get hold of one either–"

"I didn't say that," Kazul said. "I don't have a copy myself, but I know who does."

"Who?" Cimorene said impatiently.

"Morwen. I'm afraid you're not going to be able to work on that fireproofing spell of yours tomorrow. We're going to take a trip to the Enchanted Forest instead."

7

In Which Cimorene and Kazul Make a Journey Underground

Cimorene was surprised to hear that Kazul intended to take her along on the visit to Morwen, and she was not entirely sure she liked the idea. She had heard a great deal about the Enchanted Forest, and none of it was reassuring. People who traveled there were always getting changed into flowers or trees or animals or rocks, or doing something careless and having their heads turned backward, or being carried off by ogres or giants or trolls, or enchanted by witches or wicked fairies. It did not sound like a good place for a casual, pleasant visit.

On the other hand, it seemed unlikely that anything dreadful would happen to Cimorene if she were traveling with a dragon, and she was looking forward to seeing Morwen again. Besides, Cimorene was curious.

"And anyway," she said to herself, "Kazul says I'm going, and there's no point in worrying about it if I don't have any choice." Nevertheless, she decided to take one of the smaller magic swords along with her, if Kazul said it was all right. Cimorene saw no point in taking unnecessary chances.

Kazul had no objection, so Cimorene picked out a small, plain-looking sword in a worn leather scabbard that made the wearer invincible, and they started off. Cimorene had assumed that Kazul would fly through the pass, but Kazul said no.

"It's not that easy to get into the Enchanted Forest," she explained. "At least, not if you're trying to get in. Princes and youngest sons and particularly clever tailors stumble into it by accident all the time, but if one wants to go there on purpose, one has to follow the proper route."

"I didn't think dragons had that kind of problem," Cimorene said.

"Dragons don't," Kazul replied. "But you're not a dragon."

So instead of flying through the Pass of Silver Ice, Kazul led Cimorene through the tunnels. Cimorene had to walk very quickly to keep up, even though Kazul was moving slowly. It was not long before she was wishing that the tunnels were high enough for her to ride on Kazul's back. The route twisted around and up and back and forth and down and around again until Cimorene was thoroughly lost. Finally they came to a gate made of iron bars that completely blocked the passage. Cimorene studied it carefully, but she could see no sign of a handle or a lock.

"This is the entrance to the Caves of Fire and Night," Kazul said. "Be careful from here on, and don't wander away or you'll get lost."

Cimorene refrained from saying that as far as she was concerned, they were lost already. "How are you going to open it?" she asked instead.

"Like this," said Kazul.

"By night and flame and shining rock
Open thou they hidden lock.
Alberolingarn!"

As the sound of Kazul's voice died away, the iron gate swung silently open. "That's a very unusual opening spell," Cimorene commented, impressed.

"It wasn't always that complicated," Kazul said. She sounded almost apologetic. "I believe the first version was very simple, just 'Open sesame,' but word got around and we had to change it."

Cimorene nodded and followed Kazul through the gate and into the Caves of Fire and Night. For the first hundred yards or so, the only difference Cimorene could see between these caves and the ordinary tunnels on the other side of the gate was that the Caves of Fire and Night were warmer. Then, very suddenly, her lamp went out, plunging everything into complete and utter blackness.

Cimorene stopped walking immediately. "Kazul?"

"It's quite all right, Princess," Kazul's disembodied voice said from out of the darkness. "This happens all the time here. Don't bother trying to relight the lamp. Just put your hand on my elbow and follow along that way."

"All right," Cimorene said doubtfully. She groped with her free hand in the direction of Kazul's voice and scraped her knuckles on the dragon's scales. "Ow!"

"Take your time," Kazul advised.

"I'm ready," Cimorene said. Her right hand was pressed flat against the cool, rough-edged scales at the back of Kazul's left forearm. "Just don't move too fast, or I'll lose you or get stepped on or something."

Kazul did her best to oblige, but Cimorene still had difficulty in keeping up. She had to take at least three steps for every one of Kazul's, and it seemed that every time she moved her foot, she hit a rock or an uneven place in the tunnel floor. Then she would stumble, and her hand would scrape and slide against Kazul's scales, so that she was afraid she would lose contact with the dragon.

"Are you sure I shouldn't try and relight the lamp?" Cimorene asked after her fifth painful stumble-and-slide.

"Quite sure," Kazul said. "You see, it isn't–ah, there it goes." While Kazul was speaking, there was a flicker of light, and then the darkness rolled aside like a curtain being pulled. Cimorene found herself standing in a large cave whose walls glittered as if they were studded with thousands of tiny mirrors. The lamp in her left hand was burning cheerfully once more.

"*Was* it the lamp?" Cimorene asked after studying it for a moment. "Or was it me?"

"It was the caves," Kazul said. "That was one of the reasons they're 'of night' as well as 'of fire.' "

"Only *one* of the reasons?" Cimorene said thoughtfully. "I don't like the sound of that."

"You'll be quite all right as long as you're with me," Kazul assured her. "Very few things are willing to mess with a dragon, even in the dark. And the periods of darkness don't last long. It's because the magic of these caves doesn't affect us as much as other people, or so I'm told."

"You mean that blackness is likely to come back?"

Kazul nodded.

"Then let's get as far as we can before it does," Cimorene said, and started across the cave.

There were four tunnels leading out of the opposite side of the glittering cavern. Kazul took the second from the left without hesitating an instant.

"Where do all these tunnels go?" Cimorene asked, glancing at the other three openings as she followed Kazul.

"The one on the right end leads to a chain of caverns," Kazul said over her shoulder. "The first few are quite ordinary, but then you come to one full of hot sulfur pools. Some of the older dragons bathe there. They claim the water is good for rheumatism. Beyond that is a cave with molten silver dripping down the walls, and the chain ends at a deep chasm with a river of red-hot melted rock at the bottom."

"Doesn't sound very attractive," Cimorene commented.

"The dwarfsmiths find it very useful for forging magic swords," Kazul assured her. "The second tunnel on the right takes you into a maze. The tunnels and caverns constantly shift around, so that no matter how carefully you mark your way, you always get lost."

"Even dragons?"

Kazul nodded. "Though I believe there was one prince who managed to find his way out with a magic ball of string."

"Oh, bother!" said Cimorene. The lights had gone out again, just as they emerged into a small cave.

"It's quite all right. This part's easy," Kazul said.

"Next time I'm going to bring a cane," Cimorene muttered. "Where do the other tunnels lead?"

"The one on the far left goes through a couple of caverns that are pretty, but not very interesting. We're always chasing knights and princes out of it, though. They come for flasks of water from the bottomless pool at the far end."

"What does it do?" Cimorene asked. "Ow!" She had just banged her right elbow against the wall of the cave in the dark.

"It casts a cloud of darkness for twenty miles around when it's poured on the ground," Kazul replied.

"How useful," Cimorene muttered balefully, rubbing her elbow.

"And this tunnel leads to the Enchanted Forest, by way of the King's Cave," Kazul finished.

"Oh, good. I was hoping to see that," Cimorene said. The King's Cave was the chamber where the first King of the Dragons had found Colin's Stone, and the *Historia Dracorum* had not described it anywhere near well enough to suit Cimorene. "And here's the light coming back, thank goodness. Let's hurry before it goes again."

They went through three small caves and two more periods of blackness before they reached the King's Cave. Kazul pointed out various locations of interest, such as the wall of crystal with a chip in one corner where the Prince of the Ruby Throne had stolen a piece to make a magic ring and the jewel-studded cavern where the King of the Dragons met with people who needed impressing. There was one very eerie cave full of slabs of black rock. Most were standing on end, though a few had fallen over. Kazul said they were all enchanted princes.

"All of them?" Cimorene asked, appalled. There were at least forty of the stone slabs, and the cave was quite crowded.

Kazul shook her head. "No, the one on the end there is just an ordinary boulder."

"How did it happen?"

"The princes came to steal some of the Water of Healing from the well at the end of the cave," Kazul said. "There are two dippers by the well: one is tin, the other is solid gold and covered with jewels. The princes all tried to use the gold one, even though they'd been told that only the tin dipper would work. It's no more than they deserve."

Cimorene frowned, thinking of some of the princes she had known. "Well, I won't deny that they probably behaved foolishly, but–"

"Foolishly!" Kazul snorted. "Any reasonably well-educated prince ought to have sense enough to follow directions when he's on a quest, but all of these fellows were sure they knew better. If they'd simply done what they were told, they wouldn't be here."

"Still, turning them into slabs of stone forever seems a little extreme."

"Oh, they won't be stone forever," Kazul said. "Sooner or later someone will come along who has the sense not to improvise, and he'll succeed in getting the water. Then he'll use some of it to disenchant this lot, and the cave will be empty for a while until the next batch of young idiots starts arriving."

Cimorene felt better knowing that the princes would someday be freed, though she had sense enough not to try doing it herself. Since she had not been sent on a quest for the Water of Healing, it was highly unlikely that she would be able to disenchant the princes even if she succeeded in taking the water. And she knew enough about quests and enchantments and the obtaining of things with magical properties to know that she would probably get into a lot of trouble if she tried. So she tucked the matter into the back of her mind and followed Kazul through the stone-filled cavern. She was careful not to step on any of the fallen slabs.

Just outside the entrance to the next cave, Kazul stopped. "This," she said, "is the King's Cave. We have to cross it as quickly as we can. Don't stop in the middle, and don't say anything while we're inside. Understand? Good. Come on, then."

As soon as she stepped inside the cave, Cimorene understood the reason for Kazul's request for silence. The walls, the ceiling, and the floor were made of dark, shiny stone that multiplied and threw back echoes of even the smallest sound. The soft scraping of Kazul's scales against the floor sounded like thirty men sawing wood, and the tiny gasp Cimorene gave at the sight and sound of the cave was as loud as if she had shouted. Cimorene went on as quietly and carefully as she could.

Halfway across, she noticed the vibration. It began as a gentle and not unpleasant buzzing in her bones, unrelated to the loud and continually multiplying echoes of her passage, though it, too, grew stronger the farther into the cave she went. Kazul was in front of her now, and she saw the dragon's tail lash once, as if in pain or anger. Suddenly she remembered

Kazul's description of the aura that made it impossible for most dragons to carry Colin's Stone, and that this was the place where Colin's Stone had been found. No wonder Kazul was uncomfortable.

Cimorene found herself wishing she could stop and pay attention to the humming in her bones, but she remembered Kazul's directions and continued walking. She had nearly reached the exit when she saw a pebble about the size of her thumbnail, made of the same dark, shiny stone as the cavern walls. Kazul had said nothing about picking things up, so Cimorene veered a little to the right and scooped the pebble up as she passed. A moment later she was out of the cave.

"Phew!" said Kazul. "I'm glad that's over. From here on, it should be easy."

"Good," said Cimorene. She dropped the pebble into her pocket to look at it more closely later and followed Kazul down the narrow, winding tunnel.

8

In Which Cimorene and Kazul Pay a Call, and Cimorene Gets into a Fight

A few minutes later they came out of the Caves of Fire and Night into bright sunlight. Cimorene had to shade her eyes against the sudden glare. As her eyes adjusted, she saw a large clearing around the mouth of the cave. The ground was covered with short grass, so lush and dense that it made Cimorene think of green fur. Here and there a tiny flower twinkled among the blades of grass. At the edge of the clearing the forest began, but Cimorene could only make out the first row of trees. They were enormous, so large that they dwarfed even Kazul.

"Leave the lamp here," Kazul said. "There's no sense in carting it around the forest when we won't need it until we come back."

Cimorene set the lamp on the ground just inside the mouth of the cave. "Now what?" she said.

"Now we go to Morwen's," Kazul said. "And we'll get there more quickly if you ride. If you climb up on that rock over there, you ought to be able to get on my back without too much trouble."

"Are you sure you don't mind?" Cimorene said, scrambling up onto the rock Kazul had indicated.

"I wouldn't have suggested it if I minded," Kazul said. "Right there will be fine. You can hang onto the spike in front of you and you won't foul my wings if I have to take off suddenly."

Cimorene did not like the implication that there were things in the

Enchanted Forest that were nasty enough to make a dragon want to take off suddenly, but she did not say so. It was too late to back out, and she certainly wasn't going to wait at the mouth of the cave all alone while Kazul went off to visit Morwen. There was no reason to think that waiting would be any safer than going along.

As soon as Cimorene was settled, Kazul set off into the forest at a rapid pace. At first Cimorene had to concentrate on holding on, but after a while she began to get the hang of it. Soon she was able to look at some of the things they were passing. The trees were huge; Cimorene guessed that even if there were four of her, holding hands, she would not be able to reach all the way around one of the trunks. The ground was carpeted with bright green moss that looked even thicker than the grass in the clearing. Cimorene saw no flowers in it, but she spotted several bushes and a vine with three different colors of fruit.

Kazul changed course several times for no reason that Cimorene could see, but she did not like to distract the dragon by asking questions. They passed a mansion guarded by a fence made of gold and a short tower without any windows or doors. Then Kazul splashed through a shallow stream and made a sharp turn. The trees thinned a little, and Kazul stopped in front of a neat gray house with a wide porch and a red roof. Over the door was a black-and-gold sign in large block letters reading, "NONE OF THIS NONSENSE, PLEASE."

There were several cats of various sizes and colors perched on the porch railing or lying in the sun. As Cimorene dismounted, Kazul said to one of them, "Would you be good enough to tell Morwen that I'm here and would like to talk to her?"

The cat, a large gray tom, blinked its yellow eyes at Kazul. Then he jumped down from the porch rail and sauntered into the house, his tail held high as if to say, "I'm doing this as a particular favor, mind, and don't you forget it."

"He doesn't seem very impressed," Cimorene commented in some amusement.

"Why should he be?" Kazul said.

"Well, you're a dragon," Cimorene answered, a little taken aback.

"What difference does that make to a cat?"

Fortunately, Cimorene did not have to find an answer, for at that moment Morwen appeared in the doorway. She was wearing the same black robe she had worn when she visited Cimorene, or another one exactly like it, and she peered through her glasses with the air of someone studying an unexpected and rather peculiar puzzle.

"Good morning, Kazul," she said after a moment. "This is a surprise."

"Good," said Kazul. "If you aren't expecting us to be here, no one else is, either."

"That's the way of things, is it?" Morwen commented thoughtfully. "How much of a hurry are you in?"

"Not much of one, as long as no one knows we're here," Kazul replied.

"Then Cimorene had better get down and have something to drink," Morwen said in a tone that forbade contradiction. "There's cider, or goat's milk, though if you want that, you'll have the cats after you, or I can put a kettle on for tea. Good gracious, what have you done to your hand?"

While Morwen had been talking, Cimorene had turned and slid carefully down Kazul's side. It was a long slide, and when her feet hit the ground, she had to put out a hand to keep from falling. Morwen's exclamation made her blink in surprise, and she looked down. The palm of her right hand was covered with blood from half a dozen deep slashes and as many scrapes.

"Oh, dear," Cimorene said. "It must have happened in the caves, when it was so dark. I didn't realize. It doesn't hurt at all."

"Hurting or not, it needs attention," Morwen said firmly. "Come inside, and I'll see to it while Kazul tells me why you're here. You'll have to go around back this time," she added, turning to Kazul. "The front steps won't take the weight. A gnome stole one of the supports, and I haven't had time to get it fixed yet. Pesky creatures–they're worse than mice."

"Don't the cats keep the mice away?" Cimorene asked, mildly puzzled.

"Yes, but they don't do a thing about gnomes, which is why gnomes are worse. Mind the step."

Kazul started walking while Morwen shooed Cimorene up the wooden steps and into the house. Several of the cats eyed Cimorene curiously as she passed, and a tortoiseshell kitten got up and followed her in.

The front door led into a large, airy room with an iron stove in one corner. There was a good deal of furniture, but everything except the table and the stove had at least one cat on top of it. Morwen frowned at a fat and fluffy Persian that was sitting on one of the chairs. The cat stood up, yawned, gave its front paws a cursory lick or two just to show that this was all his own idea, and jumped down onto the floor. As Cimorene sat down in the vacated chair, there was a knock at the wooden door on the opposite side of the room.

"That'll be Kazul," Morwen said. She crossed to the door and opened it. "Come in. I'll get you some cider as soon as I've seen to Cimorene's hand."

Morwen's back door did not seem to get any larger, and Kazul certainly did not get any smaller, but when she put her head through the doorway, her scales did not even scrape the sides. The rest of her followed with no apparent difficulty, and somehow there was plenty of room in the kitchen even after she got inside.

Kazul settled down along the far wall, where she would be out of the way, and as soon as she stopped moving, six cats jumped onto various portions of her tail, back, and shoulders. Neither Kazul nor Morwen seemed to notice. Morwen took a small tin box from a shelf beside the stove and sat down at the table beside Cimorene. "Now, tell me what you're here for," she said, taking a roll of linen and two jars of ointment out of the box. "Apart from my cider, I mean."

"Cimorene had some interesting visitors yesterday," Kazul said.

"If they were interesting, they can't have been knights," Morwen commented.

"They weren't," Kazul said. "They were wizards, and they went to a lot of trouble to get a look at my copy of the *Historia Dracorum*. The part that describes the Caves of Fire and Night."

"And you think that's why they've been sniffing around the Mountains of Morning for the past six months," Morwen said. "How did you find out what they were looking at? Or did they ask permission?"

"I don't think Zemenar would ask permission for anything even if he was sure he'd get it," Cimorene said. "He'd consider it beneath him. No, I saw him shut the book, and he was only a little further along from where I'd left my bookmark. Ow! That stings."

"Good," Morwen said. "It's supposed to." She closed the jar of salve she had been smearing on Cimorene's palm and began wrapping the injured hand in the linen bandage. "Did Zemenar get what he was after?"

"I don't think so," Cimorene said. "He said he wanted to come back for another visit, and I don't think he'd have done that if he'd found whatever he was looking for."

"That seems like a reasonable assumption," Morwen said. "Though wizards aren't always reasonable. There, that should take care of things. Don't take the bandage off for at least four days, and if you're going to cook anything that has fennel in it, stir it left-handed."

"Zemenar's interest in the *Historia Dracorum* isn't the only thing that points to his curiosity about the Caves of Fire and Night," Kazul said, and explained about the book that had been stolen. "There have been other incidents as well, and nearly all the wizards we've caught poking around have been somewhere in or near the caves. That's why no one thought much about it at first. Ever since King Tokoz made that agreement with the Society of Wizards, they've been claiming they're supposed to have more time in the caves than we're willing to give them. Everyone thought this was more of the same."

"Not everyone," Morwen said, giving Kazul a sharp look.

"I am widely considered to be unduly suspicious of everyone and everything," Kazul said in a dry tone. "Particularly wizards."

"And what do your suspicions make of this business?"

"I think Zemenar is trying to find out something about the Caves of Fire and Night," Kazul said. "Something he hasn't been able to learn from visiting the caves in person, hence his recent interest in histories that describe the caves, however briefly."

"And you're hoping I have something in my library that will help you figure out what it is," Morwen concluded.

"I don't hope," Kazul said. "I know. Unless someone has run off with your copy of DeMontmorency's *A Journey Through the Caves of Fire and Night.*"

"If someone has, he'll regret it," Morwen said. "Wait here, and I'll check." She rose and went out. Through the doorway Cimorene could see a room full of tall, dark-stained shelves.

Cimorene blinked. "Isn't that the door you came in through?" she asked Kazul.

Kazul nodded. "Of course."

"I thought it led out into Morwen's yard."

"It leads wherever Morwen wants it to lead," Kazul said.

"I see," said Cimorene, wishing her father's court philosopher were there. He was very pompous and stuffy, particularly about magic, which he claimed was 90 percent trickery and the rest illusion. Cimorene had found him very trying. Dealing with Morwen's door would probably have given him a headache.

Morwen came back into the kitchen holding a thin red book. "Here it is. I'm sorry it took me so long to find it, but the nonfiction isn't organized as well as it should be yet."

Kazul surged to her feet, shedding cats in all directions. The cats gave her reproachful looks and then stalked out the front door with affronted dignity. Kazul paid no attention. She curled her head around to peer at the book over Morwen's shoulder.

"I suppose you'll want to borrow it?" Morwen said.

"I certainly do," Kazul said. "Is there a problem?"

"Only if it gets stolen," Morwen said. "There are very few of these around, and I'm not sure I could replace it."

"I'll keep it in the vault with the treasure," Kazul promised. "Zemenar won't think to look for it there, and even if he does, he won't get in. I've got enough anti-wizard spells on the door to stop the whole Society. They can't get in unless someone invites them."

"All right," Morwen said, handing the book to Kazul. "Is that everything you came for?"

"No," said Kazul. She looked at Morwen with limpid eyes and went on in a plaintive tone, "I still haven't had any cider."

Morwen laughed and went to one of the cupboards. She pulled out two mugs and a large mixing bowl and filled them with an amber-colored liquid she poured from a heavy-looking pottery jug. She set the mixing bowl in front of Kazul and gave one of the mugs to Cimorene, then sat down with the second mug herself.

They were in Morwen's kitchen for over an hour, drinking cider and speculating about what the wizards were up to. After a while several of the cats came back, and Morwen gave them a dish of goat's milk, which soothed their ruffled feelings somewhat.

"How is that fireproofing spell of yours coming?" Morwen asked as she returned to the table.

"I have everything I need except the powdered hens' teeth, and I'm beginning to think I'm never going to find any," Cimorene said. "Kazul has offered to let me look through the jars in the treasury, but if there isn't any there, I don't know where I'll look next."

"Really," Morwen said, giving Kazul a sharp look. "Well, if you can't find any hens' teeth, you could try substituting snake fingernails or the hair from a turtle's egg. I wouldn't try it except as a last resort, though. Altering spells is a very tricky business."

At last they had to leave. Kazul went out the same way she had come in while Cimorene watched in fascination. Then Cimorene and Morwen went onto the front porch. Kazul sidled up to the house, and Cimorene stood on the porch railing to climb onto her back. The cats were seriously affronted by this maneuver and expressed their displeasure in reproachful glances and low yowls.

"Don't take any notice," Morwen said. "It only encourages them."

Cimorene nodded. "Thank you for everything."

"You're quite welcome," Morwen answered. "Don't wait too long to come again."

"You'd better take this, Princess," Kazul said, reaching back over her shoulder to hand Morwen's book to Cimorene. "I can't carry it and run at the same time."

Cimorene took the book and tucked it into her pocket. "I'm all set," she said, and they started off.

Cimorene enjoyed the ride back to the Mountains of Morning. She was now sufficiently accustomed to riding on a dragon to be able to concentrate on looking at the forest as it flashed past. The trees seemed almost identical to one another, but Cimorene spotted quite a few odd-looking bushes and vines, and twice she thought she saw small faces staring out at her from among leafy branches.

They reached the threshold of the caves much sooner than Cimorene expected. Kazul waited while she slid to the ground, then said, "The entrance is a little narrow. I'll go first and make sure there's nothing unpleasant waiting for us."

Cimorene nodded, and Kazul vanished into the cave. Before Cimorene could follow, she heard a shrill cry above her. She looked up and saw an enormous white bird plummeting toward her, its clawed feet extended to attack. For an instant, Cimorene was frozen by surprise and fear. Then she ducked and reached for her sword.

She was almost too slow. The bird was on top of her, shrieking and slashing, before she had done more than grasp the hilt of her weapon. But the sword seemed to leap out of the scabbard as soon as she touched it, and she swung clumsily as she rolled aside. She did not expect to do any damage, just to force the bird to back away a little, but she felt the sword connect and heard a wail of pain from the bird. Thanking all her lucky stars individually and by name, Cimorene twisted and scrambled to her feet, sword ready.

There was nothing for her to guard against. The sword stroke had been more effective than she realized. The bird was dying. As she stared at it, it raised its head.

"*You* killed me?" the bird said incredulously. "But you're a *maiden.*"

"Actually, she's a princess," Kazul's voice said from behind Cimorene. "*My* princess, so you'd have been in even bigger trouble if you'd succeeded in carrying her off."

"I don't think I could have done it if I hadn't had a magic sword," said Cimorene, who was beginning to wish she hadn't. She had never hurt anyone before, and she didn't like it.

"Just my luck," the bird said disgustedly. "Oh, well, fair's fair. You killed me, so you get my forfeit."

"You're not dead yet," Cimorene said. "If you'll let me near, I can try to stop the bleeding–"

"Not a chance," the bird said. It was beginning to sound rather faint. "Do you want the forfeit or don't you?"

"Take it," Kazul advised.

Cimorene said nothing, and after a moment the bird said, "All right, then. Under my left wing, you'll find three black feathers. If you drop one and wish to be somewhere else, you'll find yourself there in the twinkling of an eye. Any questions?"

"Can I take anyone else with me?" Cimorene asked, thinking that if the bird was so determined to give her the feathers, she might as well cooperate with it.

The bird looked at her with respect. "Will wonders never cease. For once a human with sense is getting the forfeit. Yes, you can take someone with you, as long as you're touching him. Same for objects; if you can carry it, you can take it with you. You get one trip per feather. That's all."

"But–" said Cimorene, and stopped. The bird's head had fallen back, and it was clearly quite dead.

"Don't feel too bad," Kazul said perceptively. "If it had succeeded in carrying you off, it would have fed you to its nestlings."

"Fed me to its nestlings?" Cimorene discovered that she had lost her sympathy for the dead bird. "What a horrid thing to do!" She hesitated. "Won't the nestlings starve, now that the bird is dead?"

"No, one of the other birds will take over the chore of feeding them for a few weeks until they're big enough to catch their own food," Kazul said. "Now, clean that sword and take your feathers, and let's get going. I want to have a look at that book of Morwen's."

Cimorene nodded and did as she was told. The three black feathers were right where the bird had said they would be, and she put them in her pocket with Morwen's book and the black pebble from the Caves of Fire and Night. She wiped the sword on the grass several times, then finished cleaning it with her handkerchief. When she finished, she left the handkerchief beside the dead bird and followed Kazul into the Caves of Fire and Night.

9

In Which Therandil Is a Dreadful Nuisance, and Cimorene Casts a Spell

The rest of the trip home was uneventful. Passing through the King's Cave seemed easier going in the opposite direction, and the impenetrable darkness only descended once. As soon as they arrived, Kazul took the book Morwen had lent them and curled herself around a rock just outside the mouth of the cave to study it while Cimorene made dinner. She pored over the book all evening, and Cimorene found it fascinating to watch the dragon delicately turning pages with her claws. Early the next day Kazul went off to consult with Roxim.

Cimorene was rather stiff from all the dragon-riding she had done the previous day, so she decided not to do any more cleaning. Instead, she spent the morning in Kazul's treasure room, sorting through likely looking bottles and jars for those that might possibly contain powdered hens' teeth. Remembering Kazul's advice, she started by setting aside all the bottles she could find that had lead stoppers. Since the light was not very good, she took the jars and bottles that looked as if they might be worth investigating and piled them in her apron, so as to carry them outside more easily.

She had nearly finished sorting when she heard a voice calling faintly in the distance.

"Bother!" she said. "I *did* hope they'd leave me alone a *little* longer."

She bundled the last five bottles into her apron without looking at them and, not forgetting to lock the door behind her, hurried out through the maze to see who was shouting for her this time.

It was Therandil.

"What are you doing here?" Cimorene said crossly. "I told you I wasn't going to be ready to be rescued for at least a month!"

"I was worried," Therandil said. "I heard that you'd broken a leg, but you look fine to me."

"Of course I haven't broken a leg," Cimorene said. "Where did you get that idea?"

"Some knight at the inn at the foot of the mountain," Therandil replied. "He was up yesterday, talking to the princess he's trying to rescue, and he came back and warned everybody not to bother with the princess that was captured by the dragon Kazul. Well, I knew that was you, so I asked why, and he said his princess told him you'd broken your leg and wouldn't be able to walk for months."

Cimorene smiled slightly. Alianora had apparently gone through with her plan to tell Hallanna about Cimorene's "twisted ankle," and Hallanna had decided to improve the story a little in hopes of reducing the competition. "Somebody must have gotten mixed up," Cimorene said gently. "You can stop worrying. I'm fine. Is that all you came for? These jars are getting heavy, and I've got work to do."

"Cimorene, we have to talk," Therandil said in a heavy, deep voice.

"Then we'll have to do it while I work," Cimorene declared. She turned on her heel and marched into the kitchen, full of annoyance. She had been feeling almost friendly toward Therandil–he *had* been worried about her, after all–until he said he wanted to talk. Cimorene was quite sure that what he wanted to talk about was rescuing her, and she was annoyed with him for being so stupidly stubborn and annoyed with herself for being annoyed when he was only trying to do the best he could.

Therandil followed her into the kitchen. "What *is* all that?" he asked as Cimorene put the apron full of jars on the kitchen table and began lining them up.

"Some things I'm checking for Kazul," Cimorene said. She picked up a small jar made of carved jade and pried the lid off. It was half full of green salve. Cimorene put the lid back on and set the jar aside. "What was it you wanted to talk about?" she asked, reaching for another jar.

"You. Dragons. Us. That looks interesting. Can I help?"

"As long as you don't break anything," Cimorene said. "Some of these are very fragile." Maybe opening jars would make him forget about *You. Dragons. Us,* for a while.

"I'll be very careful," Therandil assured her. "This one looks like metal. I'll start with that, shall I?" He picked up one of the larger jars, made of beaten copper with two handles. He frowned at the top, then reached for his dagger, and as he tilted the jar, Cimorene saw that the neck was stopped up with lead.

"Not that one!" she said quickly. She didn't remember picking out that particular jar. It must have been one of the last four or five that she'd scooped up when she heard Therandil calling.

"Why not?" Therandil said, sounding rather hurt. "I said I'd be careful." The tip of his dagger was already embedded in the lead.

"Kazul said to leave the ones with lead stoppers alone," Cimorene said. "So put it back."

"If you insist," Therandil said, shrugging. He pulled on his dagger, but it was stuck fast in the lead. "Drat!" he said, and twisted the handle. The dagger came free, and the lead stopper came along with it.

"I should have known," Cimorene said in a resigned tone.

A black cloud of smoke poured out of the jar. As Cimorene and Therandil watched, it condensed into a dark-skinned giant wearing only a turban and a loincloth. He was more than twice as tall as Therandil, and the corners of his mouth were turned down in a stern frown.

"What is it?" whispered Therandil.

"Trouble," said Cimorene.

"Thou speakest truly, O Daughter of Wisdom," said the giant in a booming voice that filled the cave. "For I am a jinn, who was imprisoned in that jar, and I am the instrument of thy death and that of thy paramour."

"My *what?*" Cimorene said, outraged.

"Thy lover," the jinn said uncomfortably. "The man who stands beside thee."

"I know what you *meant,*" Cimorene said. "But he isn't my lover, or my fiancé, or my boyfriend or anything, and I refuse to be killed with him."

"But Cimorene, you know perfectly well–" Therandil started.

"You hush," Cimorene said. "You've made enough of a mess already."

"If he is not thy paramour, nor any of those other things, then what is he?" the jinn asked suspiciously.

"A nuisance," Cimorene said succinctly.

"Cimorene, you're not being very kind," Therandil said.

"What he is matters not," the jinn said grandly after a moment's heavy thought. "It is enough that thou and he shall die."

"Enough for whom?" Cimorene said.

The jinn blinked at her. "For me. 'Tis my will that thou and he shall die by my hand. Thou hast but to choose the manner of thy death."

"Old age," Cimorene said promptly.

"Mock me not! Thou and he shall die, and by my hand, ere this day draws to its close!" the jinn cried.

"Do you suppose he means it?" Therandil said nervously.

"Why would he keep bellowing it at us if he didn't mean it?" Cimorene said. "Do be quiet, Therandil."

Therandil lowered his voice. "Should I offer to fight him, do you think?"

"Don't be silly," Cimorene said. She saw that Therandil was distressed, so she added, "You came up here to fight a dragon. You aren't prepared for a jinn, and nobody could reasonably expect you to challenge him."

"If you say so," Therandil said, looking relieved.

Cimorene turned back to the jinn and saw that he, too, was looking perturbed. "What's the matter with you?" she said crossly.

"Dost thou not wish to know *why* I will kill thee?" the jinn asked plaintively.

"What difference does it make?" Cimorene said.

"Yes, actually," Therandil said at the same time.

"Therandil!" Cimorene said in exasperation. "Shut *up!*"

"Hear my story, O luckless pair!" the jinn said with evident relief. "I am one of those jinn who did rebel against the law of our kind, and for my crimes I was sentenced to imprisonment in this bottle until the day should come when human hands would loose me. As is the custom of my people, I swore that whoso should release me during the first hundred years of my imprisonment I would make ruler of the earth; whoso should release me during the second hundred years I should make rich beyond all dreams of men; whoso shall release me during the third hundred I should grant three wishes; and whoso should release me after any longer span of time I should grant only the choice of what death he would die."

"You're going to kill us because it's *traditional?*" Cimorene asked.

"Yes," the jinn said. His eyes slid away from Cimorene's, and she frowned suddenly.

"Just how long were you in that jar?" she demanded.

"Uh, well, actually . . ." The jinn's voice trailed off.

"How long?" Cimorene insisted.

"Two hundred and seventeen years," the jinn admitted. "But nobody *ever* releases a jinn before the three hundred years are over."

"You're trying to get around your oath!" Therandil said, plainly shocked by the very thought. "You pretended you had to kill us so you wouldn't have to give us the wishes!"

"No!" the jinn said. "Thinkest thou that the granting of wishes alone would so trouble me? Needs must I kill thee and thy fair companion, for I cannot return home and say that thou didst release me and I left thee living!

I would be a laughingstock. Never in three thousand years has such a thing occurred!"

"Then you shouldn't have sworn an oath," Therandil said sternly.

"I had to!" the jinn said miserably. "It is the custom of our kind. 'Twould be . . . 'twould be . . ."

"Improper?" Cimorene murmured.

" 'Twould be improper to do otherwise," the jinn said, nodding. "But now thou hast found me out, and what am I to do? If I kill thee, it will violate my oath; if I kill thee not, the remainder of my life will be a torment."

"You could go back in the jar for another eighty-three years," Cimorene suggested delicately.

"I could . . . go back?" The jinn blinked at her for a moment. "I could go back. I could go back!"

"And in eighty-three years we'll both be dead of old age," Cimorene said. "Since that was my choice of death, your oath will be fulfilled and you can go straight home without killing anyone else or giving them any riches or power or anything."

"Truly, thou art a jewel among women and the very Queen of Wisdom's daughters!" the jinn said happily. "Thou hast found the perfect solution to my difficulties!"

"Wait a minute!" Therandil said. "What about those wishes?"

"Therandil!" Cimorene said in a shocked tone. "I'm surprised at you! How can he give us wishes if he's going back in the jar for eighty-three years? It wouldn't be right at all."

Therandil frowned. "Are you sure? After all, we *did* let him out during his third hundred years."

"I suppose I could let thee have one wish at least, in token of my thanks for thy help," the jinn said. "As long as thou dost not tell anyone."

"I wouldn't dream of it," Therandil assured him. "And my wish is to defeat a dragon and win his princess's hand in marriage!"

The jinn waved a dark hand over Therandil's head. "There! When next thou dost fight a dragon, thou shalt surely defeat him. And thou?" he said, turning to Cimorene.

"I could use some powdered hens' teeth," Cimorene said.

The jinn blinked in surprise, but he waved his hand again, his face a mask of concentration. Then he bowed and handed Cimorene a fat brown jar. "There's thy desire. Farewell!" With an elaborate salaam, the jinn dissolved back into a cloud of smoke that poured back into the copper jar from which it had come. Cimorene leaned over and plucked the lead stopper from the end of Therandil's knife. She jammed it back into place and heaved a sigh of relief.

Therandil was not paying attention. "What did you want something like that for?" he asked, looking at the jar of hens' teeth and wrinkling his nose in distaste.

"I don't believe I shall tell you," Cimorene said, putting the jar carefully into one of her apron pockets. "It has nothing to do with you."

"Nothing to do with me? I like that!" Therandil said indignantly. "I'm going to marry you, just as soon as I beat that dragon of yours."

"I don't think you're going to beat Kazul," Cimorene said in a considering tone.

"But that jinn just said–"

"He said that if you fight a dragon, you'll defeat him. But Kazul is a her, not a him," Cimorene pointed out. "And you ought not to be trying to rescue me anyway."

"Why not?" Therandil asked truculently.

"Because there are other princesses who've been captives of dragons for much longer than I have, and they have seniority," Cimorene explained.

"Oh," said Therandil, looking considerably taken aback. "How do you know?"

"They came to visit and told me all about it," Cimorene said. "I think you should try for Keredwel. She's from the Kingdom of Raxwel, and her hair is the color of sun-ripened wheat, and she wears a gold crown set with diamonds. You ought to get along with her very well."

Therandil brightened perceptibly at this description but said, "But everyone expects me to rescue *you.*"

"As long as you defeat a dragon and rescue a princess, no one will care," Cimorene said firmly. "And Keredwel will suit you much better than I would."

"Are you sure her dragon isn't female, too?"

"Positive," Cimorene said. "Gornul's cave is two down and three over. If you follow the path outside, you can't miss it. He ought to be there now, and if you leave right away, you'll be able to get everything settled before dinner."

"All right, then," Therandil said. "As long as you're sure you don't mind."

"Not at all," Cimorene assured him fervently. She saw him to the mouth of the cave and pointed him toward Gornul's cave, then returned to the kitchen. She gathered up the jars and bottles she had been planning to check, except for the copper jar with the jinn inside, and took them back to the treasure vault. Then she fetched an ink pot, a quill pen, and a sheet of paper from the library and began writing out a warning to attach to the copper jar. She didn't want anyone else to open it until the eighty-three years were over and the jinn could go home without killing anyone.

She was just finishing when she heard Alianora's voice calling from the rear of the cave. "I'm in the kitchen!" she shouted. "Come on back!"

"You're always in the kitchen," Alianora said when she poked her head through the door a moment later. "Or the library. Don't you ever do anything but cook and read?"

"Look at this, Alianora," Cimorene said, handing her the warning she had been writing. "Do you think it's clear enough?"

" 'WARNING: This jar contains a jinn who will kill you if you let him out too soon. Do not open until at least one hundred and five years after the date when the Citadel of the Yellow Giant was destroyed,' " Alianora read aloud. "That's, let's see, eighty-four years from now. It seems clear to me. You'd have to be pretty stupid to ignore a warning like that."

"Maybe I ought to show it to Hallanna and see what she says," Cimorene said, frowning. "I wouldn't want anyone getting into trouble by accident, just because I didn't make it plain."

"It's plain, it's plain," Alianora said. "Cimorene, what on *earth* have you been doing? How do you know there's a jinn in this bottle?"

"Therandil," Cimorene said, waving a hand expressively. "I was looking through some of the bottles from Kazul's treasure room, to see if any of them happened to have hens' teeth in them, and Therandil came in and wanted to help."

"And he opened it?" Alianora said. "Oh, dear."

"Exactly," said Cimorene. "But it came out well in the end. I think I've gotten rid of him for good. I sent him off to rescue Keredwel."

"You *did?* What if he doesn't beat Gornul?"

"Oh, he'll win. The jinn gave him a wish, and he wished to defeat a dragon." Cimorene looked apologetically at Alianora. "I suppose I ought to have sent him to rescue you, but . . ."

"That's quite all right," Alianora said hastily. "Getting rid of Keredwel will help a lot. And after everything you've told me about Therandil, I don't think I'd want to have him rescue me."

"That's what I thought," Cimorene said. "Oh, and I got the jinn to give me some powdered hens' teeth, so we can finally try that fireproofing spell."

"Good," Alianora said. "Let's do it right now!"

So Cimorene got out the spell and the ingredients she had collected, and she and Alianora spent the next hour on various necessary preparations. First they had to boil some unicorn water and steep the dried wolfsbane in it. Then the mixture had to be strained and mixed with the hippopotamus oil and the powdered hens' teeth. Cimorene did most of that, while Alianora ground up the blue rose leaves and the piece of ebony.

Grinding the ebony took a long time, but fortunately they didn't need much. When Alianora finally had enough, Cimorene mixed it with the blue rose leaves and more of the unicorn water in one of Kazul's recently shed scales. Each mixture had to be stirred three times counterclockwise with a white eagle feather. Then Alianora dipped the point of her feather in her mixture and began drawing a star on the floor of the cave.

"Is this going to be big enough for both of us?" she asked, scratching busily at the stone with the tip of the feather.

"I think so," Cimorene answered. "Don't try to make it too big, or you'll run out of liquid and we'll have to start over."

Alianora did not run out, though she had used nearly all her mixture by the time she finished. "There!" she said. She sat back on her heels and studied her diagram to make sure there were no gaps, then set her dragon scale and feather aside and stood up. "Your turn."

"First we have to get into the center of the star," Cimorene reminded her. "Be careful not to smudge the lines!"

"Smudge them, after all that work?" Alianora said in tones of mock horror. She lifted her skirts and stepped carefully into the middle of the diagram. Cimorene followed, carrying a small mixing bowl half full of something that looked like brown sludge with a white eagle feather sticking out of one side. "It smells awful," Alianora said, grimacing.

"It doesn't matter what it smells like, as long as the spell works," Cimorene said. "Ready?"

"As ready as I'm ever going to be," Alianora replied, shutting her eyes and screwing up her face as if she expected to have a glass of cold water poured over her head.

Cimorene plucked the eagle feather out of the bowl and raised it quickly over Alianora's head before it could drip on the floor. She let four large drops of the brown gunk fall onto Alianora's hair, then brushed the end of the feather across her forehead twice. She finished by drawing a circle with the feather on the palm of Alianora's left hand.

"That tickles!" Alianora complained.

"Well, you can do it to me now," Cimorene said.

Alianora took the bowl and feather from Cimorene.

"You're right," Cimorene said a moment later. "It does tickle."

"Now what?" Alianora said.

"Set the bowl down and shut your eyes," Cimorene instructed. When Alianora had done so, Cimorene closed her own eyes and said:

"Power of water, wind and earth,
Turn the fire back to its birth.
Raise the spell to shield the flame
By the power that we have tamed."

"Oh!" said Alianora. "That feels *peculiar*. Can I open my eyes now?"

"Yes," said Cimorene, opening her own. "We're finished."

"Did it work?" Alianora asked, cautiously opening one eye and squinting at Cimorene.

"Well, *something* happened. We both felt it," Cimorene said. "And your hair and forehead don't have brown gunk on them any more."

Alianora promptly opened both eyes and studied Cimorene. "Neither do yours. What does that mean?"

"It means we go back to the kitchen and test it," Cimorene said. She bent over and picked up the mixing bowl. "We'll clean up later. Come on."

10

In Which Cimorene and Alianora Conduct Some Tests and Disturb a Wizard

Back in the kitchen, Cimorene and Alianora quickly determined that the fireproofing spell had indeed worked. First Cimorene, then Alianora tossed a pinch of feverfew into the air and recited the spell-verse, then put a hand into a candle flame and held it there. Neither was burned at all, though Alianora claimed that the candle tickled almost as much as the eagle feather had done.

"How long does the spell last?" Alianora asked.

"I'm not sure, exactly," Cimorene said. "At least an hour, but I'll have to do some tests to pin it down beyond that. I hope Kazul gets back soon. I want to see if it works with dragon fire."

"You're going to have Kazul breathe fire at you, just to see if the spell works?" Alianora said, horrified. "What if it doesn't?"

"Then I'll talk to Kazul, and we'll go see Morwen, and the three of us will try to figure out what to change to make the spell work for dragon fire, too. Don't look at me like that. I'm not going to stand in front of Kazul and have her breathe fire at me. I'll just stick out a finger, the way we did with the candle."

This was not enough to convince Alianora, but Cimorene was determined. "The whole point of trying this spell was to make ourselves immune to dragon fire," she said. "If it doesn't work, I don't want to find out for the first time when one of Kazul's guests gets mad and breathes fire at me because he doesn't like the way I cooked his cherries jubilee."

Alianora had to admit that this was a good point, but she was still disposed to argue. The discussion was cut short by Kazul's return. At first the dragon was more inclined to agree with Alianora than with Cimorene, but after Cimorene proved her invulnerability to candle flames, lighted torches, and the fire she had built in the kitchen stove, Kazul agreed to the trial. She insisted, however, on working up to full firepower in gradual stages, and Cimorene was forced to agree.

Before they began, Cimorene threw another pinch of feverfew into the air and recited the couplet again, just to be sure the spell wouldn't wear off in the middle of the test. Then Kazul lowered her head nearly to the ground, and Alianora watched nervously as Cimorene lowered her hand slowly into various intensities of dragon flame. Finally, Cimorene stood right in front of Kazul while the dragon breathed her hottest. The spell worked perfectly every time.

"There!" Cimorene said when Kazul stopped at last. "Now we know it works. Aren't you glad?"

"I'm glad," Alianora said fervently. "And I hope I never have to watch anything like that again as long as I live. I didn't dare blink for fear you'd go up in smoke while my eyes were closed."

"Why don't you try it yourself?" Cimorene said mischievously.

"No!" said Alianora and Kazul together.

"Watching you was bad enough," Alianora went on with a shudder. "I believe it works. I don't see any reason for me to test it."

"Besides, I've done more than enough fire-breathing for one day," Kazul added. "I'm starting to get overheated."

"All right, if you don't want to, you don't have to," Cimorene said. "If we're all done, I'd better go tidy up."

Alianora stayed to help Cimorene finish cleaning up the traces of the spell, by which time she had calmed down considerably and was very nearly her usual self again. Cimorene gave her a pouchful of dried feverfew before she left and made her recite the words that activated the spell several times, to make sure she had memorized them correctly.

"Remember, you only have to repeat the first half of the verse to get the spell going, now that it's been set up," Cimorene said. "Can you do it?"

"It's only two lines, and they rhyme!" Alianora said, laughing. "How could I forget that? My memory isn't that bad!"

"Maybe not, but say it anyway," Cimorene said. Alianora laughed again and did so. At last she set off into the tunnels, and Cimorene went back to the main cave to see what Kazul and Roxim had found out about the Caves of Fire and Night.

Kazul was somewhat out of temper, and Cimorene thought privately that she had been telling the truth about getting overheated. Rather than annoy the dragon further, Cimorene asked if she could read the book Kazul had borrowed from Morwen.

"It's in the treasure room," Kazul said. "Read it there. And I hope you see something in it that we didn't."

Cimorene nodded, picked up her lamp, and hurried off before Kazul could change her mind. The book was lying near a pile of sapphires, next to an ornate gold crown. She picked it up, went over to the table, which was large and very sturdy because it was intended for counting piles of gold and silver coins, and sat down to read.

It was even dryer and duller than Kazul had said. There were a great many "mayhaps" and "perchances" and "wherefores," strung together in long, involved sentences that compared the strange and wonderful things in the caves to obscure philosophical ideas and odd customs from places Cimorene had never heard of. After a few pages, Cimorene put the book down and went and got a quill pen, an ink pot, and some paper, so that she could write down the things she thought were important. She didn't want to have to read *A Journey Through the Caves of Fire and Night* more than once.

For the next three days, Cimorene spent bits of her spare time in the treasure room, taking notes on the DeMontmorency. It took her that long because she could never manage to read for more than a little while without getting so bored that she nearly fell asleep. Her persistence gained her several pages of notes about the caves, but nothing that seemed as if it might be of particular interest to wizards.

Alianora came to see her a few days later, looking very cheerful.

"It worked!" she announced as she came into the library where Cimorene was going over her notes. "Keredwel's gone. Therandil rescued her, just the way you said he would."

"Good," Cimorene said. "I'm glad something is going right."

"What's the problem?" Alianora asked, seating herself on the other side of the table from Cimorene.

"This," Cimorene said, waving at the paper-covered table. "Kazul is sure that the key to what the wizards are after is somewhere in that dratted book she borrowed from Morwen. I copied out everything that looked interesting, but none of it seems like anything a wizard would care about."

"How do you know that?" Alianora asked curiously.

"I don't," Cimorene said. "I'm just guessing. That's the problem."

"Oh." Alianora picked up the sheet of paper nearest her and frowned at it. "What on earth does this mean?"

Cimorene looked at the page Alianora was holding. " 'Thus these

Caves of Fire and Night are, in some sense, indivisible, whereas the Caves of Chance are, by contrast, individual, though it is preposterous to claim that these descriptions are true of either group of caves in their entirety . . .' That's one of the bits I copied word for word; the whole book is like that. I think it means that if you have a piece of something magical from the Caves of Fire and Night, you can use it in a spell as if it were the whole thing."

"I can see why you wouldn't be sure," Alianora said. "Do you think it would help you figure things out if you stopped for a while?"

"I have stopped," Cimorene pointed out. "Or did you have something more specific in mind?"

"I'm almost out of feverfew," Alianora said, looking down at the table. "I was hoping you'd come with me to pick some more."

"You're almost *out?*" Cimorene said in surprise. "How did that happen?"

Alianora shifted uncomfortably. "I've been working that fireproofing spell every hour or so for the past two days," she admitted. "Woraug has been getting more and more unpredictable, and I don't feel comfortable otherwise. Hallanna was visiting yesterday when he came in–in the middle of the afternoon!–and he was roaring and dripping little bits of flame when he breathed. She was terrified, and I don't blame her. If it weren't for the spell, I'd be scared to death."

"What's the matter with him?"

"I don't know. He doesn't tell me anything about dragon politics or wizards or what he's been getting so worked up about. He's not like Kazul."

Cimorene frowned, considering. "Maybe Kazul will have some idea what's bothering him. I'll ask her this evening. In the meantime, let's go get that feverfew. You're right to say that I could use a break."

"Oh, good," said Alianora in tones of considerable relief. "I've never picked herbs before, and I'm not sure what feverfew looks like. I don't know what I'd have done if you'd said you wouldn't come."

Cimorene put her notes away and got two wicker baskets and a small knife from one of the storage rooms. "Up or down?" Alianora asked as they left the cave.

"Up," Cimorene said. "The other way is the ledge I told you about, and I wouldn't be surprised if bits of it are still invisible."

The path through the Pass of Silver Ice twisted and turned past the openings of other dragons' caves. Most of the rocks around the caves had scorch marks, and Cimorene and Alianora didn't see much growing among them.

"At this rate, we'll have to go nearly all the way to the Enchanted Forest to find any grass, much less herbs!" Alianora complained.

"Wait a minute!" Cimorene said. "Look over there, through that crack in the rocks. Doesn't that look like something green?"

Alianora's eyes followed Cimorene's pointing finger. "Yes," she said without enthusiasm. "It looks green."

The rock Cimorene had indicated was a large boulder at the bottom of a steep slope. The slope was covered with gravel and looked as if it would be impossible to climb down without skinning a knee or an elbow at the very least. The boulder itself was in two pieces, with just enough space between them for someone to squeeze through, provided the someone was not very large.

"Come on, let's get a better look," said Cimorene. She walked to the edge of the slope and wrapped her skirts tightly around her legs. Then she sat down with her basket in her lap and slid down the slope, raising an enormous cloud of dust and sounding like an avalanche in process. She reached the bottom in safety and stood up, brushing at her skirt. The dust was so thick that she could hardly see, and when she tried to call to Alianora, she coughed so hard that she could barely speak.

"Cimorene! Are you all right?"

"It's just the dust," Cimorene said in a muffled voice. She had taken out her handkerchief and put it over her mouth and nose to keep the dust out. It wasn't perfect, but it helped a great deal. "Come on, it's your turn."

"Are you sure we shouldn't just go around?"

"Stop stalling. It's not that bad."

"That's what you say," Alianora muttered, but she wrapped her skirts around her, clutched her basket, and slid down the slope. She made even more noise than Cimorene had. When she got to the bottom, she was coughing and choking. Cimorene handed her the handkerchief, and they waited for a moment while the dust settled.

Crawling through the split boulder was easier than they expected. The crevice was wider than it had looked from the path, and the bottom of the crack was so full of dust and gravel and dead leaves that it was almost flat. Cimorene and Alianora had to walk single file, and there were one or two spots where they had to turn sideways in order to get through, but it was not really difficult.

On the other side of the boulder, the two girls found a lush, green valley. It was bowl-shaped and not very large, but flowers and grasses stood waist-high between the random clumps of bushes that dotted the valley floor. A squirrel, which had been sunning itself on a ledge near the entrance, leaped for a small tree as Cimorene and Alianora appeared.

"My goodness!" Alianora said, looking around with wide eyes. "This place looks as if no one but us has ever been here before. There aren't even any scorch marks on the rocks."

Cimorene blinked. Alianora was right. Lichens covered the weathered gray rocks that rose above the valley, and small plants grew in cracks and crevices that showed no sign of the touch of dragon fire.

"That's odd," Cimorene commented.

"Why?" Alianora asked.

"Those mountains aren't tall enough to keep dragons from flying over, and they're right in the middle of the dragons' territory. So why haven't the dragons been here? They usually keep a close eye on everything that belongs to them."

"Maybe they have been here, but they never found anything to breathe fire at," Alianora said.

"Well, I'm going to ask Kazul about it when I get back," Cimorene said as she waded into the grass. "Why don't you take that side, and I'll look over here? We'll cover more ground that way."

"First you'd better show me what I'm looking for," Alianora said apologetically. "I'm afraid I couldn't tell feverfew from carrots if there was a dragon chasing me and my life depended on it."

Cimorene nodded, and they started off. They had not gone far when she saw a patch of the white button-shaped flowers she was looking for. "Here," she said, showing them to Alianora. "This is feverfew. The younger plants are the best, the ones that haven't blossomed yet."

Alianora studied the leaves and flowers with care. "I think I'll recognize it now."

They cut some of the plants, leaving those that were blooming.

"You find the next patch," Cimorene said as they started off again.

"Let's try over there," Alianora said, pointing.

They found several more patches of feverfew, and gradually their baskets began to fill. "I think this should be enough," Cimorene said at last. "Unless you think–"

"Cimorene!" Alianora hissed, clutching at Cimorene's arm. "There's someone behind that bush!"

Cimorene turned. A dark line snaked through the grass where something large had bent and broken the plants in passing. "You're right," she said, and started forward.

Alianora hung back, still holding Cimorene's arm. "You're not going to go *look,* are you?"

"How else are we going to find out who it is?" Cimorene asked reasonably. She shook off Alianora's hand. Quietly, she walked over to the clump of bushes and peered around it. Alianora followed with evident reluctance.

A man in blue and brown silk robes was crouched on the other side of the bush with his back toward Cimorene. He was stuffing saw-edged purple leaves into a small linen bag the size of Cimorene's hand. His hair was brown, and on the ground beside him lay a long, polished staff.

"Antorell?" Cimorene said in surprise.

The man snatched up his staff and straightened as if a bee had just stung him. It was indeed Antorell, and he did not look at all pleased to see her. He stuffed the linen bag quickly into his sleeve and said, "P-princess Cimorene! What brings you here?"

"I was about to ask you the same thing," Cimorene said.

"Wizards go where they wish, answering to no one," Antorell said, waving his free hand in a lofty manner.

"Maybe outside the Mountains of Morning they do, but around here they have to check with the dragons first," Cimorene said.

"You know nothing of the matter," Antorell said, looking very put out.

"Cimorene . . ." Alianora's tone was doubtful. "You know this person?"

"I'm sorry; I should have introduced you. This is Antorell, one of the wizards I told you about. Antorell, this is Princess Alianora of the Duchy of Toure-on-Marsh. At the moment, she's the princess of the dragon Woraug."

Alianora curtsied, murmuring something polite and inaudible. Antorell, who had stiffened in surprise when he realized that Cimorene was not alone, relaxed visibly. "Woraug's princess? That's all right, then. Though he really shouldn't have sent you."

"But Woraug didn't–ow!" said Alianora. The "ow" was because Cimorene had hastily kicked her ankle to keep her from telling Antorell too much.

"Didn't what?" Antorell asked, frowning suspiciously.

"Didn't know you were going to be here," Cimorene said.

"Well, of course he didn't know!" Antorell said, looking annoyed. "That's the whole point, after all."

Cimorene would have very much liked to ask him what the point was, but she was afraid it would make him suspicious again. "I don't understand," she said instead, batting her eyes at him.

"Of course not," Antorell replied in a condescending tone that made Cimorene's teeth hurt. "But it doesn't matter. I'm not annoyed with you."

"I'm so glad," Cimorene murmured.

Antorell gave her an oily smile. "In fact, there's no need for you to tell Woraug that you met me here."

"I wouldn't dream of it," Cimorene said with perfect truth.

"Excellent," Antorell said. "Then may I escort the two of you back to the path?"

Alianora looked hopefully in Cimorene's direction.

"But we can't leave yet," Cimorene said, opening her eyes very wide.

"We haven't picked any cornflowers or daisies." Behind her, she heard Alianora making a smothered, choking noise, as if she were trying very hard not to laugh.

"Daisies," Antorell said in a flat, incredulous tone. "You want to stay and pick daisies?"

Cimorene nodded vigorously. "And cornflowers, and flax, and all sorts of things," she said, waving her hand at the flowers blooming all around. "They'll look so pretty in a bowl of water in the kitchen."

"I'm sure you're right," Antorell said. He looked as if he would have liked to object, but couldn't think of anything to object to. "Perhaps I could help you?" he said reluctantly.

"Oh, we wouldn't dream of keeping you," Cimorene said.

Antorell was clearly reluctant to leave the two girls in the valley, but Cimorene did not give him much choice. After another minute or so of conversation, the wizard was forced to go. He did not use a vanishing spell but trudged away on foot. Cimorene watched him until he was out of sight among the bushes, wondering whether he had some special reason not to use spells in the valley or whether he simply didn't know the right spells to make himself vanish.

"That's a relief!" Alianora said. "Why did you insist on staying when it was so obvious that he wanted us to leave? I was afraid he was going to turn us into toads or something."

"I wanted to see what he was up to," Cimorene said. "And I don't think Antorell is a very good wizard. He probably couldn't manage anything worse than a squirrel."

Alianora did not appear to find this very reassuring. Cimorene checked to make sure Antorell was out of sight, then went over to the place where he had been standing when she peered around the bush. At first she did not notice anything unusual. Then she saw a purplish plant oozing sap from the places where several of its spiky, saw-toothed leaves had been broken off.

"Look at this."

"What is it?" Alianora asked.

"I don't know," Cimorene said absently. "I saw a couple of other plants like this while we were picking feverfew, but I thought they were just weeds."

"Maybe it is a weed."

"A wizard wouldn't sneak into the dragons' section of the Mountains of Morning just to pick weeds. They don't even use herbs to cast spells, so what does Antorell want with this prickly looking thing?"

Alianora shrugged. "Maybe he needs it for something he can't do with magic."

"I wonder what that would be?" Cimorene reached out and carefully broke off a spray of leaves. She wrapped them in her handkerchief and put the packet in her pocket. "Let's see if we can find out whether he picked anything else."

Antorell had left a dark trail of bent and broken plants to mark the way he had come, so his path was easy to follow. Cimorene and Alianora searched carefully along it for some way, looking for signs that the wizard had picked other herbs, but neither of them saw any.

"I don't think there's anything to find," Alianora said, pushing her apricot-colored hair out of her face. "And it's getting awfully warm."

"Have you noticed that there aren't any of those purple plants along here?" Cimorene said. "I'll bet that was all he wanted."

"Then let's leave before that wizard thinks to circle around to check on what we're doing," Alianora urged.

Cimorene doubted that Antorell would think of doing such a thing, but she nodded agreement, and the two girls left the valley. Alianora was quiet and thoughtful for most of the walk back to Kazul's cave. Cimorene was grateful for her silence. She had a lot to think about herself. From what Antorell had said, it seemed likely that Woraug was helping the wizards somehow, or at least that he had known what Antorell was looking for in the little valley. Cimorene found it difficult to imagine a dragon helping a wizard, but she couldn't say with certainty that it was impossible. And if Woraug *was* involved with Antorell and Zemenar, it might explain why he had been so touchy lately.

When they arrived back at the cave, Cimorene shook herself free of her preoccupation. She and Alianora unloaded their baskets and tied the herbs in bunches to hang in a dark corner of the kitchen to dry.

"How long will it be before I can use the feverfew?" Alianora asked worriedly.

"I'm not sure," Cimorene said in a considering tone. "It will take at least a week to dry thoroughly, but you might be able to use it in the spell before then. The directions don't say how dry the feverfew has to be. We could try it every day with a pinch of leaves from one of these bunches if you like."

Alianora nodded. "I really do need it."

"I wonder if it would work without being dried?" Cimorene said. She pulled a leaf from one of the hanging plants and shredded it carefully between her fingers, then tossed it up in the air and recited the rhyme. "There! Now, light a candle or another lamp or something."

Alianora had already lit a candle and set it on the table. Cimorene moved over and stuck her finger in the flame.

"I think it's working," she said, and moved the rest of her hand closer.

The sleeve of her dress caught fire. Cimorene hastily pulled her hand away from the candle and slapped at the flames, while Alianora snatched up a bucket of water from beside the sink and poured it over Cimorene's arm. The fire went out and so did the candle, and both Cimorene and Alianora got thoroughly soaked.

"Oh, dear!" Alianora said, ignoring her soggy skirts. "Cimorene, did you burn yourself?"

"No," Cimorene said, looking at her arm with a puzzled expression. "I didn't feel a thing. I thought the spell worked, but nothing caught fire when we tested it before."

"It must be because the feverfew is fresh instead of dried. And I *had* hoped that I'd be able to use it right away!"

"If you're that low on dried feverfew, take some of mine," Cimorene offered. "Kazul's not particularly irritable. I only need to keep a pinch or two in case of emergencies."

"Thank you!" Alianora said fervently, and Cimorene turned her soggy cuffs back and went to get the bottled spices.

11

In Which Kazul Is Unwell, and Cimorene Makes a New Acquaintance

Alianora decided to return home by way of the path outside instead of through the tunnels because it was such a nice day and she hoped the sun would dry her skirt. Cimorene watched her go, swinging her basket happily and humming a little, her confidence and good humor completely restored by the possession of the fat little packet of dried feverfew in her pocket.

"I wish I had as little to worry about," Cimorene muttered, thinking of Woraug and the wizards. She held the burned patch at the end of her sleeve up to get a better look at it in the sunlight and shook her head. Even the magic wardrobe would have a hard time fixing that. A puff of wind made her shiver in her wet clothes, and she turned to go back into the cave to change.

A dark shadow fell over Cimorene, and she stopped and looked up. "Kazul!" she said as the dragon landed on the open path beside her. "Am I glad to see you. Wait until you hear what's been happening!"

"You do appear to have had a rather strenuous day," Kazul said, eyeing Cimorene's wet, stained skirt and the blackened end of her right sleeve. "Nothing serious, I trust?"

"I'm not sure," Cimorene said. "Alianora and I went out to pick some feverfew, and we ran into that wizard Antorell."

"Where was this?"

Cimorene pointed. "Up that way. There's a little round valley off to one side that looks as if dragons never go there, and–"

"You found a wizard *there?*" Kazul sounded deeply disturbed. "How did he get in? How did *you* get in?"

"We climbed through a crack in a boulder," Cimorene said. "I don't know how Antorell did it. When he left, he was heading for the far side of the valley."

"This is serious," Kazul said, getting to her feet. "I'd better warn the King. He'll have to use the crystal now."

"You'd better hear the rest of it first," Cimorene said. "Antorell wasn't too happy to see us, but when he found out that Alianora was Woraug's princess, he relaxed. He seemed to think that Woraug had sent us."

"What?"

Cimorene involuntarily stepped back a pace at the anger in Kazul's voice. "He thought Woraug had sent us," she repeated, and gave a quick summary of her conversation with Antorell.

"Woraug!" Kazul's tail lashed, sweeping a small boulder from one side of the path to the other. "But Woraug's not a fool, and only a fool would let a wizard into that valley. Unless he was sure that they didn't know . . . What was Antorell doing?"

"Cutting plants," Cimorene said. "Or rather, cutting *a* plant. It didn't look as if he took more than one."

"He wouldn't need more than one, if it was the right one," Kazul said tensely. "What did he pick?"

"It was a prickly looking purple thing, with saw-edged leaves," Cimorene said, reaching into her pocket. "I didn't recognize it, but I thought you might, so I brought a piece back for you to look–"

"What?" Kazul roared.

Flame spurted from the dragon's mouth, enveloping Cimorene. Steam hissed from her wet skirt, and the thinner material of her sleeves vanished in a crackle of sparks. The handkerchief-wrapped spray of purple leaves, which she had just taken out of her pocket to show Kazul, disintegrated into a dark, greasy-looking cloud of smoke.

Cimorene stared at the ashes in her palm, feeling very, very glad that she had decided to test the way fresh feverfew would work in the fireproofing spell. She felt a little warm, and her clothes had been reduced to a few charred rags, but that was nothing compared to what might have happened.

"Now I understand why Alianora ran out of feverfew," she muttered.

A puff of wind brushed Cimorene's arms, and she heard a choking sound from Kazul. She looked up, expecting to find the dragon laughing at her remark, and her eyes widened. Kazul's head was thrown back, and her mouth was wide open, giving Cimorene an excellent view of the dragon's sharp silver teeth and long red tongue. Cimorene skipped backward out of reach; then she realized that the dragon was gasping for air.

"Kazul! What's the matter?"

"The smoke!" Kazul coughed. Her voice was so hoarse that it was hard for Cimorene to understand what she was saying.

"What can I do?" Cimorene said, trying not to feel frightened.

"Green jar–shelf in last treasure room," Kazul managed between coughs. "Hurry."

Cimorene was already running through the mouth of the cave as fast as her feet could carry her. She did not even pause as she snatched up her lamp from the floor just inside the door. It seemed to take forever to get through the twisty passages and the first two caves full of treasure. She skidded to a halt in the doorway of the third room and stood panting, scanning the walls for the shelf and the right jar. She found it quickly and ran back at once, the jar clutched tightly in her right hand.

The sound of Kazul's coughing grew louder as Cimorene sped back the way she had come. At the mouth of the cave, Cimorene paused and set down the lamp, then unscrewed the top of the green jar. Inside was a thick, emerald-colored liquid about the consistency of honey. She looked out at Kazul. The dragon's head jerked with each cough, and the scales on her neck were beginning to turn pink around the edges. For a long, careful moment Cimorene studied Kazul's movements. Then she leaned back and threw the emerald liquid, jar and all, into the dragon's open mouth just as Kazul took another gasping breath.

The jar landed on Kazul's tongue. The dragon's mouth closed, and she swallowed convulsively. Sudden silence descended.

"Are you all right now?" Cimorene asked after Kazul had taken several deep breaths without a renewed bout of coughing.

"I will be," Kazul said. She sounded exhausted, and her movements as she slid into the cave were slow and uncertain.

"What happened?" Cimorene said, backing out of the way so that Kazul would not have to exert herself to go around.

"I got a breath of the smoke when the plant in your hand burned," Kazul said as she settled to the floor just inside the entrance. "Lucky it was only a breath. I'll need a few days of rest, but that's better than being dead."

Cimorene stared at her, appalled. "What *was* that plant?"

"Dragonsbane," said Kazul. Her eyes closed and she slept.

Kazul continued to sleep for most of the next three days. She woke only long enough for Cimorene to pour a couple of gallons of warm milk mixed with honey down her throat from time to time before she lapsed back into unconsciousness. Cimorene was very worried, but there wasn't much that she could do. Sick dragons are too large and heavy for normal nursing to be of much use.

On the afternoon of the third day, Kazul woke up completely for the first time since her collapse.

"Thank goodness!" said Cimorene as Kazul shook her head experimentally and sat up. "I was beginning to think you were going to sleep for a month."

"I might have if I'd gotten more than a whiff of that smoke." Kazul stretched her neck in one direction and her tail in the other, trying to work out some of the kinks.

"If I'd known it was so dangerous, I'd never have brought any of that purple plant back with me," Cimorene apologized. "You might have done worse than sleep for a month. You might have–" She stopped, unwilling to complete the thought.

"I might have died?" Kazul said. "Unlikely. If a dragon isn't killed outright by something in the first five minutes, recovery is only a matter of time. That applies as much to dragonsbane as to a knight's magic sword."

"Then why did you want that goo in the green jar?" Cimorene asked.

"The antidote? I wanted it because I didn't like the idea of spending a month recuperating when I didn't have to. And since–" A fit of coughing interrupted Kazul in mid-sentence.

Cimorene skipped backward out of the way. Frowning worriedly, she tossed a pinch of feverfew into the air and recited the verse from the fireproofing spell in case Kazul should lose control of her flame again. "Maybe you won't need a month to recover, but three days obviously isn't enough," she said to the dragon. "You'd better lie back down before you choke."

"I can't," Kazul said. "I have to warn the King. If the wizards have had dragonsbane for three days already–" She started coughing again and had to stop talking.

"You stay here," Cimorene said in a firm tone. "I'll warn the King."

"Tokoz won't listen to you," Kazul said, but she settled back to the ground. "Roxim will, though. Start with him."

"Roxim?" Cimorene said doubtfully. She was afraid the gray-green dragon would want to go charging out after the wizards as soon as he heard they were up to something.

"He'll listen to you, and the King will listen to him," Kazul said. "It's not ideal, but it's the best we can do."

"All right, I'll go see Roxim. You stay here and sleep."

"When you get back–"

"I'll wake you and tell you what he said," Cimorene promised. "Now, *go to sleep.*"

Kazul smiled slightly and closed her eyes. Cimorene caught up a lamp and almost ran to the exit at the back of the cave. She was afraid that Kazul would think of something else and start talking again, and she didn't think talking would be good for her.

In the tunnel outside, Cimorene paused, trying to remember the directions to Roxim's cave. She had memorized a map in the library that showed most of the twists and turns of the dragon's tunnels, but she knew from experience that in the miles of gray stone corridors it was difficult to keep track of where she was.

"Left, left, fifth right, past the little chamber, right again, on past the iron gate, two lefts to the third cave down," she muttered to herself. "I *wish* Roxim's cave were closer." Still muttering, she started off.

Though she was being very careful, Cimorene had to backtrack twice during the first part of her trip when a mistake in counting corridors led her to a dead end. When she finally saw the iron gate that led into the Caves of Fire and Night, she sighed in relief. The tricky part was over, and the rest of the trip would be easy. She held her lamp up and quickened her step, hoping to make up some of the time she had lost on her detours. Then, as she reached the bars that blocked the entrance to the Caves of Fire and Night, she stopped short. There was someone sitting on the ground on the other side of the gate.

Cimorene had almost missed seeing him, and no wonder. His clothes, though well cut, were the same dark gray as the stone of the tunnel walls, and he was curled into a lumpy, dejected ball. He looked like a large rock. If he hadn't moved his hand as she passed, Cimorene would never have realized he was alive.

The man on the other side of the bars raised his head, and Cimorene saw with shock that his hair and skin were the same dark, even gray as his clothes. His eyes, too, were gray, and their expression was apologetic.

"Forgive me for startling you," the man said, climbing ponderously to his feet. "I didn't see you coming." He made a stiff, formal bow.

"Who are you?" Cimorene demanded. "And what are you doing in there?"

"I'm a prince," the man said in a gloomy tone, "and I'm reaping the rewards of my folly."

"What folly?"

The prince sighed. "It's a long story."

"Somehow they always seem to be long," Cimorene said. "You haven't come to rescue me from the dragons, have you? Because if you have, I'm not going to let you out of there. I haven't got time to spend an hour arguing today."

"I have no interest whatever in dragons, I assure you," the prince said earnestly. "And if you would let me out, I'd be extremely grateful. Um, who are you, by the way?"

"Cimorene, princess of the dragon Kazul," Cimorene said. She studied the prince for a moment and decided that he looked trustworthy. "All right, I'll let you out. Turn around and put your fingers in your ears."

"What?" the prince said, looking considerably startled.

"It's part of the spell to open the gate," Cimorene said. She wasn't about to let him overhear the words Kazul had used to unlock the door, even if he did look trustworthy.

The prince shrugged and did as she directed. Quickly, Cimorene recited:

"By night and flame and shining rock
Open thou thy hidden lock.
Alberolingarn!"

For an instant nothing happened, and Cimorene was afraid she had not remembered the charm correctly. Then the iron gate swung silently open. The prince, whose back was to the gate, did not notice. Cimorene touched his shoulder to get his attention, and her eyes widened.

"Oh!" she said as he turned. "You're–you're *stone.*"

"I know," the prince said. "It's part of that long story I mentioned earlier. I haven't gotten used to it yet." He stepped through the gate, and it closed noiselessly behind him.

"I'm afraid I don't have time to listen to stories just now," Cimorene said politely. "I have a rather urgent errand to run, so if you'll excuse me–"

"Can't I come with you?"

Cimorene stared at him. "Why do you want to do that?"

The stone prince looked down at his feet with an embarrassed expression. "Um, well, actually, I'm lost. And you seem to know your way around down here." He glanced hopefully at Cimorene's face, then sighed. "I suppose I can just wander around some more. I'll have to find a way out eventually."

"You'll run into a dragon and get eaten."

"I don't think it will hurt stone," the prince said. He sounded almost cheerful, as if he had only just realized that being made of stone might have some advantages.

"Maybe not, but you're sure to give the dragon indigestion," Cimorene said. "Bother! I don't have time for this!"

"I could wait here if you're coming back this way," the stone prince suggested.

Cimorene brightened, then frowned and shook her head. "No, one of the dragons might need to get into the Caves of Fire and Night, or it might be the turn of those dratted wizards. You can't stay here."

"Then–"

"I know! You can wait in the serving room, just off the banquet hall," Cimorene said. "It's close, there's plenty of room, and I know no one's using it today because I checked the schedule for Alianora yesterday. I can take a shortcut out the back to get to Roxim's without losing any *more* time. Come on."

"I really appreciate this," the stone prince said as they started off. "You don't know what it's like, being lost in the dark in these caves."

"How did it happen?" Cimorene asked.

The stone prince's expression became gloomy once more. "It's all that soothsayer's fault," he said.

"Soothsayer?"

"My father didn't think it was appropriate to invite fairies to a prince's christening, so he invited a soothsayer instead," the prince replied. "The soothsayer took one look at me and said that I would grow up to do a great service for a king. I've been stuck with his blasted prophecy ever since."

"It doesn't sound so terrible to me," Cimorene said.

"It wasn't, at first," the stone prince admitted. "I had special tutors in all sorts of interesting things to prepare me for being of great service to a king. My father even sent me to a special school for people who're supposed to do special things."

"Did you do well?"

"I was the top of my class," the stone prince said with a flash of pride. His face fell again. "That's part of the problem."

"I don't understand," Cimorene said. "This way. And can you walk a little faster, please? I'm in a hurry."

"It's been three years since I graduated, and everyone's still waiting for me to do something spectacular," the stone prince said, lengthening his stride. "The rest of my classmates are already making names for themselves. George started killing dragons right away, and Art went straight home and pulled some sort of magic sword out of a rock. Even the ones nobody expected to amount to much have done something. All Jack wanted to do was go back to his mother's farm and raise beans, and he ended up stealing a magic harp and killing a giant and all sorts of things. I'm the only one who hasn't succeeded."

"Why not?"

The stone prince sighed again. "I don't know. At first it seemed as if I wouldn't have any trouble finding a king to serve. Every time there was a war, both kings asked me to lead their armies, and every king for miles around who'd lost his throne to a usurper sent a messenger to my father's court. It should have been simple. Only they were always so worried about whether I was going to side with their enemies that it was easier not to pick anyone."

"I see," said Cimorene. Privately she thought that the stone prince had been rather wishy-washy.

Some of her opinion must have crept into her tone because the stone prince nodded glumly. "You're right. It was a mistake. As long as I didn't pick a king to serve, all the messengers and ambassadors and envoys stayed, hoping to persuade me. The inns around the castle were stuffed with them. It got to the point where I couldn't show my face without at least three of them pouncing on me.

"Finally I couldn't stand it any more, and I ran away. It was a relief at first, not having everyone hovering over me waiting for me to do something great. But after a while I started feeling uncomfortable. Then I realized that even if nobody around me expected me to do anything special in the service of a king, *I* expected me to do something.

"I was so flustered that I ran up to the next palace I saw and asked whether the king needed any services done. It turned out that he was ill, and his doctors had told him that the only thing that would cure him was a drink of the Water of Healing from the Caves of Fire and Night. So I left to get it at once."

"So that's what you were doing!" Cimorene said.

The stone prince gave her another gloomy nod. "I should have known better. That king had three sons, and the first two had already gone off to get the water and failed. Anyone with sense would have seen that the youngest son was the one who would succeed; it sticks out all over. But I was too eager to do my great service and get it over with, and I didn't stop and think."

"What happened?"

"It took me a long time to find the Caves of Fire and Night, but once I did, it wasn't hard to find the Water of Healing. The chamber's getting crowded. All the princes who've tried to get the water and failed have been turned into slabs of rock."

"I know. I've seen them," Cimorene said. "Watch out for your head; the ceiling is low along here."

"Then you know what it's like, and you've seen the two dippers on the wall by the spring." The stone prince's shoulders sagged. "I *knew* I should use the tin one. It was one of the first things we learned at school. But I thought it wouldn't do any harm if I just *looked* at the gold one, so I took it off the wall. And as soon as I touched it, I started to stiffen up."

"Um," said Cimorene. The stone prince was obviously well aware of how foolishly he had behaved. She saw no reason to make him feel worse by pointing it out to him again.

"So I stuck my arm in the spring," the prince said.

"You stuck your arm–oh, I see! That was clever," Cimorene said.

"Do you really think so?" the stone prince asked anxiously. "I thought that since the water from the spring is going to turn all the slabs of stone back into princes when someone finally succeeds in the quest, then the water ought to keep me from turning into a slab of stone in the first place. Only it didn't work the way I expected," he finished disconsolately.

"I can see that," Cimorene said. "But at least you can still do things. It would be much worse to have to lie there waiting for the right prince to come along and break the spell."

"I wouldn't have had to lie there very long," the stone prince said. "That king's youngest son is going to arrive any day now, I just know it. Anyway, if I were a slab of stone, I wouldn't know about it until it was all over and I'd been turned back into a prince again."

"How do you know?" Cimorene demanded. "Have you ever *been* a stone slab?"

The stone prince looked startled. "No, I haven't. I never thought of that."

"Well, start thinking now," Cimorene said tartly. "Here's the service room. Wait here for me, and don't go wandering off if I'm late getting back. I don't know how long this errand is going to take, and it would be very awkward for me if the dragons found you roaming through their tunnels."

"I'll remember," the stone prince promised. "But what do I do if someone comes in?"

"Duck into the banquet area," Cimorene said, showing him. "And if someone comes in there, too, curl up in the corner and pretend you're a rock."

"All right," the prince said doubtfully.

Cimorene did not like leaving him, but she was even less enthusiastic about taking him to see Roxim. Roxim proably wouldn't object to the prince himself, though Cimorene suspected that there might have been some difficulty over his proposed theft of the Water of Healing. But explaining everything to the gray-green dragon would take hours. Roxim was nice, but he tended to take a simple view of things, and the prince's situation was anything but simple. So Cimorene gave the prince one more warning, just to make sure he understood, and started off toward Roxim's cave to finish her errand.

12

In Which Cimorene Calls on a Dragon, and the Stone Prince Discovers a Plot

The shortcut to Roxim's worked just as well as Cimorene had hoped, and she even made up some of the time she had lost earlier. Roxim was in, too. She could hear the scraping of his scales as he moved around inside. She stepped up to the entrance of the cave and called, "Dragon Roxim!"

Something round and shiny flew through the air, missing Cimorene by inches. It hit the wall of the tunnel with a loud clang and slid rattling to the floor. Cimorene jumped.

"Roxim!" she shouted at the top of her lungs.

"What's this?" the dragon said, poking his nose out of the cave entrance.

"I am Cimorene, princess to the dragon Kazul, and I offer you greetings and good fortune in all your endeavors." Cimorene thought it best to be particularly polite, in case Roxim were in a bad mood. She suspected he might be. In her experience, someone in a good mood did not throw things at visitors.

"Very good," Roxim said. "Nice to see you again and all that, but I haven't got time for visitors at the moment. Sorry."

"I'm not a visitor, exactly. Kazul sent me with a message for you."

"Oh, well, that's different. Just hand me that shield there, would you?"

Cimorene picked up the shield from the floor of the tunnel. There was a large dent in one side where it had hit the tunnel wall, and several smaller ones over the rest of it from banging against things on its way to the tunnel floor.

"You ought to be more careful," she said severely. "Just look at this!"

"Ha!" Roxim snorted, examining the dents. "Shoddy work, shoddy work, that's the problem. In my day, you could roll a knight in full armor down the far side of the Vanishing Mountain and bounce him off two or three cliffs without so much as scratching his surface, much less denting it. This cheap modern stuff just doesn't hold up."

"If you know it doesn't hold up, you shouldn't throw it around like that," Cimorene said. "You almost hit me."

Roxim shifted uncomfortably. "Sorry. Didn't mean anything by it."

"All right, but next time look before you throw things," Cimorene said, handing him the shield.

"I always have this problem when I try to find something," Roxim confided. "Never know where to look. Gets frustrating, and next thing you know I'm pitching armor at the walls. Bad habit, but hard to break."

"Maybe I could help," Cimorene suggested. "After I give you Kazul's message, that is."

"Don't need help to put dents in things," Roxim said. "Comes to that, I don't really want it."

"I didn't mean help throw things," Cimorene said patiently. "I meant help find whatever you're looking for."

"Oh, that. Well, come in then."

Cimorene followed the dragon into a moderately large cave, similar to the one Kazul used as a living area. Roxim's cave, however, was full of clutter. Cimorene had to pick her way past bits of armor, one half of a pair of bookends, a box of tea, a pink scroll, three mismatched kitchen pots, a small wooden statue, a broken flute, and four partially burned candles. Roxim walked straight over the mess as if it weren't there, squashing a mangy-looking stuffed pigeon and flattening a tin cup in passing. He dropped the shield on a pile of silk flowers and waved Cimorene to a seat on a large wooden chest near one wall. "Now, what's this message of Kazul's?"

"It's about the wizards," Cimorene said, settling gingerly onto the dusty surface of the chest. She made a mental note to find Roxim a nice princess as soon as she possibly could. "Alianora and I found one of them picking dragonsbane a few days ago, and Kazul thinks King Tokoz will listen to you if you tell him about it."

"So that's where they got it," Roxim said in tones of disgust. "Pity you didn't mention it sooner."

Cimorene got a sinking feeling. "What do you mean?"

"Somebody poisoned King Tokoz this morning," Roxim explained.

"Slipped some dragonsbane in his coffee. Fast-acting; nothing to be done. Now we need a new king."

"That's awful!" Cimorene said. "Do you know who did it?"

"Those dratted wizards, that's who," Roxim said angrily. "It's obvious. Stupid thing to do; has to be wizards, by George! But Woraug won't listen to me."

"Woraug? What's Woraug got to do with it?"

"He's in charge of the investigation," Roxim replied. "Taking his time about it, too, if you ask me."

"But if the King was only poisoned this morning . . ."

"What does that have to do with it?" Roxim said unreasonably. "Besides, if Woraug doesn't hurry, he won't have the culprit in hand by the time the trials start tomorrow."

"Trials? You mean with Colin's Stone, to choose the new king?" Cimorene said with some hesitation. She did not see how it could be a trial for the person who had killed the King if they hadn't caught him yet, but she was not completely certain that the dragons didn't have some way of getting around the problem and trying him anyway.

"That's it," Roxim said, pleased. "And before I leave I have to find that emerald I picked up fifty years ago. Coronation present for the new King."

"But you haven't got a new King yet," Cimorene said, feeling somewhat bewildered. "And what if *you're* the King?"

Roxim smiled broadly. "Knew you were a nice gal. Me, the King! I rather like the idea. I still have to find the emerald, though. Wouldn't do to show up at the trials without a coronation present. Rum thing to do. Overconfident."

Though she was upset and more than a little worried, Cimorene helped Roxim as best she could. After about an hour of poking through the clutter, Cimorene found the emerald, wrapped in a gold-embroidered handkerchief and stuffed into the mouth of a large brass horn. Roxim thanked her and invited her to stay to tea, but Cimorene politely declined. She was eager to get back to Kazul, to tell her what had happened and decide what to do next.

Cimorene hurried back to Kazul's cave by the shortest route, thinking so hard about Tokoz's death that she forgot everything else. She found Kazul sleeping and was forced to wake her, despite her worries about the dragon's health. She knew Kazul would want to hear about the King of the Dragons as soon as possible, and she wanted to hear what Kazul made of Woraug's involvement in the investigation.

"Back already?" Kazul said, opening her eyes. "Didn't Roxim get you in to see King Tokoz?"

"No," Cimorene said. She hesitated, uncertain of the best way to break the news. "It was too late."

"Too late?" Kazul raised her head, startled. She eyed Cimorene briefly, then said, "All right, let's have it. What's happened?"

"King Tokoz was poisoned this morning. Roxim said someone put dragonsbane in his coffee."

Kazul snorted. "Somebody knew Tokoz pretty well." Seeing Cimorene's surprised expression, she explained, "Tokoz drank Turkish coffee every morning. The stuff is strong enough to take the roof off your mouth. It's why no one ever went to talk to him over breakfast. You could boil a whole field's worth of dragonsbane in Turkish coffee without changing the taste enough to notice. Or the texture."

Cimorene tried to imagine coffee, even Turkish coffee, strong enough to take the roof off a dragon's mouth and failed. "I told Roxim about the wizard Alianora and I met, and Roxim said I ought to tell Woraug because Woraug is in charge of finding the poisoner," she said. "But–"

"But when you caught Antorell picking dragonsbane, he thought Woraug had sent you," Kazul said. "If Woraug's mixed up with wizards–" She broke off, coughing. Cimorene watched her anxiously, but the coughing spasm did not last long. "I don't like this," Kazul finished when she got her breath back.

"I don't, either," Cimorene agreed. "But what can we do about it?"

Kazul frowned and said nothing. For several minutes, the two sat and thought in silence. Then Kazul said, "We can't do anything until the new King has been chosen. Did Roxim say when the testing will be?"

"Tomorrow," Cimorene said.

"Tomorrow!" Kazul surged to her feet. "Why didn't you say so at once? If I'm to be at the Ford of Whispering Snakes tomorrow, I have to–"

"Lie down!" Cimorene commanded. Kazul looked at her in surprise and collapsed in another fit of coughing. Cimorene waited until the dragon's coughing had subsided, then said sternly, "You're in no condition to go hauling rocks all over the countryside. I'd be surprised if you can even fly as far as the end of the pass. I think you're going to have to give up on the trials this time around."

Kazul made a choking noise. Cimorene looked at her in alarm, then realized that the dragon was laughing.

"It's not optional, Princess," Kazul said. "All the adult dragons in the Mountains of Morning are required to show up, no matter what condition they're in."

"But–"

"There is *no* acceptable excuse for missing the testing of a new King,"

Kazul repeated. "None. And I have a great deal to do before I leave, so if you'll–"

"If anything needs to be done around here, I'll do it," Cimorene said firmly. "If you don't rest, you won't be able to fly at all, and then how will you get to the ford?"

"A reasonable point," Kazul said, settling reluctantly back into place. "Very well. The first thing I need is a coronation present for the new King. There's a jeweled helmet on a shelf in the second storeroom that might do. Bring it out so I can take a look at it."

Cimorene spent the rest of the evening running errands for Kazul. Besides choosing a coronation gift (Kazul rejected the helmet and two crowns before deciding on a scepter made of gold and crystal), innumerable messages had to be delivered to various dragons who were in charge of arranging the trials. This one had to be informed of Kazul's ill health, so that it could be taken into account when the order of the testing was established; that one had to be told that Kazul would not be able to join the coronation procession. Substitutes had to be found to perform Kazul's various ceremonial duties, then their names had to be approved by a surly dragon in charge of protocol, and finally the substitutions had to be recorded on all the lists of all the dragons who were managing each of the events. It reminded Cimorene strongly of Linderwall and her parents' court.

By the time the last arrangement had been made and the last message delivered, it was very late and Cimorene was exhausted. She was also very glad she had not let Kazul do all the running around. The dragon, who had slept most of the time Cimorene was out, was looking much better, even in the dim light of Cimorene's lamp. Tired but satisfied, Cimorene went to her room and dropped into bed.

Cimorene was up early the next morning, stirring a dozen ostrich eggs in a large iron kettle for Kazul's breakfast. Kazul ate all of them, then slid out of the cave and prepared to leave for the Ford of Whispering Snakes.

"Don't fret, Princess," Kazul said. "The testing doesn't start until ten. I have plenty of time to get there, even if I stop to rest now and then." Her voice sounded much better than it had the day before, and it no longer seemed to rasp her throat. "While I'm gone, why don't you visit Woraug's princess? See if she's noticed anything odd these past few days. We need to know as much as we can before we talk to the new King about Woraug and the wizards."

"All right," Cimorene said. "As soon as I'm done with the dishes."

Kazul turned and leaped into the air, her wings churning clouds of dust from the dry surface of the ground. Cimorene squinted after her and shouted, "Good luck!" Kazul's wings dipped in answer before the dragon soared out of sight behind the shoulder of the next mountain. Cimorene stood looking after Kazul, her forehead wrinkling in worry. After a moment she shook herself and went inside. She had work to do.

Washing the dishes did not take long, and as soon as she was done, Cimorene set off to visit Alianora. The tunnels and passageways were silent and empty, and Cimorene's footsteps echoed eerily through the darkness. She began to wish she had taken the longer route along the outside of the mountain. She had not realized that the dragon city would seem so strange and lifeless with all the dragons gone.

"Psst! Cimorene!"

Cimorene jumped. She whirled in the direction of the voice, raising her lamp like a club, and Alianora stepped out of the adjoining tunnel and into the circle of light. In one hand she clutched a large bucket, three-quarters full of soapy water, and she looked rather pale.

"Alianora!" Cimorene said, lowering her arm. "What are you doing out here?"

"Shhh!" Alianora said. She looked nervously over her shoulder. "Woraug told me to scrub off the table in the banquet room while everyone was away. And–and I heard someone moving around in there. Even though everyone but us is gone. And I dropped my lamp, and–"

"Oh, my goodness," Cimorene said. "The stone prince! I'd forgotten all about him."

"Who?"

"The stone prince." Quickly, Cimorene explained how she had found and hidden him the day before. "And I hadn't thought about it until now, but this is the perfect time to get him out of the mountains," she finished. "All the dragons are gone and no one will see him. Come on, before I forget again."

Alianora nodded dubiously, and the two girls headed for the banquet room. When they arrived, Cimorene went in first, holding her lamp high. "Prince?" she called. "Are you there? It's me, Cimorene."

"Yes, I'm here," said the stone prince, unfolding stiffly from a gray lump in the corner. "I'm glad you're back. Who's this you've brought with you?"

"Princess Alianora of the Duchy of Toure-on-Marsh," Cimorene said. "She's the princess of the dragon Woraug just now."

"Does her father need a great service done for him?" the prince asked hopefully.

"Not that I know of," Cimorene replied. "Unless you're good at getting rid of aunts, but that would be more of a service to Alianora than to her father."

"I can think of nothing that would make me happier," the prince said with evident admiration as he bowed stiffly to Alianora. "Good afternoon, Princess. Or should it be 'good evening'? It's hard to tell without windows."

Alianora blushed and looked down at her bucket without answering.

"Actually, it's good morning," Cimorene told the prince. "I'm sorry it took me so long to come back for you, but . . . well, a lot has been going on."

Alianora looked up sharply. "You've been sitting here in the dark all *night?*" She shuddered. "You could at least have left him a candle, Cimorene."

"Thank you for the thought, Princess Alianora, but it's just as well she didn't," the stone prince said. "If I'd been sitting here with a lit candle, they'd have noticed me right away. And an unlit candle isn't much use in the dark, is it?"

"What do you mean?" Cimorene said. "Who would have noticed you?"

"The dragon and the two men he was talking to," replied the prince. "I think they were wizards."

"What?" said Cimorene and Alianora together.

"Well, they talked as if they were wizards," the prince said. "They weren't carrying staffs, though."

"What did they look like?" Cimorene said.

"They were both tall, and they both had beards. The older one's was gray and the younger one's was brown."

"Antorell and Zemenar!" Cimorene said. "And they were talking to a dragon?"

The stone prince nodded.

"Then they wouldn't have been carrying staffs. Dragons are allergic to them. Did you hear what they said?"

"Something about a contest," the stone prince said. "The wizards were going to fix it so this dragon would win. It sounded like a kind of cross-country race, and the wizards were going to hide along the path and–and help the dragon out somehow. I'm afraid I'm not very clear about that part. Spells aren't my specialty. I'm much better at hopeless causes."

Alianora and Cimorene exchanged appalled glances.

"The trials with Colin's Stone to pick the new King!" Alianora said.

"Which dragon?" Cimorene asked urgently. "Do you know which dragon they were talking to?"

"I only heard the name once," the prince said. He sounded apologetic and a little embarrassed. "And I don't think I got it right. It's too silly."

"Tell us!" Cimorene commanded.

"Well, it *sounded* like 'warthog,' " the prince said in an even more apologetic tone than before.

"Could it have been Woraug?" Cimorene asked.

"That's it!" the prince said. "I knew it couldn't *really* have been warthog."

"What a pity you remembered," said a voice from the entrance into the banquet hall.

Cimorene whirled. Antorell stood in the doorway, staff in hand, watching them with an intolerably smug expression.

13

In Which Alianora Discovers an Unexpected Use for Soap and Water, and Cimorene Has Difficulty with a Dragon

Antorell looked past Cimorene and Alianora as if they were not there and spoke directly to the stone prince. "I told Father someone was listening. He won't be happy when he finds out I was right, but he'll feel better when I tell him I've taken care of things. He might even let me have the first look in the King's Crystal, once Woraug gives it to us."

"So that's what you're after!" Cimorene said.

Antorell favored her with a superior smile. "Quite right, Princess Cimorene. The King's Crystal will show us the whereabouts of every piece of useful and interesting magic in the world. All we'll have to do is go out and pick them up."

"Somehow I don't think it will be that easy," Cimorene murmured.

"We knew Tokoz would never give it to us, but Woraug will, as soon as he's King of the Dragons. He'll have to, or we'll tell everyone how we were the ones who made sure *he* was the new king. Of course, we can't afford to have anybody around who might make . . . awkward revelations. I doubt that dragons will listen to a couple of hysterical princesses, but he"–Antorell pointed at the stone prince–"will have to go."

"What are you going to do?" Alianora demanded. She was plainly frightened, and Cimorene could see that her knuckles were white with the force of her grip on the handle of the scrub bucket.

"Oh, gravel seems appropriate, don't you think?" Antorell said. "No one will notice a few more rocks around here."

"Ought I to be taking this person seriously?" the stone prince said in a rather doubtful tone.

"You'd better if you don't want to end up as a lot of little pebbles," Alianora answered. She still sounded frightened, but she seemed to be getting a grip on herself. "He's a wizard."

"You wouldn't be talking about gravel if *you* were the one who had to sweep the floor," Cimorene said to Antorell. She stepped forward as she spoke, hoping to get between Antorell and the stone prince before Antorell noticed what she was doing. She didn't think Antorell was a good enough wizard to do any real harm, but there was no point in taking chances.

"Stay where you are, Princess Cimorene," Antorell commanded. "I'll deal with you in a moment."

"Must you be so theatrical?" Cimorene said.

"Theatrical? You think I'm being *theatrical?"* Antorell said furiously. "I am simply showing a proper respect for the importance of this moment!"

"You're showing off," Cimorene said flatly. "And you're not doing it very well."

"He doesn't sound much like a wizard to me," the stone prince said. "Is he always like this?"

"Enough!" Antorell cried, and raised his staff. Light shimmered along its length and began to gather at the lower end. Grinning wolfishly, the wizard tilted the staff, aiming it toward the stone prince.

"Stop that!" Alianora said. Antorell ignored her. "I said, *stop it!"* Alianora shouted, and threw her bucket at Antorell's head.

Alianora's aim was off. The bucket hit Antorell's shoulder. A bolt of fire shot from the end of his staff and whizzed between Cimorene and the stone prince to strike the far wall with a whumping noise and a shower of sparks. Antorell staggered, slipped in the cascade of soapy water, and fell over the bucket, dropping his staff in the process.

Cimorene darted in and kicked Antorell's staff out of his reach. He stared up at her from a mound of soggy silk and soapsuds. "You can't *do* this to me!" he shrieked.

Something in his voice made Cimorene and her friends look at him more closely. Alianora's eyes went wide, and Cimorene blinked in surprise. "He's–he's collapsing," Alianora said in a stunned voice.

"He's melting," Cimorene corrected her.

"I can't be melting!" Antorell cried. "I'm a *wizard!* It's not fa–" His head disappeared into a small brown puddle, and his cries stopped.

There was a moment of astonished silence. "I thought it was witches who melt when you dump water over them," the stone prince said at last.

"It is, usually," Cimorene said. "What on earth did you put in that bucket, Alianora?"

"Just water and soap, and a little lemon juice to make it smell nicer," Alianora said.

"Um," said Cimorene, thinking hard. "I'll bet there's a simpler way of melting wizards, but we don't have time right now to figure out what it is. How many buckets can you get hold of in a hurry?"

"Buckets?" Alianora said. "Two, counting this one. And I suppose I could borrow one from Hallanna; that's three."

"And I've got two in the kitchen, and I expect the iron kettle is big enough. That's six altogether; two for each of us. You will help, won't you?" Cimorene added, turning to the stone prince.

"Of course," the prince assured her. "Help with what?"

"Stopping those wizards," Cimorene said. "We can't let them make Woraug the next King of the Dragons by trickery."

"I don't see how we can stop them," Alianora said. "We can't possibly get to the Ford of Whispering Snakes before the trials start, and even if we could, we don't know where the wizards will be hiding."

"If we tell the dragons that Woraug's trying to cheat, they'll stop the trials," Cimorene said with more confidence than she felt. "That will give us time to find the wizards. And I've got a way to get us to the ford. You go start collecting buckets. I'll meet you at your place after I get the things I'll need from Kazul's."

"What about . . ." Alianora gestured with distaste at the wet, messy lump of robes in the center of the puddle that was all that remained of Antorell.

"We'll clean it up when we get back," Cimorene said. "This is more important."

Alianora nodded, and the three left the banquet room. The stone prince decided to accompany Alianora since he was not a fast walker and Cimorene had farther to go. Cimorene left them when they reached the main tunnel and ran back to Kazul's cave. There she went straight to her room and opened the drawer where she kept odds and ends. In the back left-hand corner, carefully wrapped in a handkerchief, were the three black feathers she had taken from beneath the left wing of the bird she had killed in the Enchanted Forest. She shoved the whole packet into her pocket without bothering to unwrap it and went on to the kitchen to collect her buckets. Then she hurried through the tunnels to Woraug's cave, where Alianora and the stone prince were waiting.

When Cimorene arrived, she found the stone prince pumping water to fill Alianora's third bucket while Alianora mixed soap and lemon juice into the second. Cimorene set her pots and pails next to the pump and went to help Alianora.

"Now what?" Alianora said when all the buckets were full of cleaning mixture.

Cimorene reached into her pocket and dug out the package. Gently, she unfolded the handkerchief and removed one of the feathers, noticing as she did that the package also contained the pebble she had picked up in the Caves of Fire and Night. "If we each take two buckets, can we still link elbows without spilling too much?" she asked.

Alianora and the stone prince looked at each other, shrugged, and picked up two buckets each. Cimorene took the last bucket and the iron pot, holding the handle of the pot with only three fingers so that she could keep a grip on the feather with her thumb and forefinger. A series of awkward maneuvers followed as Alianora and the stone prince tried to link elbows with Cimorene without losing their balance or dropping one of their buckets. In the process, Cimorene's skirt got soaked.

"It's a good thing I'm not a wizard," Cimorene said. "Ready? Here we go." She twisted her hand toward the edge of the iron pot and let go of the black feather. "I wish we were at the Ford of Whispering Snakes," she said as the feather fell, and the room dissolved around them.

They materialized at the very edge of a river, on a flat, narrow rock that jutted out over the water, and Alianora immediately slipped on the wet stone. If the stone prince had not been so solid and heavy, all three of them would have fallen into the river. As it was, it took Cimorene and Alianora several seconds to regain their balance. When she was finally sure of her footing, Cimorene breathed a sigh of relief and quickly looked about her.

The Ford of Whispering Snakes was crowded. Dragons of all sizes and shades of green lined the banks of the river and filled the spaces beneath the towering trees of the Enchanted Forest. On the far bank, a pale dragon was poring over a parchment list that Cimorene thought she remembered seeing during one of the many errands she had run the previous night. All the dragons seemed to be talking at once, and none of them noticed Cimorene and her friends.

"Hello, dragons!" Cimorene shouted, trying to make herself heard above the noise.

"Here, now! What's all this?" an olive-green dragon on the bank demanded, turning. "Someone's trying to sneak a look at the trials."

"S-s-s-sneaksss," hissed a soft but nonetheless clearly audible voice from somewhere near Cimorene's feet. Cimorene jumped and looked down, but though she craned her neck to see all around her, she could not find the second speaker.

"Get rid of them before Troum comes back with Colin's Stone," another dragon advised.

"We aren't trying to sneak in, and we don't care about watching the trials," Cimorene said, wishing she dared to look around for Kazul. "We came to warn you about the wizards."

"Wiz-z-zardssss," the soft voice echoed.

"Wizards?" the olive-green dragon said skeptically. "There aren't any wizards here."

"No, but they've figured out some way of interfering with your choice of the next king," Cimorene said. "They're hiding somewhere. You have to put off the trials with Colin's Stone until we can find them and stop them. If you'll just tell Kazul we're here–"

"Put off the trials?" the olive-green dragon interrupted. "Impossible! They've been under way for half an hour. We can't just stop in the middle. Who are all you people, anyway?"

A flicker of motion caught Cimorene's eye, and she looked down just in time to see a thin red snake dart from one clump of weeds to the next. "S-s-s-sneaksss," whispered the soft voice an instant later. "S-s-sneaksss and wiz-z-zardsss."

"I wasn't asking you," the dragon said severely in the general direction of the snake. "And whatever they are, they certainly aren't wizards."

"They look like somebody's princesses to me," a blue-green dragon said. "Pity, that. It would be so much simpler to eat them and get them out of the way."

"Are you sure?" said a third dragon. "The one on the end doesn't look like a princess."

"I'm beginning to think this wasn't such a good idea," the stone prince said.

"He may not be a princess, but he doesn't look edible, either," the blue-green dragon pointed out. "And these other two are definitely princesses. You can't go eating them out of hand."

"Princesssessss," hissed the voice from under the rock.

"Oh, princesses," the olive-green dragon said. "No wonder they're so full of wild tales."

"It's true!" Cimorene said desperately. "If you don't believe us, take us to Kazul; she will."

"I can't do that!" the olive-green dragon said, shocked. "Kazul's third in line now, after Mazarin and Woraug. You can't talk to people who are that close to making their attempt with the stone. It would distract them."

"Woraug!" Alianora said. "Woraug's next in line?"

"Yes, he should be starting off any minute now," said the olive-green dragon. "Then comes Mazarin, and then Kazul. I don't expect it will take long, though. Nobody's carried the stone for more than a mile or two yet."

"But I'm Kazul's princess!" Cimorene said.

"I don't care who you are," the dragon replied crossly. "You can't talk to Kazul until she's done with her turn."

"That will be too late!" Cimorene cried. "You don't understand. Woraug and the wizards–"

"I've had enough of your wizards," the olive-green dragon said. "You're a confounded nuisance, and you ought not to be pushing your way in here where you're not wanted. Go away!"

"Cimorene, what are we going to do?" Alianora said as the olive-green dragon turned and stalked determinedly away.

"At hero's school we were always taught that if you couldn't persuade anyone to help you with something, it meant that you were supposed to do it by yourself," the stone prince said diffidently. "And we *are* prepared." He lifted one of his buckets slightly.

"But we don't know where the wizards are." Alianora said. "We have to find them before we can stop them, and there isn't time."

"S-s-stop the wiz-z-zardsss," whispered the soft voice.

"That's the first sensible thing you've said since we got here," Cimorene said to the hissing whisper.

"Can't you just wish to be where the wizards are?" the stone prince asked Cimorene.

"No, you have to know where you're going, or the spell doesn't work," Cimorene said.

For a moment all three were glumly silent. Cimorene stared at the water, remembering how and where she had gotten the feathers. Suddenly she raised her head.

"We may not know where the wizards are, but I'll bet I know someone who can find out. Hold this for a minute."

Cimorene handed one of her buckets to Alianora, then dug out the packet of feathers. She pulled the second feather from the packet and grabbed Alianora's elbow. "Hold tight, everybody. I wish we were at Morwen's house," Cimorene said, and dropped the feather.

The scenery shifted abruptly, and they were standing on Morwen's porch. The house was just as tidy-looking as Cimorene remembered, and the porch floor gleamed as if it had just been washed. A black and white cat, startled by their sudden appearance, fell off the porch railing. Four others left off washing themselves to stare at Cimorene with unwinking green and yellow eyes.

"I need to talk to Morwen," Cimorene said to the cats. "It's an emergency."

A lean tiger-stripped cat rose and oozed through a crack in the door. Cimorene unwound herself from Alianora and the stone prince and set her bucket on the porch floor. "I hope this works," she muttered to herself as Alianora and the prince placed their buckets beside hers.

14

In Which the Wizards Try to Make Trouble, and Cimorene Does Something about It

The door of the cottage opened and Morwen stepped out. "What sort of emergency?" she asked. She studied Alianora and the stone prince for a moment, then peered at Cimorene over the tops of her glasses and added with some severity, "I hope you weren't referring to *his* predicament. He may well find it an inconvenience, but it certainly isn't an emergency. Not by my standards, anyway."

"No," said Cimorene, "I was talking about the wizards. They've poisoned the King of the Dragons, and now they're trying to interfere with Colin's Stone so that Woraug will be the new king. We have to stop them, but we don't know where they are, and Woraug's going to try to carry the stone any minute. Can you find them for us?"

Morwen blinked twice and shoved her glasses back into place with her forefinger. "I see," she said. "You're right. It's an emergency. I'll do what I can. But if you don't tell me the whole story later, when there's a bit more time, I shall–I shall turn you all into mice and give you to the cats. Wait here."

As she spoke, Morwen disappeared into the house. She reappeared a moment later, holding a small mirror and muttering over it. "Colin's Stone," she said, and breathed on the glass. She looked up. "Any wizard in particular?"

"Zemenar, the Head Wizard of the Society of Wizards," Cimorene said, wishing Morwen would go faster and knowing she couldn't.

"I should have guessed," Morwen said. She turned back to the mirror. "Zemenar," she said, and breathed on the glass once more. Then she motioned to Cimorene to come and look.

Cimorene obeyed, and Alianora and the stone prince crowded closely behind her. The mirror showed a blurry, wavering picture of the Ford of Whispering Snakes. As Cimorene watched, the picture moved slowly along one bank of the river, past the waiting dragons and the immense trees of the Enchanted Forest and on down the river.

"Can't it go any faster?" Alianora whispered.

"There's no need to whisper, and no, it can't," Morwen said. "Not if you want to be sure of finding these wizards of yours on the first try, and it doesn't sound as if you have time to waste on mistakes."

The picture in the mirror continued to creep along the bank. Cimorene pulled the third and last feather out of her pocket and brushed it nervously across her fingers while she waited.

"What's that?" the stone prince said suddenly.

The mirror-picture stopped, then moved up the bank, away from the river toward a thicket of blackberry brambles. Cimorene saw the tip of a wooden staff poking up above the thicket. Tensely, she waited for the mirror to show the far side of the brambles.

"It's them!" Alianora said. She sounded frightened and excited at the same time. "Oh, dear!"

Cimorene took a good look at the picture in the mirror. Five wizards were standing in an opening behind the blackberry thicket, leaning on their staffs and looking at the sky. Suddenly, one of the wizards pointed. The others peered upward, nodded, and raised their staffs.

"Get the buckets!" Cimorene said. Cats scattered in all directions as the stone prince pounded across the porch behind Cimorene and Alianora. "Hang on; here we go. I wish–"

"Not without me you–" Morwen said, grabbing Cimorene's shoulder.

"–we were at the blackberry thicket where the wizards are," Cimorene said, and dropped the feather.

"–don't," Morwen finished as the porch winked out and was replaced by blackberries.

The five wizards were standing in an arc just in front of the bramble. Each of them held his staff so that the lower end was about a foot above the ground, pointing at something hidden in the moss at their feet. An unpleasant yellow-green light dripped from the ends of the staffs, and the moss where the wizards were standing was brown and dead. The wizards' backs were toward Cimorene and her friends.

"Now!" Cimorene cried. As the wizards began to turn, she set one of her buckets on the ground and lifted the other in both hands. Taking careful aim, she flung the soapy water over a black-haired wizard in the center of the arc.

"Charge!" yelled the stone prince, and threw one of his buckets at the nearest wizard.

"Take that, you cheats!" said Alianora, dumping the first of her buckets over another.

"What–this is impossible!" said one of the wizards indignantly as he began to melt.

"Too bad," Cimorene said, throwing her second load of water at the next-to-last wizard.

"Watch where you're throwing that!" Morwen said to the stone prince, who had sloshed his second bucket over the fifth wizard with such enthusiasm that water sprayed in all directions.

"Sorry," the prince apologized. "Is that all of them?"

"It's all five of the ones we saw," Cimorene said cautiously.

"Then we did it!" Alianora said.

"Not quite," said Zemenar, stepping out of the bushes behind Morwen. "You interrupted the spell, of course, but we were nearly finished anyway. And as long as the stone remains enchanted, Woraug won't have any trouble getting it all the way to the Vanishing Mountain. Look." He pointed with his staff, and Cimorene saw three dragons, high in the air, flying steadily toward the mountains. One of them had a long black stone clutched in his claws, and the other two appeared to be escorting him at a careful distance.

"Woraug and the two judges," Cimorene murmured.

Zemenar nodded. "You might as well put that bucket down," he went on, turning to Alianora. "You can't throw it at me without melting your witch friend here. What's in it, by the way?"

"I don't see why we should tell you," Cimorene said as Alianora set the last of the six buckets down.

"Because I'm interested, Princess," Zemenar said with an oily smile. "And it will pass the time until the next shift gets here, and I can decide what to do with you."

"If you're that interested, why don't you take a closer look?" said the stone prince, picking up Alianora's bucket.

"Stay where you are!" Zemenar commanded. As he spoke, he raised his staff and sidestepped so that Morwen was between him and the stone prince.

"If you insist," said the prince. He shrugged, lifted the bucket, and flung the water over Morwen and Zemenar at the same time.

"What–no!" Zemenar cried in horror as he began to melt. "Not soapsuds! It's demeaning."

"There's a little lemon juice in it, too," Alianora offered.

Zemenar glared at her. He was less than half his normal height and shrinking as they watched, while a dark puddle spread out beneath him. "Lemon juice! Bah! How dare you do such a thing? I'm the Head Wizard of the Society of Wizards!" His voice grew fainter and higher as he shrank. "Interfering busybodies! Soapsuds! Of all the undignified tricks. You'll be sorry for this! You can't melt a wizard forever, you know! You'll be sor . . ."

The wizard's voice ceased. All that remained of him was a pile of silk robes and a long wooden staff lying on some damp moss. Alianora and Cimorene stared for a moment, then Alianora turned to the stone prince.

"I'm glad he's gone," she said, "but how could you melt Morwen just to get at that wizard?"

"But I didn't," the stone prince said. "Look."

Cimorene and Alianora turned. Morwen seemed no shorter than usual, though she certainly looked very damp. She had taken off her glasses and was shaking water off them. "Don't just stand there," she said crossly to Cimorene. "Hand me a dry handkerchief."

"Just a minute," Cimorene said, checking her pockets. She found the handkerchief that had been wrapped around the magic feathers and handed it to Morwen. "Um, why *didn't* you melt?"

"Clean living," Morwen said as she began to dry her glasses on Cimorene's handkerchief.

"I thought as much," the stone prince said in a satisfied tone. "Nobody who lives in a house as clean as yours could possibly melt in a bucket of soapsuds."

"Quite right," Morwen said approvingly. "You have a good head on your shoulders, young man. What's this?" She held up a sharp-edged black pebble.

"It's a piece of stone I found in the Caves of Fire and Night," Cimorene said.

"Where, exactly?"

"In the King's Cave," Cimorene said. "Morwen, shouldn't we do something about that spell Zemenar mentioned?"

Alianora was watching the sky, shading her eyes with her hand. "Woraug's nearly halfway to the mountain," she said anxiously.

"Good," said Morwen, though neither Cimorene nor Alianora could tell which of them she was talking to. The witch shook her wet robes and walked over to the patch of dead moss where the wizards had been working, picking her way carefully past little piles of robes and staffs. Cimorene followed. In the center of the brown area was a black stone the size of Cimorene's fist. A web of yellow-green light flickered across its smooth surface.

"Sloppy," Morwen said. "Very sloppy. Though I'm not surprised. Wizards always seem to depend on brute force when a little subtlety would be far more effective." She fingered Cimorene's pebble for a moment, then reached out and dropped it on top of the wizards' stone.

There was a noise like a great deal of popcorn all popping at once, and the light that flickered over the black stone spat yellow-green sparks in all directions. Alianora jumped and backed away. Cimorene would have liked to do the same, but she did not want to give Morwen a bad impression of her courage, so she stayed where she was.

The sparks died, and the flickering light went out. From the sky high above came a faint shriek of surprise and rage. Cimorene looked up and saw three black specks in the sky. No, not three: four, and the two escort dragons were swooping to catch the speck that was Colin's Stone, which Woraug had just dropped.

Cimorene gave a sigh of relief and looked at Morwen. "So much for Woraug and the wizards," she said. "We didn't even need the fireproofing spell. What did you do?"

"And what happens now?" Alianora added.

"Duck," said Morwen, and threw herself sideways into the bushes.

"Wha–" said the stone prince, and then he and Cimorene and Alianora were engulfed by a blast of dragon fire.

The stone prince leaped in front of the two princesses, but he was much too late to protect them. Fortunately the fireproofing spell was still in effect, and neither of them even felt warm, though Alianora lost the ends of her sleeves and Cimorene's hemline rose six scorched inches.

"I knew I shouldn't have said that about the fireproofing spell," Cimorene muttered.

With a wordless snarl and a thunder of wings, Woraug landed just in front of the little group.

"You!" he shouted when he saw Cimorene. "I might have known it would be you!" Flame shot from his mouth once more, but it was just as useless as it had been the first time.

Cimorene glanced up and saw one of the escort dragons spiraling down to see what was going on. "You might as well give up, Woraug," she said, hoping to distract the angry dragon long enough for help to arrive. "You can't be King of the Dragons now."

"I'll tear you limb from limb!" Woraug raged. "Every last one of you!" One arm shot out as he spoke, and shining silver claws snapped around the stone prince's waist.

Alianora screamed.

"Hurry *up!"* Cimorene shouted at the dragon in the sky.

The dragon heard and dove toward them, but he was not fast enough. Woraug shoved the stone prince into his mouth and bit down hard. An instant later he howled in pain and spat out the prince and four teeth.

"What *is* all this?" said the escort dragon, landing carefully beside Woraug. The clearing was getting rather crowded.

"A plot to cheat on the test to see who the next King of the Dragons will be," Cimorene said. "Woraug was in it, and a lot of wizards."

"Are you all right?" Alianora asked the stone prince, who was just picking himself up. His stone was black in places from the dragon fire, but otherwise he seemed unhurt.

"More or less," the stone prince said. "But just look what that fire did to my clothes! And that dragon's put a chip in my sleeve. What am I supposed to do about that? It's not as if I can just change clothes when I get home, you know."

"That's ridiculous!" the escort dragon told Cimorene. "No dragon would cooperate with wizards. I don't see any wizards, either. I think you're making it up."

"Of course you don't see any wizards," Cimorene said, feeling very cross. "We melted them."

"Melted them?"

"Where do you think those staffs came from?" Cimorene pointed at the wizards' staffs lying across the scattered brown puddles.

The dragon backed up a pace and sniffed experimentally.

"It's all quite true," Morwen said, poking her head out of the bushes. "And we'll be more than happy to explain the whole thing to your new King as soon as you have one. Provided, of course, that you take that maniac away before he burns the whole Enchanted Forest to the ground." She gestured at Woraug. "Cimorene, I really must insist on getting a copy of that fireproofing spell. It will clearly be worth every minute of the months of hunting it will take me to find some hens' teeth, and I may as well get started as soon as I can."

"Who's that?" said the escort dragon. "Morwen? That does it! This is too much for me. I'm taking you all into custody until the trials are over and the King can sort it out. Come along."

"I assume that doesn't apply to me," Woraug rumbled. He winced as he spoke.

"It certainly does," the escort dragon said. "I said *all,* and I meant *all.* If I'd meant 'all the humans,' I'd have said 'all the humans,' or maybe 'some of you' or 'you over there' or 'all you non-dragons' or–"

"Nonsense!" Woraug interrupted. "Don't you know who I am?"

"You're the dragon who caused a ruckus just now for no reason I can see," the escort dragon replied. "And it's my duty and my job to take you into custody. When the trials are over, you can explain it to the King, and if I've done something wrong, well, I'll take what I have coming. And if I haven't, you'll take yours. And–"

"All right, all right," Woraug said. "But I warn you, you'll regret this."

"That's as may be," the escort dragon said with dignity. "Right now, though, you're in custody along with the rest of these people, and you'd better not go snacking on any of them until things are sorted out. I saw what you did to the gray one."

"Did you?" said the stone prince. "Then what are you going to do about this chip in my sleeve?"

"Tell it to the King," the escort dragon advised. "Now, off we go, the lot of you."

Morwen came cautiously out of the bushes, brushing leaves from her already wet black robes. She stopped and peered at the escort dragon over the tops of her glasses. "This has not been a good day for anyone's clothes," she said severely. "I shall send the cleaning bill to your king."

"Whatever you want," the escort dragon said impatiently. "Come *on.*"

Scowling furiously, Woraug marched off into the forest. The stone prince and Alianora followed, talking in low voices. Morwen paused to pick up the wizards' black rock and Cimorene's pebble, then went on after them. Cimorene hesitated.

"Go on," said the escort dragon.

"I will, but I think you ought to know that another batch of wizards is supposed to show up soon," Cimorene said. "Zemenar said something about a second shift. I don't know what they can do without the stone they were using, but I'm sure they'll try something."

"Wizards always do," the escort dragon said with a sigh. He studied the wizards' staffs that were lying around the clearing with a melancholy air. "All right, I'll send someone back to keep an eye on things as soon as we get to the ford. Whatever was going on here, there certainly were wizards in it, and that's enough for me."

"Good," said Cimorene. "And thank you." She smiled at the startled expression on the dragon's face and started after the others.

15

In Which the Dragons Crown a New King, and Cimorene Gets a New Job

The walk to the Ford of Whispering Snakes took longer than Cimorene expected. The trees of the Enchanted Forest grew close together in many places, forcing the dragons to take a zigzag path instead of heading straight up the bank of the river. Woraug, who was in the lead, seemed to be deliberately setting a slow pace. Cimorene was sure he was hoping that the second shift of wizards would arrive at the blackberry clearing before the dragons at the ford had been warned. She had no idea what would happen then, but she doubted that it would be good. The escort dragon was not interested in Cimorene's worries, however, and he refused to speed things up, so the group ambled on.

As they approached the ford at last, they heard cheering ahead of them. Woraug flinched visibly, and Alianora and the stone prince were startled out of their quiet conversation.

"What's that?" Alianora said.

"Sounds to me as if we have a new King," their escort said with great satisfaction. "That means I can get you lot off my hands right away. What a relief! I thought I was going to be stuck with you for hours."

Alianora looked faintly indignant at this unflattering opinion. Morwen was merely amused. Woraug's wings sagged momentarily, but then he seemed to pull himself back together, and he continued on as confidently as ever. Cimorene's concern deepened. What if Woraug managed to convince the new King that they were all lying?

They reached the edge of the cheering crowd of dragons. "Who did it?" the escort dragon asked. "Who's the new King?"

"How should I know?" the other responded. "I can't see a thing from way out here."

"You'll find out soon enough," the escort dragon said. Then he raised his voice and shouted, "Make way! Coming through! Prisoners for the King! Make way!"

The crowd of dragons parted reluctantly, and the escort dragon herded the group forward, still shouting. They made their way through the cheering dragons until they reached the edge of the river. "Stand away!" shouted someone in the crowd. "Stand away for the King!"

The nearby dragons drew back, leaving Woraug, the escort dragon, and Cimorene and her friends standing by themselves on the trampled moss. As the dragons moved away, Cimorene caught sight of Kazul, lying comfortably beside the river. "Kazul!" Cimorene cried, and ran forward. "Are you all right?"

A mottled dragon standing beside Kazul shifted and flicked his tail angrily at Cimorene. "You should say 'Your Majesty,'" he said with a warning scowl.

"Don't be ridiculous, Frax. She's my princess," Kazul said. "I'm quite all right, Cimorene. What are you doing here?"

"You're the new King of the Dragons?" Cimorene said in astonishment. "But–but when you left this morning, you could barely fly! How did you get Colin's Stone all the way from here to the Vanishing Mountain?"

"Colin's Stone apparently does more than merely pick out the right King," Kazul said. "The minute I picked it up, I felt fine."

"This is impossible!" Woraug said.

"Are you accusing me of fraud?" Kazul asked mildly.

"He'd better not," Cimorene said. "He's the one who was cheating, with the help of Zemenar and the rest of the wizards."

"Really," Kazul said in tones of great interest.

"It's all nonsense," Woraug declared. "The girl's just trying to attract attention."

"Really," Kazul said again, and smiled, displaying all her silver teeth.

"Oh, come now, Kazul. Surely you won't take a mere princess's word over mine," Woraug said.

"That depends entirely on what she says. Tell us about it, Princess," Kazul commanded.

So Cimorene told them. She brought the stone prince forward to explain what he had overheard the wizards and Woraug discussing in the banquet hall, and she made Alianora tell everyone about melting wizards with wash water and lemon juice. She told about getting to the Ford of Whispering Snakes on the first feather and being unable to convince any of the dragons to listen to her. She told about going to Morwen's house to find out where the wizards were, and about using the last feather to get to the wizards and melt them. She described Zemenar's unexpected appearance and subsequent melting, and the way Morwen had broken the wizards' spell, and she finished with an account of Woraug's futile attack.

"And then *he* landed"–Cimorene waved in the direction of the escort dragon–"and decided to bring us all back here. And I think somebody ought to go back to that clearing where the blackberries are before the next batch of wizards arrives. I don't know what they'll do when they find out what's happened, but . . ."

"Yes, I see," said Kazul. She turned to a pale green dragon beside her. "Take five or six of the younger dragons–the ones who've been talking about starting a wizard-hunt–and go have a look at this blackberry clearing."

"Yes, Your Majesty," said the pale dragon with a fierce grin.

"Surely you don't believe this!" Woraug said.

Kazul stared at Woraug without saying anything, and the dragons around the edge of the circle rattled their scales.

"Ah–Your Majesty," Woraug added hastily.

"Why should I disbelieve it?" Kazul said, still watching Woraug.

"The whole thing is preposterous!" Woraug said. "How could wizards do anything to affect Colin's Stone? Your Majesty."

Kazul looked at Cimorene.

"I'm sorry, Kazul," Cimorene said, shaking her head. "I know *what* the wizards were trying to do, but I don't have the slightest idea *how* they were doing it."

"I believe I can explain that, Your Majesty," Morwen said. She stepped forward, tossing and catching the wizards' black rock casually in her right hand. "They were using this. I believe you'll find that it comes from the Caves of Fire and Night. From the King's Cave, in fact, where Colin's Stone was found. And one of the properties of the Caves of Fire and Night is that you can use one piece to cast spells which affect similar pieces."

"Just the way that impossible book says!" Cimorene exclaimed.

"DeMontmorency? Yes, I suppose he is fairly impossible," Morwen said.

"Is this sufficiently similar to Colin's Stone that the wizards could have affected the stone through it?" Kazul asked.

"Certainly, Your Majesty," Morwen said.

"This is–" Woraug began.

"–ridiculous, impossible, and unbelievable," Kazul said. "You've said that already. But I haven't heard you say anything particularly convincing in support of that attitude."

"Oh, really, Your Majesty!" Woraug said. "Next you'll be saying I poisoned King Tokoz!"

"It doesn't seem likely," Kazul admitted, "since Tokoz was poisoned with dragonsbane, and dragons can't get anywhere near the stuff without feeling the effects."

"What if Zemenar made a . . . a dragonsbane-proof packet for him to carry it in?" Cimorene said, thinking of the bag Antorell had been carrying when she and Alianora met him in the valley. "Something that would melt when he dropped it in the King's coffee."

"I suppose it's possible," Kazul said. "But there's no evidence at all that Zemenar did any such thing."

"What would it have looked like?" Alianora asked suddenly. "Would it have been something like a very large tea bag?"

Everyone turned to look at Alianora. "I think that would have worked quite well, Princess," Kazul said. "Why do you ask?"

"Because Woraug had something like that with him when he went to see King Tokoz the night before the King was killed," Alianora said. "I saw it."

An angry muttering ran through the crowd of dragons.

"Lies!" Woraug snarled. "They're all lies!"

"Are they?" Kazul said coldly. "I don't think so. You must have wanted to be King very badly indeed."

"I–" Woraug darted a glance around the circle of dragons. What he saw did not appear to reassure him. "No!"

"Consorting with wizards, killing the King, and plotting to cheat in the trials with Colin's Stone," Kazul said as if Woraug had not spoken. "Hardly proper behavior for a dragon."

The crowd muttered agreement. Cimorene looked from Woraug to Kazul and back. Woraug appeared to be terrified of something, but Cimorene could not tell what it was. He crouched and seemed to shrink away from Kazul, drawing his wings in close and making himself as small as possible. Cimorene blinked. It was remarkable how much smaller Woraug could make himself look. In fact . . .

"He's *shrinking!*" Cimorene exclaimed.

"No!" Woraug cried again, but it was much too late. He shrank faster and faster, his wings melting into ridges along his back and his claws retracting. He was barely as tall as Cimorene's shoulder. Then, with a sudden shiver, he collapsed in on himself. A small rain of scales pattered to the ground. A moment later, an extremely warty toad with angry red eyes crawled clumsily out of the center of the pile.

"Is that–is that Woraug?" Alianora asked in a hushed tone.

The toad turned and glared at her, and she stepped back a pace. The stone prince put a protective arm around Alianora's shoulders and glared back at the toad.

"Behave, or I'll step on you," he said.

"Yes, it's Woraug," Kazul said. She sounded almost sad. "That's what happens when a dragon stops acting like a dragon."

The toad turned his glare in Kazul's direction, then hopped off and disappeared among the stones along the riverbank.

Alianora shuddered. Kazul studied her for a moment. "You were Woraug's princess, weren't you? I'm sorry about all this, but it couldn't be helped. It won't take long to find you another dragon."

"I don't think you have to worry about finding her another dragon," Cimorene said. She had been watching Alianora and the stone prince, and an idea had occurred to her.

"What? Why not?" said Kazul.

"Because the stone prince fought with Woraug, and Woraug certainly didn't win. Doesn't that mean that he gets to rescue Woraug's princess?"

"I'm not sure the rules cover this situation at all," Kazul said. "But it sounds reasonable enough, and under the circumstances I doubt that anyone will object. Unless of course she does."

"Oh!" said Alianora, and blushed a rosy red. "No, I don't object at all!"

"Are you sure?" the stone prince said anxiously. "You won't mind waiting a while to marry me? I mean, if you're willing to marry me? You needn't, you know, if the idea doesn't appeal to you."

"It appeals to me very much," Alianora said, blushing redder than ever. "But why do you say that we have to wait?"

The stone prince sighed. "I still have to find a king and do him a great service, and that's bound to take a while."

"For a young man as intelligent as you seem to be, you're remarkably foolish," Morwen commented. "What on earth do you think you've just done?"

An expression of astonishment spread across the prince's face. "You mean the king I was supposed to serve is the King of the *Dragons?*"

"Exactly," Morwen said. "And I doubt that you could do her a greater service than saving the throne from Woraug's plotting."

"That's settled, then," Kazul said. "Let's get the rest of the ceremonies finished and get back to the mountains. There's a great deal of work to be done."

The dragons all bowed, and eddies of movement began in various sections of the crowd. Shortly, two dragons came forward carrying Colin's Stone. It looked like a long black log about three times as thick as Cimorene's waist and twice as tall as she was. The dragons laid it in front of Kazul and backed away. Another dragon appeared, holding a large circlet made of iron, with six spikes poking upward at intervals around the rim. Kazul set her front feet on the black stone, and the dragon set the circlet on her head. The crowd of dragons began cheering again, and after a few minutes they began forming a line to congratulate their new King and present their coronation gifts. Other dragons set up large tubs of wine and platters of meat and cheese, which were quickly surrounded.

In the middle of the presentations, the dragons Kazul had sent off to the blackberry clearing returned, and Kazul took a short break from accepting congratulations to hear what they had to say.

"The wizards showed up before we'd been there more than ten minutes, Your Majesty," said the pale green dragon who was the leader of the group. "Six of them, just like your princess said."

"They weren't happy to see us," the youngest dragon said smugly.

"I would think not." Kazul smiled. "What did you do with them?"

"We chased five of them away," the pale dragon reported. "I don't think they'll be back, either."

"Five?"

The pale dragon shot a glance at the youngest of the group, who licked his lips and looked even more smug than before and said nothing. "Yes, Your Majesty."

"I see. Well, that's more than enough evidence to confirm what Cimorene's told us," Kazul commented. She raised her voice. "The arrangement between the dragons and the Society of Wizards is hereby canceled. From now on, wizards will not be allowed anywhere near the Caves of Fire and Night, no matter what they say." Then she went back to accepting presents and congratulations from her new subjects.

Cimorene watched the festivities with mixed feelings. She was very glad that Kazul was the new King of the Dragons, but she couldn't help wondering what effect Kazul's coronation would have on her own position. The King of the Dragons certainly wouldn't need a princess as a mark of status, and there would be plenty of younger dragons eager to cook and clean for their King, if only as a way of getting a start at the court.

Her preoccupation stayed with her for the rest of the day, through the entire coronation picnic and the flight back to the Mountains of Morning. Cimorene and Alianora rode on the back of a very large dragon whose scales were such a dark green that they looked almost black. Alianora would have preferred to ride with the stone prince, but none of the dragons were willing to take on a second passenger if the stone prince was the first. All of the dragons had paid their respects to Kazul at the coronation, so the cave was empty when the dragon dropped Cimorene off. When Cimorene said good-bye to Alianora, she promised to come over and help her pack the following morning. Then she went in and waited for Kazul to come home.

Kazul did not arrive until very late. She was still wearing the iron crown, and she looked very tired.

"Thank goodness that's over," she said, taking the crown off and throwing it across the cave. It hit the wall and bounced off with a harsh clang.

"You shouldn't treat your crown like that, Your Majesty," Cimorene said, retrieving the iron circlet.

"Of course I should," Kazul said. "It's expected. That's why we made it out of iron instead of something soft and bendable. And don't start calling me 'Your Majesty.' I've had enough of that for one day."

Cimorene began to feel a little better. "What happens next?"

"Tomorrow we start moving," Kazul said and sighed. "It will probably take weeks. It's too bad there's no way of warning a new king in time to pack everything up before the work starts."

"Everything?" Cimorene said in tones of dismay. "Even the library and the treasure vaults? But I've only just got them organized!"

"Everything," Kazul said. "And if you think straightening out things here was difficult, wait until you see the mess the official vaults are in."

"Oh, dear," said Cimorene. "Is it very bad?"

Kazul nodded. "I've just come from looking at it. You'll see for yourself tomorrow. There's a smallish cave next to the library that I think will do nicely for you, but I'd like you to look at it before we start hauling things around."

"You mean you want me to stay?" Cimorene blurted. "But I thought the King of the Dragons didn't need a princess!"

"Don't be ridiculous," Kazul said. "How am I going to get my cherries jubilee if you don't stay? And you haven't even started cataloguing the library, and how else am I going to get the King's treasure vaults arranged so I can find things? *I'm* not going to have time to do it."

"Won't the rest of the dragons object?"

Kazul snorted. "I'm the King. One of the advantages of being King is that nobody objects to whims like keeping a princess when you're not supposed to need one. If it bothers you, we'll give you a different title: King's Cook and Librarian, maybe. Stop worrying and go to sleep. Tomorrow is going to be a very busy day for both of us."

Cimorene smiled and went off to her rooms with a light heart. She slept soundly and was up early next morning. Kazul was already awake and supervising three of the younger dragons, who were packing up the treasure and the library. Since Cimorene was pressed into service at once, it was several hours before she could get away to keep her promise to Alianora.

"I'm sorry I'm late," Cimorene apologized when she arrived at Woraug's cave at last. "But it didn't occur to me that Kazul would be moving, too, and she wanted me to help."

"It's all right," Alianora assured her. "It wasn't as big a job as I'd expected, and the prince helped. I'm almost finished." She gestured at an almost-full suitcase lying open on the floor. On the other side of the room, the stone prince was stacking the empty drawers from Alianora's bureau.

"Well, at least I got here in time to say good-bye," Cimorene said.

"You're staying with the dragons, then?" the stone prince asked, straightening with a frown. "Are you sure you want to do that?"

"Of course she's sure," Alianora said. "Kazul's going to need her even more than she did before, and Cimorene wouldn't be happy in a normal kingdom."

"How did you know that?" Cimorene said, staring at Alianora.

"It's obvious. Linderwall is about as normal a kingdom as you can get. If you ran away from there, you certainly wouldn't be happy anywhere like it."

"I didn't mean that part," Cimorene said, reddening slightly. "I meant about Kazul wanting me to stay."

"That was obvious, too," Alianora said. "You're the only one who was worried about it." She studied Cimorene for a minute and shook her head. "I wouldn't like being princess for the King of the Dragons, but it will suit you down to the ground."

"I think it will," Cimorene said, smiling.

"Then maybe you can tell me something," the stone prince said. "What's being done about the wizards?"

"They've been banned from the Mountains of Morning, and there are a hundred or so dragons out checking to make sure they've gone," Cimorene replied. "They haven't had much luck, I'm afraid. Most of the wizards left after the first few got eaten."

"That's all?" asked the prince.

"What else can the dragons do? The wizards didn't actually poison King Tokoz; Woraug did that. So there's no justification for an all-out attack on the headquarters of the Society of Wizards, even if all the dragons agreed that they wanted to do it. Which they don't."

"I suppose you're right," the prince said. "But you'd better tell Kazul to keep a close eye on them. Those wizards will make more trouble just as soon as they figure out a way to do it."

"I don't know about that," Cimorene said. "I think Zemenar was behind most of it, and you melted him."

"That's it!" Alianora said, and snapped her fingers. "I almost forgot to tell you. Morwen and I talked for a long time yesterday, and she says that melting a wizard isn't permanent."

"You mean they'll all come back?" Cimorene asked.

Alianora nodded. "It will take them a while, though. And Morwen said for you to come and visit soon. She thinks that in a few days she'll have figured out a way of melting wizards without dumping soapy water over them. 'A method that's a little less sloppy' was the way she put it."

"That will be useful if the wizards start making trouble again," Cimorene said thoughtfully.

"Is this everything, Alianora?" the stone prince asked, gesturing at the suitcase.

"Yes, I think so." Alianora pulled the top of the suitcase over, and the stone prince set one foot very gently in the middle of it and pushed until the latch clicked.

"Where are you going first?" Cimorene asked. "His kingdom or yours?"

"Neither," Alianora said, smiling. "We're going to Morwen's. She said she could change him back from stone to normal. We asked Kazul last night if we could go out through the Caves of Fire and Night, and she said yes, so . . ."

"I don't know, Alianora," the stone prince said. "I'm beginning to get used to myself this way. And there are certain advantages."

"There are disadvantages, too," Alianora said, blushing slightly.

Cimorene began to giggle.

Alianora's blush deepened. "I mean–uh–how are you going to get rid of that chip in your sleeve if you can't change clothes?"

"I think I see what you're getting at," the stone prince replied, eyeing Alianora meditatively. "And you're quite right. There's no comparison. We had better see Morwen as quickly as possible."

Alianora and Cimorene looked at each other and burst into unstoppable giggles.

The stone prince blinked at them. "It's not funny!" he said indignantly, which only made them giggle harder. Shaking his head, he waited for them to stop, then picked up Alianora's suitcase. "Shall we go?"

Cimorene walked with them to the iron gate that led into the Caves of Fire and Night. A purplish dragon was waiting to guide them through the caves. Kazul was taking no chances on Alianora and the stone prince getting lost. Cimorene hugged them both and wished them a safe journey.

"And I hope you both live happily ever after!"

"I hope you do, too!" Alianora called back as she and the stone prince followed the dragon through the gate.

Cimorene watched until they were out of sight, then started back toward Kazul's cave. She thought about Morwen, and the wizard-melting spell, and about Zemenar and Antorell and the other wizards who would somehow be back soon. She thought about Kazul, and about straightening out the treasure vaults that belonged to the King of the Dragons, and about all the hundreds of books in the King's library, and of all the problems that the King of the Dragons would have to deal with. She thought about Alianora's last words and smiled.

Happily ever after? Cimorene wasn't sure about that, though she was certainly hoping to enjoy herself. She was positive, however, that life with the dragons would be interesting and busy, and in Cimorene's opinion that would go a long way toward making her happy.

"Happily ever after? I don't think it's quite what you meant, Alianora," Cimorene murmured to the empty tunnel, "but one way or another, I rather think I will."

SEARCHING

FOR

DRAGONS

I would like to thank the

RIGHT HONORABLE WICKED STEPMOTHERS'

TRAVELING, DRINKING, AND DEBATING SOCIETY

–Caroline, Ellen, and Mimi–

for kindly granting their permission

for use of their Society

in this book, and for allowing me

to inflict them with a Men's Auxiliary.

Contents

1

In Which the King of the Enchanted Forest Takes a Day Off

The King of the Enchanted Forest was twenty years old and lived in a rambling, scrambling, mixed-up castle somewhere near the center of his domain. He sometimes wished he could say that it was *exactly* at the center, but this was impossible because the edges and borders and even the geography of the Enchanted Forest tended to change frequently and without warning. When you are the ruler of a magical kingdom, however, you must expect some small inconveniences, and the King tried not to worry too much about the location of his castle.

The castle itself was an enormous building with a wide, square moat, six mismatched towers, four balconies, and far too many staircases. One of the previous Kings of the Enchanted Forest had been very fond of sweeping up and down staircases in a long velvet robe and his best crown, so he had added stairs wherever he thought there was room. Some of the steps wound up one side of a tower and down the other without actually going anywhere, which caused no end of confusion among visitors.

The inside of the castle was worse than the outside. There were corridors that looped and curled and twisted, rooms that led into other rooms, and even rooms that had been built inside of other rooms. There were secret passageways and sliding panels and trapdoors. There were several cellars, a basement, and *two* dungeons, one of which could only be reached from the sixth floor of the North-Northwest Tower.

"There is something backwards about climbing up six flights of stairs in order to get to a dungeon," the King of the Enchanted Forest said, not for the first time, to his steward.

The steward, a small, elderly elf named Willin, looked up from a hand-written list nearly as long as he was tall and scowled. "That is not the point, Your Majesty."

The two were in the castle study, going over the day's tasks. Willin stood in the center of the room, ignoring several chairs of assorted sizes, while the King sat behind a huge, much-battered oak desk, his long legs stretched out comfortably beneath it. He was not wearing a crown or even a circlet, his clothes were as plain as a gardener's, and his black hair was rumpled and needed trimming, but somehow he still managed to look like a king. Perhaps it was the thoughtful expression in his gray eyes.

Willin cleared his throat and went on, "As the center of Your Majesty's kingdom, this castle–"

"It's not at the center of the kingdom," the King said, irritated. "It's only close. And please just call me Mendanbar and save all that 'Your Majesty' nonsense for a formal occasion."

"We don't *have* formal occasions anymore," Willin complained. "Your Majesty has canceled all of them–the Annual Arboreal Party, the Banquet for Lost Princes, the Birthday Ball, the Celebration of Colors, the Christening Commemoration, the–"

"I know," Mendanbar interrupted. "And I'm sure you have them all written down neatly somewhere, so you don't have to recite them all. But we really didn't need so many dinners and audiences and things."

"And now we don't have any," Willin said, unmollified. "And all because you said formal occasions were stuffy."

"They *are* stuffy," King Mendanbar replied. "Stuffy and boring. And so is being 'Your Majestied' every third word, especially when there's only the two of us here. It sounds silly."

"In your father's day, everyone was required to show proper respect."

"Father was a stuffed shirt and you know it," Mendanbar said without bitterness. "If he hadn't drowned in the Lake of Weeping Dreamers three years ago, you'd be grumbling as much about him as you do about me."

Willin scowled reprovingly at the King. "Your father was an excellent King of the Enchanted Forest."

"I never said he wasn't. But no matter how good a king he was, you can't deny that he was a stuffed shirt, too."

"If I may return to the topic of discussion, Your Majesty?" the elf said stiffly.

The King rolled his eyes. "Can I stop you?"

"Your Majesty has only to dismiss me."

"Yes, and if I do you'll sulk for days. Oh, go on. What about the North-Northwest dungeon?"

"It has come to my attention that it is not properly equipped. When it was first built, by Your Majesty's great-great-great-great-grandfather, it was naturally stocked with appropriate equipment." Willin set his list of things to do on Mendanbar's desk. He drew a second scroll from inside his vest and began to read. "Two leather whips, one Iron Maiden, four sets of thumbscrews–"

"I'll take your word for it, Willin," the King said hastily. When Willin got going, he could read lists for hours on end. "What's the point?"

"Most of these items are still in the dungeon," Willin said, rerolling the scroll and stowing it inside his vest once more, "but the rack was removed in your great-great-grandfather's time and has never been replaced."

"Really?" King Mendanbar said, interested in spite of himself. "Why did he take it out?"

The little steward coughed. "I believe your great-great-grandmother wanted it to dry tablecloths on."

"Tablecloths?" Mendanbar looked out the window at the North-Northwest Tower and shook his head. "She made someone haul a rack up eight flights of stairs and down six more, just to dry tablecloths?"

"A very determined woman, your great-great-grandmother," Willin said. "In any case, the dungeon is in need of a new rack."

"And it can stay that way," said Mendanbar. "Why should we get another rack? We've never used the one we have." He hesitated, frowning. "At least, I don't think we've ever used it. Have we?"

"That is not the point, Your Majesty," Willin answered in a huffy tone, from which the King concluded that they hadn't. "It is my duty to see that the castle is suitably furnished, from the topmost tower to the deepest dungeon. And the dungeon–"

"–needs a new rack," the King finished. "I'll think about it. What else?"

The elf consulted his list. "The nightshades are becoming a problem in the northeast."

"Nightshades are always a problem. Is that all?"

"Ah . . ." Willin cleared his throat, then cleared it again. "There is the matter of Your Majesty's marriage."

"What marriage?" Mendanbar asked, alarmed.

"Your Majesty's marriage to a lady of suitable parentage," Willin said firmly. He pulled another scroll from inside his vest. "I have here a list of possible choices, which I have compiled after a thorough survey of the lands surrounding the Enchanted Forest."

"You made a survey? Willin, you haven't been talking to that dreadful woman with all the daughters, have you? Because if you have I'll . . . I'll use *you* to test out that new rack you want so badly."

"Queen Alexandra is an estimable lady," Willin said severely. "And her daughters are among the loveliest and most accomplished princesses in the world. I have not, of course, talked to the Queen about the possibility, but any one of her daughters would make a suitable bride for Your Majesty." He tapped the scroll meaningfully.

"Suitable? Willin, all twelve of them put together don't have enough common sense to fill a teaspoon! And neither have you, if you think I'm going to marry one of them."

Willin sighed. "I did hope Your Majesty would at least consider the idea."

"Then you weren't thinking straight," the King said firmly. "After all the trouble I've had . . ."

"Perhaps Your Majesty's experiences have given you a biased view of the matter."

"Biased or not, I'm not going to marry anyone any time soon. Particularly not an empty-headed princess, and *especially* not one of Queen Alexandra's daughters. So you can stop bringing it up every day. Do you understand?"

"Yes, Your Majesty. But–"

"But nothing. If that's everything, you may go. And take that list of princesses with you!"

"Yes, Your Majesty." With a final, fierce scowl, Willin bowed and left the room, every inch of his two-foot height reeking of disapproval.

Mendanbar sighed and dropped his head into his hands, digging his fingers into his thick, dark hair. Willin meant well, but why did he have to bring the subject up *now,* just when it looked as if things were going to calm down for a little while? The feud between the elf clans had finally been settled (more or less to everyone's satisfaction), the most recent batch of enchanted princes had been sent packing with a variety of improbable remedies, and the giants to the north weren't due to raid anyone for another couple of months at least. Mendanbar had been looking forward to a quiet week or two, but if Willin was going to start nagging him about marriage, there was little chance of that.

"I might just as well go on a quest or hire some dwarves to put in another staircase for all the peace I'm likely to get around here," Mendanbar said aloud. "When Willin gets hold of an idea, he never lets go of it."

"He's right, you know," said a deep, raspy voice from somewhere near the ceiling. The King looked up, and the carved wooden gargoyle in the corner grinned at him. "You *should* get married," it said.

"Don't *you* start," Mendanbar said.

"Try and stop me," snarled the gargoyle. "My opinion is as good as anyone else's."

"Or as bad," the King muttered.

"I heard that!" The gargoyle squinted downward. "No thanks to you, I might add. Do you know how long it's been since anyone cleaned this corner? I've got dust in my ears, and I expect something slimy to start growing on my claws any minute now."

"Complain to one of the maids," Mendanbar said, irritated. "We weren't talking about hiring a housekeeper."

"Why not? What are you, cheap or something?"

"No, and I wouldn't discuss it with you even if I were."

"King Mendanbar the Cheapskate, that's what they'll call you," the gargoyle said with relish. "What do you think of that?"

"I think I won't talk to you at all," said Mendanbar, who knew from experience that the gargoyle only got more unpleasant the longer it talked. "I'm leaving."

"Wait a minute! I haven't even gotten started yet."

"If Willin asks, tell him I've gone for a walk," Mendanbar said. As he left the room, he waved, twitching two of the invisible threads of power that crisscrossed the Enchanted Forest. The gargoyle's angry screeching changed abruptly to surprise as a stream of soapy water squirted out of the empty air in front of it and hit it squarely in its carved mouth.

Mendanbar smiled as the door closed behind him, shutting out the gargoyle's splutters. "He won't complain about dust again for a while, anyway," Mendanbar said aloud. As he walked down the hall, his smile grew. It had been a long time since he had taken a day off. If Willin wanted to grumble about it, he could go ahead and grumble. The King had earned a holiday, and he was going to have one.

Getting outside without being caught was easy, even without using any invisibility spells (which Mendanbar considered cheating). Willin was the only one who might have objected, and he was at the other end of the castle somewhere. Mendanbar sneaked past two maids and the footman at the front door anyway, just for practice. He had a feeling he might want to do a lot of sneaking in the near future, especially if Willin was going to start fussing about Queen Alexandra's daughters again.

Once he had crossed the main bridge over the moat and reached the giant trees of the Enchanted Forest, he let himself relax a little, but not too much. The Enchanted Forest had its own peculiar rules, and even the King was not exempt from them. If he drank from the wrong stream and got turned into a rabbit, or accidentally stepped on a slowstone, he would have just as much trouble getting back to normal as anyone else. He still remembered how much bother it had been to get rid of the donkey's ears he'd gotten by eating the wrong salad when he was eight.

Of course, now that he was King of the Enchanted Forest he had certain privileges. Most of the creatures that lived in the forest would obey him, however reluctantly, and he could find his way in and out and around without even thinking about it. He could use the magic of the forest directly, too, which made him as powerful as any three wizards and a match for all but the very best enchanters.

"Magic makes things much simpler," Mendanbar said aloud. He looked around at the bright green moss that covered the ground, thick and springy as the finest carpet, and the huge trees that rose above it, and he smiled. Pleasant as it looked, without magic he wouldn't have wanted to wander around it alone.

Magic came naturally to the Kings of the Enchanted Forest. It had to; you couldn't begin to do a good job of ruling such a magical kingdom unless you had a lot of magic of your own. The forest chose its own kings, and once it had chosen them, it gave them the ability to sense the magic permeating the forest and an instinct for using it. The kings all came from Mendanbar's family, for no one else could safely use the sword that did the choosing, but sometimes the crown went to a second son or a cousin instead of to the eldest son of the king. Mendanbar considered himself lucky to have followed his father onto the throne.

Uneasily, he glanced back toward the castle, then shook his head. "Even a king needs a day off once in a while," he told himself. "And it's not as if they need me for anything urgent." He turned his back and marched into the trees, determined to enjoy his holiday.

For a few minutes, he strolled aimlessly, enjoying the cool, dense shadows. Then he decided to visit the Green Glass Pool. He hadn't been there for a while, and it was one of his favorite places. He thought about using magic to move himself there in the blink of an eye, but decided against it.

"After all," he said, "I wanted a walk. And the pool isn't *that* far away." He set off briskly in the direction of the pool.

An hour later, he still hadn't reached it, and he was beginning to feel a little cross. The forest had shifted twice on him, each time moving the pool sideways or backward, so that not only was it farther away than it had been, it was in a different direction as well. It was almost as if the forest didn't want him to find the place. If he hadn't been the King of the Enchanted Forest, Mendanbar would never have known he was going the wrong way.

"This is very odd," Mendanbar said, frowning. "I'd better find out what's going on." Normally, the Enchanted Forest didn't play this sort of game with him. He checked to make sure his sword was loose in its sheath and easy to draw if he needed it. Then he lifted his hand and touched a strand of magic floating invisibly beside his shoulder.

All around him, the huge tree trunks blurred and faded into gray mist. The mist thickened into a woolly fog, then vanished with a suddenness that always surprised him no matter how many times he did the spell. Blinking, he shook his head and looked around.

He was standing right where he had wanted to be, on the rocky lip of the Green Glass Pool. The pool looked as it always did: flat and still as a mirror, and the same shade of green as the new leaves on a poplar.

"Oh!" said a soft, frightened voice from behind him. "Oh, who are you?"

Mendanbar jumped and almost fell into the pool. He recovered his balance quickly and turned, and his heart sank. Sitting on the ground at the foot of an enormous oak was a girl. She wore a thin silver circlet on her head, and the face below it was heart-shaped and very lovely. Her long, golden hair and sky blue dress stood out clearly against the oak's brown bark, like a picture made of jewels set in a dark-colored frame. That was probably exactly the effect she had intended, Mendanbar thought with a resigned sigh. Somehow princesses, even the ones with less wit than a turtle, always knew just how to appear to their best advantage.

"Who are you?" the princess asked again. She was examining Mendanbar with an expression of great interest, and she did not look frightened anymore. "And how did you come here, to this most solitary and forsaken place?"

"My name is Mendanbar, and I was out for a walk," Mendanbar replied. He sighed again and added, "Is there something I might do for you?"

The princess hesitated. "*Prince* Mendanbar?" she asked delicately.

"No," Mendanbar answered, puzzled.

"Lord Mendanbar, then? Or, belike, Sir Mendanbar?"

"I'm afraid not." He was beginning to catch on, and he hoped fervently that she wouldn't think of asking whether he was a king. It was a good thing he wasn't wearing his crown. Ambitious princesses were even worse than the usual variety, and he didn't want to deal with either one right now.

The princess's dainty eyebrows drew together for a moment while she considered his answer. Finally, her expression cleared. "Then you must be a virtuous woodcutter's son, whose deeds of valor and goodwill shall earn you lands and title in some glorious future," she said positively.

"A woodcutter? In the Enchanted Forest?" Mendanbar said, appalled. Didn't the girl have *any* sense? "No, thank you!"

"But how came you here to find me, if you are neither prince nor knight nor deserving youth?" the princess asked in wide-eyed confusion.

"Oh . . . sometimes these things happen," Mendanbar said vaguely. "Were you expecting someone in particular?"

"Not exactly," said the princess. She studied him, frowning, as if she were trying to decide whether it would be all right to ask him for help even if he wasn't a prince or a lord or a virtuous woodcutter.

"How did *you* get here, by the way?" Mendanbar asked quickly. He hated to refuse princesses pointblank, because they cried and pouted and carried on, but they always asked him to do such silly things. Bring them a white rose from the Garden of the Moon, for instance, or kill a giant or a dragon in single combat. It would be better for both of them if he could distract this princess so that she never asked.

"Alas! It is a tale of great woe," the princess said. "Out of jealousy, my stepmother cast me from my father's castle while he was away at war. Since then I have wandered many days, lost and alone and friendless, until I knew not where I was."

She sounded as if she had rehearsed her entire speech, and what little sympathy Mendanbar had had for her vanished. She and her stepmother had probably talked the whole thing out, he decided, and come to the conclusion that the quickest and surest way for her to make a suitable marriage was to go adventuring. He was amazed that she'd actually gotten into the Enchanted Forest. Usually, the woods kept out the obviously selfish.

"At last I found myself in a great waste," the princess continued complacently. "Then I came near giving myself up for lost, for it was dry and terrible. But I saw this wood upon the farther side, and so I gathered my last strength to cross. Fortune was with me, and I achieved my goal. Fatigued with my efforts, I sat down beneath this tree to rest, and–"

"Wait a minute," Mendanbar said, frowning. "You crossed some sort of wasteland and arrived *here?* That can't be right. There aren't any wastelands bordering the Enchanted Forest."

"You insult me," the princess said with dignity. "How should I lie to such a one as you? But go and see for yourself, if you yet doubt my words." She waved one hand gracefully at the woods behind her.

"Thank you, I will," said Mendanbar. Still frowning, he walked rapidly past the princess in the direction she had indicated.

The princess's mouth fell open in surprise as he went by. Before she could collect herself to demand that he return and explain, Mendanbar was out of sight behind a tree.

2

In Which Mendanbar Discovers a Problem

Mendanbar was still congratulating himself on his escape when the trees ended abruptly. He stopped, staring, and quit worrying about the princess entirely.

A piece of the Enchanted Forest as large as the castle lawn was missing. No, not missing; here and there, a few dead stumps poked up out of the dry, bare ground. Something had destroyed a circular swath of trees and moss, destroyed it so completely that only stumps and a few flakes of ash remained.

The taste of dust on the wind brought Mendanbar out of his daze. He hesitated, then took a step forward into the area of devastation. As he passed from woods to waste, he felt a sudden absence and stumbled in shock. Where the unseen lines of power should have been, humming with the magical energy that was the life of the Enchanted Forest, he sensed nothing. The magic was gone.

"No wonder that princess didn't have any trouble getting into the forest," Mendanbar said numbly. Without magic, this section of forest couldn't dodge away from her; all the princess had to do to get into the woods was cross it.

Seriously annoyed, Mendanbar kicked at the ground, dislodging more ashes. He bent to touch one of the stumps. The wood crumbled to dust where his hand met it. Coughing, he sat back and saw something glittering on the ground beside the next stump. He went over and picked it up. It was a thin, hard disk a little larger than his hand, and it was a bright, iridescent green.

"A dragon's scale? What is a dragon's scale doing *here?*"

There was no one near to answer his question. He inspected the scale with care, but it told him nothing more. Scowling at it, he shrugged and put it in his pocket. Then he began a methodical search of the dead area, hoping to find something that would reveal a little more.

Half an hour later, he had collected four more dragon scales in various shades of green and was feeling decidedly grim. He had thought he was on good terms with the dragons who lived to the east in the Mountains of Morning: he left them alone and they left him alone. Glancing around the burned space, he grimaced.

"This doesn't look much like 'leaving me alone,' " he muttered angrily. "What do those dragons think they are doing?" He began to wish *he* had not left *them* quite so much alone for the past three years. Right now it would be useful to know something more about dragons than that they were all large and breathed fire.

Absently, Mendanbar pocketed the dragon scales and walked back to the edge of the burned-out circle. It was a relief to be under the trees where he could feel the magic of the forest again. Frowning, he paused to look back at the ashy clearing.

"I can't just leave it like this," he said to himself. "If that princess came this way, *anyone* might get into the Enchanted Forest just by walking across the barren space. But how do I put magic back into an area that's been sucked dry?"

Still frowning, he circled the edge of the clearing, nudging at the threads of magic that wound through the air. None of them would move any closer to the burned section, but on the far side he found the place where the normal country outside the forest touched the clearing. He paused. It wasn't a very wide gap.

"I wonder," he said softly. "If I could *move* it a little, just around the edge . . ."

Carefully, he reached out and gathered a handful of magic. It felt a lot like taking hold of a handful of thin cords, except that the cords were invisible, floating in the air, and made his palms tingle when he touched them. And, of course, each cord was actually a piece of solid magic that he could use to cast a spell if he wanted. In fact, he had to concentrate hard to *keep* from casting a spell or two with all that magic crammed together in his hands.

Pulling gently on the invisible threads, Mendanbar stepped slowly backward out of the Enchanted Forest. The brilliant green moss followed him, rippling under his feet. The trees of the forest wavered as if he were looking at them through a shimmer of hot air rising off sunbaked stone. He took another step, and another. The threads of magic felt warm and thin and slippery. He tightened his grip and took another step. The trees flickered madly, as if he were blinking very rapidly, and the moss swelled and twitched like the back of a horse trying to get rid of an unwanted rider. A drop of sweat ran down his forehead and hung on the tip of his nose. The magic in his hands felt hot and tightly stretched. He stepped back again.

With a sudden wrench, everything snapped into place. The trees stopped flickering and the moss smoothed and lay still. The forest closed up around the burned-out clearing, circling it completely and cutting it off from the outside world. Mendanbar gave a sigh of relief.

"It worked!" he cried triumphantly. A breeze brushed past him, carrying the sharp smell of ashes, and he sobered. He hadn't repaired the damage; he had only isolated it. "Well, at least it should keep people from wandering into the Enchanted Forest by accident," he reminded himself. "That's something."

One by one, Mendanbar let go of the threads of magic he had pulled across the gap. He felt them join the other unseen strands, merging back into the normal network of magic that crisscrossed the forest. When he had released the last thread, he wiped his hands on his shirt, then wiped the sweat off his face with his sleeve.

"Are you quite finished?" said a voice from a tree above his head.

Mendanbar looked up and saw a fat gray squirrel sitting on a branch, staring down at him with disapproval.

"I think so," Mendanbar said. "For the time being, anyway."

"For the time being?" the squirrel said indignantly. "What kind of an answer is that? Not useful, that's what I call it, not useful at all. Finding my way across this forest is hard enough when people don't make bits of it jump around, not to mention burning pieces of it and I don't know what else. I don't know what this place is coming to, really I don't."

"Were you here when the trees were burned?" Mendanbar asked. "Did you see what happened? Or who did it?"

"Well, of course not," said the squirrel. "If I had, I'd have given him, her, or it a piece of my mind, I can tell you. Really, it's too bad. I'm going to have to work out a whole new route to get home. And as for giving directions to lost princes, well, it's hopeless, that's what it is, just hopeless. I'll get blamed for it when they come out wrong, too, see if I don't. Word always gets around. 'Don't trust the squirrel,' they'll say, 'you always go wrong if you follow the squirrel's directions.' They never stop to think of the difficulties involved in a job like mine, oh, no. They don't stop to say thank-you, either, not them. Ask the squirrel and go running off, that's what they do, and never so much as look back. No consideration, no gratitude. You'd think they'd been raised in a palace for all the manners they have."

"If they're princes, they probably *have* been raised in palaces," Mendanbar said. "Princes usually are."

"Well, no wonder none of them have any manners, then." The squirrel sniffed. "They ought to be sent to school in a forest, where people are polite. You don't see any of *my* children behaving like that, no, sir. *Please* and *thank you* and *yes, sir* and *no, ma'am*–that's how I brought them up, all twenty-three of them, and what's good enough for squirrels is good enough for princes, I say."

"I'm sure you're right," Mendanbar said. "Now, about the burned spot–"

"Wicked, that's what I call it," the squirrel interrupted. "But hooligans like that don't stop to think, do they? Well, if they did, they wouldn't go around setting things on fire and making a lot of trouble and inconvenience for people. Inconsiderate, every last one of them, and they'll be sorry for it one day, you just wait and see if they aren't."

"Hooligans?" Mendanbar blinked and began to feel more cheerful. Maybe he wasn't in trouble with the dragons after all. Maybe it had been a rogue who had burned out part of his forest. That would be bad, but at least he wouldn't have to figure out a way of dragon-proofing the whole kingdom. He frowned. "How am I going to find out for sure?" he wondered aloud.

"Ask Morwen," said the squirrel, flicking her tail.

"What?"

"I said, ask Morwen. Honestly, don't you big people know how to listen? You'd think none of you had ever talked to a squirrel before, the way most of you behave."

"I'm very sorry," Mendanbar said. "Who's Morwen?"

"That's better," the squirrel said, mollified. "Morwen's a witch. She lives over by the mountains–just head that way until you get to the stream, then follow it to the big oak tree with the purple leaves. Turn left and walk for ten minutes and you should come out in her backyard. That is," she added darkly, "you should if all this burning things up and moving things around hasn't tangled everything *too* badly."

"You think this witch had something to do with what happened?" Mendanbar waved at the ashy clearing a few feet away.

"I said no such thing! Morwen is a very respectable person, even if she does keep cats."

"Then I don't understand why you think I should talk to her."

"You asked for my advice, and I've given it," said the squirrel. "That's my job. I'm not supposed to *explain* it, too, for heaven's sake. If you want explanations, talk to a griffin."

"If I see one, I will," said Mendanbar. "Thank you for your advice."

"You're welcome," said the squirrel, sounding pleased. She flicked her tail twice and leaped to a higher branch. "Good-bye." In another moment she had disappeared behind the trunk of the tree.

"Good-bye," Mendanbar called after her. He waited, but there was no further response. The squirrel had gone.

Slowly, Mendanbar started walking in the direction the squirrel had pointed. When someone in the Enchanted Forest gave you advice, you were usually best off following it, even if you were the King.

"Especially if you're the King," Mendanbar reminded himself. He wished he knew a little more about this Morwen person, though. He wasn't really surprised that he hadn't heard of her. So many witches lived in and around the Enchanted Forest that it was impossible for anyone to keep track of them all. Still, this one must be something special, or the squirrel wouldn't have sent the King of the Enchanted Forest to her.

What sort of witch was Morwen? "Respectable" didn't tell him a lot, especially coming from a squirrel. Morwen could be a white witch, but she could also be the sort of witch who lived in a house made of cookies in order to enchant passing children.

"She could even be a fire witch," he said to himself. "There are probably one or two of them who could be termed respectable." He thought about that for a moment. He'd never heard of any himself.

If Morwen had lived in the Enchanted Forest for a long time, she was probably a decent sort of witch, he decided at last. The nasty ones generally made trouble before they'd been around very long, and then someone would complain to the King.

"And nobody has complained about Morwen," he finished.

Mendanbar reached the stream and turned left. Maybe it *had* been a mistake to cancel all those boring formal festivals and dinners Willin liked so much, he mused. They would have given him a chance to meet some of the ordinary people who lived in the Enchanted Forest. Or rather, he amended, the people who didn't make trouble. "Ordinary" was not the right word for anyone who lived in the Enchanted Forest, not if they managed to stay alive and in more or less their proper shape.

His reflections were cut short by a loud roar. Glancing up, he saw a lion bounding toward him along the bank of the stream. It looked huge and fierce and not at all friendly. As it leaped for his throat, Mendanbar batted hastily at a nearby strand of magic. The lion sailed over Mendanbar's head and landed well behind him, looking surprised and embarrassed. It whirled and tried again, but this time Mendanbar was ready for it. With a quick twist and pull, he froze the lion in the middle of rearing on its hind legs and stepped back to study it.

The lion roared again, plainly frustrated as well as embarrassed and confused. Mendanbar frowned and twitched another invisible thread. Suddenly the roaring had words in it.

"Let me down!" the lion shouted. "This is entirely undignified. How dare you treat me like this?"

"I'm the King," said Mendanbar. "It's my job to keep this forest as safe as I reasonably can. And I don't much like being jumped at when I'm just walking along minding my own business."

"What?" The lion stopped roaring and peered at him nearsightedly. "Oh, bother. I'm exceedingly sorry, Your Majesty. I didn't recognize you. You're not wearing your crown."

"That's not the point," said the King. "It shouldn't make any difference."

"On the contrary," the lion said earnestly. "I'm the guardian of the Pool of Gold, and I'm supposed to keep unauthorized people from dipping branches in it, or diving in and turning into statues–that sort of thing. But if you're the King of the Enchanted Forest, you're not an unauthorized person at all, and I've made a dreadful mistake. I do apologize."

"You should," said Mendanbar. He looked around and frowned. "Where is this Pool of Gold you're supposed to be guarding?"

"Just around the bend," the lion answered. He sounded uncomfortable and a little worried.

"Then what are you doing attacking people over here?" Mendanbar demanded. "I might have gone right by."

"You wouldn't have if you were a prince," the lion muttered. "They never go on by. I was only attempting to get ahead of things a little, that's all. I didn't mean anything by it."

"Yes, well, you should have thought it through," Mendanbar said in a stern tone. "Princes don't always travel alone, you know. Someone could distract you with a fight along here while a friend of his stole water or dipped branches or whatever he wanted. This far away from the pool, you wouldn't even notice."

"That never occurred to me," said the lion, much abashed. "I'm sorry."

"Stick to the pool from now on," Mendanbar told it. "And make sure that the people you jump at are really trying to get at the water, and not just wandering by."

"Yes, Your Majesty," said the lion. "Uh, would you mind letting me down now?"

Mendanbar nodded and untwisted the threads of magic that held the lion motionless. The lion dropped to all fours and shook itself, then bowed very low. "Thank you, Your Majesty," it said. "Is there anything I can do for you?"

"Does a witch named Morwen live somewhere around here?" Mendanbar asked.

"Sure," said the lion. "Her house is up over the hill where the blue catnip grows. It isn't far. I haven't ever been there myself, of course," it added hastily, "since I have to guard the Pool of Gold, you know. But sometimes one of her cats pays a call, and that's what they tell me."

"Thank you," Mendanbar said. "That's very helpful."

"You're welcome, Your Majesty," said the lion. "Any time. Is there anything else? Because if there isn't, I should really be getting back to the pool."

"That's all," Mendanbar said, and bid the lion a polite good-bye. He waited where he stood until the lion was well out of sight, then continued on. He was very thoughtful, and a little annoyed. His quiet walk was turning out to be more of a project than he had expected.

A short while later, he passed the oak the squirrel had described, and a little farther on he found a hill covered with bright blue catnip. He paused, debating the wisdom of walking around the hill rather than through the thick growth.

"You never know what things like oddly colored catnip will do if you touch them," Mendanbar reminded himself. He looked at the knee-high carpet of blue leaves, then glanced at the deep shadows below the trees at the foot of the hill.

"On the other hand, one of the easiest ways of getting lost in the Enchanted Forest is to not follow directions exactly." He looked at the catnip again. He did not want to spend hours hunting for Morwen's house just to avoid some oddly colored plants. Cautiously, he poked at the invisible network of magic that hung over the hill. It seemed normal enough. With a shrug, he waded in.

Halfway to the top, he saw some of the stalks near the edge of the patch wobble, as if something small had run through it. The wobble kept pace with him until he reached the top of the hill, but though he tried to see what was causing it, he was unable to catch a glimpse of whatever was brushing by the plants.

The patch of catnip ended at the top of the hill. Mendanbar stopped to catch his breath and look around. The hill sloped gently down to a white picket fence that surrounded three sides of a garden. A large lilac bush was blooming on one side of the gate in the middle of the fence, and an even larger apple tree loaded with fist-sized green apples stood on the other side.

Mendanbar frowned. "Aren't lilacs and apple trees supposed to *bloom* at the same time? What is one doing with blossoms while the other is covered with fruit?" Then he laughed at himself. "Well, it *is* a witch's garden, after all." He supposed he shouldn't be surprised if things behaved strangely.

On the other side of the garden stood a solid little gray house with a red roof. Smoke was drifting out of the chimney, and lace curtains were blowing in and out the open windows on either side of the back door. Below the right-hand window was a window box overflowing with red and blue flowers. The stone step outside the door was cleaner than the floor inside Mendanbar's study, and he resolved to do something about *that* as soon as he got home. Sleeping on one corner of the step was a white cat, her fur gleaming in the sun.

Mendanbar walked down the hill to the gate. A small brass sign hung on the latch. It read: "Please keep the gate CLOSED. Salesmen enter at their own risk." Smiling, Mendanbar lifted the latch and pushed the gate open.

A loud yowl from just over his head made him jump back. He looked up and discovered a fat tabby cat perched in the branches of the apple tree, staring down at him with green eyes. An instant later, a long gray streak shot out from behind a nearby tree and through the open gate. It slowed as it neared the house, and Mendanbar saw that it was actually a lean gray cat with a ragged tail. The gray cat leaped to the doorstep and from there to the sill of the open window. The white cat on the step raised her head and made a complaining noise as the gray one vanished inside the house.

"So much for a surprise visit," Mendanbar said to the cat in the tree. The cat gave him a smug look and began washing its paws. Mendanbar stepped through the gate, closed it carefully, and started across the garden toward the house.

3

In Which Mendanbar Receives Some Advice from a Witch

Before Mendanbar was halfway across the garden, the door of the cottage swung open. Seven cats of various sizes and colors trotted out, tails high. They flowed over the stoop, collecting the sleepy white cat on their way, and lined themselves up in a neat row. Mendanbar stopped and looked down at them, blinking. They blinked back, all eight at once, as if they had been trained.

"Well?" said a voice.

Mendanbar looked up. A short woman in a loose black robe stood in the open doorway. Her hair was a pale ginger color, piled loosely on her head. Mendanbar supposed she must use magic to keep it up, for not one wisp was out of place. She wore a pair of glasses with gold rims and rectangular lenses, and she held a broom in one hand.

"You must be Morwen," Mendanbar said with more confidence than he felt, for she was quite pretty and, apart from the black robe and broom, not witchy-looking at all.

The woman nodded. Giving her a courteous half-bow, Mendanbar went on, "I'm Mendanbar, and I was advised to talk to you about–well, about a problem I've discovered. I hope you weren't on your way out." He indicated the broom.

Morwen examined him for another moment, then nodded briskly. "So *you're* the King. Come in and tell me why you're here, and I'll see what I can do for you."

"How do you know I'm the King?" Mendanbar asked as the cats exchanged glances and then began wandering off in various directions. He felt disgruntled, because he had not intended to mention the fact. At least Morwen wasn't curtsying or simpering, and she hadn't started calling him "Your Majesty" yet, either. Perhaps it would be all right.

"I recognize you, of course," Morwen said. She set the broom against the wall behind the door as she spoke. "You've let your hair get a bit long, but that doesn't make much difference, one way or another. And Mendanbar isn't exactly a common name these days. Are you going to stand there all day?"

"I'm sorry," Mendanbar said, following Morwen into the house. "I didn't realize we'd met before."

"We haven't," Morwen said. "When I moved to the Enchanted Forest five years ago, I made sure I knew what you looked like. I'd have been asking for trouble, otherwise."

"Oh," said Mendanbar, taken aback. He had never thought of himself as one of the hazards of the Enchanted Forest that someone might wish to be prepared for, and he did not like the idea much, now that it had been pointed out to him.

Morwen waved at a sturdy chair next to a large table in the center of the room. "Sit down. Would you like some cider?"

"That sounds very good." Mendanbar took the chair while Morwen crossed to a cupboard on the far wall and began taking mugs and bottles out of it. He was glad to have a minute to collect his wits. He was not sure what he had expected her to be like, but Morwen was definitely not it.

Her house was not what he had expected, either. The inside was as neat and clean as the outside. The walls of the single large room were painted a pale, silvery gray. Six large windows let in light and air from all directions. There were no gargoyles or grimacing faces or wild tangles of trees and vines carved into the window ledges or the woodwork around the ceiling, and no intricate patterns set into the floorboards. One of the cats had come inside and was sitting on a big, square trunk, washing his paws; another was lying in an open window, keeping an eye on the backyard. There was a large black stove in the corner by the cupboard, and three more chairs around the table where Mendanbar was sitting. It was all very pleasant and uncluttered, and Mendanbar found himself wishing he had a few rooms like this in his castle.

"There," said Morwen as she set a large blue jug and two matching mugs in the center of the table. "Now, tell me about this problem of yours."

Mendanbar cleared his throat and began. "About an hour ago, I ran across a section of the Enchanted Forest that had been destroyed. The trees had been burned to stumps and there wasn't even any moss left on the ground. I'm afraid it may have been a rogue dragon. I found dragon scales in the ashes, and a squirrel suggested I come and see you."

"Dragon scales?" Morwen pressed her lips together, looking very grim indeed. "Did you bring them with you?"

"Yes," said Mendanbar. He dug the scales out of his pocket and spread them out on the table.

"Hmmm," said Morwen, bending over the table. "I don't like the look of this."

"Can you tell anything about this dragon from his scales?" Mendanbar asked.

"For one thing, these scales aren't all from the same dragon," Morwen said. Her frown deepened. "At least, they shouldn't be."

"How can you tell?" Mendanbar asked, his stomach sinking.

"Look at the colors. This one is yellow-green; that one has a grayish tinge, and this one has a purple sheen. You don't get that kind of variation on one dragon."

"Oh, no," Mendanbar groaned, shutting his eyes and leaning his forehead against his hands. He had so hoped that it had been a single dragon. It would have been a nuisance, sending letters of complaint to the King of the Dragons and waiting for an answer, but it would have been better than a war. If a group of dragons had attacked the Enchanted Forest, war was almost inevitable. "You're *sure* there were several dragons involved?"

"I didn't say that," Morwen snapped. "I said that these scales look as if they came from different dragons."

"But if the scales came from different dragons–"

"I didn't say that, either," Morwen said. "I said they *looked* as if they came from different dragons. Have a little patience, Mendanbar."

Mendanbar opened his mouth to say something else, then closed it again. Morwen was staring with great concentration at one of the scales, the one that was the brightest green, and she didn't look as if she would welcome an interruption. Suddenly she straightened and in one swift movement scooped the scales together like a pile of cards. She tapped the stack against the tabletop to straighten it, then set it down with an air of satisfaction.

"Ha! I thought there was something odd about these," she said, half to herself.

"What is it?"

"Just a minute and I'll show you." Morwen went back to the cupboard and took down a small bowl and several jars of various sizes. As she spooned and mixed and muttered, Mendanbar felt magic gather around her, like a tingling in the air that slowly concentrated itself inside the bowl. At last she capped the jars and carried the bowl, brimming with magic, over to the table.

"Stay back," she warned when Mendanbar leaned forward to get a better view.

Mendanbar sat back, watching closely, as Morwen spread the five dragon scales out in a line. She set the purple scale at one end and the bright green one at the other. Then she held the bowl over the center of the line, took a deep breath, and said,

"Wind for clarity,
Stone for endurance,
Stream for change,
Fire for truth:
Be what you are!"

As she spoke, she tilted the bowl and poured a continuous line of dark liquid in a long stripe across the middle of the five scales.

There was a flash of purple light, and the liquid began to glow. The glow spread outward, like fire creeping around the edges of a piece of paper, until it reached the rims of the dragon scales. Then it flashed once more and vanished.

Five identical scales lay side by side on the table, all of them bright green.

"I thought so," Morwen said with satisfaction. "These scales all came from the same dragon. Someone altered them so that they would each look different."

"Oh, good," Mendanbar said with some relief. "How did you know?"

"The scales were the same shape, and very nearly the same size," Morwen said. "Different dragons might have scales about the same size, if they were the same age, but there's as much variation in the shape of dragon scales as there is in their color."

"Really?" Mendanbar said, interested. "I didn't know that."

"Not many people do. But look at these–they're all round, with one flat edge. If they'd come from different dragons, I'd expect one to be, say, squared off, another oval, another long and wiggly, and so on."

"In that case, it shouldn't be too hard to find the dragon who destroyed that chunk of forest," Mendanbar said.

Morwen looked at him severely over the tops of her spectacles. "I'm not sure it was a dragon at all."

"Why not?" Mendanbar asked. "Because the scales were changed? But if he didn't want to be blamed–"

"If some dragon wanted to avoid being blamed for burning up a piece of the Enchanted Forest, he wouldn't have left his scales lying around, changed or not," Morwen said dryly. "Picking them up would be a lot easier than enchanting them. Besides, a healthy dragon doesn't shed scales at this rate. Unless you think your rogue dragon burned down a lot of trees and then stood around looking at them for a week or two."

"I see." Mendanbar picked up one of the scales and ran his fingertips across it.

"It's a good thing you were the one who found these," Morwen went on, waving at the dragon scales. "If it had been one of the elves, there would have been trouble for certain."

"Why do you say that? Whoever found them would have had to bring them to the castle–"

"And long before he got there, word would have been all over the forest that a lot of dragons had burned half the woods to powder," Morwen said. "Most elves mean well, but they can't keep a secret and they have no common sense to speak of. Flighty creatures."

"Do you think someone was trying to make trouble between the Enchanted Forest and the dragons, then?"

"It's possible," Morwen answered. "If you hadn't come to me, you probably would have thought the scales came from different dragons. Plenty of people know about the color variation. I doubt that you'd have figured out the transformation, though. Only people who are fairly familiar with dragons know about the differences in the shapes of their scales, and I don't think anyone at the castle understands dragons very well."

"How do you happen to know so much about dragons?" Mendanbar asked, nettled.

"Oh, Kazul and I have been friends for a long time," Morwen said. "We trade favors now and then. She lets me have a spare scale when I need one for a spell, and I lend her books from my library and pots and pans that she doesn't want to keep around all the time. In fact, Kazul was the one who convinced me that it would be a good idea to move to the Enchanted Forest."

"Kazul," Mendanbar said, frowning. "That name is familiar. Who is she?"

"Kazul is the King of the Dragons," Morwen said. "Drink your cider."

Automatically, Mendanbar lifted his mug. Then the implications of what Morwen had said sank in, and he choked. Morwen was a good friend of the King of the Dragons? No wonder she knew so much about dragon scales!

Morwen gave him an ironic look, as if she knew exactly what he was thinking. To give himself time to recover, Mendanbar sipped at his cider. It was cold and sweet and tangy, and it fizzed as it slid across his tongue. He looked at the mug in surprise and took a longer drink. It was just as tasty the second time. "This is very good."

Morwen looked almost smug. "I make it myself. You may have a bottle to take back to the castle with you, provided you take a bottle to Kazul when you go see her about these scales you found."

"Thank–wait a minute, what makes you think I'm going to see Kazul?"

"How else are you going to find out who these scales belong to? I may know more about dragons than most people, but I can't tell whose scales these are just from their color and size. Kazul can. Besides, you should have paid a call last year, when the old king died and Kazul got the crown."

"I sent a note and a coronation present," Mendanbar said. He sounded sulky even to himself, and he felt as if he were being lectured by his mother, who had died when he was fourteen. "I was going to visit, but the Frost Giants decided to come south early, and then some fool magician tried to turn a rock snake into a bird and got a cockatrice, and–"

"–and it's been one thing after another, and you've never found the time," Morwen said. "Really, Mendanbar. Haven't you learned by now that it's *always* one thing after another? Being busy is no excuse. Everyone's busy. You take those scales and a bottle of my cider and go talk to Kazul. At the very least, you'll get some good advice, and I expect you'll get some help as well. You look to me as if you could use it."

"The castle staff is very good," Mendanbar said stiffly. "And my steward does an excellent job."

"I'm sure he does," Morwen said. "But one good steward isn't enough to run a normal kingdom, much less one like the Enchanted Forest. It's perfectly plain just from looking at you that you're wearing yourself out trying to do everything yourself."

"It is?"

Morwen gave a firm little nod. "It is. And it's quite unnecessary. All you really need–"

"–is a wife," Mendanbar muttered resignedly, recognizing the beginning of Willin's familiar complaint.

"–is someone sensible to talk to," Morwen finished. She looked at him sternly over the tops of her glasses. "Preferably someone who knows at least a little about running a kingdom. An exiled prince, for instance, though they don't usually stay long enough to be useful. Someone who'll do more than make lists of things you need to attend to."

Mendanbar thought of Willin's endless schedules and could not help smiling. "You're probably right." He suppressed a sigh; he didn't have time to spend hunting for a capable adviser. "Do you know anyone suitable?"

"Several people, but they're all quite happy where they are right now," Morwen said. "Don't worry. This is the Enchanted Forest. If you start seriously looking for good help, you'll find some."

"I hope I recognize it when I see it," Mendanbar said. He took another long drink of cider and stared into the mug. "You're the most sensible person I've talked to in days. I don't suppose *you'd* consider moving to the castle?"

"Certainly not," Morwen answered tartly. "I have quite enough to do here. However, I'll have the cats keep an eye out for any more burned-out patches of forest, and if I think of anything that might be important I'll let you know. Finish your cider and go see Kazul before you talk yourself out of it."

"I won't talk myself out of it," Mendanbar said, taking another sip of cider. "It's a good idea." He picked up the dragon scales and put them back into his pocket. He hoped Kazul would be able to tell him something worthwhile. The Enchanted Forest was large, but it could disappear in a hurry if someone started punching holes in it. He frowned suddenly. "Do dragons eat magic?"

"Not that I know of," Morwen said. "Why do you ask?"

"That burned-out place I told you about," Mendanbar said. "There wasn't any magic left in it. It had been sucked dry. I've never seen anything like it."

"I don't think dragons would have done that," Morwen said. She considered for a moment, then rose. "Wait here a minute; I want to look something up."

She walked over to the back door, the one through which Mendanbar had come in. He watched, puzzled, as she opened the door and stepped through into a room full of tall, dark bookcases. Morwen left the door open and disappeared among the shelves. Mendanbar blinked. The windows on either side of the door looked out on the garden, and the one on the right still had a cat in it. *Oh, of course,* he thought. *It's one of those doors that go where you want them to.* There was a door like that in one of the castle attics, which was convenient for getting back to the ground floor without actually climbing down seven flights of stairs. Unfortunately, you still had to climb up all seven flights in order to get to the attic in the first place.

Morwen reappeared, holding a red book with the title *The Patient Dragon* printed on the cover in gold. She closed the library door behind her and sat down at the table again. She flipped rapidly through the book, then slowed and read half a page with great care.

"I thought so," she said. "Dragons don't eat magic. They generate their own, the way unicorns do."

"You're sure?"

"See for yourself." Morwen held the book out. "Austen is very reliable, and the more obscure the fact, the more reliable he tends to be. If he says dragons make their own magic, they do."

"I'll take your word for it," Mendanbar said. "But the more I find out, the less sense any of this makes."

"Then you haven't found out enough," Morwen said.

They talked for a few more minutes while Mendanbar finished his cider. Morwen told him how to find Kazul's cave in the Mountains of Morning but refused to advise him on what to do when he got there. Finally, she packed him off with two bottles of cider, the red book about dragons, and a recommendation not to waste any more time than he had to.

Mendanbar headed straight back to the castle. Visiting the King of the Dragons was going to take more preparation than simply talking to a sensible witch, and Morwen was right about wasting time.

4

In Which a Wizard Pays a Visit

When Mendanbar got back to the castle, the first person he saw was Willin, standing in the doorway looking relieved. By the time Mendanbar got within earshot, however, the elf's expression had changed to a ferocious scowl.

"I am happy to see that Your Majesty has returned safely," Willin said stiffly. "I was about to send a party out to search for you."

"Willin, that's ridic–" Mendanbar broke off as his brain caught up with him. Willin might fuss and complain about the king playing hooky, but he wouldn't send someone out looking for him without more reason than irritation. "What's happened?"

Willin unbent very slightly. "Your Majesty has an unexpected visitor." He paused. "At least, I presume he is unexpected."

"Don't frown at me like that," Mendanbar said. *"I* certainly didn't expect anyone. If I had, I'd have told you."

"So I had assumed," Willin said, relaxing a little more. "And since Your Majesty is not forgetful, in the normal way of things, I felt sure you would not have, ah, left the palace so precipitously if you had had an appointment."

"Who is it?" Mendanbar asked. "Not another complaint from the Darkmorning Elves, I hope? If it is, you can tell them I won't see them. I've had enough of their whining, and I've got more important things to attend to right now."

"No," Willin said. "It's Zemenar, the Head Wizard of the Society of Wizards."

"Oh, lord," Mendanbar said. He had only met the Head Wizard once before, at his coronation three years earlier, and he hadn't liked the man much then. Still, the Society of Wizards was a powerful group, and its members were not the sort of people it was a good idea to offend. He ran a hand distractedly through his hair. "How long has he been waiting? What does he want?"

"He's only been here for a few minutes," Willin reassured him. The elf's frown returned. "He refused to tell me his business, Your Majesty. He said it was a matter for Your Majesty's ears alone."

"He would," Mendanbar muttered. "As I recall, he's got an exaggerated idea of his own importance."

"Your Majesty!" said Willin, clearly shocked by such plain speaking. "The Head Wizard of the Society of Wizards is a person of great distinction."

"*He* certainly thinks so," Mendanbar said. "Oh, don't worry, I won't say anything improper when I'm talking to him. Where is he?"

"I asked him to wait in the main audience chamber."

"Good. I'll go see what he wants. You take these down to the kitchen." Mendanbar handed Morwen's jugs of cider to Willin. The elf blinked in puzzled surprise. Before Willin had time to collect himself, Mendanbar grabbed a handful of magic and twisted hard.

The courtyard faded into white mist. An instant later, the mist evaporated, leaving Mendanbar standing in the middle of his study. The wooden gargoyle in the corner immediately began shouting at him.

"You! You've got a lot of nerve, waltzing in as if nothing's happened. I bet you thought that trick with the soapy water was funny! You'll be sorry for it when the wood up here starts to rot from the damp, you wait and see."

"That's why you're there," Mendanbar said as he set the book Morwen had given him on the desk. "You're supposed to let us know if the wood starts to go bad or gets termites, so we can fix it before the castle falls apart."

"And look at the thanks I get," the gargoyle complained. "Water in my ears and soap in my eyes. How do you expect me to do my job if I can't see?"

Mendanbar listened with half an ear while he rummaged through the desk. The gold circlet he wore for official business was in the bottom drawer under a pile of old envelopes and out-of-date invitations to balls, dinners, birthday parties, cricket games, and teas. As he put the circlet on,

Mendanbar frowned at the drawer, wondering why he was saving all that useless paper. He resolved for the hundredth time that week to clean everything out someday soon, shoved the drawer closed, and glanced around to make sure he hadn't forgotten anything.

"Are you listening to me?" the gargoyle yelled.

"Of course not," Mendanbar said. "I never do when you're being insulting."

"Insulting? You want insulting? I'll give you insulting. You always dress funny! You've got feet like an elephant! Your nose is too big and your ears stick out!"

"Not much, compared to yours," said Mendanbar cheerfully as he crossed to the door. "Stop grousing; if you can see my nose from up where you are, there's nothing wrong with your eyes."

"Your hair is a bird's nest!" the gargoyle shouted just before the door closed behind Mendanbar. "A bird's nest, do you hear me?"

Mendanbar rolled his eyes and headed down the corridor toward the main audience chamber. He supposed he would have to apologize to the gargoyle sooner or later, unless he could figure out a way to muffle the noise while he worked. Maybe he could enchant a pair of earplugs to keep out the gargoyle's voice and nothing else. A spell that specific would be tricky, but it would be worth it just to see the gargoyle's face when it realized Mendanbar didn't mind its chatter. Mendanbar smiled and pushed open the rear door of the audience chamber.

Zemenar turned as Mendanbar entered, and the blue and gray robes he wore flared out around him. His face was just as sharp and angular as Mendanbar remembered. Giving Mendanbar a long, appraising look, Zemenar bowed his head in greeting. "Your Majesty."

"Welcome, Head Wizard," Mendanbar said, bowing slightly in return. Something tugged gently at his mind, distracting him. The strands of magic, which were always particularly plentiful inside the castle, were drifting slowly toward the staff Zemenar carried. In another minute or two, they would begin winding around Zemenar's staff like thread winding onto a spool. Before long, the wizard's staff would absorb them, leaving a tangled knot in the orderly net of magic, and Mendanbar would have to spend hours straightening it out later.

It happened every time a wizard came to the Enchanted Forest, and it was very inconvenient. Mendanbar had gotten tired of asking wizards to keep their staffs from soaking up magic. They hardly ever understood what he was talking about, and if he did manage to make it clear, they generally got upset and indignant. He didn't want to upset the Head Wizard of the Society of Wizards, but he didn't want to spend his afternoon cleaning up a magical mess in the middle of his castle, either. He reached out with a mental hand and nudged the invisible cords away from the staff.

Zemenar did not seem to notice. "I have come to see you about a matter of much urgency to the Society of Wizards," he said, stroking his long gray beard portentously. "I hope you will be willing to assist us."

"That depends on what kind of help you're asking for," Mendanbar replied. "There are some things I won't do, and a few that I can't. I'm sure you understand."

"Entirely," Zemenar said, though he sounded a little put out, as if he had hoped to get Mendanbar to agree quickly, without asking any awkward questions.

Mendanbar felt like rolling his eyes in exasperation. Everybody who lived in the Enchanted Forest knew better than to make a promise without knowing what they were promising. Did this wizard think that Mendanbar was stupid just because he was young?

"We in the Society of Wizards have been having a great deal of difficulty recently with the dragons in the Mountains of Morning," Zemenar went on. "That is the root of the problem."

"I don't think I can help you with the dragons," Mendanbar said. The strands of magic were drifting toward the wizard's staff again. He gave them another nudge. "The Mountains of Morning aren't part of the Enchanted Forest, so I can't just order the dragons to behave. If you were having trouble with elves, now, I might be able–"

"Naturally, we don't wish to involve you in our dispute," Zemenar interrupted smoothly. "However, one of the results of our quarrel is that the King of the Dragons has cut off the Society's access to the Caves of Fire and Night."

"I still don't see–"

"The caves are the source of many of the ingredients we use in our spells," Zemenar broke in once more. "They are also the only place it is possible to make certain items we need for our research." He paused and blinked, fingering his staff with one hand as if he thought there might be a rough spot somewhere along it and he was trying to find it without attracting attention. "We–the Society of Wizards–must have some way of entering the caves."

"Go on." Mendanbar tried not to sound as irritated as he felt. He did not like Zemenar's lecturing tone, he was tired of being interrupted, and he still did not see what the Society's dispute with the dragons had to do with him. On top of that, the invisible threads of magic were moving toward Zemenar's staff again, almost as if something were sucking them in. Mendanbar yanked at them hard, wishing he could do the same to the Head Wizard.

"That is where you come in, Your Majesty," Zemenar said. He sounded vaguely confused, as if he were trying to concentrate on two things at once. "You, ah, could be of great use . . . that is, you could help us enormously."

"How?" The strands of magic were gliding toward the staff more quickly than ever. Mendanbar could see that if he kept pulling at them he would soon be unable to pay attention to anything else. He thought for a moment, while Zemenar rambled, then he took hold of a fat, invisible cord and with a swift gesture threw it in a loop around Zemenar. The loop hovered three feet from the Head Wizard in all directions, spinning slowly. Other cords floated toward it and glanced off before they came anywhere near Zemenar or his staff. Mendanbar smiled slightly.

The Head Wizard broke off his speech in midsentence. "What was that?" he demanded.

"I beg your pardon," Mendanbar said with dignity. "As the ruler of the Enchanted Forest, there are sometimes matters that require my immediate attention. I have dealt with this one."

Zemenar frowned, plainly taken aback. "You have? But I didn't sense any spell–" He stopped short, staring at Mendanbar in consternation.

"You would not," Mendanbar said in an offhand manner. Inwardly, he smiled. Apparently wizards could feel normal spell-casting, but they could not sense Mendanbar's way of doing magic. He wondered why no one had ever mentioned it. Undetectable spells could be a big advantage, if he ever had trouble with the Society of Wizards. "It was not exactly a spell, just something to do with the forest forces. It need not concern you."

"Of course, Your Majesty," Zemenar said after a long pause. "If I may continue?"

"Please do."

"What we are asking is that you allow the wizards of our society to enter the Caves of Fire and Night from the Enchanted Forest," Zemenar said. "There is a way in somewhere along your eastern border, I believe."

"Yes, but it doesn't stay put," Mendanbar pointed out. "Nothing in the Enchanted Forest does, at least, not for long."

"It's always in the same *general* area, though," Zemenar said confidently. "We're willing to take whatever time is needed to find it."

Mendanbar thought of the enormous number of knots and tangles that the wizards would cause while they wandered around looking for the entrance to the caves, and he could barely suppress a shudder. "What about the dragons?"

"If you have no authority over them, they can have none over your gateway into the Caves of Fire and Night," Zemenar said, watching Mendanbar closely with his hard, bright eyes.

"That's not what I meant." Mendanbar paused, pretending to consider. "I think I must refuse your request, temporarily at least," he said in as judicious a tone as he could manage. "I have certain . . . differences of my own to settle with the King of the Dragons at the moment. From what you say, the dragons would object if I let your wizards into the Caves of Fire and Night, and I do not want to make my discussion with them any more difficult than it is likely to be already. I hope you understand."

"Ah." A fleeting expression of satisfaction flicked across Zemenar's face. "I am sorry to hear that you, too, are having trouble with dragons. I hope you will be able to settle things suitably. They are sly creatures, you know, and one can never tell what they are thinking."

The same thing could be said about the Head Wizard of the Society of Wizards, thought Mendanbar. "Thank you for your kind wishes," he said aloud.

"If you would like our assistance, the Society of Wizards would be happy to advise you," Zemenar said with a smile. "We have had a great deal of experience with dragons over the years."

"I appreciate the offer," Mendanbar replied cautiously. He did not want to offend the Head Wizard, but he doubted that the wizards' advice would help him much. After all, they seemed to be having more trouble with dragons than he was.

"Have you met the new King of the Dragons or her princess?" the Head Wizard went on.

"No, I–princess?" Mendanbar forgot his misgivings in a wave of surprised dismay. "The King of the Dragons has a princess?"

"She does indeed," Zemenar said. There was a faint frown in his eyes, and his fingers were stroking his staff again. "She's a real troublemaker, too–the princess, I mean. Our misunderstanding with the dragons is all her fault."

"Oh, lord," Mendanbar said. He raised a hand to run his fingers through his hair and remembered just in time that he was wearing his circlet. "And King Kazul listens to her?"

"Certainly. Most of the dragons do, now. Cimorene is quite the power behind the throne in the Mountains of Morning."

There was a sneer in Zemenar's voice, along with a good deal of suppressed anger. Mendanbar couldn't blame him. He'd had enough trouble with princesses himself to know the type. Cimorene must be one of the beautiful, empty-headed, ambitious bores whose only talents were the ability to stare innocently with their blue eyes and a knack for wrapping people–or, in Cimorene's case, dragons–around their fragile fingers. She was probably too stupid to realize how much trouble her manipulations caused, but if she did notice she probably liked having the power to produce turmoil.

"Oh, lord," Mendanbar repeated. Why hadn't Morwen warned him? Well, he had to talk to Kazul, one way or another. Perhaps Morwen had heard about his aversion to princesses and hadn't wanted to give him any reason to put off the visit. Mendanbar looked at Zemenar, completely in charity with the wizard for the first time. "Thank you for telling me."

"You're very welcome," Zemenar said. "You will let me know how things go, won't you? And do remember that the Society of Wizards will be happy to give you whatever help you may need. It's in our own interest, after all. The sooner you get this little matter settled, the sooner you'll be able to reconsider our request about the Caves of Fire and Night."

"Yes, certainly," Mendanbar said. "Is that all, then? I'll have Willin show you out."

"That won't be necessary." Zemenar gave Mendanbar a smile that set Mendanbar's teeth on edge. "I *am* a wizard, after all. Good day, Your Majesty."

Zemenar bowed and was suddenly and completely gone. No, not completely; Mendanbar could feel a lump of magic in the center of the looping spell where Zemenar had been standing. Mendanbar frowned. He might appreciate Zemenar's warning about Kazul's Princess, but that was no reason for the wizard to go leaving leftover bits of magic in his castle.

Mendanbar reached for the loop, to undo it, and paused. As long as he was at home, he might as well do this the easy way. He twitched a different strand of magic, and the audience chamber dissolved around him.

He materialized in the cool darkness of the castle armory. Lighting the wall torches with another twitch of the magic threads, he looked around. Willin had been hard at work since the last time Mendanbar had visited the armory. Most of the swords and shields that had been piled in one corner or another were now hanging in neat pairs on the walls. Extra swords, spears, maces, lances, and knives hung in closely spaced rows higher up. The effect was almost decorative. Mendanbar made a mental note to compliment Willin, then turned his attention toward the wooden chests along the far wall.

The one he wanted was in the center. He reached into his pocket for the key and realized he had left it in his desk. He sighed and snapped his fingers. With a small pop, the key appeared in the air level with his nose and fell into his palm. Mendanbar smiled at it and bent to open the chest. Willin was always after him to have a proper set of keys made for the various doors and drawers and chests and hiding places in the castle, but Mendanbar couldn't see any reason to waste the effort when the Key to the Castle was all you needed to open any lock in the place.

It wasn't as if Willin needed a spell to call the Key, either, Mendanbar thought as he lifted the lid of the chest. The Key had its own magic. As long as it was inside the castle, it came to whoever called it. Willin just wanted to puff up his own consequence by carrying a big bunch of keys jangling at his belt. Mendanbar looked down and forgot about Willin.

There was only one thing in the chest: a sword, gleaming in the torch-light. It was very plain, almost ordinary-looking, and it didn't have an air of magic about it at all, though anyone who looked at it closely would notice that it shone too brightly and had too sharp an edge to be an ordinary sword. Mendanbar reached in and took the hilt in his hand with a sigh of satisfaction. In the air around him, the unseen strands of power hummed in response, for this sword was linked to the warp and weft of the Enchanted Forest in ways no one, not even the Kings of the Enchanted Forest, really understood. Mendanbar always felt better when he had the sword with him, but he couldn't wear it around the castle all the time. It made Willin unhappy and visitors nervous. So he kept the sword in the armory unless he could think of an excuse to use it.

Rising, he swung the sword twice, just for fun. Then he hunted around until he found a sword belt and scabbard, put the sword in the sheath, and buckled the belt around his waist. With another wave of his hand, he was back in the audience chamber.

5

In Which There Is a Misunderstanding and Mendanbar Does Some Plumbing

The awkward lump of wizard-magic was right where Mendanbar had left it. He studied it for a moment, then drew his sword.

"Your Majesty!" said Willin from the doorway. *"What* are you *doing?"*

"Cleaning up after our visitor," Mendanbar replied. "Do be quiet for a minute, Willin. I need to concentrate."

"But–"

Mendanbar shot an irritated look at Willin. The castle steward broke off and closed his mouth into a thin, disapproving line. Mendanbar waited half a moment longer to make sure the elf was not going to say anything else, then turned back to the lump. Raising the sword, he reached over the loop of Enchanted Forest magic and stuck the point into the center of the mass.

A surge of power ran through the sword as it sucked up the wizard's leftovers and sent them to reinforce the invisible network of Enchanted Forest magic. The surge was stronger than Mendanbar had expected, and he frowned as he lifted the sword away from the now-empty space and put it back in its sheath. Perhaps it hadn't been extra, unused magic, after all; perhaps Zemenar had deliberately left a spell behind. It was too late to test it now, though. The sword was thorough, and whatever the lump had been, it was now gone for good.

"Your Majesty?"

Willin's voice sounded much more tentative than it had a moment before. Mendanbar almost smiled, but Willin was sure to get upset if he thought he was being laughed at. So Mendanbar kept his face stiff and took a little longer than necessary to undo the loop he had left to guard the wizard's magic. When he was positive that his expression was normal, he turned.

"Yes, Willin?"

"What was all that about? Has my lord the Head Wizard gone? Why are you wearing your sword? What–"

"One thing at a time," Mendanbar interrupted gently. "Zemenar has gone, yes. He cast a vanishing spell, and a very good one, too. No smoke, no whirling dust, just *poof* and he was gone. Unfortunately, he wasn't as tidy with the end of his spell, and some of it got left behind. Or at least, that's what I thought until I got rid of it a minute ago."

"I . . . see," Willin said in a tone that meant he didn't. "And that's why you have your sword?"

"Partly." Mendanbar looked at the empty patch of floor where the wizard had been, then shook his head. Whatever Zemenar might have been up to, it would have to wait. "I have to pay a visit to the King of the Dragons."

Willin's face went completely blank. "You what?"

"I'm going to the Mountains of Morning, to see the King of the Dragons," Mendanbar repeated. "And I'm certainly not going without a sword. There are lots of dangerous creatures in those mountains, and some of them wouldn't care that I'm the King of the Enchanted Forest, even if they bothered to stop for an introduction before they attacked."

"But you can't just *leave,* Your Majesty!" Willin said. "A formal embassy to the King of the Dragons will take weeks to arrange. You'll want a full escort, and–"

"I don't think there's time," Mendanbar broke in, before Willin could get too involved in planning. "Something's come up, and it needs to be dealt with *now*. So I'm going today, in another minute, and you're in charge of the castle until I get back." In a sudden inspiration, Mendanbar pulled the Key to the Castle out of his pocket and handed it ceremoniously to Willin.

"I am deeply honored by Your Majesty's confidence," Willin said. "But are you sure this is necessary?"

"Yes," Mendanbar said. "Oh, and don't let any wizards in while I'm gone. Something funny is going on, and I don't want any of them inside the castle until I figure out what, especially if I'm not here."

"But what should I tell them, if they ask for you?"

"I don't care, as long as you don't let them in," Mendanbar replied. "Is that all? Then I'm going."

He took hold of a strand of magic and pulled. When the misty whiteness cleared away, he was standing among the trees of the Enchanted Forest just outside the castle. With a bit more care, he chose another magic thread and pulled again, harder. This time, he appeared at the very edge of the forest, where the Mountains of Morning began. Two paces in front of him, the vibrant green moss stopped as if it had been sliced away, and the dry gray rock began. He checked to make sure this was the right place—Morwen's directions had been very specific—and then, reluctantly, stepped over the boundary.

Mendanbar had not left the Enchanted Forest for over three years, not since he had become King, and he had forgotten how very barren everything felt outside. He could still sense the free-floating network of magic behind him, but where he stood, the air was empty. Thin grass and scrubby bushes grew in patches wherever dirt had accumulated in low spots and cracks and corners. Ahead, the mountains rose high and sharp and dead. Many magical creatures lived here, but the Mountains of Morning had no magic of their own. Mendanbar could feel the emptiness where the magic should have been, and he shivered in spite of himself.

"At least I don't have to worry about finding Kazul," he told himself. "As long as I don't get my directions mixed up, I should be able to walk straight to her cave." He smiled suddenly. "And it will still be there when I get to it!" That was worth something. And he still had some of the magic of the Enchanted Forest along with him in the form of his sword. Even through the sheath, Mendanbar could feel the reassuring pulse of power.

"Well, there's no sense in putting it off." He shrugged, took a last look back at his forest, and started walking.

Once he got used to the dry, dead, magicless feel of the mountains, Mendanbar actually enjoyed the walk. Much as he loved the Enchanted Forest, he had to admit that it was nice to see so much sky. Since dragons liked high places, the walk was mostly uphill, but that was fun, too. With no trees to block the view, Mendanbar could see for miles, and the higher he got, the more he could see. The hills in the Enchanted Forest tended to be either low, rolling bumps that you hardly noticed, or steep mounds that were usually home to something dangerous, or magical, or both. Most of the latter were made of something strange, too—jasper or polished coal or solid silver. There was even one made of glass somewhere along the southern edge of the forest. Some king had built it in order to get rid of his daughter.

Daughter. King's daughter. Princess! Mendanbar's good mood vanished. He'd forgotten about Kazul's princess.

"And I'll have to be particularly polite to her, no matter how irritating she is," he reminded himself gloomily. If she had as much influence as Zemenar hinted, she could make things very difficult if she took a dislike to him. He wondered why Kazul had kept her. The King of the Dragons didn't normally bother with a princess, or at least, Mendanbar had never before heard of one who did.

He came around a curve and saw the mouth of a cave in front of him. There was a wide, flat, sandy space in front of the cave, big enough for several dragons to land at the same time, if they were careful about it. The mountain rose straight up behind the cave mouth. Set in the stone over the center of the opening was an outline of a spiky black crown.

As Mendanbar drew nearer, he saw a tarnished brass handle sticking out of a small hole beside the cave. The handle was level with his waist, and next to it was a sign that read: "WELCOME TO THE CAVE OF THE DRAGON KING. Pull handle to ring bell." On the line below, someone had added in neat letters printed in bright red paint, "ABSOLUTELY *NO* wizards, salespeople, or rescuers. This means YOU."

Mendanbar stared at the sign for a minute and began to smile. No wonder Zemenar didn't like Kazul's princess. Well, he wasn't a wizard, he wasn't selling anything, and he certainly didn't want to rescue anybody. He gave the handle a pull.

Somewhere inside the cave, a bell rang. "Well, it's about time," said a woman's voice, and Mendanbar's heart sank. He heard footsteps coming toward the mouth of the cave, and the same voice continued, "I was hoping you'd get here before I left. The sink is–"

The speaker came out of the cave, took a look at Mendanbar, and broke off in midsentence. "Oh, no, not *another* one," she said.

Mendanbar stared at her in utter bafflement. If this was a princess, she was like no princess he had ever seen, and he had seen dozens. True, she had a small gold crown pinned into her hair, and she was very pretty–beautiful, in fact–but she was wearing a blue-and-white checked apron with large pockets. Mendanbar had never seen a princess in an apron before. The dress under the apron was rust-colored and practical-looking, and she had the sleeves rolled up above her elbows. He had never seen a princess with her sleeves rolled up, either. Her jet black hair hung in plain braids almost to her knees, instead of making a cloud of curls around her face. Her eyes were black, too, and she was as tall as Mendanbar.

"Well?" she said in an exasperated tone. "Are you going to stand there like a lump, or are you going to tell me what you want? Although I think I already know."

"Excuse me," Mendanbar said. He pulled himself together and bowed uncertainly. "I think there's been some sort of mistake. I'm looking for Kazul, the King of the Dragons."

"I'll bet you are," the young woman muttered. "Well, you can't have her. I handle my own knights and princes."

"I beg your pardon?" Mendanbar said, blinking. He was beginning to think the mistake was his. This young woman didn't look like a princess (except for the crown), she didn't act like a princess, and she didn't talk like a princess. But if she wasn't a princess, what was she doing here?

"I handle my own knights," she repeated. "You see, I don't want to be rescued, and it would be silly for someone to get hurt fighting Kazul when I intend to stay here no matter what happens. Besides, Kazul has enough to do being King of the Dragons without people interrupting her to fight for no reason."

"You really *are* Kazul's princess"–what had Zemenar said her name was? Oh, yes–"Cimorene?"

"Yes, of course. Look, I haven't got time to argue about this, not today. Could you please go away and come back in, oh, a week or so, when things are a little more settled? Or I can direct you to a more cooperative princess, if you'd rather not wait. Marchak has a very nice one just now, and he lives quite close by."

"No, I'm afraid not," Mendanbar said. He was beginning to think Willin had been right to say he should wait for a formal audience. "You see, I didn't come to rescue you, or anybody. I'm the King of the Enchanted Forest, and I really did come to talk to Kazul. And it's urgent. So–"

"Oh, drat," said Cimorene. "Are you sure it can't wait? Kazul isn't here right now."

"I'll wait for her," Mendanbar said with polite firmness. "As I said, the matter is urgent."

Cimorene frowned suddenly. "Did you say you were the King of the *Enchanted Forest?*"

Mendanbar nodded. "My name is Mendanbar."

"Just why is it that you're so eager to see Kazul, Your Majesty?" Cimorene said suspiciously.

"I ran across a . . . problem in the Enchanted Forest this morning," Mendanbar replied, choosing his words with care. "A witch named Morwen advised me to talk to the King of the Dragons about it."

"*Morwen* sent you?" Cimorene looked surprised, then thoughtful. "It must be all right, then. Come in and sit down, and I'll see if I can explain."

"As you wish, Princess," Mendanbar said, bowing.

"Just call me Cimorene," she said, leading Mendanbar into the cave. She bent to pick up a lantern from the floor inside the entrance and added, "My official title now is Chief Cook and Librarian, so I've gotten out of the habit of being called 'Princess.' "

"Chief Cook and Librarian?" Mendanbar said curiously. "How did that happen?"

"Kazul and I decided on it between us after she became King of the Dragons last year," Cimorene said. "You see, the King of the Dragons doesn't usually have a princess, and we didn't want the other dragons grumbling about Kazul breaking with tradition. I was hoping it would discourage the knights a bit, too."

"Oh?"

"Well, it doesn't sound particularly noble and knightly to say you've rescued the Chief Cook and Librarian, does it? And it has cut down on the number of interruptions. I used to get two or three knights a day, and now there's only about one a week. And the ones who *do* come are at least smart enough to figure out that I'm still a princess even if the dragons call me Chief Cook."

"Doesn't that make them harder to get rid of?"

"Not at all. The smart ones listen when I argue with them. The stupid ones think I'm kidding. I had to offer to fight a couple of them myself before I could get them to go away."

Mendanbar peered doubtfully at Cimorene in the dim lantern-light. She didn't look as if she were joking. "You actually offered to fight a knight?"

"Four of them," Cimorene said, nodding. "*And* a prince. It was the only way to convince them." She looked at Mendanbar uncertainly. "I'm sorry if I behaved badly to you at first, but I really did think you were here to rescue me. It's the crown." She pointed to the circlet on his head. "You wouldn't believe the trouble I've had with some of the princes. Being rude is the only way to get rid of them in a hurry, and sometimes even that doesn't work. Especially if they're particularly stupid."

"I understand," Mendanbar said without thinking. "They sound a lot like princesses–stubborn, witless, and–" He stopped short in dismay. He'd forgotten for a moment that Cimorene was a princess, too. He hoped she wouldn't be insulted.

Fortunately, Cimorene didn't seem insulted at all. She nodded. "Exactly. That's why I send the knights and princes on to rescue other princesses. They mostly deserve each other. Of course, I *do* try to make sure I send the nicest knights to the nicest princesses. They can't help it if they're silly."

They had reached a side opening, and Cimorene hesitated. Then she shrugged and went in. "The kitchen's a mess today," she said over her shoulder, "but even when it's messy, it's more comfortable for human-type people than the big caves where the dragons go to chat. I can make tea, too, if you'd like some."

Before he could answer, Mendanbar emerged from the side tunnel into a large, well-lit cavern. An enormous black stove took up half of one wall, and the other walls were lined with tall wooden cupboards. A stone sink next to the door was filled to the brim with scummy gray water, and the shelf next to it was overflowing with dirty dishes. In the middle of the floor stood a large wooden table and three mismatched chairs.

"Tea sounds good," Mendanbar said, politely ignoring the dishes.

Cimorene scowled at the sink and began rummaging through the cupboards. "Do you mind having your tea in a wine glass? I know it's a little strange, but I'm afraid all the cups are dirty. The sink has been plugged up for nearly a week, and I haven't been able to do the dishes."

"I don't mind," Mendanbar said. "But you'll have to do something about that sink sooner or later, you know."

"I've tried," Cimorene said in an irritated tone. "Do you have any idea how hard it is to persuade a plumber to come look at a dragon's sink? I thought I'd finally found one, but he was supposed to get here yesterday morning and still hasn't shown up, so he's probably not coming. And there aren't any books on plumbing in Kazul's library, or I'd have fixed it myself."

"I'm sorry," Mendanbar said. "Maybe I can do something about it."

"Go ahead," Cimorene replied. "You can't make it any worse than it is already."

That didn't sound like much of a vote of confidence to Mendanbar, but it didn't matter. He went over to the sink and studied it for a moment, then backed up a pace and drew his sword.

Cimorene made a startled noise. "Your sword does plumbing?" she said, sounding interested. "I knew it was magic, but I thought it was for dragons."

"It does most things," Mendanbar said absently. Working magic outside the Enchanted Forest took a lot of concentration. He squinted down the length of the blade at the sink, feeling the power within the sword tingle against his palm. Then he whipped the sword through the air, pushing power out of it to wrap around the sink. With a final flourish, he touched the tip of the sword to the surface of the scummy water. There was a spray of magic, a loud glug, and the water swirled and began to run down the drain.

"There," said Mendanbar. "That should do it." He wiped the tip of his sword and stuck it back in its sheath.

"It certainly should!" Cimorene said. "Is your magic always that flashy?"

"What do you mean?"

"Never mind. I'll wash some cups while the tea water is boiling. Sit down while I get the kettle started."

Mendanbar sat down at the table and frowned suddenly. "Oh, bother."

"What?"

"Morwen gave me some cider to bring to King Kazul, and I was so busy cleaning up after Zemenar that I forgot to pick it up before I left. I'm sorry. I'll have to send it with someone when I get back."

Cimorene stopped short, holding the teakettle suspended in midair. "Zemenar? Not the Head Wizard of the Society of Wizards?"

"Yes, of course," Mendanbar said, a little surprised by her reaction. Then he recalled how much Zemenar seemed to dislike Cimorene. Presumably Cimorene felt the same way about Zemenar.

"And you had to clean up after him? It figures," Cimorene muttered. She finished filling the kettle and put it on the stove, then went back to the sink and washed two cups, two saucers, and two spoons with an intense concentration that made it obvious she was thinking about something else.

Mendanbar was happy to let her think. He had a few things to mull over himself. Cimorene was not at all what he'd expected. She acted more like Morwen than like a princess. He wondered where she had come from and how she had gotten captured by the dragons. He nearly asked, but pulled himself up short before the words left his mouth. He hadn't come to talk to a princess. No, indeed. "When will King Kazul be back?" he asked instead.

Cimorene did not answer at once. She set the teacups on the table, poured hot water into the teapot to brew, and sat down across from Mendanbar. She studied him for a long minute, then gave a decisive nod.

"All right," she said. "I'll tell you the truth. I don't know."

A wave of irritation swept over Mendanbar. "If Kazul didn't tell you when she expected to be back, why didn't you say so at once?"

"Oh, she told me," Cimorene said. She looked very sober. "She was supposed to be home the day before yesterday."

"And she's not back yet?"

Cimorene nodded again. "And she hasn't sent a message or anything. She's disappeared. I was just getting ready to go search for her when you showed up."

6

In Which Mendanbar and Cimorene Have a Long Talk and Mendanbar Reluctantly Decides to Embark on a Journey

Mendanbar took a deep breath. "I think you'd better tell me everything you know about this," he said. "When did Kazul leave, and where was she going?"

"She left last Monday," Cimorene replied readily. "She was going to visit her grandchildren in the northern part of the mountains. She does that whenever she gets a chance, and sometimes she stays a few extra days, but she's *always* sent word before when she's done that." She frowned worriedly.

"I–grandchildren?"

Cimorene smiled. "I know. I was taken aback when I found out about them, too. You just don't think of the King of the Dragons as a doting grandmother, but she is. In fact, I suspect she took longer than she had to about the negotiations with the Frost Giants up there, just so she'd have an excuse to stay a few more days. Anyway, she was planning to spend a couple of days with them and then swing through the Enchanted Forest on her way home."

"She was coming to see me?" Mendanbar asked, surprised.

"Not exactly." Cimorene hesitated. "We'd heard that someone was growing dragonsbane in one of the valleys along the border, and she wanted to see whether it was true. You can see why I'm worried."

"Growing dragonsbane—you mean, deliberately planting it? There have always been a few patches of the stuff here and there."

"The way we heard it, this was an entire valley full. That's hardly accidental." Cimorene lifted the lid of the teapot and peered inside, then poured a cup for each of them. "Kazul wanted to check for herself, quietly, before any of the younger dragons heard about it. Some of them are . . . impulsive. She didn't want someone tearing off in a fury to burn down the Enchanted Forest with no more reason than a rumor."

"Oh, lord." Mendanbar pushed his hair backward off his forehead and grimaced at his tea. "I'll bet that's what happened. I wish she'd sent word to me."

Cimorene studied her cup with unnecessary thoroughness. "She was afraid you might be the one doing it."

"Me?"

"The King of the Enchanted Forest. You haven't been particularly friendly since she took over, you know." She frowned suddenly. "Why *did* you turn up today, anyway? And what did you mean, 'that's what happened'? Don't tell me somebody really *has* started setting fire to the Enchanted Forest!"

"Almost," Mendanbar said. He explained about the dead area and the dragon scales he had found. "Morwen said that they were all from the same dragon, but they had been enchanted to look as if they came from several different dragons. I was hoping King Kazul would tell me which dragon they belonged to, and maybe let me ask him a few questions."

"Let me look at them," Cimorene said.

Mendanbar took the scales out of his pocket and spread them out on the table.

Cimorene made a face. "I can tell you whose scales they were, all right, but I'm afraid it won't help much. Woraug isn't around any more."

"It's a start," Mendanbar said. "You're sure these are his?"

"Very sure. But I'm afraid you won't be able to ask him any questions." Cimorene smiled, as if at some private joke.

"Why not?"

"Because the reason Woraug isn't around any more is that he got turned into a toad about a year ago. Do you know how the King of the Dragons is chosen?"

"By a test," Mendanbar replied, a little puzzled by the question. "When a king dies, the crown goes to whichever dragon can carry Colin's Stone from the Ford of Whispering Snakes to the Vanishing Mountain."

"Yes. Well, Woraug poisoned the old King of the Dragons. Then he arranged with the Society of Wizards to rig the test so he'd be the next King," Cimorene said matter-of-factly. "It was mostly luck that we found out in time to stop them. When we did, Woraug turned into a toad because of his un-dragonlike behavior." She sipped at her tea. "I think a snake ate him," she added thoughtfully.

There were so many things Mendanbar wanted to say in response to this disturbing summary that for a moment he couldn't say anything at all. He took a large swallow of tea, which gave him an extra minute to think. "Is *that* why the wizards have been banned from the Mountains of Morning?" he managed at last.

"Of course," Cimorene answered. "Kazul couldn't do anything more. Even though we knew it was all their idea, it was Woraug who actually poisoned the King. Didn't Morwen tell you about it? She was there."

"No," Mendanbar said. "It didn't come up." He shook his head. "No wonder Zemenar didn't want to talk about why the dragons don't want wizards in the mountains anymore."

Cimorene nodded. "The wizards don't talk about it because their scheme didn't work out, and the dragons don't talk about it because the wizards came so close that the dragons are embarrassed to admit it. And Morwen is too discreet to spread the story around when the dragons would rather she didn't."

"I see." Mendanbar saw considerably more than that. The disagreement between the dragons and the Society of Wizards was not a minor matter, as Zemenar had led him to believe. And Kazul's princess–or rather, Chief Cook and Librarian, he reminded himself–was nothing like the sneaky, manipulative girl Zemenar had hinted she was, either. It looked very much as if Zemenar had been deliberately trying to cause trouble between Mendanbar and the dragons, or at least get Mendanbar off to a bad start with their King. He wondered what Zemenar would have said about Morwen if *her* name had come up.

"It wouldn't surprise me if the Society of Wizards was behind this, too," Cimorene said, waving her hand at the scales. "It's exactly the kind of twisty scheme they'd come up with."

"It's possible," Mendanbar acknowledged, "but why would they want to bring the Enchanted Forest into their argument with the dragons?"

"Maybe they think you'll clean the dragons out of the mountains, or at least reduce their numbers enough so that the wizards will be able to come through without getting eaten."

Mendanbar shook his head. "If it came to a fight, the Enchanted Forest and the Mountains of Morning would be very evenly matched. A war would cut the wizards off from both places as long as there was any fighting, and it would probably drag on for ages. Zemenar must know that. He'd have to have an awfully good reason to start something like that."

"Maybe he does."

"Maybe, but I can't think what it could be. Can you?"

"No," Cimorene admitted. "But if I figure it out, I'll let you know."

"Meanwhile, is there anyone else who could have done this?" Mendanbar asked, waving at the line of scales on the table.

"There aren't many people who can get hold of even one dragon scale, much less five from the same dragon," Cimorene said, scowling at the table. "Woraug's princess might have kept one or two as a souvenir, but I don't think she'd have had this many, and anyway she doesn't know any magic." Suddenly she looked up. "Wait a minute! When Woraug turned into a toad, a whole batch of scales fell off and scattered."

"What happened to them?"

"We just left them at the ford," Cimorene said with a shrug. "Nobody thought it was important. Most of them are probably still there. Dragon scales last a long time."

"At the Ford of Whispering Snakes?" Mendanbar asked. Cimorene nodded, and he grimaced. "Then anyone who walked by could have picked up these scales any time in the past year. That doesn't narrow things down much."

"I'm as sorry about that as you are," Cimorene said.

Mendanbar's face must have shown his surprise, because she gave him an exasperated look and went on, "Hadn't it occurred to you that we'd want to know who's plotting to get dragons blamed for their mischief? Especially if it turns out *not* to be the Society of Wizards."

"But–oh. If it's *not* the Society, then you have a new enemy you don't know anything about."

Cimorene nodded again, very soberly. "I just wish I had time to look into it right now, but with Kazul missing it will have to wait."

"You'll let me know when she gets back?"

"I'll tell Roxim to send you word if she shows up while I'm gone," Cimorene assured him. "And if I find her first, I'll tell her everything you've told me. I'm sure she'll get in touch with you right away."

"Thank you."

"Now, is there anything else you want to know? Because if there isn't, I need to be going," Cimorene went on. "It's a long walk to Flat Top Mountain, and I'd like to get there before dark."

"Surely you don't plan to walk all the way to the northern end of the Mountains of Morning." He was surprised and suddenly disappointed by this evidence of princesslike behavior. From their brief acquaintance, he'd thought Cimorene had better sense.

"Of course not," Cimorene replied impatiently. "I'm not stupid. I'm going to borrow a magic carpet from Ballimore, the giantess who lives on Flat Top Mountain."

Mendanbar choked on the last of his tea. "Do you expect a giantess to loan you a carpet just because you have a dragon with you?" he demanded when he could talk again.

"I'd better not, since I won't have a dragon with me," Cimorene retorted. "Not that it's any of your business."

"You're going to wander around the Mountains of Morning *alone* looking for King Kazul?" Mendanbar said, appalled.

"Exactly. And if I can't find her there, I'll swing through the Enchanted Forest on the way back, just the way she was planning to. And it's time I got started, so if you'll just–"

"Oh, no." Mendanbar set his teacup down so emphatically that it rattled the saucer. "If you're fool enough to travel through the Mountains of Morning without a companion, that's not my concern, but you are *not* going through the Enchanted Forest alone. It's too dangerous."

"I can take care of myself," Cimorene snapped. "You forget, I've been living with the dragons for over a year."

"Maybe so," Mendanbar said, trying hard to hold on to his temper. "But the Enchanted Forest is very different from the Mountains of Morning. And what do you suppose will happen if the King of the Dragons's princess–or Cook and Librarian, or whatever–gets captured or killed or enchanted going through *my* forest?"

Cimorene opened her mouth to reply, then paused. "Oh," she said in a very different tone. "Oh, I see. That would cause just the sort of trouble we're both trying to avoid, wouldn't it? I'm sorry. I'm used to people objecting to things because they think I can't do them or shouldn't do them. It didn't occur to me that you might have a *real* reason."

"Then you won't go?" Mendanbar said with relief.

"I have to," Cimorene said in the tones of one explaining something obvious. "It's my job. Besides, Kazul is my friend. I'll just have to make sure I don't get captured or killed or enchanted, that's all."

"It's not as easy as you make it sound."

"I know. I've visited Morwen a time or two," Cimorene said. "I'll manage, one way or another."

Mendanbar started to object again, then stopped. He didn't think Cimorene was quite as sure of herself as she sounded, but she was plainly determined to go hunting for Kazul. Well, she was right about one thing: *somebody* had to find the King of the Dragons, and soon. Mendanbar didn't like to think of what might happen if Kazul stayed missing for long, especially if rumors about dragonsbane in the Enchanted Forest started floating around the mountains.

"Is there anyone you can take with you?" Mendanbar asked.

"No," Cimorene said. "Roxim and Marchak are the only dragons who have enough sense not to go off in fits when they hear that Kazul is missing. Roxim is too old for adventures, and Marchak has to stay and take care of business while I'm gone. And I hope you're not going to suggest I borrow Marchak's princess."

"I wouldn't dream of it," Mendanbar said sincerely. "Is she very awful?"

"Actually, she's one of the nice ones," Cimorene admitted. "But she's very silly. She'd try, but she wouldn't enjoy it at all, and she'd be much more of a nuisance than she's worth. I'd rather take my chances alone."

"That's almost as bad an idea as taking that princess along," Mendanbar said. He sighed. "I suppose I'll have to come with you myself."

Cimorene stared at him blankly for a moment, then began to giggle.

"It isn't funny," Mendanbar said. "I mean it." He felt a little hurt by Cimorene's reaction. He wasn't necessarily stuffy or useless or a nuisance to travel with just because he was the King of the Enchanted Forest. Cimorene ought to realize that. After all, he'd fixed the sink for her, hadn't he?

"I know you mean it," Cimorene said when she could talk again. "It wasn't what you said, it was the way you said it." She shook her head, chuckling. "You sound about as eager to come with me as I am to have company. Which isn't much."

"Maybe not, but somebody–"

"What was that?" Cimorene interrupted, holding up a hand for silence.

"I didn't hear anything," Mendanbar said.

"Shhh," Cimorene hissed. She rose and tiptoed to the door, listening. In the quiet, Mendanbar heard a faint thud outside. Cimorene's lips tightened. "Princes or wizards?" she muttered. "Wizards, I'll bet. Princes are noisier."

Still frowning, she picked up the bucket of soapy water that was sitting beside the door. As she reached for the doorknob, Mendanbar started after her. Cimorene hadn't asked for his help, but a bucket of soapy water wasn't much of a weapon against a wizard. If it was a wizard.

The corridor outside the kitchen was pitch black. Cimorene vanished into the gloom, moving with the calm sureness of long familiarity. Cursing mentally, Mendanbar picked his way after her, one hand on the cave wall for guidance, the other stretched out in front of him to keep him from running into anything.

Another muffled crash echoed from up ahead. Mendanbar took two more steps and his outstretched arm touched Cimorene's shoulder. A moment later, Cimorene's voice said calmly, "Phrazelspitz."

Mendanbar felt magic rise around him. Light flared from the walls, then settled into a steady glow, revealing an enormous cavern. He and

Cimorene stood in one of five dark openings spaced unevenly around the wall. Halfway across the cave, a tall man in blue and brown wizard's robes stood hanging onto a staff and trying to squint in all directions at once. His hair and beard were brown, and he bore a strong resemblance to Zemenar, only younger.

"Antorell," Cimorene said in tones of disgust. "I might have guessed."

"I'm glad to see you again, Princess Cimorene," the wizard said in an oily tone. "But who could fail to rejoice at the sight of so lovely a princess?"

"What are you doing here?" Cimorene demanded. Mendanbar was pleased to note that she didn't sound at all mollified by Antorell's flattery. "And how did you get in without being eaten?"

"Oh, we wizards have our little ways," Antorell said airily. "And I came because–well, because I was concerned about you, Princess."

"I'll bet," Cimorene muttered. "What do you mean?" she said in a louder voice.

"I thought you might need a friend." Antorell's voice oozed sincerity. "Especially after what Father said when he came back from the Enchanted Forest. If King Mendanbar really is getting ready for a war with the dragons . . ."

"Where did your father get that idea?" Cimorene asked in tones of mild interest.

Antorell frowned slightly, as if he had hoped for a stronger reaction. "Something the King said to him, I think. I shouldn't have repeated it, I suppose, but I was carried away by my feelings."

"Sure you were," Cimorene said. "That's why you sneaked in here without knocking and went blundering around in the dark, instead of calling me or at least bringing a lamp."

"I didn't want to disturb King Kazul, if she happened to be here," Antorell said stiffly.

Cimorene snorted. "If you'd really thought Kazul was here, you wouldn't have come at all. She doesn't like it when people ignore her rules. One of which, may I remind you, was that wizards aren't allowed in the Mountains of Morning anymore."

"But if there's going to be a war–"

"There isn't," Mendanbar said, stepping forward into the light. "At least, not if I can help it. Why are you people trying so hard to make trouble, anyway?"

Antorell's eyes widened, and he sucked in his breath. "Mendanbar? You'll ruin everything, blast you." He smiled a sudden, nasty smile. "Unless I deal with both of you now. Oh, yes, that will do very well. Father will be so pleased."

He raised his staff. Mendanbar started toward him, pulling his sword free as he ran, though he knew the wizard was much too far away to reach before he finished the spell. Cimorene followed quickly, not quite running, carrying her bucket carefully to avoid spilling. They had only gone a few steps when a swirl of smoke appeared in the air in front of them.

The smoke thickened rapidly, then congealed with shocking suddenness into the largest nightshade Mendanbar had ever seen. It was two feet taller than Mendanbar and covered with spikes of coarse black fur. Its beady black eyes glared at him as it raised a long arm and clicked its dark purple claws together. It hissed, showing a mouthful of fangs.

"There!" cried Antorell over the nightshade's noise. "Vanquish that, Cimorene–if you can!"

7

In Which a Wizard Makes a Mess and the Journey Begins

Ignoring Antorell, Mendanbar kept his eyes on the nightshade. He had a moment's useless wish that he were in the Enchanted Forest, where he could have disposed of the monster with relative ease. Here, things were going to be a lot more complicated. He shifted his grip on the sword and pulled at the power within it.

The nightshade swung at him, its fully extended claws carving a whistling arc in the air. It was very, very fast. Mendanbar barely managed to block in time. The force of the blow knocked him to one side, and he almost lost hold of the sword. The nightshade hissed in pain and shook its arm, but Mendanbar knew it was not seriously hurt. Without active magic behind it, the most damage the sword could have inflicted on a nightshade this big was a bruise.

Again he pulled at the power in the sword, then had to roll to avoid another swing by the nightshade. This time he kept on rolling until he was out of the monster's reach. He came up on one knee and pointed the sword at the nightshade, pushing power through the sword in the pattern he had pictured in his mind.

Antorell's staff struck him across the shoulders. The sword flew out of his hands and he went sprawling. His half-formed spell spun wildly in the air and then was sucked away. He heard an angry shriek from Cimorene, then a shout: "Mendanbar! Dodge left, quick!"

Without hesitation, Mendanbar threw himself to his left. He heard a rush of wind as the nightshade's claws missed him by inches. There was a splash somewhere behind him, and Antorell's voice cried, "No! No! You'll be sorry for this, Cimorene!" Then Mendanbar's hand closed on the hilt of his sword. He twisted and brought the sword up, shoving power through it recklessly.

The blast of barely formed magic caught the nightshade in midleap. The creature hung frozen in the air for an instant, then dissolved in a cloud of bright sparks. Mendanbar seized the remnants of magic and pulled them together into a tight knot, ready to throw at another nightshade or at Antorell himself. Only then did he pause to look around.

Cimorene stood a little way away, swinging the empty bucket in one hand and looking at him as if she were impressed in spite of herself.

Antorell had vanished.

"You really *do* like flashy magic," Cimorene commented as Mendanbar climbed warily to his feet. "I haven't seen anything like that since Kazul's coronation party."

"Where's Antorell?" Mendanbar asked. "Did he get away?"

"No," Cimorene said, waving her free hand at a damp area of floor to Mendanbar's right. "I melted him."

"Melted him?" Mendanbar looked at the damp patch more closely. Antorell's soggy robes were plastered to the floor in the middle of a gooey puddle. His staff lay along one side of the robes, half-in, half-out of the goo. There was no other trace of him. Mendanbar was impressed, and said so.

"It's really not hard," Cimorene said. "All it takes is a bucket of soapy water with a little lemon juice in it. A friend of mine discovered by accident how to do it, and I've kept a bucket ready ever since, just in case."

"I thought that only worked on witches."

Cimorene shrugged. "Lots of things don't work the way they're supposed to. Morwen's a witch, but she certainly doesn't melt in a bucket of soapy water."

Mendanbar thought of the shining stone step and the spotless wooden floor in Morwen's house, and nodded. "I can see that. But why does it work for wizards?"

"We don't know." Cimorene gave him a sidelong look. "I'm sorry I let Antorell wallop you with his staff, but I didn't want to throw the water at him while you were in the way."

"Why–oh, you mean you were afraid it would melt me, too?" Mendanbar blinked. "But I'm not a wizard."

"You work magic," Cimorene pointed out. "And I don't know how strict the soapy-water-and-lemon-juice trick is about defining wizards. It would cause a lot of trouble if I melted the King of the Enchanted Forest in the middle of Kazul's living room, even if it isn't permanent."

"You mean he'll be back?" Mendanbar had started to put his sword back in its sheath, but he stopped at once. "How soon?"

"Not for a couple of days, at least," Cimorene reassured him. "Antorell may be Zemenar's son, but he's never been a very good wizard."

"Antorell is the son of the Head Wizard?" Mendanbar shot a considering look at the puddle and the pile of soggy robes. "So that's what he meant when he said his father would be pleased."

"Probably." Cimorene frowned pensively at Antorell's staff. "I've *got* to find Kazul. The Society of Wizards is up to something for sure, and she needs to know right away."

"Couldn't Antorell have come here on his own?" Mendanbar asked, although he didn't really believe it himself.

Cimorene shook her head. "I don't think he'd have dared. As I said, he's not a very good wizard. He wouldn't have been able to keep himself concealed from the dragons, and he certainly must have had help to make anything as nasty and complex as that construct you took care of."

"That wasn't a construct," Mendanbar said. "That was a nightshade. They're fairly common in parts of the Enchanted Forest. Antorell didn't make it, he just snatched it from somewhere nearby."

"Snatched it?" Cimorene's eyes widened. "Yes, I suppose he could have managed that. I begin to see what you meant about traveling in the Enchanted Forest alone," she added in a thoughtful tone.

"I should hope so," Mendanbar muttered, turning away. "Then you've changed your mind about going?" he added hopefully over his shoulder.

"No, just about whether I accept your offer of escort," Cimorene said. "It'll probably be a nuisance, but nightshades would be much worse."

Slightly startled by this unflattering comparison, Mendanbar glanced back at Cimorene. There was a decided twinkle in her eyes. Mendanbar smiled and bowed elaborately. "Thank you for your kind words, Princess."

"You're welcome, Your Majesty," Cimorene said, curtsying in response. "Now, we'd better get to work, or we'll never get this mess cleaned up in time to get to Flat Top Mountain before dark."

Cleaning up the large cave took less time than Mendanbar had expected, despite the unpleasantly gummy look of the goo that Antorell had left behind. A large part of the mess turned out to be leftover soapy water, which was very convenient. Cimorene mopped most of it up with Antorell's robe, then wrapped the robe around the staff and started toward the rear of the cave.

"What are you going to do with that?" Mendanbar asked curiously.

"Hide it," Cimorene said. "There's not much else you can do to a wizard's staff. They won't break, and even dragon fire won't burn them. I know because we tried everything we could think of the last time we melted some wizards."

"We?"

"Morwen and I. Antorell will get it back eventually, of course, but hiding it will slow him down a little." She left to dispose of the staff while Mendanbar scraped up the last of the goo.

The kitchen was another matter. Cimorene insisted on doing all of the dishes that had been waiting for the sink to get unplugged, which took a while. Mendanbar offered to use his magic on the dishes, but Cimorene politely declined.

"A magic sword that does plumbing is unusual but very useful," she explained as she filled the sink. "A magic sword that does dishes is just plain silly. Besides, there have been two big flares of magic in this cave in the past hour already, and if there's a third one, someone might come to see what I'm up to."

"I didn't notice anything remarkable when Antorell brought the nightshade in," Mendanbar said, frowning. "Though I'll admit I overdid it a little when I got rid of the thing. I was in a hurry."

"Yes, of course," said Cimorene, setting a clean plate on the drain board. "But you weren't in a hurry when you unclogged the sink, were you? That was the other flare I meant, not Antorell's fiddling."

"What was conspicuous about that?" Mendanbar asked defensively. He picked up a clean towel and began drying plates. "It was a perfectly ordinary spell."

Cimorene looked at him. "Right. Just like that sword is a perfectly ordinary magic sword."

"Well, I wouldn't call it *ordinary,* exactly, but that's because it's linked with the Enchanted Forest," Mendanbar said. "Outside of that, it's nothing special."

"Nothing special." Cimorene stopped washing dishes for a moment to stare at him. Suddenly, she frowned. "You mean it. You really haven't noticed."

"Noticed what?"

"The way that sword of yours positively reeks of magic," Cimorene said. "We're going to have to do something about it, unless you want the Society of Wizards to be able to find us with their eyes closed."

Mendanbar looked at her. She was perfectly serious. He set the dishtowel down and drew his sword. It didn't look or feel any different to him from the way it normally felt, but Cimorene winced.

"Can't you . . . tone it down a little?"

"I still don't know what you're talking about," Mendanbar said, irritated. "And even if I did, I wouldn't have the slightest idea how to go about 'toning it down.' "

"Why not? It's your sword, isn't it?"

"It didn't come with directions!"

"Most of them don't." Cimorene shook her head at him and picked another dirty teacup out of the rapidly diminishing stack. "Maybe there's something in Kazul's treasury that will take care of it. I'll check as soon as we're done here."

When the dishes were finished and the kitchen tidied to suit Cimorene's exacting standards, she left Mendanbar to mull things over while she went off to investigate the treasury. Mendanbar was glad of the chance to think.

"What is the Society of Wizards doing?" he muttered. Between the misleading things Zemenar had said to Mendanbar and the downright lies Antorell had told to Cimorene, it was clear that the wizards didn't want them comparing notes. Cimorene might even be right about their desire to start a war between the Enchanted Forest and the dragons.

Starting a war, however, would take more than a misunderstanding between the King of the Enchanted Forest and Kazul's Chief Cook and Librarian. Were the wizards behind the mysterious burned area Mendanbar had found? They could have gotten hold of Woraug's scales, and they certainly could have enchanted them.

"But *why* would they do it?" Mendanbar asked the sink. "They're not stupid, at least Zemenar isn't, and a war would cause the Society almost as many problems as it would cause us. What could make them overlook the problems and try to stir up trouble anyway?" The sink did not answer.

But if it wasn't the wizards, Mendanbar wondered, who was it? Where had Kazul disappeared to? And was there really a dragonsbane farm in the Enchanted Forest, or was that just a rumor someone was spreading to add to the confusion?

He was still trying to put his questions into some sort of order when Cimorene returned. She had exchanged the apron and the rust-colored dress for a dark blue tunic with matching leggings, a pair of tall black boots, and a maroon cloak. She had taken off her crown, and her braids were wound neatly around her head. A gold-handled sword hung at her side, next to a small belt pouch. She held out a sword belt and sheath, the leather gray with age.

"I think this will do the job," she said. "Try it and see."

"I've already got a sheath," Mendanbar pointed out.

"Yes, but this one blocks magic," Cimorene explained. "It'll keep your sword from being so–so obvious all the time. At least, I hope it will."

"If you say so," Mendanbar replied, taking the scabbard. He held it a moment, testing. It didn't feel magical, but then, that was the idea. He shrugged, pulled out his sword, and put it into the sheath Cimorene had given him.

"Oh, that's much better," Cimorene said with evident relief. "I can hardly notice anything now."

"I can," Mendanbar said, touching the hilt with a frown. The pulse of the Enchanted Forest was still there, ready for him to use.

"Of course you can," Cimorene said. "It's your sword."

"Well, I suppose I don't mind using it, then," Mendanbar said. "As long as it doesn't damage the sword."

"It won't," Cimorene promised.

Mendanbar took off his sword belt and set it aside, then buckled on the belt and scabbard Cimorene had given him.

"All right," he said, "let's go."

As they left the cave, Cimorene muttered something under her breath and waved at the entrance. Mendanbar jumped as a coil of strong, hard magic sprang into place behind them. Looking over his shoulder, he saw a solid wall of rock. He transferred his gaze to Cimorene and raised an eyebrow.

"What kind of magic was *that?*"

"Just something Kazul and I worked out a while back," Cimorene said. "It's to keep wizards and knights and so forth from prowling around while I'm gone."

So Cimorene is a sorceress, as well as a cook and librarian and goodness knows what else, Mendanbar thought to himself. Every time he thought he had her figured out, she surprised him again.

"It's a good idea, but please warn me if you're going to do anything like that again," he said. "I'm not in the mood for being startled, if you know what I mean."

Cimorene nodded, frowning slightly, and asked just what it was about the spell that had startled him. This led to a long, technical discussion of the various ways of casting spells, detecting spells, and comparing spells other people had cast. Mendanbar found it both interesting and informative. He had always known that his own methods of working magic were not much like anyone else's, but he had never had time to study other styles. Cimorene knew something about most kinds of magic, and she was naturally very well informed indeed about dragon magic. She was as interested in Mendanbar's system as he was in everything else, and the conversation lasted all the way to Flat Top Mountain.

* * *

The sun had slipped behind the mountains and it was almost dark when they came to the foot of the last slope. Mendanbar could see the giant's castle at the top, large and dark and ominous against the graying sky. A broad road wrapped three times around the mountain as it wound its way to the castle gates.

"Are you sure this is the right place?" he asked.

"Quite sure," Cimorene said. "I've never been here myself, but Kazul has described it often enough. And that's certainly a giant's castle."

"Exactly," Mendanbar said. "But is it the right giant?"

"We won't find out standing here. Come on."

Cimorene marched confidently up the mountain. Shaking his head, Mendanbar followed. By the time they reached the castle gates, the stars were beginning to come out and it was getting hard to see.

"There ought to be a bellpull or a knob," Cimorene said. "You check that side of the gate, and I'll take this one."

"All right, but what–"

A loud grinding noise interrupted Mendanbar in midsentence, and the gates swung open. Yellow light spilled across the road, making Mendanbar and Cimorene squint.

"Come in, travelers," a woman's voice said, much too pleasantly. "Come in, and make yourselves comfortable for the night."

Neither Mendanbar nor Cimorene moved. "This was your idea in the first place," Mendanbar said softly to Cimorene. "What do we do now?"

"Ask questions," Cimorene replied just as softly. She raised her voice and said, "Thank you for your kind hospitality, but we're not just traveling. We're looking for the giantess Ballimore, and we're in a hurry. So if you're not Ballimore, we'll have to go on."

"I am Ballimore," said the voice, still in an artificially pleasant tone that made Mendanbar's skin crawl. "Who are you?"

"I'm Princess Cimorene, Chief Cook and Librarian to Kazul, the King of the Dragons, and this is Mendanbar, the King of the Enchanted Forest," Cimorene answered.

"Cimorene?" said the voice in an entirely different manner. "Oh, good. I've been wanting to meet you for the longest time. Come on in, you and your friend, and I'll have supper ready in a jiffy."

Mendanbar and Cimorene looked at each other. "I think it's all right now," Cimorene said after a moment.

"Well, we won't find out standing here," Mendanbar said. He held out his arm. "Shall we go in, Princess?"

Cimorene gave him a bright, almost impish smile, and laid her fingertips on his arm as if they were walking into a court ball. "I should be pleased to accompany you, Your Majesty."

Together they walked through the gate. The courtyard inside was high, wide, and empty except for two rows of blazing torches in iron holders lined up on either side of the path. Mendanbar and Cimorene paced slowly up to the door, which swung open just as the gates had, only without the grinding. As they went in, they heard the castle gates crunch shut. A moment later, the doors closed silently behind them.

They stood in a stone hall three times the size of any Mendanbar had ever seen. A wooden table, surrounded by high-backed chairs, stretched the length of the hall. At the far end of the room a large fire burned in an open hearth. High on the walls, more torches lit the room. A brown-haired woman in a pale blue dress was bending over a cauldron that hung from an iron hook above the fire. It all looked very ordinary, until Mendanbar noticed that the seats of the chairs were level with his eyes and everything else was similarly oversized.

The brown-haired woman sniffed at the cauldron, nodded to herself, and straightened. "Welcome," she said, coming forward. "I'm Ballimore. You must be Princess Cimorene. I'm so pleased to meet you at last, after all that Kazul has told me about you."

The giantess bent over to shake hands gently with Cimorene. She was at least three times as tall as Mendanbar, but she moved with a grace that suited her size. Cimorene returned the handshake gravely, and said, "I hope Kazul hasn't given you the wrong idea about me."

"Not at all, I'm sure," said the giantess. "Is this your young man? You're not running away from the dragons after all this time, are you?"

"Certainly not," Cimorene said with unnecessary vehemence. "I'm very happy with my job."

"Of course," Ballimore said, sounding disappointed. She gave Mendanbar a speculative look, then leaned toward Cimorene. "If I were you, I'd reconsider," she said in a loud whisper. "Your young man doesn't look like the patient type."

"No, no," Cimorene said, reddening. "It's not like that at all. This is the King of the Enchanted Forest, and he came to see Kazul, only Kazul has gone to visit her grandchildren and isn't home. That's why we came to see you–to borrow a magic carpet, so we can find Kazul."

"Oh, I see," said the giantess. "Strictly business. Well, you'll have to wait until after supper. Dobbilan will be home any minute, and he hates it when his meals are late."

"Dobbilan?" Mendanbar said with some misgiving.

"My husband," Ballimore said.

There was a loud crash from the courtyard outside, followed by the *thud, thud, thud* of heavy footsteps that shook the castle.

Ballimore straightened with a happy smile. "Here he comes now."

8

In Which They Give Some Good Advice to a Giant

Mendanbar and Cimorene turned to face the castle doors as the footsteps drew nearer. A moment later, the doors flew open and the giantess's husband stepped into the hall. He was a giant's head taller than she, with wild brown hair and a beard like a large, untidy broom's head. He carried a club that was as long as Mendanbar was tall.

Just inside the door, the giant stopped and sniffed the air. Then he sneezed once, scowled ferociously, and said in a voice that shook the torches in their brackets:

"Fee, fie, foe, fum,
I smell the blood of an Englishman.
Be he alive or be he dead,
I'll grind his bones to make my bread."

Ballimore shook her head. "Nonsense, dear. It's just Princess Cimorene and the King of the Enchanted Forest."

"And neither of us is English," Cimorene added.

The giant squinted down at her. "Are you sure about that?"

"Positive," Mendanbar said.

"Well–" The giant sniffed again, experimentally, then lowered his club with a sigh. "That's all right, then. I wasn't in the mood for more work tonight, anyway. Sorry about the mistake. It must be this cold in my head."

"I told you yesterday to take something for it," Ballimore scolded. "And I told you this morning to wrap some flannel around your throat before you went out. But do you listen to me? No!"

"I listen," the giant protested uncomfortably. "But I can't ransack villages with a piece of flannel around my neck. It wouldn't look right."

Cimorene snorted softly. Mendanbar got the distinct impression that she didn't think much of doing things for the sake of appearances.

"Well, really, Dobbilan," Ballimore said, "how do you think it looks if you're coughing and sneezing all over everything while you're ransacking? Have a little sense."

"I'd rather have a little dinner," said Dobbilan and sneezed again.

"If you sound like that tomorrow, you're staying home in bed," Ballimore informed her husband.

"I can't do that! I'm scheduled to pillage two villages and maraud half a county."

"You're in no condition to pillage a henhouse, much less a village," Ballimore declared. "Besides, you've earned a bit of a rest, what with all the extra time you've been putting in lately, looting and marauding and I don't know what all."

"That's not the point."

"It's precisely the point. You're just being stubborn because you think having a bad cold is un-giantlike."

"Well, it is."

Ballimore shook her head and looked at Cimorene. "Men!" she said in tones of disgust.

"And don't you say 'men' to me," Dobbilan said. "It's my job we're talking about."

"Maybe you should try a different line of work," Mendanbar suggested.

"Eh?" Dobbilan peered down at him with interest. "Like what?"

"Consulting," Mendanbar said at random, because he hadn't actually thought about it.

"Consulting?"

"You know," said Cimorene. "Giving advice to people. You could teach other giants the best ways of–of ravaging and pillaging and marauding, and you could tell villages the best ways to keep giants away. With all your experience, I'll bet you'd be good at it."

"I never thought of that," Dobbilan said, rubbing his chin.

"I don't know why not," Ballimore said. "It's a very good idea. And you wouldn't be out in all sorts of weather, catching colds and flu and goodness knows what else."

"Plundering *has* gotten to be an awful lot of work lately," the giant admitted. "It would be a relief to stop. I'm getting too old to tramp through fields."

"I understand consulting pays very well, too," Mendanbar told him.

"I'll do it!" Dobbilan said with sudden decision. "Tomorrow morning, first thing. Thank you for the suggestion. What did you say your names were?"

"If you'd listen once in a while, you wouldn't have to ask me to repeat everything," Ballimore said. "This is Princess Cimorene, the one who's been with Kazul for the last year or so and gave me that marvelous biscuit recipe you like so much. And her young man is the King of the Enchanted Forest, who she's not running away with yet."

Mendanbar choked and shot an apprehensive look at Cimorene. She rolled her eyes and made a face at him but did not say anything, having apparently decided it was a waste of effort to correct the giantess.

"Pleased to meet you, Princess," Dobbilan said solemnly. "Nice to see you, King. What brings you to Flat Top Mountain?"

"They say it's business," Ballimore said before either Cimorene or Mendanbar could answer.

"Then it will have to wait until after dinner," Dobbilan announced. "I never discuss business at dinner. Or with dinner, for that matter." He winked at Cimorene. "Besides, I'm hungry." He sneezed a third time. "Excuse me."

Ballimore began scolding again as Cimorene and Mendanbar nodded politely. Mendanbar was beginning to wonder how long they were going to have to stand next to the table, when Ballimore shooed her husband to a seat at one end and started for the other herself, saying over her shoulder, "Cimorene, dear, you and the King are on the right. Just walk around to the chair; it's all set up."

With some misgiving, Mendanbar escorted Cimorene past Dobbilan's chair toward the seat Ballimore had indicated. As they approached, he saw that the giantess had not been exaggerating. A set of normal-sized wooden steps, equipped with wheels so as to be easily movable, stood next to the giant right-hand chair, and two ordinary chairs were perched side by side on the seat at the top. The combination was, Mendanbar discovered, exactly the right height to reach the table. Apparently, Ballimore was accustomed to having smaller people at dinner, for the plates and glasses were the usual size as well. As long as Mendanbar did not look down, it was easy to pretend he was sitting at an ordinary dinner table.

The food was very good. They started with fresh greens and went on to roast pig with cranberries, mushrooms in wine, and some sort of lumpy vegetable in a thick brown sauce that disguised it completely and tasted marvelous. There was a great deal of everything. Mendanbar supposed this was only to be expected at a giant's table, but Ballimore did not seem to realize that a person who was only a third her size would have a smaller appetite as well. She filled and refilled Mendanbar's plate until he was ready to burst.

Near the end of the meal, Cimorene leaned over and whispered, "Don't take any dessert."

"Why not?" Mendanbar asked.

"Ballimore's using her Cauldron of Plenty," Cimorene said, "and it doesn't do desserts very well. So unless you *like* burned mint custard or sour-cream-and-onion ice cream . . ."

"I see," Mendanbar said quickly. "Then it's a good thing I couldn't eat another bite even if I wanted to."

When dinner was over, Cimorene brought up the question of the magic carpet. Ballimore nodded at once.

"Of course you can borrow a carpet, Cimorene dear. I'll just take a look around and see what we have."

"You won't find much," said her husband, and sneezed loudly. "That last Englishman you let in took most of them. You should have let me find him and grind his bones, like I'm supposed to."

"Nonsense," said Ballimore, frowning at her husband. "We can afford a few cheap magic harps and a coin or two. I keep the good silver and Mother's jewelry in the top cupboard, where they can't reach it. Besides, they're always such nice boys."

"Huh," said Dobbilan. "Beggars and thieves, if you ask me, and boring at that."

"What makes you say that?" Mendanbar asked curiously.

"They always do the same thing–come in, ask for a meal, hide, and then run off with a harp or a bag full of money the minute I fall asleep," Dobbilan said. "And they're always named Jack. *Always.* We've lived in this castle for twenty years, and every three months, regular as clockwork, one of those boys shows up, and there's never been a Tom, Dick, or Harry among 'em. Just Jacks. The English have no imagination."

"About the carpet," Cimorene reminded him.

"Oh, that. Well, the last Jack wasn't musical, and he cleaned us out of magic carpets instead of harps." Dobbilan sneezed again and began to cough.

"Bed for you, dear," Ballimore said firmly and shooed her husband out of the room. She followed him closely, muttering to herself about cough syrup and vaporizers and hot tea with lemon and honey. Mendanbar and Cimorene looked at each other.

"Is there anywhere else we can borrow a carpet?" Mendanbar asked.

"Not that I know of," Cimorene said with a worried frown. "We'll just have to walk. Drat. It'll take days."

"We could go back to the Enchanted Forest and–"

"There," said Ballimore, coming briskly into the room and cutting Mendanbar off in mid-sentence. "He'll be much better in the morning. I'm afraid he's right about the carpets, Cimorene dear, but I'll just have a look around and see if there isn't something stuck off in a corner somewhere. I can't believe we're completely out."

"It's quite all right," Cimorene said. "We'll manage somehow."

"Nonsense, dear," Ballimore said in the same tone she used to her husband. "It will be quite an adventure, seeing what's stuck off in corners and so on. I haven't been in some of the storage rooms in years."

It was clear that nothing they could say would shake her resolve, and after a token protest, they gave in. Ballimore showed them to a pair of comfortably furnished rooms and left them for the night. Mendanbar did not object, even though it was still fairly early. The long walk from the dragon's cave had been very tiring. He lay down on the bed and fell asleep at once.

Breakfast next morning was cinnamon-flavored porridge, milk, and toast with blueberry jam. Mendanbar found it waiting on the high table in the central hall when he left his room to look for his hosts. There was no one else around, but the giant-sized dishes and crumbs at either end of the table showed that Ballimore and Dobbilan had already eaten. Mendanbar climbed the stairs to his seat and began dishing up the porridge. Before he had finished filling his bowl, Cimorene walked into the room, peering around for the giants.

"Good morning," Mendanbar called. "Madame Ballimore and her husband appear to have been and gone, but they've left an excellent breakfast. Would you care to join me?"

"I'd be delighted," Cimorene called back, and climbed the stairs to join him. "I had no idea giants were such early risers," she said as she sat down in the second chair. "Where do you suppose they've gone?"

"Gone?" said Ballimore's voice from the hallway at the end of the room. "Dear, dear, I thought sure I'd left enough porridge for the pair of you, but it won't take a minute to make up some more."

"There's plenty of breakfast," Mendanbar said quickly. "We were talking about you and Dobbilan."

"But he was supposed to wait for you," Ballimore said, emerging from the hallway. She inspected the room over the top of the large bundle she carried, then shook her head. "Isn't that just like a man? Cimorene dear, I've found just the thing for you. I knew there would be something upstairs, no matter what Dobbilan said. Are you quite certain you have enough porridge?"

"Quite certain," Cimorene said. "What–"

"Ballimore! Ballimore, where's the inkwell?" Dobbilan's voice echoed down the corridor, interrupting Cimorene in mid-sentence. "Where are you? Why can't I find anything around here when I want it?"

"Because you never look in the right place, dear," Ballimore called. "The inkwell is in the kitchen next to the grocery list, where it's been for the past six months, and I'm in the dining room. Which is where you'd be if you'd done what I asked you to, instead of wandering off in all directions."

"I didn't wander off," Dobbilan objected, sticking his head into the room. "I went to get some paper and ink so I could write a letter. Oh, good morning, Princess, King. I didn't see you."

"You were supposed to see them," Ballimore said, exasperated. "You were supposed to be here when–oh, never mind."

"Well, if you're done scolding, could you find me that inkwell?"

Ballimore shook her head, set her bundle down on a chair, and went off to deal with her erring husband. Mendanbar looked at Cimorene, and they both burst out laughing at the same time.

"Oh, dear," said Cimorene when she got her breath back. "I hope they didn't hear."

"Are they always like this?" Mendanbar asked.

"I don't know," Cimorene admitted. "This is the first time I've been here. Kazul has always been the one who comes to talk or borrow things." The thought wiped the smile from her face. "I hope she's safe."

"You'd know if she wasn't," Mendanbar said, hoping he was right. "Being King of the Dragons is a little like being King of the Enchanted Forest; if anything really drastic happens to you, *everybody* knows."

"I suppose so," Cimorene said. "And I know perfectly well that she can take care of herself, but I'll *still* feel a lot better when we find out where she is."

There wasn't much Mendanbar could say to that. They ate in silence for a few minutes and were just finishing up when Ballimore and Dobbilan returned. Dobbilan was carrying several sheets of white paper and a pen made of a feather as long as Mendanbar's arm. Ballimore held an inkwell the size of a sink. The giantess cleared the dishes away from the far end of the table and set the inkwell gently in place, then steered her husband to the chair. When she had him settled, she picked up the bundle she had brought in earlier.

"I'll just take this outside and shake the dust out," she told Cimorene. "You and your young man can come along as soon as you've finished eating. Don't rush."

"How do you spell 'resignation'?" Dobbilan asked, nibbling on the end of his feather pen.

Mendanbar spelled it for him as Ballimore bustled out the door. He and Cimorene finished their breakfasts with only an occasional interruption from Dobbilan. Leaving the giant mumbling over his letter and chewing on the tattered end of his pen, they went out to see what Ballimore had found.

"There you are," Ballimore said as they came into the courtyard. "I've gotten most of the dust out, and it's ready to go. What do you think?"

She stepped back and Mendanbar got his first good look at the carpet. It was enormous, with a three-foot fringe on all four sides. In places it looked rather worn, and there was a hole the size of a teacup in one corner. The background was a rich cream color, dotted with teddy bears a foot long. Pink teddy bears. Bright pink.

"It's certainly large enough," Mendanbar said at last.

"Are you sure it will fly?" Cimorene asked, looking dubiously at the hole.

"Oh, yes," Ballimore reassured her. "It's the very best quality, but we haven't used it in years because of the pattern." She gestured at the teddy bears. "Dobbilan thought they just didn't look right in a giant's castle."

"I think I agree with him," Mendanbar said under his breath, eyeing the pink teddy bears with dislike. "No wonder that Jack fellow didn't take it."

"As long as it flies, I don't care what it looks like," Cimorene declared. "Thank you so much, Ballimore. I'll make sure you get it back as soon as we're through with it."

"There's no rush," Ballimore said. "It'll just go back in the attic."

"How does it work?" Mendanbar asked.

"I couldn't find the instruction manual, but it's perfectly simple," Ballimore told him. "All magic carpets are the same. You sit in the middle and say, 'Up, up, up and away' to make it take off, and you steer by leaning in the direction you want to go."

"What about stopping?"

Ballimore frowned in concentration. "I believe you're supposed to say 'Whoa,' but 'Cut it out, carpet' works just as well. I'm sorry I can't be more definite. It's been a long time."

"Right." Mendanbar looked at Cimorene. "Are you *sure* you want to do this?"

Cimorene hesitated, then nodded firmly. "We'll manage. If I could think of some other way of getting to the north end of the mountains quickly, I would. Come on." She stepped onto the carpet, and plopped down in the center.

With some misgiving, Mendanbar sat next to her.

"Oh, heavens, I nearly forgot!" Ballimore said suddenly. "Stay right there, Cimorene dear. I'll be back in a flash."

"Now what?" Mendanbar asked as the giantess hurried into the castle.

"Maybe she remembered where the instruction manual is," Cimorene said.

"Somehow I doubt it," Mendanbar said.

A moment later, Ballimore came hurrying out again, carrying a large bag. "I packed you a bit of lunch," she explained, handing Cimorene the package. "Goodness knows what you'll find out there in the mountains."

Cimorene thanked Ballimore again and set the bag between herself and Mendanbar, then said, "All right, carpet: up, up, up and away!"

The carpet shuddered, shifted and rose slowly into the air. Smiling broadly, Cimorene waved at Ballimore, then leaned forward. The carpet shivered again and began to move. It sailed up out of the castle and into the sky over the mountains, gathering speed as it went.

9

In Which They Discover the Perils of Borrowed Equipment

At first, the magic carpet ride was thoroughly enjoyable. The air was crisp and cool, and there was no noise at all except their own voices. The view was amazing, even better than looking down from a mountain. The Mountains of Morning stood in crooked, gray-blue rows below, each crack and boulder outlined in sharp black shadow. Tiny figures moved across the rocks and through the strips of greenery at the bottoms of the mountains: sheep and mountain goats and adventurous knights. Every now and then Mendanbar caught a glimpse of the lush trees of the Enchanted Forest between the peaks.

"Stop craning your neck like that," Cimorene said. "You're confusing the carpet."

"Sorry." Mendanbar sneaked a last look and sighed as the patch of green disappeared behind a rocky slope. How was Willin getting along without him?

"Mendanbar, is your sword slipping?" Cimorene said. "I thought I felt something for a minute there. Is it coming out of that sheath?"

"No," Mendanbar replied, checking it. "It's fine. And I haven't touched it. Are you sure it was the sword?"

"No," Cimorene admitted. "Maybe we flew over something magical and that's what I felt. It's gone now."

"Good," said Mendanbar. "Are you–"

The carpet gave a sudden lurch sideways, then dropped three feet. "Mendanbar!" Cimorene cried. "I told you to stop that!"

"It wasn't me!" Mendanbar protested, trying to find something to hang on to.

"Well, it wasn't *me,* and there's only the two of us up here," Cimorene shouted.

The carpet rippled alarmingly, then resumed its peaceful progress. Cautiously, Mendanbar turned his head to look at Cimorene. Wisps of black hair had come loose from her braids to blow wildly across her face. It made her look particularly lovely, even though she was scowling at him. Mendanbar blinked and pulled his thoughts together.

"I really didn't do anything," he said.

"But–"

The carpet wiggled and began to spin slowly. Mendanbar swallowed hard, wishing he had not eaten quite so much breakfast. He closed his eyes, then opened them again very quickly as the carpet bounced twice, paused, and started spinning twice as fast in the opposite direction.

"Carpet!" Mendanbar shouted. "Cut it out!"

The lurching and spinning stopped. The carpet hung motionless in midair for a long moment, then dropped like the bottom falling out of a cardboard box. Cimorene gasped, then said something that sounded like "Oof!" as the carpet froze once more, three feet lower than it had been. Mendanbar started to push himself up, then–without warning–the carpet dropped another three feet.

This time, Mendanbar stayed flat on the teddy bears. Two seconds later, the carpet dropped again. And again. And again. Mendanbar lost track of the bumps and concentrated on keeping track of his stomach. Suddenly, the carpet spun around twice and took off in a steep, fast climb.

"Whoa!" Cimorene cried. "Whoa, you stupid carpet, cut it out!"

Again, the carpet froze. Then it dropped again, but this time, instead of bumping, it fell like a stone. Mendanbar got a glimpse of the ground drawing quickly closer, and then he had both hands on the hilt of his sword. He didn't bother to pull it out of the sheath, he just yanked at the power it held and flung it around himself and Cimorene. Then he shoved with all his might.

Their speed slowed abruptly. The carpet fell away beneath them, rippling angrily, and plopped down on a rocky depression at the foot of a mountain. Mendanbar and Cimorene drifted after it, landing softly in the carpet's center. They lay there for a moment, catching their breath and collecting their wits.

Finally, Mendanbar raised his head and looked warily around. They lay in the middle of a circle of pine trees. "I think we've arrived," he said, sitting up.

"Good," Cimorene said shakily. She sat up, pushing tendrils of hair out of her face, and gave him a crooked smile. "I guess I should have asked Ballimore a few more questions about this carpet before we took it."

"Yes, well, it's too late now." Mendanbar rolled off the carpet and stood up. "How far have we come?"

"A little over halfway, I think. Too far to walk back, not far enough to walk the rest of the way there." She made a face at the teddy bears, which looked innocently back. "We may have to try the carpet again."

"We don't have to try it right away, though," Mendanbar pointed out. "There's a house over there–you can see the roof through the trees. Maybe the owner can tell us exactly where we are and the shortest way to get where we're going."

"All right," Cimorene agreed, with a swiftness that made Mendanbar think she was no more eager to get back on the carpet than he was. "We'll have to bring the carpet with us, though. If you leave magical things lying around, all sorts of dreadful things can happen."

Mendanbar had to admit that she was right, though he wasn't happy about it. They set Ballimore's lunch in the middle of the carpet, then rolled the rug around it, folding the fringe carefully to the inside. Then Cimorene took the front end and Mendanbar picked up the rear, and they started toward the house.

Weaving through three rows of pine trees, they ducked under the low-hanging branches along the outer edge of the grove and emerged in front of the house. It looked, thought Mendanbar, as if it had been put together by the same person who had built his palace, except that instead of too many towers and staircases, this house had too many windows: square windows, round windows, wide windows, tall windows, skinny windows, diamond windows, tiny windows filled with milky glass, enormous picture windows, windows with stained glass pictures of ladies in sweeping robes and birds with gold feathers, open windows with curtains blowing out of them. The roof was made of red tile and skylights, and the chimney had a square block of clear glass in the front side. Even the door had a window in it, right in the middle at about waist height. With only two floors, there were hardly enough walls to hold all the windows, in spite of the way the building sprawled in all directions.

As they drew near, Mendanbar felt a faint aura of power around the house, hanging in the air like mist. He was about to mention it to Cimorene, when he heard yells and shouts of laughter coming from behind the house. Suddenly a small blonde girl dashed around the corner and stopped short, staring. A slightly larger boy followed in hot pursuit and barely managed to stop in time to avoid a collision. The blonde child looked at him reproachfully, then turned toward the house and shrieked at the top of her voice, "Herman! Herman, there's people."

"Bah!" A deep, cross voice came carrying through the open window beside the door. "I don't want any people. Tell them to go away."

The little girl obediently turned to Cimorene. "Go away, please," she said, and stuck her thumb in her mouth.

"No, thank you," Cimorene responded. "We want to talk to your parents."

"Haven't got any," said the boy. He tilted his head to one side, as if considering, then took off for the house at a dead run. "Herman, they won't go!" he shouted as he ran. "They want *parents.* They–"

His shouting stopped as he dove headfirst through the open window and vanished inside. One of the upstairs windows scraped open, and two older children poked their heads out. At the same time, three small heads appeared at the corner of the house, gazing timidly at Mendanbar and Cimorene.

Cimorene looked at Mendanbar and set her end of the carpet on the ground. Mendanbar put his end down, too, and stepped forward to stand beside her. The children stared at them without speaking.

"ABSOLUTELY NOT!" the cross voice shouted. The front door of the house flew open and a dwarf stomped out. He was not much taller than the oldest of the children, but his long black beard and muscular arms showed plainly that he was no child. His hair looked like an upside-down black haystack. He glared angrily at Mendanbar.

"I won't do it!" the dwarf declared before either Mendanbar or Cimorene could say anything. "I don't care if it's family tradition, I don't care if you need the money, I don't care if her mother lied and now you have to convince your council, I don't care if your mother is going to turn her into a toad tomorrow if she doesn't perform. I WILL NOT DO IT AND THAT'S FINAL!"

"That's quite all right," Cimorene said. "We don't want you to. We just want–"

"I know what you want," the dwarf said, hopping furiously from one foot to the other. "You want a chance to talk me into it. Well, you won't get one, missy. You should be ashamed to even consider such a thing!"

"She *isn't* considering it," Mendanbar said. "We're travelers, and we've just stopped to get some directions."

The dwarf paused in midhop. Balancing on one foot, he peered suspiciously at Mendanbar. One of the children giggled. The dwarf glared in the direction of the sound, then turned back to Mendanbar.

"Directions? What sort of directions?" he asked with evident mistrust. "Who are you, anyway?"

"I'm Princess Cimorene and this is King Mendanbar," Cimorene said, "and we're trying to get to the cave where the dragon Falgorn lives."

"Oh, you're after a dramatic rescue," the dwarf said with relief. "I suppose that's all right. But are you sure you know what you're getting into? Dragons are tough."

"No, no," Cimorene said in the exasperated tone of someone who is very tired of correcting the same mistake over and over. "I'm Chief Cook and Librarian for Kazul, the King of the Dragons, and I'm very happy with my job, and I don't want anyone to rescue me."

The dwarf's eyes narrowed. "Then why are you looking for this other dragon?"

"Because I have an urgent message for Kazul, and she's gone to visit Falgorn," Mendanbar explained.

"Huh." The dwarf hesitated, looking from Cimorene to Mendanbar. "How do I know this isn't some sort of trick?"

"Why should we want to trick you?" Cimorene asked.

"To get me to spin straw into gold for you, you silly girl," the dwarf said. "That's why everyone comes to see me. And look at the thanks I get: children! Hundreds and hundreds of children! Bah!"

The littlest children giggled and pulled their heads back behind the corner as the dwarf spun around. The blonde girl stared solemnly at him for a moment, then took her thumb out of her mouth, ran forward, and gave the dwarf an enormous hug.

"Thank you, Herman," she told the dumbfounded dwarf. She hugged him again and skipped off, apprarently tired of listening.

The dwarf smiled foolishly after her. The expression made him look pleasant and almost handsome. After a moment, the dwarf turned back to Cimorene, and his frown returned.

"I don't see the connection between children and spinning straw into gold," Mendanbar said before the dwarf could start complaining again. "Would you be good enough to explain it to me?"

"Explain?" the dwarf fumed. "That's what the last girl said, and what happened? Twins, that's what happened! And *she* claimed she couldn't remember which one was first, so I ended up with both of them."

"I can see why that would be annoying," Cimorene said noncommittally.

The dwarf glared at her. "Yes, you say that *now,* but–oh, what's the use? You'll get it out of me one way or another."

"If you'd rather not tell us–" Mendanbar started, but the dwarf cut him off with a despairing wave.

"It doesn't matter. It's my fate, that's what it is. I should never have agreed to learn to spin straw into gold in the first place."

"Why did you?" Mendanbar asked.

"It's a family tradition," the dwarf answered gloomily. "Of course it doesn't work if you're just spinning for yourself. So, a long time ago, my great-grandfather offered to use his talent to help out a girl who was in a sticky situation. If he hadn't been such a do-gooder, I wouldn't be in this mess."

"What good did he do, exactly?" Mendanbar asked.

"The local prince had gotten a notion that the girl could spin straw into gold," the dwarf said. "Brainless young idiot, but they're all like that. If she could spin straw into gold, why was she living in a hovel? Anyway, Gramps said he'd do her spinning for her in return for part of the gold and her firstborn child. She agreed, but naturally when the baby was born she didn't want to give him up. So Gramps agreed to a guessing game: if she could guess his name, she could keep the baby. Then he let her find out what his name was. She kept the baby and Gramps kept the gold, and everyone went home happy."

"I think I'm beginning to get the idea," Cimorene said. "It's not just spinning straw into gold that's a family tradition, is it? It's the whole scheme."

The dwarf nodded sadly. "Right the first time. Only I can never make it work properly. I can find plenty of girls who're supposed to spin straw into gold, and most of them suggest the guessing game, but I've never had even *one* who managed to guess my name."

"Oh, dear," said Cimorene.

"I even changed my name legally, so it would be easier," the dwarf said sadly. "Herman isn't a difficult name to remember, is it? But no, the silly chits can't do it. So I end up with the baby as well as the gold, and babies eat and cry and need clothes, and the gold runs out, and I have to find another girl to spin gold for, and it happens all over again, and I end up with *another* baby. It isn't fair!"

"You, um, seem to be fond of the children, though," Mendanbar said.

The dwarf looked around to see whether any of the children were within hearing distance, then nodded sheepishly. "They're good kids. It's just that there are too many of them. I moved out here so it would be harder for the silly girls to find me and talk me into spinning for them, but they keep finding me anyway."

"It was a rather drastic move, wasn't it?" Cimorene said. "What about the dragons and giants and rock snakes and so on?"

"Oh, they're no problem. The house used to belong to a magician, and he left a lot of guarding spells on it. Nothing nasty can get anywhere near."

"That's why it feels magical," Mendanbar said, relieved.

"It's an odd sort of house for a wizard," Cimorene said, studying it. "Why so many windows?"

"Not a wizard," the dwarf said. "A magician. He was trying to find out which kinds of windows work best when they're enchanted."

"Did he find out?"

"I suppose so, or he wouldn't have let me buy it. Most of the windows don't work anymore, but there's a round one at the end of the attic that still shows things once in a while."

"What kinds of things?" Mendanbar asked. "Can you ask to see something in particular, or does it just show scenes at random?"

"You have to ask," said the dwarf, "and you don't always get an answer. Would you like to see it?"

"Yes, please," Cimorene said quickly.

Mendanbar looked doubtfully at the carpet, wondering whether it would be safe to leave it where it was with all the children around, and thinking how much trouble it would be to haul along if they didn't.

"Let it be," the dwarf said, following Mendanbar's gaze. "The kids won't touch it."

With some reluctance, Mendanbar nodded and followed the dwarf and Cimorene into the house. The inside was just as mazelike as Mendanbar had expected from the rambling exterior. The dwarf led them down a passage, around a corner, up a flight of creaky wooden stairs, through a room lined with pictures, up another flight of stairs, and down a long hall to a cramped, stuffy little room under the farthest slope of the roof. The only light came from a circular window about twice the size of Mendanbar's head.

"There it is," said the dwarf. "If you want to see something, ask; but I can't guarantee it'll work."

"Show me Kazul, the King of the Dragons," Cimorene commanded at once.

For a moment, nothing happened. Then Mendanbar felt a tentative swelling of magic around the window. "I think it needs a boost," he said and reached for his sword.

"No, let me," said Cimorene. She thought for a minute, then raised her right hand and pointed at the window.

"Power of water, wind, and earth,
Cast the spell to show its birth.
Raise the fire to stop the harm
By the power of this charm."

Power surged around the window, and the glass went milk-white. "What did you do?" Mendanbar said, impressed.

"It's a dragon spell," Cimorene told him, keeping her eyes fixed on the window. "It's easy to remember, and it's not hard to adapt it to do just about anything. I found it in Kazul's–look!"

The window glass had cleared. Through the circular pane, Mendanbar could see the inside of a large cave. A sphere of golden light, like a giant glowing soap-bubble, covered half the cave, and inside the glow was a dragon. She was easily four times as tall as Mendanbar, even without counting her wings. Three short, stubby horns stuck out of her head, one on each side and one in the center of her forehead, and her scales were just starting to turn gray around the edges. An angry-looking trickle of smoke leaked out of her mouth as she breathed. In front of the bubble stood two tall, bearded men in long robes, carrying staffs of polished wood.

"Wizards," Cimorene said angrily. "I knew it!"

10

In Which Mendanbar Decides to Experiment

Mendanbar stared at the window, angrier than he could remember being in a long time. In the back of his mind, he could hear a voice reminding him that the King of the Dragons was no concern of the King of the Enchanted Forest and that the Society of Wizards was a dangerous group to offend or interfere with. He could hear another voice that sounded very like Willin's, suggesting envoys and formal complaints. But he was in no mood to pay attention to either of them. Mendanbar was not going to stand by and let the Society of Wizards kidnap and imprison anyone, King of the Dragons or not.

"Huh," said the dwarf. "So you weren't kidding about looking for that dragon."

"Of course not," Cimorene snapped. Her eyes were fixed on the window, and there was a little crease between her eyebrows. "But where are they? Window! Show me where they are."

Magic rose up around the window in a great wave, and Mendanbar felt an answering surge in his sword. The window turned bright green, glowing brighter and brighter, then suddenly shattered into dust.

"Hey!" said the dwarf. "My window!"

"Drat!" Cimorene's hands clenched into fists, and she glared at the empty space where the window had been. After a moment, she shook her head and turned to the dwarf. "I'm sorry, Herman. I didn't know it would do that. And we don't really know any more than we did before."

"Oh, yes, we do," Mendanbar said. "We know that some wizards have captured Kazul, and we know that they're somewhere in the Enchanted Forest."

"We do?"

"I'm sure of it. I think that's why the window couldn't show a more general picture of where they were. Things in the Enchanted Forest move around a lot, especially if the forest doesn't like something. I'll bet my best crown that that"–Mendanbar waved at the empty window frame–"is something the Enchanted Forest doesn't like one bit."

"All right, but that doesn't help much," Cimorene said. "The Enchanted Forest is a big place. How are we going to find them?"

"That won't be a problem," Mendanbar said. "I'm the King of the Enchanted Forest, remember?"

"That makes you good at finding missing dragons?"

"It makes me good at finding out what's going on," Mendanbar said. "I can tell when places are moving around, and I can get where I want to go even when it's moving. I don't think it will be too hard, once we get back inside the forest."

"Then let's go," Cimorene said. "I didn't like the look of that bubble thing those wizards had around Kazul."

"At least they don't seem to have hurt her," Mendanbar offered.

"That's true. Oh, I *wish* I knew what they were up to!" Cimorene scowled at the broken window, then turned sharply away, almost running into the dwarf.

"I don't understand this at all," the dwarf said, looking from Cimorene to Mendanbar with a puzzled frown.

"I'm sorry we don't have time to explain," Mendanbar said. "But I'm afraid we don't."

"Thank you for all your help," Cimorene added.

The dwarf shook his head and led them back to the front door, frowning in such deep concentration the whole time that neither Mendanbar nor Cimorene could bring themselves to interrupt. In the doorway, the dwarf paused.

"Are you *sure* you don't want any gold?" he asked.

"Quite sure," Mendanbar said. "We have a long walk ahead of us, and gold is awfully heavy."

"I thought you didn't want to spin gold anymore," Cimorene added.

The dwarf looked down. "It's not the spinning, it's the rest of it," he said, not very clearly. "And spinning's the only way I know to make money, and you wouldn't believe how fast kids grow."

"Oh," said Cimorene. She bit her lip. "What if we asked you to spin some gold for us and then let you keep it?" she asked without much hope.

"No," said the dwarf. "I tried it once. It just doesn't work."

"Can you spin for the children?" Mendanbar asked.

The dwarf shook his head. "They're my responsibility, so it's the same as spinning for myself as far as the spell is concerned."

"What *are* you going to do with them all?" Cimorene asked as renewed shrieks and the sound of pounding feet came through the open door.

"Oh, most of them will grow up and save their kingdoms from something or other in the nick of time," the dwarf said. "Long-lost heirs, you know. That's what makes it so difficult. I have to see that they're properly trained on top of everything else."

"Training," Mendanbar said under his breath. He squinted into the sunlight, trying to catch hold of an idea that hovered just out of reach.

"I don't suppose their parents . . ." Cimorene's voice trailed off as the dwarf shook his head.

"A bargain's a bargain. Besides, it wouldn't be the same without them running all over. I *can't* give them back."

"Of course not," Mendanbar said, blinking. He smiled suddenly. "But you *can* charge for training them, can't you?"

An answering smile lit up Cimorene's face. "A boarding school for long-lost heirs. What a good idea!"

"A school?" the dwarf said as if the words tasted funny. "A boarding school? I don't know–"

"Why not?" Cimorene said. "It would solve your money problems for sure. Special schools are always horribly expensive. You could charge the parents of your children for just the training part, and take on a few more kids at training plus full room and board."

The dwarf's eyes gleamed at the idea, but then his face fell. "What about my spinning?" he said. "It *is* a family tradition."

Cimorene rolled her eyes. "Haven't you done enough of that already?"

"Well–"

"I have an idea about that, too," Mendanbar put in. "The problem with the spell is that you can't spin for yourself or for anyone who's your responsibility, right?"

"That's it in a nutshell," the dwarf said. "And there's nothing to be done about it."

"What if you set up a scholarship fund?" Mendanbar said. "I'll bet a really good lawyer could design one that would get around the spell's restrictions so you could spin for it."

Cimorene nodded. "A good lawyer can get around just about anything. And if that doesn't work, you could spin for other scholarship funds and only take part of the gold, the way you usually do."

"I never thought of spinning for a fund," the dwarf said in wonder.

"You think about it, then," Mendanbar said. "We have to go."

"Yes," said Cimorene. "I won't feel quite comfortable until I know Kazul is out of that bubble. Thank you again."

They left the dwarf in the doorway, muttering to himself about rooms and expenses, and walked over to the rolled-up carpet.

Mendanbar looked at it with distaste, remembering their wild ride. He hoped Cimorene wasn't going to insist on using it right away. His stomach hadn't completely settled from the last time. He turned his head. Cimorene was looking at him with a wary expression.

"Let's carry it for a while," she suggested. "The children are probably watching, and we shouldn't give them ideas."

"Right," Mendanbar said with relief. "Do you want the front end or the back?"

Cimorene took the back end, and they hoisted the carpet to their shoulders and started off. Walking with the carpet was surprisingly easy. Cimorene was a good match for Mendanbar in height, and she was quite strong. Mendanbar supposed it must be from carrying around dragon-sized servings of lamb and beef, and before he thought, he said as much.

"Actually, it's the chocolate mousse and cherries jubilee," Cimorene said.

"I didn't think chocolate mousse was particularly heavy."

"It is when you've got a bucket full of it in each hand," Cimorene retorted.

"Oh," said Mendanbar. "Yes, I suppose it would be."

He was trying to figure out how much a bucket of mousse would weigh when the carpet jerked suddenly. Mendanbar grabbed at it, thinking *Oh, no, it's going to start dancing around on its own!* Then he realized that the carpet had jerked because Cimorene had stopped. He looked reproachfully over his shoulder.

"It's time for lunch," Cimorene said. "All this talk about food is making me hungry, and I don't want to have to face a lot of wizards on an empty stomach."

Now that she mentioned it, he was hungry, too. "Good idea," Mendanbar said with enthusiasm. "And this looks like a nice spot to stop. Will you serve, or shall I?"

Cimorene laughed. They set the rolled-up carpet on a stretch of grass between two pines and got out Ballimore's package, then sat down to see what the giantess had sent along with them. It was, as Mendanbar had expected, an enormous quantity of food—seven fat pastries stuffed with chicken and herbs, a large bottle of cold spring water, a round loaf of bread and a generous wedge of yellow cheese, four large red apples, and a small box filled with a wonderful, creamy chocolate fudge.

"My goodness," Cimorene said when they had unpacked everything. "Ballimore certainly believes in feeding people well. *Look* at all of this!"

"No, no," Mendanbar said, picking up one of the pastries and handing it to Cimorene. "Don't look at it. Eat it."

"I wonder where she got the fudge," Cimorene mused. "Everything else is probably from the Cauldron of Plenty, but it doesn't do desserts very well."

"Maybe she made it herself."

"I hope so." Cimorene smiled at Mendanbar's look of surprise. "If she did, I can ask her for the recipe."

By an unspoken mutual agreement, neither Mendanbar nor Cimorene mentioned Kazul or the wizards during lunch, though they were both certainly thinking about them. Instead, they had a pleasant talk about some of the odd and interesting people they had each met over the past few years. Cimorene knew a lot of unusual folk. Many of them were dragons, of course, but her position as Kazul's Chief Cook and Librarian meant that she had also met most of the visitors from outside the Mountains of Morning who came to pay their respects to the King of the Dragons or to ask her questions.

Near the end of the meal, Mendanbar noticed that Cimorene was gazing intently at him. No, not at him: at his sword.

"What is it?" Mendanbar asked worriedly.

"Have you been doing things with that sword again?" Cimorene demanded.

"No," Mendanbar said, puzzled. "I used it on your sink, and to stop the nightshade, and when the carpet started falling, but that's all. Why?"

"Because it's leaking magic all over the place," Cimorene said. "I thought so before, but now I'm positive." She finished her second pastry and stood up, brushing crumbs from her lap. "That sheath must not be as good as I thought. Would you mind letting me look at it? Without the sword."

"Not at all," Mendanbar answered. He stood up and drew the sword. Cimorene flinched. "Is something wrong?"

"I don't know," Cimorene said. "Can't you feel it?"

"Feel what?"

"Your sword. It isn't the sheath after all; it's that dratted sword. It's gotten worse. Put it away, quickly."

Thoroughly puzzled, Mendanbar did as Cimorene asked. "All right," he said. "Now, would you please explain?"

"I'm not sure I can," Cimorene said. "You didn't know what I meant before, when I said your sword reeked of magic, so I suppose it's reasonable that you can't tell that the reek is twice as strong now. You'll just have to take my word for it."

Mendanbar looked down at the sword, thinking hard. "It's linked to the Enchanted Forest, and I've never taken it out of the woods before," he said at last. "Maybe it doesn't like it. Maybe it's trying to make the mountains more like the Enchanted Forest." It sounded silly put that way, but he couldn't think how else to say it. It would sound even sillier if he told her that he thought the sword was trying to stuff some magic into the empty, barren-feeling land around it.

"Um," said Cimorene, gazing absently at the sword. After a moment, she looked up. "I'll bet you're right. Bother. That means we *have* to use the carpet." She bent and started packing up the remains of their lunch.

"Wait a minute," Mendanbar said. "What has my sword got to do with that carpet?"

"If being *outside* the Enchanted Forest is what makes your sword behave like a–a magic beacon, then we have to get it back *inside* the Enchanted Forest as fast as we can," Cimorene explained patiently. "Otherwise every ogre and wizard for leagues and leagues around will come looking for whatever is making all the fuss. And the carpet is a lot faster than walking."

"I don't trust it."

"We managed before. It ought to be easier now that we know what to expect. Here, help me." She knelt and began unrolling the carpet as she spoke.

"*Do* we know what to expect?" Remembering the bumping, spinning, unpredictable ride, Mendanbar shuddered.

"Look, I don't like it any better than you do, but we have to do *something* about that sword. Besides, the sooner we get to the forest, the sooner you can find out where those wizards have Kazul. And do we have any other choice?"

"I could probably use the sword to get us to the Enchanted Forest," Mendanbar suggested.

Cimorene sat back on her heels, staring at him. "You can do that? Why on earth didn't you say so to begin with? We could have gone straight to Kazul's grandchildren's cave and saved a lot of time."

"I didn't mention it before because I'm not *really* sure it will work," Mendanbar said. "I've never tried that particular spell outside the Enchanted Forest before, and it wouldn't be a good idea to test it for the first time to get somewhere I've never been. Especially somewhere that isn't in the Enchanted Forest either." Actually, he hadn't tried *any* of his usual spells outside the Enchanted Forest before, for the very good reason that he hadn't *been* outside the Enchanted Forest since he'd become King and started working magic, but he didn't like to mention that in front of Cimorene. He was quite sure that if *she* had suddenly become the ruler of a magical kingdom, she would have tested all her new spells and powers and abilities immediately, under as many different conditions as she could come up with. He didn't want her to think he was careless or neglectful.

"So we can either experiment with the carpet again or experiment with your spell," Cimorene said. She scowled thoughtfully at the teddy bears, then looked up at Mendanbar and smiled. "Let's try the spell. What do you want me to do?"

"Just stand there," Mendanbar said, returning her smile. "I've never worked with another magician, and one experiment at a time is enough."

"Why haven't you?" Cimorene asked as she climbed to her feet. "Worked with another magician, I mean. From what you were telling me yesterday, you've got more than enough work for a couple of assistants."

"I've never had time to find any assistants," Mendanbar said. "Except Willin, my steward, and he's never learned much magic."

"You mean you're trying to run the whole Enchanted Forest *by yourself?*" Cimorene said. "You're as bad as the dragons!"

"What?"

"It took me six months to persuade them that the King of the Dragons didn't need to do everything all the time," Cimorene explained. "And then it took me three more months to get a system set up so they wouldn't keep running to Kazul with every little problem."

"You set up a system? How? I mean, how did you know . . ." Mendanbar's voice trailed off.

To his surprise, Cimorene flushed very slightly. "I studied a lot of unusual things when I was growing up," she said. "Unusual for a princess, I mean. Politics was one of them."

"It sounds like a perfectly reasonable thing for a princess to study to me," Mendanbar said. "Look how useful it's been for you."

"Well, it's not one of the things a princess is *supposed* to learn," Cimorene said. "You wouldn't believe the fuss they made when they found out I'd talked my protocol teacher into covering it."

"What were you supposed to be learning, then?"

Cimorene made a face. "Embroidery and dancing and etiquette and *proper* behavior."

"No wonder princesses are silly, if that's all they're supposed to know about," Mendanbar said without thinking. He blinked and added hastily, "Not you. I mean, you aren't silly, even if you are a princess. I mean—"

"Don't try to explain any more; you'll only make it worse," Cimorene said, laughing. "Now, hadn't we better try that spell? We *are* in a bit of a hurry, remember."

"Right." With some difficulty, Mendanbar pushed the discussion out of his mind and tried to remember how he had been planning to work the transportation spell. Usually he simply twisted one of the threads of power that crisscrossed the Enchanted Forest, pulling himself to his destination, but outside the forest there were no threads that he could feel. There was power in the sword, though, and it was linked with the Enchanted Forest. If he pulled on that, he should be able to move whatever he chose back to the forest.

Before he moved anything, however, he would have to indicate who and what he wanted to move. He didn't want to arrive in the Enchanted Forest with a magic carpet covered with pink teddy bears and no Cimorene. Mendanbar suppressed a sigh. Spells were so much easier at home, where he didn't have to think about them as much. He dismissed that thought and concentrated on figuring out the shape of the spell he wanted.

When he was satisfied that he knew exactly what he intended to do, and in what order, he put a hand on the hilt of his sword and looked at Cimorene. "Ready?"

"Whenever you are," Cimorene said.

Mendanbar nodded and drew his sword. He heard Cimorene suck in her breath as he raised the weapon over his head and swung it in a slow circle. Carefully, he pointed the sword at the carpet and pushed a tiny bit of power out to label it for the next part of the spell. Then he pointed the sword at Cimorene and repeated the process even more gently than before. Cimorene shivered, but she remained silent.

Turning, Mendanbar pointed the sword in the direction of the Enchanted Forest. Now for the tricky part. He drew on the power in the sword, feeling it hum through the hilt and into his hands. In his mind he pictured the giant trees of the Enchanted Forest, ranged in silent rows around the rocks that edged the Green Glass Pool, with the still water reflecting them like a green mirror. When he was sure he had the picture clear and steady in his mind, he gave the power in the sword the same twisting pull he used to move from place to place within the Enchanted Forest.

Slowly, almost reluctantly, the rocks began to blur and fade. Mist rose, wavering, to veil the mountains and sky. Then, just as the landscape was about to vanish into thick, woolly grayness, the mist stopped condensing. For a moment, everything was still. Then the mist thinned and the outlines of the rocks and mountains grew sharper.

Almost, thought Mendanbar. *It must need more power because we're outside the Enchanted Forest.* He clenched his hands around the hilt of the sword and pulled again, hard.

Gray fog slammed down around him like a window shutter dropping closed. Something hit him like a giant's hammer, and he felt himself falling. *Now I've done it,* he thought vaguely, just before everything went black. *I hope Cimorene is all right.* Then he lost consciousness completely. He didn't even feel himself land.

11

In Which Mendanbar and Cimorene Are Very Busy

Something was wrong. Mendanbar could feel it, even before he was fully awake. The magic of the Enchanted Forest floated all around him, but it seemed tenuous and tottery, almost disconnected. He thought he had better get up and fix it. He opened his eyes.

Cimorene's concerned face hovered a foot above him. Her braids had come loose from their tight crown and there was a worry line between her eyebrows. He didn't want her to be worried. He tried to say so, but all he managed was a coughing fit. Cimorene bit her lip, and her troubled expression intensified.

"Don't try to talk," she said unhappily. "Don't try to do anything yet. Your sword is safe, and I'm all right, and everything else can wait for a few minutes. Just lie there and breathe slowly."

It occurred to Mendanbar that Cimorene was anxious about *him*. That was nice, in a way, but he still didn't want her to be unhappy. In fact, it was suddenly very important to him that Cimorene should not be worried or unhappy in the slightest. He closed his eyes to consider how best to convey this and fell asleep at once.

When he woke, the sky was the pale blue of late afternoon. Rubbing his eyes, he sat up carefully, remembering what had happened earlier when he'd tried to talk. Cimorene was at his side at once.

"Are you sure you should do that?" she said.

"It hasn't hurt so far," Mendanbar replied. "What happened?"

Cimorene studied him for a moment, then relaxed visibly. "I'm not sure," she said. "One minute we were going somewhere, and the next minute we weren't. When I picked myself up, you were lying there looking three-quarters dead and as white as cracked ice, and you've been that way for over four hours. If that's your transportation spell, I think I would have preferred the carpet."

"At least it got us to the forest."

"Not exactly."

Mendanbar blinked at her, then looked around. The carpet, on which he and Cimorene were sitting, lay in the center of a twenty-foot circle of thin green fuzz. Seven saplings, pencil-thick and none more than waist high, poked randomly upward through the fuzz. Beyond the circle, patches of short, brownish-green grass alternated with mottled gray rock that rose quickly into cliffs and ridges and the sudden, sharp heights of mountains that shadowed them all. None of it looked familiar, though it still felt vaguely like the Enchanted Forest to him.

"Well, at least we went *somewhere,"* Mendanbar said after a moment.

"Yes, but where? Those are the Mountains of Morning, but this bit"–Cimorene waved at the green fuzz and the saplings–"looks as if it belongs in the Enchanted Forest. So what's it doing here?"

"It feels like the Enchanted Forest, too," Mendanbar said. He shifted, and his hand touched cool metal. Even without looking, he knew it was his sword. He picked it up and looked at it thoughtfully. "Cimorene, is this still 'leaking magic' the way you said it was earlier?"

"No," Cimorene said. "I can tell it's a magic sword, and an odd one at that, but only if I study it. It's not–not so *obvious* anymore."

Mendanbar pushed himself to his feet. It took more effort than he had expected, and by the time he finished, the worry line had reappeared between Cimorene's eyebrows.

"I'm all right," he told her. "Mostly." He waited a moment for his head to stop spinning, then walked cautiously to the edge of the circle of fuzz. He stepped over the boundary onto a patch of grass. The comforting sense of being surrounded by magic vanished, and although he had more than half expected it, he staggered slightly.

Cimorene was beside him almost at once. "What is it?"

"It was just the change. Can you feel my sword now?"

"Yes," Cimorene said. "But it's nowhere near as bad as it was this morning."

"I was afraid you were going to say that." Mendanbar looked at the circular area of green and sighed. "I hate to do this, but you're right. It doesn't belong here."

He started forward. Cimorene grabbed his arm. "Wait a minute! What are you talking about?"

"This." Mendanbar pointed at the saplings with his sword. "In a way, it really *is* part of the Enchanted Forest. That's why it feels like home to me, and that's why the sword doesn't feel 'obvious' when it's inside."

"That makes sense," Cimorene said. She still had hold of his arm. "But how did it get here?"

"I don't think it did, exactly," Mendanbar said. "I think the sword made it for us when we couldn't get through to the real forest. That's why it's so–so new-looking."

"Your sword . . ." Cimorene paused, thinking. "Yes, you told me it was linked to the Enchanted Forest." She looked at the green area. "I didn't realize it could do things on its own, without someone directing it."

"Normally it doesn't," Mendanbar said. "Unless it's picking the next King of the Enchanted Forest."

"Picking the next . . ." Cimorene's voice trailed off and she shook her head. "I think you'd better tell me about that sword. All about it, not just dribbles of information when something comes up. I have a feeling we're going to need to know."

"I don't know that much," Mendanbar said. "And I have to take care of these things first." He waved at the saplings.

"What are you going to do?"

"If the sword did it, it ought to be able to undo it," Mendanbar said. "I don't want to erase this patch, but I can't think of anything else to do with it. It wouldn't be a good idea to leave a bit of my kingdom disconnected like this."

"No, I can see that," Cimorene said, releasing his arm at last. "Just watch what you're doing with that spell. It's going to be dark soon, and I don't want to spend another four hours waiting for you to wake up."

"I don't like the idea myself," Mendanbar said. "Don't worry. I'll be careful."

"You'd better be."

Mendanbar smiled, raised the sword, and walked back into the tiny forest. He paced around the edge, getting the feel of the magic that was spread spider-web thin across the circle. Then he stopped. With his left hand, he lowered his sword so that the tip rested on the green fuzz that might one day have grown into moss. With his right, he reached out and touched the web, gathering in the threads. When his hand was full, he began to feed the threads into the sword.

It was touchy work, for the invisible strands were thin and fragile, and he knew that if he missed even one he would have to begin all over again. The task took a lot of concentration, for the sword accepted the threads with great reluctance. He was not at all sure he would have the strength to do it twice, so he worked with painstaking slowness.

When he was halfway through, the saplings began to shrink. Slowly at first, then faster and faster, the little trees grew shorter and more slender, until they disappeared into the green fuzz. For a moment, nothing more seemed to happen. Then the circle of green began to shrink. Like a drop of water being sucked up by a napkin, the green edge drew back toward the sword, leaving bare rock behind. In a moment, the retreating border was out of sight beneath the carpet.

Mendanbar continued feeding magic into the sword. There were only a few threads left, and he slowed down even more. A puddle the size of a wagon wheel was all that was left of the original circle. It shrank to the size of a dinner plate, then a pancake, then a penny. Then it was gone.

For a heartbeat longer, Mendanbar held his position, checking to be certain he had not missed anything. Finally he let go of the end of the spell and lifted the point of the sword from the ground. He felt much better than he had when he began. He looked up and smiled at Cimorene.

"That was extremely interesting," Cimorene said. She eyed the bare ground around the carpet. "Is that all of it?"

"I think so. Why?"

"Because if we don't want to spend the night here, we're going to have to leave quickly. It'll be getting dark soon." Cimorene paused, then added, "You'd better put that sword away. It's dripping magic again."

"Sorry," Mendanbar said. "Why don't we–"

With a rattle of small stones and a vicious hiss, a long, gray-black snake shot out of a crevice at the top of the nearest cliff and dropped toward Cimorene. Mendanbar jerked his sword up and sent a crackling bolt of power to meet the serpent. The hiss became a choking gurgle as the snake flared into a bright line of fire and disintegrated. Flakes of ash drifted the last few feet to fall around Mendanbar and Cimorene.

Three more snakes launched themselves from parts of the cliff, and another slithered from behind a boulder. From the corner of his eye, Mendanbar saw Cimorene yank her sword out of its sheath. He hoped briefly and intensely that she was good at fighting, and then he had no time or attention for anything except the snakes.

A second blast of magic disposed of two of the three in the air, and a single sword-stroke chopped the third in half. By then four new snakes were in the air, and Mendanbar could hear more hissing on all sides. He sent another spell skyward, and another, then swung at two snakes that had leaped from a crack barely shoulder-high above the ground. After that he lost track of how many he burned or blasted. He had no time for anything but fighting. He swung his sword until his arms were tired and his head hurt from concentration and spell-casting. And then, suddenly, there were no more snakes.

The ground was dusted with ashes and littered with pieces of snakes, and the air smelled of charred meat. Slowly, Mendanbar lowered his sword. A few paces away, Cimorene was straightening up from a fighter's crouch with the same wary hesitation. Her sword was covered with dark blood, and there were quite a lot of dead snakes around her.

"Oh, wonderful," Mendanbar said with heartfelt sincerity. "I was hoping you were good with a sword."

"You aren't bad with one yourself," Cimorene replied a little breathlessly.

"It's a magic sword," Mendanbar reminded her, but he felt absurdly pleased nonetheless.

Cimorene grinned. "So is mine. I know a little about fencing, but not enough to do me any good against most of the things in the Mountains of Morning. That's why Kazul lets me carry this." She lifted her sword, and a drop of snake blood fell from the tip. She frowned and began fishing in her pockets with her free hand. "It's supposed to make the bearer impossible to defeat."

"Sounds good to me," Mendanbar said, looking at the bits of snake near Cimorene's feet. "What's the catch?"

"Getting killed isn't the same as being defeated," Cimorene said. She pulled a handkerchief from a pocket, smiled, and began cleaning the sword with it. "Not always, anyway. And it doesn't keep you from getting hurt, either. So I still have to be careful. Do you want to use this?" She held out the stained handkerchief.

"Thank you," Mendanbar said, taking the square of cloth. He wiped his sword carefully, resheathed it, and hesitated. "Do you want it back? I'm afraid it's ruined."

"That's all right," Cimorene said. "I always carry one or two extras." She retrieved the handkerchief, grimaced, and tied it into a tight bundle, which she stowed in her belt pouch. "There. Now, let's get out of here."

"Why such a hurry?"

"We still have to rescue Kazul. And besides—do you *want* to fight more rock snakes?" Cimorene asked. "That's what we'll be doing if we stay. We've cleaned out this part pretty well, but there's sure to be several other colonies around." She pointed at a dark ridge a couple of hundred feet farther on. "There, for instance. Or there." She gestured in the opposite direction, at a wrinkled cliff.

"I don't see how we can get past them on foot," Mendanbar said, frowning.

"Well, we can't stay here. They'll slither over as soon as the last of the light goes. We'll have to take the carpet."

"I wouldn't recommend it," said a new voice.

Together, Mendanbar and Cimorene turned. The voice belonged to a dark-haired man who stood calmly next to the magic carpet, watching them with interest. He was several inches shorter than Mendanbar, with bright blue eyes and a neatly trimmed beard and mustache. He wore tall black boots, dark gray leggings, a loose-sleeved, high-necked shirt in pale gray, and an open knee-length black vest covered with pockets of all shapes and sizes. Under the vest, his wide black belt was hung with strangely shaped pouches and sheaths. The air around him crackled with magic.

"Who are you?" Cimorene asked. "And why don't you want us to use the carpet?"

"My name is Telemain," said the man, bowing, "and I have a considerable familiarity with the basic mechanics of carpets. Magic ones, that is. And this carpet"–he gestured left-handed, and three silver rings glinted in the fading light–"is plainly defective."

"Defective?" Mendanbar said suspiciously. Telemain didn't *look* like a wizard, but that didn't necessarily mean much. Wizards could wear disguises as well as anyone else.

"Oh, it will probably operate, after a fashion," Telemain said. "But not well, and not for long. I'm surprised you got this far on it."

"We didn't, exactly," Mendanbar said. "And we *have* had some trouble with it. What do you suggest?"

The sound of a pebble bouncing down a series of rocks echoed along the narrow canyon. "I suggest we talk somewhere else," Telemain said, glancing toward the sound. "This isn't a safe place, even with my defensive enchantments fully erected."

"And how do you suggest we get there?" Cimorene asked.

"Like this." Telemain raised a hand and made a circle in the air with his forefinger. As he did, he muttered something, then clapped both hands together.

The canyon flowed and melted into a sloping meadow halfway up a mountainside. "Much better," Telemain said. "No rock snakes, trolls, ogres, or other dangerous wildlife. I guarantee it."

Mendanbar was inclined to believe him. Trolls and ogres liked places where they could jump out from behind things or pop out from under rocks. An open meadow didn't have enough cover. Besides, Telemain was no longer surrounded by the hum of magic, which meant he had dropped his guarding spell.

"Now," Telemain went on, "how *did* the two of you get into a ravine full of rock snakes with a defective magic carpet? Having rescued you, I think I am entitled to some explanation."

"We were on our way to the Enchanted Forest," Cimorene said carefully, pushing wisps of loose hair out of her face. Mendanbar noticed with approval that she said nothing about their reasons for wanting to go there. "How did you happen to come by at such a convenient moment?"

"I was–looking for some people I thought might be in this area," Telemain said. "By the way, what are your names?"

"This is Cimorene and I'm Mendanbar," Mendanbar said. "Who were you looking for?"

"You, I think," Telemain said, smiling. "That is, if you're the same Cimorene and Mendanbar who visited Herman the dwarf earlier today."

"That was us," Cimorene said cautiously.

"Good! Then I can settle this quickly and get back to my work. How did you–"

"Excuse me," Mendanbar interrupted. "But how do you know Herman? And how did you find us?"

"I know Herman because he bought his house from me," Telemain said. He was beginning to sound irritated. "I also maintain certain defensive enchantments, which are especially designed to prevent incursions by noxious creatures, around the house and neighboring areas for him. When someone demolished the scrying spell I had established on the attic window, I felt obliged to investigate. Herman was in the middle of an explanation about visitors and dragons when I sensed an extremely interesting sorcerous flare to the northwest."

"I knew that dratted sword was going to get us in trouble," Cimorene muttered.

"Before I had time to locate it precisely, there was another burst of magic, which I recognized as a transportation spell," Telemain continued. He frowned disapprovingly. "A rather confused one. It has taken me all afternoon to disentangle the traces and discover your whereabouts. Does that satisfy you?"

"I think so," Mendanbar said. "I'm sorry if we seem overly mistrustful, but we've already had some trouble with one wizard and we've reason to expect more. So you see . . ."

"I am *not* a wizard," Telemain said emphatically. "I'm a magician. Can't you tell?"

"No," Cimorene said. "What's the difference?"

"A magician knows many types of magic," Telemain said. "Wizards only know one, and they're very secretive about it. I've been researching them for years, trying to duplicate their methodology, but I still haven't managed a workable simulation."

"What?" said Cimorene, looking puzzled.

"He's been trying to figure out how the wizards work their spells," Mendanbar explained, "but he hasn't done it yet."

"Why do you want to know that?" Cimorene asked Telemain with renewed suspicion.

"Because that's what I do!" Telemain said. "I just told you that. And if you'll answer a few questions for me, I can go back to doing it. How did you shatter that window?"

"We asked it to show us something," Mendanbar said. "It couldn't, so it broke."

Telemain shook his head. "Impossible! That particular glass was enchanted to reveal anything, anywhere, even in the Enchanted Forest. If it couldn't discover the object of your inquiry, the viewing plane would display an empty information buffer."

"What does he mean?" Cimorene asked, frowning.

"He means that if the window couldn't find what we were asking about, it should have just stayed blank," Mendanbar explained.

"That's what I said." Telemain nodded emphatically. "It should *not* have broken."

"Well, it did," Cimorene told him. "And we don't have time to stand around arguing. We have to get to the Enchanted Forest and rescue a friend of mine. So could you just tell us what's wrong with our carpet?"

"Nonsense," Telemain muttered. "You *must* have done more than frame a question." He intercepted a look from Cimorene and sighed. "Oh, very well, I'll examine the carpet. Spread it out so I can see all of it at once."

They unrolled the carpet the rest of the way. Telemain's eyebrow's rose in surprise at the sight of the teddy bears, but he did not comment, for which Mendanbar was grateful. When the carpet was stretched full-length on the meadow, Telemain paced twice around it, frowning and gesturing occasionally. Then he turned to Mendanbar and Cimorene and shook his head.

"The landing compensator has a gap in it, and the flight regulator has completely deteriorated," he said. "It needs more than I can do without special tools and yarn for reweaving. You'll have to take it to a repair shop."

"Wonderful," Cimorene said sarcastically. "This *would* happen with a borrowed carpet."

"Can you recommend a good place?" Mendanbar asked Telemain. "Preferably somewhere close," he added, noting the pink tint of the sky to the west. The sun would be completely down in another hour, and he didn't want to wander around the Mountains of Morning in the dark.

"Or can you send us straight to the Enchanted Forest?" Cimorene asked. "We're in kind of a hurry."

"The Enchanted Forest requires a complex and destination-specific enhancement to the basic transportation spell module," Telemain explained. "But the repair shop is simple."

He raised his left hand and made the same circular gesture he had before. "Gypsy Jack's," he said, and clapped, and the meadow and the mountain melted and flowed. The mountain bulged higher, and the meadow flattened and grew rockier. A long, rectangular section of ground squeezed upward and settled into the shape of a narrow house on wheels.

"There," Telemain said with great satisfaction. "We've arrived."

12

In Which Yet Another Wizard Tries to Cause Trouble

They were standing in front of the wheeled house. At least, Mendanbar assumed it was the front because there was a door at the end of the long side facing them. Two iron steps, black and worn with age, led up to the door. The house itself was painted a cheerful blue with yellow shutters and a yellow trim around the door. There were four windows on the side facing Mendanbar, lined up in a neat row next to the door like chicks following a hen. The roof above the windows was low but not quite flat, and covered with wooden shingles that looked brand-new. There were four pairs of wheels, too, the rims painted blue to match the house and the spokes painted yellow to match the shutters. A beautifully lettered sign on a stick had been pounded into the ground next to the door: "Ask About Our Low Prices!"

Mendanbar looked at Cimorene. Cimorene looked from Mendanbar to the wheeled house to Telemain.

"Don't do that again without asking first," she said to the magician.

"I thought you'd be pleased," Telemain said. "Look at all the time you've saved."

"Asking doesn't take much time."

"Where are we, exactly?" Mendanbar put in before they could start arguing. "And what is that?" He pointed at the house on wheels.

"That is Gypsy Jack's home," Telemain answered. "If anyone can mend that carpet of yours, he can. As to where we are, all I can tell you is that we are still somewhere in the Mountains of Morning. If you want a more precise location, you will have to ask Jack. Assuming he remembers; he moves around a lot."

"How did you find him, then?" Cimorene asked.

"Oh, Jack supplies me with unusual things now and then, when I need them for a spell or an experiment," Telemain said. "I pay him by enchanting his house for him. Any good magician can find his own spells."

"Enchanting his house?" Mendanbar said. "You mean, to keep ogres and things from bothering it, the way you did Herman's?"

Telemain shook his head. "I offered, but Jack wasn't interested. He has his own way of discouraging unpleasant company. No, what he wanted was a spell to keep the paint from fading."

"Why does he need you to put spells on his house?" Cimorene asked.

"Jack isn't a magician," Telemain said. "He does a little bit of everything–smithing, gardening, music, tailoring, pretty much any trade you can think of. For example, he designed and built his house. He has a rare knack for patching up a spell that's wearing thin, but he can't set up a complex enchantment on his own. That's why he deals with me."

One of the windows scraped open and a head poked out. "Yo! You going to stand there all night and maybe get eaten by a dragon? Not that I would dream of interfering with your plans, but if a quick exit is what you want, I got a dozen faster ways, all very cheap."

"Hello, Jack," Telemain called. "I've brought you some customers."

"Customers! Why didn't you say so? I'll be right out." The head vanished and the window screeched closed.

"Customers?" Cimorene said, looking at Telemain.

"You want that carpet fixed, don't you? Jack can–"

The door of the house flew open with a bang, and a large man leaped over the steps and landed in front of them. He had a thick black mustache, long black hair, bright black eyes, and a wide white grin. Pushing a soft, baggy cap back from his forehead, he bowed deeply.

"Welcome to my home, friends of Telemain!" he boomed. "And very welcome you are. What's the problem?"

"A little difficulty about transportation, Jack," Telemain said before Mendanbar or Cimorene had quite recovered from the man's abrupt appearance. "We were hoping you could help."

"No trouble! What do you need? Shoes? I got a barrel full–sandals, clogs, dancing shoes, walking shoes, horse shoes . . . ." His voice trailed off and he looked hopefully at Telemain.

"Nothing that simple," Telemain said. "The difficulty is magical in nature."

"Ah! You want seven-league boots! Well, you're in luck. A pair of 'em just came in this morning. They're practically brand-new, hardly been used at all. Or there's a swell pair of ruby slippers that'd be perfect for the lady. I'll throw in the magic belt that goes with 'em for free. Or—"

"No, no, Jack," Telemain interrupted. "The problem is with this." He stepped aside and let Jack get a good look at the magic carpet.

Jack's eyes narrowed to slits of concentration. He stepped forward and studied the carpet, then paced around it, much as Telemain had done earlier. "No kidding," he said at last. "That carpet's a problem, all right."

"Can you fix it?" Cimorene asked.

"Sure. Give me a week, and she'll be good as new."

"A week!" Cimorene looked at him in dismay. "Can't you fix it any faster than that?"

Jack spread his hands out and shrugged. "Maybe, but I can't promise. It depends on how fast I can get parts."

"Then we'll leave it here and go on without it tomorrow," Mendanbar said. At least they wouldn't have to carry the thing around anymore, and they wouldn't be tempted to use it in spite of its hazards. "You can send it home when it's finished, can't you?"

"Shouldn't be a problem." Jack smiled. "Where do you want it?"

Cimorene hesitated. "You're not one of those Jacks who go around killing giants, are you?"

"Lady, what do you think I am, stupid or something?" Jack asked. "I'm a businessman. I don't *do* giants."

"Then please send the carpet to Ballimore the Giantess on Flat Top Mountain when you're done fixing it," Cimorene said. "And the bill to Cimorene, Chief Cook and Librarian, in care of the King of the Dragons."

"King of the Dragons, eh?" Jack said thoughtfully.

"Yes, and don't go padding the bill, Jack," Telemain warned.

"Me? Wouldn't dream of it." Jack kicked the carpet into a loose roll and heaved it up onto his shoulder. "Anything else?"

"Is there a safe place near here where we can spend the night?" Mendanbar asked.

"Sure," Jack said. He balanced the carpet with one hand and jerked the thumb of the other at the blue-and-yellow house on wheels. "Right there. I got two spare rooms on the end I can rent you for as long as you want 'em."

"Tonight is all we need," Mendanbar said, and Cimorene nodded.

Jack bobbed his head in a way that managed to suggest a full-fledged formal bow, then started toward the house, carrying the carpet. Mendanbar turned to Telemain. "Thank you very much for your help."

"You're welcome," Telemain said, and started after Jack.

"Hey!" Cimorene said. "Where are you going?"

"To arrange for my own bed and board," Telemain explained patiently. "You didn't really expect me to leave before you'd answered my questions, did you?"

Without waiting for a reply, the magician followed Jack into the house. Mendanbar and Cimorene looked at each other, shrugged, and went in after them.

The front door of Jack's house opened into a cluttered room painted a bright green that clashed with almost everything. Fortunately, most of the walls were hidden behind piles of boxes, barrels, bales, and bundles. Jack propped the carpet in a crowded corner, where it leaned precariously against two paintings balanced on a stack of books. Then he set about fixing dinner.

Cimorene kept Telemain's attention occupied while Jack worked, and at first Mendanbar was glad of it. He wanted time to think and sort out some of the confusing things that had happened in the last two days. He was sure that a few of them were important, and if he could only concentrate for a little while he could figure out which ones.

He quickly discovered that it was not going to work. The conversation between Cimorene and Telemain was much too distracting, even though he was not particularly interested in anything they were talking about. Finally he gave up trying to think and listened instead.

"–window wasn't up to it," Cimorene was saying. "So I used a spell to boost it."

"And that broke it?" Telemain said, frowning.

"No," Cimorene replied. "It worked just fine. The window turned white, and then showed Kazul and a lot of wizards." Her face darkened. "And when I catch up with them–"

"Yes, of course," Telemain said hastily. "What happened next?"

"I told the window to show me where they were, and *then* it broke."

"I can fix up a new one for you," Jack put in over his shoulder. "I got some glass around somewhere, and it's no trick at all to cut it to size."

"I'll think about it, Jack," Telemain said. He looked at Cimorene. "The window just . . . broke? It didn't show anything at all?"

Cimorene nodded. "Not a thing. Right, Mendanbar?"

"Right," Mendanbar said. "The picture of Kazul and the wizards disappeared, and the window turned bright green, and then it broke. I think it was trying to show us a place inside the Enchanted Forest and couldn't."

"It should have been able to," Telemain said. "I tested it very thoroughly. I suppose the enchantment might have been wearing thin. What kind of spell did you say you used to boost it?" he asked, turning to Cimorene.

Cimorene hesitated, then shrugged. "It was a dragon spell I found in Kazul's library last year. It's very adaptable, and–"

A shout from outside the house interrupted Cimorene in mid-sentence. "You in there! Come out at once. There's no point in hiding."

Jack muttered something and stuck his head out the window. "Hang on!" he shouted. "I'll just be a min–"

Something exploded outside, knocking Jack back through the window and making the whole house rock. "Come out!" the voice repeated. "Now!"

"Wizards got no patience," Jack muttered, glaring at the window.

Mendanbar stiffened and looked at Cimorene.

"We'd better go out, or he'll tear the house down," she said. "Jack, can you mix up a bucket of soapy water with a little lemon juice in it, quick?"

"Huh?" said Jack.

"A bucket of soap and water and lemon juice," Cimorene repeated impatiently. "It melts wizards. Hurry up and bring it out after us. I think we're going to need it."

"Soapy water with lemon melts wizards?" Telemain said with great interest. "How did you discover that?"

Another explosion rocked the house. "Never mind that now," Cimorene said. "Come on!" She pushed the door open and darted out.

With a muttered curse, Mendanbar followed. He remembered the steps just in time to jump over them instead of tripping. As he landed, he dodged to one side and pulled his sword out. Only then did he stop to look around.

Cimorene stood with her back against the house, watching the wizard warily. The wizard was very easy to see, even though it was by now quite dark, because he was glowing as brightly as a bonfire. He was taller than the wizard who had invaded Cimorene's cave, and he wore red robes instead of blue and brown, but his staff was of the same dark, polished wood and his sandy beard was just as long and scraggly. Mendanbar wondered irrelevantly whether the Society of Wizards had a rule against its members trimming their beards.

"Cimorene!" the wizard said. "I might have guessed. What have you– no, you *haven't* got it. Where is it?"

"Where is what?" Mendanbar demanded. "And what do you mean by causing all this commotion? Didn't anyone ever teach you to knock on doors and ask for things politely?"

"So you've picked up a hero," the wizard said to Cimorene with a sneer. "He won't do you any good. Where is it?"

"I don't know what you're talking about," Cimorene said.

"Neither does he," Telemain commented from the doorway. "Unless he's even more fuzzy-headed than he seems. From the way he's been leaping to conclusions without any evidence at all, that's entirely possible."

The wizard's eyes narrowed and he pointed his staff at Telemain. "Who are you?"

"That's the first intelligent thing you've said since you arrived," Telemain said. "My name is Telemain. I'm a magician."

"A magician!" The wizard sucked in his breath. "I suppose we are after the same thing. I warn you, you had better not cross me. I represent the Society of Wizards in this matter."

"What matter?" Cimorene asked crossly.

"Yes, you have displayed a lamentable lack of precision in your account of your purposes," Telemain said. "Just what–"

Mendanbar felt the harsh swell of the wizard's magic an instant before the spell left the man's staff. Without thought, he swung his sword to parry it. As it touched the bolt of magic, the sword hummed hungrily. A shiver ran up Mendanbar's arm from the hilt of the sword to his shoulder, and the spell was gone.

"I wouldn't do that again, if I were you," Mendanbar told the wizard.

Everyone stared at Mendanbar. The wizard was the first to recover. "The sword!" he cried. "I should have seen it at once. Excellent! This makes everything easy."

He moved the end of his staff a few inches to point at Mendanbar and muttered something under his breath. Mendanbar sensed magic building up in the staff again. This time he didn't wait for the wizard to release the spell. He pushed a tendril of his own magic out through the sword and touched the wizard's staff gently with it.

Power flowed into the sword like water being soaked up by a sponge. The feeling of magic that surrounded the wizard vanished, and so did his glow. The wizard gave a squawk of surprise. He lowered his staff, staring at Mendanbar.

"How did you do that?" he demanded. "You're just a hero. How could you possibly reverse my spell?"

"I didn't reverse your spell," Mendanbar said. "I stopped it, that's all. And I'm *not* a hero. I'm the King of the Enchanted Forest."

The wizard's eyes widened. Certain that the man was going to try another spell, Mendanbar reached out with the sword's magic, hoping to stop him before he could properly begin. He wasn't quite fast enough. As the threads of the sword's magic wrapped themselves around the wizard's staff, the wizard disappeared.

There was a moment of silence. "Mendanbar, what did you *do?"* Cimorene said at last.

"Nothing," Mendanbar said. "I wasn't quick enough. I'm sorry. I should have expected him to try to get away."

Telemain walked over to the spot where the wizard had been standing. "Interesting," he muttered. "Very interesting–ah!" He bent over, and when he straightened up he was holding the wizard's staff in one hand.

"Here's your bucket," Jack said from the door of the house. "What's all this about wizards?"

"It doesn't matter now," Cimorene said. "He's gone."

"Then you won't be needing this?" Jack said, lifting the bucket.

"Don't throw it out," Mendanbar said hastily. "We might want it later. In case he comes back."

"I seriously doubt that it is necessary to worry about his return," Telemain said as he rejoined them. "Wizards depend a good deal upon their staffs. Without his, our recent visitor is unlikely to be much of a problem." He sounded very satisfied with himself, and his fingers stroked the staff lightly as he spoke.

"Then he's sure to come back for it," Cimorene pointed out.

"Yes, but how long will it take him to get here?" Telemain responded. "I assure you, he didn't transport himself anywhere close by. We'll be long gone by the time he makes his way back."

"We?" said Mendanbar.

"Of course." Telemain smiled. "I've been trying to get my hands on one of these"–he lifted the wizard's staff–"for years. You've managed to get hold of one in a few seconds. You don't think I'm going to miss an opportunity like this, do you?"

"If that's all you want, keep it," Mendanbar said. "I haven't any use for a wizard's staff."

"Neither have I," Cimorene agreed.

Telemain bowed. "Thank you both." He paused. "I would still like to join you, if you are willing. There are other matters I find intriguing about you."

Completely at sea, Mendanbar stared at the magician.

Cimorene sighed. "Mendanbar, your sword is at it again, worse than ever. I'll bet that's what he means."

"Oh." Mendanbar put his sword back in its sheath and inspected Telemain for a moment. The magician was still something of a puzzle, but he had been very helpful so far. And it was clear from the wizard's behavior that magicians and wizards did not get along, which was another point in Telemain's favor. "I can't promise I'll let you study my sword, but it's all right with me if you come along." He glanced at Cimorene.

"It's fine with me, too," Cimorene said. "But you'd better hear the whole story before you make up your mind. You might not want to come with us after all."

"If you're all done out here, come in and eat," Jack said. "Supper's ready, and if you're sure there won't be any more wizards, I'll just use this water for the dishes afterward."

13

In Which They Return to the Enchanted Forest at Last

They told Telemain and Jack the whole story over dinner and discussed it late into the night. Telemain was intrigued by their description of Kazul's imprisonment.

"You say these wizards have an enchantment capable of confining a dragon?" he said eagerly. "Are you sure?"

"That's certainly what it looked like," Cimorene said, pouring herself a cup of hot chocolate. The stew and the dinner dishes had long since been cleared away and were piled in the bucket of soapy water waiting for someone to have the time or the inclination to wash them.

Mendanbar wondered idly whether a bucket of soapy water plus lemon juice plus dishes would be as good for melting a wizard as one without dishes, and what effect the dishes would have on the process. Being melted was probably not very comfortable, but being melted while cups and plates and forks were falling on your head was likely to be even less so.

"I knew I was right to join you," Telemain said, smiling. "I might not have heard about this enchantment at all, if I hadn't. It sounds like a simple modulation of the upper frequencies of a standard reptilian restraint spell, but on an enormously increased scale. I wonder where they're getting the power."

"I don't care how they did it," Cimorene snapped. "I care about getting Kazul *out* of it as soon as possible."

"A trivial detail, once the construction of the spell is properly understood," Telemain said confidently.

"Trivial?" Mendanbar said. "Aren't you forgetting about the wizards? I don't think they'll just let us walk in and take their spell apart."

"And goodness knows what they'll do to Kazul in the meantime," Cimorene muttered.

"Nonsense," Telemain said. "I comprehend your concern, but it is highly unlikely that this episode will prove more than a minor inconvenience so far as your dragon friend is concerned."

Cimorene did not look convinced, so Telemain launched into a lecture on the political implications of the situation, the main point of which was that it would be stupid for the Society of Wizards to hurt Kazul and that wizards were not stupid. Privately, Mendanbar thought that it had been stupid of the wizards to kidnap Kazul in the first place, but saying so would not reassure Cimorene, so he kept quiet.

After a while, Telemain finished his lecture. He did not wait for Cimorene to respond, but turned at once to Mendanbar and asked about his sword. Like Cimorene, the magician could feel the sword spilling magic "like a beacon on a mountaintop," and he was amazed–and completely fascinated–to learn that Mendanbar noticed nothing unusual.

"I don't understand why I didn't spot it at once," Telemain said, shaking his head over his cup of chocolate (which looked to Mendanbar as if it had gone cold during his long speech about the relative intelligence of wizards).

"You mean when you met us?" Cimorene said. "Mendanbar's sword wasn't spraying magic all over right then. He'd just used up most of it on the rock snakes."

"It seems to recover very quickly," Telemain said with a sidelong look at the sword. "Is it always like this?"

"How should I know?" Mendanbar said, running a hand through his hair in frustration. "I can't tell when it's doing it, much less when it isn't."

"Yes, you said that before." Telemain sipped at his chocolate, staring absently into space. "I shall have to think about this for a while," he said at last, as though making a profound announcement. "It's a pity you haven't time to visit my tower for a few tests–"

"Absolutely not!" Mendanbar interrupted.

"We have to rescue Kazul from the wizards," Cimorene put in quickly. "Before this business turns into more than a *minor inconvenience*. Before those wizards decide she's too much trouble to keep around and feed her some dragonsbane."

Telemain considered this for a moment. "An excellent idea," he said at last with evident sincerity.

Mendanbar and Cimorene stared at him.

"If the Society of Wizards poisons the King of the Dragons, there is certain to be a war," Telemain explained. "Wars are very distracting. I don't like being distracted; it interferes with my work. So it would be a very good thing if we made sure there was no war."

"I'm so glad you think so," Cimorene said. Her voice sounded a little strange.

The discussion continued for a little longer, but it was getting late and everyone was tired. Finally, Jack suggested that they go to bed.

"It's all very well for you adventurous types to sit around jawing until past midnight, but *some* people have work to do in the morning," he said pointedly.

"I am not an 'adventurous type,' " Telemain said with dignity. "I am in research."

"Fine, fine," Jack said. "So go research my second-best bed. You and the King, here, take the room on the right, Princess Cimorene gets the one on the left, and I get to bunk under the kitchen. Good night, everybody."

That settled things for the evening, but the conference continued the next morning over a breakfast of flapjacks and honey.

"It seems very likely to me that you are correct about Kazul's location," Telemain said. "She is probably being held somewhere in the Enchanted Forest. Our first task, therefore, must be to find her."

"Our first task is to get back into the Enchanted Forest," Mendanbar corrected. "I don't even know which direction it's in anymore."

"It's over that way," Jack said, waving at the large mountain in back of the house. "Not far if you're flying, but a long way to walk. You have to go around, you see. Now, I've got a nice broomstick that'll get you there in a jiffy. It's extra long, so it'll seat all three of you very comfortably, and it's hardly been used at all."

"No, thank you, Jack," Telemain said firmly. "Broomsticks are only reliable transportation for witches. We will manage this ourselves. Pass the flapjacks, please."

"Here," said Cimorene, handing him the plate. "Do you mean that you're going to take us to the Enchanted Forest the same way you brought us here? I thought it would be harder than that."

"Actually, it is," Telemain said. "The Enchanted Forest is unique, magically speaking, and therefore the interface between the forest and the rest of the world is equally unique. Penetrating that interface requires a specific application."

"What's that mean, when it's at home?" said Jack.

"You need a special spell to get into the Enchanted Forest, because it's different from everywhere else," Mendanbar translated.

Telemain looked irritated. "That's what I just said."

"Is that why Mendanbar's spell dropped us into the ravine with the rock snakes instead of in the forest?" Cimorene asked.

"Possibly." Telemain frowned. "It seems unlikely, however. Mendanbar's magic is of the same variety as that of the forest. It should have worked perfectly well, assuming it worked at all."

"Well, why didn't it?" Mendanbar asked crossly. He was getting tired of puzzles, especially puzzles connected with *his* sword, *his* magic, and *his* forest.

"I'm afraid I can't answer that from your description," Telemain replied, his frown deepening. "I can think of half a dozen things that might have gone wrong, but without seeing it myself I don't know which of them it was."

"So do it again, and watch it this time," Jack said. "Hand me the honey, would you, Your Majesty?"

Mendanbar picked up the honey pot, which was shaped like a fat purple bear. Resisting the urge to throw it at Jack's head, he handed it over and said mildly, "I don't think I like the idea of repeating the spell. Last time it knocked me out for four hours, and I'm not willing to do that again just so Telemain can find out why."

"Oh, that's easy enough to fix," Telemain said. "A few wards, properly set, and there won't be any backlash worth worrying about."

"How much backlash does it take before you worry about it?" Cimorene asked, sounding dubious about the whole idea.

"A three-day headache," Jack put in before Telemain could answer. "And that's only because if his head hurts he has trouble thinking about the wherefore of the whatsit."

"That is a serious exaggeration," Telemain said stiffly. "And I don't anticipate that this experiment would result in any kind of prolonged effect, particularly if I set wards first. I have some idea of what to expect, you see, so I can customize the shielding spells to correspond to the specific variety of backlash."

"It sounds good," Cimorene said. "I think. But what happens if it doesn't work?"

Telemain began a long, involved, and somewhat indignant explanation of why his shielding spells could not fail to work. Mendanbar listened with only part of his mind; the rest was busy thinking about Telemain's suggestion. It looked to him as if the only way they were likely to get back into the Enchanted Forest was by means of his own magic. Telemain hadn't actually said he couldn't do it himself, but Mendanbar was fairly sure that was what he had meant. And from the way Jack talked, walking would take more time than they had to spare.

Even if it took Telemain two tries, or three, to figure out what had gone wrong with Mendanbar's transportation spell, it would still be much faster than walking. Of course, they could always rent some of Jack's wares, but after their experiences with the magic carpet, Mendanbar was not at all happy with that idea.

Repeating the spell would be a chance to find out more about the sword, too. His adventures since leaving the Enchanted Forest had made Mendanbar see just how little he really knew about his magic, and the sword seemed like a good place to start finding things out. The only question was, could the wards actually keep the transportation spell from knocking him head over heels again?

"Telemain, how sure of these shielding spells are you?" Mendanbar asked as soon as there was a lull in the conversation.

Telemain looked at him. "Very sure indeed. I have just spent no little time and breath telling Princess Cimorene, here, exactly how sure that is, why I am sure, and how unlikely it is that I am wrong. Obviously, you have not been attending. Do you wish me to repeat the entire explanation?"

"No, of course not," Mendanbar said hastily. "I'm sorry I wasn't listening, but I had to think for a minute."

"And?" said Cimorene.

"And I think we should do it. As long as Telemain is *sure* he can keep me from being knocked out again, that is."

"I am," Telemain said, sounding faintly put out. "I have been telling you that all morning."

"Good," said Jack. "I like to have things settled. You sure you don't want a pair of seven-league boots for backup?"

"There are three of us and you only have one pair of boots," Cimorene pointed out.

They finished breakfast quickly and helped Jack clear up. Telemain had some things to discuss with Jack, so Mendanbar and Cimorene went outside to give them a chance to talk alone. Mendanbar noticed that the worry line between Cimorene's eyebrows was back.

"What's the matter?" he asked.

"Are you sure about this?" Cimorene said. "Doing the transportation spell, I mean. After what happened before . . ."

"I'll be more careful this time," Mendanbar said. "And Telemain's wards should help. Between the two of us, it ought to be all right."

Cimorene did not look convinced. "You're still taking a big chance. There are other ways to get into the Enchanted Forest."

"Not in a hurry, there aren't," Mendanbar said. "And once we get back, we still have to find Kazul. We can't afford to waste any more time."

"I know." Cimorene chewed on her lower lip, frowning. "Look, you're the King of the Enchanted Forest. You shouldn't be taking chances like this just to help me out."

"I *like* helping you out," Mendanbar said. "But it's not just that. It's my job to take care of the Enchanted Forest. If the wizards have Kazul trapped somewhere in my kingdom, it's *my* responsibility."

"You're not responsible for what the Society of Wizards does!"

"No, but when it involves the forest it involves me, too, and I have to try to put it straight."

"No wonder you looked so tired when you showed up at Kazul's cave," Cimorene muttered. "Mendanbar–"

The door of the house slammed. Telemain came hurrying down the steps, carrying the wizard's staff. "I'm sorry I kept you waiting," the magician said. "Are you ready to start?"

"Yes," said Mendanbar.

"You aren't bringing *that* along, are you?" Cimorene demanded, eying the staff with disfavor.

"Of course I'm bringing it along," Telemain said. "I told you how long I've been looking for one. If I leave it with Jack, odds are he'll sell it to somebody before the day is out. He wouldn't be able to help it. Here, hold this for a minute while I set up the wards."

With visible reluctance, Cimorene took the wizard's staff. She grimaced as her fingers touched it, as if it felt slimy and unpleasant. At the same time, Mendanbar laid a hand on his sword and pushed a tendril of magic at the staff, to see whether there were any lingering spells, but he did not sense anything.

Raising a hand, Telemain began to mutter rapidly. Mendanbar watched with interest as the magician worked, calling up magical power and shaping it into a loose net that surrounded all three of them.

"There," Telemain said at last. "That should do it." He repossessed the staff from Cimorene and looked at Mendanbar. "Whenever you're ready."

Mendanbar studied the net uncertainly. "Is that all there is to it? Should I aim through one of the holes or through one of the threads?"

"Holes?" Telemain said. "Threads? What are you talking about?"

"This net of yours," Mendanbar said. "The warding spell. Does it matter where I aim?"

"You can *see* the warding spell?" Telemain looked and sounded considerably startled by the very idea.

"It's not *seeing,* exactly," Mendanbar said. "But I can tell where it is and how it's put together."

"Fascinating," Telemain said. "Have you always been able to do that?"

"No. It comes with being King of the Enchanted Forest."

"Does it?" Telemain's expression was all eager interest. "Can you do it for any spell? Here, let me try a listening spell, and you see if you can spot it."

"I thought we were supposed to be trying to get to the Enchanted Forest," Cimorene put in pointedly. "Can't you wait and experiment *after* we rescue Kazul?"

"Of course," Telemain said. "Do forgive me. I sometimes get carried away." He nodded apologetically, but Mendanbar thought he sounded disappointed.

"About this net–" Mendanbar reminded him.

"Oh, yes, you wanted to know about aiming." Telemain considered for a moment. "It shouldn't make the least bit of difference."

"Good," said Mendanbar. He drew his sword, and both Telemain and Cimorene jumped. Mendanbar supposed the sword must be leaking again. He pushed careful little dabs of power through the sword to mark Telemain and Cimorene, to be sure that they would come along with him. Then he raised the sword and pointed toward the mountain, where Jack had said the Enchanted Forest lay.

"I think I'll try to take us straight to the palace," he said, and began forming the picture in his mind.

"No, no!" Telemain interrupted. "Do it *exactly* the way you did before. That's the whole point of this exercise."

"I thought the point was to get to the Enchanted Forest," Cimorene muttered.

Mendanbar shrugged. The castle would be a better place from which to try and locate Kazul, since it was at the center–*near* the center–of the Enchanted Forest, but once they were in the forest, getting to the castle would be no trouble. If Telemain wanted to watch an exact duplication of the transportation spell that had dumped them in the ravine, there was no reason not to let him. Releasing his image of the palace, Mendanbar substituted a mental picture of the Green Glass Pool.

He took his time over the image, painstakingly remembering every detail of the rocks and trees and water. When the picture was as clear as he could make it, he took a deep breath and gave the power of the sword a slow, twisting pull.

The mountains and the trees and Jack's queer little house faded to gray ghosts, then melted into mist and were gone. An instant later, the mist vanished. They were standing at the edge of the Green Glass Pool.

"Absolutely fascinating!" Telemain said. "That is, without a doubt, the neatest transportation spell I have ever had the pleasure of utilizing. But I thought you said you had some trouble with it."

"He did, last time," Cimorene said.

"Well, you'd better not put your sword away, then," Telemain said. "I can't tell what the problem was until I see it. You'll just have to do the spell again."

Mendanbar, who had already stuck his sword back in its sheath, shook his head. "I never use the sword to move around the Enchanted Forest. I don't need it."

"By the way, your sword has stopped spraying magic around again," Cimorene said. "I thought you might want to know."

"So it has," Telemain said. "What an intriguing phenomenon."

"That reminds me," Mendanbar said. "The burned-out area I told you about should be right over there. Would you mind taking a look at it, since we're here?"

"Happy to oblige," Telemain replied.

"What about finding Kazul?" Cimorene asked.

"I'll try and locate her while Telemain is examining the clearing," Mendanbar said. "A locating spell takes a while to set up, anyway, so we won't lose any time to speak of, unless looking at the charred spot takes a lot longer than I expect it to."

Cimorene still did not look altogether pleased, but she nodded, and Mendanbar led the way between the enormous trees. There was the burned section, as empty of life and magic as it had been when he had first seen it. Cimorene's expression changed to one of shock and anger, and even Telemain looked shaken.

"I see why you wanted me to look at this," Telemain said.

"So do I," Cimorene agreed.

Setting the wizard's staff under a tree near the edge of the charred area, Telemain walked slowly forward until he reached the spot where the ashes began. Kneeling, he ran his fingers over the dry, dead earth. After a moment, he rose and moved on, into the burned section itself. Little swirls of ash followed him.

For a few minutes, Mendanbar watched the magician work. Then, remembering his promise to Cimorene, he tore his attention away and turned to his own task.

It was a relief to be back in the Enchanted Forest, where magic was nearly automatic. Quickly, Mendanbar sorted through the invisible threads of power, selecting the ones that ran all the way to the farthest edges of the Enchanted Forest. They made quite a bundle, but it was better to do it all at once than to split them up and risk skipping one by accident.

When he was sure he had all the threads he wanted, he looped them around his right wrist and twined his fingers through the strands as they fanned out in all directions. With his left hand, he caught a free-floating filament and wound it into a small ball. He set the ball on the web of unseen tendrils that radiated out from the bundle at his wrist. In his mind, he pictured Kazual and the wizards as he and Cimorene had seen them in Herman's window. Then he gave the invisible ball a flick and sent it rolling rapidly out along the first of the threads.

The ball picked up speed and vanished. Then it was back, bouncing to the next thread and spinning away along the new path. Out and back it went in the blink of an eye, over and over, eliminating one thread each time. And then it went out and did not return.

Mendanbar frowned. That wasn't supposed to happen. If the spell-ball didn't find Kazul, it should come back and hop to the next thread, to check along it. If it *did* find Kazul, it should come back and stop, marking the thread they should follow to lead them to the dragon. Either way, the spell-ball was supposed to come back.

"What is it?" Cimorene said.

Mendanbar looked up, startled, to find Cimorene watching his face closely. "Something's wrong," he told her. "Wait a minute while I try something."

Gently, he wiggled the last thread down which the spell-ball had vanished. He felt a vibration travel the length of the thread, and for a moment he hoped that it was the spell-ball returning. Then, with a high, thin sound like a tight wire breaking, the thread snapped, leaving a long end waving loose in the air in front of him.

"What was *that?*" Telemain said, looking up.

"Something very wrong indeed," Mendanbar said grimly. "You'd better stop that and come over here. We're going to the palace right now."

14

In Which Mendanbar Has Some Interesting Visitors

Both Cimorene and Telemain stared at Mendanbar for a moment. Then Telemain shrugged. "Very well," he said, dusting ashes from his fingers. "I was nearly finished, in any case, though I can't say that I like all this flitting around."

"Mendanbar, what happened?" Cimorene demanded as Telemain walked out of the burned area and crossed to the tree to get the wizard's staff.

"I'm not sure I can explain," Mendanbar replied. "It has to do with the way I work magic. The spell–Telemain, what is it?"

Telemain had picked up the staff and was gazing down at the ground where it had lain. "I think you'd better come and see for yourself," he said without looking up.

Feeling mildly irritated, Mendanbar went over to join Telemain. His irritation vanished when he saw what the magician was looking at. At the foot of the tree, a strip of moss had turned as brown and dead and brittle as the crumbling remnants within the burned-out area a few feet away. And the strip was the exact size and shape of the wizard's staff.

"Wizards again," Cimorene said in tones of disgust. "It figures."

"It *looks* the same as that part," Mendanbar said cautiously, waving at the dead spot. "But is it?"

"So far as I can determine from a limited visual examination, it is,"

Telemain said. "If you want absolute certainty, you'll have to give me another couple of hours for tests."

"We don't have a couple of hours," Mendanbar said. "How sure are you, right now, that this wizard's staff has done the same thing to this bit of moss as something did to that whole section over there?"

"And have you any idea how it did it?" Cimorene put in.

"The *how* is very simple," Telemain answered. "The staff is designed to appropriate any unattached magic with which it comes in contact. Magic appears to be a fundamental property of the Enchanted Forest. So when the staff rested for a few minutes in one location, it swallowed up all the magic from that location, leaving it as you see."

"What about that?" Cimorene asked, waving at the burned area. "What did they do, roll a wizard's staff around on the ground for an hour?"

"Of course not," Telemain said. "It's simply a matter of extending and intensifying the absorption spell. One couldn't maintain such an expansion for very long, but then, one wouldn't have to."

"That's it!" Mendanbar said suddenly.

The other two looked at him blankly. "What's what?" said Cimorene.

"That must be what happened to that locating spell I sent out," Mendanbar explained. "Some wizard's staff sucked it up. That's why it didn't come back."

"Come back?" Telemain said. "You mean your locating spells work on a sort of echo principle? Would you mind demonstrating just how you–"

"Not *now,* Telemain," Cimorene said. She looked at Mendanbar. "Does that mean you know where the wizards are?"

"No, but I think I know how to find out," Mendanbar said. "Ready or not, here we go."

Without waiting for a response, Mendanbar took hold of a thread of magic and pulled. Mist rose and fell, and they were standing in front of the main door to the palace.

"Willin!" Mendanbar shouted, throwing open the door. "Willin, come here. I need–"

He stopped short. Standing in the middle of the entrance hall was a boy of about ten in a blue silk doublet heavily embroidered with gold, a middle-aged man in black velvet with a pinched expression, two cats (one cream-and-silver, the other a long-haired tabby), Morwen, and an extremely harried-looking Willin. The footman who tended the front door was watching them all with the carefully blank face he kept for odd visitors and unusual events. He had had a lot of practice.

"Your Majesty! Oh, thank goodness," said Willin in tones of heartfelt relief. "This woman–these people–"

"Willin."

The elf stopped abruptly and made a visible effort to pull himself together. While he was still working at it, Morwen stepped forward.

"Hello, Cimorene, Mendanbar," she said briskly. "You're back just in time. These people have some very interesting infor–"

"Morwen?" Telemain's incredulous voice interrupted from behind Mendanbar. A moment later, the magician pushed his head between Cimorene and Mendanbar to get a better look. "It *is* you. What on earth are you doing in the Enchanted Forest?"

"Living in it," Morwen answered calmly. "As you would know if you bothered to keep up with the doings of your old friends, Telemain."

"I've been busy," Telemain said defensively.

One of the cats made a small growling noise. "Nonsense," Morwen told it. "It's perfectly normal for him to be busy. The question is, has he got anything to show for it?"

Both cats turned their heads and gazed expectantly at Telemain. Mendanbar decided it was time to take a hand in the conversation, before things got so far off track that he'd never get them back on again.

"Telemain has been very helpful," he said. "Morwen, who are these other people?"

"His Royal Highness, Crown Prince Jorillam of Meriambee," Willin said in a loud, formal tone before Morwen could reply. The elf nodded at the boy, who bowed uncertainly.

"And His Royal Highness's uncle and guardian, Prince Rupert," Willin continued. This time, the older man stepped forward to acknowledge the introduction.

"They have come with the witch Morwen"–Willin paused, obviously waiting for Morwen to curtsy. Morwen only looked at him, and after a moment the elf went on–"with the witch Morwen to beg a boon of His Majesty Mendanbar, the King of the Enchanted Forest."

"It's not a big thing, Your Majesty," Prince Rupert said hastily. "Really. If I could just have a minute or two of your time . . ." His voice trailed off in an indistinct murmur.

Mendanbar looked from Prince Rupert to Morwen and back, completely baffled. "I'm in something of a hurry just now," he said at last. "What is it?"

"If we could, ah, discuss the matter in private . . . ," Prince Rupert said with a sidelong look at his nephew.

"Oh, Uncle," said Crown Prince Jorillam in an exasperated tone. He turned to Mendanbar. "He just doesn't want to say straight out that we're lost. And he especially doesn't want to say that the whole reason we came was so he could leave me in the forest and go home and take over my kingdom."

"Jorillam!" Prince Rupert said, plainly horrified.

"Well, it's true, Uncle," the Crown Prince insisted. "And if they're in a hurry, it's better to tell them and not waste time."

"Mrow!" one of the cats agreed emphatically.

"Morwen . . ." Mendanbar said, hoping he did not look or sound as confused as he felt.

The ginger-haired witch shook her head and peered sternly over the top of her glasses at Prince Rupert. "You, sir, are here to tell these people your story with as little shilly-shallying as you can manage. You'd better get started, or I shall be tempted to do something drastic."

"Like what?" asked the Crown Prince, greatly interested. "Could you turn him into a toad?"

"I could," Morwen said repressively, "but I won't. Not yet, anyway. Provided he starts talking."

"Isn't that a bit severe?" Telemain asked, frowning.

"You wouldn't think so if *you'd* been dealing with him for the last two hours," Morwen said.

Cimorene stepped forward and gave Prince Rupert a perfectly charming smile. "Perhaps it would be best if you told us your story," she said.

"Ah, yes, of course," Prince Rupert said, rubbing his hands against each other. "I, um, we, er–"

"It's because of that stupid club Uncle joined," said Crown Prince Jorillam helpfully. "Tell them, Uncle."

"What club is that?" Cimorene asked.

Prince Rupert gave her a hunted look. "The Right Honorable Wicked Stepmothers' Traveling, Drinking, and Debating Society," he said, and sighed. "I've been a member of the Men's Auxiliary for the past fifteen years."

"That would be for Wicked Stepfathers?" Mendanbar guessed, wishing the man would get on with it.

"Yes, though we don't get many of those," Prince Rupert said. "Mostly, it's Wicked Uncles. You can even join on expectation, if you're not an uncle yet." He sighed again. "That's what I did. I never really expected to be an uncle at all. Rosannon–she's my sister–was under a curse for a hundred years, and I thought I'd be dead when someone finally broke it and married her."

"So you joined this club," Cimorene prompted.

"And it was wonderful!" Prince Rupert's face lit up, remembering. "The places we went to, and the wines, and the discussions! It was everything I dreamed. Only then a smart-alec prince figured out a shortcut and broke the curse, and he and Rosannon got married and had Jorillam here.

And *then* the two of them left on some silly quest or other and put me in charge of him."

"It isn't a silly quest!" Jorillam objected. "It's a matter of vital importance to the future of Meriambee."

"You can see my problem," Prince Rupert said earnestly. "If I don't do something really wicked soon, I'll get kicked out of the club. I only have until sunset tomorrow."

"So you brought Crown Prince Jorillam to the Enchanted Forest, intending to abandon him here," Mendanbar said.

"Actually, it was my idea," the Crown Prince put in. "After the other thing didn't work out, we needed to think of something fast."

"Other thing?" said Telemain, fascinated.

Prince Rupert looked embarrassed. "I hired a giant to ravage a village by the eastern border. He was supposed to show up yesterday, and I was all ready to send the documentation in to the club when I got a letter of resignation saying he'd quit that line of work and wouldn't be coming."

Mendanbar and Cimorene exchanged looks.

"Did he say why?" Cimorene asked.

"No, just that he'd done enough pillaging for one giant, thank you all the same, and now he was going to try something new."

"So I said Uncle Rupert should abandon me in the woods," Jorillam said. "That's *much* more wicked than hiring a giant, isn't it? And I'd get to have some adventures, too, instead of sitting home while Mother and Father are off on their quest. Only first we couldn't find the forest, and then we got chased by some wizards, and then we found the forest just in time and lost the wizards, except we got lost, too, and Uncle Rupert wouldn't leave. And then we were captured by a witch and she brought us here. Are you going to throw us in a dungeon?"

"What was that part about *wizards?*" Mendanbar demanded.

"I thought you'd be interested," Morwen said with considerable satisfaction.

"But that was *before* we got to the Enchanted Forest," Prince Rupert said in a bewildered tone. "Why would the King of the Enchanted Forest be interested in that?"

"Never mind," said Mendanbar. "Just tell me what happened."

"Well, we were just coming out of the old Pass of the Dragons," Prince Rupert said. "It cuts straight through the Mountains of Morning to the Enchanted Forest, and hardly anyone uses it these days, so I thought it would be a good choice. Only things must have changed, because when we came out of the pass we were in a wasteland, and not in the Enchanted Forest at all."

Mendanbar, Telemain, and Cimorene looked at each other. "Describe this wasteland," Mendanbar said.

"It was–it was bare," Rupert told him. "Um, well, bare. No grass or trees or anything. Just . . . just . . ."

"Just bare," Cimorene finished for him. "Did it look burned?"

"Yes, now that you mention it. I didn't examine it closely, you understand, because that was when the wizards came out of the cave and chased us off."

"We had to run for *miles,*" Crown Prince Jorillam said with relish. "They almost caught us."

"It was a long way, but it wasn't *miles,*" his uncle corrected. "And they lost us as soon as we got to the trees."

The forest must have shifted, thought Mendanbar. *Good for it.* "Thank you very much," he said aloud. "You've been very helpful."

"We have?" Prince Rupert said.

"Does that mean you're not going to throw us in a dungeon?" asked Crown Prince Jorillam, sounding disappointed.

"Not at all," Mendanbar said. "Willin, after we're gone, see that His Royal Highness, here, is made comfortable in one of the dungeons. The one under the North-Northwest Tower, I think." Mendanbar smiled to himself, thinking that it might do the overeager young prince good to climb up and down six flights of stairs to get what he wanted, and it certainly wouldn't do him any harm.

"Of course, Your Majesty," said Willin in tones of perfect understanding. He paused. "May I inquire where you are going and when?"

"To rescue the King of the Dragons," Mendanbar said, "and as soon as possible."

Willin swallowed hard, Prince Rupert choked, and even Morwen looked slightly startled.

"The only question is, what's the best way of doing it," Mendanbar continued. "Any suggestions?"

"We can't just charge in and attack the cave," Cimorene said, frowning. "The wizards could kill Kazul before we got to her. And if the area around the cave looks like that bit you showed us a few minutes ago, it simply won't be possible to sneak up on them."

"What we need is a back way in," Telemain said. "I don't suppose there is one?"

"Every cave in the Enchanted Forest has a back way in," Mendanbar said. "The problem is finding it. Do you know anything about that part of the forest, Morwen?"

"I'm afraid not," Morwen said. She turned to the cats. "Chaos? Jasper? How about you?"

The cats looked at each other, blinked, and looked back at Morwen. "They aren't familiar with the area, either," Morwen said with regret.

Willin coughed. "If I may venture a suggestion, Your Majesty . . ."

"Go ahead," Mendanbar said.

"I believe there is a list of caves, passages, vestibules, and entrances in the Royal Archives," said the elf. "Would you care to examine it?"

"Immediately," Mendanbar replied. "I might have known you'd have a list somewhere with the right information, Willin. I should have asked you at once."

The elf bowed deeply, looking very pleased. "I shall bring it without delay, Your Majesty," he said, and whisked off down the corridor.

"Hey!" cried Crown Prince Jorillam. "Are you going to fight the wizards? Can I come?"

"Yes, we are, and no, you can't," Mendanbar told him. "You're going to be locked in the dungeon, remember?"

"But a fight with wizards is *much* more interesting than being locked in a dungeon," Jorillam complained. "I want to watch."

"Maybe so," Cimorene said. "But that's how it is with dungeons. You aren't supposed to get a choice about whether you're going to be locked up in one, you know."

This was evidently a new idea for the young prince, and he did not look happy about it. "But–"

"But, nothing," Mendanbar said. "I'm the King, and I say you go to the dungeon instead of fighting wizards, and no argument."

"Yes," said Morwen. "We have much more important things to argue about. Such as how to get rid of the wizards once we find them."

"Buckets," said Cimorene. "Lots of buckets, and soap, and lemon juice. Where do you keep your buckets, Mendanbar?"

"Around somewhere," Mendanbar said vaguely. "I'll have someone bring us a few. Can the three of us carry enough buckets to get rid of all the wizards?"

"Four of us," said Morwen. The cats yowled. "Yes, I know, and of course you're coming, but you can't carry a bucket of soapy water, so for purposes of this discussion it doesn't matter," she told them.

The cats gave her an affronted look, turned their backs, and began making indignant little noises at each other.

"It seems probable that the wizards will be present in force," Telemain said. "They were certainly aware of Prince Rupert's appearance among them this morning, and they may well have detected your unsuccessful locating spell, Mendanbar. Consequently, I would wager that there will be far too many to dispose of by means of your, er, interesting methods, Princess Cimorene."

"We'll bring some buckets along anyway," Mendanbar said. "It can't hurt."

He nodded a summons to the blank-faced footman by the front door. The footman came over at once, and Mendanbar told him to bring half a dozen buckets of soapy water mixed with lemon juice out to the entrance hall immediately. The footman, who had worked at the palace for a long time and was used to peculiar requests, bowed impassively and departed.

"Any other ideas?" Mendanbar asked.

"Can't the witch turn them into toads?" said the Crown Prince.

"I certainly don't object to trying," Morwen said.

Cimorene shook her head. "I don't think it would work. The Society of Wizards has some new spell that soaks up magic. That's what makes the bare spots in the Enchanted Forest."

"I still wish I understood *why* the Society of Wizards is doing all this," Mendanbar said, half to himself. "I suppose it makes sense to try and blame the dragons for burning bits of the Enchanted Forest, but they've been deliberately trying to start a war. That would make almost as much trouble for them as for everyone else."

"Ah, well, but would it?" put in Prince Rupert timidly. "I mean, if these wizards are soaking up magic, they must want it for something."

Cimorene, Morwen, Mendanbar, and Telemain stared at one another in dismay. "Yes, what *are* they using it for?" Cimorene said after a long, thoughtful silence.

"In all probability, to intensify their general enchantments," Telemain said. "Alternatively, to enable themselves to achieve something more substantial than would otherwise be possible."

Prince Rupert looked at the magician blankly. "Oh," he said in a doubtful tone.

"Don't mind him," Morwen said. "He always gets technical when he's talking about spells."

"But what did he *mean?*" the prince asked.

"He meant that the Society of Wizards wants more magic to power their spells," Mendanbar replied. "Or maybe to use in a spell that would be too big for them to work without it."

"Yes, and *that* is an idea I don't care for at all," said Morwen, frowning. "The Society of Wizards is too powerful already, if you ask me."

"You know, if the dragons start fighting with the Enchanted Forest, any new wasted areas would be blamed on the war," Telemain commented. "The Society of Wizards could absorb considerable quantities of magic before anyone realizes what they are up to."

"That would explain why they're doing this, all right," Mendanbar said. "We have *got* to stop them." Without thinking, he put his hand on the hilt of his sword.

"Mendanbar!" said Cimorene suddenly. "Didn't that wizard say something about you reversing his spell? Not Antorell, the wizard at Jack's house. And you were using the sword. Maybe it can reverse this spell, too."

"It's worth trying," Mendanbar said.

"Not until we have a better idea of exactly what we're up against," Morwen said firmly. "If the King of the Enchanted Forest gets killed trying to rescue the King of the Dragons from the Society of Wizards, goodness only knows *what* will happen."

"We'll sneak in and take a look around," Telemain agreed. "Then we can formulate a plan of action."

"As long as it doesn't take too long," Cimorene muttered. "This isn't some kind of experiment, where we can take our time and try again. If those wizards figure out that someone is trying to rescue Kazul . . ."

Mendanbar tried to smile reassuringly at her. "I don't see how they—ah, Willin! Did you find that list? Good! Then let's all go into the parlor and look at it. The sooner we're done, the sooner we can be on our way."

15

In Which Everyone Argues

Willin's list was remarkably clear and well organized. Once they found the section headed "Caves and Caverns Near the Mountains of Morning," it was only a matter of a few minutes before they discovered the listing for the Cave of Stone Icicles, the only cave at the western end of the Pass of the Dragons. As Mendanbar had predicted, there was a back way into it. A tunnel started from the bottom of the Crystal Falls and wound around under the hills and forest until it reached a crack at the rear of the cave.

"This doesn't look as if it will be hard at all," Cimorene said. "Let's go."

"Right," said Mendanbar. "This shouldn't take long. I'll be back in an hour or so. Willin, take care of everyone while I'm gone–you know, refreshments and things."

"Wait a minute!" Cimorene said, her voice rising above startled objections from everyone else. "You're not going without me."

"But–"

"I am Kazul's Chief Cook and Librarian," Cimorene said firmly. "It's my job to help rescue her."

"I suppose so," Mendanbar said, "but all I'm going to do is sneak in and look at the wizards, and then sneak out again."

"That's all you *think* you're going to do, but what if something goes wrong?"

"Exactly," Morwen said. "You should have someone with you. Several someones, in fact."

"I'm real good at sneaking," Crown Prince Jorillam put in eagerly. "And I want to see a dragon up close."

"No, you don't," Mendanbar said. "Morwen, are you trying to tell me you want to come along as well?"

"No," Morwen said, looking at him sternly over the tops of her glasses. "I'm telling you I'm going to come whether you like it or not. Kazul is my friend, and besides, I want a crack at those wretched wizards."

"We aren't going to do anything to the wizards until we know more about what we're up against," Mendanbar said, feeling harried.

"Then how come you wanted those buckets of soapy water?" Crown Prince Jorillam demanded.

"Just in case," Mendanbar said. "This is only to find out what the wizards are doing and how many of them there are."

"Which is precisely why I must accompany you," Telemain put in.

"Not you, too!"

Telemain frowned at him. "You don't seem to realize what a priceless opportunity this is," the magician said. "It is entirely possible that we shall be able to observe the Society of Wizards in the very act of casting their magic-absorbing spells. Since they are extremely secretive about their methods, this may be the only chance we have of studying their techniques."

"It isn't worth the risk," Mendanbar said.

"Not to you, perhaps," Telemain told him. "I, however, intend to take full advantage of these circumstances. One way or another, I am going to get a look at those wizards." He leaned the wizard's staff against the wall and folded his arms stubbornly.

"Yeah, and then we melt 'em!" Crown Prince Jorillam said enthusiastically.

"You are *not* coming with us," Mendanbar told him.

"But I'm real, real good at sneaking," Jorillam said. "Tell them, Uncle!"

"He is," Prince Rupert said earnestly. "And I'll keep an eye on him so he won't get in your way."

Mendanbar stared at him. "No, you won't. Because you aren't coming with me, either. I am going to sneak into the Cave of Stone Icicles *by myself.*"

"No, you're not," said everyone at once. Morwen's two cats glanced up, then went back to washing their tails. Mendanbar got the distinct impression that the only reason they hadn't joined in the general outcry was that they thought it was beneath them to argue.

"It is inappropriate for the King of the Enchanted Forest to embark on a mission to the King of the Dragons without a formal escort," Willin added.

"You want me to take all these people along as a formal escort?" Mendanbar said incredulously. "Really, Willin–"

"Not at all," the elf replied. "They are all persons of distinction, and it would not be suitable for any of them to take a position as a formal escort to Your Majesty. Properly, only those of your subjects already in Your Majesty's employ may make up such a retinue. Due to Your Majesty's general dislike of formality, we have very few such persons available at present."

"What are you suggesting?" Mendanbar asked with a sinking feeling.

"That I am the only possible person who can accompany Your Majesty in this capacity," Willin said.

"If he gets to go, so do I!" Crown Prince Jorillam cried.

"Not without me," Prince Rupert said, setting his jaw. "I don't know anything about this business with the dragons and wizards, but Jorillam is my responsibility. Until I lose him in the forest, that is."

"And Kazul is *my* responsibility," Cimorene said.

"Like it or not, I am going to get a look at those spells," Telemain stated flatly.

"Those wizards have caused me a lot of trouble, what with one thing and another," Morwen pointed out. "I intend to cause them a bit of trouble back."

"It is necessary to Your Majesty's dignity that Your Majesty take a proper escort with you," Willin put in.

"QUIET!" Mendanbar said.

Everyone stopped talking. Willin looked utterly astonished. Jorillam had a wary expression, and Prince Rupert and Telemain both looked mildly taken aback. Morwen's eyes gleamed approvingly behind her glasses. Cimorene looked momentarily startled, but then she smiled.

Mendanbar took a deep breath. First things first. "Crown Prince Jorillam."

"Yes?"

"You are not coming on this expedition. You will stay here, at my castle, until I return. In the dungeon, just as you requested."

"But it's not fair," Jorillam said. "I didn't know *then* that you were going to go fight wizards. And that elf–"

"Willin is one of my people, and a native of the Enchanted Forest," Mendanbar said. "You aren't. Don't bother arguing; you don't get a choice. I'm the King here, remember."

Jorillam gave him a sulky nod.

"Prince Rupert," Mendanbar went on, "you were quite right to say that your nephew needs watching. You will stay here and keep an eye on him while I'm gone."

"Certainly, Your Majesty," Prince Rupert said with a relieved sigh. "If you say so."

"I'm afraid I can't bring you with me, either, Willin," Mendanbar said, turning to his steward. "Somebody has to take care of our visitors, you know, and you're the only possible person."

Willin hesitated, plainly torn. "It is my duty to serve Your Majesty regardless of the danger."

"I appreciate your willingness to accompany me," Mendanbar assured him. "I feel, however, that you would serve me better here. Now, please take these two guests to the North-Northwest Tower dungeon and see that they get some refreshments."

"As Your Majesty commands," Willin said, bowing. He gestured to Prince Rupert and Crown Prince Jorillam, and led them away.

Well, that takes care of them, *anyway,* Mendanbar thought as the three rounded a bend in the corridor and vanished from sight. The rest wouldn't be that easy. He looked over and saw Morwen, Cimorene, and Telemain standing side by side, wearing identical expressions of stubbornness, and he sighed. He supposed he could accidentally-on-purpose forget to include them in the transportation spell, but somehow he didn't think that would stop them. Not when one was a witch, one a magician, and one an experienced dragon's princess.

"Don't even bother trying to talk us out of it," Cimorene warned. "You'll only waste more time."

"You're probably right," Mendanbar said at last. "And anyway, I suspect I really *should* have some help with me, just in case."

"Very sensible of you," Morwen told him.

"Yes, well, let's get our buckets and go," Mendanbar said uncomfortably.

The four of them collected buckets of soapy water from the imperturbable castle footman. Cimorene and Telemain took two each, but Mendanbar only took one, because he wanted to keep one hand free in case he needed his sword. Morwen also took only one bucket. She did not explain, and her expression dared anyone to comment. No one did.

The footman left, removing Telemain's staff along the way. "Be sure you put that somewhere safe," Telemain called after him.

Mendanbar looked around one last time, checking to make sure everyone was finally ready, then twitched the strands of power and transported them all to the foot of the Crystal Falls.

They appeared on the slippery bank of a narrow stream. A little farther on, the Crystal Falls poured in a shining curtain down the side of a sheer cliff of black glass. The water foamed and swirled at the foot of the falls, forming a small, restless pool, then rushed down the channel at their feet and dashed on into the deeper parts of the Enchanted Forest. The noise of the falling water was tremendous, and the air had a clean, sharp smell.

Mendanbar looked around to see that everyone was there and that no one had spilled the soapy water. He noticed, without surprise, that the two cats had come along, even though he had not specifically included them in the transportation spell. Cats were like that.

"Which way is the tunnel entrance?" Cimorene asked. She had to shout to make herself heard over the roar of the waterfall.

"Over there," Mendanbar shouted back, waving at a clump of fir trees near the foot of the cliff. "Watch your step."

"What did you say?" Telemain yelled.

"He said, 'Watch your step,' " Cimorene replied at the top of her lungs.

Telemain nodded, and they moved cautiously away from the water-slick bank of the stream. The cats had already moved out of range of the mist billowing up from the base of the waterfall. When the rest of the group caught up to them, the two cats gave Mendanbar looks of deep reproach, as if to imply that he should have more sense than to set everyone down so close to such a damply uncomfortable spot.

The tunnel entrance was a narrow crack in the side of the cliff, hidden behind the clump of firs. The cats trotted through it and vanished into the darkness. Morwen gazed after them with a thoughtful expression on her face.

"I don't suppose anyone remembered to bring a light?" Cimorene said, eying the crack with evident misgiving.

Telemain smiled and said three words that crackled in the air. A small globe of golden light appeared above his head. "I'll go first, so the rest of you can see where you're stepping," he said, smiling with a trace of smugness.

"And what do you think will happen when we get near the wizards and their magic-absorbing spell gets hold of your little glow-ball?" Morwen said sharply. "You're not thinking, Telemain."

"I suppose you have a better idea?"

Morwen pushed her glasses firmly into place, set down her bucket of soapy water, and reached into one of her long, loose sleeves. She pulled out a small lantern and set it on the ground. Then she reached into the other sleeve, from which she pulled a flint striker and a long splinter of wood. Expertly, she struck a spark and lit the splinter, then used the splinter to light the lantern. She blew the splinter out, stuffed it and the flint back into her sleeve, and smiled at the surprise on everyone else's face.

"I thought we might be needing this," she said. Picking up the lantern and the bucket, she started for the mouth of the tunnel.

"Hang on a minute," Mendanbar said. "I should go first. Would you give me the lantern, Morwen?"

"Only if you don't dawdle," Morwen responded. "My cats are in there."

"Of course. You come next, then, and Telemain after you. Cimorene can come last. That way we'll have a light between every two people."

Cimorene did not look happy about these arrangements, but Mendanbar did not give anyone time to argue. As soon as Morwen nodded, he took the lantern and started into the crack. It was only wide enough for one of them at a time to edge sideways, and the ground was covered with shattered rock, which made the footing treacherous. Juggling the lantern and his bucket back and forth from hand to hand, Mendanbar tried to see what lay ahead of him while still giving Morwen enough light to follow. Progress was slow, and he began to wonder whether the whole tunnel was going to be as narrow and difficult as this beginning.

"Maybe we would have been better off charging at the main entrance," he muttered to himself.

After what seemed a very long time, but was probably only a few minutes, the tunnel widened. The piles of shattered rock became fewer, then ceased altogether. Mendanbar heaved a sigh of relief and stopped to let the others catch up.

Morwen was the first. "Good," she said as she clambered over the last of the rock piles, balancing carefully to avoid spilling her bucket. "I was beginning to think that rocky stuff was never going to end. Any sign of my cats?"

"It would be more reasonable to ask whether there is any sign of the wizards," Telemain said, following Morwen into the wider part of the tunnel. There was a large wet spot down one side of his many-pocketed vest; apparently he had not been as careful with his buckets as Morwen.

"I haven't seen a trace of the wizards," Mendanbar said, "but the cats have been by here." He pointed at two small trails of footprints leading down the tunnel.

"Thank goodness that's over," Cimorene said as she emerged from the narrow section of the tunnel to join them. "Why are you all just standing here? The Cave of Stone Icicles is a lot farther on."

As this was undeniably true, they set off again. There was still not room for all four of them to stand in a line, but at least now they could walk two by two without difficulty. Somehow, Cimorene ended up walking with Mendanbar in the front. Mendanbar was not sure whether to be glad or sorry. He enjoyed walking with Cimorene, even if they did not dare to talk much; the wizards might have someone listening for odd noises. On the other hand, being in front meant that he and Cimorene were the ones the wizards would attack first. Mendanbar did not like the idea of anyone attacking Cimorene, although he knew she could take care of herself.

He had some time to consider this, for the tunnel was long and winding, but he found it hard to concentrate with Cimorene walking so close beside him. He discovered that he wanted to put his arm around her as they walked–the one carrying the bucket of water, not the lantern–but somehow that didn't seem like the right thing to do when they were supposed to be watching out for wizards. He had never met a princess like Cimorene before. He had never met *anyone* like Cimorene before. She was smart and brave and kind and loyal, and he liked her. In fact, he liked her a great deal. In fact–

Suddenly, the light around Mendanbar dimmed. He stopped and glanced over his shoulder. The little globe that had been hovering over Telemain's head had gone out.

"Telemain?" Mendanbar whispered.

"I didn't turn it off," Telemain whispered back. "We must be getting near the wizards."

Mendanbar nodded without surprise–the atmosphere in the tunnel felt dry and magicless, and though they were still within the Enchanted Forest, he could no longer sense threads of power floating invisibly in the air. He swallowed, hoping he would not have to do any spells in a hurry.

"Keep close," he whispered to Telemain and Morwen, and slowly started forward once more.

The tunnel bent sharply to the left, then right, and without further warning opened out into a forest of stone pillars. A glimmer of light showed between the stones, and they could hear a mumble of voices in the distance.

Hastily, Mendanbar covered the lantern with a corner of his cloak, so that it only lit the area just in front of his feet. Cimorene dropped back. After a moment, she put her hand on his shoulder, and Mendanbar wondered briefly what she had done with the bucket. She gave his shoulder a brief squeeze to indicate that Morwen and Telemain had taken their places. Then he heard her pick the bucket up again.

Carefully, Mendanbar edged through the pillars toward the light and voices.

As they drew nearer, Mendanbar began to understand what the voices were saying.

"I don't like this," grumbled one. "We've wasted too much time already. We should just take her outside, dose her with dragonsbane, and leave her for someone to find."

"Stop complaining, Dizenel," replied a smooth voice, and Mendanbar frowned as he reconized Zemenar's fluid tones. "I have told you a hundred times how foolish that would be," Zemenar went on. "I am not going to tell you for the hundred and first."

"He's right, though," another voice said. "Someone is going to notice us pretty soon, and then where will all our planning be?"

"Someone already has," a fourth voice rasped. "What about those two this morning?"

"A couple of adventurers," Zemenar said dismissively. "They don't matter."

"They got away, didn't they? If they tell someone what they saw–"

"They won't," Zemenar said.

"How can you be sure of that?"

Zemenar gave a snort. "Because of who they are. Can't you recognize a Wicked Uncle when you see one? He was probably here to drop the boy somewhere in the Enchanted Forest. *He* isn't going to tell anyone about us. And even if he does, what of it? Everyone knows odd things happen in the Enchanted Forest. His story will only be one more."

Mendanbar was at the end of the stone columns, close enough to see the wizards if he peeked around a pillar. There were ten of them, grouped about a small table at one side of an enormous cavern. Zemenar and two others were seated; the rest leaned against the wall of the cave or stood in clumps close by. High above the wizards, hundreds of long, cone-shaped columns hung like stone icicles from the ceiling. Four torches dangled from iron brackets on the wall and a lamp stood in the center of the table, throwing shadows like dark fangs from the hanging rocks.

Partway across the cavern, a pale golden glow cut across the shadows like a drawn curtain. On the other side of the glow was a dragon, her wings folded along her back, her eyes narrowed to slits. Mendanbar recognized her at once, even without Cimorene's hiss. She was the same dragon they had seen in the magic window at the dwarf's house–Kazul, the King of the Dragons.

16

In Which Mendanbar Cleans Up

Mendanbar blew out the lantern and set it on the floor. They didn't need it anymore anyway. They were near enough to see by the light of the wizards' torches, even in the shadows. Carrying their buckets, Cimorene, Morwen, and Telemain slipped behind nearby pillars as another wizard came around the corner from the far end of the cave.

"Most gracious and powerful Head Wizard," he said, bowing to Zemenar. "We've checked everything at least twice. There's no one outside and no sign of anyone coming. That spell Xinamon felt before must have been some sort of normal variation."

Behind the pillars, Mendanbar winced. The wizards *had* noticed the locating spell he had sent out earlier. Cimorene frowned and shook her head at him, but he wasn't sure what she meant by that. Morwen scowled at them both and put her finger to her lips.

"Possibly," Zemenar replied. "I don't want to take any chance, though. The King of the Enchanted Forest has a certain amount of magic, and we don't fully understand it. Call in a few more wizards, just to make sure."

"If you don't want to take chances, we ought to use up the dragon now and get out of here," Dizenel said.

"I'm with you," the most recent arrival agreed. "Dragons make me nervous. Are you sure she can't get out?"

"If she could, she'd have done so right away," Zemenar said. "Don't worry about it. We've put the power of at least an acre of the Enchanted Forest into building that shield, and no one can lower it except us."

"Are you sure?" the wizard persisted.

"Take a closer look, if you're not satisfied," Zemenar said, waving at the glow.

"It *is* impressive," the wizard said, moving nearer. "But with a spell this new, how can you be positive–Say, what's that?"

At their companion's change in tone, the wizards' heads swiveled to look at Kazul. For a frozen moment, no one spoke. Then a wizard at the back said, "It's a cat."

Mendanbar glanced sideways in time to see Morwen shake her head and take a firmer grip on her bucket of soapy water. He grimaced. They had only six buckets of soapy water among them, and there were already eleven wizards in the cave. If it came to a fight, they would be badly outnumbered.

"How did a cat get inside the shield?" another wizard asked. "It wasn't there yesterday."

"It wasn't there a few hours ago," Dizenel said. "Where did it come from?"

"Spread out and search the cave," Zemenar commanded, rising. "And bring in the dragonsbane. Someone's snooping."

The wizards fanned out across the cavern and started toward the forest of pillars. There was no way Mendanbar and the others could get away without being seen, even if they had been willing to abandon Kazul to her fate. Mendanbar drew his sword. Soapy water or not, he felt better with a weapon in his hand.

As the first wizard reached the pillars, he jerked in surprise, then raised his staff. Before he could release whatever spell he had planned, a shower of soapy water drenched him from head to foot. The wizard shrieked loudly.

"Blast you six ways from next Wednesday!" he shouted as he began to melt. "This is the second time you've liquefied me! May you and your pet dragon and your triple-cursed wash water turn purple with orange spots and fall down a bottomless pit!"

The other wizards stopped in their tracks. "It's Cimorene!" one of them said nervously.

"That's *Princess* Cimorene, to you," Cimorene said, stepping out from behind a pillar. She held her second bucket in plain sight, ready to throw.

"Stay back," Zemenar ordered. "Blast her from a distance."

"Cowards!" Cimorene taunted, and ducked behind another of the stone columns. "Come and get me!"

It wasn't going to work, Mendanbar told himself, taking a firmer grip on his sword. Zemenar was too clever to let his wizards chase Cimorene into the maze of stone. They would stay at a safe distance and throw bolts of power into the pillars until they destroyed the maze or killed everyone in it, or both.

Three more wizards came running in. Zemenar stopped them with a gesture. The rest of the wizards backed away from the pillars and lined up across the width of the cave.

"Now, then," the Head Wizard said, lifting his staff and pointing it at the pillar Cimorene had ducked behind. "Like this."

Mendanbar felt magic swell around the end of the staff. An instant later, before he had time to reach for the magic himself, the spell shot forward and exploded, shattering the pillar and sending chips of rock flying in all directions.

"Ow!" Cimorene's voice cried from somewhere in the shadows.

Without thinking, Mendanbar stepped out from behind his pillar, bucket in one hand, sword in the other, into full view of the wizards. "Over here!" he called. If he could distract them for a minute or two, perhaps Cimorene could get safely behind another column.

"Mendanbar!" For an instant, Zemenar looked thoroughly startled. Then he smiled nastily. "How nice to see you. I've been hoping you would turn up, so we could finish this little business at last."

As he spoke, Zemenar stepped forward and shifted his staff to point at Mendanbar. Mendanbar raised his sword and stayed where he was. He felt magic building around the staff once more and decided not to wait to find out what Zemenar intended it to become. Instead, he reached out through the sword and touched the wizard's spell, the same way he touched the magic threads of the Enchanted Forest.

It was much easier to do here than it had been in the Mountains of Morning. The sword sopped up the spell in an instant. Mendanbar could sense the channels of power Zemenar had been using to feed his spell, and he touched those, too, and pulled. The sword obligingly drank them in.

"What are you doing?" Zemenar cried in astonishment, lowering his staff. His hair stood out around his head, as wild and tangled as the magical mess he'd left on the floor of Mendanbar's castle.

"I'm stopping you," Mendanbar said. His whole arm tingled with the power the sword had absorbed. If he could just think of the right thing to do with it . . .

"And a good thing, too," Morwen said from several pillars over. "You're too greedy for your own good, or anyone else's, for that matter."

"I am not greedy," Zemenar protested angrily. "I have every right to–"

"You're greedy, all right," Cimorene said from just behind Mendanbar. "And you wouldn't know what to do with all the power you want even if you got it. Just look at you! Your hair's like a bird's nest."

Zemenar scowled. Mendanbar stared at him without really seeing him, trying to remember why Cimorene's words sounded familiar.

"The gargoyle!" he said suddenly. "Why didn't I think of that before?"

"What gargoyle?" one of the wizards asked.

"Never mind him," Zemenar said. "He's only trying to distract us. All together, now: blast them!"

The line of wizards raised their staffs. Mendanbar grinned and twisted the mass of power in the sword, just as he had done two days earlier when he had grown tired of the gargoyle's complaints. Soapy water spurted out of the empty air in front of the wizards in a hard, fast stream, as if it were being pumped through an invisible hose. The foaming spray washed over the entire line, thoroughly soaking them all. Puddles grew rapidly on the stones underfoot, and wizards shouted and slid on the suddenly slippery floor. Several of them dropped their staffs to rub at their eyes, which had apparently gotten soap in them. None of them melted.

Mendanbar felt a moment of panic. He'd been sure that his magically created soapy water would work just as well as the buckets they had hauled with them from the castle, but it didn't seem to be doing anything. The wizards would get themselves together any minute, and what would he do then?

"Did you remember the lemon juice?" Cimorene said in his ear.

"Oh, right," said Mendanbar. He twisted the power again, and another spray of soapy water (this time smelling strongly of lemon) squirted over the wizards. To Mendanbar's considerable relief, they collapsed into gooey puddles, one after another. In another moment, there were no wizards left in the cave at all, only staffs, soggy robes, and a great deal of water and soapsuds.

Mendanbar studied the puddles, then set his bucket of soapy water on the ground. It didn't look as if he'd be needing it anymore. He kept his sword out, however, since he didn't know how many more wizards might still be outside.

"Fascinating," said Telemain. He moved forward and knelt at the edge of a puddle. "This mess appears to be mainly the liquefying agent."

"It does?" Cimorene asked.

"He means it's mostly soapy water," Mendanbar said.

"And a good thing, too, or it would take forever to clean up," Morwen said. "Wizards are a nuisance even when they're gone."

"It's a pity it isn't permanent," Cimorene said. "I'd like to get rid of that Zemenar once and for all."

"Removing their staffs will delay their reappearance," Telemain said. "I suggest we do so before we leave."

"Good idea," Morwen said. She picked her way between puddles and began collecting the wizards' staffs. Telemain went back to studying the puddle.

Cimorene turned to Mendanbar. "Now, if Kazul can just–oh, no!"

Mendanbar followed Cimorene's gaze. The glowing, golden shield spell still blocked half of the cavern, imprisoning Kazul.

There was a long silence. Then Cimorene said, "Telemain, were those wizards right when they said they were the only ones who could take down that spell?"

"What's that?" Telemain said, looking up. "Really, *must* you interrupt so constantly? I'm never going to get anything finished at this rate."

"But think of all the interesting things you're finding out," Mendanbar said. "This shield, for instance. Have you ever seen anything like it before?"

"Now that you mention it, no," Telemain replied, scrambling to his feet. "Let me look at it."

"That was the idea," Cimorene muttered.

They all watched while Telemain examined the shield. He walked from one end to the other, then put a hand gingerly against the glow and pushed. When nothing seemed to happen, he twisted one of his rings twice and touched it to the glow.

"Can you get rid of it?" Cimorene asked.

"I don't know yet," Telemain said. "I'm still checking the parameters of the primary enchantment."

"Oh."

The magician twisted a different ring and touched it to the glow. This time there was a spark. "Ah!" Telemain said in a satisfied tone. "I suspected as much."

"Well, are you going to tell us about it?" Morwen said as she dropped a load of wizards' staffs in a pile against the wall.

"It's a self-sustaining barrier produced by a recirculation of the initial power input," Telemain explained. "Because of the rotation effect, most physical substances cannot pass through the shield in either direction. Unlike the majority of spells, this one needs no exterior energy source, so the usual procedures for dismantling such sorceries would be completely ineffective."

"What does that mean?" Cimorene demanded.

"The spell keeps itself up, we can't get in or out, and we don't have any way of getting rid of it," Mendanbar translated.

"Then how did the cat get in?" Cimorene asked, pointing at Morwen's large silver-and-cream cat, which had climbed onto Kazul's back and lay curled up between her wings.

"Cats are like that," Morwen said. "When he comes out, I'll ask him how he did it, if you want me to, but don't expect too much in the way of an answer. Cats enjoy being mysterious."

"I don't care what they enjoy," Cimorene said. "We have to get Kazul out of there, and if that cat can help–"

"It is unlikely," Telemain interrupted, stepping back from the glow. "The cat's method of moving through the barrier is, in all probability, useless to anyone else. Fortunately, we have other resources."

"We do?"

Telemain looked at Mendanbar. "While I have not had a chance to make a thorough and complete examination of that extremely intriguing weapon you carry, I have observed enough to determine that its function is fundamentally antithetical to wizards and their magic. A straightforward penetration appears quite possible and would disrupt the recirculation effect, resulting in the collapse of the self-sustaining mechanism."

"What?" said Cimorene.

"Really, Telemain, must you?" said Morwen.

"Right," said Mendanbar. He took three steps forward and stuck his sword into the glowing spell.

A jolt of power ran up his arm and the globe of light flashed brighter than the sun. Mendanbar's eyes were dazzled by the flare, so he couldn't see anything except purple spots, but he heard a loud roar, the angry hiss of a cat, and the sound of scales on stone, so he was sure the barrier was gone.

"Kazul," Cimorene called from behind him. "It's all right. It's not wizards, it's us."

"And about time," a deep, unfamiliar voice said. "Hello, Cimorene, Morwen. It's nice to see you again. Who are these others?"

"This is Mendanbar, the King of the Enchanted Forest," Cimorene answered, and Mendanbar felt her hand on his shoulder. "He's the one who let you out. Over there is Telemain. He's a magician, and he figured out how to do it."

"Greetings, Your Majesty," Mendanbar said, blinking. The purple spots began to fade at last, and he found himself staring into the green-gold eyes of an enormous female dragon. He only just managed to keep himself from backing up automatically. "Pleased to meet you."

"Under the circumstances, most definitely so am I," said the dragon with a smile that showed a large number of sharp-looking silver teeth. "How did you manage it?"

"Weren't you watching?" Cimorene asked.

"Watching what?" Kazul replied. "I couldn't see a thing except what was inside that blasted bubble with me."

"We could see you."

"The shielding spell was unidirectional," Telemain put in. "The external absorptive effect would enhance its efficiency."

Kazul gave Telemain a hard look and smiled again, this time showing *all* of her teeth. "What was that again?"

Telemain looked at Kazul. Then he looked at Mendanbar. He frowned in concentration, and finally he said carefully, "The shield was a one-way spell. It soaked up everything that tried to get in from outside and used the energy to make itself stronger."

"Very good," Morwen said. "I was beginning to think you were hopeless."

"I haven't the slightest idea what you're talking about," Telemain said with dignity.

A yowl of complaint made them all turn their heads. The cream-and-silver cat was standing at the edge of the wet, soapy, lemon-scented area where the wizards had melted, shaking his front paws one at a time and eying the water with extreme disfavor.

"Too bad," Morwen told the cat. "If you hadn't sneaked in and attracted their attention, Mendanbar might not have had to be quite so extravagant with the spray. You'll have to get across it by yourself. Where's Chaos?"

The cat blinked disdainfully and began washing his right paw. Kazul snorted softly. "If you want a ride, climb up," she told the cat. "But you'd better hurry, because I'm leaving now."

Kazul rose to her feet, shaking her wings. The cat looked up from his washing, then took two bounds and leaped from the top of a projecting rock. He disappeared behind Kazul's shoulder, and there was a brief sound of claws scraping against scales. Then the cat appeared on Kazul's back, riding comfortably between the dragon's wings and looking tremendously pleased with himself.

"Wait a minute," Mendanbar said as the dragon started toward the other end of the cave. "There may be more wizards out there."

"Good," said Kazul without slowing down at all. "Four days is a long time to spend inside a blank bubble, and I owe them one. Besides, I'm *hungry.*"

"I should think so!" Cimorene said, following the dragon. "Didn't they give you anything to eat?"

"No, and I wouldn't have taken it if they had," Kazul said. Her voice became muffled as her head turned the corner at the far end of the cave. "For all I knew, those mumble mumble could have mumble dragonsbane in everything. I mumble mumble end up like Tokoz."

"But if there are more wizards–," Mendanbar began, then gave up and hurried after Cimorene. Clearly, neither she nor Kazul was going to listen to him, and if there *were* more wizards outside it would be better if he–and his sword–were there to help.

17

In Which Mendanbar Grows Some Trees and Makes a Wicked Suggestion

There were, however, no wizards outside the cave. There was only an enormous stretch of barren land that looked as if it had been burned. Morwen's long-haired tabby cat sat in the ashes several feet from the mouth of the cave, surveying the waste with evident disapproval.

"There you are," Morwen said to the cat as she joined Cimorene and Mendanbar by Kazul's left shoulder. "Any sign of more wizards?"

The cat meowed.

"Good," said Morwen. "Did any of the others get away?"

The cat made a growling noise.

"Very good," said Morwen. She turned to Mendanbar. "Can you keep them from interrupting us by accident?"

"I don't think so," Mendanbar said. "There isn't any magic here for me to work with." He was horrified at the extent of the destruction. How was he going to fix it?

"So *this* is how they did it," Telemain's voice said from behind Mendanbar. He sounded pleased, as if he had just solved a very difficult puzzle. "I'd been wondering."

"Did what?" Mendanbar asked.

"Established that shield spell," Telemain said. "The power involved was clearly several factors beyond the generating capacity of–"

Kazul turned her head and looked at Telemain.

Telemain coughed. "There weren't enough wizards to have done it by themselves."

"Power," Mendanbar said, half to himself. "They sucked all the magic out of this whole area and put it in the shield. Where did it go when the shield disappeared?"

"Into your sword, of course," said Telemain, as if that were so obvious that everyone should have realized it without his saying anything.

"And the sword is linked to the forest," Mendanbar said. "And this is part of the forest, or should be. So . . ."

"So all you have to do is use the sword to put the magic back where it belongs," Cimorene finished.

"Theoretically, that should work fine," Telemain said, frowning. "But the practical applications aren't always that easy."

"Nonsense," said Cimorene. "That sword turned a whole patch of the Mountains of Morning into a bit of the Enchanted Forest when we were having all that trouble getting here. Mendanbar pulled it back into the sword then; all he has to do now is turn that spell around and push magic out. Try it, Mendanbar."

Slowly, Mendanbar lowered the tip of the sword until it touched the ashes. He couldn't feel anything at first. Then he realized that he was trying to reach outside himself for the threads of magic that always floated around him in the Enchanted Forest. And in this wasteland there were no threads. He frowned. Closing his eyes, he concentrated on the sword instead.

That felt more promising. He could sense power crackling along the length of the blade, lots of power, but he did not think it would be enough. He stretched deeper, using his experience outside the Enchanted Forest to pull together every last bit of magic he could reach. It was still not enough.

"I don't think I can do it, Cimorene," he muttered.

"You can, too," Cimorene said, and put her hand on his shoulder encouragingly. "Try again."

As she touched his shoulder, Mendanbar felt it come–not just magic, not only power, but all the magic and power of the Enchanted Forest itself. It washed over him, and as it did he saw patterns in it, patterns that were the threads he manipulated to work magic in the forest. And he saw how to shift the pattern just a little, filling it in with the power stolen from the forest and stored in the sword, to repair the damage the wizards had done. Without thinking, he did it.

He heard an astonished gasp from Cimorene, a snort from Kazul, a low whistle from Telemain, and a surprised noise from one of the cats.

"Well!" said Morwen.

Mendanbar opened his eyes. A thick carpet of moss, greener than Kazul's scales, spread out in all directions from the cave mouth. Massive oaks and beeches with cooper leaves stood so close together that it was hard to see more than a little way into the shadows below them, packing every part of what had been a burned-out waste moments before. All around, Mendanbar could feel threads of magic hovering in the air, ready to use for more ordinary spells.

No one said anything for a long moment. Then Telemain tore his gaze away from the restored forest and turned to Mendanbar.

"Could you do that again, slowly, so I can analyze it?" he asked.

Despite Telemain's urging, Mendanbar refused to repeat the spell immediately, though he did offer to let the magician watch when he went to clean up the barren area near the Green Glass Pool. Then Telemain wanted to stay and investigate the melted wizards some more, but Morwen and Cimorene insisted that this was a bad idea, and eventually he gave in. He was inclined to be sulky about it until Morwen pointed out that he had fourteen more wizards' staffs to study, including one that had belonged to the Head Wizard. It cheered him up enormously.

"You're quite right," he told Morwen. "Those wizards will get themselves back together before long, and once they do, they'll come looking for their staffs. If I don't examine the staffs before then, I'll lose my chance. I can always melt another wizard later and study the disintegration process then." He hurried back into the cave, reappearing a moment later with his arms full of wizards' staffs.

"Be careful with those!" Mendanbar said as Telemain came out onto the moss-covered ground.

"They are unlikely to be a source of difficulty without intelligent guidance," Telemain said reprovingly. "So long as the wizards are not in contact with them, they are merely passive instruments of assimilation. There's nothing to worry about."

"Yes, there is," Cimorene put in. "If you drop them, Mendanbar will have a lot of ugly brown marks on his nice new moss. And if they can do that, there's no telling what else they might do."

"Wizards store spells in their staffs," Morwen said, nodding. "You can't always be sure what will set one off."

Telemain looked at them with annoyance. "I suppose you'd rather I left them here. Have you no spirit of scientific investigation?"

"Not where wizards are concerned," Cimorene muttered.

"Nonsense," Morwen said. "I'm just as curious as you are, Telemain, but I never heard that a spirit of scientific inquiry precluded taking intelligent precautions."

"Oh, I see," said Telemain. "Why didn't you just say so in the first place?"

While the others talked, Mendanbar studied the staffs, keeping a careful watch on the threads of Enchanted Forest magic that were nearest to Telemain. To his surprise, the threads showed no tendency to drift toward the magician or wind themselves into knots around the staffs he carried. Apparently, Telemain was right–the staffs would only be a minor nuisance as long as their wizards weren't carrying them. He resolved to mention this to Telemain later. Perhaps Telemain could even help him find a way to deal with the problems the staffs caused when they *did* have their wizards with them.

A few minutes later, when Kazul was satisfied that there were no wizards left in the area, Mendanbar took them all back to the castle with a quick spell. He was relieved that the wizards' staffs caused no trouble, and pleased to discover that transporting a dragon was no harder than transporting anyone else.

They materialized in the castle courtyard, just inside the moat. Willin, who had apparently been watching for their arrival, came hurrying out to meet them.

"Welcome home, Your Majesty," the elf said with evident relief. Mendanbar noticed that he'd dug up a formal uniform somewhere, all sky-blue velvet and dusty gold braid. "May I assume that your mission was a success?"

"Yes, you may," Mendanbar said. "Willin, this is Kazul, the King of the Dragons, and she's very hungry. See if you can scare up something in the kitchen that would do for a dragon-sized meal."

"At once, Your Majesty," Willin said, bowing. "And may I congratulate you and your companions on your great achievement and welcome King Kazul to the Enchanted Forest."

"The welcome I'm interested in is dinner," Kazul said with a smile that showed all her teeth.

Willin backed away hastily. "Of course, of course. I'll see about it immediately."

"I'd better come with you," said Cimorene. "I've been Kazul's Chief Cook for over a year, and I know what she likes."

The two of them left, heading for the other side of the castle, with Kazul trailing hopefully behind them.

Mendanbar wasn't sure whether to be disappointed or relieved. He wanted very much to talk to Cimorene, but he wasn't sure how to tell her what he wanted to say, and anyway they certainly couldn't discuss the things he wanted to talk about with all these other people around.

"Mendanbar, have you got somewhere I could work on these without being disturbed?" Telemain asked, nodding at the load of wizards' staffs he was carrying.

"I wouldn't mind examining them myself," Morwen said.

"The blue room would be best, I think," Mendanbar said. "The light is better in my study, but there's a gargoyle in the corner who can be, um, difficult."

"We'll take the study," Morwen said decisively. "Light is important, and once Telemain gets involved, he won't notice any distractions."

"What about you?" Telemain asked, nettled.

Morwen sniffed. "I can handle considerably more than a mere gargoyle."

"All right," Mendanbar said. "As long as you're sure."

He showed them to the study and helped them get settled, then went down to the kitchen to see how Cimorene and Kazul were doing. He found Kazul in the rear courtyard, eating an enormous kettle of stew that had been intended to be supper for the entire castle. Cimorene was in the kitchen, her arms covered in flour to the elbows, rolling out pie crust and giving orders to the cook. Mendanbar stayed long enough to make sure the cook would do whatever Cimorene told him to, and then Cimorene chased him away, saying that it was difficult enough to cook in a strange kitchen without people hovering over her.

"You don't have to cook anything," Mendanbar told her.

"I do if we want any dinner," Cimorene retorted. "Kazul is already eating everything that was ready for tonight, and she's going to want more as soon as she's finished. Your people aren't really prepared to cope with a visiting dragon."

"We've never had one before."

"Well, you have one now." Cimorene glanced toward the courtyard and lowered her voice. "I think we'll be staying for a few days at least, if that won't cause too many problems. Kazul needs to get her strength back before she tries to fly back to the Mountain of Morning."

"You can stay as long as you like," Mendanbar assured her. "Is there anything I can do to help?"

"You can let me get back to making dinner!" Cimorene said. She was smiling, but she obviously meant what she had said.

"All right. Call me if you need anything." Mendanbar bowed and left, feeling a little put out.

He went to the castle library, since his study was occupied, and poked about in the scrolls for a few minutes. Then he decided to check on Prince Rupert and his nephew. He found the middle-aged prince quickly enough, but he had to send someone to retrieve the young Crown Prince from the dungeon.

"Did you enjoy your stay?" Mendanbar asked when Crown Prince Jorillam arrived at last.

"It was all right," Jorillam said. He looked rumpled and vaguely dissatisfied. "But there weren't any rats. I thought there'd be rats. There wasn't a rack, either."

"Jorillam!" Prince Rupert said sharply. "It's not polite to complain about things like that. Where are your manners?"

"I don't understand," Jorillam said, frowning. "If there *were* rats and a rack, I'd be expected to object, wouldn't I? So why can't I complain when they *aren't* there?"

"It's not the same thing," Rupert told him. "I'm sorry, Your Majesty," he went on, turning to Mendanbar. "He's used to getting his own way. I'm afraid I haven't done a very good job of teaching him how to behave."

"I behave just fine," Jorillam said.

"I am beginning to understand why you wanted to abandon him in the Enchanted Forest," Mendanbar said to Prince Rupert.

Rupert flushed. "No, no, it's not that. I'm really very fond of the boy. But I have an obligation, you know, and there's no getting out of it."

"You can leave me here, Uncle," Jorillam said persuasively. "That's abandoning me in the Enchanted Forest, isn't it?"

"I don't think so," Mendanbar put in quickly. He didn't want to think about the problems the young Crown Prince could cause if he stayed at the castle. "There are too many people here for it to count as abandonment."

Prince Rupert nodded gloomily. "I'm afraid you're right. And frankly, I'm not at all sure that abandoning him is the right notion. I just can't think of anything else wicked to do on short notice."

"But you *promised* you'd abandon me in the Enchanted Forest," Jorillam protested. "And I *want* to be abandoned and have all sorts of adventures and come home covered in glory."

"You're a little young for that," Mendanbar commented, studying the Crown Prince. He smiled suddenly as an idea came to him. "What you need is some proper training."

"There isn't time," Jorillam said smugly. "Uncle has to do something wicked to me right away."

"Ah, but that's just the point," Mendanbar said. He turned to Prince Rupert, ignoring Jorillam's suddenly wary expression. "Abandoning Crown Prince Jorillam won't do you any good, because he *wants* to be abandoned. Letting him have his own way isn't terribly wicked, even if it isn't good for him."

"I'm afraid you're right," Rupert said sadly.

"But Uncle–"

"On the other hand," Mendanbar went on, disregarding Jorillam's interjection, "if you promised you'd abandon him, breaking that promise would certainly be wicked. And if you sent him off to a private school for princes–"

"I don't want to go to school!"

"Oh, my." Prince Rupert looked from Mendanbar to Jorillam–who now looked thoroughly alarmed–and back. "I think I see what you're getting at. If he hates the idea, then it probably is wicked, even if it's good for him. And there's breaking the promise, too."

"And you wouldn't have to tell anyone at home what you'd done with him," Mendanbar said. "You could rule the country just as if you really had abandoned him in the forest, and no one would know. Surely misleading all those people would be wicked enough for your society."

"I think you're right," Prince Rupert said, smiling for the first time since Mendanbar had met him. "I really think you're right." His face fell suddenly. "But how am I going to find a good school before sunset tomorrow?"

"Don't worry about that," Mendanbar said reassuringly. "I know just the place. It's up in the Mountains of Morning, where no one is likely to run across it, and it's run by a dwarf named Herman. If you like, I'll send a messenger off right away to arrange things."

"No!" said Jorillam.

"That would be wonderful," said Prince Rupert with relief. "Ah, I don't suppose this Herman person would be willing to write a letter to the Society explaining matters?"

"I don't see why not," Mendanbar said. "But what do you want it for?"

"Just to confirm that I'm fulfilling the requirements," Prince Rupert explained. "It *is* a rather unusual arrangement, you see, and I want to be sure the Society will think I've been wicked enough."

"I understand," Mendanbar told him. "Don't worry about it. If Herman won't write you a negative enough letter, I'll send one myself. I'll bet even the Right Honorable Wicked Stepmothers' Traveling, Drinking, and Debating Society will believe the King of the Enchanted Forest."

18

In Which Willin Finally Gets to Arrange a Formal Celebration

For the next several days, Mendanbar was busier than he could remember being in a long, long time. Besides arranging for Crown Prince Jorillam's schooling, a stream of messengers had to be sent to the dragons in the Mountains of Morning to explain where their King was and to warn them about the wizards.

Morwen and Telemain argued constantly about what they were finding out from the wizards' staffs, and when they weren't arguing, they were asking for obscure reference books and peculiar ingredients for their spells. Between the two of them, they kept the small castle staff busy hunting for things.

The wizards themselves seemed to have disappeared completely, but Mendanbar didn't trust them to stay gone. He spent several hours every day checking the entire network of magic that enveloped the Enchanted Forest, looking for the tangles that wizards with staffs always caused, so that he would know if any of them returned. In the process, he found several more burned-out areas where the wizards had stolen the magic of the forest. Fortunately, none of the charred spots were very big, but repairing them was not an easy task, and Mendanbar worried constantly about what would happen if a wizard sneaked into the forest and soaked up a larger patch before he could be melted.

He confided this worry to Cimorene on the third day after Kazul's rescue.

"What you really need is a way to keep them from soaking up magic in the first place," said Cimorene. "Then it wouldn't matter if they sneaked in, because they wouldn't be able to do any real harm."

"They could still cause plenty of trouble," Mendanbar said. "But you're right, it would solve a lot of problems. Unfortunately, I can't think of a way to stop them."

"Well, of course you can't," Cimorene said. "You don't know enough about wizards and that ridiculous magic-absorbing spell of theirs. Why don't you ask Telemain?"

So Mendanbar went off to find Telemain, who was with Morwen, working on the last of the wizards' staffs. At first, Telemain was a little annoyed at being interrupted, but when Mendanbar explained his problem, however, the magician nodded.

"An automatic spell to reroute any magical power should do the trick," Telemain said. "That way, anything they try to grab will just slide back where it belongs, and there will never be any new holes to fix."

Morwen looked at Telemain in mild surprise. "You're slipping," she said. "I actually understood that."

"Can you make up an automatic spell for me?" Mendanbar asked quickly, before Telemain could take offense.

"It shouldn't be a problem," Telemain said. "It'll need some sort of anchor, though, or you'll have to keep checking to see if it's still working. Any ideas?"

The three of them discussed it for a few minutes, and finally Morwen suggested tying the spell to the sword. This turned out to be an even better idea than it first appeared. Working through the sword, Mendanbar could manipulate the power of the Enchanted Forest directly, and with Telemain's help he made the new spell an integral part of the forest's magic.

"What does that mean?" Cimorene asked when he sought her out to tell her how well her idea had worked.

"It means that if any wizards come into the Enchanted Forest, their staffs won't absorb any magic, ever, for as long as they stay," Mendanbar explained. "I won't even have to check the spell very often, because it's tied to the sword. As long as the sword is anywhere in the forest, the wizards can't do a thing."

Cimorene frowned. "They could still use the spells they have stored in their staffs, couldn't they? And what if you have to leave the Enchanted Forest again?"

"I'll have to take a different magic sword, that's all," Mendanbar said.

"I ought to do that anyway, because of the way that one sprays magic around outside the forest. It's not exactly inconspicuous."

"Very true," Cimorene said with a smile.

They were silent together for a moment. Then Cimorene shook her head. "Kazul will be ready to leave tomorrow. She thinks she's ready today, but I told her not to push."

"I– That's good," Mendanbar said. He hesitated, then said tentatively, "I suppose you'll be going with her?"

"What else would I be doing?" Cimorene asked. She sounded more curious than sarcastic.

Mendanbar took a deep breath. "You could stay here. At the castle, I mean. With me." This wasn't coming out at all the way he had wanted it to, but it was too late to stop now. He hurried on, "As Queen of the Enchanted Forest, if you think you would like that. I would."

"Would you, really?"

"Yes," Mendanbar said, looking down. "I love you, and–and–"

"And you should have said that to begin with," Cimorene interrupted, putting her arms around him. Mendanbar looked up, and the expression on her face made his heart begin to pound.

"Just to be sure I have this right," Cimorene went on with a blinding smile, "did you just ask me to marry you?"

"Yes," Mendanbar said. "At least, that's what I meant."

"Good. I will."

Mendanbar tried to find something to say, but he was too happy to think. He leaned forward two inches and kissed Cimorene, and discovered that he didn't need to say anything at all.

The first person they told was, of course, Kazul. Mendanbar was a little nervous about it, because from what he'd heard, dragons tended to get testy when their princesses ran off with someone, but Kazul didn't seem to mind at all.

"Good for you," she said to Mendanbar. "And congratulations to the pair of you." Her eyelids lowered halfway, and she looked at Cimorene. "I'd been wondering how much longer you were going to stay."

"I don't know what you mean," Cimorene said indignantly. "I wasn't *planning* to leave! This just sort of happened."

"I know," Kazul said. "But you'd have gone soon in any case. Now that you've gotten things organized, there isn't really enough work to keep you busy in the Mountains of Morning. You wouldn't have stayed long, once you started to get bored."

"Living with dragons doesn't sound boring to me," Mendanbar said.

"That's because you've never done it," Kazul replied. "Being Queen of the Enchanted Forest will give Cimorene more scope for her talents."

"Then you really don't object?" Mendanbar asked.

"Why should I?" Kazul said. "You're a nice enough person, as humans go, and you've been very polite about the whole thing. That doesn't happen often. Normally, knights and princes just grab a princess and run. And most of the princesses don't even bother to say good-bye, much less give proper notice." She looked at Cimorene and sighed. "I'll miss your cooking, though."

"I can come back for a week or two, if you'd like, and train a replacement," Cimorene offered.

"I may take you up on that, once I find one," Kazul said thoughtfully.

"And in the meantime, you can come over for dinner a lot," Mendanbar said, and both Cimorene and Kazul smiled at him.

When Willin heard about the engagement, he was delighted. The wedding of the King of the Enchanted Forest was just the sort of vast formal occasion the elf had been craving, and he threw himself into the preparations with enthusiasm. He didn't even object when he learned that the bride wanted the King of the Dragons for her matron-of-honor and a witch for her bridesmaid.

"Kazul and Morwen are my best friends," Cimorene explained. "Besides, if I have them, Mother won't insist that my sisters be bridesmaids."

"You have sisters?" Mendanbar asked, somewhat taken aback.

Cimorene nodded. "Six of them. They're all perfectly lovely and sweet, and the sight of Kazul will probably scare them silly."

"Typical princesses," Mendanbar muttered, but without any active dislike. He didn't seem to mind foolish princesses much anymore, as long as he didn't have to marry one. It was amazing what a difference being engaged to Cimorene made.

"They aren't as featherbrained as they sound," Cimorene told him. "They just act as if they are."

"I don't think I like the sound of that," Mendanbar said. "Are you sure they won't want to be bridesmaids anyway? Maybe we should just elope."

"No, it's too late for that," Cimorene told him. "Don't worry about it, though. It will work out fine."

"If you say so," Mendanbar said, but he was not really convinced.

The note Cimorene's mother sent to acknowledge the engagement only increased Mendanbar's misgivings. *I am delighted to hear that you are going to be properly settled at last, Cimorene dear,* ran the note. *I am enclosing a list of relatives and family friends who ought certainly to be included in your wedding plans, however unconventional those may be. Your father wishes to know which half of the kingdom your betrothed would prefer, as he is anxious to get the paperwork out of the way as soon as possible.*

"Half the kingdom?" Mendanbar asked cautiously.

Cimorene looked more than a little put out. "It's the usual reward for rescuing a princess from a dragon. I hoped they'd forgotten about it, but I should have known better. Mother would never do anything so incorrect."

"Well, I don't want it. One kingdom is more than enough for me."

"Then you'd better write them immediately and tell them so," Cimorene advised. "Otherwise they'll have all the forms and documents and records written out, signed by twenty noble witnesses, and sealed by every member of Father's Council, and you'll never be able to get rid of it."

"I'll see to it at once."

"Good." Cimorene picked up the long list of names that had been enclosed with the note. "I'll take this in to Willin, so someone can start addressing the invitations."

"Do we *have* to invite all of them?"

"We might as well," Cimorene said. "We're asking everyone else. And most of them are family."

"I think it would be easier to elope," Mendanbar said.

The guest list was enormous. Almost all the dragons were coming, and so were a great many of their princesses, past and present. After some initial misgivings, Cimorene's entire family decided to attend, including all six of her sisters and their husbands, her fourteen nieces and nephews, her parents, three of her aunts, two uncles, seventeen cousins, and her fairy godmother. Queen Alexandra was also coming, along with all twelve of her daughters. Mendanbar couldn't help feeling a little nervous about that, out of habit. All the kings and queens and princes and grand dukes who lived around the edges of the Enchanted Forest had had to be invited, and so had most of the odd and unusual people who lived inside the forest itself. Even the ogres and trolls had agreed to behave themselves if they were allowed to be present. In fact, the only people who *hadn't* been invited were the wizards.

"This wedding will be the best and most prestigious event in years!" Willin said happily as the acceptances poured in.

"It's certainly going to be the biggest," Mendanbar said, gazing at the stacks of paper in mild amazement. "Where are we going to *put* them all?"

"You are not to worry about that, Your Majesty," Willin told him sternly. "It is *my* job to oversee the preparations, and that includes arranging an appropriate place to hold the ceremony and the reception afterward."

"I really think it would have been easier to elope," Mendanbar grumbled.

* * *

In the end, they decided to hold the wedding in Fire-Flower Meadow. The gargoyle in Mendanbar's study complained about the decision long and loudly, because it would obviously be unable to attend, but the meadow was the only open area in the entire Enchanted Forest that would be large enough for the enormous crowd of guests.

"I bet you think that makes it all right," the gargoyle told Mendanbar and Cimorene several days before the wedding. "Just because *you* want to have hundreds and hundreds of people at *your* wedding, *I'm* supposed to smile and say I don't mind being left out. Well, it isn't all right and I won't do it!"

"I wouldn't expect you to smile about anything," Mendanbar muttered.

Cimorene studied the gargoyle thoughtfully. "If you're that eager to come, I suppose we could take the molding in that corner apart and find someone to bring you down to the field to watch," she offered.

The gargoyle looked down at her in alarm. "Take me *apart?* Oh, no, you don't! I'm not stupid. I know what would happen. Even if you managed to get me out of here without damaging me, you'd forget to put me back afterward, and I'd spend centuries in a storeroom somewhere. Dust and dry rot!"

"Well, then I'm afraid all I can do is stop in before I leave for the ceremony," Cimorene said. "Unless Telemain can fix up a spell on one of the windows so you can watch from here."

"I don't want that magician messing around with anything in my—wait a minute, did you say you'd stop in? You mean, here? In this room?"

"That's what she said," Mendanbar told it.

"I wasn't talking to you," the gargoyle said. Looking back at Cimorene, it went on, "You mean, you'd come and see me *before* the wedding?"

"That's right," Cimorene said, nodding.

"*Right* before? All dressed up and everything?"

"Of course," Cimorene promised.

"Hot dog!" said the gargoyle. "I'll take it! Oh, boy, I can hardly wait! This is going to be even better than going to the wedding."

"It is?" Mendanbar said suspiciously. "Why?"

"Because *I'll* get to see her all dolled up before *you* do, that's why," the gargoyle answered smugly. "Everybody knows the groom doesn't get to see the bride on the wedding day until the ceremony. And she's going to stop in here first! Oh, boy, oh, boy!"

Mendanbar looked at Cimorene.

"He's right, you know," Cimorene said apologetically. "And I've promised."

"He's never going to let me forget this," Mendanbar muttered and left to talk to Telemain about setting up Fire-Flower Meadow for the wedding.

Despite Willin's determination to handle the wedding plans himself, there were a number of things only Mendanbar could do. Among the most important was making sure that Fire-Flower Meadow and the area around it stayed firmly in one spot on the day of the wedding, so that all the guests could find it. This was not an easy thing to arrange. Even with Telemain's help, it took Mendanbar several days' worth of work before he was positive no one would miss the wedding because of a shift in the forest.

The night before the ceremony, Mendanbar and Telemain went over the whole field an inch at a time, to make certain that all the fire-flowers had been picked (so that none of the guests would get an accidental hotfoot) and to take care of any lingering minor enchantments. They found two princesses who had been turned into pinks, a frog prince, and a hedgehog that had once been somebody's groom. All of them were grateful to be disenchanted and very happy to be invited to the wedding.

The day of the wedding dawned bright and clear. Telemain had spent most of the previous week making sure that it would, while explaining to anyone who would listen that weather magic worked best if one set it up over a long period of time, which was what made it so difficult. The guests started arriving early, and Mendanbar was kept busy greeting them.

A large corner of the field had been roped off as a landing place for dragons, and for most of the morning the sky was full of flashing green wings. Ballimore and Dobbilan–who had come the previous evening to make sure their Cauldron of Plenty would have enough time to produce a proper wedding dinner for so many guests–directed traffic, as they were the only ones large enough for the dragons to see clearly from a distance amid the growing crowd.

Jack was early, too. He parked his wagon in a corner of the field and did a brisk business selling seven-league boots, cloaks of invisibility, and magic rings (along with wrapping paper and tape) to those who had forgotten to bring wedding presents. Nearby, all nine of Morwen's cats prowled on, around, under, and through the stacks of gifts that covered the six long benches that had been set out to hold them. Whenever someone brought a new package to lay on the benches, three of the cats would converge on him and purr loudly, while the others kept a watchful eye on the rest of the presents.

Slowly, the meadow filled up. Everyone was in a good mood, everyone was on his or her best behavior, and everyone was trying to be helpful.

Even Cimorene's family seemed to be having a good time. Her father was deep in conversation with Dobbilan, discussing ways of discouraging marauding giants. Several of her sisters were comparing notes with the dragons' ex-princesses, while her mother helped Queen Alexandra and her daughters (who did not seem nearly as awful as Mendanbar remembered) set bowls of punch and trays of sandwiches on a table at the far end of the meadow for people to nibble on until dinner was served.

Herman and his flock of children–including Crown Prince Jorillam–arrived and bought several bags of walnuts from Jack to feed the squirrels. Jorillam was delighted to discover that the squirrels would give him advice about quests. He went through three bags of nuts before the ceremony began and had to be almost dragged to his seat when the time came. His uncle, Prince Rupert, showed up at the last minute, wearing a black cloak and an enormous fake mustache. He looked very wicked and thoroughly pleased with himself.

Finally, everyone was there, everything was ready, and it was time. Resplendent in deep green velvet, milk white satin, and his best crown, Mendanbar waited nervously while the musicians, a talented group of Goldwing-Shadowmusic elves, began the wedding march. Willin, who had at first argued–but not very hard–that he was not a proper person to be a groomsman because he was Mendanbar's steward, came down the long, open aisle with Morwen, who was wearing her best black robe. Following them came Kazul, the matron-of-honor, and Telemain, Mendanbar's best man. Then came Cimorene, and Mendanbar forgot about everyone else.

Instead of her usual crown of black braids, Cimorene had let her hair hang in loose, shining waves down her back. She wore a wreath of fire-flowers, specially enchanted to burn without being hot or setting anything ablaze; from the wreath hung a veil of silver lace. Her bouquet was of fire-flowers, too, and her dress shimmering snow-silk trimmed with silver. She was stunningly beautiful.

The ceremony went by in a blur, but Mendanbar was pretty sure he hadn't made any mistakes because suddenly he was kissing Cimorene and everyone was cheering. He felt like cheering himself, except he would have had to stop kissing Cimorene.

A finger poked him surreptitiously. With considerable reluctance, Mendanbar broke away from Cimorene and turned.

"Enough," Telemain said in a voice so low Mendanbar could hardly hear it over the cheering. "Now it's time for the party."

Mendanbar looked at Cimorene, who gave him a wry smile as if to say that she didn't think it was enough, either, but there was nothing they could do about it now. He looked back at Telemain.

"I *knew* we should have eloped," he said.

Cimorene laughed and shook her head at him. "You don't really mean that, any more than you mean it when you complain about the gargoyle," she said, taking his arm.

"Who told you that?"

"The gargoyle did," she admitted, and they both laughed. "Come enjoy the party."

Arm in arm, the King and Queen of the Enchanted Forest went to accept the congratulations of their guests.

CALLING ON DRAGONS

For my nieces and nephews,

with love and the hope

that they will grow up reading

Contents

1

In Which a Great Many Cats Express Opinions

Deep in the Enchanted Forest, in a neat gray house with a wide porch and a red roof, lived the witch Morwen and her nine cats. The cats were named Murgatroyd, Fiddlesticks, Miss Eliza Tudor, Scorn, Jasmine, Trouble, Jasper Darlington Higgins IV, Chaos, and Aunt Ophelia, and not one of them looked anything like a witch's cat. They were tabby, gray, white, tortoiseshell, ginger, seal brown, and every other cat color in the world except a proper and witchy black.

Morwen didn't look like a witch any more than her cats looked as if they should belong to one. For one thing, she was much too young–less than thirty–and she had neither wrinkles nor warts. In fact, if she hadn't been a witch people might have said she was quite pretty. Her hair was the same ginger color as Jasmine's fur, and she had hazel eyes and a delicate, pointed chin. Because she was very short, she had to stand quite straight (instead of hunching over in correct witch fashion) if she wanted people to pay attention to her. And she was nearsighted, so she always had to wear glasses; hers had rectangular lenses. She refused even to put on the tall, pointed hats most witches wore, and she dressed in loose black robes because they were comfortable and practical, not because they were traditional.

All of this occasionally annoyed people who cared more about the propriety of her dress than the quality of her spells.

"You ought to turn him into a toad," Trouble said, looking up from washing his right front paw. Trouble was a large, lean gray tomcat with a crooked tail and a recently acquired ragged ear. He had never told Morwen exactly how he had damaged either the tail or the ear, but from the way he acted she assumed he had won a fight with something.

"Who should I turn into a toad?" Morwen asked, looking an unusually long way down. She was sitting sideways on her broomstick, floating comfortably next to the top of the front door, with a can of gold paint in one hand and a small paintbrush in the other. Above the door, in black letters partly edged in gold, ran the message "NONE OF THIS NONSENSE, PLEASE," which Morwen was engaged in repainting.

"That fellow who's making all the fuss about pointy hats and respect for tradition," Trouble replied. "The one you were grumbling about a minute ago–what's his name?"

"Arona Michaelear Grinogion Vamist," Morwen recited, putting the final gold line along the bottom of the "L" in "PLEASE." "And it's a tempting thought. But someone worse would probably replace him."

"Turn them all into toads. I'll help."

"Toads?" purred a new voice. A small ginger cat slithered out the open window and arched her back, then stretched out along the window ledge, where she could watch the entire front yard without turning her head. "I'm tired of toads. Why don't you turn somebody into a mouse for a change?" The ginger cat ran her tongue around her lips.

"Good morning, Jasmine," Morwen said. "I'm not planning to turn anyone into anything, at the moment, but I'll keep it in mind."

"That means she won't do it," said Trouble. He looked at his right paw, decided it was clean enough for the time being, and began washing his left.

"Won't do what?" said Fiddlesticks, poking his brown head out of the front door. "Who's not doing it? Why shouldn't he–or is that she? And who says so?"

"Turn someone into a mouse; Morwen; I certainly don't see why not; and she does," Jasmine said in a bored tone, and pointedly turned her head away.

"Mice are nice." Fiddlesticks shouldered the door open another inch and trotted out onto the porch. "So are fish. I haven't had any fish in a long time." He paused underneath Morwen's broom and looked up expectantly.

"You had fish for dinner yesterday," Morwen said without looking down. "And you ate enough breakfast this morning to satisfy three ordinary cats, so don't try to pretend you're starving. It won't work."

"Someone's coming," Jasmine observed from the window.

Trouble stood up and ambled to the edge of the porch. "It's the

Chairwitch of the Deadly Nightshade Gardening Club. Wasn't she just here last week?"

"It's Archaniz? Oh, bother," said Morwen, sticking her paintbrush into the can. "Has she got that idiot cat Grendel with her? I told her not to bring him anymore, but nine times out of ten she doesn't listen."

Fiddlesticks joined Trouble at the top of the porch steps. "I don't see him. I don't see anyone but her. I don't want to see her, either. She doesn't like me."

"That's because you talk too much," Trouble told him.

"I'm going inside," Fiddlesticks announced. "Then I won't have to see her. Maybe someone's dropped some fish on the floor," he added hopefully as he trotted into the house.

Morwen landed her broomstick and stood up, just as the Chairwitch reached the porch steps. The Chairwitch looked exactly as a witch ought: tall, with a crooked black hat, stringy black hair, sharp black eyes, a long, bony nose, and a wide, thin-lipped mouth. She hunched over as she walked, leaning on her broom as if it were a cane.

Morwen put the paint can on the window ledge next to Jasmine, set her broom against the wall, and said, "Good morning, Archaniz."

"Good morning, Morwen," Chairwitch Archaniz croaked. "What's this I hear about you growing lilacs in your garden?"

"Since I don't know what you've heard, I can't answer you," Morwen replied. "Come in and have some cider."

Archaniz pounded the end of her broom against the porch floor, breaking some of the twigs and scattering bits of dust and bark in all directions. "Don't be provoking, Morwen. You're a witch. You're supposed to grow poison oak and snakeroot and wolfsbane, not lilacs. You'll get thrown out of the Deadly Nightshade Gardening Club if you aren't careful."

"Nonsense. Where in the rules does it say that I can't grow what I please in my own garden?"

"It doesn't," Archaniz admitted. "And I'll tell you right away that you aren't the only one who puts a few lilacs and daylilies in with the rampion and henbane. Why, I've got a perfectly ordinary patch of daisies in the corner myself."

"Daisies." Jasmine snorted softly. "She would."

"But I've been getting complaints," Archaniz continued, "and I have to do *something* about them."

"What sort of complaints?"

"That the Deadly Nightshade Gardening Club is too normal for witches," Archaniz said gloomily. "That all we grow are everyday plants like cabbages and apples–"

"Apples are a basic necessity for witches," Morwen said. "And everyday plants don't turn the people who eat them into donkeys. Who's complaining?"

"Some fellow with an impossible name–Arona Mc-something-or-other."

"Arona Michaelear Grinogion Vamist?"

The Chairwitch nodded. "That's the one. I've gotten six regular letters and two by Eagle Express in the past month. He says he's going to write a letter to the *Times* next."

"He would," Trouble muttered. "I *said* you should turn him into a toad."

"That idea sounds better all the time," Morwen told Trouble. Then she looked back at Archaniz, who of course had not understood a word Trouble had said. "Vamist isn't a witch," Morwen said. "He's an idiot. Why worry about what he says?"

"That's all very well, Morwen, but if he convinces people he's right, it'll ruin our image. And if people think we're not dangerous, they'll come around asking for love potions and penny curses whenever they like. We'll be so busy mixing up cures for gout that we won't have time for the things *we* want to do. Look what happened to the sorceresses!"

"I haven't seen many of them around lately."

Archaniz nodded. "They got a reputation for being kind and beneficent, and the next thing you knew everyone was begging them for help. Most of them moved to remote islands or deep forests, just to get away from the pestering. It's all very well for you, Morwen, living out here in the Enchanted Forest anyway, but I–"

A loud yowl interrupted the Chairwitch in mid-sentence. An instant later, four cats tore around the corner of the house. The one in front was a heavy, short-legged tomcat with yellow eyes and fur as black as night. Behind him came a fat, long-haired tabby tomcat and two females, one a large calico and the other a fluffy white cat with blue eyes. The black cat streaked out into the front yard, made a hairpin turn, and leapt for the porch, where he clawed his way up Archaniz's skirts to a perch on her shoulder.

The three pursuing cats jumped gracefully onto the porch railing and sat down, curling their tails around their feet, just as Fiddlesticks poked his head out of the front door.

"What's all the noise about? Who's shouting? Is it a fight? Who's winning? Can I join?" With every question, Fiddlesticks pushed a little farther, until he was entirely outside the house, staring up at Archaniz and the cat on her shoulder. "Who's *that?*"

"Mrow!" said the black cat in a complaining tone. "Yow wow mrrrum!"

"Oh, yeah?" said Trouble. "Well, *your* father wears *boots!*"

Morwen gave the black cat a speculative look. "One of these days, I am going to have to work up a spell that will let me understand other people's cats as well as my own," she said to Archaniz. "What was that about?"

"We caught him nosing around in back of the garden," the long-haired tabby growled.

"He had no business there," the white cat added primly. "He's not one of *us,* after all. So we thought we would drive him away."

"Stupid creature was babbling something about a rabbit," the calico cat said with a disdainful look at the black cat. "As if that was any excuse."

"Why didn't you call me?" Trouble demanded. "I never get to have any fun." Radiating hurt pride, he stalked to the far end of the porch and disappeared into a large clump of beebalm.

"You know, people have been trying to perfect a universal cat-translating spell for years," Archaniz said to Morwen in a dry tone. She glanced at the cats on the porch railing. "If you *do* come up with one, I'd like a copy for myself."

"Nosy old biddy," said the calico cat.

"On second thought, perhaps it would be better if I left things as they are," Morwen said.

"Being disagreeable, are they?" Archaniz said knowingly. "It's only to be expected. Who ever heard of a polite cat?"

The black cat hissed. "Grendel!" said Archaniz. "Behave yourself. It wasn't that bad, and besides, you can use the exercise."

"He certainly can," said the calico cat.

"What's all this racket?" rumbled a low, sleepy cat voice from under the porch. "Dash it, can't a fellow take a nap in peace?" A moment later, a long cream-and-silver cat oozed around the steps to blink at the growing assembly above him.

"That's another thing, Morwen," Archaniz said, scowling at the newcomer. "Cats and witches go together, I admit. And I know they're a big help with your spells, but one really ought to observe some reasonable limits."

"I do," said Morwen. All nine cats were useful, particularly when it came to working long, involved spells that required both concentration and power. Nine cats working together could channel a lot of magic. To explain all this would sound uncomfortably like bragging, however, so Morwen only added, "Anyway, I like cats."

"She is simply jealous because we're all smarter than *he* is," the white cat informed Morwen with a look at the black cat on Archaniz's shoulder.

"What, all of you?" Morwen said, raising an eyebrow.

"All of us," the white cat said firmly. "Even Fiddlesticks."

"I'm very smart," Fiddlesticks agreed. "I'm *lots* smarter than Fatso there. Don't you think I'm smart, Morwen?"

Grendel hissed and bunched together as if he were preparing to launch himself from Archaniz's shoulder. Hastily, Archaniz put up her free hand to hold him back. "Perhaps I had better leave now," she said. "We can finish our discussion some other–"

"There's a big garden show coming up in Lower Sandis," Morwen said thoughtfully. "Why doesn't the Deadly Nightshade Garden Club enter an exhibit? If we all work together, we should be able to put together something quite impressive."

Archaniz considered. "Monkshood and snakeroot and so on? In a large black tent."

"And if everyone sends one or two really exotic things–"

"Morwen, you're a genius! People will talk about it for years, and that Airy McAiling Grinny person won't have a leg to stand on."

"I don't think it will be that simple," Morwen cautioned. "But an exhibit will buy us time to find out why he's so interested in making witches do things *his* way. And stop him."

"Of course," the Chairwitch said happily. "Let's see–Kanikak grows Midnight fire-flowers, and I have half a dozen Giant Weaselweeds. If I can talk Wully into letting us use her smokeblossoms . . ."

"I'll contribute two Black Diamond snake lilies and an invisible dusk-blooming chokevine," Morwen said. "I won't keep you any longer now; just let me know when you've got things arranged. Chaos, Miss Eliza, Scorn, wait for me inside, if you please."

The three cats sitting on the railing looked at each other. Then Chaos, the long-haired tabby, jumped down and sauntered past Fiddlesticks into the house. The white cat, Miss Eliza Tudor, followed, tail high, and Fiddlesticks fell in behind her, apparently without even thinking about what he was doing. Scorn sat where she was, staring stubbornly at Morwen.

"I'm not leaving while that idiot of hers is still here," Scorn said with a sidelong glance at Grendel and Archaniz. "There's no telling *what* he might get up to."

As this did not seem unreasonable, for a cat, Morwen let it pass. She walked Archaniz out into the yard, where there was plenty of room for a takeoff, and bade her a polite good-bye. As soon as the Chairwitch was out of sight above the trees, Morwen turned to go back inside. Jasper Darlington Higgins IV was sitting in front of the porch steps, watching her.

"Was that a good idea?" he said. "Invisible dusk-blooming chokevines aren't exactly easy to find, you know. Much less to grow. And you haven't got any, unless you've added them to the garden since early this morning."

"I'm well aware of that," Morwen said. "But I've been wanting some for a long time, to put along the fence by the back gate. Now I've got a good excuse to hunt them up."

"As long as you know what you're getting into," Jasper said. "Can I go back to sleep now, or is there going to be more noisy excitement?"

"Go to sleep," said Morwen. As she climbed the porch steps, she gave Scorn a pointed glare. Dignity dripping from every whisker, Scorn jumped down from the railing and walked into the house. Morwen shook her head, picked up her broomstick and her paint can, and followed.

2

In Which Morwen Encounters a Rabbit

Miss Eliza, Scorn, and Chaos were sitting in the kitchen, trying to look as if they were waiting for something interesting to happen and not as if they were doing as Morwen had told them. The only one who managed it was Scorn, who had jumped up onto the bench below the side window and begun washing her face. When Morwen entered, she looked up briefly and then returned to washing. In contrast, Chaos jumped guiltily and Miss Eliza Tudor looked away. There was no sign of Fiddlesticks.

"Archaniz has left, and Grendel has gone with her," Morwen said, setting the paint on the table. "Now, which of you three would like to begin?"

"Begin what?" Chaos asked warily.

Scorn stopped washing and snorted. "Don't be dense. She wants to know about our chasing Grendel."

"We have already explained that," Miss Eliza said.

"Not to my satisfaction," Morwen said. "You know better than to pick a fight with another witch's cat. At least, I thought you did."

"It's our job to keep things out of the garden," Chaos said, looking up with his green eyes wide. "That's all we were doing."

Morwen sighed. "Well, at least I don't have to ask who started it. What happened, exactly?"

The cats exchanged looks. "We were out by the back fence, the three of us and Aunt Ophelia and Murgatroyd," Miss Eliza said. "Chaos was in the apple tree–"

"As usual," Scorn put in. "You'd think it belonged to him."

"–and he saw that witch swoop down over the hill behind the house. He said he saw her cat jump off the broomstick–"

"Probably looking for that blue catnip that grows on the far side," Scorn said. "Grendel's a little too fond of his nibbles, if you ask me."

"Nobody did," said Chaos.

Miss Eliza glared at the other two and lashed her tail. *"If* I may continue . . . ?"

"Nobody's stopping you," Scorn said, and to show her complete indifference she bent sideways and began washing her side.

"We were concerned," Miss Eliza went on. "It seemed unusual. A minute or two later, while we were discussing whether to do anything about it, that black cat came tearing over the hill and down toward the garden, shouting about some rabbit."

"Stupid excuse for a cat," Chaos muttered. "Running away from a *rabbit!* I ask you!"

Scorn merely snorted expressively.

Miss Eliza looked at them. "While I do not like all these interruptions, I must confess that I agree with you. It is *not* the kind of behavior one hopes for in a cat."

"So you couldn't resist tearing off after him." Morwen shook her head.

"He was heading for the garden," Chaos said, avoiding her eyes. "We were just doing our job."

"Murgatroyd and Aunt Ophelia stayed in back, in case the rabbit showed up," Miss Eliza Tudor offered.

"At least that much was well done," Morwen said. "I think–"

"Morwen? Morwen? Open the door and let me in. Morwen?" The new cat voice floated in through the back window.

With a faint frown, Morwen crossed to the far door and opened it. Immediately, Aunt Ophelia, a spiky tortoiseshell cat, shot through the opening and bounded onto a chair. "Thank goodness! I was afraid you weren't going to hear me."

"I thought you and Murgatroyd were watching for rabbits," Morwen said.

"We found one," said the tortoiseshell. "And I think you had better go look at it."

"I suppose it's got fangs," Scorn said, looking down her nose. "Or webbed feet."

"You needn't sneer at Ophelia," Miss Eliza said. "The last one I chased out of the sweetpeas had both."

"Where is this interesting rabbit?" Morwen asked.

"Heading for the back fence," Aunt Ophelia said with poorly concealed relief. "Murgatroyd is in Chaos's apple tree, keeping an eye on it."

Morwen nodded and went out onto the back step. The garden seemed neat and peaceful, the square beds of vegetables on the left, the more exotic plants and herbs on the right. A shoulder-high row of new apple trees marched along the rear of the vegetable beds, just inside the picket fence. The first was just beginning to leaf out, the second was speckled with white blossoms, the third held a half-dozen marble-sized green fruit, and the fourth was beginning to drop its dark, rust-colored leaves as if in preparation for winter. At the far end of the garden stood a much older tree, heavily laden with apples that were just turning red. Below it, the back gate led out onto a grassy hill. An enormous lilac bush, nearly as tall as the apple tree, leaned over the fence on the right side of the gate.

There was no sign of Murgatroyd or of the interesting rabbit, so Morwen started toward the gate. Halfway there, she heard a thump and the top of the lilac thrashed violently.

"Murgatroyd?"

A loud hiss from the apple tree was followed by more thrashing in the lilac. "Get back, you, you–you *rabbit!"* snarled Murgatroyd's voice. "I warn you! Watch out, Morwen, it's in the lilac!"

"I suspected as much," Morwen said. "Exactly where–"

"Here," said a deep, mournful voice. "I'm stuck."

"If you break any of those branches, Morwen'll turn you into a lizard," Murgatroyd yelled from the apple.

"Lizards?" said Fiddlesticks from behind Morwen. "But I thought she was doing mice now."

"Quiet," Morwen said without looking back. "You in the lilac, hold still. Murgatroyd, stop making him nervous." She opened the gate and went slowly around the end of the lilac. "Now, then–good heavens."

Standing on the far side of the lilac was an enormous white rabbit. He was at least six feet tall, not counting the ears that drooped miserably down his back. Apart from his size, he did not seem unusual to Morwen: he had bright black eyes, a pink nose, and long whiskers. His front paw was caught in the branches of the lilac bush.

"I don't suppose you can do anything about this," the rabbit said gloomily. He tugged at his paw and the top of the lilac waved wildly to and fro.

From the apple tree, Murgatroyd hissed again. The rabbit cringed. "Stop that, both of you," Morwen commanded. "I think I can help if you'll hold still. What is your name, by the way?"

"Killer," said the rabbit in the same melancholy tone.

Morwen blinked, then shook her head. Rabbits had the oddest ideas about appropriate names. Perhaps it was because they had to come up with so many of them. She peered into the tangled heart of the lilac, then reached through the outer branches and tapped one of the fat trunks at the center. With a reluctant creak, the trunk bent slowly outward, freeing Killer's paw.

"My goodness," said the rabbit. He looked at his paw as if he were not quite sure it was properly attached, then shook it, then wiggled its toes. "My goodness gracious. Thank you very much, ma'am."

"Morwen. And I would still like that explanation."

A low, warning growl of agreement came out of the apple tree, and a moment later Murgatroyd scrambled down through the apple's branches to the fence rail.

Killer gave the cat a nervous look and began backing away. "It isn't a very interesting story. I'm sure you all have better things to do."

"All?" Morwen glanced back over her shoulder. Fiddlesticks, Miss Eliza, Aunt Ophelia, Jasmine, Trouble, Chaos, and Scorn were lined up in a long row at the bottom of the garden, staring at the rabbit. They made an intimidating picture. When Morwen looked at Killer again, he had retreated another couple of feet. Morwen glared.

"I, ah, was just going," said the rabbit. "You see, I'm late."

"For what?" Morwen demanded.

"Something important, I'm sure. Not that it matters. I'm always late, you see. It runs in the family; my brother even got himself a big gold pocket watch, and he still can't get anywhere on time."

"In that case, it won't matter if you're a little later. How did you happen to get caught in my lilac bush?"

The rabbit sighed. "I wanted something to eat, and this thing–you say it's a lilac?–looked large enough for a meal. It takes a lot to fill me up, now that I'm so big. Only I couldn't reach the bit I wanted, and when I tried, the branches twisted around and I got stuck, and then *he* snarled at me–" Killer broke off, cringing, as Murgatroyd demonstrated the snarl for Morwen's benefit.

Morwen frowned at the rabbit. "How long have you been six feet tall?"

"Seven feet, eleven inches," corrected Killer, "counting the ears. Since this morning. And it's no fun, believe me. I'm hungry all the time, and I don't fit in my hole, and I can't hide under bushes the way I used to."

"And how did you happen to grow so large so quickly?"

"I don't know." Killer sighed again and his ears lifted and dropped expressively. "I was just nibbling at my clover patch when all of a sudden everything started shrinking. The next thing I knew, I was nearly eight feet tall–counting the ears–and there wasn't enough clover for a snack, much less breakfast. It didn't even taste right," he finished sadly.

"Before or after you started growing?"

The rabbit's ears stiffened as he frowned in concentration. "The taste? Before. Definitely before. The leaves were a little sour and the stems didn't crunch right."

It sounded as if some enchanted seeds had gotten mixed in with the clover, and Killer had eaten the sprouts. If Morwen was lucky, he wouldn't have eaten all of them. A plant that increased one's size would be a valuable addition to the garden, even if it only worked on rabbits. "I'd like to see this clover patch."

"Well . . ." Killer hesitated. "Do you have to bring *them?* I don't like cats."

"I don't think I'll need everyone," Morwen said. "Aunt Ophelia, Trouble, and Miss Eliza will be quite enough."

"Why can't I come?" Fiddlesticks trotted up to the gate and inspected the rabbit through the slits. "I didn't get to chase Fatso, and I didn't get to chase the rabbit. My, he's big. And I didn't get any fish."

"You talk too much, that's why," Trouble told him.

"Perhaps you should go tell Jasper what's happened," Miss Eliza put in.

"Right," said Fiddlesticks. "Maybe he's caught a mouse while we've been out here talking to rabbits. Maybe he'll share!" And he bounded off.

"Optimist," said Scorn, looking after him.

"If we are going to look at *vegetables,"* said Aunt Ophelia in tones that conveyed her poor opinion of the entire undertaking, "perhaps we should get it over with."

"Are you done for now, Morwen?" Jasmine asked. "Because if you are, I'm going back to the window before someone else grabs it."

"Go ahead," Morwen told her. Immediately, Jasmine and Scorn took off at a dead run for the house. Morwen turned to the rabbit. "Now, about this clover patch . . . ."

Killer dropped to all fours, which brought his head nearly level with Morwen's. He sniffed the air twice and cocked an ear to the right. "That way." He started off, and Morwen and the three chosen cats followed.

After ten minutes, Morwen was wishing she had brought her broomstick. Killer set an extremely uneven pace, taking two or three long hops that would nearly carry him out of sight and then pausing to sniff the air and twitch his whiskers nervously. It would have been much easier to follow him by air, Morwen thought, but she did not say anything because it would only encourage the cats to complain. Trouble, in particular, was extremely put out at having to let a rabbit lead. To make up for it, he pretended to stalk Killer, slinking around trees like a gray shadow and muttering under his breath. Aunt Ophelia and Miss Eliza contented themselves with making malicious remarks. Fortunately, Killer was usually too far ahead to hear any of them.

When they finally reached the clover patch, Morwen was nearly as cross as her cats. Killer did not seem to notice. He sat back on his haunches, waved proudly, and said, "Here we are!"

"This is it?" Trouble said, staring at an irregular mat of small green plants. It was no more than four feet across, and a third of the plants had been nipped neatly off, leaving only short, bare stems. "That's *all?*"

"It's much larger when I'm my normal size," Killer said in an apologetic tone. "And it's got much better flavor than the one by the little pond or the one by the currant bush. At least, it used to."

Morwen suppressed a sigh of irritation. As long as she'd come this far, she'd better have a look at the thing, even if it didn't seem particularly promising. Pushing her glasses firmly into their proper position–they had slid down her nose a little on the walk–she knelt beside the clover patch.

At first glance, nothing looked out of the ordinary. Trouble came up beside her and sniffed at the plants. "Don't nibble on any of them," Morwen said.

"I'm not *stupid,*" said Trouble.

"No, but you've done things like that before," Aunt Ophelia put in. "Don't interrupt Morwen while she's working."

Trouble licked his front paw twice, displaying his unconcern to the world at large, then pounced on an imaginary mouse in the middle of the clover patch.

"Morwen, there's something rather odd over here," Miss Eliza said. She was crouched at the opposite edge of the clover patch, and her tail was lashing back and forth in a way that belied her casual tone. "When you have a moment, you may wish to look at it closely."

"I'll take a moment now," Morwen said, rising. "What is it?"

"These." Miss Eliza sat back and waved a paw at the moss in front of her. A six-inch strip next to the clover patch was peppered with small brown spots, as if someone had pushed the end of a pencil into it several times.

"You're quite right," Morwen said. "This is odd. Killer, do you remember which part of this patch you were nibbling on when you started to grow?"

"Not really. Does it matter?"

"It might. Trouble, would you please look around and see whether you can find any more of these spots?"

"Oh, all right," said Trouble, but his yellow eyes gleamed with pleasure as he circled the clover patch.

"What are they?" Aunt Ophelia asked, joining Miss Eliza at Morwen's side. "Besides odd."

"I don't know. They *look* like a small version of–"

"Morwen!" Trouble yelled from the foot of a nearby tree. "Here's a big one!"

With a sinking feeling, Morwen crossed to Trouble's side, followed by the other cats. In the moss at the foot of the tree, just where someone might have set the end of a staff to lean against the trunk, was a dead brown circle about two inches across.

"A wizard!" Morwen said. "I was afraid of this."

3

In Which Morwen Makes a Discovery and Some Calls

There was an instant of silence, and then all of the animals tried to talk at once.

"One at a time, please," Morwen said. "Or I won't understand a thing any of you are trying to say. Killer first."

"The *rabbit?*" Trouble curled his lip back, showing his fangs in an expression that wasn't quite a snarl. "Why *him?*"

"Courtesy to a guest," Morwen replied. "Killer?"

"It's just a hole in the moss," said the rabbit. "It doesn't look like a wizard to me."

"Of course *that's* not a wizard," Aunt Ophelia said. *"That* is what a wizard's staff does when it touches a part of the Enchanted Forest. I thought everyone knew that."

"He obviously hasn't been paying attention to the news for at least a year," Miss Eliza said. "Possibly longer." She switched her tail. "Are you even aware that the King of the Enchanted Forest has been married for nearly fourteen months?"

"Stop badgering," Morwen said to the cats. "And remember that you are in something of a privileged position when it comes to news from the castle." She turned to Killer. "Queen Cimorene has been a friend of mine since before the wedding, and we still keep in touch."

"You knew about the wizards' staffs long before then," Miss Eliza objected.

"Knew what about wizards' staffs?" Killer's ears swiveled from the cats to Morwen. "That they make holes in the forest?"

"Exactly," Morwen said. "Wizards' staffs absorb magic from anything that happens to be around. Unfortunately, in the Enchanted Forest *everything* is magical, one way or another, and when a staff soaks up enough magic it kills part of the forest."

"And this certainly looks like the kind of thing that happens when a wizard sets down the end of this staff," Miss Eliza said. "Careless creatures."

"Well, if this bit is from a wizard's staff, what made all those tiny dots back by that clover patch?" Aunt Ophelia said. "Miniature wizards?"

"Quite possibly," Morwen replied. "If a wizard worked a size-changing spell in this area and let a little spill over into the clover patch, it would explain Killer's unusual growth very nicely."

Miss Eliza's nose twitched as if she smelled something unpleasant. "I *said* they were careless."

"Yes, but look, Morwen, this can't be wizards," Trouble said. "The King chased all of them out of the forest before he got married."

"One of them seems to have come back," Morwen said, looking pointedly at the bare spot. "And I think we had better notify the King immediately."

"Couldn't you just, uh, plant something new in the hole and forget about it?" asked Killer nervously. "I mean, the King must have more important things to do than worry about my clover patch."

All three of the cats swiveled their heads and stared at him with disapproval.

The rabbit's ears wilted under their combined gaze. "It was just a thought."

"On the contrary," said Miss Eliza.

Aunt Ophelia shrugged. "What do you expect from a rabbit?"

"It's the wizards that are important, not your clover," said Trouble. "If there *are* wizards."

"Nothing else I know of does *that."* Morwen pointed at the hole.

"Just because you don't know of it doesn't mean there isn't something," Trouble retorted.

"Mmhmph. I suppose you're right." Morwen considered for a moment. She couldn't tell whether the holes had been made by a wizard's staff or not, but she knew at least three people who could. The first two were the King of the Enchanted Forest and his Queen, Cimorene. The third . . . "I'd better give Telemain a call, then, as well as Mendanbar and Cimorene. If we're lucky, he'll think it's a fascinating challenge."

"And if we're not, he'll prose on about it for hours," Trouble muttered.

"Who's Tele-whatsis?" asked Killer.

"An old friend and magical theoretician," Morwen said. "He's interested in wizards."

"Among other things." Trouble poked his nose into the brown spot, then pulled it back very quickly and sneezed. "Can we go now?"

Morwen started back toward the clover patch. "As soon as I take a sample of Killer's clover."

"I guess I'll be going, then," Killer said, backing away as he spoke. "Nice meeting you and all that."

"Don't be silly," Morwen said over her shoulder. "You're coming with us. I want you to tell your story to Telemain and the King. And how else are you going to get a decent meal?"

The rabbit didn't answer, and Morwen stopped paying attention to him. Kneeling next to the clover patch once more, she reached into the loose left sleeve of her robe, which she used as a sort of enchanted backpack. The spell on her sleeves allowed her to carry around all kinds of useful things, but it required a certain amount of concentration to retrieve them. And, of course, she had to remember what she had put into the sleeve in the first place.

"Sample jars," she muttered to herself. "Small sample jars with the lids that clamp down–ah!" With a smile of satisfaction, she pulled a glass jar the size of her fist out of the sleeve. The glass had a faint purple tint, and the lid was a glass bubble that was attached to the jar with a complicated-looking wire clamp. Morwen flicked the wire with her thumb, and the lid popped up. She could hear Killer and the cats arguing in the background, but she refused to listen. Reaching into her sleeve once more, she took out a small pair of herb snips and began cutting clover.

By the time the jar was half-full, the argument had stopped and the animals had joined her. Half a jar was enough, for now, Morwen decided. She clamped the lid down and put the jar and snips back into her sleeve, then rose, dusting bits of clover off her hands.

"Are you all ready to go now?" she asked.

"Yes," said Miss Eliza.

"No," said Killer. Trouble glared at him. "I mean, yes. I suppose so. Oh, I don't *like* cats!"

"That's what comes of being a rabbit," Aunt Ophelia said. "Size makes no difference whatsoever."

"Come along, then," Morwen said, and started briskly off in the direction of the house. The sooner she got home and relayed her news to the King, the better.

* * *

When they arrived home, the other cats were lined up in the garden, waiting for them. Chaos was loudly surprised to see that the rabbit was still tagging along, and Fiddlesticks demanded explanations and fish in the same breath, while Jasmine pretended to find the whole affair boring beyond expression.

"You'll just have to wait a bit longer," Morwen said over the racket. "I've work to do. In the meantime, try to remember that Killer is a guest."

"Killer?" said Fiddlesticks. "Who's Killer?"

"The rabbit, you idiot," Trouble told him as Morwen went into the house.

The closing door cut off whatever else Trouble might have had to say. Morwen shook her head but did not go back outside. As long as the cats left Killer alone and didn't damage each other too much, it was better to let them settle matters among themselves. Frowning in concentration, Morwen reached into her sleeve and pulled out the sample jar of clover. She set it on the kitchen table, then turned around and went out through the door by which she had just entered.

The door now led into her study. Making that door–and the various rooms it led to–had taken Morwen a great deal of time and effort, considerably more than her sleeves, but it had been worth every minute. She had added a library, a study, several bedrooms for visitors, a magic workshop, and a large storage area since she moved in, and all without using up any of the garden. And there was still space for three or four more rooms, if she needed them, before she'd have to add a second magic door.

Frowning slightly, Morwen skirted the cluttered desk and stopped in front of an oval mirror in the corner. The silvered glass was the size of a serving platter, and it was surrounded by a gilt frame three inches wide. The effect was a little too elaborate for Morwen's taste, but when someone makes one a present of a state-of-the-art magic mirror, one doesn't turn it down simply because it doesn't fit in with one's decor. *I suppose I'll get used to it eventually,* she thought. *After all, I only got around to hanging it this morning.*

"All right, let's see if this thing works as well as he said it would," she muttered. Taking a deep breath, she said clearly,

"Mirror, mirror, on the wall,
I would like to make a call."

Immediately, the mirror turned milky white and a pleasant voice from somewhere inside the glass said, "What party are you calling, please?"

"The King of the Enchanted Forest," Morwen answered, impressed in spite of herself. Telemain had been right; this was an enormous improvement over the mirrors Morwen had used in the past. And on top of that, it was polite.

"One moment, please," said the mirror.

Almost before it finished speaking, the glass cleared. Morwen blinked, startled. The face looking out at her was dark brown, with bulging eyes and a wide mouth full of crooked teeth. "This is the castle of the King of the Enchanted Forest, you lucky person," said the face with a leer. "Nobody else is here to answer the mirror, so you're gonna have to leave a message with–oh, it's you."

By this time, Morwen had recognized the bad-tempered wooden gargoyle that occupied the upper corner of King Mendanbar's study. "Good morning, gargoyle. Do Mendanbar and Cimorene know how you answer their mirror?"

The gargoyle snorted. "It was her idea. She thought it might cut down on the stupid questions people ask."

"I might have guessed. Where are they? I've got some news they should hear right away."

"They've gone to the beach with Kazul," the gargoyle said in tones of disgust. "Work's piling up, but do they care? No! Do they even ask if it's a good idea? No! They just pack a bag of towels and take off. Poof!"

"I see. In that case–"

"He humors her too much," the gargoyle went on confidentially. "She's healthy as a horse, but you wouldn't know it, the way he fusses over her. And I'm going to have to put up with it for another six or seven months, at least! What he'll be like when the baby actually arrives–well, all I can say is that I'm going to have a full-time job trying to see that the kid isn't spoiled rotten."

"I expect Cimorene will help," Morwen said. "How soon will they be back?"

"How should I know? I'm not a secretary."

"Well, as soon as they arrive–*either* of them–tell them that I've reason to think that there's a wizard running around in the forest."

The gargoyle's eyes widened, making him look even uglier than before. "A wizard? Hoo boy!"

"I'm going to call Telemain next," Morwen went on. "If we're not here when they call back, tell them to come on out anyway. The cats can show them how to find us."

"I bet," the gargoyle muttered. "Anything else? 'Cause if there isn't, I'm going back to sleep."

"That's all," Morwen said, and the mirror clouded over. As soon as it cleared, she repeated the rhyme and snapped, "Telemain," in response to the mirror's polite question.

This time it took much longer for the glass to clear. When it did, Telemain's face scowled out of the mirror. His ferocious expression lightened only fractionally when he saw who was calling.

"Oh, hello, Morwen! Will this take long? I've just set up an exceedingly sensitive spell to test the stability quotient of–"

"It's wizards," Morwen interrupted. "Well, one of them, at the very least, though in my experience whenever one turns up a half-dozen more are sure to follow. They're worse than cockroaches."

"You're in a poor humor this morning." Telemain ran a hand across his neat black beard, a sure sign that he was interested but didn't want to show it. "What about this wizard?"

"He appears to have been poking around near my home," Morwen said. "Or so I conclude from the splotches his staff left in the moss."

Telemain shook his head. "That is quite impossible. The warding enchantment that Mendanbar and I worked out keeps wizards from absorbing, manipulating, utilizing, or controlling any portion of the magical basis on which the Enchanted Forest is founded. So even if a wizard were unwise enough to enter the forest, his staff could not possibly leave, er, 'splotches in the moss.' "

"I know it's *supposed* to work that way," Morwen said. "But the splotches are there. So is a six-foot rabbit–this wizard is careless as well as nosy and impossible. If you don't believe me, come and look at them yourself."

"I believe I shall," Telemain said. "It'll only take me a few minutes to set up the transportation spell, and firsthand observation is always superior to reports from even the most reliable of witnesses. Now, let me see; I had better bring the microdynometer, and some detection instruments, and–"

He turned away, muttering to himself, and the mirror blanked abruptly. Morwen rolled her eyes.

"He's in rare form today," said Aunt Ophelia from behind her. "What was that about 'reliable witnesses'?"

Turning, Morwen saw the tortoiseshell cat standing just inside the open study door. "Since it came from Telemain, I'd have to say it was a compliment."

"Someone should take him in hand before he talks himself into a real mess."

"He can take care of himself," Morwen said. "If he couldn't, someone would have murdered him years ago. I've been tempted a time or two myself." Out of habit, she glanced around the study to see if there was anything she needed. Then she walked out to the kitchen and picked up the can of paint she'd abandoned there after Archaniz's visit. With a little luck, she could finish touching up the sign over the door before any of her visitors arrived.

4

In Which Morwen and Telemain Argue and Killer Discovers the Perils of Mixing Cosmetics and Magic

By the time Telemain appeared in the front yard, Morwen had finished the sign and was cleaning her brush. He did a tidy transportation spell, Morwen had to admit, even if her own taste ran more to flying. The passage hadn't even ruffled his dark hair. He'd clearly come prepared: The many pockets of his open knee-length black vest were bulging, and so were the pouches that hung from his wide black belt. Seven magic rings glittered on his fingers, three on his left hand, four on his right. His bright blue eyes were alight with anticipation.

"Well, it's about time," Aunt Ophelia said acidly as he walked up the porch steps.

"Hello to you, too," Telemain said, nodding far more politely than he would have if he'd understood her comment. "There you are, Morwen! Where are these hypothetical wizards of yours?"

"I bet he doesn't even know which one of us you are," Scorn said from the porch rail. "Hypothetical wizards, indeed!"

"What's that?" Fiddlesticks shouted from inside the house.

On the window ledge, Jasmine yawned, curling up her tongue and stretching her head back. Then she called back, "Telemain's here."

"Who's here?" Fiddlesticks poked his head around the edge of the door. "Telemain! Chaos, Murgatroyd, Trouble, Telemain's here!"

"Chaos and Trouble are watching that *rabbit,*" said Miss Eliza, in a tone that indicated clearly that she would have liked very much to call it something else but was far too polite to actually do so.

"If I knew where the wizards were, I wouldn't need your help," Morwen said to Telemain. "The dead spots in the moss are about twenty minutes' walk from my back garden, if the forest hasn't moved them."

"Twenty minutes! Morwen, I don't have time–"

"I'd have told you to transport straight there, but I don't think you've been to the place before, and there's no sense in taking chances. Besides, it'll only take two minutes by broomstick, even riding double and with an extra load."

Telemain shook his head. "No. No. Absolutely not. I have no intention of riding on that uncomfortable contraption of yours ever again. Once was quite enough."

"Wimp," said Scorn.

"You only think broomsticks are uncomfortable because you insist on riding astride," Morwen said to Telemain. "If you'd sit sidesaddle, the way you're supposed to–"

"No!"

"Well, if you really want to hand-carry a bucket of soapy water mixed with a little lemon juice on a twenty-minute walk–"

"What? Morwen, you didn't say anything about buckets."

"Water?" Fiddlesticks sat up very straight, his nose twitching. "Buckets of water? With *soap?* Maybe I won't come with you this time, either, Morwen."

"I thought the buckets were obvious," Morwen told Telemain. "If there are wizards around, I want to be able to get rid of them in a hurry." And the only way to do that, so far as anyone knew, was to dump a bucket of soapy water mixed with a little lemon juice over the top of them. For some reason, this made them melt into a gooey puddle, and it usually took several days for them to put themselves together again. Cimorene had discovered the method by accident, back when she was living with the dragon Kazul.

"Soapy water," Telemain muttered. "Buckets. I still say it's terribly inelegant."

"If you'd finish working out a spell to do the same thing, the buckets wouldn't be necessary," Morwen pointed out.

Telemain flushed. "I've designed a prototype, but it requires the immediate accessibility of a target. It has therefore been impossible for me to run the necessary tests to ascertain its effectiveness."

"What?" said Fiddlesticks.

"He's invented a spell for melting wizards, but he can't tell whether it works because there aren't any wizards around to try it on," Miss Eliza said.

"Oh. Why couldn't he just say that?"

"Because that's how he is," said Aunt Ophelia.

"We still need the buckets," Morwen said to Telemain. "I haven't the slightest objection to your testing your new wizard-melting spell on any wizards we run across, but I want to bring something that I *know* works, in case your spell needs some adjusting."

"Reasonable." Telemain rubbed his chin thoughtfully. "But I still categorically refuse to travel on that broomstick of yours."

"Morwen?" Even muffled by the front door, Trouble's tone was clearly far too casual, and when he strolled out onto the porch Morwen felt a strong twinge of misgiving. Every whisker dripped the kind of deliberate unconcern that usually meant he'd been living up to his name.

"Excuse me a moment, Telemain," Morwen said. "What is it, Trouble?"

"You know that rabbit you wanted us to watch?"

Morwen's misgivings deepened. "Yes?"

"Well, he's kind of upset," Trouble said. "Murgatroyd thought I'd better come tell you."

If Murgatroyd thought Morwen should be told about it, it was probably serious. Not urgent, though, or he'd have come himself, at a dead run. And he didn't expect Morwen to be happy about it, or he wouldn't have sent Trouble. Morwen sighed. "What is Killer upset about?"

"Oh, things. I wouldn't have bothered you if Murgatroyd hadn't insisted."

"Such a fuss about a *rabbit.*" Aunt Ophelia sniffed.

Trouble studied the porch roof, as if he were hoping to spot a fly. "Not exactly."

"I see." Morwen turned to Telemain. "I appear to be needed in the garden. You're welcome to come along."

"Certainly."

All of the cats followed them, except Jasmine, who had fallen asleep on the window ledge, and Jasper, who was presumably still napping under the porch. When they reached the garden, they found the grass inside the gate trampled flat and a six-foot donkey with a blotchy brown-and-white coat standing next to the vegetable patch. The donkey wore a mournful expression, and half a cabbage leaf was stuck to the side of his muzzle. The green cabbage directly in front of him was missing a large chunk from its left side.

"Hello, Killer," Morwen said to the donkey.

"I thought Killer was a rabbit," Telemain said, frowning in mild puzzlement.

"He was, until he started eating my cabbage." Morwen eyed the donkey reprovingly.

"He *ate* a *cabbage?*" Fiddlesticks said, horrified. "Why would he do *that?*"

"I was hungry," said the donkey. His tail switched and he jumped, startled.

"Hmph," said Aunt Ophelia. "Just what I'd expect from a rabbit."

"Yes, you'd think anyone would have more sense than to nibble on plants in a witch's garden," Miss Eliza said.

"I thought the gray cat said it was all right. And it tasted very nice. Almost spicy. And the crunch–" The donkey stopped as all the cats glared, and his ears drooped. "I must have misunderstood."

Morwen glanced around. Trouble was nowhere in sight. "I don't think you misunderstood him at all." She looked sternly at Chaos and Murgatroyd. "Why didn't you stop him?"

"You've got plenty of donkey-cabbages," Chaos said. "And donkeys are nearly as stupid as rabbits, so it's not as if Killer lost anything by it."

"I think it's a definite improvement," Murgatroyd said, nodding.

"A six-foot donkey doesn't look nearly as silly as a six-foot rabbit," Aunt Ophelia put in.

"Seven feet, eleven inches, counting the ears," said the donkey, twitching them. "I always know how big I am."

"That is not the point," Morwen told the cats. "You were left here to prevent any untoward happenings. This is an extremely untoward happening. I am seriously displeased."

"And you know what that means," Scorn said. "No fish in the food bowl tonight."

"No fish?" Fiddlesticks looked up at Morwen with large, distressed eyes. "Not even for me?"

"I'm sorry about this, Killer," Morwen said. "Those cabbages aren't supposed to work on rabbits." She paused, considering. The red cabbages on the other side of the row were an antidote, but she wasn't sure she wanted to mention that. It was entirely possible that they wouldn't work, or that Killer would end up turning into a twelve-foot-tall rabbit or something even more inconvenient.

"Can't you do anything?" the donkey said. "It's not that I mind being a donkey, exactly, but I don't like what it did to my coat."

"He *is* awfully blotchy," Scorn said.

"Interesting," Telemain murmured. "You say these plants aren't supposed to work on rabbits, Morwen? And this rabbit was already under the influence of a magnifying enchantment. So the layered interaction of the two magical energies produces a synergistic effect . . ."

Killer looked at Telemain, and his ears twitched forward. "Is that why my coat is all funny?"

"Highly unlikely," Telemain said. "The two spells seem to affect primarily the parameters of form and stature, rather than coloration."

Morwen stared at the donkey. Suddenly her eyes narrowed. "Killer, do you dye your fur?"

"I, um–well, actually . . ."

"I thought so. That's what your problem is. Spells are hard on cosmetic changes. The dye job lasted through one spell, but now that you've been enchanted twice it's wearing off."

"Oh *no,*" said Killer. "You mean if you turn me back into a rabbit, I'll look even *worse?*"

"Probably," Morwen said. "And you won't be able to redye it until the residue of the spell wears off. That usually takes about six weeks."

"How do you know all this?" Telemain asked her.

Morwen gave him a look. "Why do you think witches never color their hair?"

"This is terrible." Killer's ears waggled in distress, and several of the cats snickered. "I won't be able to hold up my head. This is *awful.* Can't you do anything?"

"Not right now," Morwen said. "We have some wizard hunting to do. And if you're willing to help, you may have solved a little problem for us."

"I don't mind being helpful," said Killer. "What problem?"

Morwen turned to Telemain. "You can ride *him* instead of the broomstick. He knows how to find the clover patch, and at that size he ought to move fairly quickly. I'll take the broomstick and a bucket and meet you there. And you can study the interaction of the size- and shape-changing spells on the way."

Less than ten minutes later, Morwen, Telemain, and Killer met at the half-eaten patch of clover. As Morwen landed her broomstick–with some care, so as not to spill the bucket she had hung on the front end–Scorn and Fiddlesticks slid out of the bushes and sat down at the foot of the nearest tree. The two cats wore identical smug expressions.

"What are you doing here?" Morwen said.

"We all discussed it and decided you might need help," Scorn replied. "Aunt Ophelia and Miss Eliza came last time, Trouble and Murgatroyd and Chaos are in disgrace because of the cabbages, and Jasmine didn't want to be bothered. So it came down to the three of us."

"Three of you?"

"Jasper's around somewhere."

"I came because I'm very brave," Fiddlesticks announced. He rose and sauntered over to the clover patch. "Don't you think I'm brave, Morwen? What's all this prickly stuff?" He sniffed at the bare stalks on the eaten portion of the patch.

"That's Killer's clover patch," Morwen said. "Don't eat any of it."

"Eat it?" Fiddlesticks looked up, green-gold eyes wide. "Why would I eat it? It's some kind of *plant."*

"We know," Scorn said. "Shut up."

Telemain slid down from Killer's back, stepped quickly to one side, and shook himself as if to check that everything still worked. Then he walked over to Morwen. With a glance over one shoulder to make sure Killer was out of hearing distance, he said in a low voice, "Morwen, this is absolutely the last time I agree to one of your . . . your ideas. That beast has a gait that would rattle the teeth out of a troll."

"It's not my fault," Killer said. "I'm supposed to be a rabbit."

Telemain looked startled, then chagrined.

"You forgot how long his ears are," Morwen said. "Never mind. The tracks I told you about are over here."

She led the way to the cluster of brown pencil-sized holes at the far side of the clover patch. When he saw them, Telemain immediately lost interest in the rest of his surroundings.

"Fascinating," he murmured. He pulled something that looked like a bright metal tube in a wire cage from one of his pockets and began twisting and pulling and unfolding. In less than two minutes, he held a small telescope attached to three long, spidery legs. He jabbed the legs into the moss and peered through the end of the telescope. "Absolutely fascinating. The residual energy displays the characteristic spiral, but its concentration–"

"Tell me about it when you decide what it is," Morwen said. She was in no mood for one of Telemain's long digressions into magical theory, even if she was one of the few people who actually understood most of what he said. Besides, listening only encouraged him.

Telemain peered through his telescope again, then pulled out several other peculiar instruments and poked at the holes. Finally he looked up. "Where's the other one?"

"Other one?" Morwen said. Even when he was being simple, Telemain didn't seem to be able to make himself clear.

"The full-sized, er, splotch. I believe you said there was one?"

"Trouble found it." Leaving Killer to nibble disconsolately at the moss and the cats to wander as they pleased, Morwen led Telemain to the two-inch circle of brown moss. "There."

"This is really amazing. Look here, Morwen, along the perimeter. There's no regeneration occurring at all. And–"

"Yes, of course," Morwen interrupted. "But all I want to know is, is it wizards?"

"Oh, certainly. That's what I was saying," Telemain replied with maddening innocence. "And it looks as if they've figured out how to evade the enchantment the King and I worked out. You were quite right to call me."

"Quite right?" Scorn said with considerable indignation. "That self-centered, conceited idiot! Of course you were quite right. Magicians, bah!" Tail stiff with disapproval, she stalked off.

"Exactly," said Morwen. "Now, what was the bit about that enchantment of yours?"

"Of mine and the King's." Telemain was a stickler for accuracy, even when it meant sharing the credit for a major magical achievement. He pointed at the brown spot in front of him, then waved back toward the clover patch. "None of these should be here."

"Well, obviously. Wizards aren't supposed to come into the Enchanted Forest any–" Morwen stopped short. "That isn't what you meant. Very well. Explain what you *did* mean, and none of your jargon. I've too much on my mind already without trying to unravel your sentences."

Telemain looked hurt. "I'm only trying to be precise."

"Right now I'll be quite content with fast and sloppy. Now, why shouldn't there be any dead patches in the moss?"

"Because the spell Mendanbar and I worked out should–should repair them as soon as they're made," Telemain said carefully. "As long as the spell is working, the absorptive properties of the wizard's staff should be balanced immediately by the recirculation of–"

"Telemain!"

"I'm trying," Telemain said in a plaintive tone. "There just isn't any other way to say it."

"No?" Morwen thought for a minute. "How about this: When a wizard's staff sucks up magic from the forest, your spell sucks it back. And it works so fast that the moss shouldn't die this way."

"Or it should regenerate," Telemain said, nodding. "This has obviously not done either."

"Can you tell how they did it?"

"Not without an examination of the primary linkages." Telemain frowned down at the dead moss. "If something has damaged one of them, it might account–"

A loud cat squall erupted from behind a nearby bush, followed by a high shriek. Morwen started forward, but before she had taken two steps,

Fiddlesticks came trotting around the left side of the bush. He held his head very high, and his tail was a long brown exclamation mark. Dangling from his mouth by a bunched-up wad of blue-and-brown wizard's robes was a man about six inches tall.

5

In Which the Plot Thickens

Fiddlesticks halted just in front of Morwen's feet. The man he was carrying kicked, then tried to punch backward and overhead at the cat's nose. Fortunately, he missed. Fiddlesticks growled and shook his head, and the man shrieked as he swung back and forth.

"How interesting," Telemain said. "Morwen, your cat appears to have captured a miniature wizard."

"So I see," Morwen said. "What did you do with his staff?"

"Mmmph hmmmph uff," said Fiddlesticks, and jabbed his tail back toward the bush.

"Good. Don't let him anywhere near it." Morwen turned and started for the clover patch.

"Where are you going?" Telemain said.

"To get the bucket," Morwen called over her shoulder. There was another high-pitched shriek from the wizard and a jumbled protest from Telemain, both of which she ignored. Having collected her bucket, she returned to find the wizard on his feet with Fiddlesticks standing guard. Telemain sat cross-legged in front of them, holding something that looked like a silver watch with an orange dial and four hands. He kept looking from the watch to the wizard and back.

"Has he told you what they're up to yet?" Morwen said, setting the bucket down a little to one side, where it would be handy but out of the immediate way.

Telemain looked up, frowning. "I haven't asked. Do you realize that this is the first opportunity I have had to observe a wizard *in situ?* Of course, the magical connections would be clearer if his staff were a little closer."

"You leave that staff where it is," Morwen said. "Fiddle, if either of them tries to go get it, stop them. I don't care how."

"You don't? That's easy, then." Fiddlesticks curled his lips back, showing most of his teeth. "Did I do good? Does this mean I can have fish for dinner?"

"It certainly does," Morwen said. "And possibly a bowl of cream as well. Where's Scorn?"

"With Jasper, watching the staff. Do they get fish, too?"

"Yes, if they want it." Morwen transferred her attention to the six-inch wizard. He had a sharp, angular face half-covered by an untidy brown beard, and he seemed a little young compared to most of the wizards Morwen had met. Not to mention short. "If it won't interfere with your observations, Telemain, I'd like to ask this fellow a few questions."

"Hmmm? Oh, not at all." Telemain did not even glance up.

"Good. Now, wizard, who are you and what are you doing in the Enchanted Forest?"

The wizard drew himself up to his full height, which brought his head about even with Fiddlesticks's nose. "I am Antorell, and if you know what is good for you, you will not meddle with me!" he said in a shrill voice.

"I might have known," Morwen said.

"What's that?" Telemain said, looking up. "Morwen, these readings are absurd. This fellow can't be very good."

Antorell's face turned bright red. Morwen smiled. "He isn't. This is Antorell, Telemain."

"Antorell, Antorell. Oh. The son of Head Wizard Zemenar?"

"That's right," Antorell said. "And you'll regret–"

"Isn't he the one Cimorene keeps melting?" Telemain said. "And shouldn't he be larger?"

Antorell's face became downright purple. Curious about the change, Fiddlesticks leaned forward, and his whiskers brushed the side of Antorell's head. The wizard shrieked and jumped away, the cat pounced, and bits of moss flew in all directions. After a moment, the rapidly moving tangle resolved into Fiddlesticks crouched over the wizard. One front paw, with claws fully extended, rested on each of Antorell's shoulders. Antorell looked terrified.

"He's the one," Morwen said to Telemain. "Very good, Fiddle. You may back up now. I don't think he'll do that again."

"Fascinating," Telemain murmured, his eyes fixed on the cat. "Did you see the sparks, Morwen? He cast a basic warding-off spell, but it didn't affect the cat at all!"

Morwen frowned in concern. "Fiddlesticks?"

"Well, of course it didn't do anything to me." Fiddlesticks eased slowly off Antorell's chest and sat down very close beside him. "Wizards don't know how to handle cats. I don't think they're very smart."

"Get that beast away from me!" Antorell cried as Fiddlesticks raised a paw and flexed his claws.

"See?" said Fiddlesticks, and began washing wizard germs out from between his toes.

"Calm down," Morwen told Antorell. "Fiddlesticks won't hurt you. Unless I tell him to, of course. What are you doing in the Enchanted Forest?"

"I won't tell you." Antorell was plainly trying to sound defiant, but all he managed was sulky.

"Morwen?" Scorn wound her way around the far edge of the bush. "How long are we going to have to watch this staff? It's not doing anything, and Jasper wants to take a nap."

"I'll be there as soon as we finish with Antorell," Morwen said.

"What is it?" Telemain asked.

"Scorn wants the staff taken care of," Morwen told him. "Antorell–"

"That presents no difficulty," Telemain said. "If you'll just fetch it here, Scorn, I'll do it for you."

Scorn gave him a long look. *"Dogs* fetch." She turned her back and lay down, her tail thrashing indignantly.

"That means 'no,' I take it," Telemain said with a sigh.

"It does. And I told you I didn't want the staff anywhere near the wizard," Morwen said.

"A proper spirit of scientific investigation–"

"I'm more interested in self-preservation. Study the staff later. Antorell–"

"Ha!" said Antorell. "You are too late! Behold!"

With a flourish, he raised his right arm. As he did, he began to glow. Fiddlesticks pulled his head back in surprise, and the glow began pulsing, first bright, then dim. After three pulses, Antorell started growing. He gained an inch on the next pulse, two on the one after that, and then he had grown to a foot in height.

"Bother," said Morwen, and grabbed for the bucket.

"Argelfraster," said Telemain, and pointed at Antorell.

"Eeeaugh!" said Antorell, his expression changing from sinister to shocked. He continued to glow and pulse, but he was no longer getting taller. A puddle of brown goo began to spread out from under his robe where his feet should have been. "No! Help! You can't *do* this to me!"

"Wow!" said Fiddlesticks. "Look at him go!"

Morwen nodded, but she kept the bucket of soapy water ready to throw, just in case. Antorell was now melting faster than he was growing. In another minute, all that was left were his robes and the puddle of goo sinking slowly into the moss. Fiddlesticks edged up to it and sniffed, then backed away rapidily.

"What was all that noise?" Killer said from behind Telemain. "Part of it sounded like another donkey."

"No, it was a wizard, though in this case it's much the same thing," Morwen said. "You needn't worry. He's gone now." She set her bucket down once more and gave Telemain a nod of approval. "Congratulations. It works."

"Yes, and did you notice the echo effect on the size-amplification spell?" Telemain shook his head. "Remarkable. The theoretical ramifications–"

"Are very interesting, I'm sure," Morwen said. "How permanent is this?" She waved at the gooey robes.

"Not very, I'm afraid," Telemain said. "He'll be back in a day or two."

Killer ambled over to the puddle. "Is this edible?" he asked in a doubtful tone.

"No!" said Morwen and Telemain together.

"What an awful idea," said Fiddlesticks, wrinkling his nose.

"What a mess," said Scorn.

"Don't touch it," Morwen said to Killer. "With two spells on you already, you shouldn't take any chances with wizard residuum."

"Oh," said Killer. He looked at the puddle again and sighed. "But I'm *hungry*. And thirsty. What do donkeys eat?"

"We'll take care of you in a minute or two," Morwen promised. "Finish up quickly, Telemain. We're leaving." Beach or no beach, King Mendanbar and Queen Cimorene had to be found and informed as soon as possible. Morwen started back toward the clover patch to collect her broomstick.

"Don't forget about that staff!" Scorn called after her.

Getting ready to leave didn't take long. Morwen picked up the staff–and Jasper, who was still guarding it–on her way back to Telemain. She noticed with interest that the staff was over three feet long and expanding slowly. Apparently the shrinking spell was wearing off it even without Antorell's help.

When she reached him, Telemain was just stowing the last of his shiny instruments back in one of his pockets. "Have we got everyone?" the magician asked.

"Everyone but the wizard," Scorn said. "And good riddance to *him*, I say."

"Yes," Morwen replied to both Telemain and Scorn. "If you'll take the staff, Telemain–"

"I wouldn't do that," Jasper said, jumping down from Morwen's shoulder.

Morwen paused, frowning, then saw Killer standing by the bucket of soapy water. He lowered his head and sniffed experimentally. "Why not? It smells nice."

"That's the lemon juice," Morwen said.

"It's got *soap* in it," Fiddlesticks said, lashing his tail. "It's for *melting wizards.*"

"There aren't any wizards around, and I'm thirsty." Before anyone could stop him, Killer took a large slurp. His ears stood straight up and he reared back, shaking his head. "Blea-eea-eaugh! That tastes terrible."

"Fiddle warned you," said Scorn, with a visible lack of sympathy. "So did Jasper. Serves you right for not listening."

"What's it doing to his nose?" Fiddlesticks said, poking his own nose forward until he had to stand up and follow it. "Look at his nose, Morwen. It's turning blue."

"Not just the nose." Jasper stared in fascination. "His whole face is changing color."

Killer gave a frightened snort and shook his head, sneezing soap bubbles in all directions. The color went on spreading. Soon his head and neck were a bright, clear sky blue that continued to inch up his ears, down his forelegs, and across his back.

"Help!" Killer cried. "Morwen, you're a witch. Make it stop!"

"That would be inadvisable," Telemain said. He, too, was watching Killer's changing color with great interest. "The synergistic action of the original wizardly enchantment, which was itself an unstructured mechanical surplus and therefore liable to produce unpredictable side effects, and the secondary vegetation-based enchantment has rendered you vulnerable to the wizard liquefication fluid while also, fortunately, mitigating its effects."

"What?" said Killer.

"You've got a leftover bit of a wizard's spell on you and you don't know what all it may do. You're lucky you aren't melting, the way the wizard did," Scorn summarized.

"But just *look* at me!"

"I think it's an improvement," Morwen said. "Much better than being blotchy."

"Blue? *Blue* is better than blotchy?" The color had spread to Killer's hindquarters. Only his tail and his back legs were still a patchy white-and-brown.

"Not much," said Scorn.

"Settle it later," Morwen said. "We have to go. Telemain–"

"Everyone still here? Good." Telemain raised a hand and made a circle in the air with his left forefinger. The wide silver band on his finger sparkled as he said in a low voice,

"Convey this crowd
On wind and cloud
To the castle of the King
By the power of this ring."

On the last word, Telemain clapped his hands together loudly. The trees melted and ran like soft wax on a hot stove. To her surprise, Morwen felt no sensation of movement. It was more as if she were standing still while everything around her shifted. As she nodded in approval, the blur flowed into a new shape and solidified.

They now stood on the paving stones of the castle courtyard, in the relatively narrow strip between the moat and the main door. A large dragon lay along the left side of the castle, basking in the sun. Her head, with the three stubby horns that proclaimed her a female, rested at the edge of the moat; most of her body was hidden by a tower with two staircases running around its outside. Her wings were partway open to catch the sun, and her green scales glittered, even where they were beginning to turn gray at the edges.

"Eee-augh!" Killer brayed in terror. "A dragon!"

"Oh, good," Morwen said at the same moment. "That will save some time."

"Good?" Killer seemed to be trying to hide behind Telemain and to watch the dragon at the same time. "A *dragon* is good?"

"Not *a* dragon, you idiot," said Scorn. "That's Kazul, the *King* of the Dragons."

Killer edged away. "Does he eat rabbits? Or donkeys?"

"She prefers cherries jubilee," Jasper said.

"She?" Killer looked thoroughly confused, as well as alarmed. "But– the 'King of the Dragons'?"

" 'King of the Dragons' is the name of a job," Jasper said. "It has nothing to do with gender."

"Dragons are very sensible about things like that," Fiddlesticks put in, nodding. "Almost as sensible as me. But they don't like fish."

"I'd be happier if they didn't like donkeys."

"Don't worry about King Kazul," Morwen said to Killer. "She doesn't eat friends of friends."

"Not even if she's hungry?" Killer's ears pricked forward nervously. "She looks hungry to me."

Before Morwen could respond, the castle door creaked open. From the dark hallway inside, a voice called, "Madame Morwen! Magician Telemain! Welcome to the castle."

6

In Which the Plot Positively Curdles and the King of the Dragons Loses her Temper

As everyone turned to look, a three-foot elf wearing a gold lace collar and a crisp white shirt under a green velvet coat with gold buttons, white silk hose, and green shoes with chunky gold heels stepped into view in the doorway of the castle. "Welcome, all of you," he added, bowing low.

"Hello, Willin," Morwen said. "We need to see King Mendanbar and Queen Cimorene right away."

"In regard to what?" the elf asked.

"Technical difficulties," Telemain said. "We have discovered a possible disruption in the obstructive enchantment fabricated by King Mendanbar and myself, and–"

"Er, yes, of course," said Willin. "I'll tell the King immediately. You needn't give me the details."

Telemain caught Morwen's eye and winked. Morwen suppressed a smile and said, "And while we're waiting, Killer's hungry." She nodded at the donkey. "If your kitchen could put something together that would suit him . . ."

"Certainly," Willin said. "Just trot around back, er, Killer, and the cook will take care of you." He waved toward the left, where Kazul was sleeping.

"I'm not *that* hungry!" Killer said.

"Go around the other way, then," Morwen told him. "It doesn't really matter. Just *go.*"

"I'll show him!" Fiddlesticks bounded across to Killer. "The kitchen is this way. They have cream, and butter, and fish, and . . ." His voice faded as they rounded the crooked tower by the stone bridge.

Scorn stood up and stretched. "What a pair of idiots." She looked at Jasper. "Maybe we should go after them and make sure they don't get into trouble."

"An excellent idea," Jasper agreed. With an air of determined casualness, the two cats strolled off, following the donkey.

Willin looked after them with a worried frown. "Did I offend them?"

"Not at all," Morwen assured him. When his expression did not clear, she added, "They're hoping the cook will give them some cream. Now, we'll just go have a word with Kazul while you let Cimorene know we're here. Oh, and would you put this bucket somewhere? I've enough to carry without it."

"Very good, ma'am," Willin said stiffly. He accepted the bucket and vanished into the castle, closing the door carefully behind him.

"Morwen, Mendanbar's the one we really need to see," Telemain said softly. "King Kazul–"

"Has good reason to be just as interested in the doings of wizards as the rest of us," Morwen said. "Besides, it wouldn't be polite to go in without at least saying hello."

"I suppose not," Telemain said, and the two walked across the courtyard to talk to the dragon. Up close, Kazul was an even more impressive dragon than she looked from a distance. Standing, she was at least six times Morwen's height, even without her wings, and every inch was muscle and armor scales. The sleepy, contented expression on her face vanished as Morwen and Telemain drew nearer, and by the time they were close enough to talk, the dragon was wide awake and ready for them.

"Hello, Morwen, Telemain," Kazul said. "Wizards again?" She flicked a claw in the direction of the staff Morwen held.

"Hello, Kazul," Morwen said. "It's *a* wizard, at least."

"I thought you'd shut them out of the forest," Kazul said to Telemain.

"What one magician can do, another can find a way around," Telemain said with a shrug. "Unless the quantity of energy involved reaches a magnitude that renders–"

Kazul cleared her throat pointedly. Telemain stopped. "Unless *what?*" asked the dragon.

"Um. Unless you . . . put so much power into a spell that nobody can, er, examine it closely enough to, um, figure out how to break it without getting fried by the backlash," Telemain said carefully.

"Ah. Well, I suppose nothing's perfect."

A bell chimed, and all three turned to look at the castle. The door swung open, and Willin marched out. "Their Majesties King Mendanbar and Queen Cimorene of the Enchanted Forest," he announced, and bowed low.

"Hello, Morwen, Telemain. We were just trying to get you on the magic mirror." The speaker was a tall young woman in a loose cream-colored shirt and a pair of baggy gray pants tucked into short leather boots. Her black braids were wound around and around her head like a crown, and her face was both lovely and intelligent.

As she came down the steps and into the courtyard, a man emerged from the door behind her. He was equally tall and dark-haired, and he wore a plain gold circlet that he had pushed back off his forehead. It gave him a rakish look.

"Yes, the gargoyle said something about wizards," the man said, coming forward. "Is it urgent?"

"Important, certainly," Morwen said. "Urgent, possibly. I don't think it's an emergency. Not yet. Hello, Cimorene, Mendanbar."

There was a brief round of greeting, and then Mendanbar said, "I thought something was wrong in the forest. It's been niggling at me ever since we got home."

Cimorene frowned. "You didn't say anything."

"I didn't want to worry you."

Cimorene rolled her eyes. "Mendanbar, I haven't suddenly turned to glass just because I'm going to have a baby."

"Well, but–"

"I believe that can wait," Morwen interrupted tactfully. "The wizards shouldn't."

"Yes, now that we're all here, tell us where you came across *that.*" Kazul waved at the wizard's staff in Morwen's right hand.

Morwen nodded and launched into a summary of the events following Killer's appearance in her back garden. Cimorene, Mendanbar, and Kazul listened without interrupting, though their expressions grew more and more serious. When she finished, Mendanbar turned to Telemain.

"These dead spots. I thought the spell we worked out prevented them."

"It should have," Telemain said, nodding. "And since the spell has worked perfectly well for over a year, it seems unlikely that the breakdown is due to an inherent flaw; nonetheless, I think the initial phase of our investigation should involve an examination and analysis of the primary linkages."

Cimorene blinked and looked at Mendanbar.

"He doesn't think there should be anything wrong with the spell, but he wants to check and make sure," Mendanbar translated. "In that case, we'll need the sword, won't we? I'll go get it." He snapped his fingers, and a small gold key materialized out of the air in front of him and dropped into his hand. An instant later, Mendanbar and the key vanished. A quiet huff of air rushed in to fill the space he had vacated.

"Now *that* is a transportation spell that has everything," Telemain said with a touch of envy. "Power, elegance, and economy of style. I wish I could determine exactly how he does it."

"I wish he could get it to work properly outside the Enchanted Forest," said Cimorene. "It would make visiting Kazul much easier."

"A little walking in the mountains is good for you," Kazul said.

Cimorene looked at the dragon with fond exasperation. "It may be a little walk to *you,* but it takes a good deal longer for *us.* And as I recall, you usually fly most of the way. You shouldn't give advice you don't follow."

"When I was your age, I did follow it."

"When you were Cimorene's age, you were a rambunctious dragonet barely out of the egg," Morwen said. "None of which has anything to do with our present problems."

Air puffed outward as Mendanbar reappeared. His face was set in grim lines and his hands were empty. "It's gone," he said. "The lock on the chest has been melted to a puddle, the lid is up, and the sword is gone. And there are tangles of wizard magic all over the armory. It'll take me a week to straighten them out."

There was a moment of stunned silence. Then Kazul made a low growling sound and a small flame flickered around her jaws. Cimorene's eyes went wide and she stepped quickly in front of Mendanbar, muttering something under her breath as she moved.

Probably the fire-proofing spell she discovered when she was Kazul's princess, Morwen thought. *I hope it still works.* Dropping the wizard's staff, Morwen grabbed Telemain's arm and hauled him forward.

"Morwen, what are you–"

Kazul sat back on her haunches, snapped open her wings, and roared, sending bright streams of fire shooting across the courtyard. The flames missed Telemain's head by inches, and the near edge engulfed Cimorene and Mendanbar.

"Kazul, stop that immediately!" Cimorene cried from the center of the fire. She didn't sound as if she were in pain, so the fire-proofing spell must be working.

"Yes, you don't want to finish those wizards' work for them," Morwen said as loudly as she could. "And I'm sure they'd be delighted if you roasted the King and Queen of the Enchanted Forest for them."

The roaring and the flames did not stop, but Kazul tilted her head so that the stream of fire shot harmlessly up into the air. As the flames lifted away from Cimorene and Mendanbar, Morwen breathed a sigh of relief. Cimorene's creamy shirt was now closer in color to toast, and the ends of Mendanbar's hair had crinkled visibly from the heat, but they both seemed unhurt. They ran forward to join Morwen and Telemain next to Kazul's right shoulder. Windows were flying open and closed all over the castle as people looked out to find out what all the noise was and then quickly ducked back inside.

"I've never seen her like this before, not even when the wizards kidnapped her!" Cimorene shouted over the roaring.

"I hope I never see her like this again!" Mendanbar shouted back. "I'd have been roasted if it hadn't been for that fire-proofing spell of yours. It's a good thing you're so tall."

"Fire-proofing spell?" Telemain lowered his hands from his ears and leaned forward. "What fire-proofing spell? Why hasn't anyone mentioned this before?"

"Later, Telemain," Morwen yelled.

Finally, Kazul paused for breath. In the sudden silence, Cimorene yelled, "Kazul! For goodness' sake, calm down!"

"I will not calm down!" Kazul said, but at least now she was shouting and not breathing fire indiscriminately. "This time the Society of Wizards has gone too far, and I'm not settling for throwing them out of the Enchanted Forest or limiting their power. *This* time I'm going to see the end of them, I swear I am, even if it takes two centuries. By my fire, I swear it!"

"Ah, Kazul." Mendanbar tapped one of the dragon's shoulder scales. "It's *my* sword they've stolen."

"Yes," Cimorene said, "and the first thing we have to do is get it back. The Enchanted Forest needs it."

"Very well," said Kazul. "You may help me exterminate the Society of Wizards." Slowly, she settled back to the ground, scales rattling faintly as she let her wings close.

"First things first," Morwen said. "Cimorene's right; we have to get the sword back, and quickly. Otherwise, the Society of Wizards can walk into the Enchanted Forest and soak up pieces of it until there's nothing left."

"That's probably why they took it," Cimorene said.

"No, no," Telemain put in. "The sword is only *one* of the primary foci. Its physical removal does not invalidate . . ." He paused, glanced at Kazul, and cleared his throat. "Ah, that is, the King's sword just helps maintain the spell. Taking the sword out of the forest doesn't destroy the whole spell. It just weakens it. That's why the dead spots Morwen showed me didn't fill in right away. But the spell is still strong enough to keep the wizards from gobbling up large chunks of the forest."

"Does that mean that if we recover the sword, the forest will be fully protected again?" Mendanbar asked.

Telemain nodded.

"Good. Give me a minute or two to explain to Willin, and I'll be ready to go."

"Go?" Telemain blinked. "But–"

With a huff of air, Mendanbar vanished.

"But what?" asked Cimorene.

"Mendanbar shouldn't go anywhere right now," Morwen said. "It's bad enough that the sword's missing, but no one will know about that for a while unless we tell them. But if the King of the Enchanted Forest goes tearing off on a quest while mysterious things are happening in the forest, people are bound to notice."

"There's more to it than that," Telemain said. "Mendanbar *can't* go after the sword, not if he wants to keep what's left of the antiwizard spell working. He's the other main focus."

"Oh, dear." Cimorene looked back toward the castle, and her lips twitched. "He's not going to like that at all."

"I'm certain that Morwen, Telemain, and I will be able to handle it," Kazul said.

Cimorene frowned. "Don't *you* start fussing at me, Kazul. I'm perfectly capable of–"

"I'm sure you are," Morwen said. "But the Queen of the Enchanted Forest shouldn't go tearing off any more than the King should. You have responsibilities."

"Bother my responsibilities!"

"If I thought you meant that, I'd be worried."

"Retrieving the sword is much more important than anything else I have to do right now. Thank goodness it won't be hard to find."

Morwen frowned, puzzled. "Why do you say that?"

"Well, the wizards have taken it out of the forest, haven't they? Otherwise Telemain's antiwizard spell would still be working." Cimorene smiled briefly at Telemain. "The last time that sword was outside the forest, it started leaking magic the minute it crossed the border."

"Leaking magic?"

Cimorene shrugged. "I don't know what else to call it. And it gets worse and worse the longer the sword is outside the forest. By the end of the week, anyone with any magical ability at all will be able to find that sword with his eyes closed."

"I don't think we can afford to wait that long," Telemain said slowly.

"What? Why not?" Cimorene looked at the magician in alarm. "You don't think the Society of Wizards will try to destroy it, do you?"

"It's not that." Telemain began to pace up and down beside Kazul. "It's the magic leakage. I'd forgotten about it, and of course it didn't matter as long as the sword was inside the forest, but now–"

"Now the wizards have it," Morwen said. "And wizards' staffs absorb magic. If they absorb all the magic the sword leaks, and the leak keeps growing, it won't be long before they're more than we can handle."

"That, too," Telemain said, nodding. "But the real problem is the source of the magic the sword leaks."

"The source–oh. Oh, dear." Morwen looked at Telemain. "You mean the Enchanted Forest itself?"

Slowly, Telemain nodded again. "I'm afraid so. Mendanbar and I linked the sword directly to the heart of the forest's magic. The defensive enchantment will inhibit the, er, leakage for a while, but after a few days–"

"–the pressure will build up and the sword will start leaking. And all the magic of the Enchanted Forest will drain out of the sword," Morwen finished.

"But that will kill the forest!" Cimorene said. "We have to get that sword back right away."

"Not quite," Kazul said. A thread of smoke continued to trickle angrily out of the corner of her mouth, but otherwise she seemed to be in complete control of herself again. "From what Telemain said, it will take another day or two for the sword to start leaking. Right?"

Telemain nodded. "As near as I can tell."

"Then we don't have to learn to fly by jumping off a cliff. There are still a few things I want to know before we go chasing off."

"Such as?" Morwen asked.

"How the Society of Wizards got inside the castle to steal the sword without anyone noticing, whether they're likely to be back soon, and what we can do about it if they are."

Morwen, Telemain, and Cimorene looked at each other. Then Telemain looked at Kazul. "Commendably methodical. And now that you mention it, I'd better teach all of you the wizard-liquefying spell before we leave."

"You mean you've come up with a better way of melting wizards than soapy water with lemon juice in it?" Cimorene's smile was only a little forced. "Wonderful!"

"I don't know that it's *better,"* Telemain said. "However, it appears to have the same effect, requires far less preparation, and is considerably more portable."

"He melted Antorell with it," Morwen said.

Kazul shook herself and stood up. "Enjoy the lesson. I'm going to ask your cook to pack us something for dinner."

"Don't you want to know how to melt wizards?" Cimorene said.

"No." Kazul smiled fiercely, showing all her sharp, silver teeth. "If I run into any wizards, I'm going to eat them."

"Then why are you bothering about dinner?" Telemain asked, frowning.

Kazul's smile broadened. "That's for the rest of you," she said, and glided off.

7

In Which Killer Rises in the World

Mendanbar returned just as Telemain began his explanation of the wizard-melting spell. "You'll want to know this, too, Mendanbar," Telemain said, and went right on with his lecture. The enchantment was typical of the magician's spare spells: it required a lot of preparation and a complicated ritual to set it up, but once that had been done, you could use it several times simply by pointing and saying a trigger word. According to Telemain, you didn't even have to *say* the trigger word aloud.

"Theoretically, a mental recitation would be just as effective," Telemain said. "This theory, however, remains unverified, as no opportunity for experimentation has–"

"Telemain, if you don't stop babbling gobbledy-gook, I'm going to bring Kazul back to listen," Morwen said. "Mendanbar and I know what you're saying, but Cimorene hasn't the slightest idea what you're talking about."

"Yes, and I'd appreciate it if somebody would translate that last bit," Cimorene said. "It sounded important."

"Just thinking the trigger word ought to be as good as saying it," Mendanbar explained. "But he doesn't know for sure because he hasn't had a chance to test it on a wizard yet."

"Well, you'll probably get one soon," Cimorene said. "Have we got all the ingredients you need for the ritual? Because I think everyone ought to be prepared to melt wizards before anyone goes sword hunting. It's all very well for Kazul to say she'll eat them, but if they have any dragonsbane . . ."

"Good idea," Mendanbar said. "What will we need?"

"I brought the rarer components with me," Telemain said. "If you have seven lemons, a book that's missing half its cover, and three pints of unicorn water, I can start working on it at once."

Mendanbar pursed his lips. "I don't think we have any unicorn water."

"Yes, we do," said Cimorene. "It's in the cupboard by the buckets, in a jug marked 'Magic-Mirror Cleaner.' Don't look at me like that. It was the safest place I could think of. Ever since we put the gargoyle in charge of answering the mirror, nobody but me dares to clean it."

Mendanbar laughed. "I don't blame them."

"Why don't you and Telemain check the library and start setting up in the Grand Hall?" Cimorene suggested. "Morwen and I will get the other ingredients and meet you there."

The two men agreed to this plan, and the group split up. As the castle door closed, Cimorene gave a sigh of relief.

"How do you stand it?" she asked Morwen.

"The way Telemain complicates things when he talks?" Morwen shook her head. "I don't have to, much."

"I thought you were old friends."

"We are. That doesn't mean we see a lot of each other, though I'll admit that he drops by much more often now that he lives in the Enchanted Forest, too."

"Even so . . ."

Morwen thought for a minute. "The only thing you can do is avoid talking about magic with him," she said at last. "He's reasonably clear when it comes to normal conversation, but as soon as anyone mentions spells he gets technical. Or you could make sure Kazul is always with you."

"Yes, I'd noticed that Telemain doesn't–"

A distant bray interrupted Cimorene in midsentence. "Good heavens," she said. "What on earth was that?"

"Killer," Morwen said, walking more quickly. "Unless you've acquired a donkey since the last time I was here."

"A donkey? No, but–"

As they rounded the last corner and came in sight of the kitchen, Cimorene stopped short. The cook stood in the half-open kitchen door, brandishing a copper frying pan to keep Killer from forcing his way inside, while Scorn and Jasper watched from the safety of a nearby window ledge. Midway between the kitchen and the moat, Kazul sat on her haunches, smiling down at the terrified blue donkey in amusement. Since the smile showed a fair number of teeth, it wasn't helping Killer's state of mind at all.

"Killer," Morwen said sternly. "Stop that this instant."

"But it's a *dragon!"* Killer wailed. "And it's *right there!* Eee-augh!"

The cook glanced toward them, gasped, and dropped the frying pan. "Your Majesty!"

Taking full advantage of the cook's distraction, Killer flung himself forward. He hit the door with a thud, shoving it wide and knocking the cook over backward. As his head and front feet disappeared inside the kitchen, a cat yowled loudly in surprise and pain.

"Fiddlesticks!" Morwen said. "That does it." She raised her arms.

"Sky and sea and whirling sands,
Stop that creature where he stands!"

On the final word, she brought both hands down in a swift chopping gesture. Killer stopped moving and gave a startled bellow. An instant later, Fiddlesticks shot out from between the donkey's legs. Morwen breathed a quiet sigh of relief.

"He stepped on my *tail!"* Fiddlesticks said with great indignation. He sat down at Kazul's feet and began energetically washing the offended part.

"I'm surprised it wasn't your nose," Scorn said. "You poke it into enough peculiar places."

"Help! Hee-eeau-elp!" Killer cried. "I'm going to be eaten!"

"Get this creature out of my kitchen!" the cook yelled as he scrambled to his feet.

"Quiet, all of you," said Cimorene, edging her way through the narrow gap between Killer's rear end and the door frame. Since Fiddlesticks seemed more or less unharmed, Morwen followed Cimorene inside. Killer continued to moan and whimper despite Cimorene's order, but he at least stopped braying.

Inside, Cimorene glanced around the kitchen, which was nearly as clean and tidy as Morwen's, and nodded to the cook. The cook bowed deeply. Cimorene turned to Killer. "Nobody is going to eat anyone here unless I say so. Now, how did this happen?"

"Just how you'd expect," Scorn said from the window. "Killer was being stupid again."

"I'm not stupid," Killer said. "Eee-eeaugh! Oh, help!"

"I said *quiet,"* Cimorene said.

"But I can't move, and there's a dragon–"

"I can arrange it so you can't talk, either," Morwen said. "And if you don't start behaving yourself, I'll do it. Cimorene, this is Killer. He ought to be a rabbit of the usual size and color, but he's had some trouble with wizards lately. This is Cimorene, the Queen of the Enchanted Forest. I think you should answer her question."

Killer rolled his eyes and waggled his ears, managing to look foolish and terrified at the same time, but after a few more minutes of reassurance, coaxing, and stern commands, he calmed down enough to explain. He had been waiting for the castle cook to mix up his promised lunch, and hadn't noticed Kazul's arrival. When the cats pointed her out to him, he had been nervous, but he hadn't really started to worry until Kazul asked the cook to pack provisions for a journey. What had really panicked him, though, had been the dragon saying, in answer to a question from the cook, that the provisions should be for human people only, because she would find her own meals.

"There, you see?" Scorn said, lashing her tail. "He was being stupid."

"I can see why it might make you nervous," Cimorene said to Killer. "Kazul can be a bit intimidating up close." She considered for a moment. "Kazul won't eat you once you've been properly introduced. Let him loose, Morwen, and I'll take him over and present him."

"Are you sure?" Killer asked.

"Positive," Cimorene told him. "Dragons are very polite. Morwen?"

Since all the cats were out of danger and Killer seemed to have settled down, Morwen nodded agreement. Bringing her hands together at waist height, she said,

"Fire and cloud and rain and snow,
Lift the spell and let him go!"

As she spoke, she raised her arms in a slow reversal of the movement she had used to freeze Killer where he stood.

For a long moment, nothing seemed to happen. Morwen frowned, wondering if the wizards' size-changing spell was interfering with her witchcraft. Then a ripple ran across Killer's back, like heat rising from an iron stove. He shivered, shook himself, and pranced backward several steps, ducking his head to clear the top of the doorway.

"Thanks," he said. "Um, could we just sort of skip the part about presenting me to the dragon for now?"

"That wouldn't be a good–Killer, are you growing again?" Morwen asked. "You look taller."

Jasper yawned widely and jumped down from the window ledge. "He's not taller," the cat said, strolling forward. "He's just farther up."

Automatically, Morwen, Cimorene, and the cook glanced down, following Jasper's movement. Morwen blinked. Between Killer's front hooves and the flagstones of the courtyard stretched a long inch of empty air.

"I wonder if he'll still leave footprints?" Cimorene said, half to herself.

"What is it?" Killer asked nervously. "What are you all staring at?" He looked down and his ears stiffened. "Eee-augh!" He pranced backward, out of sight, and Cimorene and Morwen hurried out after him. With every step, he gained a little more height, until he was a good four inches above the ground. "Help! I'm falling!"

"You're not falling," Scorn said. "You're floating."

"He is, isn't he?" Fiddlesticks said, walking over. "And it's a very good idea. He can't step on anybody's tail now."

"Hold still," Morwen said to the donkey. "Every time you take a step, you get farther up. If you keep moving, you'll be over the castle in no time. And if the spell suddenly wears off . . ."

"Eee-augh!" Killer rolled his eyes and planted his feet firmly in thin air. "Now what?"

"Now you wait," Morwen told him. "This looks like another side effect of mixing different kinds of magic, and that's really Telemain's specialty. I'll send him out as soon as we're done inside."

"Tell him to hurry!"

Cimorene shook her head. "I'm afraid it will take a while, but we'll bring him as soon as we can. In the meantime, Evim will get you some lunch." She looked back over her shoulder at the cook, who nodded and vanished into the kitchen.

Behind Killer, scales scraped noisily against stone. "This is very entertaining," Kazul said, "but haven't we got more important things to do than argue with an oversized blue donkey with avian ambitions?"

Killer rolled his eyes and choked back another bray. Cimorene smiled but shook her head. "It's not quite as silly as it looks. Kazul, this is Killer; Killer, this is Kazul, the King of the Dragons. Killer is the one who found out that the wizards are back in the forest, Kazul."

"He is?" Kazul came around in front, where she could see Killer more clearly. "Have you got any idea how they got into the palace?"

"N-no, sir–I mean, ma'am," said Killer.

"The size-changing spell must have had something to do with it," Morwen said. "If they shrank themselves small enough to sneak through the door without being seen–"

"That would be hard," Cimorene said. "Our regular doorman is on vacation, so Willin's been handling it. And he's not all that big himself. Those wizards would have had to shrink awfully small to get past him."

"There are other doors," Kazul pointed out. "This one, for instance." She waved a claw at the kitchen entrance.

"Yes, but there's a spell on them that rings a bell in the footman's room whenever someone who doesn't belong here comes through one of them."

"However they did it, we aren't going to figure it out standing here," Morwen said. "Either we should go down to the armory and investigate, or we should get those lemons and go meet Mendanbar and Telemain the way we planned."

"Good heavens, I almost forgot," Cimorene said. "Lemons and unicorn water it is. I'm sorry, Kazul, but we can't do everything at once."

Cimorene and Morwen said good-bye to Kazul and went back into the kitchen, where they collected the lemons and unicorn water. Just as they were leaving, Jasper slipped out from behind a large basket of apples that was leaning against a corner wall.

"Morwen?" said the cat. "I've got something to tell you."

"All right," Morwen said. "Would you mind waiting a minute, Cimorene? Jasper wants to talk to me, and he wouldn't interrupt if it weren't important."

"Of course," Cimorene said. "But do try to be quick, Jasper. We've already taken more time than we should have."

Jasper favored Cimorene with a slow blink of approval. "I like her. She understands cats better than most people do."

"Very likely," said Morwen. "Now, what was it you wanted to tell me?"

"I know how the wizards got into the armory."

"Well?"

The cat coughed and looked around to make sure none of the other animals were within hearing distance. "Plumbing and mouse holes," he said very softly. "There's an old drain that goes under the moat and comes out in the forest. The wizards used it to get into the castle and then wandered around in the walls until they found a mouse hole into the armory. Once they had the sword, they used a transport spell to leave."

"How do you know all this?"

Jasper hunched his shoulders in embarrassment. "I asked the castle mice. A couple of them are friends of mine, and they gave me the whole story. Don't tell anyone, will you? If Scorn finds out, I'll never hear the end of it."

"If Scorn or anyone else says one word about it, you let me know," Morwen said. "That was very well done, Jasper. Thank you."

Jasper raised his chin and arched his back proudly. "You're welcome. But I'd still rather you didn't tell Scorn."

"I won't," Morwen promised. "All right, Cimorene. Let's go."

"What was that about?" Cimorene asked as they left the kitchen.

"Jasper found out how the wizards got in," Morwen said, and explained as well as she could without mentioning Jasper's friendship with the mice.

Cimorene frowned. "Mouse holes? That's awful. We'll never find them all, and even if we did, the mice would just make new ones. And no one has *ever* invented a spell to keep mice out. Not one that works, anyway."

"And if you can't keep the mice out, you can't keep the wizards out, either. It's a problem." Morwen thought for a minute. "Why don't you ask the mice to help?"

"Ask the mice?" Cimorene looked startled, then nodded. "Of course. Even if they won't tell us where their holes are, they can let us know if any more wizards try to use them. But who should we get to talk to them?"

"Your gargoyle. I'll wager my best broomstick that the mice will talk to him, and Telemain can rig up some portable magic mirrors so he can warn you when you're in other parts of the castle."

"Can Telemain make portable magic mirrors?"

"I don't know," Morwen said. "But we can ask."

They turned down the last long corridor that led to the Grand Hall, and Morwen's eyes widened. "Impressive," she said after a moment.

"Haven't you been to the Grand Hall before?" Cimorene said.

"No," Morwen said positively. "I'd remember."

The door to the Grand Hall was made of gold. It was twice as wide and three times as tall as a normal door, and it was covered with relief patterns that moved and twisted if you looked at them too long. Cimorene smiled at Morwen, tapped at the door with one finger, and waited. After a moment, the door swung smoothly open.

"We're here," Cimorene said, stepping forward. "Are you ready to start?"

8

In Which Telemain Does a Spell and Morwen Misses a Call

The Grand Hall was as large as a ballroom, with a high ceiling and a green marble floor. Sunlight streamed through a dozen windows in the upper half of the walls, and two branches of unlit candles hung below each window, ready for evening or a cloudy day. Mendanbar and Telemain had pushed the few pieces of furniture–five high-backed wooden chairs and a long low-backed couch–up against the far wall. In the empty center of the room, Telemain had set up a large iron brazier, about three feet high and nearly five feet across.

"Where on earth did you get that?" Cimorene asked.

"I ordered it from the dwarfs," Telemain said, stooping to squint across the rim of the brazier. "And I had to send it back twice. The wizard liquefication spell requires extraordinary precision in the initial stages." With considerable difficulty, he shoved the brazier half an inch to the right and stooped to check its position once more.

"I made a quick trip to his house just now to bring it," Mendanbar said. "I don't need the sword for a spell that simple."

Cimorene smiled at him. "Thank you. How long will this take?"

"Not long," Telemain said, rising. "You've got the lemons and the unicorn water?"

Morwen handed them to him. "I don't think I've seen a setup quite like this before. How did you think of it?"

"The design was not difficult, once the theoretical basis for the spell was determined." Telemain carefully set the lemons on the floor and opened the bottle of unicorn water. It glowed with a faint silver-white light as he poured it into the brazier. "The efficacy of the cleansing solution in liquefying wizards suggested the operation of an antithetical principle, which–"

"Did you have to get him started?" Cimorene asked reproachfully.

"Yes," said Morwen. "I want to know how this works. Talk to Mendanbar, if you'd rather not listen."

From one of his many pockets, Telemain produced a small envelope. As he mixed and poured and arranged the various elements of the spell, he explained each procedure in detail. Morwen was impressed in spite of herself. The spell was clearly a major magical achievement.

Finally the preparations were finished and the brazier was half-full of white, foamy liquid. "That's enough," Telemain said. "Now, would all of you come here and hold your right hands over the brazier, please." Frowning, he watched the bubbling liquid until the foam reached the lip of the brazier. Then he said,

"Over and under, in and out.
Back and through and roundabout.
Send them away when we wish them to go.
Argelfraster!"

The liquid spattered upward as if someone had thrown a large rock into it. Three icy droplets fell on Morwen's extended hand, and several more sprinkled her robe and glasses. It was all she could do not to flinch. Then, with a burbling hiss like a giant steam bubble bursting, the liquid exploded into a dense white cloud and rolled over them. The clean parts of Morwen's glasses fogged up immediately. Beside her, she heard Mendanbar cough.

"That's right, take a deep breath." Telemain's voice sounded very far away. Somewhere in the thick fog, Cimorene gasped and started coughing.

Warily, Morwen sniffed. The fog was bitterly cold and smelled strongly of lemons and bleach. "Bother," she muttered, and breathed in as Telemain had directed. As she had expected, she began to cough. A moment later, the fog cleared.

"Very good," Telemain said, beaming at the three of them as they gasped for air. "You can put your hands down now."

"You might have warned us," Cimorene said when she could talk again.

"About what?" Telemain sounded genuinely puzzled.

"Any number of things," Morwen said, taking off her glasses. Concentrating briefly, she reached into her sleeve, pulled out a clean handkerchief, and carefully wiped the lenses. "The temperature of that concoction, the fact that we were supposed to breathe that steam, and the presence of bleach in the mixture, for example."

"Why the bleach?" Mendanbar asked, in a tone nearly as puzzled as Telemain's.

Morwen settled her glasses back on her nose and scowled at Telemain. "Take a good look at my robe." She held out her arms so that he could clearly see all the pale purple-gray dots where his magic fluid had spattered across the black fabric.

"I'm sorry, Morwen," Telemain said. "I didn't realize it would do that."

"Obviously." Tucking her handkerchief into her sleeve, Morwen shook her head. "At least the spell worked."

"You're sure?" Cimorene asked. "I didn't feel anything when it went off. Except like coughing."

"An unfortunate but necessary side effect," Telemain said, nodding. "It may be possible to eliminate the discomfort in the future, but this time I thought it best to use a proven method."

"Didn't you have to adjust for the number of people involved?" Morwen asked.

"A simple matter of altering the balance of ingredients," Telemain assured her.

"And the trigger word is *argelfraster?"* Morwen went on. "For all of us?"

Telemain nodded. "Say it, or think it very clearly, and point your finger at the wizard. It's quite effective."

"How did you pick a word like *argelfraster?"* Cimorene asked.

"I wanted something memorable."

"It is that," Morwen murmured. "Telemain, if you are quite finished, I am going home. I want to change clothes and make arrangements with the cats before I go sword hunting. Oh, and take a look at Killer before you leave, or he's likely to float off and starve."

"Float off?"

Cimorene shook her head. "Morwen, in your own way you can be just as bad as he is. It's like this, Telemain . . ." She began explaining what had happened in and around the kitchen.

Frowning, Mendanbar moved closer to Morwen. "I understand why you want to stop at your house before we leave," he said, "and I know you can get yourself back there somehow–"

"I have my broom with me," Morwen said. "It's outside, by the front door where we arrived."

Mendanbar nodded. "Still, I'd like to get this expedition under way as fast as I can. If I send you home on a quick spell, you'll get there much sooner than if you fly."

"That would be fine, as long as you're willing to send my cats and my broom with me," Morwen said. "And make sure someone remembers about Killer. He's a nuisance, but it isn't his fault that he's turned into a six-foot blue floating donkey. Well, mostly it isn't."

"Of course." Mendanbar's eyes got a faraway look, as they always did when he was drawing on the magic of the Enchanted Forest. His right hand moved, as if he were plucking a string, and Fiddlesticks, Jasper, and Scorn appeared on the green marble in front of Morwen. All three were crouched around a bowl-sized circle, and Fiddlesticks had cream on his nose.

"Hey!" said Fiddlesticks. "I wasn't *finished!*"

"I'll give you something more when we get home," Morwen said. "I believe that's everyone, Mendanbar."

"I'll see you later, then," Mendanbar said, and raised his hand. "Telemain and Kazul and I will meet you at your house. We won't be long." His fingers twitched and the room started to fade.

As the walls blurred into gray mist, Morwen heard Telemain say, "Ah, about this expedition, Mendanbar, I don't think . . ." His voice grew faint and faraway, then was swallowed in the mist. A moment later, the mist cleared, leaving Morwen standing in the large open area in front of her house.

"Remarkably convenient," Morwen said, bending to pick up her broom.

"He could have set us on the porch, if he'd wanted to." Jasper strolled forward and paused at the foot of the steps. "Do you need me for anything now, Morwen?"

"I didn't mean the transportation," Morwen said. "I was referring to the timing. And no, I won't need you for a while."

"Then I'll just take a nap until you do. All this running around is exhausting." Jasper vanished under the porch.

"What timing?" Fiddlesticks asked. "Do you mean it's time for some fish?"

"No, I mean that I won't have to help explain to Mendanbar why he can't leave the Enchanted Forest to look for his sword." Morwen walked briskly up the steps and set her broom against the wall next to the door, where it would be handy. "Scorn, please get everyone together in the garden in about half an hour."

"Half an hour? I thought you were in a hurry."

"We are, but it'll take at least that long for Cimorene and Telemain to convince Mendanbar that he can't go. Run along, now. I've got to pack." With that, Morwen pushed open the front door and went inside.

* * *

Slightly less than half an hour later, Morwen walked out the back door into the garden. The sleeves of the bleach-speckled robe had been emptied and disenchanted, and the robe itself dumped into the rag basket. She had transferred the sleeve spell to her new robe (identical to the old one, except for the bleach speckles) and packed both sleeves with magic supplies and a variety of everyday items that might come in handy, including several lemons, a small collapsible bucket, and a bottle of liquid soap. Spells or no spells, Morwen did not intend to take unnecessary chances. Since she did not know how long they would be gone, she added an extra robe, a blanket, and several chicken-salad sandwiches. She considered putting in a few bottles of cider as well, but there were limits to what the spell would hold, and her sleeves were growing heavy, a sure sign that the limits were close.

The cats had already collected in the garden, lolling in patches of sun, perching in the branches of the largest apple tree, or stalking along the garden rows, as if they had all intended to be there for reasons of their own. Smiling slightly, Morwen sat down on the back step next to Miss Eliza. In a few minutes, the other cats drifted over to join them.

"I'm glad you're all here," Morwen told them. "There's been some trouble, and there'll probably be more."

"Scorn and Jasper told us," Murgatroyd said. "Wizards."

"Revolting creatures," Miss Eliza said.

"I'll kill one for you, if you want," Trouble offered.

"I don't think that will be necessary," Morwen said. "Telemain and I hope to retrieve the King's sword and put a stop to this nonsense once and for all. Trouble and Scorn will come with me. The rest of you will stay here and guard the house and garden."

"How long will you be gone?" Aunt Ophelia asked.

"I'm not sure. At least a week, I expect, unless we're very lucky."

"You should take us all," Chaos said, crouching and lashing his tail fiercely. "You might need us. Wizards are tough."

"Hah," said Trouble. "Wizards aren't tough. You just have to know the right place to dig in your claws. Ogres, now, ogres are–"

"We are well aware of your talents, Trouble," said Miss Eliza. "This is not the time to brag."

"I would prefer that you stay here," Morwen said to Chaos. "It's possible that Telemain will be bouncing us around with his transport spells, and he's not used to dealing with a crowd. I'd worry about someone getting left behind."

"I'm staying," Jasmine announced with an enormous yawn. "Telemain's spells give me motion sickness."

"Moving gives you motion sickness," Trouble muttered. "But the rest of us–"

"Several of you should stay here in case the wizards show up while I'm gone," Morwen pointed out.

"I'll be ready for them." Fiddlesticks jumped onto the window ledge, where he balanced precariously, trying to look fierce and watchful without stepping on Jasmine. "I won't let them in, even if they offer me some fish!"

"You are an example to us all," Miss Eliza said. It was impossible to tell from her tone whether or not she meant it to be sarcastic.

"He'll do better than Jasmine would," Murgatroyd said. "She didn't hear a thing when the mirror went off a bit ago."

Morwen frowned. "Someone called while I was out? Why didn't you mention it?"

"It was that fellow you don't like," Trouble said. "The one with the long name that you won't turn into a toad."

"Arona Michaelear Grinogion Vamist?" Morwen said incredulously.

"That's him. He was annoyed when he didn't see anyone but us." Trouble's tail whipped sideways, up, and then down onto the ground with a thump that showed what he thought of such lack of taste.

" 'Us'? How many of you were in my study when he called?"

Several of the cats shifted uncomfortably and looked away.

"Oh, never mind," Morwen said. "Vamist will have to wait; I haven't time for him now. The fate of the Enchanted Forest is much more important than his idiotic notions."

"She sounds cranky," Fiddlesticks said to Jasmine. "Do you think she'll turn him into a toad after all?"

Before anyone could answer, there was a loud *thwump* from the other side of the house. Fiddlesticks fell off the window ledge, and all of the rest of the cats except Jasmine jumped. The moment he landed, Trouble leapt for the back door with an angry growl, Chaos and Murgatroyd close behind.

"Wait for me!" Fiddlesticks yelled, scrambling to his feet. "Wait–"

"Morwen!" The shout came from the front yard as Morwen rose unhurriedly to her feet.

"That sounds like Kazul," Scorn said.

"I suspect it is," Morwen said. "Come along, Scorn. It's time to leave."

9

In Which the Expedition Leaves the Enchanted Forest at Last

The rest of the cats, even Jasmine, followed Morwen and Scorn through the house and out onto the front porch. Kazul was standing in the center of the yard, along with Telemain and Killer. The donkey was still floating a good six inches above the ground, and he looked extremely uncomfortable. Standing beside him was Mendanbar, who was frowning ferociously, and Cimorene, who seemed to be trying to suppress a satisfied smile. With some dismay, Morwen noted that Cimorene now had a small pack slung over one shoulder and a slim sword belted to her waist.

The cats flowed across the yard and converged on Kazul. Making little noises of satisfaction, all nine of the cats scrambled up the dragon's sides. Their claws rasped against Kazul's scales, making Cimorene wince, but neither they nor the dragon seemed to notice.

Morwen looked at Telemain while the cats draped themselves contentedly all over Kazul. "I thought you were going to explain to him why he couldn't come along," she said, nodding sideways at Mendanbar.

"I did," Telemain said grumpily.

"Then what is he doing here?"

"Making trouble?" Scorn suggested from a comfortable perch on Kazul's left shoulder.

"He'd better not be," Trouble said. "That's my job." He stretched himself full length along the lower part of Kazul's neck, beside her spinal ridges, his tail and one front paw dangling lazily.

"I'm taking you to the edge of the Enchanted Forest," Mendanbar said. "I can do that much, at least, even if I can't come with you. My magic will get you there faster than anything else, and you'll be safe from most of the things that live in the forest if you're with me."

"I see." That explained Telemain's bad mood: he hated having to admit that anyone's magic was better than his, even the King's. Morwen looked at Cimorene. "What about you?"

"I'm coming with you," Cimorene said. Mendanbar scowled fiercely as if he wanted to object, but before he could, Cimorene hurried on, "I *have* to. Otherwise you'll have as much difficulty with the sword as I hope those blasted wizards are having right now."

Kazul snorted angrily, sending out a large ball of smoke, which made everyone in front of her cough. "If they aren't having trouble now, they will soon."

Morwen gave Kazul a stern look over the tops of her glasses. "We are going on this expedition to recover Mendanbar's sword, Kazul. We aren't trying to destroy the entire Society of Wizards."

"Yet," said Trouble.

"You be quiet, or I'll leave you at home," Morwen said. "Now, would someone explain to me just *why* Cimorene has to come along?"

"Resonance and half-hard deflection mechanisms," Telemain said. "Which are–"

"–as clear as mud," Kazul put in.

Telemain looked annoyed. "I wasn't talking to you. Morwen understands what I mean."

"Most of the time," Morwen said.

"I think he means that Mendanbar's sword is painful to touch, unless you happen to belong to the King's family," Cimorene said. "And the longer it stays outside the forest, the harder it is to handle."

"The deflection increases exponentially," Telemain said. "Rather like the magic leakage we discussed earlier, only the defense spells won't slow down the deflection. By this time, it is undoubtedly past the transfer-resonance point."

"So the Society of Wizards can't use the sword against us." Morwen smiled grimly. "Good. I'd been wondering about that."

"Unfortunately, *you* can't use it, either," Cimorene said. "If Telemain is right about the timing–"

"And I am."

"–then in a day or two nobody but a member of the Royal Family will be able to pick up the sword at all, much less carry it back to the Enchanted

Forest. So since Mendanbar and I are the only members of the Royal Family right now, and since Mendanbar has to stay in the forest–"

"–you *have* to come with us to retrieve the sword," Morwen finished, raising an eyebrow. "I see."

Cimorene grinned. "Telemain explained it at least three times at the castle, and by the time he and Mendanbar finished arguing, I had a pretty good idea what he meant, even if he never did say it straight out."

"I did, too!" Telemain said indignantly. "Several times."

"Not so I understood."

"That is unfortunately not very surprising," Morwen said. "Mendanbar, your sword is very inconveniently designed."

"Don't blame *me,*" Mendanbar said. "The blasted thing came with the kingdom."

"Hmph." Morwen glanced around. "What about Killer? Why is he here?"

Killer's ears twitched anxiously forward. "They told me I was supposed to come. Is it all right?"

"Once we're away from the interference patterns of the Enchanted Forest, we should be able to trace the residual energy in the morphological field trap," Telemain said. "At that point, a standard locus delimiter should–"

"Telemain," Kazul said in a warning tone.

Morwen rolled her eyes. "He thinks we can use what's left of the size-changing spell on Killer to find the wizards. But are you sure there's enough, Telemain?"

"I can't tell until we're out of the forest," Telemain said. "The interference–" He glanced at Kazul and stopped.

"I understand," Morwen said. "But remember: bringing him along was your idea, so you're responsible for keeping him out of trouble."

"And he'd better do a good job," Trouble said. "If that overgrown blue idiot steps on *my* tail, he'll wish he'd never left his rabbit hole."

"I *already* wish I'd never left my hole," Killer said. "Rabbits aren't supposed to have adventures. Our temperaments aren't suited to them."

"Are you people going to stand around talking all day?" Kazul asked pointedly. "Or are we going wizard hunting?"

"*Sword* hunting, Kazul, if you please," Morwen said. "And I am ready to leave as soon as we decide which way we're heading."

There was a pause while Cimorene, Telemain, and Mendanbar looked at each other. Scorn snickered. "Look at them! They didn't even think of that."

"The central office of the Society of Wizards is in the Brown Forest," Telemain said at last. "We should probably start there."

"Why waste time?" Kazul said. "The wizards wouldn't be stupid enough to take Mendanbar's sword to their main office."

"Antorell would," Cimorene said.

"Where is the Brown Forest?" Killer asked timidly. "It doesn't sound very . . . appetizing."

"It's worse than it sounds," Telemain told him. "The Brown Forest is actually a corner of the Great Southern Desert."

Frowning, Cimorene looked at Telemain. "I always thought the Brown Forest was a dead woods. Are you sure it's really a desert?"

Telemain nodded. "I've been there."

"You have?" Kazul said. "Why?"

"I wanted to learn wizardry, and the school the Society of Wizards runs is the only–"

"You wanted to be a *wizard?"* Kazul said, outraged.

"No," Telemain said in the too-patient tone of someone who has had to give the same explanation far too many times. "I didn't want to *be* a wizard. I wanted to *study* them. Their magical methods are unique, and magicians have been attempting to figure them out for a long, long time."

"And you thought they would tell you if you asked politely?" Cimorene said.

Telemain shrugged. "It was worth a try. Anyway, I've been to the Brown Forest in the Great Southern Desert. I can probably even find the area where the central office of the Society of Wizards was when I was there."

"The area where it *was?"* Kazul said.

"They move the building every couple of months," Telemain explained. "I don't know whether they do it to stay hard to find or whether they take turns practicing the relocation spell."

"No wonder they keep trying to steal other people's magic," Kazul muttered. "They waste what they've got moving buildings around."

"South, then?" Mendanbar said, glancing around. "Very well." He raised a hand, then paused. "Morwen, are you taking *all* your cats along on this expedition?"

"Phooey," said Murgatroyd. "I was hoping no one would think of that."

"Just Trouble and Scorn," Morwen said, giving the cats a stern look. "The rest of you should get down now."

Cats flowed along Kazul's back and off her shoulders, until only Trouble and Scorn remained. When the whole crowd had reached the porch, Morwen nodded to Mendanbar. An instant later, gray mist rose, thickened to hide the house and forest, then faded to reveal a grove of slender young trees, none of which were much taller than Kazul. They looked odd and spindly, and it was a moment before Morwen realized that they only seemed scraggly by comparison to the giant oaks that surrounded her house.

"This is as far as I can take you," Mendanbar said unhappily. "The edge of the Enchanted Forest is over there."

"What about getting back in, once we leave?" Telemain asked.

"If we recover the sword, getting into the forest won't be a problem," Cimorene said. "If we don't–"

"I'll keep an eye on the border," Mendanbar said. "As soon as I see you, I'll come out to meet you."

"Don't worry about watching for us," Morwen said. "Worry about the wizards. We'll call on the magic mirror when we're ready to come back."

"And a couple of times before then, just to say hi," Cimorene put in.

Mendanbar looked at Cimorene for a long minute, then turned to Telemain. "Are you *sure* I can't leave the Enchanted Forest?"

"Not without destroying the energy loop that prevents the Society of Wizards from primary absorption inside the forest," Telemain said.

"Then can't you transfer the spell's focus from me to Cimorene?"

"Hey!" said Cimorene, frowning. "Who says I want to be a focus?"

"No," Telemain said to Mendanbar. "The top links connect directly to the central–"

" 'No' is quite enough," Morwen said. "Didn't you go over all this at the castle?"

"Yes," Cimorene said. "Mendanbar is just trying to keep me out of this." She stepped forward and drew Mendanbar a little away from the others. "Look, dear, there's nothing you can . . ." Her voice faded to a murmur.

"How far is the Brown Forest from here?" Morwen asked Telemain.

"Three transports and a two-day walk." Telemain looked at Kazul and frowned suddenly. His gaze traveled down the dragon's neck, across her wings and massive back, and out along her tail. "Make that five transports and a two-day walk. I didn't have quite so much to move last time."

"I could stay here," Killer offered hopefully.

"No, you couldn't," Morwen said. "Telemain needs you to find the wizards. Why a two-day walk, Telemain?"

"Because the Society of Wizards has established an interference pattern around the Brown Forest."

"So?" said Scorn.

"So that means it isn't safe to use transportation spells anywhere near the forest," Morwen said.

"I bet you could break it," Trouble said. "Wizards are wimps.

"Maybe," Morwen said. "And maybe you would end up with Killer's ears and Scorn's tail. Even simple interference patterns are tricky, and this one has the whole Society of Wizards behind it."

"Committees never do a good job," Scorn said, but she did not pursue the issue.

"Are you sure you need the donkey?" Kazul asked. "Because I think I can carry everyone else for at least a little way, and that would cut down on the travel time."

Killer's ears pricked up, then drooped as Telemain shook his head. "Without Killer we'd have to hunt for the Society of Wizards' building. We'd probably lose more time than we gained."

Kazul shook her head irritably. "Well, if you human people didn't waste so much time arguing, we'd–oh, good, Cimorene's finished."

Turning, Morwen saw Mendanbar and Cimorene coming toward them. Mendanbar's expression was even more unhappy than before, and Cimorene looked equally sober. "Ready to go?" she asked as they reached the group.

"Whenever you are," Telemain replied.

"Cimorene . . . ," said Mendanbar.

"Don't start," Cimorene said in a gentle tone. "One of us has to go, and you can't."

"If Telemain and Morwen weren't with you, I'd say let the wizards have the blasted sword," Mendanbar muttered. "It isn't worth the risk."

"Telemain and Morwen?" Kazul muttered. "What am I, diced troll food?"

Cimorene kissed Mendanbar's nose. "You'd say 'let the wizards have the sword,' but you wouldn't mean it. Don't worry, I'll be all right." She turned to Morwen, her eyes suspiciously bright. "Come on, let's go before he thinks of another objection."

Morwen nodded and started off. The edge of the Enchanted Forest was only a few yards away, clearly visible as a sharp line where the bright green moss stopped and ordinary grass began. At the border, Morwen waited a moment for everyone to line up, then they all crossed at more or less the same time. Telemain had them walk several yards, to get away from the "field influences," before he was satisfied that his transportation spell would work properly. Then, frowning in concentration, he made a circling gesture and muttered under his breath. The trees melted and shifted, then solidified into an open field.

"One down, four to go," said Telemain.

10

In Which Telemain Works Very Hard

Telemain had to stop and rest for a while after the second transportation spell, and after the third he looked so pale that Morwen said, "We don't *have* to go on immediately, you know. We've got at least one more day, and probably two, before the sword reaches the critical point."

"It *is* getting late." Telemain puffed as if he had been running hard for a long time. "Still, I'm quite capable of casting another spell or two."

Cimorene glanced at the tall pines that surrounded them and dug an experimental toe into the spongy accumulation of needles underfoot. "If you're sure it won't be too much–"

"We're going to have to spend the night somewhere, and this looks like as good a place as any," Morwen broke in quickly. "Better than some."

"Boring," said Trouble. "It looks boring. Jasmine would love it. Let's try for somewhere more interesting."

Kazul coiled her tail loosely around the base of one of the trees and stretched herself out on the ground. "It's comfortable, and there's plenty of room."

"I thought you were in a hurry," Telemain said irritably. "Do you want to find Mendanbar's sword or not?"

"If you wear yourself out doing transports, you won't be able to do the locating spell," Morwen said as Cimorene opened her mouth to speak.

"I'm not worn out!"

Cimorene closed her mouth and gave Telemain a long, thoughtful look.

Good, thought Morwen. *Now if I can just get Telemain to agree to stop transporting before he falls over . . .* "If we go on, where will we land next?"

"I'm not sure," Telemain admitted. "Normally, I transfer from here straight to the edge of the Great Southern Desert, but the interval is incompatible with the number of people and the mass I'm transporting on this occasion. Given the ratios, I would approximate a landing site at three-fifths of the normal distance."

"Do you know what we'd find there?" Morwen asked, ignoring Cimorene's puzzled expression.

"No."

"Then we're better off here," Morwen said in a tone intended to discourage further discussion. "It looks comfortable and quiet, and the next stop might not be either." She stepped closer to Telemain and murmured, "And we should be careful not to let Cimorene get too tired."

"Oh!" Telemain sighed in relief. "Of course. Very well, we'll camp here, and go on in the morning."

Cimorene glanced at Morwen suspiciously, but all she said was, "That's settled, then. Why don't you rest for a few minutes while we set things up?"

Killer's nose twitched. "Does that mean we'll get dinner soon? Because I'm hungry."

"Again? All those layers of spells must be affecting your metabolism," Morwen said. "Or didn't Cimorene's cook feed you properly before you left the castle?"

"Oh, he had plenty to eat," Scorn said. "He was gorging himself when we left, and he had nearly half an hour after that before Telemain brought him and the others to the house. You should have seen him, Morwen. He's worse than Fiddlesticks with a plate of fish."

"It's not my fault," Killer said in a plaintive tone. "I can't help being hungry. I just *am.*"

"Well, we can't get anything for you to eat until after we've set up camp," Morwen said. "Telemain, is there a source of water around anywhere?"

Telemain directed her to a small pool a short distance away. As Morwen set off, Cimorene fell into step beside her. Once they were too far from the others for anyone to hear, Cimorene said, "I'm sorry I wasn't more help with Telemain, Morwen. I was so worried about Mendanbar's sword that I didn't see how tired he was until he snapped at you. How did you convince him to stay here?"

"I told him you needed to rest."

"You told him *I* needed to–Morwen! I'm not sick. I'm going to have a baby, that's all. I feel *fine.*" Cimorene hesitated. "Well, mostly. Sometimes in the mornings my stomach gets a little queasy. But that's not the point."

"No. The point is that *Telemain* needs rest." Morwen pushed aside a low-hanging branch and looked at Cimorene. "Do you really want an over-tired magician transporting you? I let someone do that. Once."

"What happened?"

"I ended up forty leagues west of where I wanted to be, and I had an upset stomach for a week afterward. No one had a spare broomstick, so I had to fly home on a borrowed rake. All forty leagues. In the rain. It's the only time in my life I've been airsick."

Cimorene shuddered. "I can see why you'd want to keep Telemain from overextending himself. I just wish you'd thought of some other way to do it."

Pushing through a sweep of long, prickly pine branches, they found the pool Telemain had described. Morwen pulled the collapsible bucket out of her sleeve and filled it, and they started back to the others.

Just before they reached the camp, Cimorene paused. "Morwen, how tired *is* Telemain?"

"He could probably do one more transport without any problems," Morwen admitted. "Two more are definitely out of the question. And if we land in the middle of a battle or on top of a troll's hill–"

"I see."

Morwen nodded. "I prefer not to take chances."

"But a smaller spell wouldn't be a problem for him, would it?"

"What did you have in mind?"

Cimorene blushed slightly. "Well, I did promise I'd call Mendanbar whenever I could. And even if I'd had room for a full-sized magic mirror in my pack, I wouldn't have brought one because they're too breakable. I was hoping Telemain . . ."

"I understand." Morwen thought for a minute. "The hardest part of Telemain's magic-mirror spell is making it permanent. He shouldn't have any difficulty with a temporary speaking spell, especially if he has a chance to rest first. Ask him about it after dinner."

"I will," Cimorene said with a smile.

Cimorene's cook had provided plenty of food for the people and cats, so dinner for them was fairly straightforward. After some initial grumbling, Killer nibbled at low-hanging pine branches and even admitted that they didn't taste too bad, once he got used to them. Since there was not enough of anything to make a dragon-sized meal, Kazul left to forage for herself.

As soon as she finished eating, Cimorene broached the subject of the speaking spell with Telemain. The magician frowned and patted his pockets.

"I believe I have the necessary materials," he said. "All I need is an object."

Waving at her pack, the various cups and containers Morwen had produced from her sleeves, and the half-empty water bucket, Cimorene said, "Aren't there plenty of things around?"

"No, I mean an object for the *enchantment*. Something with the correct reflective properties. To be compatible with the existing enchantment on the castle mirror, a provisional communications spell must employ the same similarities and reversals of congruence as the original. Therefore–"

"You need a mirror, right?" Cimorene guessed.

"No," Morwen said. "He needs something *like* a mirror. Something you can see your reflection in."

"Maybe if we polish the dishes?" Cimorene said, eyeing the dented metal dubiously.

The castle cook had sent along four of the oldest tin plates Morwen had ever seen. They were suitable for camping, but not, Morwen thought, for spell making.

"What about this?" Scorn said, circling the water bucket.

"Yes, that might do." Hastily, Morwen picked up the bucket, barely in time to keep Trouble from setting his paws on the rim to peer in and collapsing it. "What do you think, Telemain?"

"Between the metallic surfaces and the water, the reflective properties appear to be adequate," Telemain said after a moment's inspection. "As long as there is no previous enchantment, it should do."

"Does carrying it in my sleeve count?"

"Since the bucket is no longer inside the spell's sphere of influence, it should have no impact on the application of a transitory enchantment."

"What does he mean?" Killer asked.

"It doesn't count–as long as the bucket isn't in my sleeve when he tries to enchant it," Morwen said. "How long will the spell last, Telemain?"

"About a quarter of an hour." Telemain set the bucket in front of him and began removing things from his pockets. "It should return to its base state by dawn tomorrow."

Setting up the speaking spell did not take long. Morwen watched Telemain closely as he crouched over the bucket, for he still seemed unusually tired, but he had no difficulty in casting the enchantment.

"There," he said finally, sitting back on his heels. "You can go ahead now, Cimorene. Just don't move the bucket."

"All right, then," Cimorene said, though she looked as if she felt a little silly.

"Mirror, mirror, on the wall,
I would like to make a call."

The water in the bucket turned white. "Tell it who to find," Morwen said softly.

"I wish to speak to Mendanbar, the King of the Enchanted Forest," Cimorene said.

With a swish and a gurgling noise, the milky color cleared. "Who's there?" snarled the wooden gargoyle. "Nobody's home and they can't be bothered, so–oh, hello, Your Majesty."

"Hello. *Is* Mendanbar at home?" said Cimorene.

"Sure. Hey, King! There's somebody on the mirror you should talk to!" the gargoyle shouted.

"Tell him who it is," Cimorene commanded.

"Aw, you spoil all my fun," grumbled the gargoyle, but it yelled, "It's Queen Cimorene!"

An instant later, the picture in the water shifted rapidly, then steadied to show King Mendanbar. "Cimorene! Is everything all right?"

"Everything's fine," Cimorene said. "We're halfway to the Great Southern Desert–"

"About three-fifths of the way, actually," said Telemain.

"–and we decided to stop for the night. How are things at home?"

"I caught a couple of wizards prowling around the forest right after you left," Mendanbar said. "You can tell Telemain that his wizard-melting spell works just fine."

"Kazul will be disappointed," Cimorene said. "We haven't seen any traces of wizards, and I think she's been hoping for a good fight."

"Well, tell her to be careful if you do run across them," Mendanbar said. "One of the ones I melted was carrying dragonsbane."

"Oh, dear. Maybe I should send Kazul home."

"You can try."

They both paused. In the brief silence, Morwen caught Telemain's eye and nodded toward the far side of the clearing. Telemain looked puzzled, then suddenly his expression changed and he rose hastily and joined her.

"We might as well give them a few moments' privacy," said Morwen when they were out of earshot. "Unless you have to stay nearby to maintain the mirror spell?"

"No, the spell is self-maintaining once it's established," Telemain said. "If someone wants to make another call, I'll have to reset everything, but she and Mendanbar can talk as long as they like without worrying about any sudden termination."

Trouble appeared around the trunk of a pine and leaned against it, scratching his back against the bark. "Well, I hope they don't go on much longer. You wouldn't *believe* how mushy they're getting."

"I don't want to hear about it," Morwen said.

"What's that?" Telemain asked. "Is something wrong?"

"Only a cat's usual refusal to let morals interfere with satisfying his curiosity," Morwen said. "Don't ask. It only encourages him."

Fortunately, Cimorene and Mendanbar did not chat for very much longer. Later, when Cimorene reported the conversation to Kazul, the dragon refused to consider leaving.

"I want some wizards, and one way or another I am going to get them," Kazul said. "If I don't go on to the central office of the Society of Wizards, I'll go back to the Enchanted Forest and hunt up a few of them there, dragonsbane or no dragonsbane."

"I don't think that's necessary," Cimorene said quickly. "Mendanbar seems to have everything under control."

"For now," said Scorn.

Not for the first time, Morwen was glad that Cimorene and Telemain, at least, could not understand what her cats were saying.

11

In Which They Make an Unexpected Detour

The next morning, much to Morwen's relief, Telemain appeared to have recovered: Without tiring, he walked briskly to and from the stream to wash up, and his color was nearly normal. After breakfast, he arranged everyone to his satisfaction and muttered the transportation spell.

They materialized on a sunny, grass-covered hillside, and as soon as their feet were firmly planted, Telemain sat down.

"Telemain?" Morwen said with concern. The magician looked a little gray.

"I'm all right," Telemain said. "I just need a minute to catch my breath."

Killer's long blue ears pricked up. "How long a minute? Have I got time for a snack? Because I think I smell a patch of clover off to the left there, and I'm hungry."

"I don't know what you're complaining about," Kazul said. "*You* had plenty of breakfast. Four cheese sandwiches aren't much of a meal for a dragon."

"Five," said Trouble.

"Pine needles are not very filling," Killer said with dignity. "Besides, I want to see what the clover is like outside the Enchanted Forest. I may not get the chance again."

Flicking a look at Telemain, Morwen said, "Go ahead, Killer. Just don't get out of sight."

Killer ambled off, his hooves just grazing the tips of the waving grasses.

"What a good thing you got him stabilized," Morwen said to Telemain. "Otherwise he'd be walking around Kazul's head by now."

"It would serve him right," Scorn said, switching her tail. "That idiot rabbit is worse than Fiddlesticks."

"Nobody's worse than Fiddlesticks," said Trouble.

Scorn gave him a green glare, then bounded over to Kazul. Two seconds later, both cats were perched on the dragon's back, basking in the sun. Smiling slightly, Morwen found a sun-warmed rock and sat down. Cimorene joined her at once, and though Telemain gave them both a suspicious frown, he did not comment.

"It's so nice to be able to just sit down, without worrying about what you're sitting on," Cimorene said. "In the Enchanted Forest, you have to be careful that you don't land on someone who's been transformed into a flower or a rock."

"Or sit on something that will transform *you* into a flower or a rock," Telemain added. He appeared to have his breath back, but he still looked a little pale so Morwen did not suggest that they continue.

The drowsy silence was broken by an earsplitting bray. "Eee-augh! Go away!" yelled Killer. "Morwen said I could eat this, and I'm going to. Leave me alone!"

Morwen looked up. The curve of the hill hid the donkey from sight, along with whatever he was shouting at.

"Blast that creature," Morwen muttered, getting to her feet. "I told him to stay in sight. No, you stay here, Telemain," she added as the magician started to follow. "There's no need to let him inconvenience both of us."

Nodding, Telemain settled back.

He must really be tired, or he'd disagree, Morwen thought. *Perhaps I can get Kazul or Cimorene to override his objections to staying here, or—no, it will be better if Trouble gets conveniently lost for a few hours. I'll have to speak to him as soon as I'm done with Killer.*

As she came around the hill, she saw a tall, grayhaired man in baggy blue overalls with a length of rope in one hand and an empty bucket in the other. Standing at the far edge of the clover patch, he stared expressionlessly at Killer and Morwen.

"This your donkey, ma'am?" the man asked.

"Not exactly," Morwen said. "What seems to be the problem?"

"He says I can't eat any more," Killer complained. "And I'd only just figured out how to get at it, too."

Morwen glanced down. Below Killer's front hooves, a double handspan of grass and clover had been trimmed several inches below the surrounding meadow. "So I see. How did you manage it?"

"Well, if I kneel down and stretch way out—"

"Excuse me, ma'am," said the man in the overalls, setting his bucket at his feet, "but if this ain't your donkey, whose is it?"

"He doesn't belong to anyone in particular," Morwen said. "And he's not actually a donkey. Why?"

The man in the overall, who had begun uncoiling the length of rope, paused. "Not a donkey, eh?" He studied Killer intently for a moment. "Blue *is* kind of an unusual color for a donkey."

"What's he getting at, Morwen?" Killer's ears waggled nervously.

"Quiet, Killer," Morwen said.

"And I got to admit that donkeys don't normally talk much," the man added. "So what is he? Enchanted prince? Knight? Circus sideshow performer?"

"Rabbit," Morwen said. "Judging from his behavior, a permanently hungry rabbit."

"Huh." The man in the overalls eyed Killer speculatively. "A rabbit named Killer. Amazing, the things people come up with. How'd he end up a blue donkey?"

"It's a long story," Morwen said. "Killer, why don't you go back to the others?"

"But what about the clover? I was just getting started. And it *is* different–not so crunchy, and not as sweet, and there's sort of a cinnamon undertaste that–"

"Not now, Killer. Go let the others know what's happening."

"Oh, all right." Muttering sullenly, Killer started back around the hill.

"What's this about others?" demanded the man in the overalls as Morwen turned back to him. "How many of you are there?"

"Seven, altogether," Morwen said.

"There are *seven* of you trampling across my fields and ruining the harvest?" the farmer asked, plainly appalled.

"Not exactly. Killer couldn't trample anything right now if he tried, and the rest of us haven't moved around much."

The farmer shook his head. "It was bad enough having that donkey or rabbit or whatever eating up my crops, but this! I want the lot of you out, right now."

"Crops?" Morwen looked pointedly to the left, then to the right, then raised her chin and stared directly at the man in the overalls. "Grass and clover?"

"Hay," the man said, unperturbed.

"Hey what?" said Cimorene's voice. "Morwen, who is this and what is going on? Killer said something about trespassers, but then he got into an argument with your cats, and it's a little hard to follow when you can't understand half of the conversation."

"This appears to be the man who owns this hill," Morwen said.

"Name of MacDonald, ma'am," the man said, nodding politely. "And this is my farm, and I'd appreciate it if you'd take your friend and your donkey and your cats elsewhere."

"I'm Cimorene, the Queen of the Enchanted Forest," Cimorene said. "Pleased to meet you, Farmer MacDonald. And we'll be leaving just as soon as our magician recovers a bit more. I'm sorry if we've caused a problem."

"Queen, eh?" MacDonald's eyes narrowed speculatively. "Little unusual to find a queen out adventuring. Mostly it's princes and younger sons, and once in a while a princess."

"So I'm unusual," Cimorene said.

"I wasn't criticizing," MacDonald said peaceably. "I just wondered if you'd be in the market for some vegetables."

"Vegetables? Why would I–"

"I got a full line of specialty crops," the farmer went on. "My peas are perfectly round, and hard as rock. I sell 'em by the bag if you want to scatter them on the floor for maidens disguised as huntsmen to walk on, or you can buy one at a time for sticking under the mattress of a visiting princess."

"I don't think I–"

"Then there's straw, first quality, for spinning into gold. I can deliver as much as you want, on a regular schedule. I grow four kinds of grain–oats, barley, millet, and wheat–on the same plants, so it's harvested premixed. I sell it by the bushel, to people who want to test someone by making them sort out the different kinds. And beans, naturally. I got the kind that jump and the kind that grow giant stalks. I've got apples, poisoned or gold, in several varieties; extra-large pumpkins for turning into coaches; and walnuts with anything you want inside, from a miniature dog to a dress as shining as the stars."

"I appreciate the offer," Cimorene said, "but I don't think I need any of those things."

"You wouldn't happen to have any invisible dusk-blooming chokevines, would you?" Morwen asked.

"No, I don't grow ornamentals," MacDonald replied. "I stick to vegetables, fruit, and nuts. Farm things. I'm hoping to branch out into livestock soon."

Cimorene blinked. "What sort of livestock?"

"Oh, little dogs that laugh, winged horses, geese that lay golden eggs, that sort of thing. That's why I'm growing hay." The farmer waved at the hillside. "I want to have it on hand when the horses arrive."

"It's not enchanted hay, is it?" Morwen asked with sudden misgiving.

"Not exactly. Why?"

"Killer tends to react . . . oddly when he's exposed to new enchantments." Nothing seemed to have happened yet, though. At least, Morwen hadn't heard any horrified braying since Killer disappeared over the hill. Perhaps it would be all right.

MacDonald shrugged. "I use enchanted fertilizer to help it grow, but the hay itself is nothing special. Winged horses eat pretty much the same thing as regular horses, plus a little birdseed."

"You sound as if you've thought about it quite a bit," Cimorene said.

"Had to," MacDonald said, nodding. "This farm's been in the family for a long time, but I couldn't make a living running it the way my dad did. Here a horse, there a pig—that just doesn't work anymore. These days, you have to have a plan. So I decided to specialize. Sure you don't need anything?"

"Not right now," Cimorene said, "but I'll keep you in mind."

"Thanks." The farmer hesitated. "About that blue donkey—"

"He isn't a donkey," Morwen reminded him. "He's an enchanted rabbit."

"Oh, that's right. Pity. He'd make an interesting start at stocking the barnyard." Fingering his rope thoughtfully, MacDonald stared off in the direction Killer had taken.

"I don't think you'd want him," Cimorene said. "He doesn't seem to be good for much."

"And he eats a great deal," Morwen added. "Most of it unsuitable, inconvenient, or both. Besides, it's time we were leaving."

"What about my hay?"

Morwen glanced at the nibbled clover and raised an eyebrow. "Killer hardly touched it. In a couple of days, you won't be able to tell which part of the patch he got at."

"Well . . ."

"Then that's settled," Cimorene said in a tone that somehow reminded everyone that this was the Queen of the Enchanted Forest talking, and if she said it was settled, it had better *be* settled. "It's been nice meeting you, Mr. MacDonald, and I shall certainly mention your special crops to my friends. Now, we really must be going." She turned and swept off.

Nodding a brisk farewell to MacDonald, Morwen followed. Halfway around the hill, she glanced back and saw MacDonald frowning uncertainly after them. *At least he isn't chasing after us,* she thought. *Goodness knows how he'd react if he saw Kazul.*

The same thought had apparently occurred to Cimorene. "We need to leave right away, if we can," she said as soon as they reached the others. "Can you manage it, Telemain?"

"Of course," the magician said. "But what's the problem?"

"Nothing dangerous, but if we stay we're likely to waste the whole afternoon arguing. I'll explain later."

"Wait a minute," Morwen said as Telemain climbed to his feet. "Where's Scorn?"

"She went after you," Trouble said.

"Bother," said Morwen. "I'm sorry, Cimorene, but–"

A narrow path of grass stirred and shifted. An instant later, Scorn leapt for Morwen's back. Her claws dug into the folds of material, and with another brief effort she pulled herself the rest of the way up to Morwen's shoulder, where she perched, purring smugly.

"No wonder you wear loose robes," Cimorene said.

Balancing carefully, Scorn stretched. Then the purring stopped and she said, "That farmer is coming after you, Morwen. I thought you'd want to know."

"Scorn says MacDonald is on his way," Morwen said to the rest of them. "If you really want to avoid him, Cimorene, we should go now."

"Then let's *go.*" Cimorene looked at Telemain.

"Everyone here? Very well, then." Eyes narrowed in unwonted concentration, Telemain raised his hands and recited the spell.

The hillside wavered like a reflection in a suddenly disturbed pool. Reluctantly, it began to melt and shift. Morwen caught a glimpse of MacDonald's face, too distorted to tell whether his expression was one of astonishment or fear, before the scene became unrecognizable.

Suddenly, everything froze. For an impossibly long instant, they hung between greenish blurs and brown blobs. Then, with a painful jerk, everything darkened and slammed into proper shapes once more. Morwen dropped two inches into a puddle of mud. The landing jarred her glasses loose and tore Scorn from her shoulder. Morwen managed to catch the cat, but her glasses vanished into the mud. Behind them, there was a squishy *thwump* as Kazul landed, followed by a yowl from Trouble and various startled noises from Killer and Cimorene.

"Drat," Morwen muttered, swallowing hard. "I knew I should have brought a stomach remedy." The air was damp and smelled like rotten eggs, which didn't help any.

"And boots," Scorn said, relaxing in Morwen's hands.

"Definitely boots," Morwen agreed. The mud was cold, soft, and ankle deep, and between the gloom and her missing glasses she could not spot a better place to step to. Assuming, of course, that there *was* a better place to stand.

"Morwen?" Cimorene called. "Where are you?"

"Where are *we,* is the question," Scorn said.

"Quiet," said Morwen. "Over here, Cimorene. Scorn, I'm going to hunt for my glasses, and I'll need both hands. If you don't want to walk around in this, you'd better climb up on my back."

With a disdainful snort, Scorn scrambled out of Morwen's grasp and back to her shoulder. Slowly, Morwen bent forward, giving Scorn time to adjust her balance. Holding her sleeves out of the way with one hand, she fished in the mud with the other.

A series of sucking noises and squelches came near. "Morwen, *what* are you doing?" Cimorene asked. She was muddy to the elbows, and she held her drawn sword in one hand.

"Looking for my glasses," Morwen replied. "Unfortunately, I don't seem to–Wait a minute." Carefully, she worked her hand free of the mud. "There. Now all I have to do is clean them."

"Easier to say than do, in this muck," Cimorene said. "Didn't you bring an extra pair?"

"Chaos broke my extra pair last week." Morwen squinted at the mud-covered glasses, then shrugged. Pinching a fold of material from her robe, she began wiping the lenses. "The replacements haven't been delivered yet."

"Well, I'm afraid I can't help. I slipped when we landed, and even my handkerchiefs are full of mud. Morwen, where *are* we? This doesn't look like the edge of a desert."

"No kidding," said Scorn.

"Ask Telemain," Morwen said, putting on her glasses. "He should have some idea where we were when he lost control." The lenses were still streaky, but at least she could see.

A worry line appeared between Cimorene's eyebrows, below the mud that smeared her forehead. "I don't know where Telemain is," she said. "I was hoping he was over here, with you."

12

Which Is Exceedingly Muddy

Morwen looked around. Here and there, tall, thin trees shot upward from the omnipresent mud. High in the air, they suddenly sprouted a wide, dense mat of twisted branches. Long, fuzzy gray-green strips of moss dangled from the branches, shutting out most of the light, and patches of dirty white fog drifted among the trunks. Between the fog and the shadows, it was hard to be sure of seeing anyone. Even Kazul seemed to melt into the gloom. Only Killer's vivid blue stood out against the muddy colors of the swamp.

"Is everyone else here?" Morwen said. Her stomach was already settling down, which was a relief. The last time this had happened, it had taken much longer.

Cimorene nodded.

"Then I'll look for Telemain. There's bound to be some residue from the transportation spell for me to trace. The rest of you stay together so I can find you again. If we split up in this mess, we're likely to lose someone permanently."

"I suppose that's best," Cimorene said, but she did not sound happy.

Morwen was not very happy about the arrangement, either, but she did not say anything more as Cimorene squelched back to Kazul. Then, with a resigned sigh, she reached into her left sleeve and pulled out a ball of red yarn and a shiny metal plate three inches across with a small hole near the rim. Focusing her attention on her most recent memories of Telemain's magic, she tied the yarn to the plate. She bent and breathed on the metal, clouding it over, then said quickly,

"Green and growing, show me.
Swift and silent, show me.
Damp and dingy, show me.
Deep and shining, show me what I would see."

With her last words, she released the plate so that it hung free. It spun wildly on the end of the yarn, and she felt it tug lightly to the right, well away from the others. Carefully, she turned, letting the faint pull guide her. It took considerable concentration to follow the spell while slogging through the cold, sticky mud.

"I *thought* something smelled different over this way," Scorn said.

Morwen spared a moment for a glance at the cat. "You might have told me."

"You were busy."

"True. Next time, tell me anyway." The tug was growing stronger. Morwen dodged around a tree trunk and almost stepped on Telemain. He lay face up in the mud, his eyes closed and his skin an unhealthy grayish white. Morwen had to look twice to be sure that he was still breathing.

Stuffing her yarn and the metal plate back into her sleeve, Morwen shouted for Cimorene to come at once and bring the others. Then she crouched next to Telemain to see what she could do for him. Unfortunately, what he needed most was to be warm, dry, and somewhere he could sleep in comfort.

He must have been even more tired than I thought he was, or the backshock wouldn't have affected him this badly, Morwen thought. *He should have said something.*

"Stubborn fool," she said aloud.

"This comes as a surprise?" Scorn said.

"Morwen, what–oh, my." Cimorene squished over as quickly as she could, followed by Killer and Kazul. Trouble, somewhat muddy and damp looking, was clinging with grim determination to a spot high on Kazul's back. The moment the dragon stopped moving, Trouble extended a rear leg and began washing it vigorously. Killer looked unusually pleased with himself, probably because floating six inches off the ground had kept him the only completely dry and unmuddy member of the group.

"What happened?" Kazul asked as Cimorene joined Morwen. "That was *not* one of the most enjoyable experiences I've ever had."

"I'm not completely sure." Morwen reached into her right sleeve and began fishing around. "I'm a witch, not a magician. But I think it's backshock from that transportation spell."

"Backshock?" said Killer.

"If you pull a rubber band too hard, it breaks and snaps your fingers," Cimorene explained. "The same sort of thing can happen when someone loses control of a spell, only it's usually more serious than stinging fingers."

"Oh." Killer looked at Morwen. "Rubber band?"

"Never mind," Morwen said. "Ah, there it is." She pulled her heavy-duty wool camping blanket out of her sleeve, glanced around for a dry spot to put it, and ended by draping it across Killer's back. "Cimorene, we have to get Telemain out of this mud. Help me lift him onto Killer."

"What? Wait a minute!" said Killer, taking two hasty steps backward. "I'm not supposed to do things like this. I'm a *rabbit.*"

"You used to be," said Morwen. "Now you're a six-foot floating blue donkey. Hold still."

"But you'll get mud all over me!"

Trouble glanced up from his washing. "Good idea. Can I help?"

"If you do, you'll get muddy, too," Scorn said. She looked at Trouble. "Muddier."

"The mud will get on my blanket," Morwen said. "And I can tell you already that Mendanbar is going to get a really enormous cleaning bill when this is all over."

"But–"

"Don't argue," Kazul said to the donkey. "I'm feeling cross enough already, and my stomach is bothering me."

"The stomachache is a side effect of snapping the transportation spell," Morwen said. "The bad temper is probably from waking up too early. Ready, Cimorene?"

Killer did argue, of course. It took nearly as long to convince him as it took to pry Telemain's unconscious body out of the mud, wrap him in Morwen's blanket, and hoist him onto the donkey's back.

"There," Cimorene panted, steadying Telemain with one hand. "That's done."

"And it looks pretty useless to me," Scorn said. She had joined Trouble on top of Kazul and was watching the whole procedure with an expression of disapproval. "Now that you've got him there, what are you going to do with him?"

Killer shifted his feet in evident unease. "This is really uncomfortable. Isn't there *somewhere* else you could put him?"

"He doesn't care much for riding on you, either," Morwen said. "Don't worry, we'll try to keep it short. Kazul, can you see anything that looks like a way out of here?"

Stretching up to her full height, Kazul peered into the fog. "No. The fog's getting thicker, and the trees all look the same."

"Hey, warn me before you do that," Trouble said reproachfully. "I almost fell off."

Kazul lowered her forelegs and glanced over her shoulder. "That can be arranged."

"It wouldn't matter," Scorn said to Trouble. "All that washing hasn't done much good. You still look like something the dog dragged in."

"You've got wings," Killer said to Kazul. "Why don't you fly up and look around?"

"Because there isn't enough room between the trees for a proper take-off, because flying in a fog is dangerous, and because I probably couldn't find you again once I got up above the treetops," Kazul said. "The tops of forests all look the same."

"Oh."

"You found Telemain," Cimorene said to Morwen. "Can't you use the same method to find a way out of here?"

"I could if there were any magic left to trace," Morwen said. "Unfortunately, there isn't. Pick a direction."

"That way," said Cimorene, and they started off.

Walking through the swamp was hard work. With every step, the ankle-deep mud sucked at their feet. Twice, Cimorene almost lost one of her short leather boots, and even Kazul had difficulty making headway. The only one who had no problem was Killer. Telemain's added weight did not pull him down at all; his hooves stayed a dry six inches above the muck no matter what. Morwen found herself wondering a little sourly whether the donkey could walk across water the same way he did across the endless mud.

Around noon, Morwen passed out chicken-salad sandwiches to everyone. Her sleeves had protected them from the mud, which was doubly fortunate since Cimorene's pack had leaked and the remains of breakfast were inedible. Unexpectedly, no one complained of a stomachache (though Killer complained about the taste of the lettuce and the bread), and the sandwiches disappeared rapidly.

When they finished eating, they went on. Morwen kept a close but unobtrusive eye on Telemain. Though he did not stir, he did not appear to grow any worse, either, which surprised her a little. She kept both her surprise and her worries to herself.

On and on they waded, until the shadows began to thicken as did the fog. Beads of moisture glistened on Kazul's scales, and the cats complained loudly of the damp. Morwen gave up trying to keep her glasses from clouding over. Telemain remained unconscious, and the worry line between Cimorene's eyebrows grew deeper.

"It'll be dark soon," Cimorene said at last. "We should find somewhere to camp. If there is anywhere. We haven't seen a dry spot since we got here. Killer, where do you think you're going?"

"I'm hungry," Killer said. "If you're going to make me haul people around, the least you could do is let me eat. It's been a long time since lunch."

"There isn't anything *to* eat," Cimorene said.

"Not for you, maybe, but those things over there look edible to me."

"What things?" Feeling slightly annoyed, Morwen took off her glasses and began hunting for a clean patch of robe to wipe them on.

"Those things wrapped around the trees," Killer said, cocking a bright blue ear to his left. "The viney things with the silver leaves. There was one patch of clover back home that had silver leaves sometimes, and it was especially good. Sweet and tart at the same time, and quite strong."

"You're seeing things," Cimorene said. "There aren't any vines on those trees."

"There are, too. You must be looking in the wrong place. Here, I'll show–"

Morwen shoved her glasses back onto her nose and snapped, "Killer, stop right where you are. Don't you take another step toward those vines of yours. If they're really there, they could be very dangerous."

Killer looked at her in disbelief. "They're just *plants.*"

"Possibly. Kazul, do you see anything?"

"Trees, fog, and mud," the dragon replied. "Lots and lots of mud. And I agree with Cimorene. We should be trying to find somewhere to camp, not arguing about imaginary vines."

"Not imaginary," Morwen corrected. "Invisible. To be exact, invisible dusk-blooming chokevines." She peered at the trees, wishing she had time to collect one or two of them. Then she shook her head. Cimorene and Kazul were right, and they'd wasted enough time already.

"They don't *look* dangerous," Killer said stubbornly. "And I'm *hungry.*"

"The last time you said that, you drank Morwen's wizard-melting water and turned blue," Scorn said.

"Quiet," said Trouble. "Go on, Killer. I would if I were you."

"You hush," said Morwen. "Keep away from those plants, Killer. They're called 'chokevines' for a very good reason. Try to remember you're carrying Telemain, and avoid anything dangerous. And let us know if you see any more of those vines."

"Oh, there are patches of them all over," Killer said. "We've been walking by them for the last hour. You really can't see them at all? None of you?"

"I can," Trouble said.

Morwen gave him a look. "We'll discuss it later."

As she turned away, a soft globe of light blossomed from the side of one of the trees Killer had pointed out. "What on earth is that?" Cimorene said.

Another light appeared, and another, and suddenly the swamp was full of ghostly radiance. "Invisible dusk-blooming chokevines, all right," Morwen said. "The sun must be setting."

"It's beautiful," Cimorene said. "How long will it last?"

"An hour, maybe two." As she spoke, Morwen moved to Killer's side to check on Telemain's condition once more. His color was no better, and the skin of his wrist was cold and clammy where she touched it to take his pulse. Of course, everything was cold and damp after hours of laboring through the mud. At least his pulse was strong.

"Will he be all right?" Cimorene asked, joining her.

"Probably," Morwen said with more confidence than she felt. The worst case of backshock she had ever seen prior to this trip had regained consciousness in a little over an hour. Telemain had already been out more than twice that long and showed no sign of awakening. Bouncing about on Killer's back should not have delayed his recovery *this* long.

"Look at the bright side," Scorn said. "As long as he's unconscious, he can't go on about things no one else understands."

Realizing that Cimorene and Kazul were watching her anxiously, Morwen shook herself. "What he really needs is warmth, rest, and a bowl of hot broth . . ."

". . . and we aren't going to find them standing here," Cimorene finished for her. "Come on, Killer. We'd better keep moving while we can still see."

In one way, the next half hour of walking was easier than the last couple had been. The invisible dusk-blooming chokevines lit the swamp with a silvery glow, like the light of a hundred miniature moons. As the group went farther along, the vines grew more and more thickly, and their blossoms shone more and more brightly, until even the mud seemed to glisten like liquid silver. Not only was it pretty to look at, but it also made it much easier to see where they were stepping.

After a while, they paused to rest. Morwen checked on Telemain again, with no better results. Frowning, she turned away. If they didn't find somewhere dry and warm soon . . .

"Cimorene, Morwen," said Kazul, "look at these lights."

"I have been, all the time we were walking," Cimorene said. "They're useful as well as pretty."

"No, I mean *look* at them." Kazul stretched out her neck and swiveled her head from one side to the other. "They aren't just growing at random. They're in rows."

Morwen studied the lights. "Not quite. The trees aren't in rows, so the vines can't be, either. But they're close."

"It's as if someone arranged them to light a path," Cimorene said after a moment. "I don't know if I like this."

"I do," Morwen said. "Paths lead somewhere. And if someone has gone to the trouble of lighting this one up, there's a good chance it leads somewhere useful."

"In that case, why didn't they pave it?"

"Maybe they like mud. Come on, we've only got another hour or so before the lights go out."

With renewed energy, they went on. Less than a quarter of an hour later, they reached a dead end. The invisible dusk-blooming chokevines covered the trees on either side and hung in swirls of glowing silver across the trunks ahead. The only way out was the way they had come.

"Useful, huh?" said Scorn.

"This doesn't make any sense," said Cimorene. "Why would anyone make a path that leads nowhere?" She drew her sword, eyeing the vines doubtfully. "Can we cut our way through, do you think?"

"I don't know," said Kazul, "and I don't care." Her tail thumped into the mud for emphasis, spattering thick, sticky gobs in all directions.

"Uh-oh," said Trouble. "Hang on, Scorn."

The dragon sat back and arched her neck. "I am *not* going to spend another two hours fighting the same mud we just came through. If I must wade through mud, it is at least going to be *new* mud. Get out of my way, the rest of you."

"If you're thinking of diving through the vines, don't," Morwen said, moving sideways. "Invisible dusk-blooming chokevines are very strong, and there are enough of them here to kill even someone as large as you are."

"Not if they've been toasted first." Stretching her head forward until it was only a few yards from the chokevines, Kazul opened her mouth and blew. Long streamers of bright orange fire shot between the trees. Kazul's head moved back and forth, sweeping the flames across the end of the path.

Steam hissed from the mud, and glowing silver blossoms winked out in puffs of ash. As Kazul's flame moved across the tree trunks, it left smaller flickers of fire behind hanging in midair. On the second pass, the flickers spread, outlining leaves and stems in tongues of flame. Blackened spirals slowly materialized around the trees as the fires burned upward and the charred vines lost their invisibility.

"I think that's enough, Kazul," Cimorene said at last.

The fire died. "Good," said the dragon, sounding a little out of breath. "Shall we go on?"

"I think we'd better wait until the mud cools off," Morwen said. "You got a trifle overenthusiastic, I'm afraid."

"No kidding," said Scorn. "Next time, warn us before you do that."

"Killer!" Cimorene shouted. "Come back here!"

"Why?" said the donkey. He stood in the middle of the path Kazul's flame had cleared through the chokevines, flecks of ash drifting through the air around him. Beyond, the fog and darkness closed in once more. "You said it was the vines that were dangerous, and they're gone."

"Even so, we shouldn't split up," Morwen said. "There may be other dangerous things around."

"We haven't seen any so far."

"And that's supposed to mean it's safe?" Scorn shook her head. "Rabbit logic."

"Isn't that a contradiction in terms?" Trouble said.

Morwen sighed. "We may not have seen anything but the chokevines, but that doesn't mean there aren't other dangers."

"All right," Killer said. "But I thought you wanted to get this wizard of yours somewhere dry."

"He's a magician, not a wizard," Morwen said automatically. "And just because Kazul dried out some of the mud–"

"No, no, I'm talking about that tall building in the open space." Killer pointed both ears into the gloom ahead of him and a little to the right. "It looks dry. Why don't we take him there?"

13

In Which They Make a New Acquaintance

Gingerly, Morwen moved forward to take a look at whatever Killer had found. The acrid scent of burned chokevines made her stomach feel queasy again, but the mud turned out to be cool enough to wade through without discomfort. Where Killer stood, it was almost dry enough to be solid ground, and the warmth that remained to filter through her shoes was very welcome.

"Now, where–ah, I see." Dimly visible in the foggy dark, a white tower stood among the trees ahead of them.

"Yes, that looks promising. Let's go." Morwen started forward, and the others followed.

Less than five minutes later, they stood at the foot of the tower. It was at least four stories high, and made of something smooth and pale that did not feel like stone. Ten feet from the base of the tower, the mud changed to hard, bare ground. This gave Morwen and Cimorene a comfortably wide area on which to stand, though Kazul was a little cramped.

"There's no door," Cimorene announced after circling the tower. "No stairs on the outside, either, but there are four windows at the top. One of them is showing a light, so somebody's home."

"But how could anybody get in?" Killer asked.

"Through the windows," Morwen said. "What a pity I didn't bring my broomstick."

"Maybe whoever lives here has some other way of getting inside," Cimorene said.

"There's one way to find out," said Kazul. With Morwen, Cimorene, and Killer in line after her, the dragon edged around the tower until she stood below the single lighted window. Then she sat back and stretched her neck upward, until her head was halfway up the side of the tower.

"Here we go again," said Trouble, wrapping all four paws tightly around one of Kazul's back spines.

"Hello, the tower!" Kazul bellowed. "Who's home? Come out and meet your visitors!"

The window flew open with a force that ought to have shattered the glass. "Go *away!"* shouted someone inside the tower. "She doesn't live here anymore, and if you keep pestering me, I'll burn you to cinders!"

Cimorene's eyes narrowed and she muttered something Morwen could not hear. Then she motioned Morwen and Killer to move back. After a moment's consideration, Morwen stayed where she was. If there were any real danger of being burned, her cats would not still be clinging to Kazul's spikes; their instinct about such things was very good.

"Come out and talk!" Kazul roared again.

A man's head appeared at the window, silhouetted against the light. "I don't want–Good lord, a dragon."

"Don't go away!" Cimorene shouted. "We need to talk to you."

"I wasn't going away," the man yelled down. "Not yet, anyway. What is a dragon doing in the middle of the Smoking Swamp?"

"So that's where we are," Trouble said.

"We missed our way," Morwen called. "And we have an injured companion who needs to rest in a warm, dry place. We were hoping you could help."

"Another one?" The man leaned precariously out, peering into the gloom. "How many of you *are* there?"

"Three humans, a donkey, two cats, and a dragon," Cimorene said. "Are you going to help or not?"

"Help." The man sounded mildly surprised by the idea. "I suppose I could. Since you didn't actually come looking for me."

"What's that got to do with it?" Killer whispered. "I don't understand this person at all."

"I expect we'll find out in a little while," Morwen said. Raising her voice, she called, "Are you going to let us in or not?"

"I think so. Yes, I believe I will. Hold on a minute while I get the laundry basket."

"Basket?" Killer's ears waggled. "I don't like the sound of this."

"Neither do I," said Kazul.

"Don't be unreasonable," Cimorene said to the dragon. "You can't expect everyone to be able to accommodate a dragon on short notice."

"This place doesn't look as if it could accommodate a dragon on *any* notice," Kazul said.

"Here it comes," said the man's voice above them. "Look out below."

Something large and dark poked out of the window, trembled, and fell. Kazul ducked, and her rear legs slid back into the mud. An instant later, a large straw laundry basket jerked to a stop a foot from the ground, bounced once, and swung twisting in the air. Three short ropes stretched from metal anchors around the basket's rim to a much longer rope that extended upward into the dark.

"One at a time, please," the man called. "And send somebody light first."

"I don't like the sound of that at all," Kazul said.

Morwen studied the laundry basket, nodded, and reached into her left sleeve. "One person at a time? Nonsense. There is no reason to drag things out." She withdrew a fat round jar and opened it. "Trouble, Scorn, I'd like your assistance, please."

Alerted by her tone, the cats slid down Kazul's sides and bounded over. Purring loudly, they took up positions on either side of the laundry basket without further instructions.

"What's that?" Cimorene asked, nodding at the jar Morwen was holding.

"Flying ointment," Morwen said. "It's a standard spell for broomsticks, but it should work equally well on a straw basket. Be quiet for a moment, please."

"What's going on down there? Hurry up, or I'll haul it in without you!"

"Kazul, would you mind?" Morwen flicked a finger at the rope.

"Not at all." Kazul took hold of the knot where all the ropes met, inserting her claws carefully in the gaps between ropes so as not to damage anything.

Satisfied that the laundry basket wasn't going anywhere, Morwen dipped a finger in the flying ointment and smeared it along the basket's rim. The straw soaked it up much faster than a broom handle, so it took longer than she had expected to work her way around the basket. Overhead, the man in the tower shouted again, but Morwen did not bother to listen. Suddenly, as she neared the spot where she had started, Scorn hissed and the laundry basket swayed wildly.

Her concentration broken, Morwen looked up. A palm-sized semicircle had disappeared from the rim of the laundry basket in front of her, and Killer was backing rapidly away. A ragged fringe of straw stuck out around the edges of his mouth.

"Killer!" said Morwen.

"I'm sorry," Cimorene said. "I should have been watching him, but I got too interested in what you were doing."

"Mm hmph *hmphrmph,"* said Killer. He swallowed and tried again. "I was *hungry*. You wouldn't let me eat those vine things."

"Straw has no nutritional value," Morwen said. "And after all that's happened to you already, I'd think you'd know better than to take a bite out of something while I'm casting a flying spell on it."

"Oh, I was careful," Killer said. "I aimed for the part you hadn't gotten to yet."

"I think you missed," said Kazul.

Killer's ears pricked up, then dropped. "What? No, I'm sure I–ouch! Oh no, now what? Morwen, this *hurts!"*

"What hurts?"

"My back. Owww! Can't you do something?"

"In a minute," Morwen said. Whatever was happening to Killer, it was unlikely to damage him seriously. Finishing the spell was far more important. To break off now might cause difficulties, and even if it didn't, there wasn't enough of the flying ointment to start over from the beginning.

Morwen turned back to the laundry basket. With two more swipes, she covered the rest of the rim, including the part Killer had bitten out. She wiped her fingers carefully on the side of the laundry basket, nodded to the cats, and said,

"One of fire, two of light,
Three from ground at dead of night.
Four in strands of deep sea foam,
Five that sings and brings them home."

The cats stretched upward and dug their claws into the straw. With a faint *pop,* a spark of dim purple light appeared on the rim of the laundry basket. It rolled around the edge, then spread down along the sides to where Scorn and Trouble held on. The cats meowed in harmony, and the light winked out, leaving a smell of burned nutmeg.

"There," said Morwen. "Now, Killer–"

"Hurry!" said the donkey. "It's getting worse. Owww! None of the other things hurt like this."

"That doesn't surprise me," Morwen said after a quick look. "You're growing wings, and Telemain's lying across the top of them. Cimorene, give me a hand, please."

"Wings?" Killer sounded stunned. "Me?"

Trouble snickered. "A bright blue six-foot donkey with wings. What an idea."

Together, Morwen and Cimorene got Telemain off Killer's back and into the laundry basket. Killer sighed in relief as the weight lifted, then he craned his neck backward to get a look at his new appendages.

"They're awfully large," he said after a stunned moment.

"They're not just large," Cimorene said. "They're enormous."

"And they're still growing," Trouble pointed out.

"Fertilizer," Morwen said resignedly. "Magic fertilizer. I *thought* there'd be trouble over that hay."

"Can't you stop them?" Killer asked nervously.

"They'll stop growing on their own, when they run out of–of the fertilizer magic," Morwen said. "It shouldn't take too long. You didn't eat much of MacDonald's hay. Now, Kazul, if you'll let go of the rope and tell our future host to give it a tug–"

Fire ran down the rope from the window to the knot, then flared brightly and died. When Kazul opened her hand, the charred ends of the three short ropes fell into the laundry basket, along with a few horrible-smelling flakes of black ash. There was nothing left of the long rope. Above them, the window slammed shut.

Shaking her hand as if it stung, Kazul said, "I think he's changed his mind."

"Too late," Morwen said. "Trouble, Scorn, let's go."

"Do we get a raise?" Trouble asked as he leapt into the laundry basket.

"Move over," Scorn said, following.

"Morwen, what are you going to do?" Cimorene asked in a worried tone.

"Get Telemain inside where it's warm and dry," Morwen replied. "I'll send the basket back for you and Killer."

"Are you sure you should–"

"I'm sure." Morwen settled herself against the side of the laundry basket and took hold of the rim. Tapping three times with her left forefinger, she said, "Onward and upward."

The laundry basket shuddered, then slowly began to rise. Morwen made no attempt to speed it up. The broomstick spell was stretched a little thin as it was. As they passed Kazul's nose, Trouble stuck a long gray paw over the rim and waved. The laundry basket wobbled in response, and Trouble scrambled back toward the center.

"Hold still," Morwen told him. "You could dump us over if you aren't careful. This isn't a broomstick."

"Now she tells me."

"I should think it was obvious."

To this Trouble made no reply. Morwen sat motionless, watching the pale surface of the tower glide past. Finally, the laundry basket reached the window. "Stop," said Morwen.

The laundry basket obliged. Peering in, Morwen saw a thin young man with bright red hair standing beside a fireplace, his back to the window. *A fire-witch?* thought Morwen. *In the middle of a swamp?* Well, not all red-haired people were fire-witches. Morwen glanced around the rest of the room. On the far side, a staircase led downward next to the wall. A stone bench, a small desk, and three comfortable-lookng chairs were the only furnishings.

With great care, Morwen leaned forward and tapped on the glass. The young man jumped and whirled, and his eyes got very large. When he did not come any nearer, Morwen tapped the window again.

"Just break it," said Trouble. "It would be less work."

Scorn snorted. "You are thinking about as much as that blue winged imbecile down below. If she breaks the window, some of the glass might fall on top of them." She waved her tail at the figures of Kazul, Cimorene, and Killer beneath them. "She can't count on *all* of it falling inside, even if she's careful."

For the third time, impatiently, Morwen rapped at the window. The red-haired man blinked, as if he were coming out of a daze, and then walked over to the window.

"Who are you?" he said, his voice slightly muffled by the glass.

"My name is Morwen, and I have an injured friend here who needs rest and warmth. Open this window immediately, please."

"I suppose I might as well." The redhead unlatched the window and swung it open, narrowly missing Morwen's head. "Sorry."

"And well you should be," Morwen told him. "Are you always so careless?"

"Mostly," said the man. "How did you get up–That's my laundry basket!" He stared for a moment, then hit his forehead with the palm of his hand. "Stupid, stupid, stupid. You enchanted the basket. Why didn't *she* think of that years ago? Why didn't *Rachel* think of it? Why in heaven's name didn't *I* think of it?"

"Because you're stupid?" Scorn suggested.

"When I think of all the effort I could have saved, hauling that thing up and down and up and down and–"

"Yes, of course," said Morwen. "Now, if you could just give me a hand with–Trouble! Not yet." The cat had crouched, preparing to spring out of the laundry basket.

"What's that?" said the man. "What sort of trouble? And why do you want a hand with it?"

"Cats," said Morwen. "And I don't want a hand with them. It's Telemain who–"

As if the sound of his name had partially awakened him, Telemain grunted and stirred. The laundry basket swung sideways, throwing Trouble off his feet. This made the basket swing even more wildly. Morwen bent forward and grabbed the window ledge, which helped stabilize things a little. Then Telemain moaned and tried to sit up. The laundry basket wobbled violently, nearly spilling everyone out. The cats wailed, and Morwen was only just able to keep hold of the window ledge.

"Blast the man!" Morwen said. "Why does he have to pick just this instant to start recovering? Telemain, hold *still.*"

The red-haired man leaned out of the window and grabbed the rim of the laundry basket. "Stop that immediately," he said sternly. "Stay *put.*"

The laundry basket froze. Trouble yowled and leapt from the bottom of the laundry basket to the young man's bent-over back, and from there into the room. "Good idea," said Scorn, and followed.

"Oof! Oof!" said the man. "What was that?"

"Cats," Morwen said again. "Help me get Telemain out of here before he dumps us over."

Between the two of them, they wrestled Telemain out of the laundry basket and through the window. To Morwen's mild surprise, the basket remained perfectly stable throughout the entire operation, but as soon as the red-haired man turned away the basket began to wobble once more.

"There's another person and an oversized donkey at the foot of your tower as well," Morwen said when Telemain was safely inside, lying comfortably on the floor in front of the fireplace. They'd have to wait to do anything about the mud that covered him from head to foot, but fortunately the red-haired man did not have much in the way of carpeting. The stone floor would sweep up easily enough. "I'd like to bring the others up as soon as possible. The donkey will be a bit tricky."

"I'll be glad to–" The young man broke off, and his expression darkened, as if he were remembering something that annoyed him. "No. I shouldn't have let you in. You had your chance."

Morwen looked at him sternly over the tops of her glasses. "If you are sulky because we didn't allow you to haul us up immediately, you are being unreasonable, unmannerly, and overly bad tempered, even for a fire-witch. Enchanting that basket of yours has saved you a good deal of effort, now and in the future, and you ought to thank us for it."

"How do you know I'm a fire-witch?" the man demanded angrily.

"You have red hair, a touchy disposition, and an instinctive control over magic, even other people's spells," Morwen said. "And from the way you burned that rope, you've some affinity for fire as well. It's obvious. Now, are you going to let me bring up those people or not?"

"I don't–"

"Morwen, company," said Scorn.

Morwen turned. Outside the open window, enormous wings flapping furiously, Killer was coming in for a landing. Cimorene lay low along his back to avoid the wings, her arms wrapped around his neck.

"Have you found something we can have for dinner?" Killer asked.

14

In Which They Trade Stories

The red-haired man stared at the apparition in disbelief. Morwen didn't blame him. Killer looked nearly as unsteady as the laundry basket, which was still hovering just outside the window.

"What on earth is that?" the man demanded.

"My friends," Morwen said. "You'd better back up. There's not much room to spare, coming through that window, and Killer's never done this before."

"Killer?" The man backed up hastily. "Good grief, it's *blue.*"

"Oh, really?" said Scorn, her voice dripping sarcasm. "We hadn't noticed."

"You know, I don't think his wings will fit through the opening unless he folds them," Trouble said. "I wonder how he'll manage?"

Killer flapped higher, then dove for the window, folding his wings at the last minute. His momentum wasn't quite enough to carry him through, and for an instant his front hooves flailed uselessly against air inside the tower while his back legs hung outside. Then he kicked, wiggled, and tumbled into the room, where he sprawled six inches above the floor, panting loudly. The sudden jerk tore Cimorene loose, and she landed next to Killer with a thud.

"Ow!" said Cimorene. "Morwen, are you all right? When the basket didn't come down again, I got worried."

"Everything is fine," Morwen said. "Telemain is even beginning to come out of the initial stages of backshock."

"Then what took you so long?" Cimorene demanded.

"I was chatting with our host . . ." Morwen turned expectantly to the red-haired man.

"Brandel," the red-haired man supplied. He still sounded sullen, but there was an undercurrent of interest, too. "I suppose that, since you're in, you can stay." He looked from Morwen to Killer to the cats to Cimorene. "But you're going to have to explain yourselves."

"In a minute," Morwen said. "First, we have to tell Kazul what's been going on. Unless you want a worried dragon tearing your tower apart." Without waiting for Brandel to answer, she leaned out the window and began shouting reassurances.

Explaining to Kazul took some time, and after that they had to haul the laundry basket back inside. Once it was in, they discovered that Killer had kicked a hole in the side in his last desperate lunge through the window. This put Brandel out of sorts again.

"I should throw you all back out the window immediately," he grumbled. "You're nothing but a lot of vagabonds."

"That doesn't sound right," Killer said, climbing to his feet. "Unless *vagabonds* is a word for a witch and a magician and the Queen of the Enchanted Forest and the King of the Dragons and some cats. And me. Is that what it means, Morwen?"

"Not exactly. Brandel is just grouchy."

"Oh." Killer shook himself, which made his wings flop open. He had to flap them once to keep his balance and then again to get them back in position. "I thought having wings would be interesting, but they're just a big nuisance."

"What was that about queens and kings and magicians?" Brandel asked Morwen.

So Morwen made a round of formal introductions, which soothed everyone's feelings. Then, just when they were getting ready to sit down and talk, Telemain stirred again and Morwen had to quiet him.

"I thought you wanted him to wake up," Killer said.

"I do, but thrashing around won't help him recover," Morwen said. "He needs to keep quiet."

"No problem," said Trouble. He stood up, stretched, strolled over to Telemain, and draped himself down the center of the magician's chest. "How long do you want him like this?"

"Thank you, Trouble," Morwen said, feeling relieved. Not only would Trouble's efforts hasten Telemain's recovery, but keeping Telemain quiet would also keep Trouble from getting into trouble. Given a specific job, the cat was quite reliable. "Two or three more hours should do it, now that he's warm. Then we can wake him, feed him some broth, and put him to bed."

"I bet he won't want to go," said Scorn.

"Three hours. Right." Trouble yawned and put his head down on his paws.

"I thought regular witches were supposed to have black cats," said Brandel, looking from Trouble to Scorn. "Unless–are you a fire-witch, too?"

"No," said Morwen. "But I don't see why that should limit me to black cats."

Brandel started to ask something else, then stopped, frowning. "No. I'll ask you about that later. Right now, you're here and you're all settled, and I want my explanation. Before something *else* happens."

"First, I'd like to know how you feel about wizards," Morwen said.

"I've never met one," Brandel replied. "And I'm not sure I want to. They don't have a very good reputation."

"Good," said Cimorene. "It's like this . . ." And she launched into the explanation.

Brandel listened with interest, but when Cimorene reached the end of her tale, he frowned. "How did you get by the invisible dusk-blooming chokevines? I thought I'd gotten all the openings near the tower filled in."

"Kazul burned a path through them."

"Mmph. Must be handy, traveling with a dragon."

"Sometimes," said Morwen. "Other times it's an inconvenience."

Suddenly, Scorn's ears pricked up and her whiskers twitched forward. "Well, *well.* What's this?"

Morwen glanced sideways to see what Scorn was watching so intently. On the top step of the staircase, a large, fluffy cat stood gazing at the newcomers. He was mostly black, with a white chin, white front paws, and a white tuft at the very end of his tail, and his expression was wary and disapproving.

"So you've finally decided to come see what was going on, have you?" Brandel said to the cat.

"Mrrow," said the cat.

"We have visitors," Brandel said. "Morwen, Cimorene, Killer, this is my cat, Horatio."

"Well, hel-lo, handsome," said Scorn. Her tail lashed once each way, and she sat up and began washing her face with great unconcern.

"He doesn't look that great to me," Trouble snarled.

"Behave yourself," Morwen said sternly. "We're guests."

Horatio eyed the group a moment longer, then came slowly forward. Halfway across the room, he stopped, studying Scorn with an intensity that matched hers. "Mmmrrr," he said at last. "Mrow yow eiou?"

"No, she won't!" Trouble shift uneasily, as if longing to jump up and pounce on this intruder. Then Morwen caught his eye, and he settled back into place on Telemain's chest, muttering under his breath.

Scorn looked from Trouble to Horatio and made a show of considering. "You don't need me for anything right now, do you Morwen?"

"No," said Morwen.

"Then I'll be happy to look around," Scorn said to Horatio. "See you later, folks."

"Watch your step," Trouble growled. "You can't trust him."

"I should hope not," said Scorn. "After all, he's a cat." Tail high, she sauntered over to Horatio. The two cats exchanged sniffs, then Horatio led the way to the staircase and they disappeared.

"She's going to regret this," Trouble said. "So is he, as soon as I–"

Morwen caught his eye again, and he stopped short. "I don't expect to have to warn you twice," she said.

"All right, all right, but you wait and see."

"Quiet," said Morwen. "Brandel, we've told you what *we're* doing here. Now suppose you tell us what *you're* doing here."

"Living," said Brandel. "Staying out of trouble. At least, that's how it was supposed to work," he added sourly.

"Of course," said Cimorene with considerably more patience than Morwen could have mustered. "But how did you come here in the first place? The middle of a swamp is an unusual place to find a fire-witch."

Brandel sighed. "It's a little complicated. I come from a family of fire-witches. Both my parents are fire-witches, and so are most of my aunts and uncles and cousins. My eldest sister is a fire-witch, and my younger brother. Everyone, in fact, except my younger sister, Rachel."

"That must have been difficult for her," Cimorene said. "Being the only different one in the family is hard."

"My parents thought the same thing," Brandel said. "So when Rachel was very small, Mother brought her to the sorceress who lived in this tower, to be apprenticed."

"A sorceress chose to live in a swamp?" Cimorene said skeptically.

"They like inaccessible places," Morwen said. "Though I'll grant you, this is a little extreme. Go on, Brandel."

"The sorceress agreed to take Rachel in and teach her magic, and once every five years or so we would come and visit. Since there wasn't a door in the tower, the sorceress lowered a chair on a long rope and hauled us up to the window one at a time." Brandel shook his head. "The laundry basket is a lot safer; it's not so easy to fall out of.

"In any case, the sorceress asked us to keep the arrangement a secret, and we tried, but that sort of thing always seems to get out somehow. Some of the rumors were pretty wild: one of the stories said my mother sold Rachel to a wicked witch in exchange for some vegetables."

"I think I've heard that one," Cimorene said.

"Anyway, there wasn't much we could do. By the time Rachel was sixteen, all sorts of people were showing up in the swamp to rescue the beautiful princess from the wicked witch."

Cimorene nodded. "I know what that's like. When I was Kazul's princess, the knights and heroes made themselves a dreadful nuisance. You wouldn't believe how stubborn some of them could be."

"Want to bet? They're still coming around, and half the time they won't listen when I say she isn't here any longer." Brandel looked down. "That's what I thought you were, at first: a group of heroes."

"Sounds like a reasonable description to me," said Trouble.

"Is your sister beautiful?" Morwen asked.

Brandel shrugged. "She's pretty enough, I suppose. For a while, she was flattered by all the attention, but the constant interruptions just irritated the sorceress. Finally, she gave the tower to Rachel and moved somewhere else, just to get away from it all."

"I can't say I blame her," Cimorene said, nodding.

"I don't know," said Killer, who had been listening with great interest. "It must have taken a lot of work to build a place like this. Couldn't she have just kept them away somehow?"

"They're very persistent," Cimorene said. "You have no idea."

"And besides, heroes weren't the only problem with this location," Brandel said. "Just the main one."

Killer snorted softly. "I still think–"

"About the tower," Morwen said to Brandel. "The sorceress gave it to your sister . . ."

"And she lived here for a while, until she couldn't stand having strangers stand outside and shout, 'Rachel! Rachel, send down the chair' any longer. Half the time they didn't even get her name right. So when Arona started making life difficult for me, she–"

Morwen stiffened. "Hold on a minute. *Who* did you just say was making life difficult for you?"

"Arona Vamist." Brandel's eyes narrowed and his fists clenched. "He is the meanest, lowest, most obnoxious, narrow-minded, opinionated . . ." With every word Brandel's voice rose, until he was shouting at the top of his lungs. Then, abruptly, his hair burst into flames.

After a shocked instant, Morwen relaxed. Fire-witches were supposed to be immune to fire, among their many other gifts, and she found this demonstration extremely interesting. Cimorene, too, seemed more surprised than frightened, but Killer was not so sanguine. He reared back in surprise, forgot to allow for his wings, and almost overbalanced. To keep his footing, he had to flap several times, filling the room with the wind from his wings. The flames brightened briefly, but then the breeze distracted Brandel from his angry tirade, and a moment later his hair went out.

"That was interesting," said Trouble.

"Interesting isn't the half of it," said Morwen. "That wouldn't by any chance have been Arona Michaelear Grinogion Vamist you were railing at a moment ago, would it?"

"That's the one," Brandel said, nodding vehemently. "And if I ever get my hands on the sneaking little–"

"Yes, of course," Morwen interrupted hastily, hoping to forestall another outburst. "If talking about it won't upset you too much, would you mind telling me exactly how Arona Michaelear Grinogion Vamist was 'making life difficult' for you?"

"Not just for me. That weasel has it in for the whole family." The ends of Brandel's hair began to glow like embers in a high wind. With a visible effort, he controlled himself and went on. "He'd been going on about *true magic* and *traditional forms* for a long time, but nobody ever paid much attention. Then he petitioned the Town Council to outlaw all 'nontraditional' magic, and somehow he got them to do it."

"And fire-witches aren't on his traditional list," Morwen said.

Brandel nodded. "He got us thrown out of our home, and there wasn't a thing we could do about it."

"Nothing?" Cimorene raised an eyebrow. "From what I've heard about fire-witches–"

"Using our magic against him would only have made his arguments to the Town Council sound more reasonable," Brandel said.

Cimorene and Morwen just looked at him.

"All right, we tried!" Brandel hit the arm of his chair with one fist, and little flames flickered in his hair. "Somebody was helping the little creep. He has a really first-class protective spell, one the whole lot of us couldn't get a handle on. When we found out we couldn't get at him, the others went to visit my uncle in Oslett. I came here, hoping Rachel would know where the sorceress had gone. I thought maybe she'd help."

"Rachel didn't know, I take it?" said Morwen.

"No, but she let me have the tower. She even warned me about all the knights and heroes before she left, but I didn't believe her." Brandel sighed. "I do now. That's why I filled in the end of the sorceress's walkway."

"Walkway?" said Cimorene.

"The one lined with invisible dusk-blooming chokevines. Didn't you notice?"

"We noticed the vines. We didn't notice a walkway. Just mud."

Brandel shrugged. "I don't think she got out much, and when she did, she usually flew."

"So you've been living here ever since you got thrown out of your hometown?" Morwen asked.

Brandel nodded.

"How long is that?"

"Around four months, I think. I lose track. Not a lot happens, except knights, and the days sort of blur together. I don't even know what's been happening outside the swamp."

"Arona Michaelear Grinogion Vamist seems to have decided to move on from fire-witches to regular witches," Morwen said. "As near as I can tell, he's trying to get everyone to wear pointy hats and cackle a lot."

"You watch out," Brandel said. "He's up to something."

"I'm beginning to regret missing his call," Morwen said.

"*You* got a call from this Vamist person?" said Cimorene. "What did he want?"

"The cats didn't say."

Trouble let his eyelids close almost to slits. "Nothing important."

"That reminds me," Cimorene said. "Brandel, have you got a magic mirror around that I could use? I promised Mendanbar I'd let him know how things were going every once in a while."

"I think the sorceress left an old one in the storage closet," Brandel said. "I'll check."

The fire-witch disappeared down the staircase. Morwen and Cimorene looked at each other.

"This is *not* going well," Cimorene said.

"I wouldn't say that," Morwen replied. "We have somewhere dry to spend the night. Under the circumstances . . ."

"That's just it. The circumstances. We're goodness-knows-how-many leagues from where we ought to be, Telemain's hurt, and we still don't have any idea where Mendanbar's sword is. And we've wasted a whole day. Any minute now, that sword may start leaking magic and–"

"–and fretting yourself into fits won't help a bit," Morwen said. "Magical pressure takes time to build up, and it's only been a day and a half since the sword was stolen. We probably have at least another day before the magic of the Enchanted Forest starts draining out."

"Probably. But what if we don't?"

Morwen sighed. "Perhaps we're approaching the problem from the wrong direction. Let me think about it."

"With Telemain to take care of, when will you have time?"

"I'll manage," Morwen said.

A muffled *thump* echoed from the stairwell. Another followed, then some scraping noises. "Ow!" said Brandel's voice. A moment later, the carved wooden rim of an enormous old mirror thrust up out of the stairwell.

"My goodness, it's large." Cimorene rose hastily and went over to help. "You should have said something."

"I'd forgotten how big it is," Brandel panted.

Together, they hoisted the mirror the last few feet up the stairs and propped it against the wall. "Will it do?" Brandel asked.

"I don't see why not," Cimorene said, but she sounded doubtful.

Morwen couldn't blame her. The sorceress's magic mirror was so old that the glass had uneven areas that distorted the reflection. Tarnish mottled the silver backing like black moss, and the wooden frame had deep cracks.

"Well, there's no point in waiting," Cimorene said.

"Mirror, mirror, on the wall,
I would like to make a call."

Leaning forward, she waited eagerly for the mirror's response.

15

In Which They Have Difficulties with a Mirror

Slowly, the splotchy reflection of the room faded into a smooth, even white. Then a voice from the mirror said, "Really?" It sounded hoarse, as if it hadn't been used in a long time. "Are you sure you don't want to leave me down in that storeroom for another twenty or thirty years, gathering dust and cobwebs and talking to the magic cloaks for company? Not that I'm complaining, mind, but cloaks don't have much in the way of conversation."

"I wish to speak to Mendanbar, the King of the Enchanted Forest," Cimorene said firmly.

"You're supposed to specify that in the verse, you know," the mirror said. "Though I guess I can make an exception, this once. Especially since you know exactly who you want to talk to. None of this 'fairest of them all' silliness. I hate that. I have to hunt through seven or eight hundred people, and in the end it's a matter of opinion anyway, and nobody is ever happy with the results. Now, you are clearly a woman of decision. 'I wish to speak to Mendanbar, King of–' Wait a minute. King? Are you sure?"

"Quite sure," said Cimorene. "Put me through to him, please."

"If you insist," said the mirror, "but I should warn you that in my experience kings don't talk to just anyone."

"He'll talk to me. I'm his wife."

"Well, sorry, Your Majesty," said the mirror in a huffy tone. "I'll get right to it. I suppose you know that there's mud on your cheek."

Before Cimorene could reply, the mirror filled with slowly swirling colors, and from it came the sound of someone humming a soft melody ever-so-slightly off key. "Mirror!" said Cimorene. "Mirror?"

The mirror did not respond. "I think you just have to wait until it comes back," said Brandel.

"Isn't there some way to make it stop humming?" said Cimorene. "Morwen? You know about magic mirrors."

"Not enough to do that," Morwen said regretfully.

Finally, the humming stopped and the mirror cleared, but instead of the grinning face of the gargoyle in Mendanbar's study, or Mendanbar himself, they saw only the same milky whiteness as they had before. "I'm sorry," said the mirror. "I don't seem to be able to get through."

Cimorene and Morwen stared at the mirror for a moment in appalled silence. Then Cimorene said, "Can't get through? Why not?"

"How should I know? I'm just a mirror."

"Try again," said Morwen.

"And no humming this time!" Cimorene added, but she was too late. The swirling colors–and the humming–were back.

This time the wait seemed interminable. Cimorene paced back and forth in front of the mirror, frowning and biting her lower lip. Finally, the humming stopped and the mirror cleared.

"Nope," it said. "There's nothing to communicate with. Are you sure he has a magic mirror?"

"He did when we left," Cimorene said.

"Maybe someone broke it," Killer suggested.

"Unlikely, but possible," Morwen told him. "Still, I think the difficulty is probably at this end."

"There's nothing wrong with me!" said the mirror indignantly. "I've had no complaints, not one, in all the years since I was first enchanted."

"That was, however, a long time ago." Morwen turned to Cimorene. "Telemain did the spell on the mirror at the castle, didn't he?"

Cimorene nodded. "Last year, as a wedding present. He updated it just a few weeks ago."

"Then it is possible that the two mirrors are incompatible," Morwen said.

"Ridiculous," said the mirror. "I'm very easygoing. I get along with everyone, even that dreadful woman who spied on her stepdaughter all the time. Now, *that* woman was incompatible with everyone. Honestly, the things she did–"

"Go to sleep," Morwen said.

"Phooey," said the mirror, and the milk white surface faded back into blotchy silver.

"Do you really think it's just a problem with the different spells?" Cimorene asked doubtfully, but her expression had lightened a little already.

"It doesn't happen often, but it does happen," Morwen said. "We can ask Telemain about it tomorrow morning. Maybe he'll have some suggestions."

"I don't know." Cimorene chewed gently on her lower lip. "I think I need to talk to Kazul. Killer–"

"Oh no," said the donkey. "Not me. Flying is too much work. And I haven't had any dinner yet."

"He does sound like Fiddlesticks," said Trouble.

"I suppose I should get you something," Brandel said without much enthusiasm. "What would you like?"

Killer's eyes lit up. "Clover. With sweet flowers and slightly tart leaves, for a nicely balanced mix of flavors, and maybe a little parsley as a palate cleanser. Not the kind of parsley that crinkles up, the kind with the flat leaves."

"I'll see what I have," Brandel said, sounding slightly stunned.

"Well, if Killer won't help, I'll have to take the laundry basket," Cimorene said with a shrug. "Will you show me how to use it, Morwen?"

"Certainly," Morwen said. "Just bear in mind that the balance is a little tricky."

"It can't be any worse than the magic carpet Mendanbar and I had to ride when we were looking for Kazul," Cimorene replied. "I'll manage."

Morwen nodded, and she gave Cimorene the short list of basket-control commands. Together, the two women wrestled the basket out the window and set it hovering. Then Morwen held it while Cimorene climbed carefully into it. To make sure nothing went wrong, Morwen watched as Cimorene started down, then she turned away from the window with a smile. Cimorene was right. She could manage.

A new series of thumps and scrapes echoed up the stairwell, and Brandel appeared, carrying a bushel basket heaped full of clover.

"Now, where did you find that?" Morwen asked.

"The sorceress didn't like running to town for groceries," Brandel said, setting the basket in front of Killer. "So she enchanted her pantry so it would always have whatever she needed, for herself or for any visitors who happened to stop by."

"I thought she didn't have visitors," Morwen said.

"She didn't have many. I suppose she thought having company was bad enough without having to go shopping to feed them, too."

Killer's ears stiffened, and he paused in midbite. "Enchanted?" he said around a mouthful of clover. "This is more enchanted food?"

"No, no, it's the *pantry* that's enchanted. The *food* is perfectly normal," said Brandel. "Weren't you listening?"

"You'll have to pardon him," Morwen said. "He's trying to be cautious because he's had a bad experience. A series of bad experiences."

"You're *sure* this is safe?" Killer said anxiously. "I'm getting tired of all these changes."

"It's a little late to worry about it now," Trouble told him. "You've already eaten some. I don't suppose Brandel thought to bring a saucer of cream along with all that rabbit food?"

"Yes, about the rest of us . . . ," Morwen said.

"Oh, sorry." Brandel looked embarrassed. "I guess I'm not used to having company. What would you like?"

"Let's see what you have," said Morwen, and started for the stairs.

By the time Cimorene returned, Morwen and Brandel had laid out a substantial supper, including roast boar, baked potatoes, carrots, green beans and tiny onions, and spring water for the people; and sardines with cream for the cats. Killer had finished his first basket of clover, the second was half gone, and he was beginning to slow down. It looked as if he might, for once, have enough to eat at a meal.

"Did you have a nice chat with your dragon?" Brandel asked as Cimorene pushed the laundry basket into a corner where it would be out of the way.

Cimorene rolled her eyes. "Kazul is not, and never has been, *my* dragon. I was *her* princess for a while, but now we're just friends."

"Oh. Well, did you have a nice chat with your friend, then?"

"Sort of." Cimorene looked at Morwen. "Kazul is leaving."

Morwen considered. "When? And why?"

"Right away. She–"

Something large *whooshed* past the window outside. "There she goes," Cimorene said.

"That still leaves why." Morwen pulled a chair up to the table and sat down. "You can explain over dinner."

"Something smells good up here," Scorn said from the staircase, poking her black nose over the top of the last step. "Hey, Horatio, there's cream!"

"If I don't get any, I will be *very* upset," said Trouble, lashing his tail for emphasis as the other two cats bounded out of the stairwell and headed for the bowls Brandel had left on the floor.

Cimorene smiled absently at the cats and joined Morwen at the table.

"It's–well, dragons aren't very patient at the best of times. And we haven't run into any wizards yet, and Kazul wasn't sure your enchanted pantry would be up to feeding a dragon. So since I was worried about Mendanbar–"

"And since Mendanbar said something about wizards in the Enchanted Forest when you talked to him last night–" Morwen said.

And since there's not much dragon food in the swamp–" Killer put in.

"–Kazul offered to go home and–and see what's going on." Cimorene took a large helping of the roast boar and dug in with relish.

"It may be just as well." Morwen took a much smaller portion of the boar and looked at it doubtfully, wondering whether her stomach was up to it. "Once we have the sword, we'll want to return to the Enchanted Forest immediately. Telemain won't be fit for much for a day or so, but–"

"Oh no! Morwen, we can't afford to sit around here for a whole day!"

"If you have a better idea, I'd like to hear it," said Morwen. "Besides, we haven't got the slightest idea where we're going, so rushing off won't get us there any quicker. We'll be better off if we take time to plan."

"I suppose so," Cimorene said, but she didn't sound happy about it.

"As I was saying: By tomorrow morning, I'll have some idea when Telemain will be able to do a proper transport spell again. Without Kazul, he can take us considerably farther each time and still stay within the safety limits."

Cimorene swallowed a mouthful of potato. "That's good. The faster we go, the sooner we'll get the sword back to the Enchanted Forest."

"Exactly." With some regret, Morwen set down her fork. "For tonight, the best thing we all can do is rest. Brandel, will you help us with Telemain?"

"I don't need help," Telemain said unexpectedly from the floor in front of the fire. "I need dinner. Where are we, and why is there a cat on my chest?"

"He was supposed to be making sure you stayed asleep," Morwen said, turning to give Trouble a reproving look.

"It's not *my* fault," Trouble said. "He doesn't react right. I've never had to use that spell on a magician before; maybe that's why." He rose and stepped carefully down from Telemain's chest. "Are there any sardines left?"

Telemain sat up and looked at Trouble with dislike. "That animal is remarkably heavy for something that looks that skinny."

"That's gratitude for you," said Trouble. "He should be glad I'm not Chaos."

"How are you feeling?" Cimorene asked Telemain anxiously.

"Squashed," said Telemain. "And may I point out that as yet no one has answered my first question. Where are we?"

"The Smoking Swamp," Morwen told him. "And this is Brandel. We were fortunate enough to find his tower in time to spend the night, or you'd be sleeping in mud."

"I appear to have done that already," Telemain said, picking flakes of dried mud from the left shoulder of his vest. Suddenly, he looked up, frowning. "Spend the *night?*"

"You got an unusually heavy dose of backshock when you lost control of the transportation spell," Morwen told him. "You've been unconscious all day."

"Ridiculous," said Telemain. "I did not lose control of the transportation spell, and I am not suffering from backshock."

"Well, this certainly isn't the edge of the Great Southern Desert," Cimorene said. "And *something* knocked you out for most of the day."

"I had to carry you," Killer said, bobbing his head up and down for emphasis. "You're heavy."

Morwen's eyes narrowed. "If it isn't backshock, what is it?"

"The opposite of backshock," Telemain said. "I don't believe there is a word for it."

"Explain."

"Backshock occurs when the accumulated magical energy contained within an enchantment-in-process rebounds upon the magician casting the spell due to his inability to maintain control," Telemain said.

"He's feeling better, all right," said Trouble, glancing up from the sardines.

"Mrrow vrow?" said Horatio.

"Yes," said Scorn. "Sometimes he's even worse."

"In this instance, both the disruption of the transportation spell and the prolonged unconsciousness that followed resulted from an expropriation of magical energy as a result of the partial absorption of my enchantment-in-process by a similar but much more extensive enchantment."

"What?" said Brandel.

"You're sure?" Morwen said, frowning.

"Positive," said Telemain. "The sensation was quite unmistakable. And I must also point out that the normal secondary consequences of backshock are not in evidence."

"What does *that* mean?" Cimorene said.

"It means I'm starving," Telemain said, climbing to his feet. "Can we finish this discussion over dinner?"

"Most of us have eaten," Morwen said. "You can have dinner while the rest of us discuss. About this other spell–"

"*What* other spell?" Cimorene said. "Morwen, will *one* of you please explain what you're talking about?"

"Sorry," Morwen said. "Telemain said that he didn't lose control of the transportation spell. Somebody else was transporting at the same time–"

"A very large somebody else," Telemain said, piling a plate with slices of roast boar and heaps of vegetables. "Or possibly someone moving a moderately large house."

"–and the second spell sucked up enough of Telemain's magic to break his spell right in the middle of things."

"Sucked up Telemain's magic?" Cimorene scowled. "That sounds an awful lot like wizards."

"Aren't you jumping to conclusions?" Brandel said. "I know wizards have a bad reputation, but they aren't *thieves.*"

"They took Mendanbar's sword."

"And they've been stealing magic on a small scale for years," Morwen said. "Just ask the dragons."

"But if it *was* wizards, where were they going?" Cimorene tapped her fingers nervously against the arm of her chair. "And what were they planning to do when they got there? Oh, I *wish* I'd been able to reach Mendanbar."

Telemain made a questioning noise, so Morwen explained about Brandel's magic mirror. "I thought the spell might be incompatible with the one in the castle," she finished. "Do you feel up to checking, once you're done eating?"

"I can certainly try," Telemain said. "If that's the problem, though, I doubt that I'll be able to do anything about it until tomorrow. It takes time to rebuild magical reserves."

But when Telemain examined the mirror, he shook his head. "It's an old universal-application single-unit enchantment. Quite an impressive antique, and I can see that it's been well maintained. The connective interface is pretty basic, therefore–"

"Can you fix it to get through to Mendanbar or not?" Cimorene asked.

"I was getting to that." Telemain looked at the expression on Cimorene's face and sighed. "I'm afraid it doesn't need adjusting," he said with unusual gentleness. "There's nothing wrong with the spell, and it shouldn't be incompatible with the castle mirror. The problem is somewhere else."

"I knew it," Cimorene said. She rose and began to pace in front of the fireplace. "Something is wrong at home."

16

In Which They Learn Something Worth Knowing

Both Morwen and Telemain agreed with Cimorene, at least in part, but even if they had wanted to, they could not have done anything that night. Telemain was much too drained to cast another transportation spell, and they had no other way of getting back to the Enchanted Forest in a hurry. Furthermore, there was not much point in going back without the sword.

"Mendanbar has all the magic of the Enchanted Forest to use against the wizards," Morwen said. "He doesn't need more magicians. He needs his sword, so he can stop all of the wizards at once instead of attacking them one or two at a time."

"Yes, but there are so *many* of them," Cimorene said. "And there's only one of him. And what if the sword has started draining magic out of the forest? The wizards will be getting more powerful and Mendanbar will be getting less."

"If the sword has started leaking Enchanted Forest magic, the best thing we can do is to get it back to the forest quickly," Morwen said.

"And anyway, there are only three of us," Telemain pointed out. "That wouldn't change the odds much."

"There are six of us," Trouble said indignantly. "What's the matter, can't he count?"

"I'll admit that the rabbit isn't good for much, even as a donkey," Scorn said. "*We,* however, are another matter entirely."

"Kazul will be far more help to Mendanbar than we would," Morwen told Cimorene. "Our job is to get hold of that sword. And you are the only one who can do that."

Cimorene sighed. "I know. I just wish I could be there with him."

"Then we had better stop worrying about what Mendanbar is doing and start figuring out how to find his sword in the shortest possible time, so we get back as soon as we can," Morwen said.

Everyone agreed that this was an excellent idea, but though they discussed the matter for another hour, no one had any suggestions. Finally, Morwen put an end to the discussion. "We are all getting too tired to think," she said. "We will do much better in the morning." Brandel supplied them each with a room and a warm bath–which the cats declined–and Morwen made certain that the others were settled in before she retired herself.

The following morning, Morwen rose early. Even so, Telemain was up before she was. She found him in the topmost room of the tower, sitting in front of the dead ashes of the fire and staring at Brandel's magic mirror with an expression of concentration on his face. On the far side of the room, Killer slept with his head down and his oversized wings flopped awkwardly across his back.

"Good morning," Morwen said as she climbed the last few stairs. "How are your magic levels?"

"Much better," Telemain said absently. "Morwen, how much do you know about these old universal-application units?" He waved at the mirror.

"Using them or enchanting them?"

"Using them."

"Quite a bit," Morwen said. "Forty years ago they were standard equipment for witches, and learning to use them is still considered part of a witch's basic education. Why?"

"How universal is the universal application?" Telemain asked.

"It depends on the mirror. Can't you figure it out from looking at the underlying enchantment?"

Telemain frowned. "Probably, but it's not a good idea to take a working antique apart unless you absolutely have to. They're old and fragile, and if I popped one of the main core links it could take days to repair."

Morwen suppressed a sigh of irritation. There was no point in snapping at Telemain when he was in this mood. He wouldn't notice. "It would help if you told me what you want to do with it."

"I was considering the possiblity of using the mirror as a locating device," Telemain said. "If the universal-application portion of the enchantment is truly universal . . ."

". . . then we can use it to find Mendanbar's sword," Morwen said.

"What an excellent suggestion. I should have thought of it myself. Back at the castle, perhaps, when it would have saved us some time."

"It wouldn't have done any good then." Telemain bent over the mirror, oblivious to Morwen's sarcasm. "The enchantment on the castle mirror is limited to animate, sentient beings, and while Mendanbar's sword is occasionally temperamental, it is neither animate nor sentient. Now, if you'll just show me where the external connectors are, I'll hook this to a low-level identification spell and–"

"If all you want to do is find Mendanbar's sword, you shouldn't need an identification spell. The mirror is quite capable of handling the whole thing itself, if it's approached correctly."

"Who's approaching what, and why do you have to be correct about it?" Cimorene asked, climbing the last few stairs into the room. Trouble, who seemed to have been escorting her, bounded over the last step and stopped dead in his tracks. Cimorene did not quite trip over him, but it was a near thing.

"Telemain wants to use Brandel's mirror to find the sword," Morwen said, giving Trouble a reproving look. Trouble looked away and wandered casually toward Killer, who raised his head and blinked sleepily at the cat.

Dubiously, Cimorene examined the mirror. "Can it do that?"

"I see no reason why not," Morwen said. "You heard what it said last night about hunting for the fairest in the land. If it can do that, it ought to be able to look for a sword."

"Good," said Cimorene.

"Mirror, mirror, on the wall,
I would like to make a call."

Nothing happened. "What's the matter?" said Cimorene. "Is it broken?"

"Possibly," Telemain said. "Antique spells are easily disrupted."

"They're also cranky," said Morwen. Stepping forward, she tapped the mirror briskly on the left side.

Immediately, the mirror turned white, as if someone had thrown a large bucket of milk at the reverse side. "Now what?" it said, sounding extremely cross.

"I want to see where Mendanbar's sword is," Cimorene told it.

"Too bad," said the mirror. "I told you yesterday, that has to be specified in the verse. Get it right, or don't bother asking. I really can't make any more exceptions." Without waiting for an objection, the mirror turned its usual blotchy silver.

"Come back here!" said Cimorene, but the mirror remained obstinately silver.

"Hmph," said Morwen. "I suppose I should have expected this. My first magic mirror used to be irritable in the mornings, too."

"What can we do about it?" Cimorene asked.

"Give me a minute to think."

"I could constrain a certain level of performance," Telemain said, frowning. "However, the accuracy of the information obtained might leave something to be desired. On the other hand–"

"Better think fast," Trouble said to Morwen.

Footsteps sounded in the stairwell. "You're all up early," said Brandel. "Would you like some breakfast?"

"I'd like your blasted mirror to cooperate," Cimorene muttered under her breath.

"Got it," Morwen said. "Move over, Cimorene."

"Mirror, mirror, on a hook,
Where's the sword the wizards took?"

As the mirror's surface reluctantly faded to white, Telemain stared at Morwen in disbelief. "You call that a spell?"

"It rhymes and it scans," Morwen said. "What more do you want at this hour of the morning? And on the spur of the moment, too."

"I agree with him," the mirror said. "That was a *lousy* couplet."

"If you'd found us the sword to begin with, you wouldn't have had to listen to it," Morwen said, unperturbed. "Do your job."

Cimorene leaned forward. "And this time, please don't–"

Whirling colors filled the mirror, and a soft but penetrating off-key hum echoed through the room.

"–hum," Cimorene finished, half a second too late. "Bother!"

"As long as it finds the sword for us, I don't care if it sings an aria backward," Morwen said. "If it annoys you that much, put your fingers in your ears."

Trouble jumped onto the window ledge and curled his tail around his feet. Two seconds later, Scorn and Horatio tore out of the stairwell and raced around the room, startling Killer into wakefulness. A loud bray drowned out the mirror's humming, and Brandel winced. As the cats settled onto various pieces of furniture for their morning wash, Cimorene nudged Morwen's side. "Look! It's working."

Morwen turned back to the mirror and smiled in satisfaction. The glass had cleared to show a large, ramshackle house with two chimneys and a steeply pointed roof. The windows were made up of small glass rectangles, and ivy covered most of them so thickly that it seemed unlikely that anyone could see out.

"That's the central office of the Society of Wizards?" Cimorene said.

"No," Telemain replied. "Apparently I was wrong, and they aren't keeping the sword at the central office. It's a good thing I thought to check." He sounded extremely smug. "Now all we have to do is find out where that house is."

"It's about five miles past the edge of the swamp," Brandel said. "Right outside the town where I grew up. But I don't think knowing that does you much good."

"Why do you say that?" Morwen asked.

"Because you said the Society of Wizards stole this sword you're after. *That* house belongs to Arona Michaelear Grinogion Vamist."

"What?"

"You mean it's the wrong *place?"* Cimorene said. "After all that?"

"It is *not* the wrong place!" the mirror said indignantly. "I've been a magic mirror for one hundred and forty-seven years, and I haven't made a mistake yet. Look here!"

The scene in the glass swooped and whirled dizzyingly, and then the view plunged through one of the ivy-covered windows into a dimly lit room. Inside, two men sat at a dusty table, drinking black coffee and contemplating a shiny sword lying on the table between them. One of them was bald and sharp faced, while the other–

"That's Antorell!" Cimorene said. "He's gotten himself back together awfully fast this time. It must be all the practice he's had."

"That's Arona!" Brandel said at the same instant, staring at the bald man. "Is that the sword you're looking for?"

"It appears to be," said Telemain.

Cimorene nodded. "That's Mendanbar's sword, all right. See how it looks twice as bright as anything else? I bet it's leaking magic all over."

"Leaking magic?" said Killer, poking his long nose over Morwen's shoulder to peer at the mirror. "You never said anything about that sword leaking magic. It doesn't sound very safe."

"It isn't," Cimorene told him. "Which is another reason why we have to get it back to the Enchanted Forest quickly. The longer it's outside the forest, the worse it gets. That sword *belongs* in the Enchanted Forest."

"Don't worry about it," Morwen said to Killer. "It won't hurt you unless you try to eat it."

"That would be fun to watch," said Trouble, cocking his head to one side.

"Mrow?" said Horatio.

"Probably not," Scorn said with some regret. "Even Killer isn't *that* stupid."

Brandel was still staring at the mirror with a grim expression. "So that's it. That no-good, interfering, lousy little troublemaking weasel has gotten the Society of Wizards to help him!" His voice rose steadily until he was shouting, and on "troublemaking" his hair burst into flames.

"Yow!" said Killer, jumping backward. "Ouch! That was my *ear*. Whoops!" As he recoiled from Brandel's blazing head, his wings flopped open, catching air and throwing him off balance. Twisting frantically to keep his left wing tip away from the fire, Killer flapped twice and fell over in a tangle of legs and ears and feathers. The cats bounced away from him, startled and bristling.

"Hey, watch what you're doing," said Scorn. "You could hurt someone." Horatio gave her neck a reassuring lick.

Slowly, Killer settled his wings into place and climbed back to his feet. "I think I sprained something," he said mournfully. "And my ear is singed." He gave Brandel a reproachful look.

Brandel didn't notice. Hair still burning merrily, he turned to Cimorene. "If you want some help getting that sword back, just ask. That sneaking, repulsive little–"

"Are you done?" asked the mirror. "Or do you actually want to watch these two have breakfast?"

"Possibly," said Morwen. "Telemain, is there any way we can hear what they're saying?"

"I doubt it," Telemain said. "In any event, it would require considerable time to determine the precise adjustments appropriate to the subcategory. Antiques are not my area of specialization."

"Watch who you're calling antique, buster," the mirror said. "I'll have you know that I found that sword in less than half the time it'd take some of your new-fangled hotshot mirrors."

"And a good job you did of it," Morwen said. "We're finished. Go to sleep."

" 'Antique,' " muttered the mirror as the reflection faded into white and then cleared to show the tower room once more. "Bah phooey to 'antique.' I'm just as good as I was a hundred years ago. Better! I've got more experience. *And* I give personal service. 'Antique!' Some people . . ."

"I think he hurt her feelings," Scorn said.

"What about *my* feelings?" Killer said loudly. "My ear is burned, I've bent three feathers and pulled a muscle in my back, and I'm *hungry.*"

"So are the rest of us," Trouble said. "But you don't hear *us* complaining." He glanced at Scorn and Horatio, and then all three cats looked up at the humans with matching expressions of starvation being nobly borne in a good cause.

Morwen sighed. "Brandel, would you be good enough to calm down, stop flaming, and see about a morning meal? Or if you'd rather not be bothered, at least tell us how to work the pantry spell?"

Setting up breakfast took nearly half an hour, mostly because everyone except Killer and the cats had other preoccupations. Brandel and Cimorene kept getting sidetracked into a discussion of Arona Michaelear Grinogion Vamist and his involvement with the Society of Wizards and the theft of the sword. Telemain was more interested in studying the mirror than in talking or food, and Morwen made a mental note to make sure he didn't skip breakfast. Backshock or not, he was still recovering, and he'd be a great deal more use if he ate well before they left. Morwen herself would have liked to join either Cimorene's discussion or Telemain's investigation, but for the most part she forced herself to stay out of them. After all, *someone* had to keep the others moving.

Finally, everything was ready, and they sat down to eat. "I still can't believe it," Brandel said, tipping three sausage patties onto his plate and handing the platter to Cimorene. "Vamist never liked the idea of wizards. They weren't traditional enough for him."

"Don't start on that again," Morwen said. "You'll use up all your energy burning your hair."

Cimorene swallowed a bite of toast and said, "Yes, what we need now is a plan. Can you give us directions to this Vamist person's house, Brandel?"

"I'll do better than that. I'll show you." Brandel scowled and a wisp of smoke rose out of his hair. "The idea of that pompous, overbearing skunk helping wizards after he got *us* kicked out of town for being nontraditional . . ."

"I wonder what they offered him?" Telemain said.

"How about a warding spell powerful enough to protect him from half a dozen fire-witches?" Morwen suggested.

"You mean he was working with them all along?" Brandel said. "That little–"

"We don't know that for certain," Cimorene said hastily. "Yet. And if you still can't go home, you can come back to the Enchanted Forest with us after we get the sword. I'm sure Mendanbar would be happy to have you, and the rest of your family, too."

"It's *lots* nicer than a swamp," Killer put in. "There's plenty of clover– at least, there's plenty for rabbits. I don't know if there's enough for six-foot donkeys with wings." His ears drooped at the thought.

"We'll worry about that later," Morwen told him. "Eat your breakfast. Brandel, how long will it take us to get to Vamist's house? And does anyone have any suggestions as to how we should proceed once we get there?"

"That's easy," Cimorene said. "It looked like Vamist and Antorell were the only ones there. Brandel and Telemain can go to the front door and distract them while you and I sneak in through the back and grab the sword. And if Antorell tries to stop me, I'll melt him. Pass the salt, please."

17

In Which There Is Much Excitement

Although they discussed the matter for the rest of the meal, Cimorene's plan was the best idea they had. Since only Cimorene could carry the sword, she had to be the person who sneaked in and took it. Morwen had to go with her because the cats were going to act as lookouts and no one else could understand them. Brandel was the logical person to distract Arona Vamist, and Telemain had to be with him in order to melt any wizards who might show up.

"What about me?" asked Killer.

"You get to stand outside the back door and stay out of mischief," Morwen told him. "You'd be safer here, but we'll probably want to transport home right from Vamist's house."

"You're *sure* you can manage that part, Telemain?" Cimorene asked.

"Quite certain," Telemain said a little crossly. "The last error was due to a cross-matrix interference that is not at all likely to be repeated."

"I might agree with you if we knew exactly what caused the interference in the first place," Morwen said. "Since we don't . . ."

"If it will make you feel better, I'll put a screening mechanism in the bypass module." This time, Telemain made no attempt whatsoever to hide his annoyance.

"Temperamental, isn't he?" said Scorn.

"A screening mechanism sounds like a very good idea to me," Morwen told Telemain. "And we aren't questioning your competence, so stop frowning. Getting the sword back to the Enchanted Forest is too important to take chances, even small ones."

"Then you'd better help me figure out what kind of adjustments to make to the springbase loader so that it won't ignore Brandel," Telemain said. "Since I assume you don't want to leave him behind for the wizards."

Brandel looked at Telemain with alarm. "Leave me behind? Why?"

"Fire-witches are immune to most spells," Morwen said. "Including ordinary transportation spells. Telemain is quite right; if we don't make a few changes, you'll undoubtedly find yourself standing alone in the middle of Arona Michaelear Grinogion Vamist's yard when the spell goes off."

"We can't let that happen!" Cimorene said. "If the Society of Wizards catches him, they'll do something awful."

"But you just said he's immune to spells," Killer said in a puzzled tone. "So what can the wizards do to him?"

"Break his legs, tie him to a tree for the nightshades to eat, stick him in a dungeon with no food," said Trouble. "Wizards don't need magic to do nasty things."

Horatio hissed. Killer's ears went stiff and the hair along his neck bristled. "No food! They wouldn't. Not really."

"Yes, they would," said Morwen. *"If* they caught him. Which they won't, because before we leave here, Telemain and I are going to make sure the transportation spell works on Brandel."

Killer bobbed his head up and down in vigorous agreement. "That's good. We don't want to leave anyone behind. No food! Those wizards really *are* horrible."

"You two work on the spell," Cimorene said. "I'll get everything else ready to go. How far away did you say this place is, Brandel?"

"Two or three hours' walk," Brandel said. "It'll take us an hour or so to get out of the swamp, but after that it should be easy."

Trouble lowered his head and lashed his tail in disgust. "More mud. And no dragon to ride on this time, either."

"Dibs on Morwen's shoulder," said Scorn.

"Mrrow!" said Horatio in an emphatic tone.

"Will you need me for the changes you want to make in the transportation spell?" Brandel asked Telemain. "Because if you won't, I'd like to make a few calls. The rest of the family ought to know that the Society of Wizards is behind Vamist."

Telemain removed a silver globe the size of a tennis ball from the pouch at his belt and studied it. "What? Yes, of course. Go ahead. Morwen, I think we should start with the shift alignment linkages. We'll have to add two or three interrupt vectors, and we may have to modify the invisible channel connection as well."

"We'll need you when we test our work," Morwen said to Brandel, "but that won't be until we're finished. You'll have plenty of time for your calls; this will take at least half an hour, possibly more."

Brandel nodded and left. Morwen turned back to Telemain. "I don't see the point of adding interrupt vectors. All we really need is a temporary change in the definition section so that it includes fire-witches."

Telemain's face went blank for a moment as he considered the idea. Then his nose wrinkled and his mouth twisted as if he had bitten into something very sour. "Temporary changes. How inelegant."

"As long as it's effective, who cares? Think of it as a trial run. You can study the ways all the various pieces interact, and do a permanent redesign later."

"True." The magician began to look more cheerful. "In that case, where do *you* suggest we start?"

Changing the transportation spell was simple, compared to keeping Telemain from putting in various extra things he wanted to test. Morwen insisted on doing the last few checks, since she was still a little worried about Telemain's condition. When they were sure everything worked properly, they called Cimorene, who had vanished down the stairwell while they were working.

"Coming." A moment later, Cimorene appeared at the head of the stairs, carrying her pack over her left shoulder and a long-handled straw broom in her right hand. "Morwen, have you got any of that flying ointment left? Because if you do, I think you should use it on this. We'll get to Vamist's house a lot faster if we don't have to slog through all that mud."

"I am *not* riding on that thing," Telemain said. "Mud or no mud."

"He wouldn't say that if *he'd* spent most of yesterday wading through the stuff," Scorn observed.

"You should talk," said Trouble. "Between riding on Morwen's shoulder and riding on Kazul's back, you never even got your paws dirty."

"I was going to suggest that you and Brandel ride in the laundry basket anyway," Cimorene said to Telemain. "There isn't room for all of us on the broomstick."

"There's a flying mortar and pestle in the basement," Brandel offered. "It's too heavy to use every day, and it's a little small, but if you'll help me haul it upstairs you can use it."

"It sounds nearly as uncomfortable as a broomstick," Telemain said. "No, thank you. I'll take the laundry basket."

"What about *us?*" Trouble demanded.

"You will come on the broomstick, where I can keep an eye on you," Morwen told him as she fished in her sleeve for the jar of flying ointment.

"Scorn and Horatio should probably go in the laundry basket, or possibly on Killer's back. We don't want to overload anything."

"I don't know," Killer said, ruffling his wings nervously. "I still don't like cats. And they've got *claws.*"

"You bet we do." Trouble held up a paw and flexed it, displaying five wickedly curved and sharply pointed claws.

Killer shuddered. "Couldn't I go by myself?"

"No," Cimorene said firmly. "We all have to do what we can, and what you can do is carry the cats."

"Well, I'm not doing any more flying," Killer said, planting his feet for emphasis. "It's too hard, and it scares me."

"I bet he gets airsick, too," said Scorn. "Rabbits!"

While Morwen enchanted the broomstick, Brandel picked up the laundry basket and shoved it through the open window. Cimorene set it hovering and helped steady it as the two men climbed in. Then she sent Killer and the two cats out after the basket and turned to Morwen and Trouble.

"All done," Morwen said. "I hope the laundry basket holds together, because that was the last of the flying ointment."

"Then let's go. We don't want Telemain and Brandel to get too far ahead of us."

"Not to mention that rabbit," Trouble said.

They climbed onto the broomstick and took off. Cimorene had to duck as they went through the window.

"Excuse me, Cimorene," Morwen said as they swooped out and down. "I forgot how tall you are."

"Better watch for low branches," Trouble said.

"There aren't any low branches," Morwen told him, setting the broomstick to fly about ten feet off the ground.

A moment later, they caught up with Killer and the laundry basket, and the whole group continued on together. Their speed was limited to Killer's trotting pace, but with all the trees to dodge they could not have traveled much faster, even without him. Following Brandel's directions, they reached the edge of the swamp in fifteen minutes.

"It's straightforward from here," Brandel said. "Head west, toward those hills. At this rate, we should be there within half an hour."

"Half an hour!" Killer shook his mane, drawing yowls of protest from Scorn and Horatio. "You want me to keep running like this for another half an *hour?* I can't do it. And don't ask me to fly. That's even more work."

"Maybe if you didn't eat so much you'd be in better shape," Scorn said.

"Hrmrrrr," agreed Horatio.

"I do not!" said Killer. "It's all very well for the rest of you. *You* all get to ride. I want a rest and a drink and a snack to keep my strength up."

Morwen landed the broomstick. "That sounds reasonable enough, if you don't take too long. Five minutes now, and we'll stop again halfway there." She looked at Cimorene, who was frowning impatiently.

"I suppose we don't have much choice," Cimorene said. "And it really isn't fair to make Killer work so hard when it's so easy for the rest of us. But I do wish there were some way to–to speed things up. I'm worried about what those wizards might be doing at home."

"I'll think about it," Morwen said. "Now, as long as we're stopping for a few minutes . . . Killer, are there any invisible dusk-blooming chokevines around?"

"I can see two of them right over there." Killer pointed with his right ear. "Are you going to let me eat one?"

"No, I'm going to collect them for my garden," Morwen said. "Goodness knows when I'll get another chance." She began rummaging in her sleeves for a trowel and some specimen bags.

"Is this an appropriate time to be gathering plants?" Telemain said.

"We've promised Killer a five-minute rest. I may as well use the time constructively. You're going to analyze Brandel's magic again, aren't you?"

Telemain glanced at Brandel and shifted uncomfortably. "Given the necessity of a transportation spell and the possibility of unpredictable interactions between it and fire-witch magic, it seems wise to repeat–"

"Then don't fuss about my plants." Morwen turned to Killer. "Show me exactly where the vines are, and I'll give you the last bottle of cider. Don't get too close; they're dangerous, remember."

"How are you going to collect them, then?" Killer asked.

"Watch."

Puzzled but willing, Killer described the exact positions of the two chokevines. Cautiously, Morwen edged closer, until Killer said she was just within three feet of the plants. Then she stopped and took a spray bottle and a paper packet of powdered slowstone from her right sleeve.

"What's that?" Cimorene asked, interested in spite of herself.

"The bottle is plain water." Morwen pumped the top to get the spray working, then aimed it at the tree in front of her and covered as much as she could reach with a fine mist. Shining drops of water collected in midair, outlining invisible leaves and stems that shifted restlessly as if trying to reach Morwen and her friends.

"That's pretty," said Killer.

"That's wet," growled Trouble, shaking his fur as if he were the one who had been sprayed.

Morwen slipped the spray bottle back into her sleeve, then carefully opened one corner of the packet. Checking the direction of the wind, she shifted position until the slight breeze came from behind her, blowing toward the invisible dusk-blooming chokevines. "Everyone else, stay back," she said, and sprinkled the slowstone over the vines.

The gray powder settled over the dampened leaves, outlining them even more clearly than before. Slowly, the restless movement of the plants died down, until it was only a sluggish tremor. Morwen smiled in satisfaction. She hadn't been altogether certain that slowstone would work the same way on plants as it did on animals and people.

"What was that?" Telemain asked, breaking off his conversation with Brandel in midsentence.

"Powdered slowstone," Morwen said.

"It smells good," Killer said. "Like fresh dandelion greens with cinnamon bark."

"You wasted powdered slowstone on a couple of *plants?*" Telemain sounded completely outraged.

"I had to do something to calm them down," Morwen said. "This should keep them quiet for a day or two–long enough to transplant them in my garden, at any rate."

"Does that mean they're safe now?" Killer asked.

"Temporarily," Morwen replied, reaching for her trowel. "That is, they won't bother you if you get close, but I wouldn't eat them if I were you."

"Oh." Killer's ears drooped. "Why not? They smell awfully good, especially with that powdered stuff all over them."

"Weren't you listening at all?" Scorn said with a superior sniff. " 'That powdered stuff' is slowstone. It's magical, and it does just what it sounds like it ought to do. We'd be lucky to get to Vamist's house by tomorrow night if you ate any of it."

Killer looked at Morwen. "You mean it would slow me down? I thought you said it made those plants safe!"

"Safe to walk near, not safe to eat." Morwen knelt next to the chokevines and began to dig. "And I don't know whether you'd slow down or not. So far, you haven't reacted with any particular consistency to any of the things you've eaten."

"It's possible that the slowstone would inhibit the onset of any alteration resulting from the consumption of invisible dusk-blooming chokevines," Telemain said. "There is precedent for such an eventuality in Killer's response to the growth-enhancing qualities of MacDonald's fertilizer, although the parallel is not perfect."

"What did he say?" Killer asked anxiously.

"That the slowstone might slow down your reaction to the invisible dusk-blooming chokevines, instead of slowing *you* down." Having dug all the way around the roots of both plants, Morwen slid her trowel under the clump of dirt and carefully lifted the first paralyzed chokevine into a sample bag. "Unfortunately, the only way to tell for certain would be to try it and see what happens."

"You mean the vines might do something to me, too, if I ate them? Why didn't you warn me?"

"I did."

"You told me they were dangerous! You didn't say they were magical."

Trouble gave Killer a look of deep disgust. "You think normal plants get named *invisible* dusk-blooming chokevines?"

"But they aren't invisible!" Killer protested. "Not to me."

"Then maybe nothing would happen to you if you ate one," Cimorene said. "You can experiment later. Morwen, are you finished? We've been longer than five minutes, and I'd like to get going again."

"I'm done." Climbing to her feet, Morwen tucked the sample bags and trowel into her sleeve and smiled. "And I believe I've thought of a way to speed up the rest of the trip. Have you got any rope in your pack?"

18

In Which They Concoct a Plan

Cimorene looked at Morwen, frowning. "Rope? I think so. Why?"

"So we can tow Killer," Morwen said. "Between the laundry basket and the broomstick, we should have plenty of power, and we'll be able to go a lot faster, now that we're out of the trees."

"Good idea," Brandel said. "It's a pity you didn't think of it sooner. I've got plenty of rope back at the tower."

"I don't know about this," Killer said. "It doesn't sound very comfortable."

"Do you want to run all the way to Vamist's house?" Morwen said. "That's your other choice. Take it or leave it."

Killer took it, but not without grumbling the whole time they spent rigging a harness for him and tying it to the laundry basket and broomstick.

"This is undignified," he complained as they prepared to start off once more.

"What's so dignified about a six-foot floating blue donkey with oversized wings?" said Scorn.

"I'm very . . . very . . . Eee-augh! Help! Slow down! Oh, I knew this was a bad idea. Rabbits weren't meant to go this fast."

Morwen glanced back and almost laughed. Killer hung at the end of the tow ropes, all four feet braced against the air (which did him no good whatsoever). His wings and ears streamed behind him in the wind. On his back, barely visible between the blue ears and feathers, Scorn and Horatio lay flat with their front claws dug into the rope harness.

Smiling, Morwen turned back to concentrate on flying the broomstick. Despite Killer's loud complaints, by her standards they were not traveling particularly fast. Between the extra weight on both broom and basket and the energy it took to pull Killer, Morwen estimated their speed at about a third of her usual rate. Still, it was much faster than walking, especially over the open meadows that stretched ahead of them.

They had gone several miles and Killer's objections had degenerated into occasional terrified brays when Brandel slowed the laundry basket. Morwen matched his reduction in speed, and a moment later they landed in a small stand of trees near the top of a hill.

"That's enough of that!" Killer said. "I don't care if you want to get there quickly, I don't care if I have to run, I don't care if those wizards turn me into a pancake and eat me for breakfast. I'm *not* doing that again."

"You won't have to," Brandel said, climbing out of the laundry basket. "Vamist's house is over this hill and down the road about a quarter of a mile." He looked at Cimorene a little apologetically. "I know you'd rather be closer, but with him making all that noise–"

"You'd make noise, too, if you were being hauled along three times as fast as any reasonable rabbit should go," Killer said unrepentantly.

"Well, you're not being pulled anywhere now, so be quiet," Cimorene said. "If you do anything that messes up our getting Mendanbar's sword, I'll . . . I'll turn you into a pancake and eat you myself."

"You can't do that!" Killer's ears jerked nervously. "Can you?"

"I can try."

"Killer will behave himself." Morwen looked at her cats. "Scorn and Trouble will see to it." And between keeping Killer out of mischief and acting as lookouts, the cats might actually have so much to do that *they* wouldn't get up to anything unfortunate. She hoped.

Cimorene nodded and turned to Brandel. "How easy will it be to sneak up on this house without being seen?"

"It shouldn't be too difficult," Brandel replied. "There are a lot of trees and bushes around the house."

"Let's go, then."

"What about these?" Brandel asked, waving at the empty laundry basket and broomstick.

"Leave the basket here," Morwen said. "It's too awkward to carry, and I can always enchant another one for you when this is all over. I'll take the broomstick in case Cimorene and I need to get away quickly."

"Then we're ready," Cimorene said. "Let's *go.*"

Twisting his rings absently, Telemain nodded and started up the hill. The rest followed in silence. No one seemed to feel much like talking as they went up over the hill and down the tree-lined lane on the other side.

A few minutes later, Brandel stopped and looked at Cimorene. "Vamist's house is just around the bend. If you and Morwen cut through these bushes and head off to the right, you should come out in his backyard."

"Good," said Morwen. "Scorn, Trouble, run ahead and find out which room the sword is in and where Antorell and Vamist are. Don't forget to come back and let me know."

"We aren't *amateurs,"* Scorn said, switching her tail.

"Right," said Trouble. "And Kazul's not here, so I get first crack at the wizard." He stood up and stretched to show that it wasn't all that important, then vanished into the bushes.

"I don't know why you care so much about the wizard," Scorn said, following. "That obnoxious idiot with no hair is the one I want dibs on. The things he said . . ."

Frowning, Morwen looked after the cats. "When we get back I'm going to have to make one of them tell me just what Arona Michaelear Grinogion Vamist said when he called the other day. Scorn is really annoyed."

"Yow mrow," said Horatio, and began washing his left front paw.

A few minutes later, the two cats returned. "Vamist and Antorell are in a big room with glass doors at the side of the house," Trouble reported. "They've got the sword on the table and they're arguing."

"Arguing?" said Morwen.

"About what to do with the sword. Vamist thinks the Society of Wizards should stick it into a rock and leave it somewhere because that's traditional, but Antorell says that's only for important swords that are supposed to be found again. I don't think he knows what that sword does."

"Or else he doesn't want it found," said Scorn.

"Hmph. We'll see about that." Morwen turned to the others. "Trouble says things haven't changed much since we saw them in the mirror. Cimorene and I will leave now; Killer, you come with us." She looked at Telemain. "You two get ready, and I'll send Scorn to signal you when to knock on the door."

"Good luck," Telemain said, and the two groups started off in different directions.

Sneaking up on Arona Michaelear Grinogion Vamist's house was much easier than Morwen had expected. The garden at the rear of the house was wildly overgrown, so there were plenty of shrubs to hide behind, and most of the windows were covered with dense vines. As far as Morwen could tell, all anyone would be able to see out of those windows were the back sides of leaves.

As they approached, Scorn vanished under a scraggly chrysanthemum.

She returned a moment later. "They're still arguing. The doors are over here on the left."

Morwen translated for Cimorene, who nodded and murmured, "Good. Killer, you stay here. And don't eat anything. Arona Vamist consorts with wizards, so there's no telling what he has in his garden."

Weeds, mostly. It looks as if he hasn't paid attention to it for years, Morwen thought, but this was no time to say so. She looked at Scorn and said softly, "As soon as we're next to the doors, go around to the front so Telemain and Brandel will know when to knock."

"No problem," said Scorn.

"And don't forget to come back when they've seen you," Trouble said. "You don't want to get left behind."

Scorn looked at him. "I won't be left behind. Telemain's the one who's doing the transport spell."

"Enough," said Morwen. "Do your jobs and argue about it later." She started toward the corner of the house.

"Are you going to be long?" said Killer.

"Keep your voice down," Cimorene whispered. "I don't know, so stay alert. We're going to be leaving in something of a hurry."

Trouble snorted. "There's an understatement."

Cautiously, they edged up to the corner, leaving Killer to watch anxiously from among the vines. Long ago, someone had built a stone patio along the far side of the house, with a flower border along the south edge and a row of tall bushes to the west for privacy. Now, weeds and grass grew in the cracks between stones, the bushes were an untidy mass of prickly twigs, and the flower border was full of thistles. Cimorene and Morwen had to step carefully to avoid being stuck.

Scorn directed them to a spot that was in easy reach of the glass doors but still out of sight. As soon as they were in position, Trouble insinuated himself between the vines and the wall of the house and crept around the corner and out of sight.

"He's ready," said Scorn after a minute. "See you later." She threw Morwen a slow blink of affection and disappeared into the unpruned hedge.

The wait that followed seemed to last hours. Morwen could feel Cimorene's tension, and she was not exactly calm herself. Planning to avoid a direct confrontation with any wizard–even if it was only Antorell–was all very well, but there was no guarantee that the wizard would cooperate. She fingered her sleeves, wishing that witches' spells did not take such a long time to perform, or that there were some way of storing them for quick use, the way wizards did.

The ivy trembled, and an instant later Trouble appeared. "They've left the room. Both of them. And the sword is just sitting on the table."

"Did you spot any alarm spells?" Morwen asked.

"Nope." Trouble lashed his tail.

"This sounds too easy." But Morwen turned to Cimorene anyway and said, "They're gone."

"Then let's go." Cimorene stepped over a patch of gigantic dandelions onto the ruined patio, and Morwen followed. Together they crossed to a set of double doors made of small rectangular windowpanes, eight down and four across on each door.

Cautiously, Morwen tried the handle. With a sharp click, the latch opened and the right-hand door popped half an inch inward.

They looked at each other, and without a word they leaned forward to peer through the nearest windowpane. The room looked just as empty of people as Trouble had claimed, though it was rather full of other things. Ornate chairs lined the walls, and most of them had things piled on their seats. One held a stack of books; another, a clay pot filled with dirt; a third, a stuffed pigeon sitting on a stringless violin. Two dusty suits of armor holding spears stood on either side of the far door, and the walls were covered with cobwebby pictures. In the center of the room was a large table, with two chairs pulled out crookedly from opposite sides, as if the occupants had gotten up quickly.

In the center of the table, shiny and positively reeking of magic, lay an unsheathed sword.

Cimorene looked at Morwen and sighed. "It must be a trap. But that's Mendanbar's sword in there, for certain, and we have to try to get it. And I don't think we're going to have much time. Any suggestions?"

"Quit fussing and go get the silly thing," Trouble said.

"Are you volunteering to be first in line?" Morwen asked.

"Why not?" Trouble rose on his back legs and set his front paws against the unlatched door. As it swung inward, he dropped to all fours once more and sauntered through. He paused just out of reach, glanced around, and then took a short running start and leapt onto the table. Looking very smug, he twitched his tail and sat down on the hilt of the sword.

"I should have known better," Morwen muttered. "Well, at least we know he was right about the alarms. If there were any, that performance would have set them off."

"Then let's–"

From the front of the building came a loud, angry yowl, carrying easily over and around the intervening walls. Trouble jumped to attention, straddling the sword, and Morwen took a worried half step toward the sound before she caught herself. *The sword is the important thing right now,* she reminded herself, but she couldn't quite make herself believe it.

"That's torn it." Shoving the door the rest of the way open, Cimorene darted inside. Morwen had no real choice except to follow.

"Drat," she said, and did so.

As Cimorene ran across the two yards of open space that separated the doors and the table, Morwen felt a ripple of magic in the air. "Cimorene, stop!" she said, but she was not quite in time. The ripple hit Cimorene and froze her motionless, one hand stiffly extended toward the hilt of Mendanbar's sword.

"Oh!" said Cimorene. "I can't move. Morwen, what's happened? Can you do something about it?"

"*I* am what has happened!" said a new voice, and one of the suits of armor shifted and began to change. Its hard edges blurred and darkened, and its feet and legs spread out into a long robe. The spear it held lost its head and shrank a foot and a half. Last of all, the face came clear.

"Antorell!" said Cimorene.

"Exactly," the wizard said with an evil grin. "And I don't think there's anything at all that your witchy friend can do about me."

Morwen's eyes narrowed. "We'll see about that." She pointed at him and said firmly, "Argelfraster."

Nothing happened.

19

In Which They Confront the Villains

A startled expression crossed Antorell's face. Then he smiled smugly and said, "You see? I have taken care of your little spell."

Hmph, thought Morwen. *I certainly don't believe* that. *He's probably just out of range. Now, how can I get close enough to melt him before he gets suspicious and freezes me?*

"How interesting that Mendanbar sent the two of you to retrieve this"–Antorell waved his free hand at the sword, and Trouble bristled–"instead of coming himself. It must not be as important to him as Father thought it was. Not that it matters now. Even if Father and the others haven't taken control of the castle yet–"

"Taken control of the castle?" Cimorene sounded thoroughly alarmed. "I *knew* there was something wrong at home."

"And just how was the Society of Wizards planning to take over the castle of the King of the Enchanted Forest?" Morwen asked in as politely skeptical a tone as she could manage.

Antorell flushed angrily. "One man is no match for the combined might of the Society of Wizards."

"He has been until now," Morwen said. *Of course, until now he's had the sword. It's a good thing Cimorene sent Kazul back last night; it sounds as if Mendanbar can use the help.*

"Until now, we have not acted in concert," Antorell said. "But yesterday morning, all of the wizards of the Society of Wizards, led by my father, the Head Wizard Zemenar, transported themselves to the Enchanted Forest to take the magic that rightfully belongs to us. By this time, they should be finishing up their work."

"Yesterday morning?" Morwen blinked. "So that's what disrupted Telemain's transportation spell! He must have gotten caught in the backwash of the Society of Wizards transporting *en masse.*"

"Mendanbar and Kazul are quite capable of handling your society between them," Cimorene said to Antorell, putting up her chin.

The wizard frowned. "I doubt that. Father is prepared for anything."

"It's hard to be prepared for the King of the Dragons."

Antorell seemed to have forgotten Morwen for the moment. Hoping to move close enough for the melting spell to work, she stepped sideways around the end of the table. Unfortunately, the movement attracted his attention.

"Halt!" Antorell raised his staff and pointed it at her. "Stay where you are, or I'll see to it that you can't move, either."

"Try it," Trouble growled. "Just try it."

Muffled noises filtered through the door beside Antorell. A moment later, it swung open. Antorell glanced over and moved away as Telemain entered, supporting Brandel with one arm. Brandel's face was a grayish white, and his eyes were glassy. Even across the room, Morwen could smell a burned odor.

Telemain's eyes met hers. "He lost his temper, and the reflective sidewash from the shielding enchantment on Vamist produced a temporary circulating phase inversion at the energy source. He'll be all right in a few minutes."

"His own magic bounced back and stunned him," Morwen translated for Cimorene's benefit. Then she looked past Telemain and stiffened. Behind Telemain and Brandel, the bald, sharp-faced man they had seen in the mirror entered, carrying Scorn at arm's length by the scruff of her neck. He had reason for caution: his hands were covered with scratches. Scorn's eyes were narrowed to slits and she was panting for breath, but she still managed an occasional swipe with a paw. Unfortunately, she wasn't close enough to the bald man to connect.

"Put that cat down immediately," Morwen said. "You're suffocating her. Adult cats aren't meant to be carried that way."

"Oh, is it yours?" said the bald man. "You should train it better. It's not very well behaved."

Trouble bunched himself together and growled. If Telemain and Brandel had not been between him and Scorn's captor, Morwen thought, he would have leapt to the rescue at once.

"You seem to have had some difficulty after all, Vamist," said Antorell to the bald man. "I did warn you."

"It was nothing I couldn't handle," said Vamist.

"Put that cat *down,"* Morwen repeated, sliding her hands into her sleeves in search of something to throw.

"You'd better do it," Cimorene said. "Hurting one of her cats is the only thing I know of that makes Morwen lose her temper."

"Morwen!" Vamist's eyes widened, and he brandished Scorn as if she were a banner. "The so-called witch? Then you should thank me for–ow!"

Suddenly, Vamist jumped and flailed his arms in a desperate attempt to keep his balance. Morwen glimpsed a black-and-white blur between his feet. Then Trouble launched himself from the table, ricocheted off Brandel's shoulder, and landed, claws extended, on top of Vamist's bald head. Vamist howled and dropped Scorn, who landed heavily and dragged herself under the table, wheezing audibly. As he grabbed at Trouble, Morwen pulled the collapsible bucket from her sleeve and threw it.

The bucket hit Vamist in the shoulder just as he got a grip on one of Trouble's legs. The impact wasn't heavy enough to do any real damage, but it startled him into losing his hold. Trouble took a final swipe at the back of Vamist's neck and dropped to the floor, where he joined Horatio under a chair.

"You little–" Vamist bent and grabbed at the cats, only to trip over Telemain's conveniently extended foot. He went sprawling, and Telemain smiled slightly.

"You all right, Scorn?" Trouble asked, his voice slightly muffled by the table and chairs.

"I will be in a minute," Scorn said. She sounded hoarse but angry. "Save some of that creep for me."

"Grrrow," said Horatio, and he wound between the chair legs to Scorn's side, where he began washing her neck.

"Nothing you can't handle, eh, Vamist?" said Antorell. "No wonder you needed our help. You did fine as long as all you had to deal with were ordinary townspeople, but you can't handle even one witch's cats."

"I don't–yowch!" When Vamist looked up to answer Antorell, Horatio had reached out and calmly dug his claws into Vamist's hand. Vamist pulled back out of reach, glared at Horatio, and said, *"Traditional* witches have *one* black cat. These are clearly not proper witches' cats, and there are far too many of them. Had we had the opportunity to discuss it, I would have advised that witch to dispose of these–these mongrels and find a more suitable companion."

"Is *that* what you called about?" Morwen said. "No wonder the cats were furious!"

"Do you blame us?" said Trouble. " 'Dispose of these mongrels,' indeed!"

"I can see how successful your persuasion would have been," Antorell said to Vamist.

"There are always those who insist on ignoring the great traditions," Vamist said with an attempt at dignity. "They are foredoomed to failure."

"Of course. You're doing this"–Antorell waved at the sword–"out of the goodness of your heart. You don't need us to protect you from the fire-witches, because they're doomed to failure. Right?"

"You're as bad as he is," Brandel said, scowling at the wizard. He still leaned heavily on Telemain, but his color was improving rapidly and his eyes had lost their glassy look.

For the first time, Antorell took a good look at Brandel. "A fire-witch! How fortunate. My staff can use a little more magic, and yours will do very nicely." Antorell stepped forward and raised his staff.

Morwen's lips tightened. She was no closer to Antorell than she had been, so she still couldn't make Telemain's melting spell work. Telemain was near enough, but he was very sensibly saving what was left of his magic for the transportation spell that would take them all back to the Enchanted Forest. Brandel didn't know the melting spell, and Cimorene was close enough but couldn't move to point her finger because of Antorell's spell. *Antorell's spell–wizard's magic. Mendanbar's sword automatically counters wizard's magic. The sword . . .*

Morwen leaned forward and grabbed the hilt of Mendanbar's sword. It felt as if she had grabbed the hot end of a poker, but she hung on. *Only for a minute, only long enough to swing it,* she thought, and swept the flat of the blade up against Cimorene's arm. A jolt of magic shook her hand loose as the sword absorbed the wizard's spell, and the blade clattered to the table. At exactly the same instant, Antorell's staff exploded.

Everyone ducked, including Cimorene. "Ow! My staff!" yelled Antorell. "This isn't poss–Cimorene!"

Cimorene pointed at him. "Argelfraster. Argelfraster, you nasty little thief."

Antorell began to melt. "Noooo! Cimorene, this is all your fault. I spent months making that staff! I'll get you for this, I swear I will. If it takes me twenty years, I'll get you. You'll be sorry. You'll be . . ." His voice trailed off into a gurgle. Arona Vamist leaned forward, staring incredulously at Antorell's empty robe and the spreading puddle of brown goo on his floor.

"Well, that takes care of *him,*" Cimorene said with considerable satisfaction. "Who blew up his staff?"

"I think it was Mendanbar's sword," Morwen said, gesturing.

"No," said Telemain with utter certainty. "The sword was not responsible. I was observing with great care, and the necessary connections for such a serious shift interference were not present."

"Then who did it?" Brandel asked.

"I suspect you did." Telemain let go of Brandel, waited a moment to make sure the fire-witch would not fall over, and then began picking up splinters of Antorell's staff. "At this point, it is only speculation, but a fundamental incompatibility between your magic and that of a wizard would account for the phenomenon very nicely. I will be able to say for certain after I do a few tests."

"Good," said Cimorene. "Do them after we get back." Gingerly, she leaned forward and picked up Mendanbar's sword. Morwen's hand still felt sore and she could not help flinching, but although Cimorene held it with obvious care, the sword did not appear to bother her. "And now that we've got this, we can–"

"Not so fast!" Arona Michaelear Grinogion Vamist had straightened and edged around the table as Antorell melted. Now he picked up a clay pot filled with dirt from the seat of a nearby chair and held it poised to throw. The angry red scratches that covered his hands and head made him look very fierce. "Put that sword down at once and leave."

"No," said Cimorene. "It's my husband's sword, and I'm taking it home. Telemain, how soon can you do that transportation spell?"

"The initial preparations require a mental effort that–" Telemain paused, looked at Cimorene, and then said carefully, "I'll be ready in a minute or two."

"Thank you," Cimorene said, smiling. "Then let's–"

"Cimorene, duck!"

Cimorene dodged in response to Morwen's shout, and Arona Vamist's clay pot flew over her left shoulder. For a moment, it looked like a clean miss. Then Cimorene yelled in surprise and clawed at her face with her free hand. Even before Morwen saw the pot dangling from nothing at all down Cimorene's back, she knew.

"It's an invisible dusk-blooming chokevine," she said. "Stay back, everyone, or it'll grab you, too."

"I warned you," Vamist said. "*Now* will you leave?"

"Get that thing off Cimorene."

"No. Not until you leave."

"I bet he doesn't know how," Trouble said.

"He kept it from attacking him when he threw it," Scorn objected. "He must know *something.*"

"Well, why don't you shove him into it and see what happens?" Trouble emerged from underneath the table and approached Vamist.

"Good idea." Morwen stalked around the table to join Trouble.

"What's a good idea?" Vamist said, backing away from them along the far side of the table. "You get out of my house, all of you!"

"Aren't you finished yet?" said Killer from the doorway. "I thought this wasn't supposed to take long."

"What is *that?"* said Vamist, looking wildly over his shoulder.

"Killer!" said Morwen. "Get in here and eat this vine immediately."

"Isn't that one of those things you say you can't see?" Killer said doubtfully, shoving his way through the partly open double doors. "You said before that they weren't safe. And what if there are side effects?"

"Eat it!" Morwen said. "I'll take care of the side effects later. Hurry up!" Cimorene had kept her grip on the sword and she was still on her feet, but she was beginning to turn blue.

"If you say so." Killer stretched out his neck and bit at the air in back of Cimorene. The clay pot crashed to the floor and shattered, spewing dirt and shards of clay, while Killer munched thoughtfully. "Not bad. It's much more delicate than I'd expected from the way it smells, though. And I can't quite place the flavor." He nibbled delicately next to Cimorene's ear.

Cimorene choked, gasped, and began to regain her proper color. Taking two or three deep breaths, she made a series of brushing and pulling motions around her head and shoulders.

"Hey!" said Killer. "You're knocking it all over the floor!"

Cimorene coughed and glared at him. "That's the idea."

"But it'll get all dusty!"

"You won't have time to worry about that," Vamist said. "I have other snares in my house for criminals and thieves!"

Dodging between two chairs, he jabbed his thumb against a wooden flower carved into the wall. With a high-pitched screeching of metal against metal, the suit of armor next to the door raised its spear to throw.

"Telemain," cried Morwen, "get us out of here!"

The suit of armor let fly. Cimorene evaded the missile easily, but Killer was too large to avoid it quickly. As the edges of the room blurred and ran together in the beginning of Telemain's transportation spell, the spear struck the left side of Killer's chest.

"Eeee-augh!"

Killer reared back, wings flapping. As the mist of transportation cleared, he sat down on the air six inches above a clump of violets. The spear fell to the ground below him with a loud thump, flattening a strip of moss.

"Killer!" said Cimorene. "Oh no! Morwen–"

With the back of her mind, Morwen noted that Telemain had managed to transport them all the way back to the Enchanted Forest in one jump, and that for some reason he had brought Arona Michaelear Grinogion Vamist along. Most of her attention, however, was centered on Killer, who was flopping around in a manner that would have looked exceptionally silly if she had not been so concerned.

"Stop floundering about like that," Morwen said to the donkey. "I can't do anything to help if I can't get near you."

"Waugh!" Killer rolled sideways and struggled to his feet. "That was uncomfortable. Am I dead?"

"No such luck," said Scorn.

Everyone stared at Killer. There was not a mark on him to show where the spear had struck, though they had all seen it hit him. Then Trouble sauntered forward. Reaching up, he batted at Killer's front hooves. His paw went right through them as if there were nothing in the way but air.

"That's a handy trick," Trouble said. "How'd you do it?"

"Do what?" Killer asked. He looked down in time to see Trouble jump through his right leg. "Eee-augh! I'm a ghost! Oh, help."

"You can't be a ghost," Cimorene said. "It's the middle of the day. Ghosts only come out at night."

"Most of them," Morwen corrected. "I knew a ghost once who was afraid of the dark, so he always appeared at noon. He had a terrible time scaring anyone. Still, I believe you're right about Killer."

"If I'm not a ghost, why is that–that *cat* prancing through me like this?" Killer demanded.

"Side effect," said Morwen. "An extremely opportune side effect, in fact. Eating that invisible dusk-blooming chokevine seems to have made you insubstantial."

"Shouldn't it have made him invisible?" Brandel asked.

"Not necessarily," Telemain said. "The pattern of interactivity among the various layers of enchantment affecting Killer is such that the precise effect of additional incidents is not subject to the usual predictive methods."

"Eeeeee-aaauugh!" Killer's wail of distress was louder and longer than any of his earlier complaints. "If I'm insubstantial, how am I going to *eat?"*

"We'll take care of that as soon as we return Mendanbar's sword," Morwen told him. "Telemain, if you're quite recovered, we should–Arona Michaelear Grinogion Vamist! Where do you think you're going?"

"Somewhere else," Vamist said. "You have no right to kidnap me like this."

"And *you* have no business aiding and abetting the theft of important magical items from the King of the Enchanted Forest," Cimorene said.

"Besides, I'm a witch," Morwen put in. "Isn't it *traditional* for witches to steal people away?"

"Not people like me!" Vamist said. "Babies and princesses."

"Babies and princesses are of no practical use whatsoever," Morwen said. "Most of them, anyway. And the ones that are useful don't need to be kidnapped."

"That's not the point!"

"No," said Cimorene. "The point is that we have more important things to do right now. We'll deal with you later; until then, you stay with us. Telemain, can you take us to the castle now?"

"It will be simpler if you will all stand a little closer together," Telemain said. "That's better." He gestured, and the familiar mist rose around them.

When it cleared, they found themselves in a large empty area. Forty feet ahead of them, the enormous trees of the Enchanted Forest rose in massive splendor, but where they stood were only ashes and bare, blackened ground. For a moment, Morwen thought Telemain had made a mistake. Then she turned her head and saw the castle, with its improbable towers and windows and staircases, shimmering inside a giant ball of golden light.

"Good heavens!" said Cimorene, speaking for them all. "What's *happened?*"

20

In Which Disaster Strikes

For a long moment, no one answered. Then Morwen said, in a voice that sounded grim even to herself, "The Society of Wizards happened. I just wonder where they've all disappeared to."

"Good riddance, wherever it is," Scorn said. *"What* a mess."

"Maybe they're inside the castle?" Brandel suggested.

"No," said a pleasant female voice behind them. "Outside the forest. At least, that's what the dragons tell us. Hello, Brandel; it's nice to see you again."

"Amory!" Brandel spun around, kicking up a small cloud of ash, and hugged the slender red-haired woman standing in back of him. "So Marli passed my message on."

"Yes, and we've certainly had an interesting time of it." The red-haired woman smiled over Brandel's shoulder at the rest of the group. "I'm Brandel's cousin Amory. You must be Queen Cimorene and the others King Kazul told us about. She wants to see you right away."

"I should hope so," said Trouble.

"What's been going on here?" asked Cimorene. "And where's Mendanbar?"

"Who?" said Amory.

"The King of the Enchanted Forest," Brandel said. "Her husband."

"Oh. I'm afraid I don't know anything about him. I think King Kazul does, though."

"Then take us to Kazul right away," Cimorene said.

Telemain took hold of Vamist's shoulder–the bald man had been trying to slip off again, although there was nowhere near to slip off to–and they followed Amory around the castle. As they walked, little eddies of ash followed everyone except Killer. The cats were very unhappy about the way the fine gray particles stuck to them; Trouble even tried to jump onto Killer's back to get out of the dust, having forgotten about the donkey's lack of solidity.

A quarter of the way around the castle, they saw the first few dragons walking purposefully along the boundary between the forest and the ashy area. As they went on, they saw more dragons, some walking, some flying above the trees. A number of red-haired people–presumably more of Brandel's fire-witch relatives–were standing guard near the edge of the glow that surrounded the castle. Amory nodded to them in passing and cut across the open area to the forest on the far side.

Kazul was just inside the forest, talking with another dragon and two more fire-witches.

". . . and now it seems to have stopped growing completely, Your Majesty." The second dragon had a deep, clear voice that carried plainly to the approaching party. "Nobody's sure why."

"Well, it's a good thing, whatever the reason," Kazul said. "Send someone over to–"

"Kazul!" Cimorene quickened her pace. "What's been happening? Where's Mendanbar?"

"I think he's still in there," Kazul said, nodding at the castle, which was partially visible through the trees. "I see you got the sword. I'm glad *something's* gone right lately."

Trouble and Scorn ran ahead and jumped onto Kazul's tail, but Horatio hung back.

"Mrow?"

"If Kazul doesn't care, I don't see why you should," Scorn told him, and began to wash the ashes off of her back.

"You *think* Mendanbar's in the castle?" Cimorene paled slightly. "Why don't you know? Kazul–"

"Stop flapping your wings over it and let the dust settle," Kazul said. "I'll explain in a minute. Marchak, send someone to notify the air patrol about this area, and tell them that if they find any other ashed-out spots they're to check whether the spots are stable before they report in. Let them know that Cimorene's back, with Mendanbar's sword."

"Right away, Your Majesty," said the other dragon. With a cheerful wave in Cimorene's direction, he walked off.

Cimorene took a deep breath. "Kazul, tell me right away. Is Mendanbar all right, or . . . or . . ."

"Mendanbar is *not* dead," Morwen said firmly.

"Why are you so sure of that?" Kazul asked.

"I've lived in the Enchanted Forest for a long time. I was here four years ago when the old King, Mendanbar's father, died. Believe me, when a King of the Enchanted Forest dies, the forest makes sure everyone knows it. I didn't get a good night's sleep for a week, and neither did anyone else."

Trouble looked up from washing his tail. *"Including* cats," he said in tones of deep disapproval. "I remember that."

"That's good," Kazul said. Then her head turned to look at the castle and the sphere of gold light that surrounded it. "I think." She glanced at Cimorene and sighed. "It was the Society of Wizards."

"Of course it was the Society of Wizards," Cimorene said shortly, and Killer backed away from her, ears twitching nervously. "But what, exactly, did they *do?"*

"Well, when I got here late last night, they had the castle surrounded," Kazul said. "They must have been using their staffs a lot, because there was a good thirty yards of dead forest around the castle already. I thought it would be better to head back to the Mountains of Morning for reinforcements."

"I should think so!" said Amory. "Even a dragon can't take on the whole Society of Wizards single-handed. 'Scuse me, Your Majesty."

"We attacked at dawn," Kazul continued. "About fifteen minutes after the fight started, that bubble went up around the castle and no one could get in. A couple of wizards came out, but I'm afraid they, ah, got eaten in all the excitement, and no one thought to ask them any questions first. So we don't know what happened inside."

"Isn't there some way of finding out?" Cimorene turned to Telemain. "Can't you adjust your magic mirror spell to get through that bubble, now that you know it's there? If I could talk to somebody inside–"

"There isn't anybody inside, Your Majesty," said a new voice, and everyone turned to see Willin, the castle steward, standing by the base of a nearby oak. The normally immaculate elf looked awful: his gold lace collar was torn and blackened; his crisp white shirt was wrinkled, dusty, and smeared with ashes; his velvet coat was ripped in several places and was missing most of its buttons; his white silk hose were torn and dirty; and his left shoe had lost its gold heel.

"Willin!" said Cimorene. "Sit down–you look exhausted. What happened? How do you know there's no one in the castle?"

"I should say, no one other than His Majesty," Willin said. "When he realized that the Society of Wizards intended to attack the castle, he sent the staff away. Including me. I wouldn't have left, Your Majesty, only he insisted . . ."

"You mean Mendanbar was all alone in there when the wizards got here?"

"An unusual strategy, but quite possibly an extremely effective one," Telemain said thoughtfully. "I doubt that anyone but Mendanbar really knows all the passages in that castle, and with everyone else gone, he could use his magic full force, without worrying about hurting someone on his own side."

"Well, it doesn't seem to have worked very well, does it?" Cimorene snapped.

"Kazul, did you manage to catch Head Wizard Zemenar?" Morwen asked. "If anyone knows what the Society of Wizards did, he does."

Kazul shifted in evident embarrassment. "I'm afraid I ate Zemenar myself. I caught up with him coming out of the Caves of Chance just a little while ago, and by then I was so angry . . ."

"It's a good thing you did," Amory put in. "That was what set the rest of them running. Before then, we were barely holding our own."

"I'm confused," Killer said. "And this talk about eating is making me hungry. Somebody explain it all so we can have lunch."

"You can't have lunch," Trouble said. "You're insubstantial."

"So somebody can fix me, and *then* we can have lunch," Killer said.

"I'm confused, too," Brandel said. "Even if I'm not particularly hungry."

"Then let us take things in a proper order," said Telemain, for all the world as if he were talking about laying out a new spell. "Willin, you are the reasonable person to begin. What happened at the castle after we left?"

Willin glanced at Cimorene to make sure it was all right to let this unofficial person take charge. When she nodded, he began to speak. At first, the others interrupted him frequently with questions, but Telemain insisted that answers wait until the whole tale had been told. Once they realized that he meant it, everyone except the cats stopped interrupting.

The first wizards, Willin said, had turned up almost as soon as Cimorene and her party had left the Enchanted Forest. Mendanbar had melted them with Telemain's spell, but they had damaged several sections of the Enchanted Forest before he caught up with them. Without the sword, he could not repair the harm they'd done, and he had been very concerned. To help minimize the problem, he'd called in several tribes of elves and asked them to keep watch.

"The elves could melt some of the wizards with soapy water and lemon juice," Willin said, "and if they couldn't get close enough, or if there were too many wizards, they could let the King know right away. Then he'd come and take care of the wizards before they did too much damage."

Unfortunately, the wizards were well prepared. The following morning, the entire Society of Wizards had appeared outside the castle. Before anyone had realized what was happening, they had destroyed a wide patch of the forest, leaving the elves no way of getting near them with buckets of soapy water.

"That was when King Mendanbar sent us away," Willin finished sadly. "I tried to make him let me stay, I really did, but–"

"I understand," Cimorene said. "You did your best."

"Did you see what happened outside the castle after you left?" Telemain asked.

"Some of it. The wizards cleared a twenty-foot ring around the castle and then spent most of the day working some spell; I wasn't close enough to see what. Around the middle of the afternoon, the circle they'd cleared started to expand. Fortunately, it didn't grow very fast, and those of us who were watching had plenty of time to move back. Then about ten of them walked across the main bridge into the castle. That's all I can tell you, I'm afraid. It got harder to see what was going on because I kept having to move back to stay out of sight."

"Was Head Wizard Zemenar one of the group that went into the castle?" Morwen asked.

Willin nodded.

Turning to Kazul, Telemain said, "So when you got here that night, Zemenar was inside the castle and the rest of the Society of Wizards were camped in the burned-out area just outside."

"Right," said Kazul. "I called in the rest of my people, and we attacked in the morning. Four or five wizards came out of the castle, the shield spell went up–"

"Wait a minute," said Brandel. "Shield spell?"

"That glow around the castle," said Telemain. "The Society of Wizards invented it, and it's really a remarkable piece of work. Nobody can get in or out while it's up, not even a dragon–remember, Morwen?–and they're the only people who can take it down."

"Not quite," Morwen said. "Mendanbar's sword got rid of the last one we ran into."

"Mmmm, yes. Cimorene, how well can you use that sword?"

"I can't use it at all really, the way you mean," Cimorene replied. "From what Mendanbar said, the sword has to . . . to agree to work for you somehow before you can use it for magic, and it'll only do that for the Kings of the Enchanted Forest and their direct descendants. I'm a member of the family, so it will let me hold it as a sort of courtesy, but I'm not a direct descendant of any of the Kings of the Enchanted Forest, so I can't use its magic."

"Blast. It's probably got a selectivity module in the central linkage generator, and if it's braided to the spell core . . ." Telemain's voice trailed off into muttering.

Morwen frowned. The last time they had encountered the Society of Wizards' shield spell, the wizards had been using it to hold Kazul prisoner. And if she remembered correctly . . . She caught Trouble's eye and motioned to him. Tilting his head, Trouble considered for a moment. Then he jumped down from Kazul's back and sauntered over.

"What is it?"

"Do you think you could get inside the shield spell around the castle?" Morwen asked in a low voice. If the answer was no, she didn't want Cimorene getting her hopes up.

"I don't see why not," Trouble said. "Jasper did it last time, and I'm as good at that sort of thing as he is."

Morwen didn't bother to ask what sort of thing he was talking about. If it was a cat sort of thing, as was likely, Trouble wouldn't explain anyway, and questioning him might make him refuse to help at all. "I'd like you to go inside and see if you can find out what's happened to Mendanbar."

Trouble's ears pricked up in interest. "Sounds amusing," he said in a tone that tried to be casual and failed. "I'll do it."

As he walked off toward the castle, Morwen hid a smile. Now that he'd realized he could get inside, it would take more than wizards to keep him from satisfying his curiosity. She turned her attention back to the main conversation as Amory said, ". . . doing very well when we got here."

Kazul snorted. "You're being generous. We weren't doing well at all." She looked at Cimorene. "It's hard to fight when you're having an allergy attack, and with all those wizards' staffs in one place every dragon for miles was sneezing so hard they could barely see straight."

"I understand perfectly," Cimorene said. "And thank you both for trying."

Kazul must have heard something in her tone that everyone else missed, because she lowered her head almost to the ground so she could look at Cimorene eye to eye and said, "It will be all right, Cimorene. If he's not dead–and if Morwen says we'd know, then we'd know–then he's probably perfectly all right. All we have to do is get him out of the castle."

"And how are we going to do that?" Cimorene said crossly. "The sword is the only thing that can get rid of that shield, and he's the only one who can use the sword."

"We'll think of something," Kazul said.

"In the meantime, what are you going to do about *him?*" Brandel asked with a dark look in Vamist's direction.

"If he's a wizard, I'm sure I can find someone to eat him once you're finished with him," Kazul offered. "*Everyone* can't be full yet."

Vamist turned white, making the cat scratches on his head look even redder. "You can't do this to me!"

"Why not?" Morwen said. "It's *traditional* for dragons to eat people, isn't it?"

"Princesses!" Vamist said in the tones of someone grasping desperately for a straw. "It's traditional for dragons to eat princesses, not people."

Cimorene frowned. "Princesses are people. Some of them aren't very sensible, but they're still people."

"And anyway, dragons don't eat princesses," Kazul said. "We never have. I don't know how that silly story ever got started."

"I'm afraid you're mistaken, madam," Vamist said. "Rathenmor Quillen says quite clearly in his *Observations of Magical Beasts* that–"

"Rathenmor Quillen was an idiot," Kazul said. "And so, it seems, are you."

"Got it in one," said Scorn. "He's as dumb as that rabbit."

"I'm not dumb," said Killer. "I'm hungry. I just thought I'd mention it, in case you'd forgotten."

"Rathenmor Quillen, an idiot?" Vamist's outrage got the better of both his terror and his good sense, and he drew himself up stiffly and glared at Kazul. "How dare you say such a thing about the greatest scholar of the past two hundred years! Who do you think you are?"

"I say it because it's true." Kazul smiled, starting slowly and letting the corners of her mouth draw back farther and farther until all of her sharp, shiny silver teeth were exposed in a fierce grin. "And I'm the King of the Dragons."

"Ah, er–oh, ah–" said Vamist, deflating abruptly.

"Cimorene, when you're finished with this fellow, whoever he is, I believe I'd like to see how he tastes," Kazul went on. "Unless you want to save him for later, of course."

"I don't know," said Cimorene. "He's certainly caused a lot of trouble, but I'm not sure he deserves to be eaten."

"He hasn't got any manners," Kazul said. "That's enough for me. And I could do with some dessert."

"Could you stop talking about food?" Killer said plaintively.

"So if you haven't got any better ideas . . ." Kazul said.

Morwen smiled suddenly. "I think perhaps I have one that's more . . . appropriate. If you'll forgo your dessert, Kazul, I'd like to–"

"What dessert?" asked Trouble, strolling into the center of the group. "I thought all the wizards were gone. Oh, and does anyone want to know what I found in the castle, or are you busy with other things right now?"

21

In Which Nobody Is Satisfied

No one except Morwen and the other animals–Killer, Kazul, Scorn, and Horatio–understood what Trouble had asked, but everyone, even Vamist, could tell by their reactions that it was important.

"All right, hotshot, what did you find in the castle?" asked Scorn, switching her tail in annoyance at having to admit to so much curiosity in public.

"One moment, please," Morwen said. Quickly, she explained to Cimorene, Telemain, Brandel, and Amory where Trouble had been and what he had just said. Cimorene bit her lip, glanced at Vamist, and turned to Willin. "Willin, can you keep this fellow under control and out of the way? He was working with the wizards, and I don't think he should hear this."

"He may have some insight to offer, Your Majesty," said the elf. "However, if you wish it, I will do my best."

"I'll get his insights later," Cimorene said grimly. "Get him out of here."

"I'll help," Amory offered.

"Me, too," said Brandel. "I'd be quite happy to help, in fact."

Vamist looked at the two fire-witches, who were eyeing him the same way Murgatroyd and Chaos tended to eye a particularly plump mouse, and blanched.

"Thank you," Cimorene said to Brandel. "Just leave enough of him for me to get some answers out of later."

"I think we can manage that," said Brandel.

Willin bowed and the three of them marched Vamist off into the forest. Cimorene turned back to Trouble. "Morwen . . ."

Morwen nodded at the cat. "Go ahead now, but slowly, so I can translate."

"Couldn't you just let them wonder?" asked Trouble. "Oh, all right. The castle is empty, except for the usual furniture and a couple of gooey wizards' robes. I'd guess Mendanbar melted a few of them before they got him."

"Got him?" Cimorene said after Morwen's translation. "What does he mean by that, Morwen?"

"If she doesn't interrupt, I'll tell you." Trouble was plainly enjoying all the attention. "I didn't see any trace of Mendanbar, so I asked the gargoyle in the study–the one that answers the magic mirror–if it knew what happened. Apparently, the wizards didn't notice that it was intelligent, so they did quite a bit of talking in front of it."

"What did they say?" Killer asked with the air of someone interested in spite of himself.

"Oh, this and that. Most of it wasn't very interesting."

Kazul put one forearm down next to Trouble and flexed claws that were almost as long as the cat's tail. "Little one, tell your story without these digressions, or I may lose what little patience the Society of Wizards has left me."

"If you insist." Trouble stretched, to show that even a dragon couldn't impress *him,* then went on. "The gargoyle said I was right about the robes: Zemenar and his group lost four wizards before they managed to corner Mendanbar. The gargoyle knew about it because they all came into the study afterward to decide what to do next. Seems that the wizards found out that they couldn't kill a King of the Enchanted Forest outright without messing up what they were doing to the forest. And Zemenar didn't want to just hold him prisoner, because he was afraid we would come back any minute." Trouble shook his head in admiration. "You know, Mendanbar's almost as good as a cat."

"At what?" asked Morwen. "Oh, never mind. What did they do with him?"

"Zemenar put him in storage," said Trouble.

"What does *that* mean?" Cimorene asked once Morwen had translated this.

Trouble shrugged. "He sent Mendanbar somewhere where he couldn't make any difficulties while the wizards finished up with the forest. 'I'll put him through a door and then hide the door,' is what the gargoyle heard him say. Too bad Zemenar didn't work the spell in the study where old wooden-head could watch, or I might have been able to tell you what it means."

"This doesn't make any sense." Cimorene sounded thoroughly frustrated.

"Of course it doesn't make sense," Scorn said. "Wizards don't *have* sense. If they did, they wouldn't make all these problems."

Morwen did not translate Scorn's comment. Instead, she asked Trouble, "Where did the wizards do their spell? Could you tell?"

"Piece of cake," Trouble said. "In the Grand Hall. The place reeked of recent spell casting, and–"

"Did you check the rest of the castle?" Morwen interrupted. "The Grand Hall is where Telemain did his wizard-liquefication spell, and you may have been sensing the residue from that."

"Give me credit for some sense," Trouble said. "Besides, it's not that hard to tell Telemain's magic from a wizard's. Even though they used some of his equipment."

"I still don't understand," Killer complained. "And–"

"And you're hungry," said Scorn. "We know."

"I don't understand either," said Cimorene. "What does 'put him through a door and then hide the door' *mean?*"

"Telemain?" said Morwen.

"Mmmm. It sounds as if someone did a partial transportation spell, looped it, bound the residual to a temporary construct, and then–"

Kazul cleared her throat pointedly. Telemain paused, frowned, and said crossly, "I don't know any other way to explain it."

"They used a transportation spell to send Mendanbar somewhere, only they stopped in the middle," Morwen suggested.

"No, that would be unstable," Telemain said. "The field would collapse unless they looped it and bound the ends to something. It's theoretically possible, but it takes an enormous amount of power."

Cimorene glanced over her shoulder at the destruction that surrounded the castle. "As much power as you'd get from soaking up a big chunk of the Enchanted Forest?"

"I think they used most of that for the shield spell," Telemain said. "But if anyone could have done a looped transport, Zemenar could. After all, he was Head Wizard of the Society of Wizards."

"I don't care if he was First Minister to the Grand Poobah of the Great Cathayan Empire," Cimorene said. "How are we going to get Mendanbar *out?"*

"We can't," Telemain said.

"What?"

"To dismantle the spell, we would need to be inside the castle. To get into the castle, we would have to get through the wizard's shield spell. The only thing–besides the Society of Wizards themselves–that can take down that shield spell is Mendanbar's sword. And none of us can use it."

Cimorene looked appalled. "Then Mendanbar's stuck *forever.*"

"Or until he starves to death," Killer put in gloomily.

"Not necessarily," Morwen said. Everyone turned to look at her. "In the first place, if Telemain is right about what they did, Mendanbar won't starve. A looped transportation spell makes it temporarily unnecessary to eat."

Telemain nodded, pleased. "Hershenfeld's experiments proved it. They were quite definitive."

"In the second place, it is only true that none of us can use the sword *yet.*" Morwen pushed her glasses firmly up and gave Cimorene a significant look.

"What–oh, Morwen, you can't mean the *baby!*" said Cimorene.

"Sounds reasonable to me," said Killer.

"It would," said Scorn.

Telemain frowned. "I don't think it will work, Morwen. The sword requires a certain level of deliberate control, and I doubt that a baby could provide coherent directions."

"We'll wait for him to grow," Kazul said. "It won't take long."

"Maybe not by dragon standards," Cimorene said. "But fifteen or sixteen years is a long time for people. I don't want to wait. And what if he's a she?"

"That shouldn't make any difference," Telemain said. "What's important to the sword is the bloodline and the–the personality. Or perhaps it's attitude that counts. I've never actually seen the linkage process that enables someone to use the sword, so I can't say for sure."

"No," said Cimorene. "Absolutely not. It would take too long, and it's too iffy. And what if one of the wizards decides to come back and sneak into the castle to finish Mendanbar off?"

"Have you got any better ideas?" Kazul asked.

"How about lunch?" Killer said pointedly. "Aren't people supposed to think better when they've eaten? I do."

"It wouldn't take much," Scorn said. "You're a rabbit."

"Not anymore." Killer's ears went limp and his wings drooped at the thought. "Now I'm a–a something else."

"Lunch sounds like a very good idea to me," Kazul said. "Especially since we needn't rush right in to rescue Mendanbar."

Looking suddenly uneasy, Killer backed away from the dragon. All at once, he stopped and his eyes got very big. "You *can't* eat me! I'm insubstantial." His muzzle twitched. "I never thought there'd be anything good about that."

"I'm not interested in eating you," Kazul said. "What I want is six gallons of Morwen's cider and a big helping of cherries jubilee."

Morwen frowned. "I thought you were full."

"I'm never too full for dessert," said the dragon. "And chasing wizards is thirsty work."

"I suppose we might as well," Cimorene said. "It doesn't look as if any of you will make much sense otherwise."

"Does that mean someone is going to fix me?" said Killer.

"I thought you wanted to stay insubstantial," Trouble said with a sly glance in Kazul's direction.

"Not if it means I can't eat."

Since this was an eminently reasonable attitude, and since Killer had been very patient, all things considered, Telemain agreed to take a look at the spells afflicting Killer. While Kazul called in various dragons and fire-witches to set up lunch, Telemain unloaded a large number of peculiar-looking implements from his pockets and began stalking around the donkey, muttering under his breath. Morwen, after a moment's consideration, chose to help Telemain rather than assist with lunch. It gave her a fighting chance of keeping the magician from getting so absorbed in studying the interconnecting layers of enchantment that he forgot about removing them.

They were, it turned out, just in time. The various enchantments seemed almost to have taken on a life of their own, linking and intertwining with each other until there was no separating them. Fortunately, Killer's insubstantiality had only just begun to be incorporated into the main mass, but even so it took the combined efforts of Morwen and Telemain to nullify it. The process was slow, and by the time they finished they stood in the center of a circle of interested observers attracted by the spectacle of a six-foot-something blue donkey with wings blinking on and off as bits of the spell came loose.

"Whew!" said Telemain when the last of the insubstantiality had been removed and canceled out. "That was more of a job than I expected."

"Can you stop now?" Cimorene asked. "Lunch is ready. If you could leave the rest of the spells for afterward–"

"I think we're going to have to leave the rest of the spells for good," Telemain said, stowing his implements back in their appropriate pockets.

"What?"

"Killer has so much magic stuck to him that the bottom layers have melted together," Morwen said. "It's practically impossible to undo the spells he's under. We were lucky to get the top layer off."

"You mean I'm going to be a seven-foot, eleven-inch–counting the ears–bright blue floating donkey with oversized wings for the rest of my *life?"* Killer wailed.

"Count your blessings," said Scorn. "At least you're not insubstantial anymore."

"And you're not a rabbit," Trouble pointed out. "That's a plus."

"But I'm *supposed* to be a rabbit!"

"Quiet," Morwen told them sternly. "As I was saying, *undoing* the spells is next to impossible. But *moving* them . . ."

". . . is elementary magic," Telemain said, nodding. "We won't even need any special equipment. But who were you thinking of moving them to?"

Morwen smiled. "Cimorene, would you ask Willin to bring Arona Michaelear Grinogion Vamist over here for a moment, please? This won't take long, and then we can relax and have lunch."

For a moment, Cimorene and Telemain stared at Morwen, and then they began to smile, too. "It will be my pleasure," Cimorene said, and called Willin over. A short time later, Vamist appeared, flanked by Brandel and Amory.

"What do you want now?" Vamist asked. "I *demand* that you send me home at once."

"In a minute," Morwen said. "Stand over here by Killer. Trouble, Scorn–"

"Right here," Scorn purred. "Go ahead whenever you're ready."

"Good." Morwen raised her left hand, palm up, then flipped it over.

"Front to back,
White to black,
Young to old,
Silver to gold."

As she finished speaking, Killer began to glow green. The glow pulsed once, brightly, far enough for the edge to touch Vamist. "Whoops!" said Vamist, and "Eek!" said Killer, and then an ordinary brown rabbit with a few faded patches of white-dyed fur dropped to the ground next to an oversized blue floating donkey with wings.

"Look," said Scorn. "He's got a little bald patch between his ears."

"What–eee-augh!" said Vamist. "No! You can't *do* this to me!"

"Want to bet?" said Trouble.

"Goodness, he looks silly," said Killer, twitching his nose. "Is that really what I was like?"

"Except for the bald patch," said Scorn.

"You can't mean to leave me like this!" Vamist cried. "You wouldn't make me stay a *donkey!"*

"You're not just *a* donkey," Morwen said, letting her smile grow.

"You're a seven-foot bright blue floating donkey with oversized wings. And as far as I'm concerned you can stay that way for the rest of your life. Telemain, have you got enough energy left to send him to the main square in his hometown?"

"I believe I can manage that," Telemain said.

"No! I'll be the laughingstock of the whole countryside! And how will I get people to pay attention to what I say?"

"You won't," Brandel said with considerable relish. "No one will listen to someone who looks that silly. Morwen, it's perfect."

"It certainly is," Cimorene said. "How on earth did you think of it?"

"It came to me a while back, when Scorn said he was 'as dumb as that rabbit.' Now all that's left is the problem of what to do about the castle."

But though they discussed it over lunch, after lunch, and through the afternoon until dinner, no one could think of anything that might work. Telemain spent an hour studying the shield spell, but he could not find any way to get rid of it. The dragons could not get close to it because the spell was too similar to the one on the wizards' staffs and made them sneeze. The fire-witches' magic just bounced off. In desperation, Cimorene even tried to stick Mendanbar's sword into the spell, but it stopped at the edge of the glow and refused to penetrate it.

"I think we're going to have to wait for the baby," Telemain said finally.

"I'm not giving up yet," Cimorene said. "There's *got* to be some way to get in, or to get Mendanbar out."

"Don't be so sure," Morwen said. "Barrier spells frequently come with a time delay, rather than any specific sort of key. I believe a hundred years is the usual period, though that normally applies to hedges of briars, not glowing magic shields. Still . . ."

"I'm not giving up," Cimorene repeated. "And I'm certainly not waiting a hundred years!"

And she didn't. For the next two months, while Telemain and Morwen disposed of Vamist the donkey and sent Killer the rabbit back to his clover patch, while the dragons combed the Enchanted Forest for stray wizards, while the fire-witches finished helping out and went home (or, in some cases, built new homes in the Enchanted Forest), Cimorene tried everything anyone could think of to get herself through the wizards' shield. She had dwarves dig tunnels and birds dive at the top of the shield; she sprayed it with soapy lemon water and sprinkled it with powdered dragon scales (donated for the purpose by Kazul); she cast spells alone at midnight and at noon in combination with Morwen, Telemain, all of the fire-witches, and several dragons.

Nothing made any difference.

Kazul left a squad of dragons to keep watch for wizards near the castle, and she herself visited frequently. Eventually, she persuaded Cimorene to slow down, at least until the baby was born. Since none of the other attempts had shown any sign of success, Cimorene's child seemed more and more to be their best hope of getting into the castle, rescuing Mendanbar, and defeating the wizards once and for all. Rumors began circulating, each purporting to give the real truth about the battle and the whereabouts of King Mendanbar.

The Society of Wizards was too busy with its own affairs–choosing a new Head Wizard and recovering from the unexpected onslaught of dragons and fire-witches–to make new trouble for the time being. So the pause in the fighting stretched out longer and longer until it became a sort of uneasy, unofficial peace.

And everyone waited.

EPILOGUE

Which Hints at Things to Come

Motherhood suits Cimorene, Morwen thought as she watched the Queen of the Enchanted Forest and the King of the Dragons making peculiar noises over the infant Prince Daystar, aged two months, six days, and some-odd hours. On the moss beside them, at the foot of an ancient and enormous willow, lay Mendanbar's unsheathed sword.

"Telemain says he melted another wizard in the eastern part of the forest yesterday," Morwen said aloud. "They're getting bolder."

Cimorene looked up, her face clouded. "I know. Antorell found me this morning. It's all right. I melted him," she added quickly. "But he was very angry. I think he blames me because Kazul ate his father."

"Antorell never was very strong on logic," Kazul said. "Ooochy-ooo. *What* a fine big boy you are!"

Since this last was directed at the baby Prince, Morwen only smiled. "It's a good thing none of my cats are here, or you'd have to make an equal fuss the next time one of them has kittens."

"As long as I don't have to be their godmother, I'll be happy to fuss," Kazul said.

"I didn't know your cats were expecting kittens," Cimorene said.

"None of them is, yet." Morwen smiled again. "Though the way Scorn and Horatio are behaving, it's only a matter of time. You should hear some of the things Trouble says about them–'mushy' is probably the kindest."

"It's a good thing you like cats," Cimorene said.

"Yes, it is." Morwen looked at Cimorene, and her smile faded. "You're avoiding the real subject, which is, *What are you going to do now?* It will be a long time before Daystar is old enough to use Mendanbar's sword, and if the Society of Wizards is looking for him–"

"I don't think they are," Cimorene said. "I don't think they even know Daystar exists. Mendanbar and I hadn't officially announced it before they attacked, and afterward it seemed like a good idea to keep quiet about it. So they haven't heard, and they're not looking for Daystar. They're looking for the sword, and they're looking for me."

"It amounts to the same thing," Morwen said. "And doesn't Antorell know about Daystar, if he found you this morning?"

Cimorene snorted. "Antorell was so mad at me that he didn't notice anything else. He walked right by the sword and tripped over Kazul's tail before I melted him."

"Still, if he found you, it's only a matter of time before the rest of the Society does, too. Isn't it?"

"Not quite." Cimorene glanced sideways at Kazul and took a deep breath. "I've thought about this a lot, and I have an idea how to outsmart them. I want to know what you think of it."

"You know what *I* think of it," Kazul rumbled. "I don't like it one bit. The idea of–"

"Hush, Kazul, you'll upset Daystar. It's like this, Morwen: The Society of Wizards knows I've brought Mendanbar's sword back to the Enchanted Forest, because they can't swallow big chunks of the forest's magic anymore and they know that the sword is what keeps them from doing that. So they're poking around here, looking for me and the sword. If I leave the forest–"

"But you can't take the sword out of the Enchanted Forest or the Society of Wizards will start destroying it again," Morwen said. "Or else the sword will leak all the magic out of the forest, which amounts to the same thing."

"I'm not going to take the sword out of the Enchanted Forest," Cimorene said. "I'm going to hide it in here, and then I'm going to take Daystar and settle down outside the forest somewhere. Not with the dragons; the wizards will expect that."

Morwen frowned, forcing herself to consider the proposal carefully. "So the Society of Wizards will look for you inside the Enchanted Forest, because they'll expect you to be with the sword and they'll know that the sword is still inside the forest. And since you'll be *outside* the forest, you and Daystar will be relatively safe. And things won't get any worse *inside* the forest, because the sword will keep the wizards from destroying new bits. Very neat. But what if they find the sword?"

"I don't think they will," Cimorene said. "Telemain did some experiments with a wizard's staff, and he says that as long as the sword is inside the Enchanted Forest, it's invisible to wizards' magic. If I hide it well, they'll have to search the whole forest, inch by inch, on foot, in order to find it."

"And I doubt any of them have the patience for that. But are you sure that the wizards won't think up a way to get around it?"

"Telemain says that the only way a wizard could use magic to find the sword would be to use a spell that finds the person who's carrying it. And for *that* to work, the person carrying it has to know that what he's got is Mendanbar's sword. That's why I can't give it to you or Telemain."

"I see. So by the time the wizards think of casting that type of spell, if they ever do, the sword will be hidden and you'll be outside the forest."

Cimorene nodded. "I'd like to have you or Telemain check on the sword once in a while to make sure it's all right, but if the wizards start looking for someone who knows what it is–"

"That shouldn't be a problem as long as we don't try to carry it." Morwen's right hand tingled, remembering the way it had burned when she held it. "And I certainly don't intend to try!"

"Oh, that only happens outside the Enchanted Forest," Cimorene said, then frowned. "At least, I'm fairly sure that's what Telemain meant when he explained. Inside the Enchanted Forest, the sword does different things."

"Well, I'm not giving it the chance to do them to me," Morwen said. "If you want to be certain the wizards won't catch us checking, I'll send one of the cats."

"That should work. Not too often."

"No, we wouldn't want to lead the Society of Wizards right to it." Morwen shook her head. "I don't like it any more than Kazul does, but it sounds as if it will work. As far as it goes."

"As far as it goes? What do you think I've forgotten?"

"The Society of Wizards put up that shield spell. What if they decide to pull it down in a year or two and take over the castle? We can't keep a guard on it for the next sixteen or twenty years. Not an effective one, anyway."

"Speak for yourself," Kazul said. "Sixteen or twenty years of guarding a castle is nothing to a dragon."

"And Kazul and Telemain have already solved that problem anyway," Cimorene said. "You must not have come by the castle, or you'd have seen it."

"Seen what?" said Morwen.

"The second shield spell, the one the dragons put up." Cimorene's eyes sparked. "Telemain analyzed the wizards' shield spell, and then Kazul got all the dragons to duplicate it. It works the same way the Society's spell does: only the people who put it up can take it down."

Morwen pursed her lips. "So we can't get at the castle because of the wizards' spell, and the wizards can't get at their spell because of the dragons' spell. You do seem to have thought of everything."

"Thank you," said Kazul. "Now convince Cimorene that she'll be safe in the Mountains of Morning with the rest of us, and we'll be all set."

"I don't think I can do that," Morwen said. "In the first place, Cimorene is stubborn as a pig when she wants to be, and in the second place, she's right. As soon as the Society of Wizards figures out she's not in the Enchanted Forest, they'll look for her with dragons. And they're sneaky enough to find her, and that would ruin everything." She sighed. "When do you intend to leave, Cimorene?"

"This afternoon, as soon as I hide this." Cimorene picked up the sword. "It's a pity I can't put it in a sheath, but Telemain says that with Mendanbar . . . unavailable, a sheath would obstruct some of the sword's spells that interfere with wizards."

"Would you like some help?" Morwen said.

"It can't hurt. Kazul, will you watch Daystar for an hour or two?"

"I suppose so. Since you seem determined."

"Good." Cimorene patted the dragon's shoulder. "And thank you. Bye, Daystar."

As she bent forward to kiss him, the flash of light on the blade of the sword caught the child's attention, and he reached for it with both hands. "Ah-ah-ah!" he demanded.

"No, Daystar," Cimorene replied gently. "Not now. This is for later, when you're older."

"Ah-ah-*ah!"* said Daystar emphatically.

"When you're older," Cimorene said again. "Come on, Morwen, let's get started." Together they walked through the trees to find a place to hide the sword against the time when Daystar would be old enough to use it.

TALKING TO DRAGONS

For NATE *(who started it),*

and for the rest of the Scribblies:

STEVE, PAM, KARA,

WILL, AND EMMA

Contents

1

In Which Daystar Leaves Home and Encounters a Lizard

Mother taught me to be polite to dragons. Particularly polite, I mean; she taught me to be ordinary polite to everyone. Well, it makes sense. With all the enchanted princesses and disguised wizards and transformed kings and so on wandering around, you never know *whom* you might be talking to. But dragons are a special case.

Not that I ever actually talked to one until after I left home. Even at the edge of the Enchanted Forest, dragons aren't exactly common. The principle is what matters, though: *Always* be polite to a dragon. It's harder than it sounds. Dragon etiquette is incredibly complicated, and if you make a mistake, the dragon eats you. Fortunately, I was well trained.

Dragon etiquette wasn't the only thing Mother taught me. Reading and writing are unusual skills for a poor boy, but I learned them. Music, too, and fighting. Don't ask me where Mother learned to use a sword. Until I was thirteen, I didn't know we had one in the house. I even learned a little magic. Mother wasn't exactly pleased; but growing up on the edge of the Enchanted Forest, I had to know some things.

Mother is tall–about two inches taller than I am–and slender, and very impressive when she wants to be. Her hair is black, like mine, but much longer. Most of the time she wears it in two braids wound around and around her head, but when she really wants to impress someone she lets it hang straight to her feet. A lot of the disguised princes who stopped at our cottage on their way into the Enchanted Forest thought Mother was a sorceress. You can't really blame them. Who else would live at the edge of a place like that?

Sometimes I thought they were right. Mother always knew what directions to give them, even if they didn't tell her what they were looking for. I never saw her do any real magic, though, until the day the wizard came.

I knew right away that he was a wizard. Not because of his brown beard or his blue-and-brown silk robes—although no one but a wizard can walk around in blue-and-brown silk robes for very long without getting really dusty. It wasn't even his staff. I knew he was a wizard because he had the same *feel* of magic that the unicorns and griffins have when you catch a glimpse of them, farther on in the forest.

I was surprised to see him because we didn't get too many wizards. Well, actually, we'd never gotten any. Mother said that most of them preferred to go into the forest through the Gates of Mist and Pearl at the top of the Crystal Falls, or through the Caves of Fire and Night if they could manage it. The few that went into the forest in other ways never stopped at our cottage.

This wizard was unusual. He turned off the road and walked right past me without saying anything, straight up to our cottage. Then he banged on the door with the head of his staff. The door splintered and fell apart.

I decided that I didn't like him.

Mother was cooking rabbit stew in the big black pot over the chimney fire. She didn't even look up when the door fell in. The wizard stood there for a minute, and I sneaked a little closer so I could see better. He was frowning, and I got the impression he wasn't used to being ignored. Mother kept stirring the stew.

"Well, Cimorene, I have found you," the wizard said at last.

"It took you long enough," Mother said without turning. "You're getting slow."

"You know why I am here."

Mother shrugged. "You're sixteen years too late. I told you, you're getting slow."

"Ha! I can take the sword now, and the boy as well. There is nothing you can do to stop me this time," the wizard said. I could tell he was trying to sound menacing, but he didn't do a very good job.

Mother finally turned around. I took one look at her face and backed up a couple of steps. She looked at the wizard for a minute and started to smile. "Nothing, Antorell? Are you sure?"

The wizard laughed and raised his staff. I backed up some more. I mean, I wanted to see what was going on, but I'm not *stupid.* He paused a moment—for effect, I think—and Mother pointed at him.

"Argelfraster," she said, and he started to melt.

"No! Not *again!*" he screamed. He shrank pretty quickly–all but his head, which was shouting nearly the whole time. "I'll get you, Cimorene! I'll be back! You can't stop me! I'll–"

Then his head collapsed and there was nothing left but a little puddle of brown goo and his staff.

I stared at the puddle. All I could think was, *I never knew Mother could do that.* Mother let me stand there for a while before she told me to clean it up.

"Don't touch the staff," she said. "And don't forget to wash your hands before you come to dinner."

I went to get a bucket. When I came back, the staff was gone and Mother was stirring the stew as if nothing had happened. She didn't mention the wizard again until the next morning.

I was out by the remains of our door, trying to fix it. I didn't think my chances were very good. I picked up the hammer, and as I looked around for nails I saw Mother walk out of the Enchanted Forest. I was so surprised I dropped the hammer and nearly smashed my foot. Mother never went into the Enchanted Forest. Never. Then I saw the sword she was carrying, and if I'd still been holding the hammer, I'd have dropped it again.

Even from a distance, I could tell it wasn't an ordinary sword. It was about the same size and shape as the one I practiced with, but it shone too brightly and looked too sharp to be ordinary. Mother brought it over to me and set it down on top of the boards I'd been working on. "Don't touch it," she said, and went into the house.

I had a hard time following Mother's instructions. The more I looked at the sword, the more I wanted to pick it up and try a few of the passes Mother had taught me. It was such a beautiful weapon! Just looking at it made me shiver. But Mother always had good reasons for the things she told me to do, so I waited.

I didn't have to wait long. She came back almost immediately, carrying a sword belt and a sheath that I'd never seen before. They were old–so old that the leather had turned nearly gray–and very, very plain. I was disappointed; the sword deserved something more impressive.

Mother went straight to the sword and put it in the sheath. She relaxed a little then, as if she'd been worried about something. Mother almost never worried. I started wondering just what that weapon did. I didn't have much time to think about it, though. As soon as she had sheathed the sword, Mother turned and gave me her You're-not-much-but-you'll-have-to-do look. *I* started to worry.

Mother picked up the sword belt. "This is for you, Daystar." I reached for it, but she shook her head. "No, I'll do it this first time. Hold still."

She bent down and buckled the belt around my waist, then hung the sheathed sword on the belt. I felt a little strange letting her do all that, and my elbows kept getting in the way.

Finally she straightened up. "Now, Daystar, I have a few things to tell you before you leave."

"Leave?" I was shocked. Mother had never mentioned leaving before. It occurred to me that she'd said "you," not "we." I swallowed hard. "By myself?"

"Of course. You're sixteen; it's time you left, and I'm certainly not coming with you. Now pay attention." She gave me one of her sharp looks.

I paid attention.

"You have a sword, and you know as much as I can safely teach you. I don't want to see you back here again until you can explain to me why you had to leave. Do you understand?"

I nodded.

Mother went on, "Start with the Enchanted Forest. One way or another, things will happen more quickly there. Don't lose your sword, and don't draw it unless you need to use it. Oh, and watch out for Antorell. It'll take him a couple of days to get himself back together and find out where I put his staff, but once he does he'll try to make trouble again. All right?"

"But you haven't explained anything!" I blurted. "Why did that wizard come here yesterday, anyway? Why should he want to make trouble for me? And if he's so dangerous, why are you sending me–"

"Daystar!"

I stopped in midsentence.

Mother glared at me. "What happened to the manners I've tried to teach you?"

"I–I'm sorry, Mother," I said. "I was upset."

"Being upset is no excuse," Mother said sternly. "If you're going to be rude, do it for a reason and get something from it."

I nodded.

Mother smiled. "I know it's hard, and it's rather short notice, but this will probably be the best chance we get. I can't waste it just to give you time to get used to the idea of leaving home. Besides, if I tell you too much now, it could ruin everything. You'll just have to work things out for yourself."

I was more confused than ever, but I could see Mother wasn't going to tell me anything else. She looked at me for another moment, then bit her lip as if she wanted to say something and couldn't. Abruptly, she turned and walked away. At the door of the cottage, she stopped and looked back. "Good luck, Daystar. And stop wasting time. You don't have much of it." Before I could say anything, she disappeared inside.

I started off toward the Enchanted Forest. Mother's advice was always good. Besides, I was afraid she'd melt me or something if I hung around very long.

I didn't bother to follow the road. It isn't particularly useful, anyway–it disappears as soon as you cross into the forest. Or at least, it usually does. At any rate, I wanted to start with the section of the Enchanted Forest that I knew.

The Enchanted Forest comes in two parts, the Outer Forest and the Deep Woods. Most people don't realize that. The Outer Forest is relatively safe if you know what you're doing, and I'd gathered herbs there a few times. I'd never gone more than an hour's walk from our cottage, and nothing particularly interesting had ever happened, but I'd always known that something might. The way things were going, I was pretty sure that this time something would.

I felt the little tingle on my skin that marks the border between the ordinary woods, where our cottage was, and the Enchanted Forest. Some people have trouble getting in and out of the Enchanted Forest, but I never did. I was feeling excited and adventurous, and maybe a little scared. I mean, for years I'd watched all those princes and heroes and so on go into the forest, and now it was my turn. I looked back over my shoulder to see if Mother was watching. The cottage was gone.

That shook me. You just don't expect the place you've lived in for sixteen years to vanish like that. I looked around. The trees were huge–much larger than the ones by our cottage. I couldn't reach more than a quarter of the way around the trunk of the smallest one. The ground was covered with dark green moss that ran right up the bases of the trees and stopped short. I could see a couple of bushes, including one that had three different colors of flowers on it. Everything felt very dark and green and alive, and none of it looked familiar at all.

I shivered. This wasn't the Outer Forest. This was the Deep Woods.

I waited for a couple of minutes, but nothing happened. Somehow, I wasn't reassured. Being lost in the Enchanted Forest does not do much for one's peace of mind.

After a while I started walking again. I felt much less adventurous and considerably more scared.

I walked for a long time. Eventually I quit being scared, at least mostly. Finally I started looking for a place to rest; my feet hurt and I was getting very tired. I was careful, though. I didn't want to sit on a flower that used to be someone important. After about fifteen minutes I found a spot that looked all right, and I started to sit down. Unfortunately, I'd forgotten I was wearing the sword. It got tangled up in my legs and I sort of fell over.

Somebody giggled. I looked around and didn't see anyone, so I decided to get untangled first. I straightened my legs out and sat up, making sure the sword belt was out of the way this time. Then I took a second look around. I still didn't see anyone, but the same somebody giggled again.

"Sir or madam or–" I stopped. What was the proper honorific for something that wasn't male or female? I was pretty sure there was one, but I couldn't remember it.

"Oh, don't bother," said a high, squeaky voice. "I've never cared for all that fancy stuff."

I still didn't see anyone. "Forgive my stupidity, but I can't seem to find where you are," I said.

The giggle came again. "Down here, silly."

I looked down and jumped. A little gold lizard was sitting right next to my hand. He was about twice as long as my middle finger, and half of that was tail.

"Hey, watch it!" said the lizard. "You might hurt someone if you keep jumping around like that. Me, for instance. You big people are so careless."

"I'm very sorry," I said politely.

The lizard lifted his head. "You are? Yes, you are! How amazing. Who are you, anyway?"

"My name is Daystar," I said, bowing slightly. It was a little awkward to do from a sitting position, but I managed. Being polite to a lizard felt peculiar, but there are only two rules of behavior in the Enchanted Forest: Don't take anything for granted, and Be polite to everyone. That's if you don't live there. The inhabitants have their own codes, which it's better not to ask about.

"You're Daystar?" The lizard did something very tangled very quickly and ended up balanced on his tail. "So you are! Well, my goodness. I hadn't expected to see you around here for a while yet."

"You were expecting me?"

"Of course." The lizard looked smug. "I know everything that goes on in the Enchanted Forest. Absolutely *everything!* I've seen you in the Outer Forest. It was only a matter of time before you got this far, though I thought it would take longer. I'm Suz, by the way."

"Pleased to meet you," I said.

"You are?" The lizard leaned forward and almost lost his balance. "Yes, you really are! How positively extraordinary. Whatever are you doing in the Enchanted Forest?"

"I don't know," I said.

"You don't know!" The lizard did a back flip and scurried up onto a fat tree root, where he would have a better view. He balanced on his tail again and looked at me thoughtfully. "If you don't know what you're doing, why are you here?"

I thought for a moment. "Do you really know everything that happens in this forest?"

"Of course I do." Suz looked offended. An offended lizard is an interesting sight.

"I didn't mean to hurt your feelings or anything," I said hastily. "I just wondered if you could tell me where this came from." I touched the sword Mother had given me.

The lizard squinted in my general direction. "What? It's on the wrong side of you, silly. Bring it over where I can see it. If it came from the Enchanted Forest, I can tell you about it."

I lifted the sword, sheath and all, and twisted it around so it was on the same side of me as Suz. The lizard promptly fell over backward.

"Oh dear me my gracious goodness my oh," he squeaked. "Do you know what that *is?*"

"I wouldn't have asked you if I knew," I said. "It's a sword. I think it's magic."

"It's a sword! He thinks it's magic!" Suz ran around twice in a small circle, then did the tail-balancing trick again. "Where did you get it?" the little lizard demanded.

"My mother gave it to me. She got it out of the Enchanted Forest somewhere." I was getting a little tired of this. "Are you going to answer my question?"

"Your mother gave it to you. The Sword of the Sleeping King, that everyone in the world has been looking for for fifteen or twenty years, and *your mother gave it to you.*" The lizard got so agitated he fell over again. "That isn't right. That isn't reasonable. My dear boy, that simply isn't done! Even in the Enchanted Forest there is a proper order for these things! Someone will have to notify them at the castle immediately. Oh, dear, what a stir this will cause!"

"I'm sorry, I didn't know. What's the Sword of the Sleeping King?" I'd never heard of it before, which rather surprised me. After Mother made me memorize all those pages of names and titles and peculiar weapons, I'd thought I knew the name of every magic sword in the world.

"You don't know?" The lizard froze in the middle of getting back up on his tail. He looked like a golden pretzel. "No, you don't! Oh, my. You'd better go to the castle at once. Kazul will know what to do with you. I'd better go there myself, right away." Suz untwisted and darted off into the undergrowth.

"Wait!" I shouted. "What castle? Who is Kazul? And why–"

The lizard looked back. "I don't have time for that! And even if I did, I couldn't tell you. You have to find out yourself. Magic swords always work that way. Don't you know *anything?*"

"Do you want me to recite the names of the Four Hundred Minor Swords of Korred the Spellsmith? . . . I know lots of things. I just don't know about this. How do I find out?"

"Follow the sword, silly," Suz said, and disappeared among the leaves.

2

In Which Daystar Is Polite to a Bush and Makes a Friend

I didn't try to chase the lizard. For one thing, there wasn't much point in it. Suz was small enough to hide practically anywhere. For another, I didn't want to go running through the Enchanted Forest. People get killed that way, or enchanted, or other unpleasant things. Besides, I wanted to think.

I settled back against the tree and looked down at the sword, a little unhappily. "Follow the sword," Suz had said. But Mother had told me not to draw it unless I meant to use it, and I didn't think "following" it was the kind of use she meant. Besides, I wasn't sure I wanted to draw a magic sword in the middle of the Enchanted Forest, especially one I didn't know anything about. I decided to try something else.

I stood up and looked around. Over on my right there was a little gap in the trees, not enough to call a clearing, just a place where the trees were farther apart than usual. I went over to the middle of it and stood there while I tried to unfasten the sheath. That was a lot more complicated than it looked, and in the end I had to take the whole belt off. I wrapped the belt around the sheath and set it down in the middle of the open space. I backed up a couple of steps and sat down on the ground with the hilt of the sword close to me and the end of the sheath pointing away from me.

The woods had gone very, very quiet. I didn't like that, but after all the trouble I'd had getting out of the belt, I would have felt stupid if I'd just picked up the sword again without doing anything. Besides, I'd started setting up for a spell, and leaving things like that half-finished can be awfully dangerous.

I took a deep breath and spoke as steadily as I could:

"Sword of the Sleeping King,
I conjure thee:
By stream and starlight,
By sun and shadow,
By song and storm wind,
Show me thy tale!"

It was the simplest spell I knew–almost the only one, in fact. It's supposed to let the spell caster know more about the nature of whatever object is named in the first line of the chant. I didn't think the spell would work quite the usual way on a magic sword, but it wouldn't do any harm, and I was hoping to find out something useful.

I finished the spell, and everything was quiet for about two heartbeats. *Fast* heartbeats. I was nervous. Then the world turned over.

That's what it felt like. The ground started shaking, and the part under the sword pushed up until it made a mound taller than I was. I didn't have much of a chance to look at it, though, because I was rolling all over the open space and trying to grab hold of something. Then everything went dark, and I was falling, and a huge, deep voice said solemnly, "All hail the Bearer of the Sword!"

And then it was over and everything was back to normal. I was lying on the ground in the Enchanted Forest, trying to dig my way through the moss. I stopped and waited. Nothing else happened, so I sat up and looked around. I was still sitting in the same not-quite-a-clearing, with the sword and sheath in the middle. The sword . . .

The sword was standing upright, half-buried in a knee-high mound that hadn't been there before. The blade was about a handspan out of the sheath, and it glittered when the sun got far enough through the trees to hit it. I stood up and walked over. The mound was covered with moss, just like the rest of the forest floor. It could have been there forever. I shivered, wondering how I was going to get the sheath out of the ground.

I put one hand on the hilt, intending to shove it back down into the sheath. When my hand touched it, my whole arm started to tingle. I jerked my hand away and stared at the sword. It just sat there. I reached out again, this time for the sheath.

As soon as I touched it, the sheath slid out of the ground. The belt was still wrapped around it, and no dirt clung to either of them. I touched the hilt again. My arm tingled, but this time I was ready for it, and I shoved the sword back into the sheath. Then I stuffed the sword belt under my arm and started walking. I was sure *somebody* must have noticed what had just happened, and I didn't want to be around when they came to find out what was going on.

I didn't stop again until midafternoon. By then I was hungry as well as tired. I hadn't brought any food with me, and even if I'd known how to get home it was much too late to go back for some. I sighed and sat down under another tree to rest and think, but I didn't get much thinking done. Mostly, I stared at the sword.

Finally, I gave up. Sitting under a tree wasn't going to teach me anything. I stood up and buckled on the sword belt. As I adjusted it, my hand touched the hilt of the sword again. *Three* little tingles ran up my arm before I pulled my hand away. I looked at the sword for a moment, then shrugged and reached for the hilt with my right hand, as if I were going to draw it.

As soon as my hand touched the hilt, I felt the tingling. This time, instead of letting go, I concentrated on the way it felt. I got three distinct impressions. One was a low sort of background vibration, like a kitten purring in its sleep; one was a deep rumble; and one was a bright buzz, like a bee in a jar. Almost as soon as I figured them out, they started to fade. In another minute they were completely gone, and they didn't come back.

I took my hand off the sword's hilt, then put it back. I didn't feel anything. I tried a couple more times, but whatever it was had stopped. Finally I gave up and started walking again. I wasn't getting anywhere trying to figure out the sword, and I had to find somewhere to spend the night.

At least I didn't have to worry about giants; they live farther east, in the Mountains of Morning. It occurred to me suddenly that I didn't know where I was. I might *be* in the Mountains of Morning. It wasn't a particularly cheerful thought. I started walking more quietly.

I'd been walking for nearly half an hour when I realized that I knew where I was going. Unfortunately, I didn't know where I'd be when I got there. It was very odd, and I was a little uneasy until I realized that I didn't *have* to go that direction. I could have turned around and walked the other way, or gone sideways. In fact, I did go sideways for a while, just to prove I could.

After that I felt better, so I stopped avoiding whatever it was and started walking toward it again. I wasn't going to get anywhere if I kept avoiding things, and I might miss something important. Besides, there isn't any way you can avoid *everything* in the Enchanted Forest. This way, at least I knew something was coming.

I was still walking very quietly when I heard somebody crying. I headed toward the sound, wondering what I was getting myself into. You can't just ignore things like that, especially in the Enchanted Forest. On the other hand . . .

I stopped, staring at a thick, prickly hedge. It was taller than my head and impossible to see through, much less to shove through. The crying was coming from the other side.

I bent over. The bushes were much too close together for me to crawl through them. I could make out sunlight and long red hair and a brown tunic on the other side, but not much else. I stood up and walked to one side, looking for a thin spot in the hedge. It wasn't long before I realized I was going in a circle. *Terrific,* I thought. *I bet it goes all the way around without breaking.* I kept walking anyway, just in case.

It didn't take long to make the full circle. I bent over and peered through the bushes again. Suz might be able to get through, but I never would. I stood up and tapped lightly on the outside of the bushes.

"Excuse me, please, but would you mind letting me through?" I asked as politely as I could.

The bushes rustled and pulled apart. I stared at them for a minute. I hadn't really thought it would work. The bushes rustled again. Somehow they managed to sound impatient.

"Ah, thank you very much," I said, and stepped through.

The hedge closed behind me with a prim *swish,* and I looked around. Inside the hedge was a circular clearing full of sunlight and the feel of magic. A red-haired girl in a brown tunic was lying at one side of the clearing. She sat up as I came in; her face was tearstained.

"Who are you?" she demanded fiercely, as soon as she saw me. "And what do you want?" She looked about my age, but I never have been very good at guessing how old people are, especially people who aren't in disguise or enchanted.

"My name is Daystar," I said. "I heard you, um, crying, and I wanted to see if I could do anything."

She looked at me suspiciously. "You just walked through that hedge? Ha! I've been trying to get out of here all day. It's not that easy. I bet you're a wizard." I noticed some scratches on her arms and some fuzzy places in the tunic where it might have caught on branches or trees.

"I'm not a wizard. Maybe it's easier to get in than it is to get out," I offered.

The red-haired girl sat back. "That could be true," she said a little less belligerently. She eyed me skeptically, and I tried to look trustworthy. "Well, you don't *look* like a wizard," she said at last. "Can you get out again?"

"I don't know," I said.

"Well, try!" she said. "No, wait. I'll stand next to you so I can get out, too. Then we'll both be rescued." She jumped to her feet. "What are you waiting for?"

"I'm sorry, but I don't really think I need to be rescued," I said. "I was looking for a place to spend the night and this seems pretty safe. I'm not sure I want to leave just yet. Besides, I don't know anything about you. Maybe I don't want to rescue you."

"Oh, rats." The redhead sat down again. "I thought you might be a hero. You can talk them into anything. Stupid creatures."

"Who are you?" I asked. "And why are you worried about wizards?"

"I suppose it won't matter if I tell you," she said after thinking for a minute. "They're chasing me. My name's Shiara," she added.

"Wizards are chasing you? More than one?" I was impressed. Wizards usually don't cooperate much, even the ones who belong to the Society of Wizards. At least, that's what Mother always told me. "What did you do?"

Shiara hesitated, then threw her hair back over her shoulder with a toss of her head. "I," she said defiantly, "am a fire-witch."

"You're a fire-witch?" Well, she had the red hair for it, but that doesn't always mean someone is a fire-witch.

She must have heard the doubt in my voice, because she scowled at me. "I *am* a fire-witch! I am!"

"I didn't say you weren't," I said hastily. That only seemed to make it worse.

"You don't believe me! But I am *so* a fire-witch! I am! I am!" By the time she finished, she was shouting. She glared at me, and her hair burst into flame.

That settled it. "I believe you, I believe you," I said. "Uh, shouldn't you do something about your hair?"

Shiara burst into tears and her hair went out.

I stood there feeling silly and useless. Finally I remembered my handkerchief. Mother made me carry one all the time, even to chop wood, so I actually had it with me. I pulled it out and offered it to her.

After a couple of sniffs, she took it and mopped her face, but she didn't say anything.

"I'm sorry," I said finally. "I didn't mean to make you mad."

"Well, you did," she snapped. She crumpled the handkerchief into a little ball and threw it at me.

I caught it and stuffed it back into my pocket. "I *said* I was sorry."

"I can't *help* having a temper," Shiara said crossly. "All fire-witches do."

"Really? I've never met one before. I've met heroes and princes, but no fire-witches. Does your hair always do that when you get mad?"

"No," she said. She looked like she was going to cry again.

"Why are the wizards chasing you?" I asked hastily, hoping it was a safer topic.

"I burned the Head Wizard's staff," Shiara said matter-of-factly.

My jaw dropped about a foot. A wizard's staff is the source of his power, and furthermore, most wizards store spells in them. Sort of an emergency reserve. A lot of the staffs get passed down from one wizard to the next, accumulating magic as they go. They're practically indestructible. Sometimes they get lost or stolen and then found in the nick of time under peculiar circumstances, but I'd never heard of one being destroyed before. And the Head Wizard's staff . . .

"You *burned* a *wizard's staff?*" I managed finally.

"You bet." Shiara's eyes glinted at the memory. "He deserved it, too. But the rest of them got mad. So I ran away while they were arguing about what to do with me."

"And you came to the Enchanted Forest? On purpose? Isn't that a little extreme? I mean, you could get, well, enchanted. Or killed or something. This place is dangerous."

"Having the whole Society of Wizards mad at you isn't exactly safe," she snapped.

I thought about it. She was right. "Why did you burn the Head Wizard's staff?" I asked after a minute.

"I didn't like him," Shiara said shortly. I got the distinct impression she didn't want to talk about it, so I decided to change the subject again. Besides, my feet hurt.

"Would you mind if I sat down?" I asked. "I've been doing a lot of walking today."

"Go ahead."

I moved the sword out of the way and sat down. This time I didn't fall over the sheath; I was starting to get the hang of it.

Shiara saw the weapon and frowned. "Are you sure you're not a hero or an apprentice hero or something?"

"I don't think I am," I said cautiously. "I'm not really sure."

"You're not sure? Don't you know who you are?"

I blinked. I'd never really thought about it that way. "I know who I *am,*" I said. "I just don't know what I'm supposed to be *doing*. Except finding out what I'm supposed to be doing."

Shiara stared at me. "I don't believe it. Nobody comes to the Enchanted Forest without some kind of reason."

"What's yours, then? Besides running away from wizards." I was getting a little tired of people and animals and things not believing me.

"None of your business!" Shiara glared at me again. Then she jumped up and glared down at me. "I want to leave," she announced. "Right now."

"All right," I said. "But I thought you couldn't get through the hedge."

Shiara stamped her foot, and a little flame flared up from it. "I can't! Open it for me! Right now!" She was really mad, but at least this time her hair wasn't burning. I was glad. Watching someone glare at you with her hair on fire is a little unnerving.

"I don't want to open the hedge yet," I said reasonably. "I don't even know if I can. Besides, it would be dangerous. There are wolves in this forest. And it's getting dark. There could be nightshades out there already. That may not bother a fire-witch, but–"

"I hate you!" Shiara cried. She sounded like she meant it.

"Just because I don't want to get eaten by wolves or driven mad by a nightshade or something?" I said, puzzled. "What's wrong with that?"

Shiara just turned her back on me. I watched her for a minute, then sort of settled back on the ground. Things were getting very complicated. I was lost in the Enchanted Forest, with no food or water. I had a magic sword I didn't want to use because it did strange things to the ground. In another day or so I would probably have a wizard looking for me. I didn't have any idea how I was going to figure out why Mother wanted me to leave home. And then there was Shiara.

Fire-witches are rare. Nobody can learn to be one. You're either born one or you're not. They're very powerful. They can burn anything, of course, and fire doesn't hurt them at all. Fire-witches can learn almost any kind of magic there is. They're immune to most spells, too, which is why wizards don't like them. Fire-witches can even summon Elementals and get them to listen. Well, sometimes. And Shiara was a fire-witch. With enough power to burn a wizard's staff. The Head Wizard's staff.

I didn't think I wanted her to be mad at me.

I didn't know what to do about it, though. I didn't even know what I'd done wrong, and I wasn't at all sure what to do next. What do you say to a mad fire-witch?

Right about then I heard snuffling noises. I looked up. Shiara was crying again. I sighed and dug out my handkerchief.

"I don't mean to make you mad," I said as I watched her mop her face again. "I just keep doing it by accident. It'd make things a lot easier for both of us if you would tell me what I'm doing wrong so I can stop."

Shiara looked at me over the top of the handkerchief, which was starting to look sort of damp and wrinkled. "You want to talk to me? You're not scared?" She lowered the handkerchief and stared at me. "You mean it!"

"Of course I mean it," I said. "Why shouldn't I? And why should I be scared?"

"I guess I'd better tell you," she said with a sigh.

3

In Which They Meet a Wizard and Get Wet

The problem was, Shiara was a fire-witch who couldn't do anything. On purpose, I mean. Things happened when she got mad, and once in a while a spell worked for her, but most of the time she couldn't make anything happen, which was why she hadn't just burned her way out of the bushes before I got there. She didn't have very many friends because everyone was afraid of her. I could understand that. I mean, with a temper like hers and no way of telling what would happen when she lost it, people had reason to be nervous.

On top of that, everyone kept telling her all the things she ought to be able to do because she was a fire-witch. Like not worrying about nightshades. That was why she got mad at me. She was awfully sick of being told what fire-witches could do, especially when she couldn't, and she thought I was starting, so of course she lost her temper.

And then the Society of Wizards heard about this fire-witch who couldn't cast spells or anything. They decided it would be a great chance to find out more about fire-witches, so a whole bunch of them came and grabbed Shiara right out of the middle of town. Shiara didn't like it. She liked it even less when she found out they wanted her to stand in the middle of a circle of wizards while they threw spells at her to see what would work.

"I said no," Shiara told me. "And they said I didn't have any choice. That's when I burned the Head Wizard's staff. I don't like wizards."

"I don't blame you," I said.

She nodded and went on, "Anyway, it turned out that the wizards had brought me to the edge of the Enchanted Forest. So as long as I was here, I decided to see if there was somewhere in the forest I could find out how to use my magic. Only then I stumbled in here and I couldn't get out. I was afraid the wizards would catch up with me, and I was tired and hungry and mad, and I couldn't make my fire magic work enough to burn even a little hole in those bushes. That's why I was crying."

I wished she hadn't mentioned being hungry. Until then I'd almost forgotten that I hadn't eaten since breakfast. But there wasn't any food inside the hedge, and I wasn't going to try opening it. I'd already done enough experimenting for one day, and besides, it was getting dark.

"Your turn. What are you doing in the Enchanted Forest?" Shiara asked when I didn't say anything.

"I don't know," I said.

"How can you not know?" she demanded. "I told you why I came!"

So I explained about Mother and the wizard. Shiara was very interested.

"I want to meet your mother," she said. "After I learn how to use my magic. Do you think she would teach me how to melt a wizard?"

"I don't know."

Shiara thought for a minute. "I don't see how you can find out what you're supposed to be doing just by wandering around the Enchanted Forest."

"Well, *you're* planning to wander around until you find out how to use your magic, aren't you?" I said. "I don't think I really see the difference."

"I know what I'm doing," Shiara said. "That's the difference."

"If you knew very much about the Enchanted Forest, you wouldn't have gotten caught by this hedge."

Shiara scowled, then looked suddenly thoughtful. "Is it more dangerous to wander around the forest alone than with someone?"

"It depends," I said. "Two people attract more attention than one, but sooner or later everyone in the Enchanted Forest runs into something dangerous. And when you do get into trouble it's sort of nice to have someone around to help."

"Why don't we stay together, then? After we get out of this stupid hedge, I mean. As long as neither of us knows exactly where we're going, we might as well wander in the same direction."

"All right." It sounded like a good idea, especially since it's hard to run into someone completely by accident in the Enchanted Forest.

Then Shiara made me describe Antorell in detail, and she decided that he wasn't one of the wizards who had kidnapped her. I wasn't sure whether that was good or bad. Shiara was nice when she wasn't mad, and I was beginning to like her. But if we were going to stick together, we would have two sets of wizards looking for us, and that didn't sound too good. Shiara was still curious, so I wound up telling her about the sword and the lizard and everything.

"The Sword of the Sleeping King," she said thoughtfully when I finished. "Well, it *sounds* important. Can you do that spell again? I'd like to watch. Maybe I could figure it out."

"I could do it, but I won't," I said. "Once was enough."

"You scared or something?" Shiara said scornfully.

"I'm not scared, I'm being sensible. That was no minor magic I set off. Are you *trying* to attract attention?"

"No, I suppose you're right. Will you let me see the sword, at least?"

"Sure, if you promise not to take it out of the sheath or say any spells at it or anything," I said. I stood up and started trying to unbuckle the belt. It was hard to do in the dark. Finally Shiara got tired of waiting and came and helped. It still took a while, and my elbows got in the way again, but finally we managed to get the sword belt off. Shiara took the sheath and squinted at the parts of the sword that showed.

"I can't see anything," she complained.

"There isn't much to see," I said. "Besides, it's dark. Maybe we should wait until tomorrow."

"I wanted to see it now. Oh, all right." She handed it back, hilt first. I took it and nearly let go again right away. The tingling was back, the one that reminded me of a bee, and it was a lot stronger than it had been before.

"Watch out!" Shiara said. "You almost dropped it."

"It's tingling again," I said.

"It is? Let me see." I handed the sword back, and Shiara touched the hilt. "I don't feel anything. Are you sure?"

"Of course I'm sure." I reached out and put my hand on the hilt, next to Shiara's.

"Ow!" I said, and Shiara went, "Oh!" and we both dropped the sword. We looked at each other for a minute.

"What did it feel like to you?" I asked finally.

"Like something pulling at me." Shiara eyed the sword warily. "You can have it back now. I don't want to look at it anymore."

I picked up the sword and put it back on. I still wanted to know what it was doing, but I wasn't going to mess around with it in the dark. Shiara and I talked a little, but we were both tired, and finally we decided to just go to sleep. We would have plenty of time to experiment in the morning if we still felt like it.

* * *

Spending the night in the Enchanted Forest sounds awfully exciting, but it isn't really. Either you stay up all night so the wolves and nightshades and things won't get you and they don't, or you fall asleep and they do, or you find someplace safe and sleep there and never know. We slept all night–at least, I did–and when we woke up in the morning the hedge was still there.

By that time I was really hungry, and since there wasn't anything to eat inside the hedge I was ready to leave. So was Shiara. She was still worried about the Society of Wizards. We brushed most of the moss off our clothes, and I checked the sword, just to be safe.

"Will you quit fussing with that and come open this stupid hedge?" Shiara said.

I walked over to the bushes. They looked very dense and very prickly.

"Excuse me," I said to the hedge. "I would like to thank you for keeping the wolves and things out all night, and I would very much appreciate it if you would let us through now."

"That's the dumbest–" Shiara began, and the bushes rustled and parted. I grinned and stepped through. The branches shut behind me with a snap. "Ow!" said Shiara. I turned around. She was still on the other side of the hedge.

"What happened?" I yelled.

"What do you think happened? And you don't have to shout. I'm not that far away."

"Sorry."

"Make it open up again!"

"I'll try," I said doubtfully. I addressed the bushes again. "Excuse me, but you seem to have a friend of mine inside, and she can't get out. Will you please let her through?"

The bushes rustled smugly and didn't move apart at all. "I'd really appreciate it if you would let her out," I said. "She's nicer than you think."

The bushes rustled again. This time they sounded skeptical. They still didn't open.

"Well?" said Shiara's voice.

I sighed. "They won't open up. I'm afraid you'll have to apologize."

"Apologize? To a *bush?*" Shiara sounded outraged. "I won't! I'll burn this hedge to cinders! I'll–Ow!"

"I really think you'd better apologize," I said. "Otherwise you probably won't get out before the wizards come."

There was silence for a while. Finally Shiara said, "Oh, all right. I'm sorry I said you were a stupid hedge." She paused. "Now will you please let me through?"

Reluctantly, the bushes pulled apart. Shiara sighed with relief and stepped through.

She almost didn't make it. The bushes closed again so fast they caught a piece of her tunic.

"Hey!" she said. "Stop that!"

"I hate to mention this," I said as I helped Shiara work her tunic free, "but you really ought to be more polite."

"To lizards and bushes? Ha!" She jerked her tunic free and glared at the hedge.

"I mean it," I said. "It only gets you into trouble when you're not."

"I'm a fire-witch," Shiara said sullenly. "People are supposed to be polite to *me.*"

"I thought you didn't like having everyone scared of you," I said. I turned to the bush. "Thank you very much."

The branches rustled politely. I turned back to Shiara, who was watching me with her mouth open. "If you act that way all the time, I don't think people would like you much even if you weren't a fire-witch. Good-bye." I turned around and started walking.

"Wait!"

I stopped. Shiara ran up beside me. "I–I'm sorry. I guess I'm not used to being nice to people."

"That could really get you in trouble in the Enchanted Forest," I said.

Shiara looked back over her shoulder at the hedge and shuddered. "No kidding. Well, I'll try."

"All right. Let's find something to eat."

That was easier to say than do. We found a bush that had some berries on it, but half of them were blue and half were red. I wasn't quite hungry enough to take a chance on them, and neither was Shiara.

"If my fire magic doesn't always work, my immunity to magic might not always work, either,"she said. "I'd hate to turn into something awful just because of a few berries." I thought that was very sensible. We kept going.

Eventually we found a clearing full of blackberry brambles. It was so ordinary that it looked very odd sitting there in the middle of the Enchanted Forest. The berries were full of seeds, but we ate a lot of them anyway. I picked some extras and tied them up in my handkerchief for later. When we finished, we started walking again.

It wasn't a very exciting walk. The trees didn't get any smaller, the moss still covered the ground, and every once in a while there was a peculiar bush growing next to one of the trees. It would have gotten boring if Shiara hadn't been there. It was nice to have someone my own age to talk to. I'd never had any friends. Most people don't want their children getting close to the Enchanted Forest, so Mother and I had never had any visitors except the princes and heroes and so on. I told Shiara about living at the edge of the forest, and she told me about the town she lived in. I thought it was very interesting.

By the middle of the morning we were both hungry again. Blackberries don't stick with you for long. We stopped and ate the berries I'd saved in my handkerchief. They were squashed and messy, but they tasted fine. When we finished, we walked some more. It was a warm day, and by the time we saw the stream we were both very thirsty.

"Water! Oh, great!" Shiara said as we reached the bank. It was a small stream, ankle deep and a little too wide to jump. I could see the pebbles on the bottom. Shiara knelt on the bank and reached down.

"Wait a minute!" I said. "You shouldn't just drink that. You could turn into a rabbit, or lose your memory, or disappear, or something."

Shiara looked at me. Then she looked at the stream. "I don't care," she said finally. "I'm thirsty." She leaned toward the water again.

"But what if–Watch out!" I grabbed Shiara and pulled her away just as a huge swirl of muddy water came rushing down the stream. She scrambled back and stood up, and we watched the stream for a minute. It was now almost a river, deep and fast and angry.

Shiara looked at me. "Thanks."

"You're welcome. I guess we'll have to go back–" I started to turn back toward the woods and stopped. There was dark water on that side of us, too. We were standing on an island. A very small island. It was getting smaller every minute.

I stared at the churning water, and my hand went to my sword. I don't know why–most swords aren't any good against floods. As soon as I touched the hilt I knew that it wasn't in the nature of this particular stream to do this sort of thing. I didn't know how I knew, but I was sure someone was creating the flood.

Right about then I heard a chuckle. Not a nice chuckle. I was looking around for the chuckler when Shiara grabbed my arm. "Daystar! Over there!"

I turned. A man was leaning against one of the trees. He had blue robes and black hair, and he held a wizard's staff in one hand. I didn't like the way he was watching Shiara.

"Well, little fire-witch, I seem to have caught you again," he said.

"You leave me alone!"Shiara shouted. "Or I'll burn your staff, too."

The wizard chuckled again. He really had a nasty chuckle. "Oh, I don't think so. I've taken precautions, you see." He waved at the water that surrounded us and smiled patronizingly. "Or weren't you aware that fire magic won't cross water?"

"Magic may not cross water, but we can," I said. I was beginning to share Shiara's dislike of wizards. "Come on, Shiara. It can't be very deep."

"Where did you find the hero?" the wizard asked. Shiara just glared at him. The wizard laughed. I didn't like his laugh any better than his chuckle. "I should give him something to do, don't you think? A monster, perhaps. Heroes like monsters." He waved his staff in the general direction of the flooding stream.

The water on one side of our island bunched up and began to solidify rapidly. I didn't even have time to step back before the thing finished growing. When it was done, it looked sort of like a giant snake's head that dripped. The outlines kept changing because it was made out of water that wasn't completely solid, but it was pretty clearly a snake.

It lunged at me. I dodged, barely in time, and drew my sword. Shiara yelled, and steam puffed from the snake head. The snake didn't seem particularly hurt. Some of the stream water bunched up around it, but that was all. I heard the wizard laugh again.

"I'm afraid that won't work very well, young lady," he said. "You'd have to boil the whole stream away to get rid of my monster, and I don't think you can. Pity, isn't it? Be patient. You'll have your turn in another minute, and then the Head Wizard will owe me a favor."

The head lunged again. By now I was ready for it, but it was awfully fast. I dodged and struck at it with the sword, even though I wasn't sure what good it would do me to wound something that wasn't even alive.

The sword made a humming noise. I heard the wizard shout, and then a sound like an explosion. The snake head made a bubbly noise and collapsed in a wave of muddy water that swept over the little island Shiara and I were standing on, soaking everything. In another minute, the flood water drained away, leaving a lot of wet moss. And Shiara yelled again.

I whirled around. Shiara was pointing. It took me a second to realize what she was pointing at. It was the big tree that the wizard had been leaning against. A couple of short branches were lying at the foot of the tree. The wizard was gone.

4

In Which They Learn the Perils of Inspecting a Wizard's Broken Staff

I stood where I was, panting, and dripping. When I got my breath back, I went over to the tree. There was no sign of the wizard, except for the "branches" I'd noticed. There were three of them, and they weren't branches. They were pieces of a staff.

I looked at Shiara. "That's two wizards' staffs you've broken. They're really going to be after you now."

"I didn't break it," Shiara said indignantly. "You did."

"I did not," I said. We looked at each other for a minute.

"If neither of us broke it," Shiara said finally, "who did?"

"Me," said a voice. I looked up. A little man was sitting in the branches of the tree. He was about two feet tall and dressed entirely in green. His eyes were black and very bright, and his ears were slightly pointed. He had to be an elf.

"I think you mean 'I,' " I said automatically.

"I shouldn't wonder if you're right." The elf tilted his head to one side. "Does it matter?"

"Can you get down from that tree?" Shiara said. "You're giving me a crick in my neck."

The elf looked from me to Shiara and back to me again. "Introduce me to your charming companion."

"Oh, excuse me," I said. I told the elf our names and thanked him for taking care of the wizard. I was a little curious about that. I'd never met an elf, but they didn't have a reputation for altruism. I wasn't sure I wanted to trust one, either. Elves can be very tricky.

"You're welcome," the elf said. "I've never cared much for wizards. Unfortunately, it's very difficult to do anything permanent to them. This one will be back in a day or two."

"If there is anything we can do for you in return, I would like to hear what it is," I said. If someone in the Enchanted Forest does you a favor, you have to offer to do one for them. Well, you don't have to, but if you don't, things seem to go wrong a lot after that. You have to be careful, though. If you promise to do a favor before you hear what it is, you can end up in more trouble than you started with. I wasn't going to promise anything without finding out first what I was promising.

"Consider the debt canceled," the elf said politely. I thought he sounded disappointed, and I didn't like the way he was looking at my sword. Suddenly I was very glad Mother had told me about making promises in the Enchanted Forest.

"Thank you," I said. "You did a very neat job." He had, too; the staff had been sliced cleanly into thirds. I began to wonder how he had done it. I hadn't thought elves were powerful enough to break a wizard's staff. I didn't want to offend him by asking about it, though.

"You may have the staff, if you want it," the elf said, waving at the pieces.

"What good is a busted wizard's staff?" Shiara asked. "You can't *do* anything with it."

"Nonsense," said the elf. "Wizards' staffs are just as powerful in pieces as they are whole, and they're fairly easy to put back together. Please, take it with you."

I didn't like the way he kept suggesting that, though it sounded reasonable enough. "Are you sure you don't want it?" I asked finally.

"What would an elf do with a wizard's staff? If you don't take it, I'll just have to get rid of it somewhere."

That sounded reasonable, too, but I wasn't going to commit myself. He was too insistent. "Thank you for the suggestion," I said. "We'll think about it."

"Do," the elf said. His black eyes twinkled. "Perhaps I'll see you later. Good-bye." Before I could say anything he had disappeared into the treetops. Elves move very quickly.

"What was that about?" Shiara demanded.

"I don't know about that elf," I said slowly. "I think something funny is going on. He was trying too hard to get us to take that staff."

"Well, we have to do something with it," Shiara said.

"Why?" I said. "*We* didn't break it. And I don't want to mess with a wizard's staff, even a broken one."

Shiara frowned. I made a gesture toward the pieces and realized that I was still holding the sword in my hand. I started to put it back in its sheath, then stopped. The sheath was as wet as everything else I was wearing. I couldn't put the sword in that. I mean, not all magic swords are rustproof, and even if you have one that is, putting your sword away without cleaning it is a bad habit to get into. I checked my pockets, just in case, but even my handkerchief was wet.

"Shiara, do you have anything–no, you wouldn't, you were in the middle of that stream, too."

"What? What are you mumbling about?" Shiara said.

"I need something to dry off my sword," I said. "Everything I have is soaked. But you're just as wet as I am . . ." My voice trailed off, because right then I really looked at her, and she wasn't. Wet, I mean. Her shoes were steaming a little, but her hair and her clothes weren't even damp.

"Fire-witches dry off fast," Shiara said in a smug tone.

"Then can you give me something to clean my sword?" I asked. "Everything I have is soaked."

"What does that have to do with the wizard's staff? Oh, give it here. I'll fix it." She held out her hand a little reluctantly. I could see she didn't really want to take the sword. After what had happened the last time she'd touched it, I couldn't blame her.

"That's all right, I'll do it," I said. "It's my job. All I need is something dry to wipe it with."

Shiara glared at me. "All I have is my tunic, and I am not going to take it off just so you can dry your stupid sword! If you won't give it to me, it can rust."

My face got very hot. "I, um, I'm sorry, I didn't mean . . . I mean, I didn't think . . ."

"Oh, shut up and give me the sword."

I held it out. Shiara took it a little gingerly, but neither of us felt anything unusual. While she wiped it dry on the front of her tunic, I walked over to the stream. I was pretty sure, now, that the water was safe to drink. I'd swallowed some of it when the wizard's wave hit me, and nothing had happened to me yet. I bent over and took a drink.

The water was clean and cold, with just a hint of lime. It tasted awfully good, though I prefer lemon-flavored streams myself. I think I like lemon because Mother and I got most of our drinking water from a lemon-flavored stream just inside the forest. It was much nicer than the well water we used for washing, even if it was more work to haul the buckets that far.

Shiara came over just as I finished. She looked at me for a minute, then handed me the sword. "Here." I took it, and she sat down and started trying to drink out of her cupped hands. Most of the water ran out, but she kept trying.

I stood holding the sword and wondering what I was going to do with it. I mean, walking through the Enchanted Forest with a sword in your hand is just *asking* for trouble. On the other hand, I couldn't put it away until the sheath dried out, and that would probably take hours.

Shiara finished drinking and sat up. "Now, what are we going to do about that wizard's staff?"

Neither one of us wanted to take it with us. Shiara suggested hiding the pieces before we left, and finally I agreed. We walked back over to the tree. I started to put my sword down, then changed my mind. One of the easiest ways of losing important things in the Enchanted Forest is to put them down while you do something else. Then you have to go to all the bother of finding whoever took your things before you can get on with whatever you really want to do. I shifted the sword into my left hand and looked around for the nearest piece of staff.

"Daystar! Come see!" Shiara was waving a piece of the staff to attract my attention.

"You really shouldn't do that," I said as I walked over. "You might set off a spell or something. This used to be a wizard's staff, remember? We ought to at least *try* to be careful."

"Yes, but look what it did," Shiara said, pointing. I looked down. There was a brown patch in the moss, just the size and shape of the stick Shiara was holding. I bent over and looked more closely. The moss was so dry and brittle that it turned to powder when I touched it.

"But this is the Enchanted Forest," I said to no one in particular. "You aren't supposed to be able to *do* things like this."

"Well, this wizard's staff did," Shiara said. "I bet it'll do it again, too." Before I could stop her, she laid the stick down on the moss. She picked it up almost immediately. The moss underneath it was brown and dead.

I stared. "I don't like this," I said. There aren't very many things you can be sure of in the Enchanted Forest, but I'd never seen a dead plant there, not even in the Outer Forest. The whole place felt too alive to put up with that sort of thing. "I wonder if all wizards' staffs do that."

"I don't know about other staffs, but we can check the other pieces of this one," Shiara said. She walked toward one of the other two sticks. I sighed and started for the last one.

"This one's the same," Shiara reported after a minute. "What about yours?"

"Just a minute," I said. I bent over and picked it up in my right hand. . . .

When I woke up, Shiara was dripping water on my face. "You can stop now," I said. "I'm wet enough already."

Shiara shook her head. "Are you all right? I mean, you're not enchanted or anything, are you?"

I thought about it for a moment. "I don't think so, but if I am, we'll find out pretty soon." I sat up and realized I'd been lying on the moss at the foot of the tree. "What happened?"

"How should I know? One minute you were standing there with that sword, and then there was some kind of explosion and when I turned around you were lying here and that piece of the wizard's staff was over there, burning. I don't think anyone's going to put that staff back together again. It was the middle piece." Shiara scowled. "But I think you were right about that elf."

"Where's my sword?" I asked. All of a sudden I was sure someone had taken it while Shiara and I weren't paying attention.

"In your hand," Shiara said. She sounded a little exasperated. "You wouldn't let go of it."

I looked down. My left hand was still clenched around the hilt. When I relaxed my hand, the fingers started to tingle. I'd been holding on so tightly that my hand had fallen asleep.

Well, at least I hadn't lost it. I started to shift the sword back to my right hand, then stopped and swallowed hard. The hand was burned black. I couldn't even feel it. I looked away, feeling sick. Shiara was staring, too.

"Daystar, I didn't notice, I was so worried about waking you up I didn't even see–" She stopped. She tilted her head back until she was looking up the tree trunk, and her eyes flashed. "I'm going to find somebody who can fix this," she said grimly. "And then I'm going to find that stupid elf and make him sorry he ever mentioned that wizard's staff." The way she said it made me very, very glad I wasn't an elf, particularly the elf she'd be looking for.

"It doesn't really hurt or anything," I offered. As soon as I said it, my arm started to throb. Not the hand; it was my wrist and arm that hurt. As far as I was concerned, that was more than enough.

"That's bad," Shiara said. She looked worried. "I know a little about burns, from the times when I . . . Are you sure you can't feel anything?"

"Not in my hand," I said. "And I'd really rather not talk about it. It might help me not notice the way my arm feels."

"Well, let me look at it, then, and I won't have to ask questions," Shiara said.

I stuck my right hand out in her direction and stared at my sword for a couple of minutes. I didn't succeed in ignoring the sensations that were coming from my arm, but I tried awfully hard. Finally Shiara said, "You can put it down now." I looked back in her direction.

"It's bad," she said. "I don't know what to do for it, either. We have to find help, and pretty soon, too. There has to be someone in this forest who knows something about healing. Can you walk?"

"My legs are all right," I said. I started to stand up and discovered I was very dizzy. I made it on the second try, but only by using the sword as a prop.

Shiara picked a direction and we started walking. After about twenty steps I stopped worrying about which way we were going and concentrated on walking and hanging on to the sword. It was hard; I really had to work at it. I was still dizzy, and I was beginning to feel cold, too–all but my arm, which felt as if it were on fire, and I wondered whether the wizard's staff had done more than just burn my hand.

I don't know how far we went before we stopped. By that time, Shiara was holding my good arm, trying to help me walk. She couldn't help as much as she might have, because she had to keep out of the way of the sword. As soon as we quit walking, I sat down.

"Daystar, are you sure you can't put that sword away yet?" Shiara asked. "It gets in the way a lot."

"The sheath is still wet," I said hazily.

"Well, can we at least put the sheath in the sun so it'll dry faster?"

I looked around, feeling sort of light-headed as well as dizzy. On top of everything I was getting thirsty. "We can't do that," I said. "The cat has the only patch of sun around here."

"What cat?"

"That one." I pointed at the large, dignified, black-and-white cat that was cleaning its face in the middle of a puddle of sunlight. It didn't even strike me as odd that I hadn't noticed it until I started talking about it.

Shiara turned her head. As soon as she looked at it, the cat stopped washing itself. It stared at her for a minute, then stood up. The tip of its tail twitched three times, and it turned around and started walking away. After a minute, it stopped and looked back over its shoulder. It was obviously waiting.

Shiara jumped up. "Come on, Daystar. We're going to follow the cat. I think somebody sent it."

"That doesn't make sense," I said, but I wasn't in very good shape to argue. Eventually, Shiara got me back on my feet. The cat was still waiting for us, but as soon as we moved in its direction it started walking again. I decided Shiara was right and concentrated on walking.

I don't know how far we followed the cat. It seemed like a long way, but anything would have seemed like a long way at that point. My arm hurt, and every muscle in my body felt shaky. I never quite dropped the sword, but a couple of times I came close. After a while I stopped thinking about it.

Finally Shiara stopped moving.

"I was about ready for another rest," I said fuzzily. "Is the cat still around?"

"This isn't a rest," Shiara said. "We're here."

I looked up. We were standing in front of a neat gray house with a wide porch and a red roof. A wisp of smoke was coming out of the chimney, and whatever was cooking smelled delicious. Over the door was a black-and-gold sign in block letters that read, "NONE OF THIS NONSENSE, PLEASE."

I'm going to like whoever lives here, I thought.

The door of the house was closed, but the black-and-white cat jumped up on the porch and scratched at it. A moment later, the door swung partway open and the cat disappeared inside.

5

In Which They Meet a Witch

We stayed where we were for a minute, waiting. I don't think either one of us really knew what to do next. A few seconds after the cat vanished, the door opened the rest of the way and the owner of the house appeared.

She wore a very loose black robe with long sleeves and a small pair of glasses with rectangular lenses. She was considerably shorter than I was, though she obviously wasn't a dwarf; she managed to look down her nose at both of us anyway. Standing on the porch helped, I think. "It's about time you got here," she said.

"Do you know anything about healing?" Shiara demanded.

"Of course I do, or I wouldn't have sent Quiz out to get you," said the woman.

"Quiz?"

"The cat. Do you plan to stand there all day? I certainly can't do anything for you while you're outside."

So we went inside. The porch steps didn't creak. Neither did the porch, and the hinges of the door didn't squeak at all. I didn't think they would dare.

The inside of the house seemed to consist of a single large, airy room full of cats. I counted five before I stopped. Several of the cats had furniture under them, and there was a table in the middle of the room and another door next to the stove in the corner.

The woman in the black robe shooed two cats off of chairs, and Shiara and I sat down at the table. Shiara looked at me. "You can put that stupid sword down now. No one's going to take it."

"No." I didn't know why I wanted to hold on to the sword, and I didn't have enough energy to explain it if I had known. I just knew I wanted it in my hand.

"Sword?" said the woman in black. "Oh, *that* sword. It's quite proper of you to keep it for now. If I may see your hand?" She came over next to me and examined my right arm while I carefully didn't watch. Oddly enough, it didn't hurt when she touched it. After a minute or so, she nodded.

"Just as I thought. This could have been very bad, but you got here in plenty of time." She went over to a cupboard by the stove and took out a piece of something that looked like dried vine. She brought it back to me and tied it around my arm, muttering something as she did. Suddenly my head wasn't fuzzy anymore.

"That should take care of things for the time being," she said, "and in a little while I can take care of the magic. Then we can pack the burns with salve. Would you like some cider while you wait?"

I nodded.

Shiara frowned. "Can't you do anything right away?"

"I have done something," the woman said. She set three mugs on the table, all different. "Several things, in fact. I sent Quiz out to bring you here, and I have stopped the damage from spreading. I have also made gingerbread, which should finish baking any minute now."

"Gingerbread?" Shiara blinked. "Daystar is hurt! Why are you baking gingerbread?"

"For you to eat," Morwen said. "Why, were you expecting me to make a house out of it?"

"Well, no, but–Oh, never mind the gingerbread! How did you know to send a cat out for us? Who are you, anyway?"

The woman looked through her glasses. "I know a lot of things. I'm a witch. My name is Morwen. And you?" She stopped. The cats looked at us.

"Pleased to meet you," I said. "This is Shiara, and I'm Daystar."

"Why do we have to wait?" Shiara asked again.

"Mixing magic and cooking is *never* a good idea," Morwen said. "Don't worry, the gingerbread won't take much longer." She got out a large jug and began pouring the contents into the mugs. "There!" she said as she set the jug down. "Help yourselves. I'll be back in a minute."

Morwen went over to the second door and opened it. I got a glimpse of a small yard with a square garden, a well, and two more cats. Then the door closed with a swish of black robe. I stared at my mug, wondering how I was going to pick it up without putting my sword down. Then I heard a sniffle and turned my head. Shiara was not crying. Much.

"What's wrong?" I said.

"It's all my f-fault!" Shiara said miserably. "If you hadn't been with me, you wouldn't have run into that wizard at all, and if I hadn't insisted on hiding that stupid staff, your hand wouldn't have gotten . . ." Her voice trailed off into snuffles. I sighed.

"If you want my handkerchief, you'll have to get it out yourself," I said. "And it's probably still pretty wet. But you can have it if you want it."

That made Shiara look like she was really going to burst into tears. Fortunately, just then the door opened and the witch came back in. When she saw Shiara, she set down the plants she was carrying and produced a large black handkerchief from somewhere inside her sleeve.

"That is *quite* enough of that," she said, handing the handkerchief to Shiara. "It does nothing constructive, it makes everyone else feel bad, and it is extremely self-indulgent. Drink your cider. You'll feel much better."

Just then one of the cats made a loud noise, sort of a cross between a purr and a meow. "Good, the gingerbread is done," Morwen said. She got it out of the oven and gave us each a piece. Shiara looked much better by that time, even if she still didn't seem really happy.

Morwen put a large pot of water on the stove and then started sorting through the plants she had brought in. After a minute, she frowned.

"Two sprays or three?" she muttered. "I suppose I'd better look it up." She put the plants down and went out again. A few seconds later, she came back holding a book. I saw a roomful of shelves behind her before the door closed.

I blinked. My head didn't feel fuzzy, but I was sure that a minute ago that door had led out to the yard. I looked around the room, but there weren't any other doors, except the one we'd come in through. Finally I decided to ask.

"Excuse me, Morwen, but would you mind telling me where that door leads?"

Morwen stuck a finger in the book and looked up. "Wherever I want to get to. What good is a door if you can't get somewhere useful by walking through it? Within reason, of course." She went back to the book.

I thought about it for a minute. Then I decided not to think about it. I was afraid it was going to make sense. Instead, I looked at my cider and gingerbread. I was just about ready to put the sword on the floor so I could eat when Morwen set the book down next to the plants and looked over at me.

"Daystar, you aren't–Oh, of course, you're still holding the sword. No, don't put it down yet. This will only take a few more minutes." She picked up a handful of plants. "Come here, please, both of you."

We got up and walked over. Morwen had me stand next to the stove, holding the sword across the front of my chest so that the tip of it rested on the pot of water. Shiara was behind me, with one hand on my right arm just above the dried vine. It took a while before Morwen was satisfied with our positions, but finally she stepped back. "Very good. Stay just like that until I'm finished, please."

She reached inside one of her sleeves and brought out a silver knife. She dipped the knife in the pot of water, then began muttering over the plants she was holding. Immediately, all the cats jumped down onto the floor and formed a half-circle around the stove, with Morwen and Shiara and me in the middle. They just sat there with their eyes glowing and only the tips of their tails moving, in tiny twitches. Suddenly, there was a sizzling noise from my right. The water was boiling.

Morwen gave a shout. Then she held the plants high over her head and said loudly,

"By the darkness of the stone's heart,
By the silence of the sea's tears,
By the whisper of the sky's breath,
By the dawning of the star's flame,
Do as I will thee!"

Just as she finished she threw the plants into the boiling water.

A cloud of steam puffed out of the pot, smelling of herbs and magic and gingerbread, and I sneezed. The steam spread out around me and got thicker. It smelled more and more like herbs and magic and less and less like gingerbread. My right arm started to ache, and my left arm started to tingle. The ache got stronger, but it stayed where it was; the tingle spread. In another second or two I was tingling all over, except for the arm that was aching.

By now the steam was so thick I couldn't see anything, but I could still feel Shiara's hand and the vine Morwen had tied around my arm. For what seemed like a long time, nothing else happened. Then one of the cats yowled. I saw Morwen's hand, the one holding the silver knife, come out of the mist.

"In the King's name!" Morwen's voice said, and the knife cut the vine from my arm and pulled it away.

My sword flashed once, very brightly. Most of the steam settled on my right arm and turned black. The ache started to creep upward, and something that felt like lightning or wind ran up my left arm and down my right one. I heard Shiara gasp. The black steam stuff dropped off my arm into a slimy blob on the floor. My right arm stopped hurting, and my other arm stopped tingling, and everything felt normal again. I let my breath out and looked around.

Morwen was looking in my direction with an expression of extreme distaste. "That," she said, "was an exceptionally nasty wizard. He deserves what's coming to him."

"What's coming to him?" Shiara asked hopefully.

"I don't know, but he certainly deserves it," Morwen said. "Anyone who would keep a spell like that in a staff . . ." She shook her head and looked down. "I do hope it doesn't disagree with the cats."

I followed her gaze. The cats had formed a small mob and were playing with something I'd rather not describe in detail. I looked up again very quickly and took a step backward. I bumped into Shiara and remembered that Morwen had said not to move until she was finished. "I'm sorry," I said to both of them.

"It's quite all right. You can sit down again now," Morwen said. "And if you don't want to put your sword in your sheath, you can lean it against the wall. You won't need it for the time being."

I followed Morwen's instructions and sat down at the table again. I didn't realize until I reached for the gingerbread that although my right hand felt better it didn't *look* any better. I didn't have time to worry about it, though, because Morwen was already standing by my chair with some oily-looking salve and bandages. She worked on my hand while I ate gingerbread and cider left-handed. We finished about the same time, and I thanked her.

"You're welcome," Morwen said. "Now, perhaps you would explain how you got into such an uncomfortable situation? I have a general idea, but I would appreciate a few details."

I told her about the wizard and the elf, and then Shiara explained how the staff had exploded.

"Of course the staff exploded!" Morwen said severely. "That sword doesn't like wizard's staffs. Next time, make sure it's sheathed before you touch one."

"I knew it!" Shiara said angrily. "That elf was *trying* to get Daystar hurt!"

"Not necessarily," Morwen said. "He may simply have been trying to make sure the wizard found you again. If you'd taken the pieces of the staff with you, the wizard would have had no trouble locating you once he got himself back together, because the first thing he'd do would be to look for his staff."

"If that elf wanted the wizard after us, why'd he get rid of the wizard in the first place?" Shiara objected.

"I doubt that he did," Morwen said calmly. "It's more the sort of thing the sword does. I wouldn't depend on it in the future, though, particularly since you still haven't learned how to use it properly."

I wanted to ask more questions about the sword, but I was pretty sure Morwen wouldn't answer them. "What if the wizard couldn't find his staff when he came back?" I asked instead.

"Wizards always know where their staffs are. And it's almost impossible to keep wizards away from their staffs for any length of time. One can slow them down a bit by putting the staffs somewhere hard to get at, but they usually manage in the end."

"That's why Mother hid Antorell's staff!" I said.

"I shouldn't wonder," Morwen murmured. "Now, I strongly suggest that you rest for a while, Daystar, and while you are doing so I will talk with Shiara in the library." She stood up and nodded to me.

Shiara frowned and opened her mouth to say something. Then she looked at me and seemed to change her mind. "All right," she said.

Morwen went to the door, followed by Shiara and most of the cats. It was the room of books again. Trying to be careful of my bandaged right hand, I lay down on a bench that had had three cats on it before they went into the library with Morwen. I fell asleep almost immediately.

When I woke up, I could tell by the way the sunlight was slanting in through the windows that it was late afternoon. There wasn't anyone else in the room, except for the black-and-white cat who had led us to Morwen's house. It was sitting in the middle of the table, washing its tail.

"Hello," I said. "And thank you very much for bringing Shiara and me here."

The cat looked up briefly, decided I was uninteresting, and went back to cleaning its tail.

I shifted a little; the bench was hard. I felt much better than I had when I lay down. Then the back door opened–this time it was the door to the yard–and Morwen came in.

"You're awake. Good. Shiara has been waiting for you."

I sat up just as Morwen saw the cat on the table. She frowned at it. "Child of Scorn," she said sternly, "you are *not* allowed on the table."

The cat looked at Morwen. Morwen looked at the cat. After a minute, the cat jumped down to the floor, where it did its best to pretend that the floor was exactly where it had wanted to be all along. Morwen shook her head.

"You'll have to excuse the Grand Inquisitor. He knows he did me a favor when he brought you here, and he's inclined to take advantage of it. I would have sent Cass, but I was afraid you wouldn't pay attention to her."

"Cass?"

"Cassandra." Morwen nodded at a small gray cat that I hadn't noticed before. "She has much better manners than Quiz, but she tends to be overlooked. Nobody overlooks Quiz."

I studied the cats. They both ignored me. I glanced back at Morwen. "I don't think I've thanked you yet for–for fixing my arm." I wasn't really sure what else to call whatever she'd done.

"Yes, you have," Morwen said. "And if you insist on repeating yourself, you'd better wait until you take the bandages off tomorrow. Time enough for thanks if it's healed properly. Not that I have any doubts, mind, but it's better to be sure."

"All right," I said. "Did you say Shiara was waiting for me?"

Morwen went over to the stove. "Yes, I did. She's out by the garden," she said over her shoulder. She reached up and lifted a large kettle down from a hook on the wall.

"Thank you," I said. I got up and opened the back door. There was a room on the other side, with a bed and a large bookshelf and, of course, a cat. I shut the door and tried again. This time I got the library. Morwen had more books than anyone I'd ever heard of. I shut the door and looked back at Morwen.

"How do I get out to the garden?" I asked.

"Through the door," Morwen said without turning. "Just be firm. Sometimes it's a little contrary with strangers, but that won't last long."

I turned back, wondering how to be firm with a door. I opened it again. Still the library. I closed it, wondering how long it would take me to get to the garden. I didn't really want to spend the rest of the afternoon opening and shutting Morwen's door, but what else could I do? I sighed and opened the door again.

This time it worked: The door opened onto three steps going down into the yard. I went through quickly, before the door could change its mind. Shiara was sitting on a stone bench by the corner of the house. She looked a lot happier than she had earlier, but all she would say was that she'd been talking to Morwen.

"She's been showing me some things," Shiara said. "And she's going to give me a kitten."

"That's nice," I said. Actually, I wasn't sure it would be a good idea to have a pet with us while we wandered around the Enchanted Forest. On the other hand, if it was one of Morwen's cats, it could probably take care of itself.

Shiara and I sat and talked for the rest of the afternoon. I discovered that somehow she and Morwen had decided that we would be spending the night here. Shiara was very pleased about it. Evidently Morwen had promised to show her some interesting magic. I wasn't sure we should stay, even though I liked Morwen. After all, neither of us had ever met her before. I had to admit, though, that it sounded a lot better than sleeping out in the open. We were still discussing it when one of the cats came to bring us in to dinner.

6

In Which Daystar Makes a Mistake

Dinner was a stew that smelled and tasted awfully good, though it didn't look like much. Morwen had made a large pot of the stuff. Half of it she put in a big pan and set on the floor for the cats, and the rest we ate. By the time we'd finished, we had decided to spend the night with Morwen and the cats.

I was a little worried, at first, about what to do with the Sword of the Sleeping King. I didn't want to leave it leaning up against Morwen's wall all night. Finally, I decided to keep it with me. It wasn't that I didn't trust Morwen, but Mother had given the sword to me and it was my responsibility. Once that was settled, I started wondering where Shiara and I were going to sleep.

I shouldn't have worried. Morwen had several extra bedrooms behind her magic door, and she simply put each of us in one of them. By that time I was starting to wonder how many rooms she had in her house and where she kept them all when they weren't needed. That isn't the sort of question you ask people in the Enchanted Forest, though. So I didn't.

Besides, I was tired again. As soon as Morwen showed me to my room, I stuck the sword under the bed and went to sleep. I was pretty sure the sword would be safe there.

I was right, too. When I woke up in the morning, a cat was asleep on top of it.

After breakfast, Morwen took the bandages off my hand. The burns were gone and it felt fine, but she examined it carefully anyway. When she was finished with my hand, she helped me get my sword belt on. The sheath was dry, so I put the sword back in it. While I was doing that, Morwen produced a couple of bundles and a small black kitten with one white paw. She gave Shiara the kitten and one bundle and turned to me.

"This is for you," she said, handing me the other bundle. "It should make your travels a little easier. Now, come outside."

She opened the front door and went out onto the porch. I let Shiara leave next and started to follow her, but one of the cats darted in front of me and I nearly tripped. I had to grab for the door frame to keep my balance.

"Watch out!" Shiara said, then, "Daystar! What's the matter?"

I almost didn't hear her. I was staring down at my sword. My hand had brushed it when I'd tripped, and I'd felt the tingling again. Only this time there was even more of it. I reached over and took the hilt in my right hand. The rumbling tingle hadn't changed, but the buzzing tingle and the purring tingle were considerably stronger than they had been, and they'd been joined by a brisk vibration I hadn't felt before. I concentrated on the new feeling, trying to figure out where it had come from, and found myself looking at Morwen.

I looked back at the sword. I hadn't let go, and my arm was still tingling. I tried to pick out one of the other vibrations. Suddenly I was feeling mostly the purring tingle and looking out into the woods. I blinked and tried again. This time I got the buzz, and I was staring at Shiara. Suddenly I understood.

"It's magic!" I said.

"Of *course* it's magic," Shiara said. "Honestly, Daystar–"

"No, I mean that's what it does," I said. "The Sword of the Sleeping King finds magic!"

"Among other things," Morwen said in a satisfied voice.

"Finds magic?" Shiara said skeptically.

"That's what the tingling is," I said. I was completely sure of myself, though I didn't know why. "Different tingles mean different kinds of magic, and the tingles get stronger when the sword gets closer to the magic." I looked at Shiara. "No wonder it gave me such a jolt when we both touched it at the same time."

Shiara had been reaching for the hilt, but she pulled her hand back hastily. "If the sword finds magic, how come I couldn't feel anything until you touched it? And if the tingles are the way it finds things, why can't you feel them all the time?"

"I don't know," I said. The tingling was fading again, the same way it had when I held onto the sword before, so I let go of the hilt.

Morwen considered me through her glasses. I couldn't tell what she was thinking from her expression. Finally she nodded very slightly. "I see.

There is considerably more to you than I had expected, Daystar," she said in a thoughtful tone.

I was still trying to figure out what that statement meant when Morwen turned away and said briskly, "However, it is time for you to be going. You see those two trees? Walk straight between them and keep on until you get to a stream, then follow the stream northward. You'll get to something eventually, and you should be able to figure out what to do from there."

My eyes turned in the direction Morwen was pointing. It was the same way I'd been looking when I'd been concentrating on the purring tingle from the sword. I looked back at Morwen.

"Exactly," Morwen said.

"What?" said Shiara.

"Let's go," I said. I was feeling a little unsettled by the whole thing, and I didn't want to talk about it anymore. Shiara scowled, but she didn't insist on an explanation.

We said good-bye and thank-you to Morwen and started walking toward the trees. Shiara carried the kitten for a while, but pretty soon the kitten decided it wanted to walk. We slowed down a lot after that, until the kitten got tired enough to let Shiara pick it up again without scratching her.

Shiara and I spent most of the walk talking. I hadn't realized how little she knew about the Enchanted Forest, and I wound up telling her a lot of things. Like about being polite to people and why you shouldn't promise things without knowing what they are first.

Morwen hadn't told us how far away the stream was, and eventually I started wondering how much longer it would take us to find it. I was also curious about where we were going. Right about then, I noticed that the trees we were walking past were larger than the ones I'd seen the previous day. At least, I *thought* they were larger. I studied them as we walked, trying to decide whether it was my imagination or whether they really were larger. I was just getting ready to mention this to Shiara when I heard a cough. I stopped and looked around.

"Ahem," said a voice.

This time I located the speaker. It was the little gold lizard, Suz. He was sitting on a branch at just about eye level, watching me.

"Oh, hello, Suz," I said. Shiara looked around. I nodded toward the lizard and said, "Shiara, this is Suz. You remember, I told you about him. Suz, this is my friend Shiara."

The lizard ignored the introduction and continued staring at me. "Why," he demanded in an aggrieved tone, "didn't you tell me Cimorene was your mother?"

"You didn't ask," I said.

Suz looked at me reproachfully. "It would have saved me a great deal of trouble if you'd mentioned it."

"I'm sorry," I said. "I didn't know it mattered."

"You didn't?" Suz ran down the branch and peered at me. "No, you really didn't! How amazing. I can't understand how it happened."

"What are you talking about?" Shiara said.

The lizard appeared to see her for the first time. He leaned outward in Shiara's direction and I thought he was going to fall off, until I saw that his tail was wrapped tightly around a sturdy twig on the far side of the branch. "You've brought someone with you? Dear me, this will never do. Who is this?"

"I've already introduced you once," I reminded him. "You weren't listening."

"You did? Yes, of course, you did. How perfectly dreadful." Suz ran around the branch very fast, and for a minute I was afraid he was going to try to stand on his tail. If he did, I was sure he'd fall off, because the branch wasn't very wide.

"What's so dreadful?" Shiara demanded. "There's nothing wrong with me."

"No, of course, there isn't. Oh, dear, Kazul will be terribly unhappy about this."

"Who is Kazul?" I asked.

Suz looked at me in astonishment. "You don't know? No, you don't. I haven't told you yet. Kazul is who you're going to see." He cocked his head to one side as if that explained everything.

"Why should I want to see Kazul?" I asked. "And why should he care about me, or Shiara, or anything?"

"She," Suz said. "And of course you want to see her. You have the Sword of the Sleeping King, don't you? I'm afraid she'll be dreadfully upset if you bring someone with you, though."

"Well, I'm not going to leave Shiara alone in the middle of the Enchanted Forest," I said firmly.

"No, no, you couldn't possibly do that," the lizard agreed. "That wouldn't be right at all. Dear me, whatever are we going to do?"

"You don't have to worry about me," Shiara said indignantly. "I'm a fire-witch. I can take care of myself."

"You are?" Suz turned his head and looked at Shiara so intently that his eyes crossed. "You really are! How convenient! Everything's quite all right, then. Kazul won't mind a fire-witch at all."

"Who," I said very slowly and carefully, "is Kazul?"

The lizard stared thoughtfully at me for a long time. "I don't think I ought to tell you any more," he said at last. "You're quite safe, you really are, but it wouldn't do at all for Kazul to lose her temper with me. Oh, dear, no."

"Quite safe? In the middle of the Enchanted Forest, with wizards after us?" Shiara said sarcastically. "You're crazy."

"I am? No, I'm not at all! How very rude." He turned his back, looking extremely offended. Shiara stared at him. As I said, an offended lizard is an interesting sight.

I sighed. "Shiara."

Shiara looked at me. I just stood there. After a minute, she looked down. "Well, it *is* dangerous to be out here, even if you do have that stupid sword," she said defensively. "What's wrong with saying so?"

"It wasn't very polite," I said. "And you promised you'd try."

Shiara glanced up at me, then sighed. "Oh, all right. I'm sorry, Suz."

The lizard twisted his head around. "You are?" He ran around the branch again and peered at her upside down from underneath the limb. "No, you're not at all. How disappointing. I accept." He ran back up on top of the branch.

"Accept?" Shiara said.

"Your apology," the lizard said with dignity. A dignified lizard looks even odder than an offended one.

"Oh." Shiara looked at Suz doubtfully.

"If you won't tell us who Kazul is, will you at least tell us how to find her?" I asked hastily. I didn't want Shiara to say anything that would offend Suz again, and she looked like she was going to. Besides, I was curious.

"You won't have any trouble," the lizard assured me. "Just head for the castle. Kazul will–" He broke off in midsentence, staring at the kitten Shiara was holding. "What is that?" he asked disapprovingly.

"A kitten," Shiara said. "What does it look like?"

"You're sure it's under control?" Suz seemed a little nervous. I looked at the kitten. It was watching Suz with a great deal of interest.

"What do you mean, under control?" Shiara said. "She's a perfectly well-behaved kitten. Morwen wouldn't have given her to me if she wasn't."

"Cats are not–Did you say Morwen?" Suz peered at Shiara.

"Yes, I said Morwen. Can't you finish a sentence?"

Suz ignored her. "You've been to see Morwen? I didn't know that. Oh, dear me, I must be dreadfully behind. Why, all sorts of things could be happening that I don't know about! How perfectly dreadful. I must really get back to work at once. Oh yes, indeed I must."

The lizard ran down the branch and disappeared behind the tree trunk. "Wait a minute!" I said. I ducked around the back of the tree, but Suz was nowhere in sight. I shook my head and went back to where Shiara was standing.

"He's gone again," I said. "And he still hasn't told me what castle he's talking about."

"So what? Nobody else has told us anything either." Shiara glared at the branch where Suz had been sitting. "I don't think *he's* very polite. He didn't even say good-bye."

"He keeps going off like that," I said. "I think that's just how he is."

"Well, I can't say I'm sorry he left," Shiara said. "Come on, let's find that stream Morwen was talking about. I'm thirsty."

We started walking again. Shiara put the kitten down, and we took turns keeping an eye on her. She had a marvelous time jumping on leaves and attacking bushes while Shiara and I talked about what Shiara was going to name her. Finally she decided on Nightwitch. I didn't think that was a very good name, but Shiara liked it, so I didn't say anything.

By the time we found the stream, Shiara and I were tired and hungry as well as thirsty, so we stopped. We each took a drink, and then we sat down and opened the bundles Morwen had given us. Just as I had expected, there were packets of food right on top–meat pies and apples and gingerbread. Shiara and I each ate some, and we gave one of the meat pies to Nightwitch. There was a little left over, so we wrapped it up and put it back in my bundle before we started off down the stream.

We stayed as close to the bank as we could. It's easy to get lost in the Enchanted Forest, especially if you don't really know where you're going. If we got out of sight of the stream, we might never find it again.

In a couple of places the trees grew in thick clumps, right up to the water's edge, and we had to choose between wading and going around. I didn't like the dark look of the forest near the tree clumps, and the water was only ankle deep, so we waded. Nightwitch did *not* approve.

The forest got darker as we went along. I was sure, now, that the trees were bigger, and they were certainly closer together even when they weren't growing in tight clumps. We spent more and more time in the stream, but the water wasn't very cold and the pebbles on the bottom were smooth, so it wasn't particularly unpleasant. Even so, I was glad when the woods started to open up again.

Then I saw the clearing a little ahead of us. A minute later, I saw the person sitting in it.

She was a princess. She had to be. Her hair was long and golden and not tangled at all, and her eyes were very blue, and her skin was very white, and she was very, very beautiful. One dainty foot was peeping out from under her blue silk gown. Her hands were folded in her lap, and she was looking at them with a sad expression.

Shiara poked me. I realized that I was standing in a stream with my shoes in one hand and Morwen's bundle in the other and my mouth hanging open. I swallowed and waded over to the bank. I wanted to put my shoes back on before we got any closer. I had seen at least two princesses before, that I knew of, but both of them were enchanted and hadn't looked at all like their usual selves when I met them. When I finished with my shoes, the Princess was looking in our direction.

I stood up hastily and hurried toward her. Shiara followed. As soon as I was within speaking distance, I stopped and bowed. The Princess smiled sadly.

"I bid you such poor welcome as I may," she said in a musical voice. "Alas! That I can offer you no refreshment. For I am in great distress."

"I'm sorry to hear that," I said. "Is there anything I can do to help?"

"I fear not," said the Princess. "For you are as yet a youth. Alas! and woe is me! For I am in great distress."

"All right, all right. So tell us about it," Shiara said. She sat down on the ground and looked at the Princess expectantly.

I frowned. I didn't think that was the proper way to address a princess, though I wasn't positive. Mother had taught me a lot more about dragons than she had about princesses.

"You are kind to inquire of my sad tale," the Princess said. "It is not long to tell. My father was a king, much beloved of his people, and I his only daughter. Being lonely after my mother's death, my father remarried, to a woman comely but proud, and under her influence have I suffered these seven years. And now the King my father is dead, and my stepmother hath cast me out, to wander alone and friendless through the world. Alas! For I am–"

"In great distress. We know. You said that before," Shiara said. "Why didn't *you* throw *her* out when your father died? It would have saved you a lot of trouble."

The Princess's blue eyes filled with tears and she bowed her head. " 'Twas not within my power to work harm against her, alas. And now I seek some prince or hero who will take pity on my destitute state and return me to my proper place. Woe is me! That I should be without help in such distress."

"Sounds like a lousy excuse to me," Shiara muttered under her breath. Fortunately, the Princess didn't hear.

"I'm afraid we can't help you get your kingdom back," I said. "I'm very sorry. But if there's any other service I can do for you, I'd be happy to try."

"Daystar!" Shiara's voice was horrified, and suddenly I realized what I'd said. I swallowed. At least I'd only promised to try.

"There is one thing," the Princess said. She raised her head, and her eyes were very bright. I went cold. The Princess smiled sweetly.

"Give me your sword," she said.

7

In Which There Is a Good Deal of Discussion

I stared at the Princess. Then I shut my mouth and swallowed again, hard. *Mother isn't going to like this at all,* I thought. I was just about to draw the sword and give it to her when Shiara said, "Wait a minute, Daystar."

I stopped and looked at her. She looked at the Princess. "Daystar hasn't got a sword."

"What?" the Princess and I said at the same time. The Princess frowned. "I am not blind, to be so easily deceived. See, there it is." She pointed to my scabbard.

"That," said Shiara triumphantly, "is the Sword of the Sleeping King. So it belongs to him, not to Daystar, and Daystar can't give it away."

The Princess looked very puzzled. I thought for a minute. Shiara was right, but she was wrong, too. I mean, it was obvious what the Princess had *meant,* even if she hadn't said it right. I sighed and reached for the hilt.

Shiara turned on me. "Daystar, what are you doing?"

"Giving her the sword," I said, tugging at it. The sword wouldn't come out of the sheath. "You know as well as I do what she meant."

"Well, if all those wizards and sorceresses can be picky about the way people say things, why can't you?" Shiara was so mad I expected her hair to start burning any minute. "You can't even get it out of the sheath! You only said you'd try to do what she wanted. Well, you've tried. Isn't that enough?"

I sighed. "I'm sorry, Shiara, but it's my sword, and I'm not a wizard. I just have to do it."

"Daystar, you . . . you . . ." Shiara gave up and just glared.

I tugged at the sword again, and Shiara turned her back. The Princess still looked puzzled. I shook my head and unbuckled the whole sword belt. I stared at it for a minute, then held it out toward the Princess. "Here. Take it." My voice seemed too loud, and I realized that the woods had gotten very quiet. The Princess smiled and took hold of the scabbard. I let go of the sword.

There was a rumbling noise, and the Princess said, "Oh!" very loudly and dropped the sword belt. The point of the scabbard hit the ground, and there was another rumble, and an enormous geyser of water shot up into the air.

I saw the Princess cringe, and Shiara fell backward. Then I couldn't see anything but white spray. A voice said, "All hail the Holder of the Sword!" The words echoed hollowly around me as the fountain vanished.

Shiara and the Princess were both staring at me, wide eyed. All of us were dripping. The sword was standing upright in front of me, in the middle of a pool of water about four feet across. It was about halfway out of the sheath, and the blade shimmered in the sun.

The Princess burst into tears. "I knew not that this weapon was of such potency," she said between sobs. "Alas! For I cannot hold the sword, and who now will be my help? Alas, and woe is me!"

"You mean you don't want the sword anymore?" Shiara demanded.

The Princess nodded. She was weeping too hard to say much.

"And Daystar can have it back now?"

The Princess nodded again. She was still weeping.

I sighed and dug out my handkerchief. It was wet. I squeezed it out and offered it to the Princess anyway. She took it without thanking me and cried some more.

"What am I to do?" she kept saying. "Who now will be my help? Alas! For I am in great distress!"

"Oh, help yourself," Shiara said crossly. "Daystar, are you going to take that stupid sword?"

I hesitated, then reached out and took hold of the hilt. The blade flashed once, and a brief shock ran through me as the hilt came to rest. I ignored the feeling and pulled at the scabbard. It came free almost at once, and the water closed silently behind it. I took a closer look at the bottom part of the sheath. I wasn't even surprised when I saw that it wasn't wet.

I looked up. The Princess had just about stopped crying. I looked at the sword. Then I looked back at the Princess. "Are you sure you don't want this?" I asked finally.

"Daystar!" Shiara sounded like she wasn't sure whether to be mad or horrified.

The Princess didn't seem to hear her at all. "I cannot take it!" she cried. "Oh, indeed, I cannot! Alas! That I am so helpless in my time of need!"

"Well, if you didn't want the sword, why did you ask for it in the first place?" Shiara said angrily.

"I fear I have deceived you," the Princess said tragically. "Yet I myself have been misled. Alas! I beg of you, forgive me! For indeed, I am–I am in great distress."

"Distress? Ha!" said Shiara. "You better tell us the truth, right now, or you'll find out what distress is."

"Shiara–" I began.

Shiara turned. "You shut up. You obviously don't know anything about handling princesses, so let me do it. Now," she said to the Princess, "explain. And it better be good."

"I am a king's daughter," the Princess said. "My father would have me wed the prince of a neighboring kingdom, to bring us wealth. Yet I could not, for I love not him but another. My father listened not, for all my pleading, so my love and I fled into the forest. We wandered far, and great was our suffering, yet we were happy, for we had each other. But I, being unused to travel, became tired, and my love at last set me here and bade me wait for him. And here have I stayed these two long days, and I fear me some evil may have befallen him. Alas! That we are parted!"

"What," said Shiara, "does all this have to do with Daystar's sword?"

The Princess sighed again. "I was seated here, as you see me, bewailing my bitter fate, when lo! a man appeared, most wise and powerful of aspect. He told me my love was imprisoned by a mighty sorceress, and at that news I wept bitterly. Then he bade me desist from my grief, for the means of delivering my love was at hand, to wit, a sword most magical. And he himself made promise of aid, if I would but attain the sword. And this have I attempted, and I have failed. Alas, and woe is me!"

"I don't think I understand," I said. "Why didn't you tell us this to begin with?"

The Princess began to weep again. "My unknown friend instructed me in what I was to say and told me that all would be well once I had the sword in my own hands. And in this he deceived me, for the touch of the sword burns so that I cannot hold it. And the cause is that I deceived you, and tricked you into offering me the sword, and the sword knew, and it will not abide in my hand, and now am I utterly without hope."

"What did this person look like?" Shiara asked unsympathetically. "The one you were going to give the sword to."

The Princess seemed a lot more interested in explaining how wise and powerful and helpful the man had been than she was in giving a simple description, but eventually we managed to get some idea what he looked like. Tall, dark haired, blue eyed, and carrying a staff–

"It sounds a lot like Antorell," I said finally.

"Antorell?" Shiara asked.

"The wizard that Mother melted. She said he might try to make trouble for me in a day or two."

"Oh, great. All we need is another wizard looking for us."

The Princess didn't seem to be following the conversation at all. "Alas!" she said finally. "There is nothing left for me but grief. I have no means now to save my love, so I shall die with him. I shall fling myself in yonder stream and make an end."

"You are even dumber than Daystar," Shiara informed her. "That stream isn't deep enough to drown in. You'll only get wet. Besides, if that stupid wizard lied about the sword, how do you know he didn't lie about your love? Who is this person you ran off with, anyway?"

"He is a knight," the Princess said, her eyes lighting up. "Poor in goods, yet rich in spirit, of most pleasing aspect. His eyes are a hawk's, his arms are mighty, and his sword is bright and–"

"He sounds like he can take care of himself," Shiara said. "I don't think you have to worry about him."

Shiara's words had a marvelous effect on the Princess. "Truly, you believe this?" she said, and her face lit up even more. "Then here will I await his coming, for surely he will return to me. Ah, joy! That we shall soon be once more together!"

Shiara looked disgusted. "I'm sure you'll be very happy. Come on, Daystar, let's go." She stood up.

"I don't think we should leave her here by herself," I said.

"Daystar, you're impossible!" Shiara was still mad. "She tried to trick you! Besides, she's been here two days already, and nothing's happened to her yet."

"Alas! I did indeed attempt to deceive you," the Princess said. "And for that I beg forgiveness. Yet consider my unhappy plight, and be not harsh with me."

"Oh, shut up," Shiara told her.

"What if Antorell comes back?" I said. "Somebody ought to take care of her. Besides, I made a promise."

"Well, I didn't!" Shiara said. "And I'm not going to sit here doing nothing just because of a stupid princess! I'm leaving."

"You can't do that!" I said. I was really upset. Shiara didn't know very much about the Enchanted Forest, and she was going to go tramping off into the middle of it with no one but Morwen's kitten. I couldn't let her do that, but I couldn't leave the Princess sitting there alone, either.

"Want to bet?" Shiara said. She picked up the bundle Morwen had given her. "Come on, Nightwitch. Let's go."

"Nightwitch? What an unusual name for a cat," said a new voice.

Shiara stopped and both of us turned. An old man was standing at the edge of the clearing, in front of a clump of scruffy lilacs that were almost tall enough to be considered trees. His beard and what was left of his hair were quite white, and he was stooped over and leaning on a staff. Even without the way my skin prickled, I knew he was a wizard.

The Princess was the first to recover from the surprise of seeing him there. "Ah, sir, have pity on my sad state!" she said. "Have pity, and if you have seen a knight, bright armored, hawk eyed, most fair and pleasing in speech and semblance, then tell me speedily where he may be found. For he is my love, and we are parted, and thus am I in great distress! Alas!"

"That's quite all right, my dear," the wizard said in a kindly tone. "You've nothing to worry about. In fact, he should be here before very much longer. That's why I hurried. Just sit there and wait quietly, like a good girl."

"Oh, joy! Oh, bliss!" said the Princess rapturously. "To be with my love again!" She started happily explaining how strong and handsome and generally wonderful her missing knight was. Since she didn't seem to be speaking to anyone in particular, the rest of us ignored her.

Shiara, Nightwitch, and I were edging backward. I had my right hand on the hilt of my sword, and my whole side was tingling with the feel of the wizard's magic. The wizard noticed us and smiled.

"Take your hand from your sword," he said, looking at me. "I am not here to engage in a vulgar physical contest with you."

"Are you from the Society of Wizards?" Shiara demanded. Her voice sounded a little shaky, but I don't think anyone who didn't know her would have noticed.

"No," the wizard said. "Why? Are you looking for one of them?"

"Then why are you here?" I said.

"Why, to assist you," the wizard said.

"Assist *us?*" Shiara said. "But you're a *wizard!*"

"I am not at all concerned with your baseless prejudices," the wizard told her. "I have come to offer to help your companion, and I will thank you to cease interfering."

I stared at him. "I don't want to be impolite," I said before Shiara could say anything else, "but why do you want to help me?"

"Why, because you deserve it, of course," the wizard said. "You made a foolish promise to this other young lady," he went on, nodding toward the Princess, who was still talking to the air. "You could have gotten out of it several times, but you refused to behave dishonorably. I think that is deserving of a reward."

"Thank you very much," I said. I didn't really know what else to say. After all, there are people in the Enchanted Forest who go around rewarding heroes and princes for noble deeds. Why else would all those heroes come here?

"Well, what would you like?" the wizard said after a moment.

"Like?"

"As a reward." He sounded a little impatient.

I thought about it for a moment. "I appreciate the offer," I said finally. "But I really don't need anything. Thank you very much all the same."

"What? Isn't there anything you want?" he asked sharply. He didn't look nearly as friendly as he had at first.

"No, I don't think so," I said.

For a moment the wizard looked very disconcerted. Then he seemed to relax a little. "Perhaps I did not make myself clear enough," he said. "You need not ask for something material. Information will do just as well. The word for *sorcery* in the tongue of the giants, or the location of the Well of Silver Storms, where the unicorns drink. There must be something you want to know, even if there is nothing you want to have."

The only thing I wanted to know was what I was supposed to do in the Enchanted Forest. Somehow, I didn't think Mother had told him. "No," I said. "I don't think there is anything."

The wizard looked at me, and his eyes narrowed. "Come, come! You need to know the name of your father, do you not?"

"No," I said, puzzled. I'd wondered about my father a few times, but I'd never asked Mother about him. She would have told me if she'd thought I ought to know. And I certainly couldn't think of any reason why I *needed* to know. "Why should I?"

"You're looking for him, aren't you?" the wizard snapped.

"No, not really." That might be one of the things Mother wanted me to do, but it certainly couldn't be the only one. Furthermore, I couldn't see how knowing his name would help much, even if I were looking for him. In the Enchanted Forest, looking for someone usually isn't the best way of finding him. You're much more likely to run into people by accident.

"You aren't? Then you must know! She *told* you! Who is it?"

"I thought *you* were going to tell Daystar that," Shiara said. "Don't you know?"

"Silence, fool! I have waited too long for this." The wizard turned back to me. "You will tell me now or regret it deeply: Who is your father?"

"I don't know," I said. "And if I did, I don't see why I should tell you."

"There are other ways of learning what I wish to know," the wizard said. He straightened abruptly. The Princess squeaked and fell silent. Nightwitch hissed. Shiara started edging backward again. And the wizard changed.

He got a little taller and a lot younger; his beard and hair darkened and filled in. His eyes changed from brown to blue, but they still glared.

"Antorell!" I said, and drew my sword.

The steel rang as it came out of the sheath, and the blade shimmered and flashed in front of me. It made the whole clearing seem brighter. Antorell's lips curled into a sneer.

"Fool! What use is a sword against a wizard?"

He raised his staff, and a globe of green light appeared at the lower end of it. A thread of green, dark and bright as the shine of a snake, reached out toward me from the staff. I raised the sword.

The green light touched the Sword of the Sleeping King. The sword hummed a little and the ray of light vanished, and that was all.

Antorell frowned, and another, larger ray of green reached out. This time, the humming was a little louder, and the light around the end of Antorell's staff vanished, along with the ray touching the sword. The jangling feeling lessened a little. I was considerably relieved. Antorell looked shocked.

"You cannot! Not possibly! That sword can't . . ." His eyes moved to my face, then back to the sword, and he took a deep breath. "So! She must have known all along. But now I will have that weapon. I *must* have that weapon!"

"No," I said. "Mother wouldn't like it."

Antorell's eyes narrowed. "Cimorene has had her way long enough. If you will not give me that sword, I will take it." He started to raise the staff again.

The lilacs behind Antorell rustled noisily, and the wizard shifted. "You, there!" he called over his shoulder. "Show yourself at once!"

"Ach–ach–" said someone behind him, and the tops of the lilacs rustled again. I looked up at them, wondering how tall whoever-it-was was. The branches that were rustling were a good ten feet off the ground.

Antorell frowned and turned around, raising his staff. "I will teach you to interfere–"

The angry look on Antorell's face changed abruptly to one of mingled surprise and fear. He stepped backward very quickly and waved his staff through the air in front of him.

"Achoo!" said the voice, and an enormous ball of fire demolished the lilacs and enveloped Antorell. The wizard screamed and disappeared, and we could see the person who had been behind the bush.

It was a dragon.

8

In Which They Meet Their First Dragon

It was about twelve feet tall, which is not very large, as dragons go. But it was definitely a dragon. It sneezed again, which took care of the remains of the lilac bush, and slid forward over the ashes into the middle of the clearing. The Princess fainted.

I put my sword away. Walking through the Enchanted Forest with a drawn sword is bad, but talking to a dragon with a sword in your hand is much worse. Fortunately, the dragon hadn't noticed it yet. As soon as the sword was sheathed, I looked up again, and my stomach went hollow.

The dragon was eyeing Shiara, and I didn't like the gleam in its eyes. I didn't like the militant way Shiara was glaring back, either. There wasn't very much I could do, though. You just don't interrupt a dragon when it's busy with something else. They don't like being distracted.

The dragon slid closer and bent its head until it was staring at Shiara from about a foot in front of her face. Shiara jumped. The dragon blinked.

"Are you a princess?" it asked hopefully.

"No. I'm a fire-witch," Shiara said. "And if you bite me, I'll burn your nose off."

"Oh. I thought you were a princess." The dragon lost interest in Shiara. It looked around the clearing again and saw me. Its head moved over in my direction.

I bowed. "Sir or madam," I said, trying to recall all the proper ways of addressing a dragon, "I offer you greetings in the name of myself and my companions, and I wish you good fortune in all your endeavors."

"I beg your pardon?" said the dragon. Its voice reminded me of one of those wooden wind instruments, the deep kind that you have to stand on a chair to play. It eyed me doubtfully. "Are *you* a princess?"

"I–" I stopped and stared. Dragons just don't beg people's pardon. Then I realized that this must be a very young dragon, and I relaxed a little. Dragons don't usually insist on formality until they get old enough to decide which sex they're going to be. "I'm very sorry, but I'm afraid I'm not a princess. My name is Daystar, and I'm very pleased to meet you."

The dragon sat back. "I had no idea princesses were so hard to find." It blinked and seemed to look at me for the first time. "I'm sorry I burned your bush, but I couldn't help it."

"Oh, please don't worry about it," I said. "It really doesn't matter in the least."

"It was the wizard," the dragon said confidentially. "I'm allergic to them. All dragons are."

"I'm sorry to hear that," I said.

The dragon looked at me. "You're very polite, Daystar." Its head swiveled back toward Shiara. "Say–you weren't polite at all!"

Nightwitch poked her head out from behind Shiara's ankle and hissed. The dragon started and then peered down at the kitten. "You aren't polite, either," it said.

I nudged Shiara. "Offer to do something for him," I hissed.

"What? Why?"

"If you insult a dragon, you have to do him a favor," I said. "Hurry up!" If she didn't say something quickly, the dragon would probably eat both of us. Unfortunately, the dragon might eat Shiara anyway. The favor most dragons want is dinner. I couldn't tell Shiara that, though, without offending the dragon. I wondered whether I could talk the dragon out of eating us, if it came to that. I didn't think so. Dragons are stubborn.

The dragon's eyes glittered. Shiara looked at it. "Can I do anything for you?" she asked finally. She sounded a little sullen, but dragons aren't very good at tone of voice. Besides, it's the offer that counts.

"Find me a princess," the dragon said promptly.

I breathed a very quiet sigh of relief. I didn't think there was a polite way to kill a dragon, and I hadn't been able to think of any other way of stopping it from eating Shiara and me if it wanted to. It was nice to know I wouldn't have to try.

"You want a princess?" Shiara looked thoughtful. "Why?"

"Dragons are supposed to have princesses," the dragon explained. "I can't be considered a proper dragon until I have one. But I've been looking for two days, and I haven't seen even a *smell* of a princess, and I'm tired of it. So you do it."

"You aren't going to eat her or anything, are you?" Shiara asked.

"Eat her?" The dragon sounded horrified. "And waste a perfectly good princess? Of course not! There aren't enough of them to go around as it is. What kind of barbarian do you think I am?"

"Well, I've never met a dragon before," Shiara said. "How was I supposed to know? I didn't mean to hurt your feelings."

"All right," said the dragon. "But you have to get me a princess. It doesn't have to be a large one."

"Do you want any particular kind of princess?" Shiara asked. "I want to be sure you'll be satisfied."

"Oh, young and beautiful, of course," the dragon said. "Are there other kinds?"

"There are enchanted princesses," Shiara pointed out. "Especially around here."

"That's right. Say, maybe that's why I haven't found one!"

"I wouldn't be surprised," Shiara said. "But will you take an enchanted princess?"

The dragon thought for a minute. "No, I don't think so. Spells make things too complicated."

"And does it matter how long it takes me to find her?" Shiara went on.

The dragon considered. "I don't want to wait too long, but I really don't want to be unreasonable, either. How about a week? You bring the princess here by a week from today, otherwise you owe me another favor." It licked its lips with a long red tongue.

"That sounds reasonable," Shiara said. "But what if I'm early?"

Suddenly I realized what Shiara was planning to do. I edged around the clearing, toward where the Princess was lying, but I wasn't quite fast enough.

"The earlier the better," the dragon said.

"Then, there's your princess!" Shiara said, and pointed.

"My, you do work fast," the dragon said. It turned and looked at the Princess. "She's certainly beautiful enough, but are you sure she isn't enchanted?"

"I'm quite sure," Shiara said.

"Then why is she asleep in the middle of the day? I didn't think princesses were nocturnal creatures."

"She just fainted when she saw you," Shiara said reassuringly. "It's nothing to worry about. It happens to princesses all the time. Will she do?"

"Quite well." The dragon nodded. "You're very prompt. Thank you very much."

Shiara nodded. I waited until the dragon turned away, then I frowned at Shiara.

"Why did you do that?" I whispered. "That was a terrible thing to do!"

"Would you rather I got eaten?" Shiara whispered back. "*She* won't get eaten. The dragon said so. And I bet it won't want her for long. Dragons are smarter than some people."

I didn't know what to say to that, so I looked back at the dragon. As it bent its head to inspect the Princess more closely, the Princess opened her eyes. She gave a small scream, and the dragon frowned.

"You don't have to be frightened," it said. "Really. You're my princess now, and I'm going to take proper care of you, and you can clean my scales and cook for me. I believe that's the standard arrangement."

The Princess burst into tears. The dragon pulled back, eyeing her uncomfortably. "Did I say something wrong?"

The Princess just cried harder. "Alas! Ah, woe is me! So recently was I happy, awaiting the coming of my love to rescue me from this dismal forest! And now am I a prisoner of a monster, and when my love arrives he will be eaten by this awful beast, and I abandoned to my fate! Alas, that I should come to this!"

The dragon looked considerably taken aback. It turned to Shiara and me. "*This* is a princess?"

"Yes, she is," I said, and Shiara nodded.

The Princess had heard the question, too, and she raised her head. "Indeed, I am a princess, and the daughter of a king, and see to what misery I have been brought!" she said tragically. "Alas, the day I left my father's house! Yet would I flee again, and endure with patience all the trials and woes which have come upon me, only to be with my love once more!"

The dragon backed up a pace. "Are you *sure* this is a princess?"

"Alas! Now even my birth is doubted, and to whom shall I turn in my distress? Ah, pity my sad state! For I am alone and friendless, and parted from my love. Ah, woe! That ever I let him leave my side! For he is mighty among men, most brave and fearsome in battle, and of a fair and pleasing appearance in all things, and he would not leave me thus, did he but know my fate." She went back to crying.

"If this *is* a princess, I'm not sure I want one after all," the dragon said. It looked at the Princess speculatively. "Maybe I could eat her instead."

"Ah, help!" said the Princess.

"I really don't think you should eat her," I said. "After all, you did say you wouldn't."

"That's right, I did." The dragon looked at the Princess, who was crying again, and sighed. "Nobody told me princesses were like this," it said in an aggrieved tone. "And who is this love she keeps talking about?"

"We haven't met him yet, I'm afraid," I said. "She says he's a knight that she ran away with because her father wanted her to marry someone else."

"A knight?" The dragon backed up a little farther. "I don't think I'm ready for knights yet. They're so unpredictable. I don't suppose you could find me a princess without a knight?"

"All really good princesses have knights," Shiara said firmly. "And you wouldn't want a second-rate princess, would you?"

"All of them?" the dragon asked plaintively.

"Well, not all of them," I said. "Some of them have princes instead."

"Princes are much worse than knights," Shiara said thoughtfully. "They have magic rings and sorceresses for godmothers and things like that. With knights you only have to worry about their armor and weapons, and maybe once in a while an enchanted sword."

"My love has no need of magic!" the Princess broke in indignantly. "For he is most strong and skilled, and never has he been beaten in combat with sword or spear. Woe that he is no longer at my side!"

"I don't like the sound of this," the dragon said uneasily. "Maybe if I just–"

There was a loud crash from the bushes at the edge of the clearing, and then a rather tinny-sounding voice said, "What ho! A dragon?"

The Princess stopped crying very suddenly and sat up quite straight. "Hark! My love approaches! Now shall you see his prowess for yourselves!"

There were more crashing noises. The dragon backed up again, looking nervous. A moment later a knight in a dented suit of armor fell through the middle of the thickest clump of bushes, right in front of the dragon.

"On guard, monster!" the knight said as he picked himself up. "Prepare to die!" He pulled out a sword and waved it at the dragon. Well, actually, he waved it a couple of feet to one side. His helmet had slipped a little, and evidently he couldn't see very well. The dragon looked at him, and then back at Shiara.

"This is a knight?" it said.

"My love is the bravest and best of knights!" the Princess cried.

"If this *is* a knight, maybe I can handle him after all," the dragon said. "He doesn't look so bad."

"Ah, hideous reptile! No longer do I fear you, for my love will defend me! Yea, he will defend me even unto death!"

"Now, wait a minute, Isabelle," the knight said. He pulled off his helmet, looked at it disgustedly, and threw it on the ground behind him.

"I'm perfectly willing to kill dragons for you, but who said anything about dying?"

"You are my knight, and my brave love!" the Princess said dramatically. "Oh, save me from this awful monster, who would carry me off and eat me!" She sprang up and threw her arms around the knight.

"It's going to be a bit difficult for me to save you if you hang about my neck like that," the knight said apologetically. "It's quite awkward. If you'll just sit down, I can see about doing this properly."

The Princess only hung on to him more tightly, which made his aim almost as bad as it had been when he was wearing his helmet crooked. The dragon was watching them closely, and its eyes were starting to glow. "You certainly aren't very polite," it said.

"My love is the soul of courtesy!" the Princess said from behind the knight. "For he is a knight most gentle and well spoken, much given to–"

"I say, Isabelle, must you go on like that?" the knight said. "It's embarrassing. Do, please, sit down and let me fight the dragon. Then you won't have to worry about being eaten, you know."

The Princess gave a small scream. "Alas!" she said in a quavery voice. "Behold my sad state! For now must I watch a bloody battle, and perhaps see my love slain before my eyes, and become a captive of this monster."

"This is ridiculous," said Shiara, and before I could stop her she marched over to stand between the dragon and the knight. I followed her, hoping I could get her out of trouble if I had to.

"Ah, save me!" the Princess said as we got closer. I wasn't sure whether she wanted to be saved from the dragon or from Shiara.

Shiara glared at her. "You shut up," she told the Princess. "You've caused enough trouble already."

"I say," said the knight. "If we're going to discuss politeness–"

"We aren't," said Shiara. "We're going to discuss battles. Battles between dragons and knights. Why do you want to fight this dragon?"

"Knights are sworn to do battle with the beasts that ravage the fields, carry off innocent maidens, and generally make a nuisance of themselves," the knight said. He sounded as if he were reciting something, and he didn't look very pleased about the idea, but the Princess nodded approvingly.

"Well, this dragon isn't ravaging anything, and it doesn't even want your stupid princess," Shiara said.

"I do, too!" the dragon broke in. "If I'm not going to carry her off I could eat her, after all. And if I fought a knight no one could say I'm not a proper dragon, even if I don't have a princess."

"I really don't think that's a good idea," I said. "Princesses aren't all that common, after all."

"Besides, you promised me you wouldn't," Shiara said.

"I did not!" the dragon said. "I only said I wouldn't waste a perfectly good princess, and this one's not so great. Eating her wouldn't be much of a waste."

"I don't think that would be very polite," I said. "Especially when you've talked to her this long without bringing it up. You really ought to ease into these things gradually, you know."

"Are you sure?" the dragon said.

I nodded.

"Oh, all right," said the dragon. "I won't eat her, then. But couldn't I fight the knight anyway? Just for practice?"

"I say, that sounds like an excellent idea," the knight said, brightening perceptibly. "A sort of exercise for both of us."

"A tourney!" the Princess cried. "Oh, brave and clever, to think of such a thing!"

The knight looked pleased. So did the dragon. It nodded, then whispered to Shiara, "What's a tourney?"

"It's like a battle, only no one gets hurt. Usually."

"Not even a little?" the dragon said. The knight started looking worried again.

"Of course not!" Shiara said to the dragon. "It's a show of skill."

"If you were trying to hurt each other, it wouldn't be a tourney," I added. Actually, it wasn't going to be a tourney anyway. There are very specific rules about what a tourney is, and a practice fight between a dragon and a knight just doesn't qualify. I decided not to say so.

"Oh, all right, then," the dragon grumbled. "I don't know why I'm letting you talk me into this. How do we start?"

9

In Which There Is a Fight, Sort of, and They Find Out Where They Are Going

The hardest part was getting the dragon and the knight to agree about rules. The Princess was no help at all. She kept talking about the marvelous tourneys she'd seen, and which knights had been wounded. Whenever she did, the dragon would start looking at the knight, and pretty soon it would want to know why it couldn't bite off one of the knight's arms, or at least a hand. The knight would get worried, and the Princess would start crying, and Shiara and I would have to talk the dragon out of it. As soon as the dragon agreed, the Princess would cheer up and start talking about tourneys again.

Finally, Shiara told the Princess to shut up. It wasn't very polite, but it worked. Well, sort of. The Princess didn't stop talking, but as long as she was complaining about Shiara and not talking about tourneys we didn't have any more problems getting the dragon and the knight to agree.

When we finally decided on the rules, we had to draw a circle in the middle of the clearing for them to fight in. It was harder than it sounds. For one thing, a circle has to be pretty big if a dragon is going to fit inside it, even if it's a small dragon. Also, the moss in the Enchanted Forest grows awfully fast. By the time we finished drawing the circle, the first half of it had already disappeared. Shiara watched for a minute, then looked at the knight.

"Are you sure you *have* to have a circle to fight?" Shiara said.

"I really do think so," the knight said apologetically. "It wouldn't be a proper tourney without it, don't you see."

"I'm sick of proper dragons and proper princesses and proper tourneys," Shiara said under her breath. Fortunately, the dragon didn't hear her.

We started redrawing the circle, trying to make the line wider this time. The knight scratched at the moss with his sword. Shiara used a stick. So did I; I didn't think Mother would approve if I used the Sword of the Sleeping King to cut moss. Nightwitch and the dragon sort of dug at the ground. The Princess sat under a tree.

Eventually we finished, and the knight and the dragon stepped inside the circle. "Well, what are you waiting for?" Shiara demanded.

"Someone has to say, 'go,' " the knight said in a reasonable tone.

"Go!" I said quickly.

Shiara gave me a disgusted look, but she didn't say anything, because as soon as I shouted, the dragon and the knight got started. They were fairly evenly matched. The dragon was much larger, of course, and it had a very good sense of timing, but it didn't have much experience. The knight was wearing armor, which helped, and he was obviously used to fighting, but he was a little awkward most of the time. They were both good at dodging, though, and they each managed to take three or four swings without hitting the other. The dragon was just starting to take another swipe at the knight when a little tree sprouted up in front of him and hit him in the nose.

I was surprised. I mean, even in the Enchanted Forest, trees don't usually grow that fast. The dragon was even more surprised than I was. It sort of reared back, and its tail came around very fast to balance it. Nightwitch was a little too close and had to scramble back out of the way.

"Hey, watch out!" Shiara said.

The dragon jumped and swung around, looking as if it expected another tree to pop up behind it. Its tail swung in the other direction, and the end of it caught the knight right in the middle of his chest plate as he was trying to back out of the way. The dragon yelped, the Princess screamed, and the knight fell over backward into the pool of water that my sword had made when the Princess had tried to take it.

Evidently the pool was a lot deeper than it looked, because the knight sank right out of sight. We all forgot about the fast-growing tree and leapt forward. The Princess was faster than either Shiara or I. By the time I got to the pool, she had hold of the knight. She wasn't quite strong enough to pull him out, but she wasn't letting go, either.

Shiara got to the pool about the same time I did, and together the three of us managed to get the knight out of the water. He was unconscious, and he had a large dent in his armor where the dragon's tail had hit him. The Princess checked to make sure he was still alive, and then she burst into tears.

"Alas! See now how sad is my fate! For my love has been grievously injured and I am without protection in this awful place. Ah, woe is me!"

"Is he dead?" asked the dragon from right behind me. I jumped. It peered curiously over my shoulder at the knight.

"Monster!" said the Princess. "Your base attempt to slay my love has failed! No second chance shall you have to harm him while I can stand between you! For if my love be slain, I care not whether I live or die, and thus I now defy you." She threw herself across the knight's chest.

The knight coughed, moaned, and opened his eyes. "I say, Isabelle," he said weakly, "that really is a bit uncomfortable."

The Princess sat up and started weeping all over his face. It didn't seem to make him much more comfortable.

The dragon was still peering. "That was a very good fight," it said to the knight. "Except for the last part. My tail still stings. I think I may have sprained it. Is armor always that hard?"

The knight tried to answer and started coughing instead. The Princess cried harder, until Shiara said pointedly, "I don't think all that water is doing him much good." The Princess stopped crying and glared at Shiara for a minute, then turned back to the knight. Somehow, she looked a lot more unhappy now that she wasn't crying. I felt sorry for her.

Finally the knight managed to get his coughing under control. He looked up at the dragon and said, "I do believe I agree with you about the fight. That trick with the tail is quite good. I don't recall seeing it before. I really must remember it."

"Actually, it was something of an accident," the dragon said modestly. "But I think I could do it again if I tried. Did you really think it was good?"

"Oh, quite," the knight said. I got the feeling that he would have tried to bow if he hadn't been lying on his back. "I think perhaps you broke one or two of my ribs."

"I'm sorry," said the dragon. "Is that bad?"

"It is certainly a bit uncomfortable," the knight said. "I don't really blame–"

A coughing spasm interrupted him. The Princess looked alarmed, but she didn't start crying. I saw Shiara watching the Princess with a surprised look on her face, and right about then Nightwitch sprang up onto the knight's chest.

"What is this? Go hence, and leave my love in peace!" cried the Princess.

"You let my kitten alone," Shiara warned.

The Princess stopped in midreach and looked over at Shiara. "And shall I neglect aught that may bring comfort to my love in his hurt?" she said.

"Nightwitch isn't going to hurt–" Shiara started, then paused. "I guess it doesn't matter. Go ahead."

I stared at Shiara in surprise, but she was watching the Princess and Nightwitch. The Princess got scratched a couple of times before she finally managed to pick the kitten up and move her. By then, the knight wasn't coughing quite so hard anymore, but he still didn't seem up to talking. Shiara frowned at him. "You don't sound very good," she said.

The dragon stuck its head farther over my shoulder. "If you can't fix him, can I eat him?" it asked hopefully.

Nightwitch hissed. The knight looked alarmed and tried to say something, but all that came out was more coughing. The Princess said, "No!" very loudly and looked as if she wanted to throw herself on top of the knight again.

"Of course not," Shiara said. "You promised."

"It wouldn't be polite," I added. "After all, that was why you had the tourney."

The dragon looked hurt. "I was just *asking.*"

"Ah, what are we going to do about them?" I asked hastily, waving at the Princess and the knight. "They can't stay here, not when the knight's been injured like that."

"It's not so bad, really it isn't," the knight said, looking at the dragon nervously. He started coughing again right away, but it didn't sound as bad as it had before and he stopped fairly quickly.

"I suppose you could come with us," I said after a minute.

"That's frightfully kind of you," the knight said. He looked uncertainly at the dragon. "Very kind, to invite us to come with you. *All* of you?"

"I don't know," I said. "I haven't asked the dragon about its plans yet. But you're quite welcome to join us, if you want to."

"Yes," said Shiara. "I'm sure you'll be very useful when the wizard comes back."

"Wizard?" said the knight. He was so alarmed he almost started coughing again. "What wizard?"

"Well, actually, there are several of them," I said. "Every now and then one of them shows up and tries to do something to us. The last one left when the dragon showed up."

"I'm sure he'll be back in a little while," Shiara said. "Or one of the others will. They've been chasing us all over the Enchanted Forest."

"You know," the knight said, "I really don't believe it would be a good idea for me to join you. I should almost certainly be a bit of an inconvenience, you see. Wet armor rusts, and with that and the ribs I'm afraid I'd be a little slow. Thank you terribly, all the same."

"If you don't come with us, what will you do?" I asked.

"Mrow," said Nightwitch.

"Morwen!" Shiara said. "They can go to Morwen! She'll know what to do for them." Nightwitch started purring loudly, sort of like a pepper grinder with rocks in it.

I thought about it for a minute. "It sounds like a good idea, but will she want to?"

"Morwen seems to like helping people," Shiara said. "And I'm sure she can take care of both of them."

"You know Morwen?" said the dragon. "I like her. She gives me apples out of her garden."

I tried to imagine a dragon eating apples and failed. I could imagine Morwen giving them to a dragon, though.

"Who is this Morwen?" asked the Princess, clasping her hands in front of her. "Think you that she could help my love, indeed?"

"Morwen's sort of a friend of ours," I explained. "She lives back that way, with a lot of cats, and her house has kind of a strange door."

"I didn't have any trouble with it," Shiara said. "And she has nine cats. She told me while you were asleep."

"Nine cats?" said the Princess, looking puzzled. "But what has that to do with my love, who is so grievously hurt?"

"I said it wasn't that bad, Isabelle," said the knight uncomfortably. "Really, I wish you wouldn't make such a fuss. I shall be quite all right in a little, I'm sure."

"If this woman with the many cats can help you, then we shall go to her," the Princess declared with more spirit than she had shown about anything else. "For you are my love, and I will have you whole and well."

"Oh, but really, Isabelle–"

"I'm sure Morwen won't mind," Shiara put in. "She fixed Daystar up just fine. She's even good with wet swords."

The Princess looked thoroughly confused, but the knight brightened a little. "Are you quite sure? Because I'm frightfully wet, sword and armor and everything, and it would be very nice if I could keep it all from rusting. It's rather expensive, you see."

"I'm sure she could manage that," Shiara said. "Of course, you don't have to go. You could stay here and wait for the wizard to come back."

The knight didn't argue. I don't think he liked the idea of staying around the dragon, especially if a lot of wizards were going to show up any minute. As soon as he agreed, the Princess started telling him how wise and brave and wonderful he was. Shiara looked disgusted, but the knight seemed to like it. He sat up and even managed not to cough very much.

Shiara and I gave the knight directions back up the stream and through the woods to Morwen's house. He and the Princess said good-bye and started off.

"That's a relief!" Shiara said when they were out of earshot. "For a while I thought you were going to make us go with that stupid princess. It was bad enough having to listen to her here without following her around."

I blinked at her. "But I thought you changed your mind about her! You were being a lot nicer to her after the knight got hurt."

Shiara snorted. "So I feel sorry for her. She really cares about that klutz in the tin can. I could tell. That doesn't mean I like her! I still think she's dumber than you are, but I'm glad they're going to see Morwen."

I wasn't sure whether Morwen would object or not, but I didn't say anything else about it. By then, the knight and the Princess were completely out of sight anyway. I turned around to see where I'd put the bundle of food and things Morwen had given me. The dragon was staring at me.

"Why," it said, "do you have wizards chasing you?"

"It's a long story," I said. "I'll be glad to explain, but you might want to make yourself comfortable first."

The dragon sighed. "Have you ever tried to be comfortable with a sprained tail?"

Shiara giggled. I ignored her. We waited while the dragon tried curling into a couple of different positions. One of them looked sort of like Suz when he was halfway through getting up on his tail. Finally, the dragon curled itself around the little tree that had sprouted up in the middle of the tourney. "That's better," it said. "Enchanted trees are always more comfortable than regular ones."

"Enchanted trees?" Shiara said.

"Of course," the dragon said. "What else do you expect to find in an enchanted forest? I'm going to have to remember to tell someone about this, though. There haven't been any new ones in a long time."

I looked at the tree a little more closely. It was nearly six feet tall now, and it seemed to have stopped growing. It didn't look very different from the other trees in the Enchanted Forest, except that it was a lot smaller than most of them. And, of course, none of the other trees had dragons wrapped around them.

"You were going to tell me about the wizards," said the dragon.

So I explained about Mother and Antorell, and the Sword of the Sleeping King, and everything. It took a long time. The dragon didn't say anything at all while I talked, but its tail twitched a couple of times. Whenever that happened, the dragon winced.

"That's very interesting," the dragon said when I stopped. "Where are you going now?"

"Morwen told us to follow the stream," Shiara said. "And Suz said we should go talk to someone named Kazul."

"It's the same thing," the dragon said.

"What do you mean?" I asked.

"The stream goes to the castle, and Kazul lives right outside it. I wonder why she wants to see you?"

"What castle?" Shiara said in an exasperated voice. "And who is this Kazul person, anyway?"

"It must have something to do with that sword," the dragon said, ignoring her questions completely. "Especially if it really does belong to the Sleeping King."

"You mean you know something about it?" Shiara said. "Well, then, tell us what the stupid thing does!"

The dragon looked sheepish. Dragons just weren't meant to look sheepish. "I don't know. I'm not old enough yet," it said.

"Not old enough?"

"That's why I wanted a princess," the dragon said. "Otherwise, Kazul won't tell me anything important until I'm two hundred. She says that before then dragons are irresponsible, unwise, and talk too much." It looked faintly indignant. "I don't talk too much."

"Who is Kazul?" I said. I was getting a little nervous about meeting her. I hadn't ever known anyone who could tell a dragon what to do, even a young one. Well, Mother might have been able to get away with it.

"Oh, I thought you knew," the dragon said. "Kazul is the King of the Dragons."

10

In Which They Take a Shortcut and Run into an Obstacle

Shiara and I looked at each other. "Terrific," Shiara said. "And I thought wizards were bad."

"Did I say something wrong?" the dragon asked.

"No, not at all," I said hastily. "We were just a little surprised, that's all."

"Hey!" Shiara said. "How can Kazul be King of the Dragons if she's a she? That doesn't make sense."

"It does too!" the dragon said. "What else would you call her?"

"How about Queen?" Shiara said sarcastically.

"Queen?" The little dragon wrinkled its nose. "Why would you want to call her Queen? That's not the same thing at all! You're the one who doesn't make sense."

"I do too make sense!" Shiara said. "Queens do the same things Kings do."

"Not for dragons," I said hastily. I didn't want the dragon to get offended again. "Dragons have a king, period. The King of the Dragons is whichever dragon can move Colin's Stone from the Vanishing Mountain to the Ford of the Whispering Snakes. It doesn't matter whether the dragon is male or female."

"It's silly to have two names for the same job," the dragon said complacently. "People get confused."

"Oh." Shiara looked skeptical, but at least she didn't object anymore. I decided I was going to have to explain a few things to her soon, before she got us both in real trouble. For about a minute, no one said anything. Then Shiara looked over at me.

"Daystar," she said, "*why* are we looking for the King of the Dragons?"

I started to say something, then stopped because I wasn't really sure what to say. I mean, it would sound a little odd to say that I was looking for a dragon because a lizard told me to. Especially since the dragon was apparently King of the Dragons. I thought some more.

"I don't know," I said finally. "But I think we have to. At least, *I* have to."

Shiara sighed. "I was afraid you were going to say something like that."

The dragon looked puzzled. "What's the matter? It doesn't sound particularly unusual to me, but I suppose it'll be at least as interesting as running away to find a princess."

Shiara and I looked at the dragon, then at each other, then back at the dragon again. "You ran away?" Shiara said finally.

"It was the only way I could think of to get a princess." The dragon sighed. "It didn't work out the way I thought it would, though."

Shiara and I exchanged glances again. "You're sure you really want to come?" I said to the dragon. "I mean, there are wizards after us, and it might be a little inconvenient if they showed up again. And I doubt that we'll run into any more princesses."

The dragon looked thoughtful for a moment, then it shook its head. "I'm coming with you, wizards or no wizards," it said stubbornly. "Sneezing isn't so bad."

It was my turn to sigh. Dragons are awfully hard to talk out of things. "We'd better go, then," I said. "I'm sure Antorell will be back as soon as he thinks it's safe, and I'd sort of like to be gone by then."

Shiara grabbed Morwen's bundles and shoved one at me. "You're absolutely right. Here. Let's go."

I nodded and started toward the stream. "Not that way!" said the dragon. "It takes too long."

"How else are we going to find the stupid castle?" Shiara demanded. "We don't even know what it looks like!"

The dragon looked smug. "I do. And I'm very good at shortcuts."

"Morwen told us to follow the stream," I said doubtfully.

"Morwen didn't know you were going to meet me." The dragon looked at us for a minute. "I thought you were in a hurry."

"Come on, Daystar," Shiara said. "I don't care which way we go, but let's go!"

I decided not to argue. I still didn't like the idea of leaving the stream, but it didn't seem worth fighting over. Not with a dragon, anyway. Besides, if we didn't leave soon, the wizards would catch us. We started off, following the dragon.

Traveling with a dragon was rather nice, in a way. Nothing bothered us at all. When it started to get dark, we stopped and opened Morwen's bundles again. There was obviously something magic about them, because the leftovers from lunch had turned into a fresh packet of food, and there was plenty for everyone, even the dragon.

Nothing dangerous came near us all night, either. I stayed awake for a while, just to make sure, but evidently nightshades and wolves and things don't want to annoy a dragon any more than people do. Finally, I went to sleep, too.

We started off again as soon as we woke up next morning. The dragon went first because it knew the way, and we followed. After about an hour, I noticed that I didn't feel quite comfortable for some reason. I touched the hilt of the Sword of the Sleeping King a couple of times, but I didn't feel any new magic tingles, just the same familiar ones. I started watching the trees as we walked. Finally, Shiara noticed.

"What's the matter, Daystar?" she said.

"I don't know," I said. "But I feel as if I'm being watched."

"Watched?" Shiara looked at the trees quickly. "Who's watching us?"

"I don't know," I said. "I'm not even sure someone is. I just feel uncomfortable."

"You're being a little slow," the dragon called back over its shoulder, and Shiara and I stopped talking and ran to catch up. We didn't have a chance to discuss it again, but I noticed Shiara looking uneasily at the forest from time to time. Even Nightwitch seemed to notice something wrong; she stopped jumping at leaves and stayed close to Shiara. In fact, Shiara almost stepped on her once. After that, Shiara carried her.

In spite of all the worrying, nothing happened until late that morning. The dragon was moving on through the forest, ignoring all the little branches and things that happened to be in its way. Suddenly it gave a smothered yelp and stopped. Shiara and Nightwitch and I ran forward to see what was the matter.

The dragon was sitting back, rubbing its nose and glaring at a large open space in front of it. I looked around, but I didn't see anything else. "What happened?" I asked.

"I ran into something," the dragon said, glaring at me for a minute instead of the open space.

"But there isn't anything–Ow!" Shiara had started to wave toward the clearing, but her hand stopped about halfway through the wave, as if it had hit something. She rubbed her fingers, then put out her hand more cautiously. It stopped in midair, right where it had before. Nightwitch hissed and backed away.

I reached out, very carefully. It was a little strange to feel something where I couldn't see anything. It was cool and smooth, like stone, and it went up as far as I could reach. "It's an invisible wall," I said.

"No, it's an invisible castle," Shiara said. Then she jerked her hand away and stared at the air in front of her as if she could make herself see something by trying hard. "Hey! How do I know that?"

"I don't know," I said. "When did you figure it out?"

"I didn't! I was just standing here, wanting to know what it was, and all of a sudden I did."

"That sounds like fire magic!" I said.

"I don't care what it is," the dragon said crossly. "I want to know where it came from. It wasn't here last time I came this way."

"No, I mean what Shiara did sounds like fire magic."

"Really?" The dragon looked at Shiara. "Then use your fire magic to find out what this invisible thing is doing in the middle of my shortcut."

Shiara looked doubtful, but she put her hand back on the castle. "It's an invisible castle, all right. Hey, I even know how to do it!"

"Do what?" asked the dragon. "Put your hand on a castle?"

"No, no, how to make things invisible," Shiara said.

"I don't want to know how to make things invisible," the dragon snapped. "What's it doing here?"

For once, I wasn't paying much attention to the dragon. I was staring at Shiara. Analyzing spells is *hard*. "You figured out how to turn a castle invisible just by touching it?"

"No, you have to do a lot of other things to it." Shiara's face changed, as if she had just remembered something she didn't like, and she stared at the open area for a minute. Then she swallowed so hard I could see it. "Let's leave, Daystar. I don't think I want to meet anyone who would live in an invisible castle."

I looked at Shiara, then at the open space. I looked back at Shiara and opened my mouth to ask another question, but I stopped before I said anything. Shiara looked a little white, and a little sick, and a lot scared. I hadn't seen Shiara look like that before, not even when the wizard tried to catch us with his snaky water monster. Especially not then.

"All right," I said. "Let's go."

"But I want to know what it's doing in the middle of my shortcut," the dragon complained.

"We can talk about it somewhere else," I said.

Shiara was already backing into the trees, her eyes fixed on the open space where the castle would be if we could see it. I glanced back at the dragon. It shrugged. "Oh, all right. But I don't see what all the fuss is about."

Right then Shiara gave a half yell that stopped in the middle. I whirled around. There was a woman standing where Shiara had been. She was very tall, and she had long hair that was so red it was almost black. She was dressed in something green and shining and elegant that hung from a deep red jewel at her throat, and she was very beautiful. More beautiful than the Princess, even. I didn't care.

"Where's Shiara?" I said.

She smiled, the same way a very satisfied cat smiles, except that cats don't look evil. Well, most cats don't. "Shiara–is that your little friend's name? She's right here, my dear." She stepped aside, and I went cold. Behind her, where it had been hidden until she moved aside, was a gray stone statue that looked exactly like Shiara.

"That can't be Shiara!" I said. I was too upset to even think about being polite. "Shiara's a fire-witch, and fire-witches are immune to magic!"

The woman smiled another unpleasant smile. "Not to the magic of another fire-witch. I've been waiting a long time for someone like her to come by. I need her for something."

"How is turning her into a statue going to help?" I asked. I was hoping I could talk her into changing Shiara back. Then maybe I could do something to keep Shiara that way.

The fire-witch glanced at the statue. "It's an excellent way of storing people until you need them. I have quite a number in my garden. They're ornamental as well as useful."

"That doesn't sound nice," the dragon said.

The woman seemed to see it for the first time, which I thought was a little odd. After all, dragons aren't exactly easy to overlook. "I am not concerned with being nice," she said.

"Why not?" I asked.

The fire-witch turned and looked at me. Suddenly her eyes narrowed. "Who are you, boy?" she asked sharply.

"My name is Daystar," I said, "and I would appreciate it if you would change Shiara back."

"No," she said flatly. "Why should I?" She was still staring at me, as if she were trying to figure something out. "You're very interesting, Daystar," she said abruptly. "I think perhaps I'll let you go. I haven't done anything like that in a long time. It might be an interesting experience. I think you had better leave before I change my mind."

"I'm sorry, but I'm not leaving until you turn Shiara back," I said.

"Then I am afraid you will grow rather bored." The woman looked at me thoughtfully for a moment, then shook her head. "No, I don't have any use for you, and I can't be bothered storing things that aren't useful. Pity; you'd make a nice fountain." She lifted one hand and snapped her fingers.

I had just enough time to realize that I hadn't drawn my sword. I grabbed for it and pulled, knowing I wasn't going to make it. There was something like an explosion just in front of me, and a wave of heat, and then I was holding the Sword of the Sleeping King up in front of me and watching the fire-witch cursing and stamping at something. She didn't look at all elegant anymore.

Suddenly I realized why the fire-witch had missed. "Nightwitch!" I yelled. A small bundle of black fur darted out from under the witch's skirts and vanished under a bush. The fire-witch glared after the kitten, then turned back to me. "You'll suffer for–"

Right next to me there was a sound like someone blowing out several very large candles all at once, and a stream of fire shot out and enveloped the fire-witch. She laughed.

"Fire, to harm me? Even a dragon should know better! I'll see to you in a moment. Or do you think I am fool enough to grow a garden without dragonsbane?"

The dragon shuddered, and the fire-witch laughed again. Then she looked at me, and her eyes glittered. "I want you first, though. Now!" She pointed at me, and I raised the Sword of the Sleeping King a little higher, holding on to the hilt with both hands and hoping it could handle fire-witches as well as it handled wizards.

Something hit the sword, and pain ran through my whole body. It felt a little like the shock I'd gotten when Shiara and I had tried to pick up the sword at the same time, except it went on and on. The Sword of the Sleeping King began to get hot. I felt as if boiling lead were running down the sword and into my arms. I think I screamed; I know the fire-witch did, because I heard her.

The Sword of the Sleeping King glowed dull red in my hands. It wasn't behaving at all the way it had when it stopped Antorell's spell, and I got the distinct impression that this wasn't very good for it. It wasn't very good for me, either; the sensation of boiling lead was oozing farther up my arms.

I knew that if I didn't do something I was going to drop the sword. I shouted and *pushed.* At least, pushing is the only way I can describe what I did. I wasn't really thinking too clearly by then. I just wanted the lead to go back into the sword and quit hurting.

I heard a wail from the fire-witch that kind of died out, and the pain stopped very suddenly. I noticed that the sword wasn't glowing anymore, and then I fell over. It wasn't that I felt particularly tired or weak. I just couldn't stand up anymore. The last thing I remember thinking was that I had to hang on to the sword, no matter what.

I woke up because something small and warm and rough was rubbing my chin. I opened my eyes. Night-witch was sitting on the ground in front of me, licking my face. I was lying face down on the moss. I could feel the Sword of the Sleeping King underneath me. It was very uncomfortable, but I didn't feel like moving. I closed my eyes again.

Nightwitch hissed and dug her claws into my shoulder. Kittens have surprisingly sharp claws, and I opened my eyes again very quickly. The dragon was staring at me from beside Nightwitch. At least, its head was beside Nightwitch. The rest of it wouldn't fit. It blinked at me.

"Are you dead?" it asked.

"No," I said. I thought about saying something else, but I didn't have the energy.

"Oh." The dragon sounded almost disappointed for a minute. Then it brightened. "I think that fire-witch is."

"That's nice." I had the feeling I should remember something, but I didn't want to think hard enough to figure out what.

Nightwitch hissed and dug her claws into me again.

"Stop that!" I said, and I rolled onto my back.

"What?" said the dragon.

"Nightwitch," I said. Rolling over had taken all the energy I had, and I didn't want to talk anymore. I didn't even want to think anymore. I wanted the dragon to just leave me alone, but I couldn't say so without being rude, so I closed my eyes and started drifting off to sleep instead. Then Nightwitch jumped onto my chest and dug her claws in hard.

I yelled and sat up. Nightwitch jumped down to the ground and ran off. I tried to see where she'd gone and saw Morwen's bundle instead. Suddenly I realized that I was very hungry. I started to reach for the bundle, then remembered that I was still holding the sword. I also remembered the boiling lead, and I was almost afraid to look at my hands. I was sure that this time I'd burned both of them worse than when I'd picked up the wizard's staff.

I looked down. There wasn't anything wrong with me–at least, not that I could see. I let go of the sword with one hand. It didn't hurt. I heaved a sigh of relief and put the sword back in its sheath, then got out some of Morwen's gingerbread and started eating. It was a good thing the food was right on top of the bundle, because I didn't have the strength to hunt for it.

The dragon watched me for a few minutes with a puzzled expression. "You're a very good magician," it said finally. "Where did you learn that spell?"

"Spell?" I was having a little trouble remembering the details of the fight. I wasn't sure whether it was because it had hurt so badly or because I was too busy eating.

"The one you shouted right before the witch went up in smoke," the dragon said, "You said,

'Power of water, wind, and earth,
Turn the spell back to its birth.' "

"Oh, that," I said, feeling a little silly. "It's just part of a rhyme Mother taught me when I was little. I don't know why I said it."

"Your *mother* taught you? But that's a dragon spell! Your mother couldn't teach you dragon spells!"

"You don't know my mother," I said. I'd eaten most of the gingerbread, and I was feeling much better. "She taught me two more lines to the rhyme," I offered. "They go,

'Raise the fire to free the lord
By the power of wood and sword.' "

The dragon looked at me suspiciously. "Where did your mother learn dragon spells?"

"She didn't tell me," I said. I finished the gingerbread and looked around. "Where did Shiara . . ." My voice died in midsentence as I remembered exactly where Shiara had been when I saw her last. I didn't want to look, but I had to. I took a deep breath and turned my head.

Sometimes, when witches or wizards die, all of their spells die with them. If the witch or wizard is skillful, sometimes the spells last.

The fire-witch had been skillful. Shiara was still a statue.

11

In Which a Lizard Suggests a Solution

I sat there for a minute, staring at the statue and wondering what to do. Finally I looked at the dragon. "Do you know anything about magic?"

"Of course I do!" the dragon said. "Everyone who lives near the Enchanted Forest knows something about magic."

I sighed. "I mean, do you know anything about turning statues that used to be people back into people again? Because I don't, and we have to figure out some way to fix Shiara."

"Oh." The dragon looked doubtfully at the statue of Shiara. "We could take her to the Living Spring and drop her in," it suggested. "That would bring her back to life."

"You *know* where the Living Spring is?" I said in surprise.

"No," said the dragon. "But I bet if we found it, it would work."

I shook my head. "I don't think we have time. There are wizards looking for us, remember?"

"Oh, that's right. I keep forgetting. I don't like to think about wizards." The dragon blinked. "What about your sword? You could say that spell again."

I nodded. I walked over to Shiara and pulled the Sword of the Sleeping King out of its sheath. I felt a little uncomfortable, partly because I hadn't thought of using the sword and partly because the dragon spell was still just one of Mother's nursery rhymes to me. The idea of standing in the middle of the Enchanted Forest holding a magic sword and reciting a nursery rhyme made me feel very silly. I looked at the statue of Shiara again and decided I'd try it anyway. Slowly, I lowered the point so that it touched the statue's shoulder, and I said,

"Power of water, wind, and earth,
Turn the spell back to its birth.
Raise the fire to free the lord
By the power of wood and sword."

For a minute I thought nothing had happened, but then three or four little tingles ran up my arm from the sword. I hadn't even realized they were missing until they started again. When I finally did notice, I was relieved. Mother wouldn't have been at all happy with me if I'd ruined the Sword of the Sleeping King.

Unfortunately, Shiara was still a statue. "I suppose we're going to have to look for the Living Spring," I said. "Unless you have some other ideas."

"No," the dragon said. "I've never been on an adventure before. How are we going to find the Spring?"

"I don't know," I said. Half of the heroes who stopped at our cottage had been looking for the Living Spring, but I'd never heard of anyone finding it. I tried to think of someone who might know where the spring was. "Suz!" I said suddenly.

"What?" the dragon said.

"Suz is sort of a friend of mine," I explained. "He says he knows everything that goes on in the Enchanted Forest, so he ought to know where the Living Spring is. I wish he were here."

"You do?" said a squeaky voice by my right foot. "Yes, you really do! How intriguing. Why do you?"

"Suz!" I said. I looked around until I saw him, then carefully sat down on the ground. "I'm awfully glad to see you. Do you know where the Living Spring is?"

"The Living Spring?" Suz said. "Dear me! Why do you want to know?"

"What's that?" asked the dragon, who had finally managed to find the source of the squeaky voice. "It looks like a little dragon."

"Oh, I'm sorry. This is Suz. I was just telling you about him. He's not a dragon, he's a lizard."

"A lizard of extremely good family." Suz frowned at the dragon, but the dragon didn't seem to notice. Suz gave up and looked back at me. "Now, why do you want to know about the Living Spring?"

"Because Shiara got turned into a statue by the fire-witch who lived in the invisible castle," I said.

"She did?" The lizard peered around until he saw the statue, then scurried over. He cocked his head briefly and stared upward, then ran up the gray stone in a spiral until he was sitting on one of the statue's shoulders. "She really did! How exceedingly distressing. What are you going to do about it?"

"We thought if we dropped the statue in the Living Spring, it would, well, fix Shiara," I said. "But we don't know where the spring is."

"You don't? No, of course you don't. It's a secret." Suz peered at me from Shiara's shoulder. "I suppose you want me to tell you where it is." He considered for a moment. "I couldn't possibly do that, so you needn't bother asking."

"But, Suz!" I said. "How else can we fix Shiara? I've tried the only other thing we could think of, and it didn't work."

"That is extremely obvious," the lizard said severely. He ran down the side of the staue and stopped right in front of me. "If it had worked, she wouldn't be a statue anymore, and you wouldn't be asking me silly questions." Suz did whatever the thing was that he did to balance on his tail. "People who are looking for things in the Enchanted Forest have to find them for themselves. You really ought to know that, you really ought."

"Well, what are we going to do about Shiara if you won't tell us where the spring is?"

"My goodness gracious, you certainly are persistent," Suz said. "Have you tried kissing her?"

"Kissing her?" I said incredulously.

"Kissing the statue," Suz explained condescendingly. "It's one of the standard cures for being made to sleep for years, or being turned into a frog or a statue or such. Have you tried it?"

I felt my face getting hot. "Um, well, no."

"Well, then," Suz said pointedly.

I thought about it for a minute or two. Shiara might not think much of my kissing her, but I didn't really object, especially if it would break the spell. In fact, I sort of liked the idea. At that point, I stood up very quickly because my face was getting even hotter and I could feel Suz staring at me.

I was right next to the statue, and as soon as I was all the way standing I leaned forward and kissed it. I didn't want to take time to look before I did it, because I didn't really want to think about it. First I felt cold stone, but it warmed up right away. A second later Shiara jerked away and said, "Hey! Daystar, what on earth do you think you're doing?"

"It worked!" I said. I was awfully relieved. If we hadn't been able to break the fire-witch's spell, we'd have had to bring the statue with us, and carrying a statue around would have been a lot of work. Besides, having Shiara back felt good, even if she *was* glaring at me.

"What worked?" Shiara demanded suspiciously. "And where did that witch go? She was here a minute ago."

"You were a statue," the dragon informed her. "The fire-witch did it, but Daystar got rid of her. I'm glad he did," it added thoughtfully. "I didn't like her. She wasn't polite at all, and she . . . and she . . ." The dragon leaned forward and said in a loud whisper, "And she grew dragonsbane!"

Shiara stared at the dragon, but before she could say anything there was a loud squeak from behind me, and Suz's voice started shouting. "Help! Murder! Wild beasts and dangerous lunatics! Oh dear oh my help help goodness gracious help oh!"

I turned around. Nightwitch had come out from wherever she'd been hiding and sneaked up on Suz while I was, well, kissing Shiara. Suz was rolled into a tight golden ball, and Nightwitch was batting him back and forth between her paws in wide-eyed fascination. I didn't think she'd ever played with a ball that yelled at her before.

I bent over to pick up Nightwitch, but before I actually got hold of her the lizard uncurled very quickly, slapped his tail sharply against the kitten's nose, and curled up tight again. He didn't stop yelling the whole time. The kitten jerked her head back so fast that she sat down hard on her tail, and I grabbed her.

"It's all right now, Suz," I said.

The lizard poked his nose out of the ball. "You're quite certain?" he said.

"Yes, of course," I said.

Suz uncurled a little more. "This sort of thing is quite unsettling," he said. "I do not approve at all. Dear me, no, not at all."

"I'm very sorry," I said. "I'm afraid I didn't know she was there."

"People who keep wild animals ought to know where they are so they don't go around eating other people," the lizard said. He uncurled the rest of the way and lay on the moss, peering reproachfully up at me.

I bent down, and Suz scooted back a couple of feet. "You keep that—that beast away from me!"

"Nightwitch isn't a wild animal, she's a kitten," Shiara said indignantly. "And I don't believe she meant to eat you. She just wanted to play."

"She's too young to know better," I said. Shiara glared at me, and I added hastily, "Nightwitch, I mean."

"She is?" The lizard squinted at Nightwitch from a safe distance. "Yes, I suppose she is," he said reluctantly. "How unfortunate. I really do think I had better leave. Dear me, yes, I really must."

Suz nodded and headed off into the woods.

"Suz, wait!" Shiara called.

The lizard stopped and looked back over his shoulder. "What is it?"

"I'm sorry Nightwitch scared you," Shiara said.

"You are?" Suz turned around and ran back to where Shiara was standing. He cocked his head at her, then did his tangled tail-balancing trick and stared up at her. "Why, you really *are!* How astonishing! How extraordinary! How extremely unexpected!"

I was a little surprised myself, but I decided I'd better change the subject before Shiara got offended. "Suz?"

The lizard turned his head and looked at me.

"What's the best way to get to the castle where Kazul lives?" I asked.

"Why, it's–" Suz paused. "Dear me, there seems to be an invisible castle in the way. How ridiculous. I'm afraid you'll just have to go around."

"That's what I thought," I said. "But thank you anyway."

"It's quite all right. And I really must be going now, I really must. Good-bye." Suz bowed politely, then did a quick back flip and scurried off into the woods.

"And thank you for telling me how to change Shiara back!" I called.

Suz didn't answer. I turned back to find Shiara glaring at me again.

"All right, Daystar, explain. What's all this about statues and getting rid of witches?"

"I already told you all that," the dragon said in an injured tone. "Why do you want him to tell you again?"

"Because I didn't understand it when you told it," Shiara said. She sounded a lot like Mother. "And I want to know what's been going on." She sat down on the ground and looked at me. "So explain."

I explained. Shiara let me talk until I started to explain how we'd finally turned her from a statue back into Shiara, but then she interrupted. "You don't have to keep going," she said. She gave me an odd look. "I remember that part."

"Oh. I'm sorry," I offered. My face was getting hot again. "But no one could think of anything else, and it did work."

Shiara wasn't paying much attention. "Daystar, did your sword burn your hands when Antorell tried to throw that spell at you?" she asked suddenly.

"No," I said, relieved by the change of subject. "It didn't do anything at all."

"It did, too!" Shiara said. "It ate Antorell's spell. And it didn't do anything to you. Why didn't it work like that on the fire-witch's spell?"

"Who's Antorell?" asked the dragon.

"The wizard you were sneezing at when we met," I said. "He's not very pleasant."

"Wizards aren't," the dragon said.

"Daystar, this is important!" Shiara said. "Why didn't your sword work the same way on the fire-witch as it did on Antorell?"

"Fire-witches and wizards are different," I said. "It makes sense that the sword does different things to them. I wish it *would* get rid of Antorell, though. Then I could stop worrying about him."

Shiara said something else, but I missed it. All of a sudden I had the same itchy feeling I'd had earlier, as if someone were watching me. I looked over my shoulder, but there wasn't anyone there. Just trees.

"Daystar?" Shiara almost sounded worried.

"I'm all right," I said. "But can we get started and talk about this somewhere else? We still have to get to see Kazul, and there's an invisible castle in the way."

"Shouldn't we do something about the people she turned into statues for her garden?" Shiara said, looking nervously at the clearing where the castle ought to be.

"Why?" said the dragon in a puzzled tone.

"Because it wouldn't be right to just leave them there," I said.

No one seemed to like the idea of going into the castle. No one wanted to leave the fire-witch's statue people there, either. We spent a little while trying to figure out how to get into the castle. Shiara wanted to climb over the wall, but I didn't think that was a very good idea if we couldn't see the wall or what was on the other side. Finally, she agreed to help me look for a door or a gate or something.

We stretched our hands out in front of us and walked carefully toward the castle. It wasn't there. We went a little farther. It still wasn't there. We walked around the clearing for a few minutes while the dragon watched with interest. Eventually, we gave up.

"I don't understand," Shiara said as we came back to pick up Nightwitch and Morwen's bundles. "Where did it go?"

"Maybe the fire-witch moved it while she was talking to me," I said.

"A whole castle? That fast? Besides, didn't Suz say it was still in the way? It must have moved since he left." Shiara stopped, and her eyes widened. "Daystar, you don't think she could still be around, do you?"

"She isn't around anywhere," the dragon said positively. "She went up in smoke. I saw her."

"Good," Shiara said savagely. I must have looked awfully surprised, because Shiara glared at me and added, "She deserved it. You don't know what she had to do to make that castle invisible."

"What was it?" the dragon asked curiously.

Shiara glared at it, too. "I don't want to talk about it."

"Why not?" said the dragon.

"Because she tortured people to death!" Shiara shouted. "It was part of the spell, and I know how to do it, and I don't want to think about it!"

"I told you she wasn't a nice person," the dragon said.

Shiara snorted. She picked up Nightwitch and her bundle and walked straight across the clearing. After a couple of seconds, the dragon and I followed.

Once we got across the clearing, the dragon took the lead again. Nobody said much for the rest of the morning, which was fine with me; I still felt as if someone was watching me, and I didn't like it. Finally even the dragon noticed.

"You look a little strange," it said. "Is something wrong?"

"I don't think so," I said. "I just feel like someone's watching me."

"You're imagining things," Shiara said. "I've been looking since you told me about it this morning, and I haven't seen anyone."

"Someone's following us?" the dragon said. It blinked at me, then turned in a slow circle, eyeing the trees. "You're right," it said finally. "Someone is following us. That's not polite."

Before Shiara or I could say anything, the dragon's head shot out toward one of the trees. I'd never seen anything move so fast. There was a loud yell from someone who wasn't the dragon. Then the dragon yelped and a bunch of leaves came drifting down to the ground. I heard a couple of crashing noises and another, louder yell, and then the dragon reappeared. Dangling by the seat of his pants from the dragon's mouth was an elf.

I stared for a minute, trying to decide whether this was the same elf we'd met before. He *looked* the same, but all elves look alike. Besides, he was yelling and kicking, and every now and then the dragon would shake its head, which made it hard to see the elf clearly.

I almost laughed; the dragon looked a lot like a very large cat with a very small mouse.

Nightwitch evidently thought so, too. She eyed the wriggling elf with some interest, then glanced up at me. "Mrrow?" she said.

"I'm afraid he's too big for you," I said.

"He certainly is!" yelled the elf. "Put me down! Let me down at once!"

"Mrof!" said the dragon through a mouthful of cloth.

"I don't think he wants to," I said to the elf. "Why were you following us?"

"Hey!" said Shiara. "Are you the elf we ran into before? Because if you are, I want to talk to you."

The elf stopped struggling and looked down at Shiara. Then he twisted around and looked at the dragon. "On the other hand, maybe I'm better off up here," he said.

"Mmnuf!" said the dragon, and shook its head violently.

"Yow!" said the elf. "Help! I surrender!"

"Really?" Shiara said skeptically.

"Really!" said the elf. "Absolutely! Completely and without question. Will you put me down?"

"Maybe you should," I said to the dragon. "I don't think he can get away from all of us, and it will be a lot easier for you to talk."

The dragon looked at me for a minute, then slowly lowered its head and dropped the elf in a heap in front of us. The elf lay there breathing hard while Shiara and the dragon and I closed in around him. As soon as we stopped moving, he bounced to his feet and spun rapidly in a circle, bowing to each of us. Then he sat down cross-legged and looked up at us with bright black eyes.

"Now," said the elf, "what can I do for you?"

12

In Which They Ask Many Questions

We looked at each other and then at the elf. "What you can do," said Shiara, "is answer some questions."

"My dear lady, I would be delighted," the elf said. "What do you want to know?"

"Why were you following us?" the dragon rumbled.

"I thought *she* was asking the questions," said the elf.

"We're *all* asking questions," Shiara told him. "So you can just stop dodging and answer that one."

"What one?" the elf said. The dragon growled and made a snapping motion at the elf, who jerked back hastily. "Yes, ah, of course," he said. "*That* question. I was, um, looking for information."

"Information? Ha!" said Shiara. "What kind of information?"

"Who you are, where you're going, and what you're going to do when you get there," the elf replied promptly. He was pointedly not looking at the dragon.

"That's all?" Shiara said sarcastically. "It sounds a lot like what we want to know about you."

"How nice," the elf said, beaming. "We have something in common."

"Excuse me," I broke in. "But who exactly are you?"

The elf looked at me with a pained expression. "I'm an elf."

"I can see that," I said politely. "But would you mind telling me your name? I mean, I'd sort of like to know to whom I'm speaking."

"My dear boy, I would be delighted." The elf rose and bowed with a flourish. "My name," he said, "is Janril." He sat down again and looked at me expectantly.

"Pleased to meet you, Janril," I said. "This is Shiara, that's Nightwitch . . ." I hesitated a moment. Dragons don't pick their names until they're old enough to pick what sex they're going to be, too, and I wasn't quite sure how to introduce one. I couldn't leave it out, though. "This is a dragon–"

"Somehow I guessed," the elf muttered.

"–and I'm Daystar," I finished.

Shiara was frowning at me, but before she could say anything the elf bounced to his feet and said, "Daystar! Not Cimorene's son? My dear boy, I can't tell you how glad I am you've finally come. It's about time things got straightened out a little."

"I don't trust elves," Shiara said. "And why should we listen to you, anyway?"

"My dear girl, if you expect me to answer questions, you're going to have to listen to me," said the elf. "Otherwise there's no point in it. Why don't you trust elves?"

Shiara didn't want to tell him anything, but I was beginning to like him. Also, I didn't see any good reason not to explain, so I told him about the first elf and the wizard's staff. When I finished, Janril nodded solemnly.

"That," he said, "makes your position entirely understandable. I'm afraid you ran into one of the Darkmorning Elves. They're a rather disreputable lot. They've been running wild since the King disappeared, so of course they'd cause you trouble."

"Why 'of course'?" said Shiara suspiciously. "And what king are you talking about?"

"The King of the Enchanted Forest," the elf said. "The Darkmorning Elves don't want him to come back. They like the way things have been run since he disappeared. Since you have his sword, of course they want to get rid of you. If they can," he added thoughtfully. "Personally, I don't think they really know what they're doing."

"How do you know about Daystar's sword?" Shiara asked suspiciously.

"My dear girl, everyone who lives in the Enchanted Forest knows something about the Vanished King's Sword," Janril said. "It–"

"Wait a minute!" I said. "I only have one sword, and I thought it was called the Sword of the Sleeping King."

"Sleeping, vanished, run away–what difference does it make?" Janril said. "He's *gone.*"

"I don't care about the sword," the dragon said. "I want to know why you were following us."

The elf looked annoyed. "My dear . . . ah . . . dragon," he said, "I told you already, I wanted to find out more about you. I believe that's the usual reason for following people around."

"But that doesn't explain anything," the dragon complained.

Shiara's eyes narrowed suddenly. "All right, then, why did you want to know more about us?"

Janril considered for a moment, then grinned reluctantly. "Because I'm trying to find out what the Darkmorning Elves are up to."

"What does that have to do with us?" I asked.

"If I knew that, I wouldn't have to follow you," the elf said reasonably. "But the Darkmorning Elves have been very active in this part of the woods for the past few days, and we thought it might be you they were interested in. And of course, if they're interested, so are we."

"Who do you mean by 'we'?" I said.

"The Goldwing-Shadowmusic Elves," Janril said with a touch of pride. "*We* are on the side of the King, even if he is missing right now. We follow the sword."

"What does that mean?" Shiara demanded. "And how many kinds of elves are there?"

"Quite a few," said Janril. "But the only ones you have to watch out for are the Darkmorning Elves and the Silverstaff Elves. Fortunately, the Silverstaff Elves don't know the sword is back yet, but I doubt that your luck will hold much longer."

"How do you know these Silverstaff Elves don't know about Daystar's sword?" Shiara asked.

"My dear girl, if they did, you'd have wizards all over the place. The Silverstaff Elves are in league with them. Undiscriminating, that's all I can call it." Janril looked prim. A prim elf is almost as odd looking as a dignified lizard. I found myself wishing Suz were still around so I could compare them.

"How do we know you're telling the truth?" Shiara said.

"I suppose you don't," the elf said cheerfully. "But it doesn't really matter. We'll still be glad to help you."

Shiara snorted. "The last elf who said he was going to help us almost got Daystar killed."

"I'm sorry about that," Janril said politely. "But I simply can't take responsibility for the Darkmorning Elves. Now, I must be going; I have to let the rest of the Goldwing-Shadowmusic Elves know what's going on. We'll see you at the castle."

"Just a minute!" Shiara said. "What makes you think we're going to let you go?"

"Can you think of anything else we could do with him?" I said.

"I could eat him, I suppose," the dragon said dubiously. "I don't think I want to, though. Elves don't taste very good."

I decided not to ask how the dragon knew that. "You don't have to eat him," I said. "I think we should just let him go."

"But Daystar–" Shiara stopped and thought for a moment, biting her lip. "Oh, all right. If you want to let him go, let's do it."

"Are you sure?" I said, surprised. "I thought you didn't like the idea."

"I don't," Shiara said, glaring at me. "But we'll be here all day if we start arguing. Besides, it's *your* sword."

"All right," I said to Janril, "You can go, as long as you don't follow us around anymore."

"But of course!" The elf bounced to his feet again, bowed to each of us–including Nightwitch–and whisked off. Shiara scowled after him and opened her mouth, then apparently decided not to say anything.

"Well, let's go," I said after a minute. We picked up our bundles and started walking again. The dragon and I both watched the trees for a while, but Janril kept his promise.

Shiara walked just behind the dragon, looking thoughtful. "Do you really believe that elf?" she finally asked me.

"I'm not sure," I said. "I don't think it makes much difference, though. I'd still be going to see Kazul, no matter what he said. I want to find out about this sword and what it does and what's really going on around here."

I must have sounded annoyed, because Shiara frowned at me and asked, "What's the matter with you?"

"I'm getting sort of tired of people chasing my sword," I said. "I'd like to know why they want it so badly." I was also beginning to realize that I didn't know nearly as much about the Enchanted Forest as I thought I did, which made me very nervous. I wasn't going to mention that to Shiara just yet, though.

"Oh." Shiara looked thoughtful again. "Well, you could–"

The dragon looked backward over its shoulder. "You're slowing down," it said. "Can't you two talk and walk at the same time?"

We made fairly good time for the rest of the afternoon, and we were just beginning to think about finding a place to spend the night when we came to a clearing. The dragon stopped right at the edge of it, very abruptly. Fortunately, Shiara and I were back far enough to stop before we ran into it or stepped on its tail or something. Bumping into a dragon is not a particularly good way to end a day.

"What's the matter now?" asked Shiara.

"This looks just like that last clearing," the dragon said. "The one that had the castle in it."

"You mean we've been going in circles?" Shiara said.

"No," said the dragon. "I know my way around the Enchanted Forest better than that. I just don't like this."

"Why are you worried?" Shiara said. "*You're* not the one who got turned into a statue."

"Well, if you think banging into something you can't see is fun, you go first," said the dragon.

I put my hand on the hilt of my sword and felt a nice, strong rumble, like a cart full of bricks on a bumpy road. There was definitely a lot of magic in the clearing, or at least close by. I said so.

"If it's invisible, I don't want anything to do with it," Shiara said decidedly. "Can't we just go around?"

"No," said the dragon grumpily. "I want to know who's putting all these invisible things in my shortcut. If there's another one here, I'm going to find out about it." It stalked cautiously out into the clearing, heading straight through the middle.

Nothing happened. The dragon walked all the way across, then turned and looked at us. "Are you *sure* there's something here? I can't find anything."

I touched the sword again. "It feels like there is," I said. I looked at Shiara. She looked dubiously across the clearing. "Hurry up," said the dragon.

I sighed and started forward. I kept one hand on the hilt of my sword, just in case, and I walked across the same part of the clearing the dragon had. Shiara shook her head and started around the edge of the clearing.

I got about five steps. Then there was a *whooshing* noise and a wall of flames shot up around me, very hot and bright. I yelled, because I couldn't see where I was going, and I yanked at my sword. I think I had some vague idea that the sword might keep me from burning to death; I certainly couldn't see to fight anything.

Something hit me in the middle of my back just as the sword came out of its sheath. I felt a wave of anticipation from the sword followed very closely by a surge of disappointment. I was so surprised I nearly dropped it. Then I realized that it wouldn't matter if I *did* drop it, because I was lying on the ground. I was also much cooler than I had been a minute ago, and someone was pounding on me.

"Stop it!" I said.

The someone sat back, and I saw that it was Shiara. "Are you all right?" she asked.

"I think so," I said. "Why were you pounding on me?"

"Your clothes were on fire," Shiara said. "I was trying to put them out. If I'd known you were going to fuss about it, I'd have let them burn."

I apologized and thanked her, then looked around. Shiara and I were sitting on the ground, just inside a ring of fire. In the center of the ring was a short, round building with a pointed roof. It wasn't quite tall enough to call a tower, but it wasn't short enough to call a house, either. I moved away from the flames, which were uncomfortably warm, and looked at Shiara. "What happened?"

"How should I know? One second you were walking across the clearing, and the next second there was all this fire and you were yelling," Shiara said. "And when I tried to shove you out of it, we both got in here instead, and that thing was sitting there." She waved at the not-quite-tower.

"At least it isn't invisible," I offered. Shiara gave me a disgusted look, but she didn't say anything.

"Hello?" called the dragon's voice from the other side of the wall of fire. "Are you there?"

"We're here," I called back. "Both of us."

"How did you do that?" the dragon shouted.

"I don't know," I said. "And I don't want to stay here to find out." I picked myself up off the ground and put the sword back in its sheath. "I think maybe we'd better go," I said to Shiara. "Before something comes out of that house."

"It isn't a house," Shiara said. "But for once I agree with you."

"Achoo!" said the dragon from the other side of the fire.

"Just a minute, there!" a voice said behind me.

I turned around. A medium-sized man was standing about ten feet away, leaning on a staff that was about three feet taller than he was. He had black hair and three rings on each hand, and he was frowning irritably at Shiara and me.

"Oh, rats," said Shiara disgustedly. "Another wizard!"

"You," said the man, ignoring her statement completely, "are trespassing. I don't know how you got in here, but it was a great mistake for you to do so."

"We didn't exactly do it on purpose," I said. "We were just trying to get across the clearing."

"Young man, I surround my home with a wall of fire for a reason," the wizard said. "And the reason is that I do not like to be disturbed. I wish to know how you penetrated it, or I would not be wasting my time talking with you."

"I'm a fire-witch, that's how!" Shiara said. "And if you don't want to be disturbed, you ought to be more careful with your stupid wall. We would have gone right by if it hadn't jumped up all over Daystar when he tried to cross the clearing!"

"A fire-witch?" the man said. He gave Shiara an extremely odd look. "You haven't mislaid an invisible castle recently, have you?"

"No!" said Shiara. "It isn't mine!"

The wizard looked even angrier. "You know of it!"

"Well, sort of," I said. "It isn't ours, but we ran into it this morning."

"Did you," said the wizard. He sounded skeptical and very dangerous. I decided I didn't want to talk about the castle anymore.

"I think we ought to be going now," I said. "We're really very sorry to have bothered you."

"I'm not!" Shiara said.

"Shiara!"

"Well, I'm not," Shiara said. "He ought to apologize to us, not the other way around. And anyway, I'm not apologizing to any wizard, especially not one that messes around with invisible castles!"

The man with the staff frowned, but this time he looked more thoughtful than angry. "What is your complaint against wizards?"

"Ha!" said Shiara. "You should know."

"No," said the man, "I should not. I am not a wizard."

"ACHOO!" came the dragon's voice, and the wall of fire bulged inward on that side.

"Excuse me, but if you're not a wizard, why are you carrying a staff?" I asked. "And why is the dragon sneezing?"

The man looked startled. "Dragon? You travel with a dragon?"

"No, it travels with us," I said. "Does it make a difference?"

"Perhaps," the man said. He looked at the wall of fire and made a pass with his staff. The flames began to die, and a moment later we could see the clearing again.

13

In Which They Learn the Difference Between a Wizard and a Magician

The dragon was still sneezing in medium-sized puffs of flame. The man with the staff examined it and shook his head. "That certainly is a dragon." He made another pass with his staff.

The staff vanished, and the dragon stopped sneezing abruptly. It sniffed a couple of times in an experimental way, looking surprised, as if it expected to start sneezing again any minute. I was surprised, too. I mean, wizards *never* let go of their staffs–not willingly, anyway.

The man bowed politely to the dragon. "I apologize for inconveniencing you," he said. "I offer you greetings and welcome to my home, and I wish you good fortune when you leave."

"What?" said the dragon.

The man looked a little startled and peered at the dragon more closely. "Oh, I see," he said after a moment. "Well, you're welcome. Come and make yourself comfortable."

Shiara scowled at him and bent to pick up Nightwitch, who had come running toward her as soon as the flames had died. The dragon looked suspiciously at the man.

"I don't like wizards," it said. "And I don't like people who put invisible things in the middle of my shortcut."

"I am not a wizard," the man said with a sigh. "And my tower has been here for years, and it isn't invisible. Now, come in and talk. There hasn't been a dragon by for a long time, and I'm a bit behind on the news."

"If you're not a wizard, what *are* you?" Shiara said, petting Nightwitch and glaring at the man.

"I'm a magician," the man said. "And my name is Telemain."

"Pleased to meet you," I said.

"Mrrow," said Nightwitch, and started purring loudly.

Telemain looked at the kitten, and suddenly he began to laugh. He had a nice laugh, sort of deep and friendly. I started thinking that I might be able to like him after all, even if his fire wall had nearly burned me to a cinder.

"I don't believe I have ever seen a group quite like this one," Telemain said when he finished laughing. "Please, tell me who you all are."

I introduced everyone, and Telemain nodded courteously to each of us. He gave me a sharp look when I told him my name. "I thought that was what your friend called you," he said. "Welcome to my home."

"Some welcome!" Shiara said. "You nearly got Daystar killed, and you started the dragon sneezing again. And how come the dragon was allergic to you if you aren't a wizard?"

"Dragons aren't allergic to wizards," Telemain said, sounding surprised. "What gave you that idea?"

"I did!" the dragon said. It came forward and sat down emphatically, right next to me. "All dragons are allergic to wizards. I should know: I sneeze every time I get near one." It eyed Telemain belligerently.

"Oh, I don't doubt that at all," Telemain said. "But the hypersensitive reaction results from the indiscriminate absorption of magical energy through the enchantments fixed in their staffs."

"What?" said the dragon.

Telemain sighed. "It's not wizards you're allergic to, it's their staffs. You stopped sneezing as soon as I got rid of mine, didn't you?"

The dragon looked startled. "I did, didn't I?" it said after a minute.

"If you aren't a wizard, what are you doing with a wizard's staff?" Shiara asked.

Telemain raised his eyebrows. "Why do you ask?"

"We've been having some trouble with wizards," I said before Shiara could answer. I didn't want her to make him angry. We had enough people mad at us already.

"Really." Telemain looked as if he were going to laugh again. "All of you?"

"Well, mainly just Shiara and me," I said. "We've been sort of worried about them. Most of them are after Shiara," I added.

"What would the Society of Wizards want with a fire-witch?" Telemain said. "I can see that I shall have to invite you in, if only to hear your tale."

"How do you know about the Society?" Shiara said angrily. "And why should we trust a wizard, anyway?"

"Anyone who knows much about magic can tell you're a fire-witch, and the only reason I can think of for a fire-witch to have several wizards after her is if she has done something to offend the Society of Wizards," Telemain said. He still sounded amused. "And for the third time, at least, I am a magician, not a wizard."

"What's the difference?" Shiara demanded.

"Magicians deal with many ways of magic," Telemain said. "Wizards with only one. Now, will you come in and sit down?"

Shiara was still looking at him doubtfully. Telemain smiled. "Will an oath content you? If you mean no harm, I am not your enemy, and I will do you no harm while you are my guests, save in self-defense. I swear by the sword."

I felt a kind of popping at my side, even though I wasn't touching the sword, and a ripple ran through the clearing, like a shimmer of light in the air. I thought it kept on going out into the forest, but I couldn't be certain. Shiara started and dropped Nightwitch, who landed on her feet with a yowl. The dragon stretched its neck, looking almost as if it were trying to purr.

Telemain suddenly looked very intense.

"That is the way of it, then?" he said when the ripple passed. "I don't think I blame you for your caution." He looked pointedly at my sword.

Shiara scowled again, but I thought she looked a little more doubtful than the last time. "If you're so smart . . ." she began, and stopped. Nightwitch was rubbing against Telemain's leg and purring. *"Nightwitch?"* said Shiara.

"An intriguing name for a cat," Telemain said, bending over to pick up Nightwitch. "Even more interesting for a kitten. Where did you come by her?"

"She was a present," Shiara said grudgingly. "From a witch named–"

"Morwen?" said Telemain. Nightwitch purred louder. "I suspected as much. Now, will you come in? Or do you wish to continue this discussion where anyone may hear?"

We went in. The door of Telemain's home looked like an ordinary, normal-sized door, but it couldn't have been, because the dragon fit through it without any trouble. The room inside was made of stone and very bare. In the center of the floor, two iron staircases twisted around each other in a spiral and disappeared into the ceiling. The whole place seemed much taller from the inside. If I hadn't seen it before we came in, I would have been sure we were in a tower.

As the door closed behind the dragon, Telemain waved his hand. A table and three chairs materialized beside the stairs. "Sit down and tell me more about yourselves."

We sat down, except for the dragon, who sort of curled itself around the edges of the room. I started explaining about Mother and Antorell and everything that had happened in the Enchanted Forest. I even told him about the Sword of the Sleeping King, because I was pretty sure from the way he looked at it that he already knew something about it. The questions he asked made it pretty clear that I was right, although sometimes he got so technical that I had to ask him to repeat something. He sounded as if he knew exactly what answers he expected, too. When I told him about the voice that had said, "All hail the Bearer of the Sword," he nodded in satisfaction.

Then I explained how Shiara and I had met, and why the wizards were after her, and about the one who'd tried to get us at the stream. Shiara frowned at me, but she didn't interrupt. When I told him about meeting Morwen, Telemain seemed very interested.

"I haven't seen Morwen in a long time," he said. "How is she?"

"You know Morwen?" Shiara said.

"We grew up together," Telemain said. "Now, exactly what did she have you do to repair the damage to your hand?"

Telemain asked a lot of questions about the things the Sword of the Sleeping King had done, but he didn't seem particularly interested in the wizards. He wasn't interested in the Princess at all. Then I told him about the invisible castle and the fire-witch.

"So that's how you knew about it," Telemain said. "I wondered."

"That's how *we* knew," Shiara said. "How did *you* know?"

"The castle landed in my clearing sometime around noon," Telemain said dryly. "I was understandably curious as to why someone would go to all the trouble of making a castle invisible and then drop it on top of a magician who can't help noticing it."

"It's not there now," Shiara said.

"Of course not! What would I want with an invisible castle? When I found no one home, I cleaned the place up a bit and got rid of it."

"Cleaned it up?" I said, puzzled.

"The most recent owner had a number of unattractive habits," Telemain said even more dryly than before. "In addition to casual petrification of passersby, she indulged in seven varieties of involuntary metamorphosis, as well as necromancy and demonology. I don't believe you would be at all interested in the technical details."

"Oh." He was right; I didn't really want to know about it.

Telemain looked at Shiara again. "I owe you an apology," he said. "I knew that the castle was the property of a fire-witch, and I'm afraid that when you showed up, I thought you had some connection with it."

"Well, I don't, but I suppose I can see why you might have gotten mad." Shiara sounded a lot friendlier than she had before. I think she would have been friendly to anyone who didn't like that other fire-witch. Then she frowned. "How did the castle get into your clearing, anyway?"

Telemain shrugged. "As far as I can tell, the unit transportation spell operated on a set of totally random parameters, both in terms of time and location."

"What does *that* mean?" said the dragon.

"The castle was designed to move around the Enchanted Forest more or less randomly. It's a rather unusual spell to put on a building, particularly an invisible one, because if you happen to be outside when it moves, you get left behind."

"Then why on earth would anyone put a stupid spell like that on a castle?"

"Presumably this fire-witch didn't expect to have any problems finding the castle again. I don't believe it occurred to her that someone else might find it first." He smiled. "I left a few surprises for her. I doubt that she'll be pleased."

"Oh, that's all right," the dragon said. "Daystar got rid of her."

Telemain looked at me. "Really. How did you manage that?"

"She threw some sort of spell at me, but Nightwitch scratched her, so she missed," I said. "And after that, I had the sword out."

"You used the Sword of the Sleeping King on a fire-witch?" Telemain said. He sounded somewhere between shocked and horrified.

"I couldn't think of anything else that might work," I said apologetically. "And it did work, sort of. I mean, it got rid of the fire-witch."

"She went up in smoke," the dragon said with considerable satisfaction. "I watched."

"She went up in smoke," Telemain repeated in tones of fascination. "And what were you doing while this was going on?"

"I was trying to hang on to the sword," I said. "It was glowing red, and my hands felt like they were burning or something, so it was sort of hard to do. But as soon as the fire-witch was gone, it stopped."

"You are extremely fortunate," Telemain said. "You might have gotten yourself killed and ruined everything. I don't recommend that you try that again. Stick to wizards. That's what the sword was meant for."

"It was?" said Shiara. "How do you know? What else does it do?"

Telemain looked at her. "Magicians know many kinds of magic." He turned back to me. "Please, continue."

I was curious about what the sword did, too, but Telemain obviously didn't want to talk about it, so I didn't ask. Instead, I explained about fixing Shiara and not finding the castle and meeting the second elf. Telemain listened carefully, then shook his head.

"So the war is beginning again," he said, half to himself. "I had best make my own preparations. I wonder why no one let me know?"

"War?" Shiara and I said together.

Telemain looked up, almost as if he had forgotten we were there. "The war between the dragons and the wizards," he said in the tones of someone trying to be patient.

The dragon, who had been falling asleep, suddenly came awake. "War with the wizards?"

"It is obvious," Telemain said a trifle crossly. "The elves are choosing sides, the dragons are restless, the wizards are coming into the Enchanted Forest in large numbers, and the Sword of the Sleeping King has returned. What more do you need to know?"

"What does the Sword of the Sleeping King have to do with a war between the dragons and the wizards?" I asked before the dragon could take offense.

"The sword is what started the war in the first place," Telemain said, and then he refused to say any more. "If Cimorene didn't see fit to explain, I certainly won't," he said. "When you meet Kazul, I am sure she will tell you whatever you need to know. I'm afraid I don't have time at the moment. I must see to things at once, if we are to win this war at last."

"Who do you mean, 'we'?" Shiara asked suspiciously.

"The dragons," Telemain said, "and the rest of us who follow the sword. Now, if you will excuse me?" He rose and started for the stairs.

"Wait a minute!" Shiara said. "What about us?"

"What? Oh, of course," Telemain said. He waved his hand again and muttered something, and suddenly the table was full of plates and bowls of food. I jumped. Telemain didn't seem to notice. "Help yourselves while I am gone," he said. "I don't expect to be long." He turned away and went up one of the iron staircases.

Shiara and I looked at each other. "Now what do we do?" Shiara said.

"*I'm* going to eat," I said. "Would you like something?"

Shiara snorted, but she reached for one of the bowls. There was plenty for all of us, including Nightwitch and the dragon. About the time we finished, Telemain came back.

"I was right," he said to no one in particular. Then he looked at me. "You'd better stay here for the night. It will be much safer for everyone, and it will give me time to look into things a little more. You've been extremely lucky so far, but there's no reason to take any more chances until you must."

I started to nod, then looked at Shiara. Shiara looked at me, then at Nightwitch, who was curled into a small ball on Telemain's chair. She shrugged. "Let's stay."

"You will find rooms upstairs, on the second floor," Telemain said. "Just pick one and go in." He turned to the dragon. "I think you'll be more comfortable down here."

"I think you're right," said the dragon, eyeing the iron staircases a little dubiously.

"And thank you very much for your hospitality," I said.

Telemain nodded. Shiara and I started for the stairs. Shiara got there ahead of me and started climbing, but she didn't get anywhere. "What's the matter?" I asked.

"There's something wrong with this stupid staircase!" Shiara said. "I keep trying to climb up, but I don't go anywhere!"

Telemain, who had been talking quietly to the dragon, turned. "I'm sorry; I should have warned you. You'll have to take the other staircase. That one incorporates a unidirectional matrix focused groundward."

"Say that again, in English," Shiara said.

"That stairway just works going down."

"That's ridiculous!" said Shiara. "How can a staircase only work going in one direction?"

"He's a magician," I said.

We didn't have any trouble getting up the other stairway. Telemain's tower really was a lot taller than it looked from the outside; the stairs kept going after they got to the second floor. Shiara and I didn't climb any farther, though. We got off on the landing at the second floor and looked around.

We were standing on a narrow circle of wooden floor around the hole where the two staircases came through. Around the edge were six identical wooden doors.

"Well, he said to just go in," Shiara said.

Each of us picked a door and opened it. The rooms were all the same and very comfortable looking. They each had a bed, a table, a lighted lamp in a bracket on the wall, a padded chair, and a small set of drawers with a mirror above it. Shiara looked thoughtful. "I wonder if he keeps lights going in all these rooms?"

"He might," I said. "I mean, he *is* a magician. Does it matter?"

Shiara glared at me and went into the room she'd picked, slamming the door behind her. I stood there for a moment, wondering whether to knock on the door and apologize. In the end I decided to wait until morning to talk to her, since by then she probably wouldn't be mad anymore, and anyway I wasn't sure what I should apologize for.

I kept the Sword of the Sleeping King with me all night. It was a little uncomfortable sleeping that way, but I felt better knowing where it was. It wasn't that I didn't trust Telemain. I was just getting more and more worried about the sword. Everyone I met seemed to know about it, or want to know about it, or just want to get hold of it. I spent a lot of time thinking instead of sleeping.

Telemain served breakfast the next morning on his magic table. He was very quiet while we were eating, but as soon as we finished he looked at me and said, "I have watched the Enchanted Forest all night, and there are some things you should know, but I do not wish to detain you against your will."

"What things?" Shiara demanded.

Telemain smiled slightly. "I fear you will have some difficulty in reaching the castle," he said. "I found no less than twelve wizards searching the area between it and you."

"Oh, great," Shiara said disgustedly. "Just what we need–more wizards!"

"I don't think it's very good," the dragon said. "Why do you?"

"I don't," Shiara said.

"Then why did you say so?"

"What can we do about them?" I asked Telemain.

"I think you can avoid them if you go through the Caves of Chance," Telemain replied.

14

In Which the Dragon Has an Allergy Attack

We all stared. "Ha!" Shiara said finally. "The Caves of Chance are even more dangerous than the wizards!"

"I don't think so," Telemain said. "I have been through them, and they're not as bad as most people think. Furthermore, there is an entrance to the caves within half a day's travel, and an exit that is very close to the castle. And once you are inside the caves, the wizards will not be able to find you."

"Why not?" Shiara asked.

"The Caves of Chance do not welcome wizards' magic."

"Can you give us directions?" I asked.

Telemain nodded and pulled a large map out of his sleeve. Most people don't even *try* making maps of the Enchanted Forest because things change so fast that an ordinary map is only good for a few days, so I'd never seen one before. This map must have been magical, because it seemed fairly accurate. At least, all the things Shiara and I had seen were in the right places.

Telemain showed us where his tower was and where the castle was, and he pointed out several places he'd found wizards. Then he showed us the entrance to the caves. It really did look a lot closer and safer than trying to get by all those wizards. Even Shiara looked less doubtful.

Then Telemain turned the map over, and on the back was a map of the

Caves of Chance. He went over the routes from the entrance to the exit we wanted and what to do about some of the things we might run into inside. It was very interesting. I knew that trolls are allergic to milk, but I hadn't known that rock snakes like mirrors enough that they'll stop squeezing someone in order to look at their reflections. He also told us to hold anything we really didn't want to lose in one hand until we were out of the caves.

When Telemain was satisfied that we knew our way, he rolled the map up and put it back in his sleeve. We went outside to say good-bye.

"When you meet Kazul, tell her I will be coming for the battle," Telemain said. "I called her last night on the magic mirror to let her know that you're on your way, so she's expecting you."

"I'll remember," I said. "And thank you again for your help."

"Yes," said Shiara. I looked at her, a little surprised, but she was watching Telemain with an odd look on her face. "I think I ought to apologize to you," she said finally. "I wasn't very nice last night."

This time I really did stare, but she didn't seem to notice. Telemain bowed. "Neither of us was blameless," he said. "I shall forget it, if you will."

Shiara nodded and turned to me. "Let's go, then."

I shut my mouth and picked up the bundle Morwen had given me. Shiara already had hers. We waved good-bye to Telemain and started off into the forest again.

Nothing much happened all morning. Shiara and I were both nervous anyway, thinking of all those wizards ahead of us. The dragon didn't seem bothered, though, and Nightwitch certainly wasn't. We found the first few landmarks Telemain had told us about, and we were fairly close to the entrance to the Caves of Chance when the dragon stopped and demanded lunch.

As soon as the dragon mentioned food, Shiara and I realized that we were hungry, too. We started looking for a good place to sit down and eat. Almost immediately, we found a huge tree lying on the ground in the middle of a small clearing.

The dragon wrapped itself around a medium-sized tree in front of us; it said it was much more comfortable that way. Nightwitch wandered around investigating the interesting holes and crannies around the fallen tree. Shiara and I sat down and passed out gingerbread and meat pies from Morwen's bundles.

"How much farther is it to the castle?" Shiara asked the dragon, handing it a slice of gingerbread.

"Oh, not very far," the dragon said. "About another day, if we weren't going through the caves. I've never been in the caves, so I don't know how long that will take."

"I thought you said this was a shortcut," Shiara said.

"It *is* a shortcut," the dragon said in a hurt tone. "How was I supposed to know a fire-witch was going to get in the way? Not to mention an elf and a magician."

"Do you think Kazul will tell us anything about the sword?" I asked. Nobody else seemed willing to explain, and I didn't see why Kazul should be any different.

"I'm sure she will," the dragon said reassuringly. "That is, if you're polite to her. Kazul is very particular about . . . about . . . *ahh . . . ach . . .*"

Shiara and I dropped our lunches and ducked hastily to either side.

"Achoo!" said the dragon. A large spurt of flame shot across the clearing, just missing us, and the dragon's tree shook. *"Achoo!* Oh, bother. *Achoo!"*

"Daystar!" Shiara shouted. "Over here!"

I ran around behind the dragon, who was now sneezing almost continuously. I pulled out my sword as I went. When my hand touched the hilt, I felt the same jangling that I'd gotten from Antorell earlier. Then I came around the tree, and even before Shiara pointed, I saw the wizards.

There were two of them right in front of Shiara, leaning on their staffs and looking from Shiara to the dragon and back.

"Hurry up," one of them said nervously. "We don't want this to get out of hand."

"I'm afraid you'll have to wait," another voice said from behind him. The first wizard jumped, and Antorell stepped out of the bushes. His beard and hair were several inches shorter than they had been, and his staff had a scorched streak near the top, but getting caught in the little dragon's fireball didn't seem to have done much to him otherwise. He smiled and went on, "You see, I want him, too."

"Um, can't we discuss this somewhere else?" said the nervous wizard, eyeing the dragon.

"Oh, you needn't worry about that," Antorell said, following his gaze. He smiled nastily. "I came prepared." He held up his free hand so that all of us could see the spray of spiky, saw-edged purple leaves he was holding. "Dragonsbane," he said unnecessarily.

The other wizards relaxed a little. "Such forethought," murmured the tall one. He exchanged glances with his companion, then bowed to Antorell. "Under the circumstances, we will be happy to split the reward with you."

"I am afraid that is out of the question," Antorell said over the dragon's sneezes. "The boy and his sword are mine."

"The boy!" said the nervous wizard. "But–" The tall one frowned at him, and he stopped.

The tall wizard turned back to Antorell. "As you say, the boy is yours. I trust you have no objection if we take the girl?"

Antorell frowned. He turned toward Shiara and stared at her for a minute, then shrugged. "She's no use to me. Of course I have no objection."

I started moving very, very slowly toward Shiara, so that when the wizards started throwing spells at us I could try to stop them with the sword. The wizards didn't notice, and neither did Shiara. By the time the wizards finished deciding what to do with us, I was almost over to her.

"It's settled, then," Antorell said. "We help each other. The girl first?"

"Ah, why not start with the dragon?" the nervous wizard asked.

Antorell smiled condescendingly. "Very well." He stepped forward and started muttering over the dragonsbane. Right away the dragon started yelling.

"Yow!" it said. *"Achoo!* I hate wizards. Ouch! *Achoo!* Help!"

"You stop that!" Shiara said to Antorell. The wizards ignored her, and Antorell kept mumbling.

I started forward. If I could knock the dragonsbane out of Antorell's hand, the spell would stop. I wasn't sure whether it would be completely broken, but at least he wouldn't be able to hurt the dragon anymore. Unfortunately, I'd forgotten about the other wizards. I didn't even realize one of them had done something until my feet stuck to the ground and suddenly I couldn't walk forward anymore. If I hadn't been stuck, I'd have lost my balance. It was very disconcerting. Antorell was still out of reach.

I took a quick glance back over my shoulder. The dragon was sneezing much too hard now to say anything at all. I could see its coils going slack, and it was losing its hold on the tree. Here and there, its scales were turning pink around the edges. Even the tree looked wilted.

"Shiara!" I yelled. "Get the dragonsbane!" I didn't think I could get loose in time, but the wizards wouldn't be able to stop a fire-witch.

I didn't wait to see what she did. I leaned forward a little and tried to lay part of the Sword of the Sleeping King across my feet. It hadn't helped Shiara when she was a statue, but this was a wizard's spell, not a fire-witch's spell, and Telemain had said the sword was meant to be used on wizards. Besides, I couldn't think of anything else.

It worked. I straightened up just in time to see a little tongue of flame shoot up from Antorell's hand. Antorell yelled and dropped the dragonsbane, which was burning brightly. Before it even hit the ground, there was nothing left of the plant except ashes.

I looked behind me. Shiara was standing with a surprised look on her face and one finger pointing at Antorell. The dragon was still sneezing, but the green was already starting to come back to its scales. I sighed in relief.

"This is the assistance you give us?" the tall wizard said to Antorell, who was brushing ashes off the front of his robe. "The dragon still lives!"

"Did I say anything about killing it?" Antorell said. I got the feeling he was trying to sound haughty, but he only managed to sound annoyed. "You need have no more fear of it. It will take some time to regain its strength, and by then we shall be finished. What next?"

"The girl, I think," said the tall wizard. "That is, if you're sure you can handle her?"

Antorell glared. "That is the least of my problems," he said grandly.

"Ha!" said Shiara loudly. I moved back over to her, holding the sword in front of me. The three wizards looked at us, then at each other. "Let us begin," said the tall one.

All three of them raised their staffs, but instead of pointing them directly at us, they brought them together, so that they made a kind of star about a foot from their ends. There was a bright flash as the three staffs touched, and I felt a shock from my sword. I jumped, and suddenly I realized that I could feel the forest. The magic of the forest, I mean; it was all around me, waiting. I felt almost as if the whole Enchanted Forest were watching me.

Right in front of me, I could feel the wizards' power growing and building. There was a kind of pattern in it that kept getting clearer and more complicated, and I knew I had to do something about it before the wizards finished. I stepped forward and swung the sword right through the middle of the pattern.

I felt a huge jolt of power from the sword, but it didn't hurt the way the fire-witch's spell had. In fact, it didn't hurt at all. The pattern collapsed in an invisible tangle. Antorell's eyes started to narrow; the other two wizards just looked stunned. And then something exploded.

I couldn't see anything. It wasn't that things had gone dark, and it wasn't that the light had blinded me. It was more as if the whole world had suddenly become invisible, so there was nothing left to see. There was a rushing noise all around me, and I felt as if I were floating. I heard a chorus of voices cry, "All hail the Wielder of the Sword!" and then the noise and the voices vanished, and I was standing in the clearing with the Sword of the Sleeping King shining in my hand and three very surprised wizards in front of me.

I stared at the wizards. The wizards stared at me. Antorell recovered first.

"Enough of this!" he cried, and raised his staff. As he did, the ground in front of him humped up a little bit. A second later, a tree shot up about twelve feet into the air. It reminded me of someone opening an umbrella very quickly. The branches shivered once as the leaves unrolled, and then it burst into bloom with a sound like a hundred little bells tinkling.

Antorell looked even more surprised than before, then he scowled angrily and pointed his staff at me again. The tall wizard next to him grabbed his arm. "Wait, fool! Don't you know what that sword *is?*"

"Of course I know, oaf." Antorell's eyes sparked. "It is mine! I will have it!"

"You will be dead, you mean," the tall wizard said, but he let go of Antorell's arm. "This is a matter for the whole Society of Wizards. There may still be time to stop him if we can bring them quickly enough."

"More wizards? *Achoo!* Oh, no you don't! *Achoo!* Oh, drat, *achoo!"* said the dragon. It dove out of its tree, unwinding itself like a spool of string, very quickly. Its head shot past me, and I got a fleeting glimpse of green scales and golden eyes and a very, very red tongue. One of the wizards yelled, and the dragon sneezed again. I jumped forward just in time to see all three of the wizards vanish hastily. Antorell looked a little white and he had one hand clutched around a dark, wet-looking spot on his other arm as he disappeared.

I looked at the dragon. It snapped its teeth together twice, swallowed something, and sat back, looking very pleased with itself. "Wizards," it announced, "taste *much* better than elves."

I swallowed hard and decided I didn't really want to finish my lunch. The dragon looked at Shiara. Shiara scowled.

"Don't you look at me like that!" she said. "I'm not a wizard, I'm a fire-witch."

The dragon looked thoroughly shocked. "But I wouldn't eat you! You're my friend. It wouldn't be polite at all!"

Shiara looked suspiciously at the dragon, then nodded. "I just wanted to make sure you remembered."

"I think we'd better get going," I said. "Those wizards sounded like they were going to come back with reinforcements."

"Oh, terrific," said Shiara. "Let's go, then. Where's Nightwitch?"

"Mrow," said a kitten voice from somewhere above me.

I looked up. Nightwitch was perched on a branch of the tree that had sprouted up in the middle of the fight. She was washing her paws. She stopped and looked down at me for a second, then went back to washing.

"Nightwitch, come down!" Shiara said. "Those wizards might come back any minute!"

Nightwitch ignored her. The dragon came over and peered curiously at the tree. "Where did this come from?" it asked.

"It grew," I said. "I think you were sneezing when it happened."

"Kazul is going to be surprised about this!" the dragon said happily. "Two new trees in a couple of days!"

"What are you talking about?" Shiara said. "It's just a tree."

"No, it isn't," the dragon said. "It's a *new* tree. And it's the *second* new tree I've seen in two days, so it's important. The other one hit me on the nose," it added in an aggrieved tone.

"You mean it's been a long time since there were any new trees?" I asked.

The dragon nodded. "Kazul mentioned it once. She sounded worried. *I* think they're a nuisance, popping up like that."

"But where do they come from?" Shiara asked. "And why do they show up when we—" She stopped short, and we looked at each other.

"Daystar," said Shiara finally. "It's the wizards."

"It can't be," I said. "What about the first one?"

The dragon tilted its head to one side and looked at us. "What are you talking about?"

"The trees," Shiara said. "Both of them grew in places where a wizard threw a spell at us. . . . But there wasn't any tree when the first wizard tried to drown us, so it can't be wizards."

I looked down, trying to think, and saw the Sword of the Sleeping King in my hand. "It's the sword!" I said. "It stopped Antorell's spell the first time, and a little while later a tree sprouted. This time it stopped a bigger spell, and we got a bigger tree. It didn't stop any spells when the first wizard made that water monster, so no new trees grew. It *has* to be the sword."

"You didn't get a tree when you fought the fire-witch," Shiara objected, but she sounded half-convinced.

"Well, Telemain told us the sword was meant for wizards. It probably only does that for wizards' spells."

"Your sword grows trees?" the dragon said skeptically.

"It does sound a little silly," I said.

"Mmmrrrow!"

We all looked up. Nightwitch launched herself at Shiara, who just barely managed to catch her.

"Good," said Shiara. "Now, if you're all done fussing about trees and swords, how about leaving? Before the wizards come back."

The dragon and I looked at each other and nodded. We picked up our things and started off.

15

In Which They Take a Chance

The entrance to the Caves of Chance wasn't very difficult to find. That worried me a little, partly because Antorell and the other wizards would probably figure out where we had gone, and partly because it isn't usually that easy to find something in the Enchanted Forest. Especially if you're looking for it.

Not that the way into the Caves of Chance looked as if it would move around easily. It was a large, smooth, circular hole in the ground with moss growing right up to the edge of it, and it was very dark. The dragon and Shiara and I stood around the edge, staring down into it.

"How are we going to get down there?" Shiara asked finally. "I can't even tell how deep it is."

"We'll have to use the blankets Morwen gave us," I said. "We can tie them together."

"What about me?" said the dragon. "*I* can't climb down blankets."

"I don't know," I said. "Maybe we'll think of something once we know how far it is."

"What if you can't think of anything?"

"Hey!" Shiara had opened her bundle to get the blankets out, and now she was staring at it as if she'd never seen it before. "Daystar, look at this!"

The dragon looked a little put out. It usually isn't a good idea to interrupt someone's conversation with a dragon, but for once I decided not to say anything, because I was glad Shiara had yelled. I didn't *know* what was going to happen if I couldn't think of a way to get the dragon into the Caves of Chance, and I didn't really want to say so.

I said, "Excuse me," to the dragon and went over to Shiara. "What is it?"

"This," said Shiara. She pulled a coil of rope out of the top of the bundle. "It wasn't here before."

"Are you sure?" I asked.

"Of course I'm sure!" Shiara said. "Look in your pack. Maybe you have one, too."

Shiara was right: There was another coil of rope in my bundle, along with a little silver lamp and a set of flints, and I didn't remember seeing any of them before. We tied the ropes together, then looped one end around the tree closest to the hole. The dragon watched, grumbling the whole time.

When we finished, Shiara and I argued about who was going to get to climb down first. We wound up tossing a coin, and I won.

I stuck the flints and the lamp into my belt, right next to the Sword of the Sleeping King, where I could find them easily. Then I lowered myself over the edge of the hole and started to climb down the rope. It wasn't easy. The rope kept twisting around, which made me dizzy, and I kept bumping into the side of the hole. I'd gotten about three feet from the top of the hole when the lights went out.

I stopped climbing for a minute and just hung there. I couldn't see anything except a circle of sky right above me, and that looked much farther away than it should have. Then I realized that I had to start climbing one way or another because my arms were going to get tired very quickly if I didn't move. I looked up at the sky. I knew I'd only come down a couple of feet, and it shouldn't have been difficult to climb back up. On the other hand, I knew it could be extremely dangerous to start things and not finish them in the Enchanted Forest. I started down again.

Climbing in the dark is not pleasant. I couldn't see where I was going; I couldn't even see the rope. It seemed like years before my feet finally touched something flat below me. I felt around to make sure what I'd found wasn't just a narrow ledge, then I let go of the rope and called to Shiara that I was at the bottom.

The next thing I did was to get out the lamp and light it. I had a little trouble, since I was doing everything by feel, but I finally got it going. At first all I could see was the tiny yellow flame. Then the lamp made a popping noise and suddenly I could see the cave.

Actually, it was more like a tunnel. Where I was standing, the walls were a smooth, speckled stone, but as soon as the tunnel got out from under the hole the walls looked rough. It was cool and dry and dusty, as if no one had been there in a long, long time.

"That's not so bad," said a voice above me. I looked up. The dragon was peering over the edge of the hole. "I can jump that far."

"I think you should wait until Shiara climbs down," I said. "Then you can untie the rope and bring it with you."

Shiara's head appeared beside the dragon's. "You're right; it's not nearly so bad when you can see the bottom."

"If you drop the bundles Morwen gave us, I can catch them," I said. "Then you can climb down and we can get started."

"All right." Shiara's head vanished for a few seconds, then reappeared, along with a pair of hands and a bundle. "Ready? Catch."

Nightwitch was more of a problem than the bundles. I got a few scratches catching her. As soon as I had everything, Shiara climbed down. We picked up our things and moved into the tunnel while the dragon took care of the rope, and then the dragon jumped down.

"That was easy!" it said.

I thought about sliding down the rope in the dark and didn't say anything.

Shiara looked from me to the dragon and back. "Well? Are you going to stand there until the wizards show up again?"

"We have to decide what we're going to hold on to first," I said.

"Daystar, we have to carry everything ourselves anyway," Shiara said. "What difference does it make?"

"I don't think that's what Telemain meant," I said. "There are all sorts of ways to lose things in the Caves of Chance if you aren't paying attention, but if you have something in your hand all the time and never set it down, it's less likely to disappear."

"If you really believe that, you'd better carry the sword," Shiara said. "The only thing *I* don't want to lose is Nightwitch, and she can take care of herself."

"You're right," I said doubtfully. I didn't really want to march through the Caves of Chance with the Sword of the Sleeping King in my hand, but I certainly didn't want to lose it. Finally I decided to take the sheath off my belt and carry the sword and sheath together. I had some trouble doing it, though, and Shiara had to help.

"Are you sure this is necessary?" she asked. "Why can't you just wear it?"

"Magic things are particularly easy to lose here," I said. "And Mother told me to take care of this sword." I tucked the sheathed sword under my arm and picked up the silver lamp and the bundle Morwen had given me. "Let's go."

* * *

The tunnel slanted down for a long way, then leveled. Every now and then we came to a dark opening in the wall that led to a side passage, but we ignored all of them. Telemain had been very specific about that. Not that they were particularly tempting. The silver lamp had no difficulty lighting up our part of the tunnel, but it didn't penetrate into the side passages at all.

After a while, the tunnel we were following jogged sharply left, then right again, and suddenly it opened out into an enormous cave. The walls were crystal, and they seemed to have hundreds of different-colored lights shifting behind them. I stopped abruptly, staring, and the dragon bumped into me from behind.

"Excuse me," I said automatically.

"You shouldn't stop so fast," the dragon complained. It craned its neck to see around me. "Hey! This is nice!" It stretched upward, and a minute later it was clinging to the crystal wall several feet above us.

I backed away hastily. I didn't want to be underneath if the dragon slipped.

"Where are we supposed to go from here?" asked Shiara, ignoring the dragon.

"This must be the Cave of Crystal Lights," I said. "Telemain said to walk straight across. There ought to be three passageways on the other side, and we want to take the left one."

"I see them," the dragon said. It squinted across the cave, then climbed down and sat beside us. "They aren't straight across. They're over that way a little." It waved toward the right.

I looked at the dragon. "I think we should follow Telemain's directions. The Caves of Chance are even trickier than the Enchanted Forest. I don't want to risk getting in trouble if we don't have to." I didn't mention that the last time we had taken the dragon's advice we'd run into the fire-witch and Shiara had gotten turned into a statue, but I was thinking it. Shiara nodded in agreement.

"All right," the dragon said sullenly. "But I think you're being silly."

We started walking again, trying to go straight across the cave. The walls curved in and out, and the floor humped up in low mounds and ridges. Between that and the shifting colored lights, it was hard to be sure we were going straight. Shiara and I backtracked a couple of times, just to check, and every time we did the dragon grumbled.

Finally we got to the other side and saw the three openings. The dragon stared at them, then looked around suspiciously. "Where did these come from? These aren't the ones I saw!"

"Well, then, it's a good thing we followed Telemain's directions," Shiara said. "Otherwise, we'd be lost. Come on, let's go." She scowled and headed for the left-hand passageway.

I started after her, and right away I tripped and fell.

"Ow!" I said. Shiara looked around, then came back to help me up.

"What happened now?" she asked.

"I tripped," I said. "I've still got the sword, but I dropped the lamp. Where is it?"

"I don't see it." Shiara sounded a little worried. She had reason to be. Without the lamp, we wouldn't be able to see anything once we got out of the Cave of Crystal Lights.

"It can't be very far away," I said, and we started hunting. Shiara went one way and I went the other. About half a minute later, I saw something glittering. "There it is!"

"No, it's over here," said Shiara. She bent over and picked something up from behind a rock. "It's still burning," she said, sounding surprised.

"It lights up more space than it ought to, too," I said over my shoulder. "Morwen probably put a spell on it."

"Where are you going?" Shiara said.

"I saw something over here, and I want to know what it is," I said. "Especially since it obviously isn't the lamp."

Shiara started to object, but right then I saw the glittering thing again and I bent to pick it up. "Here it is," I said. "See?" My fingers touched metal, and a fountain of sparks shot up from the floor of the cave where my fingers were.

I yelled and fell backward. The fountain hissed and sizzled angrily, getting bigger and brighter and hotter every minute. I scrambled back toward the others. Blue and white and purple sparks started falling around us, and all of us ran for the left-hand tunnel. Nightwitch yowled as one of the sparks hit her, and Shiara scooped her up and kept on running.

We made it to the tunnel, but no one stopped until we were well inside, not even the dragon. When we finally got out of reach of the falling sparks, we stopped and panted for a while. Fortunately, Shiara had hung on to the lamp as well as to Nightwitch. When she set Nightwitch down, the kitten glared back toward the mouth of the tunnel, then began determinedly washing a spot on her back where the fur was a little singed.

"What was that?" Shiara asked as soon as she had her breath back.

"I don't know," I said. "I was just trying to–" I stopped. I was holding something in my right hand. I didn't even remember grabbing it. "It went off when I picked this up," I said, and I opened my fingers.

I had three pebbles of various sizes, a little sandy dirt, and a small gold key. A tingle ran down my back as I looked at the key, and I jumped. "Now what?" said Shiara.

"I felt something," I said. "Sort of like the sword when it's finding magic, but not the same."

"Is it magic?" the dragon asked.

"I don't know."

"Well, find out!" Shiara said impatiently. "I thought that was what the stupid sword was for."

I sighed a little and shifted all the things I was carrying until I could put my left hand on the hilt of the Sword of the Sleeping King. I didn't feel any tingles, but the key started to glow.

We all stared at the key for a minute.

"I knew it was magic!" the dragon said happily.

"I don't feel anything from the sword, though," I said. I took my hand off the hilt, and the key stopped glowing.

"So? The sword makes it glow, doesn't it?" Shiara said. "It *has* to be magic. What are you going to do with it?"

"I'm going to keep it, at least until we talk to Kazul," I said. "She may know what it's for, or who it belongs to."

"It b-b-belongs in the c-c-cave," something said in a bubbly voice behind us.

I jumped and turned around. There wasn't anyone there. Shiara and the dragon and I all peered into the darkness. Nightwitch looked up from washing her back long enough to hiss, then continued washing.

"Who said that?" Shiara demanded.

"M-m-me. You b-better put that k-k-key back right away," said the same voice.

I still didn't see anyone.

"Why?" I asked.

"B-because it b-belongs there!" the voice said. It sounded like water hitting a hot frying pan. "Gug-give it to me, and I'll put it back."

"If you want it, you'll have to come out here where we can see you," Shiara said firmly.

There was an unhappy bubbling noise from the dark part of the tunnel, then a series of unpleasant squishing sounds. A moment later something wobbled into the light from the silver lamp. It was about four feet tall, and it looked like a slightly sloppy pillar of very dark blackberry jelly.

"There!" it said. "Now, gug-give me that key!"

I was so busy trying to figure out how it could talk when it didn't have a mouth that I didn't answer. I was still trying when Shiara asked, "How do we know it's your key?"

"It isn't my key. I just take care of it. Gug-give it to me!" The jelly was shaking angrily and bobbing up and down like the lid on a teakettle. Every time it bobbed up, the pillar of jelly stretched thin; and when it bobbed down, the jelly made a sort of flattened lump; and every time it moved at all, it wobbled.

The dragon, who had been standing behind Shiara, poked its head over her shoulder to see better. "That stuff reminds me of something," the dragon said. "I can't think what, though. What is it?"

"I," huffed the jelly, "am a quozzel." It leaned forward as if it were trying to peer at us and asked haughtily, "What are *you?"*

"It's a dragon," Shiara said, a little nastily. "Can't you tell?"

The pillar froze in midwobble. "There are n-n-no dragons under-gug-ground," it said. "None!" It leaned cautiously in Shiara's direction for a minute, then started bobbing again. "You aren't a dragon. I want that k-k-key! It belongs in the cave, and it's g-going to stay there!"

"Of course she's not a dragon!" the dragon said. *"I'm* a dragon. And I've never heard of a quozzel before."

The quozzel bent a little, then froze again. "Glurb," it said.

The dragon tilted its head to one side. "I don't think you're very polite," it said.

The jelly burbled unhappily to itself. It looked as if it were boiling. The little dragon kept staring at it, and suddenly the dragon's eyes started to glow. "I know what this reminds me of!" it said triumphantly. "Dessert!"

The quozzel shrieked and collapsed backward into the darkness just as the dragon's head shot toward it. The dragon kept going, knocking Shiara and me out of the way as it went past. We heard several squishing noises, then an angry snort from the dragon, followed closely by a small puff of flame that lit up the dark end of the tunnel. I got a brief glimpse of the dragon before the light died, but I didn't see the quozzel anywhere. There was a disgusted-sounding growl, and a moment later the dragon stalked back into the light from the silver lamp. "It got away."

"Well, I'm glad it's gone," Shiara said. She frowned. "You shouldn't go around trying to eat things all the time, especially if you don't know what they are. I wouldn't be surprised if quozzels were poisonous or something."

"Dragonsbane is the only thing that poisons dragons, and that quozzel wasn't polite, and I'm *hungry,"* the dragon said. It shook its head sadly. "Wizards taste good, but they aren't very filling."

I put the key in my pocket and rummaged in Morwen's bundle. I was sure I still had some meat pies, and I didn't like the idea of traveling with a hungry dragon. I found the food and offered it to the dragon, who brightened up a little and accepted.

"We ought to keep going," Shiara said as the dragon sat back against the wall of the tunnel and started eating. "Suppose that quozzel thing comes back?"

"I don't think it could really do much to us," I said. "It didn't look very dangerous."

"You can't always tell by looking," Shiara said darkly. "And if that marmalade mess wants the stupid key badly enough, it'll think of something."

"Marmalade is orange," I said. "The quozzel looked more like blackberry jelly to me. And I still don't think it's going to come back. Not while the dragon is around."

"Well, you'd better carry that key in your hand," Shiara said. "I think it's important, and it might fall out of your pocket or something."

"All right, but you'll have to keep the lamp. I don't think I can manage the sword *and* the things Morwen gave us *and* the lamp, *and* still hold the key." I dug the key out of my pocket again. Maybe it did belong to the quozzel, but the more I thought about it, the less likely that seemed. And if the key had something to do with the sword, I wanted to hang on to it.

"You won't have to juggle things until we start walking again," Shiara said, but she kept the lamp.

Just then the dragon looked up. "I'm done," it said. "Where do we go now?"

16

In Which Things Get Very Dark for a While

We started walking again. I don't know how far we went or how long it took us. The tunnel forked and we turned right, then it forked again and we went left. We walked through a large cave with walls like black mirrors, and a damp one that dripped water onto our heads, and an unpleasant slimy one with gray moss on the walls. I was very glad that Telemain had told us which way to go. We would have gotten lost very quickly without his directions.

A few times I thought I heard squishing noises behind us, but I wasn't sure enough to say anything. I was a lot more worried about remembering all the things Telemain had told us than I was about the quozzel.

Just when I was beginning to think we had taken a wrong turn somewhere, we came to another cavern.

This one was long and narrow, full of orange light and very hot. The tunnel came out halfway up one wall, about a hundred feet above the floor of the cave. A narrow path ran along one wall from where we stood to a dark opening on the opposite side of the cave.

"Are you sure we're going the right way?" Shiara asked, eyeing the path dubiously.

"I am now," I said. "This was the last cave Telemain mentioned. Once we're on the other side, it shouldn't take long to get to the castle."

"We have to get to the other side first," Shiara pointed out. "That doesn't look very safe."

"The Caves of Chance aren't supposed to be safe," I said. "I'm surprised we haven't run into something a lot more dangerous than the quozzel."

"I suppose–Nightwitch!" Shiara shouted, a minute too late; the kitten was already halfway across the narrow path. Shiara sighed. "Well, now we *have* to go across."

Shiara insisted on going first, because Nightwitch was her cat. I didn't argue much. I went next, and the dragon came last. I had to hug the wall to keep from losing my balance and falling, which was hard to do with the key in one hand, Morwen's bundle in the other, and the sword under one arm. The dragon didn't have nearly as much difficulty as I did, even though it was a little too large for the ledge. It just dug its claws into the rock and kept coming.

When we finally made it to the other side, Shiara and I were covered with black rock dust. We took turns brushing each other off while Nightwitch sat far enough back to avoid getting any of it on her and the dragon looked superior. Evidently rock dust doesn't cling to dragon scales, which was very nice for the dragon but didn't do much to improve Shiara's temper.

"How much farther is it?" Shiara asked as we started off.

"I don't know," I said. "But it shouldn't take much longer."

"I hope not," said the dragon. "I don't like this tunnel."

"Why not?" Shiara asked.

"It isn't finished," the dragon said.

I looked around. The tunnel was a lot rougher than the others we'd come through, and there were rocks sticking out at odd angles from the walls and the roof and even the floor. Every now and then it narrowed into a crooked little passage. If the dragon had been much bigger, it wouldn't have been able to fit through sometimes. We still saw side passages once in a while, but they seemed smaller and farther apart than they had in the first part of the tunnel.

"It does look sort of incomplete," I said. "I think somebody–"

"Daystar, look out!" Shiara yelled. A large rock fell out of the ceiling, just missing my head. Along with the rock came a shower of pebbles that didn't miss.

I heard a creaking noise and felt more pebbles.

"Get back!" I shouted. I dropped Morwen's bundle and shoved Shiara. "Run!"

Shiara stumbled backward. Nightwitch yowled and made a tremendous leap right onto the dragon's nose. The dragon jerked in surprise, and

Nightwitch made another jump and vanished into the darkness behind it. I heard more rumblings, and I shoved Shiara again, just as the roof came down on top of us.

When I woke up, it was very dark and I was lying face down on the tunnel floor. Somehow I'd managed to keep hold of the sword and the key. I could feel them, one halfway under me and the other digging into my left palm. I ached all over. I tried to move, but my legs were pinned under something heavy, and I couldn't drag them free. I pushed myself up a little and stared into the darkness. "Shiara? Nightwitch? Dragon?"

No one answered. They couldn't all have gotten caught in the cave-in. I'd been closest to the falling rocks, and only my legs were pinned. I started wishing I had the lamp, and then I remembered that the key glowed when I touched the Sword of the Sleeping King. I pushed up farther and felt around under me for the hilt, and something very moist and heavy hit me in the middle of my back.

I slammed back into the floor and almost lost consciousness again. The thing on my back bubbled, "The k-k-key! Let go, drop it, gug-give it to me!" Instinctively, I shoved my right hand farther under my chest, groping for the sword.

My fingers touched the hilt, and the key started to glow. It wasn't quite as good as the lamp, but at least I could see. I heard a muffled shriek, and the weight left my back very suddenly. An instant later, I saw the quozzel bending over my hand, and I tightened my grip on the key.

The quozzel bounced angrily. "You're still alive! I don't want you alive. I want that k-k-key. That's why I fixed the rocks."

I shook my head to clear it. *"You* made the tunnel cave in? Just to get a *key?"*

"Of c-c-course!" the quozzel spluttered. "I'm supposed to take c-care of it. I'll get it, too. All I need is m-m-more rocks."

The quozzel wobbled backward, toward the caved-in part of the tunnel. I rolled onto one elbow and looked back over my shoulder, trying to see what it was doing.

A medium-sized rock came crashing down beside me. The quozzel made an angry whistling noise. "H-hold still!"

"So you can drop rocks on me?" Out of the corner of my eye, I saw a long pile of something that seemed to end in a tangle of red hair. Shiara hadn't been buried under the rocks, then. Unfortunately, she didn't look like she would be able to help me with the quozzel anytime soon, and I still didn't know where Nightwitch or the dragon was. I twisted sideways, moving off the sword as much as I could with my legs pinned, and started working the Sword of the Sleeping King out of its sheath. It's not easy to draw a sword when you're lying on top of it, but I thought I might need it if the quozzel came any closer.

There was a sizzling noise from somewhere behind me, and a dozen or so rocks of assorted sizes came rolling down on top of me. Some of them hit places that had already been battered by the cave-in, and I yelled. The quozzel bubbled happily, and a few more rocks went by on one side. I shoved myself up on my hands as far as I could and yanked the sword the rest of the way out of the sheath and out from under me at the same time. I twisted around, just as two more large rocks came rolling down.

Awkwardly, I swung at the rocks with the flat of the sword, trying to deflect them a little. There was a bright flash as the sword hit them, and the rocks went flying toward the far wall of the tunnel. I heard a low humming sound that changed suddenly into a rumble, and the light in the cave went out. For some reason, I thought of the clearing where I'd said the spell at the Sword of the Sleeping King, when everything had gone dark and the voice had called me the Bearer of the Sword.

This time I didn't hear any voice, but the rumbling got louder and louder, and suddenly I realized that my legs were free. I curled them up under me, so I wouldn't be trapped again if the quozzel started another cave-in or something. The rumbling began to die down, and I heard faint shouts mixed in with it, and the bubbling noise that the quozzel made, and someone groaning. Then the rumbling stopped, and I could see again.

Carefully, because my legs felt kind of rubbery, I stood up and looked around. I could still hear the shouting; it sounded faint and far away, and after a moment it faded completely. Shiara was the person who had groaned. As I looked at her, she moved a little, and suddenly I felt a lot better about things generally. Then I heard squishing noises from in back of me, and I whirled.

Behind me, the tunnel was completely blocked by a sloping pile of rocks and dirt. At the base of the pile, where I had been trapped, was an empty space that looked as if something had sliced cleanly through the rocks and lifted them out of the way. Midway up the slope was the quozzel. It was wobbling hastily toward the tunnel floor. I pointed the Sword of the Sleeping King at it, and it stopped abruptly.

"Just a minute, you!" I said. "You have some questions to answer."

"I d-d-d-didn't know," said the quozzel. "I still don't. K-k-keep the k-key. Nice to m-m-meet you. Glug-gug-good-bye."

"Oh, no, you don't." I stepped in front of it, so that if it wobbled forward any more it would get stuck on my sword.

"I'm gug-gug-gug-going," said the quozzel. It seemed to be stammering a lot more than it had before. I found myself hoping it was even more nervous than it looked.

"You aren't going anywhere until you explain why you want this key so badly," I said. "And maybe not then. I don't think I ought to leave something as sneaky and treacherous as you running around loose." I tried to sound intimidating, even though I had no idea what I was going to do with the quozzel. I didn't think I could just kill it, and I certainly didn't want to bring it along with me, but I wasn't about to tell the quozzel any of that. After what it had tried to do, I thought it deserved to worry a little.

"Daystar?" Shiara's voice distracted me from the quozzel, which was bubbling and popping worriedly to itself. "Daystar, what happened?"

"The quozzel made the tunnel cave in," I said. "It was trying to kill me so it could get the key. Are you all right?"

"Of course I'm–yow!" said Shiara. I looked quickly around and saw her sitting up very carefully. She looked a little pale. "I think I broke my arm," she said.

"Can I do anything to help?" I asked.

"You can keep that stupid quozzel away from me!" Shiara said. "I'll be fine as long as I don't move much."

I didn't believe her, but I couldn't have done much to help anyway. I didn't know anything about setting broken arms, except that you can make things a lot worse if you don't know what you're doing. And if Shiara wanted me to keep watching the quozzel instead of trying to help her, she would probably get mad if I didn't. I doubted that that would be good for her arm, either. Besides, I didn't want the quozzel to get away and try dropping the roof on us again.

"Where's Nightwitch?" Shiara asked after a while. "And the dragon?"

"I don't know," I told her. "I haven't seen them since the tunnel fell in."

"You miserable little blob!"

I looked around in surprise and was very relieved to see Shiara glaring at the quozzel and not at me.

"If anything's happened to Nightwitch because of your stupid cave-in, I'll–I'll melt you into a puddle!"she went on.

"You'd better not try," the quozzel said, starting to bounce. "The w-w-wizard will gug-get you if you do!"

"What wizard?" I said.

The quozzel bubbled unhappily. "I can't tell you."

"Oh no?" Shiara said. She stood up slowly and came over beside me, holding her right arm carefully in her left one. "I guess I'd better just melt you, then, and save some time."

"No-n-*no!*" said the quozzel. Little ripples ran over it, and it seemed to shrink.

"Then you'd better tell us what wizard you're talking about," I said.

"The one who gug-gave me the key," the quozzel said unwillingly. "He told me to take care of it until he came back for it."

"How long ago was that?" I asked, ignoring Shiara, who was rubbing her bruises and muttering to herself.

"A long time," the quozzel said. "He never came back, so it's still m-m-my responsib-b-bility."

"Not if I melt you, it isn't," Shiara said, and the quozzel subsided very suddenly.

"What is it the key to?" I said. "And why did the wizard leave it here?"

"D-d-don't know," the quozzel said sullenly. "He said people would come look for it and try to take it. That's why he wanted m-m-me to look after it. You aren't supposed to take it. No one's supposed to take it b-b-but the wizard!"

"What did this wizard look like?" I asked, although I had an unpleasant feeling that I knew already.

The quozzel's description sounded a little like Antorell, but he was definitely older and he'd been wearing blue-and-gray robes instead of blue and brown. I was extremely relieved. Shiara didn't recognize the description, either, but she wasn't as relieved as I was.

"How do we know this stupid thing isn't lying?" she said. "I think we should–what's that?"

I could hear something far down the tunnel, but it echoed too much for me to be able to tell what it was. It seemed to be getting louder.

"I think something's coming," I said to Shiara; then, "You stay where you are!" to the quozzel, who had been trying to wobble a little closer to the bottom of the rock pile.

The quozzel froze again, and Shiara gave me a disgusted look. "I know *something's* coming, but what is it?"

I didn't answer. The noise came closer, and I saw a flickering light partway down the tunnel. I shifted position so I could watch the quozzel and still see some of the rest of the tunnel. The light got brighter, and a moment later a bunch of people came through one of the side passages. They were all short and sort of squashed looking, bigger than the elves we'd met, but considerably shorter than a normal person. Most of them were carrying picks or shovels or long, pointed iron poles, and a couple of them had torches. They seemed to be following something, but they were too far away and the light was too bad for me to be sure.

"Dwarves!" I said. They must have heard the echo, because two of them looked up and saw us. One of them shouted something, but I couldn't make out the words.

"Terrific!" Shiara muttered as they started in our direction. "What'd you have to do that for?"

"They'd have seen us anyway," I said. "I mean, we'd be sort of difficult to miss, with the key lighting up the tunnel like this. And maybe they'll help us. Dwarves do, sometimes; Mother had me study a whole lot of examples two years ago, after the prince came through looking for the glass coffin."

"I thought princes looked for glass *shoes,* not coffins," Shiara said. She squinted into the dark part of the tunnel between us and the dwarves. "They're coming this way. What's that in front of them?"

I didn't have to answer, because a second later Nightwitch came bounding out of the darkness with her tail held very high. She looked extremely proud of herself. She went straight to Shiara and started rubbing against her legs and purring.

"I'm glad to see you, too," Shiara said. She started to bend over and winced. "Sorry, kitten; you'll have to wait to get petted until somebody does something about this stupid arm."

Nightwitch stopped rubbing and looked up. "Mmrew?"

"Well, I said I was sorry," Shiara said. "I didn't *ask* to break it."

The dwarves had reached the edge of the key's glow, and the whole tunnel was lit up by their torches. It made things a lot more cheerful, as well as letting me get a good look at the dwarves. There were seven of them, five males and two females, all carrying shovels and picks. I could see the dragon in back of the dwarves, looking almost as smug as Nightwitch had.

"Look!" it said when it got close enough to talk without shouting. "I found a whole lot of dwarves!"

"I see that," I said. I bowed to the dwarves as well as I could while trying to watch the quozzel at the same time. "My name is Daystar, and that's Shiara. We're very pleased to meet you."

"They're going to dig through the part of the tunnel that came down," the dragon said.

"Hold on just a minute!" one of the dwarves said. "I didn't say I'd help. Not exactly. I said I'd look at this cave-in of yours."

"Me too," said another. "Proper mess it looks."

"Not natural," said a female dwarf. She looked at Shiara and me suspiciously.

"How do you know?" Shiara said belligerently.

"We made this tunnel," still another dwarf said. "And dwarf-made tunnels don't just fall in."

... first one.

... 'The quozzel made the tunnel cave in. It was

... out of the Caves of Chance."

... gon said, looking interested. "That dessert

"You can't eat it until we find out if it knows anything else," I said. "Besides, you had plenty of lunch."

The dragon sighed. "I suppose so. All right, I'll wait."

I looked at the dwarves. "We'd be very much obliged to you if you would help us get through this, or show us a way around it, or something," I said.

"Now, why should we do that?" one of them said.

"I don't see any reason," said another.

"Lot of work for nothing," added a third.

"And I don't like dragons!" said a voice from the middle of the group. The dragon glared, but it couldn't pick out the dwarf who'd spoken.

"Could you at least set Shiara's arm?" I asked.

One of the female dwarves started to reply, but she was cut off by a yell from Shiara. "Daystar! Behind you!"

I raised the sword and spun around just as the quozzel bunched itself together and jumped at me. It came flying through the air, and I ducked. Something dark and purple shot out of it toward me, and I slashed at it with the sword. I got most of the purple stuff and part of the quozzel as well. I heard it shriek, and then it had landed and launched itself again, straight for the wall of the tunnel.

"I'll kill all of you!" it whistled angrily. "Key stealers! Cannibals! I'll kill you d-d-dead!"

I lunged for it, but I was too late. The quozzel hit the tunnel wall, and instead of bouncing, it vanished into the rock like water being absorbed by a sponge, only faster. An instant later a shower of rocks fell out of the roof of the tunnel, and I heard the walls creaking ominously.

"Run!" I yelled. I started to follow my own advice but saw a large rock shifting in the wall of the tunnel just above Shiara's head. I shouted again and swung the sword at it, hoping it would be deflected like the other rocks the quozzel had tried to drop on me.

The flat of the sword hit the rock, and everything seemed to slow down suddenly. There was a lot of creaking, and the top of the tunnel started to sag, as if it were trying to fall in again but couldn't quite manage it. The sword got very heavy, and then there was an angry-sounding rumble and the whole tunnel shook. The rock that had been heading for Shiara went bouncing off the opposite wall of the tunnel, and all the creaking and rumbling stopped very abruptly.

I didn't move for several seconds at least. I didn't think the quozzel would give up this easily. Then I saw a thin trickle of dark purple stuff dripping down the wall of the tunnel where the quozzel had disappeared. I watched it for a minute or two and decided that we probably didn't have to worry about the quozzel anymore. I looked at Shiara.

"Are you all right?"

"That's a stupid question," Shiara said. "My arm is broken!"

"I mean, you didn't get any more hurt than you were already, did you?"

"No," she said. She looked at me. "Thanks."

I was so surprised that I couldn't think of anything to say for at least a minute.

"Um, you're welcome," I said finally. I realized suddenly that my sword still had some wet purple stuff on it from hitting the quozzel, and I started digging in my pocket for my handkerchief so I could wipe off the sword.

I couldn't find it. I sighed. It had probably fallen out of my pocket somewhere on the trip through the caves. I didn't really mind losing it, except that now I didn't have anything to get the purple goo off my sword with. I turned to the dwarves. "Excuse me, but do any of you–"

I stopped. The dwarves were standing in a tight group, and all seven of them were staring at the sword.

"Now, why didn't you think to mention you had that?" one of them said.

17

In Which They Get out of the Caves and into Even More Trouble

Shiara and I looked at the dwarves. "He's been holding it since before you got here!" Shiara said finally. "Why should he have mentioned it?"

"It would have saved a lot of bother," one of the female dwarves said in an aggrieved tone.

"Time, too," said another.

"Inconsiderate, I call it."

"Well, not inconsiderate, exactly," said one of the male dwarves, eyeing the dragon. "A little thoughtless, maybe."

"Thoughtless?" The dragon looked puzzled. "Why? What difference does it make if Daystar has a sword?"

"A sword is one thing. *That* sword is something else again."

"Someone should have told us."

"Someone should *definitely* have told us."

"After all, we aren't elves."

"Of course you're not elves," the dragon said. "Anyone can see that! What does that have to do with Daystar's sword?"

"It's not his sword!" one of the dwarves objected. "It's the King's!"

"And elves can recognize it just by *looking* at it," a female dwarf said in a resentful tone.

"So can some other people," said another darkly.

"But not dwarves."

"Unless we get a good look at it, of course. Which we couldn't, because of the light, not to mention the fact that you were standing there talking and distracting our attention."

"Which is why you should have mentioned it," a dwarf in the back finished triumphantly.

"I didn't mention it because there seem to be a lot of people who want it," I said. "One of them is a wizard."

About six of the dwarves started talking so fast it was hard to tell whether they were all speaking at the same time or whether they went one after another.

"Of course there are a lot of people who want it!"

"*Particularly* wizards."

"It *is* the King's sword, isn't it?"

"Maybe it isn't; he hasn't said."

"It has to be the King's sword, silly. There aren't any other swords that the earth obeys."

"What about Delvan's blade?"

"That's not a sword, it's an ax."

"And the earth doesn't *obey* it, it just shakes a lot."

"So this has to be the King's sword."

"Wait a minute!" I said. "What do you know about my sword?"

"It's the *King's* sword," one of the dwarves said indignantly. Another dwarf shushed him, and a dwarf near the front of the crowd stepped forward and bowed.

"We follow the sword," she said, as if it explained everything.

The other dwarves all smiled and nodded. I sighed and gave up. Either none of them really knew anything else, or they knew and weren't going to tell me, and I didn't think it mattered much which it was. "If you aren't going to tell me about my sword, could one of you do something about Shiara's arm?" I asked. "And after that, we'll be going."

"Going where?" the dragon said.

Some of the dwarves jumped. Evidently they'd forgotten the dragon was behind them. I was surprised; if a dragon were standing behind me, I certainly wouldn't forget it was there.

"We have to find another way out of the Caves of Chance," I told the dragon. "I don't really think we can dig through this one."

"That will not be necessary," said the dwarf closest to me. "Had we known you were the Bearer of the Sword, we would not have objected to your request."

"Not at all," said the dwarf next to him. She turned and waved at the others. "Lord Daystar requires this tunnel cleared. Begin!"

I stood and stared while the dwarves all grabbed their picks and shovels and things and started toward the rocks that were blocking the tunnel. In a few minutes they were all digging furiously–except for one, who came over to Shiara and bowed.

"I am Darlbrin," he announced.

"That's nice," Shiara said sarcastically. I sighed, but I didn't say anything. You can't really expect a fire-witch with a broken arm to be particularly polite.

Darlbrin didn't seem to notice. "I have some skill at mending things," he said, and bowed again. "If you will permit it, I would like to examine your arm." He looked at Shiara a shade anxiously and added, "To see if I can mend it."

Shiara rolled her eyes, but she walked over to the edge of the tunnel and sat down so the dwarf could see better. Nightwitch followed, alternately purring reassuringly and meowing anxiously.

I watched for a minute or two, then turned away. I couldn't do anything to help, and I wanted to think.

I didn't get the chance. As soon as I turned, the dragon stuck its head over a couple of dwarves and said, "I didn't know you were a lord. Why didn't you tell me?"

"Because I'm not a lord!" I said. I think I sounded a little desperate, and I know I felt desperate. I didn't have the slightest idea what was going on, except that it had something to do with my sword. *Everything* seemed to have something to do with my sword. I was getting tired of it, and more than a little worried.

"Well, if you aren't a lord, why did they call you one?"

"Because he has the King's sword," said a dwarf who was walking under the dragon's chin with a boulder more than half as big as he was. The dragon pulled its head back far enough to eye the dwarf, who ignored it and kept walking.

"I really wish you'd explain a little more," I yelled after the dwarf, and then I thought of something. "Why did you call me the Bearer of the Sword?"

"I didn't call you anything," the dwarf said without stopping. "That was Cottlestone." He set the boulder down and headed back toward the pile of rocks, which was beginning to look smaller already.

"Excuse me," I said loudly, in the general direction of the crowd of dwarves, "but would one of you tell me which of you is Cottlestone? I'd like to talk to him, please."

"Cottlestone!" shouted half a dozen voices.

For a minute I thought the roof was going to cave in again, but all that actually happened was that one of the dwarves stepped out of the crowd and bowed to me. He looked as if he really meant it, not as if he were just being polite.

"Don't do that," I said.

"As you wish," the dwarf said, bowing again. "What do you want to know from me?"

"Why did you call me the Bearer of the Sword?"

Cottlestone looked surprised. "It's obvious. When the Bearer of the Sword holds the King's sword, the earth obeys it. So when you held up the sword and the earth obeyed, we knew you were the Bearer of the Sword."

"Oh." I thought for a moment. "Have you ever heard of the Holder of the Sword? Or the Wielder of the Sword?"

"Who?"

"Never mind," I said. "How does someone get to be the Bearer of the Sword?"

"No one knows," Cottlestone said, looking at me curiously.

"Oh," I said again. I was trying to think of something else to ask when there was a shout from the top of the caved-in section of the tunnel. Cottlestone bowed again. "If you will excuse me, I think they've gotten through to the other side. I ought to go help. It's my job."

"All right," I said uncomfortably. Cottlestone turned away, and I watched him melt into the crowd of dwarves. I wasn't sure what I'd found out, except that I didn't like people bowing to me. I found myself hoping that the rest of the dwarves wouldn't imitate Cottlestone.

"Did he say they're almost finished?" asked Shiara from behind me. "Wonderful! I can't wait to get out of here."

I turned. Shiara was standing, holding Nightwitch in the crook of her left arm. Her right arm was covered from her fingers almost to her shoulder in something smooth and gray and shiny. She looked a little white, but that might have been the torch light. "Well, what are you staring at?" she demanded.

"I wasn't staring," I said. "I was just checking to see if you were all right."

Darlbrin stepped up beside Shiara and bowed. "Not quite all right. But not bad, not bad at all."

"I wouldn't call a broken arm 'not bad,' " Shiara said sourly.

"Oh, I didn't mean that!" Darlbrin said hastily. "I was referring to the mending."

"I'm sure you did a very good job," I told him. "And I really appreciate it."

"I suppose I do, too," Shiara mumbled. "Thanks."

"It isn't really mended yet, you know," Darlbrin said with a touch of anxiety. "People aren't as easy to fix as ax handles. It'll be a month before you can take the sheath off."

"Yes, I know. I've had a broken arm before." Shiara scowled at the sheath.

"Then you're very welcome!" The dwarf beamed. "Happy to be of service!"

Shiara snorted, but quietly. Darlbrin didn't notice. He bowed to each of us and went off to help the rest of the dwarves finish clearing the tunnel. I looked at Shiara. "I didn't know you'd broken your arm before."

"That's because I didn't tell you about it," Shiara said. She looked at me for a minute, then sighed. "I was stealing apples from the Prince's gardens and fell out of the tree, all right?"

"Oh. What prince, and why were you taking his apples?"

"The Prince of the Ruby Throne," Shiara said after a minute. "He had a house and garden just outside town, and he never picked any of the apples. He just left them to rot. And I was hungry. So I sneaked over the wall and climbed the tree, but there was a big snake in it, with wings. So I fell out of the tree and broke my arm, and the snake went away."

"Shiara," I said, and stopped. She obviously had no idea what she had almost done. I sighed and changed what I was going to say. "Shiara, the Prince of the Ruby Throne raises magic apples. All kinds of people have been trying to steal them for years and years, but he's a very powerful sorcerer, and there are hundreds of spells protecting his gardens."

"That must be why he was so upset," Shiara said in a tone of sudden enlightenment. "I'm pretty sure he was the one who told the Society of Wizards about me. I *thought* it was a lot of fuss to make about a few apples."

I looked at her for a minute. "I don't want to be nosy or anything, but I'd really appreciate knowing if there's anyone *else* who's mad at you."

"I don't think so," Shiara said, frowning.

"Good. I don't think I want any more people chasing us. Particularly people with powerful magic. It wouldn't be so bad if you could use your fire magic."

"She can!" said the dragon, and Shiara and I both jumped and turned around. "She burned the dragonsbane, and she can make her hair burn."

"When did *you* see Shiara's hair burning?" I asked. The only time I'd ever seen Shiara's hair on fire was when she'd gotten mad at me right after we'd met, and the dragon hadn't been there then.

"Just a few minutes ago," the dragon said. "You were fighting that dessert thing, so you might not have noticed."

I looked at Shiara, and she blushed. "I was trying to do something to the quozzel. I thought it would work because it worked on the dragonsbane."

"It worked on the dragonsbane," I repeated slowly. "And that first wizard, the one who made a water monster out of the stream–you did something to that monster, too. That's at least twice that you've made your fire magic work properly. Can you think of any others? Maybe we can figure out why it happens."

"She used it at the invisible castle," the dragon offered. "The one where that *other* fire-witch lived."

"I did not!" Shiara said. "I didn't have time. We ran into the castle, and she came out, and *bang!* I was a statue."

The dragon sat back, looking smug. "You said you wanted to know what the castle was, and then you did. That's fire magic, isn't it?"

"I suppose it is," Shiara said slowly.

"Then that's three," I said. "Can you think of any more? Before you came to the Enchanted Forest, for instance?"

Shiara frowned and was silent. "No," she said finally in a very positive tone. "Those are the only times I've ever gotten my magic to do what I wanted it to, ever."

"So it's only been happening since you came to the Enchanted Forest," I said.

"And met you and got bitten by that stupid sword," Shiara added, and stopped. We looked at each other for a minute.

"Not again!" I said. I thought for a minute. "It can't be the sword alone, or you would have been able to do something to the quozzel. There has to be something else, too."

"Like what?"

"I don't know. Did you do anything differently when it worked?"

"No."

"Well, then did you do anything differently right before it worked?" I said. "There has to be some–" I stopped, remembering. "Oh," I said.

"What is it?"

"I think I know what makes your magic work." I didn't think Shiara was going to like it much, but I couldn't just keep quiet about it. "I think you have to be polite to people."

"That's *stupid!*"

"It makes sense," I said. "You apologized to me after we got out of the hedge, and then when the first wizard came along your magic worked against the snake thing. You were nice to the Princess because you felt sorry for her, and right after that you knew about the invisible castle. And you said thanks to Suz and apologized to Telemain, and then you made the dragonsbane burn."

"But that other fire-witch wasn't polite!" Shiara objected.

"I didn't say *all* fire-witches have to be polite to people before their magic will work," I said. "I only said *your* magic works that way. And I'm not positive. I mean, it could be something else."

"Well, I'm not going to go around being nice to people just so I can do magic!"

"I don't think it would work, anyway," I said unhappily. "I mean, I don't think you can just say things. I think you have to really mean them. You meant it when you apologized to me, and when you were nice to the Princess, and when you were talking to Telemain."

"Oh, great," Shiara said disgustedly. "I bet this is all that stupid sword's fault." She glared at me for an instant, then turned her back.

I sighed.

"Excuse me, Lord Daystar," said a voice by my elbow. I looked down, and the dwarf bowed.

"Don't *do* that," I said.

"Certainly, my lord," she said, and started to bow again, then stopped and looked confused. "The tunnel is clear. You may continue your journey whenever you wish."

I looked around. The pile of rocks that had been blocking the tunnel was nearly gone. A few boulders were left along the sides, but there was plenty of room to walk through, even for the dragon. "Thank you very much," I said. "But I really ought to tell you: I'm not a lord."

The dwarf smiled tolerantly. "Of course not, my lord. Is there anything else we can do for you?"

"I'd appreciate it if we could borrow one of your torches," I said. "Our lamp got lost in the cave-in."

"We would be pleased to offer you a torch," the dwarf said. "You can leave it by the exit, and someone will get it later. The exit isn't far."

We gathered up what we could find of Morwen's bundles, and the dwarves did some more bowing. One of them handed Shiara a torch. She grumbled a little because she had to put Nightwitch down in order to take it, but she was the only one of us who could carry it. I had the sword in one hand and the key in the other, and the dragon couldn't hold a torch. Fortunately, Nightwitch didn't seem to mind walking. We thanked the dwarves and said good-bye, and they all bowed again, and finally we started off.

The tunnel started slanting upward almost as soon as we were past the cave-in, and shortly after that we stopped seeing side passages. Eventually we came to a wide flight of stairs that curled around and around until all of us were dizzy. Just when I didn't think I could climb anymore, the stairs ended against a hard, rocky surface, like a trapdoor made of stone.

I shoved against it, but it didn't budge. "It's too heavy."

"Really?" said the dragon. "It doesn't look so bad."

I looked down at the dragon, who was last on the stairs because neither

Shiara nor I had wanted to be behind it if it slipped. "It probably isn't too heavy for you. Why don't you try it?"

The dragon agreed, and Shiara and I squashed ourselves against the side of the stairs so it could climb past us. There were a couple of minute's worth of grunts, and the dragon's tail whipped back and forth, which made Shiara and me retreat farther down the stairs. Finally there was a loud noise like extremely rusty hinges, and the dragon started moving upward. A moment later, it stopped. "Uh-oh," it said.

"What's the matter?" Shiara called.

The dragon didn't answer, but it moved out of the way so we could climb up. Shiara and I got to the head of the stairs at almost the same time and looked around.

We were standing at the top of a small rise. The sun was starting to set, but there was still enough light to see the castle clearly. It was quite close, not more than a few minutes' walk from where I was, and it fascinated me. At first, I thought it was made of something shimmery, like mother-of-pearl; then I realized that it wasn't the castle that was shimmering, it was something around the castle, like a giant soap bubble. I was still trying to figure out what it was when Shiara poked me, and I looked down.

There were approximately two hundred dragons sitting on the ground around the little hill we were standing on. Watching us.

18

In Which the King of the Dragons Does Some Explaining

I swallowed hard, and for a moment I wished I were wearing my sword instead of carrying it under my arm. Every dragon from inside the Enchanted Forest had to be there, and quite a few from the Mountains of Morning as well. They were spread out in all directions, so I couldn't even see the ground. The forest encircled the castle at a distance, and there seemed to be something *wrong* about the trees. I couldn't tell what, though, and besides, I had other things to worry about right then. Two hundred dragons, for instance.

I stepped forward and bowed carefully in all directions. One of the first things Mother taught me about dragons was that they expect a new arrival to make the first move. They always allow you one chance to convince them that you're too polite or too important to eat. I didn't think I could convince two hundred dragons that I was particularly important, especially since I didn't believe it myself, so I was going to have to rely on being polite. I took a deep breath.

"Sirs and madams, I apologize most profoundly for intruding upon you in this fashion, and I hope we have not inconvenienced you in any way," I said, trying not to shout while still talking loudly enough for all the dragons to hear. "Nevertheless, I offer you greetings in the name of myself and my companions, and I wish you good fortune in whatever endeavors are most important to you."

The dragons stirred briefly, then settled back again. After a moment, an old gray-green male slid forward. "We greet you and wish you well," he said. "May we know your names?"

I bowed again, the half bow of respect for a dragon of great age and uncertain status. "I thank you for your greeting," I said. "I am called Daystar, and my companions are Shiara and Nightwitch. This young dragon has graciously accompanied us for part of our journey." Since some of them presumably knew the little dragon already, I didn't have to introduce it.

I didn't ask for the dragons' names. It's perfectly acceptable not to, and I didn't feel like standing there through two hundred introductions, especially since the dragons would expect me to remember them all.

"Well met, Daystar," the old dragon rumbled. "We've been expecting you since early this afternoon."

"I'm sorry if I kept you waiting," I said. "We had problems with some wizards, and a cave-in, and a quozzel, and I didn't really know you were all here."

"Of course not. Telemain only told Kazul yesterday that you were coming. Silly way to do things, making everyone gather in such a hurry." He looked at me for a minute, then nodded approvingly. "Well, come along; no sense wasting any more time. You might as well bring the girl and the cat, too. This way."

Our dragon lifted its head. "What about me?" It looked much smaller next to the full-grown dragons all around us, and it sounded considerably younger as well.

"*You* had better keep quiet," the older dragon said indulgently. "You're in quite a bit of trouble already. I wouldn't make it worse if I were you."

"I don't have to keep quiet!" our dragon said. "I found a princess, even if I did decide not to keep her, and I fought a knight and bit a wizard. I can talk if I want to!"

The crowd of dragons shifted again, very slightly. Shiara shivered and held Nightwitch closer. I thought about wiping my hands on my tunic, but I didn't want to look too nervous. The older dragon just stood and stared at our dragon, which finally shook its head and settled back, watching the crowd below us with a sulky expression.

The old dragon smiled slightly. "What do you think?" he asked the crowd of dragons behind him.

All of the dragons roared at once. I couldn't tell what they were saying, or even if they were saying anything, but the old dragon nodded again and looked at the little dragon. "You'll get your wish, then. Well, don't just stand there."

I nodded and stepped forward as the old dragon turned. Shiara followed behind me, very closely, and our dragon came behind her.

"Where are we going?" Shiara whispered to me.

The old dragon looked back over his shoulder, and his eyes glinted with amusement. "You're going to see Kazul."

"Oh," Shiara said. We stepped down from the little hill, and there was a loud clattering and rumbling as the dragons moved out of our way. I stopped short in shock.

The ground around the hill was dry and brown and bare. It looked even worse to me than it would have normally because I'd spent several days looking at the rich green moss in the Enchanted Forest and the contrast was striking. Then I remembered that we were still *in* the Enchanted Forest, and I started being worried as well as shocked. I knew from experience how fast the moss grew and how hard it was to clear off even a small strip of ground. I didn't like to think about what had stripped the moss from the area around the castle.

Shiara poked me, and I moved forward again. Fortunately, the dragon ahead of us hadn't noticed my pause. A few of the ones at the edge of the crowd had, but they seemed more amused than anything. I walked a little faster, trying to ignore the large shapes on either side of me. With two hundred dragons around, I could waste a lot of time worrying if I wasn't careful.

The old dragon led us toward the castle. As we got closer, I could see that there were two shimmerings in the air around the castle, one a few feet inside the other. The outer one looked like a shifting green-and-silver veil, very thin and transparent. The inner one seemed to be a pale golden glow, but I couldn't be sure because the one on the outside kept shifting around, interfering with my seeing the inner one clearly. After a few minutes, I gave up on trying to look *at* the shimmerings and tried looking *through* them instead.

The shimmerings didn't get in the way at all, so I could see quite a bit of the castle. There was no wall around it, only the shimmerings and a water-filled moat just inside them. The castle itself was a wonderful, rambling-looking place, with six towers of various sizes, large square windows, and four balconies. I could see several stairways running up to oddly shaped doors or around the outsides of towers, and a lot of walls that seemed to be there just to confuse people. I was so busy studying the castle and the shimmerings that I almost didn't notice when the old dragon stopped. I was lucky not to step on his tail.

We were about halfway around the castle, and there seemed to be fewer dragons around. I was trying to guess which one was Kazul when the old dragon who had been leading us stepped a little to one side and bobbed his head respectfully.

"King Kazul, these are the travelers who wish to see you. That one's Daystar, the other one's Shiara, and the cat is Nightwitch."

Right away I bowed very deeply, and so did Shiara. I was relieved. I hadn't been completely sure Shiara would do any of the things I'd suggested. As I straightened up, I got my first look at Kazul.

Even lying on the ground, she looked large for a dragon. Her scales were just beginning to turn gray around the edges, which surprised me; I'd expected someone older. Her eyes were hypnotic, green-gold ovals. She was the most dangerous-looking dragon I'd ever seen.

Kazul smiled broadly. Dragons have a *lot* of teeth.

"So," she said, "you are the people Telemain sent through the Caves of Chance, and you have the Sword of the Sleeping King."

"Yes, Your Majesty," I said. I took the sword out from under my arm and held it up so she could see it better. "Mother gave it to me a few days ago, and I was told you would want to know about it."

"Ahhhhhh." As she looked at the sword, Kazul's eyes glowed. Literally. The light from them was a little like firelight, except it didn't flicker. After a minute, she transferred her gaze to me. "And you got it here safely. Well done, Cimorene's son."

"Thank you, Your Majesty," I said. "You know my mother?"

Kazul smiled again. "Cimorene was the best princess I ever had."

Shiara choked, and my jaw dropped.

The little dragon said, "So *that's* how she knew dragon magic!" in a pleased tone.

I closed my mouth, swallowed hard, and bowed to Kazul. "Excuse me, Your Majesty. I was, um, startled. Mother is a princess?"

"She certainly was once," Kazul said. She looked at the sword again. "I'm glad she managed to keep it safe. We didn't have a lot of choice at the time, but it's still worrying to have to take a risk like that."

I wasn't certain what to say. Kazul didn't seem to be talking to me, but it isn't a good idea to ignore a dragon. So, just to be safe, I bowed again.

Kazul looked up from the sword. "You needn't be quite so formal. I have a lot to tell you, and the conversation will go faster if you're not so stiff."

Before I could reply, Kazul turned toward the old dragon, who was still standing beside me. "It will be tomorrow morning. Let everyone know."

The old dragon nodded and left. Kazul looked back at us. "Come with me." She started to rise.

"What about me?" the little dragon demanded.

Kazul sighed. "Yes, you may come, too." She stood, which made her look twice as big as she had before, and started walking. Shiara and I looked at each other, then followed.

By this time the sun was completely down, but there was still enough light in the sky to see where we were going. Kazul led us a little farther around the castle, then turned away from it. As we walked along, the other dragons slid out of the way for Kazul and bowed their heads respectfully. Then Shiara and I walked by and bowed respectfully to the dragons. It kept us too busy to see much of where we were going.

Kazul led us to what looked like a jumbled pile of rocks a little way from the castle. There was a dark opening at one side of the pile, and Kazul went right in. Shiara and the little dragon and Nightwitch and I followed.

It was very dark inside, almost as black as the Caves of Chance. I stopped immediately, since I didn't want to step on Kazul's tail in the dark or run into her accidentally. Shiara bumped into me, squeezing Nightwitch between us. Nightwitch said, "Mrowww!" in a complaining tone, and Kazul's voice came out of the darkness.

"I suppose you human people need some light."

"Only if it won't be inconvenient," I said.

"Not at all," Kazul replied, and added about five hissing words.

Silvery light sprang up all around us. I squinted, and then I blinked. The inside of the pile of rocks looked a lot like a cave. I looked for the source of the light and realized that the light was coming from the rocks.

That shook me. Dragons don't usually do magic casually. In particular, the King of the Dragons wouldn't normally work a spell just for a visitor's convenience. I looked at Kazul, wondering exactly what was going on.

"Sit down," said Kazul, nodding toward a row of rocks. We did. The little dragon sat down by the entrance, looking half-sulky and half-defiant. Kazul ignored it.

"I think you had better tell me your story first," she said, looking at me intently. "Start at the beginning, when Cimorene gave you the sword."

"I'm sorry," I said. "I'll start with the sword if you want me to, but I think the beginning is the wizard."

"Wizard?"

"His name's Antorell, and he came to our cottage the day before Mother gave me the sword. Mother melted him."

"Oh, him." Kazul shook her head. "Sounds like he hasn't learned anything since the last time he tangled with Cimorene. Yes, start with him, by all means."

So I told Kazul everything that had happened to me since Antorell had walked up to our cottage and knocked the door in. It took a long time—especially the part after Shiara and I met the little dragon, because then the dragon kept adding things. Finally, Kazul told it to either be quiet or go away. It looked terribly offended, but it quit talking.

Kazul didn't ask any questions at all. Once, when I mentioned finding the key in the Caves of Chance, she made a noise that sounded like an astonished snort, but she apologized for interrupting and told me to go on. I did, once I got over the shock of having the King of the Dragons apologize to me.

When I finished, there was silence for a minute or two. Then Kazul stirred. "So. You have accomplished a great deal in a short time, Daystar."

"It doesn't seem like much to me," I said.

"A great deal," Kazul repeated. She sounded as if she were talking to herself.

Shiara shifted restlessly. "Are you going to explain about Daystar's sword?"

"Shiara!" I said, horrified. *Nobody* talks to the King of the Dragons in that tone of voice.

Except Shiara. "No," said Kazul. "Or at least, I'm not going to tell you as much as you want to know. The Society of Wizards has more than a hundred spells hunting for that sword right now, and all of them depend on finding someone who knows what he's carrying. Fortunately, wizards' magic can't detect the sword itself. If Daystar finds out too much about that sword, we'll be up to our wings in wizards in no time. I don't want that to happen yet."

"I don't like wizards," the little dragon said suddenly. "They make me sneeze."

Kazul's head turned and she eyed the little dragon for a minute. "I think it is time you made yourself useful," she said at last. "Go find Marchak and tell him to bring us dinner. Then go back to your teacher and apologize for running off, and after that you can start getting ready for tomorrow."

"What happens tomorrow?" the little dragon said suspiciously.

"We have a war," Kazul said. "Which you *might* live through, if you're ready for it. So go!"

"Yes, ma'am!" The little dragon disappeared out the door of the cave.

Kazul looked after it for a minute, then shook her head. "That is undoubtedly the most irritating grandchild I have."

"Who are you going to be—*'Grandchild?'* " said Shiara.

"Yes, of course." Kazul looked mildly surprised. "It's an annoying youngster, but precocious children frequently are. I'm hoping it will grow out of it."

"Oh." Shiara stared out the entrance thoughtfully.

"I enjoyed its company, most of the time," I said honestly.

"I'm glad," Kazul said.

After another minute, I went on, "Um, if you wouldn't mind telling us, I'm sort of curious about whom you expect to be fighting tomorrow." I was also wondering whether Kazul thought Shiara and I were going to be included in this. I wasn't particularly anxious to get involved in a war between dragons.

Kazul smiled; I got the feeling she knew what I was thinking. "Wizards," she said. "There will be a few elves, of course, and maybe some ogres and trolls, but mostly we'll be fighting wizards."

"Oh. Of course." I was even less interested in getting involved in a war between dragons and wizards. Dragons alone might overlook Shiara and Nightwitch and me, but wizards certainly wouldn't.

"I'm afraid you already are involved," Kazul said.

"Because of the sword?" Shiara asked while I tried to remember whether I'd said anything out loud about not wanting to get involved.

"Yes," said Kazul. "The sword and other things. It's a long story. I hope you're comfortable."

We both nodded, and Kazul smiled again. "Well, then. There are two types of magic in the world: the kind you're born with, and the kind you get from something else. Dragons"–Kazul looked smug–"elves, unicorns, and fire-witches are born with magic. Ordinary witches and magicians get their magic from objects or from rituals involving things that have magic, which works quite well and doesn't upset things.

"Wizards, on the other hand, get their magic from everything around them that happens to have magic. Those staffs of theirs absorb little bits of it constantly, and the suction gets worse every time a wizard stores a new spell in his staff. That, by the way, is why dragons are allergic to wizards. Whenever those staffs get near us, they start trying to soak up some of our magic and we start sneezing."

"Telemain said something like that," I said.

Kazul nodded. "Wizards' staffs create other problems, too."

"You mean those stupid wizards have been grabbing my magic every time they come near me?" Shiara said indignantly.

"Not yours," Kazul said. "Wizards can't use fire-witches' magic; it's too different. Their staffs explode if they try."

"Good!" Shiara's face grew thoughtful. "I wonder if I could learn to do that on purpose?"

Kazul looked as if she agreed with Shiara. "Wizards get most of their magic from the Enchanted Forest, but if they absorb too much magic in any one place, things die."

"The moss!" I said. "That's why it turns brown when a wizard's staff touches it."

"Yes," said Kazul. "The King of the Enchanted Forest had a way of reversing the process, taking magic out of a wizard's staff and putting it back in the forest, so wizards weren't too much of a problem until about seventeen years ago. The fellow who was Head Wizard then decided he was tired of stealing magic in bits, so he stole the tool that the King used to keep wizards from swiping magic in large chunks."

"The sword?" I said. "Telemain said it was supposed to be used on wizards."

"Telemain talks too much," Kazul said a little sourly. "Almost as soon as they had the sword, the wizards attacked the castle. They thought that without the sword the King would be easy to take care of. They forgot that the King of the Enchanted Forest has friends." She smiled fiercely. I felt almost sorry for the wizards.

"They wound up in a full-fledged battle, and while we were all fighting, the sword got stolen again. A few wizards managed to get inside the castle, but without the sword they couldn't actually kill the King. So they found some way of keeping him out of action while they hunted for the sword."

"They put the King to sleep?" I said doubtfully. It sounded a bit unlikely. Sleeping spells are very effective on guards and princesses, and even a kingdom now and then, but they can't usually do much against a good magician. And whatever else he was, the King of the Enchanted Forest had to be a master magician.

"We don't know exactly what they did," Kazul admitted. "We know the King isn't dead, because the Enchanted Forest reacts very strongly when a King dies. We know they did something, though, because the seal they have around the castle wouldn't hold the King in by itself."

"You mean those shimmerings around the castle?" I said.

"The outer one is ours," Kazul said with a grim smile. "The wizards put up a spell to keep everyone but themselves out of the castle, so we put up one to keep the wizards out. Without the sword, there wasn't anything more we could do."

"Then how did Daystar's mother get hold of the sword?" Shiara asked.

Kazul smiled again. "Cimorene was the one who stole it back from the wizards in the first place. They've been trying to get hold of it again ever since. They'll show up as soon as we break through their barrier tomorrow, but by then we should be ready for them."

"Uh, you expect Shiara and me to help you fight wizards?" I said.

"Of course not," Kazul replied. "Shiara may help us if she wishes, but you, Daystar, will be going into the castle to break whatever spell the wizards put on the King seventeen years ago."

19

In Which the Battle Begins

That took some explanation. What Kazul meant was, the dragons would lower the barrier they had put up around the castle. Then I would draw the Sword of the Sleeping King and put it into the wizards' barrier, which, according to Kazul, would bring it down. The wizards would know immediately that something was happening, and they would start trying to get to the castle. The dragons and their various allies would hold off the wizards and whomever they brought to help them while I ran into the castle, found the King, and broke the spell.

I didn't like the sound of it at all, but I couldn't say much. After all, Mother had given me the sword, and I was pretty sure this was what she'd wanted me to do with it. Besides, Kazul seemed to think I was the only one who could use the sword to break the spell. And how do you tell the King of the Dragons that you won't do something she wants you to do?

Shiara, on the other hand, had a lot to say. She thought it would be stupid for me to go into the castle by myself. Kazul asked if she was volunteering, and Shiara said that she wasn't going to be left out just when things were getting interesting. Kazul pointed out that Shiara's arm was broken, and Shiara told her that being inside the castle with me sounded safer than being outside with a lot of wizards and dragons fighting.

Finally Kazul said Shiara could go with me if she wanted to. Shiara said, Good, and were the dragons going to be able to keep all of the wizards out of the castle, or were some of them going to sneak in after us? They kept on like that for quite a while. I was very glad when a middle-sized dragon arrived with dinner and interrupted. I couldn't see why Kazul was being so patient with Shiara, and I was getting worried that her patience wouldn't last much longer.

Dinner was excellent. Kazul spent most of the meal lying on the floor and watching us inscrutably. Dragons are very good at being inscrutable. I found it a bit unsettling, but it didn't seem to bother Shiara. Or Nightwitch.

After dinner we talked some more. Kazul told us about the castle and what the floor plan was. She also told us about a lot of things to watch out for. Most of them were magical items that would be dangerous only if we accidentally did something to them, but there were a few traps, too.

"This castle sounds awfully big," Shiara said after a while. "How are we supposed to find this King, anyway?"

"You look for him," Kazul said. "I'm afraid I can't tell you exactly where. The only people who knew where the King was were the wizards who went in and put the spell on him, and as far as I know they're all dead."

"As far as you know?" I asked.

"Some of them didn't come out of the castle."

"But you're sure that the ones who *did* come out are dead?"

"Positive." Kazul smiled reminiscently and licked her lips.

"So what?" said Shiara. Kazul and I looked at her. "I don't care about the wizards who came *out,*" she went on defensively. "I'm worried about the ones who might still be *in* there."

"They have to be either dead or enchanted," Kazul said. "Even a wizard can't live seventeen years without food."

Shiara relaxed a little. "I suppose not. All right, then, what does this King look like?"

"You'll know him when you see him. Besides, he's the only other person in there."

"Oh, great." Shiara wrinkled her nose disgustedly. "We have to hunt through an empty castle for someone we don't even know while a bunch of wizards try to get in and stop us."

"It shouldn't be that bad," Kazul said. "The sword and the key should both help considerably."

"The key?" I said.

"Of course, the key!" Kazul said impatiently. "It can open any door in the castle; that's what it was made for. You could have managed with the sword alone, but it will be much faster with the key as well."

"Are you saying I just picked up the key to the castle by *accident?*"

"Accidents like that happen all the time in the Caves of Chance," Kazul said dryly. "Where do you think they got their name?"

"How do you know it's the right key?" Shiara demanded. "The quozzel said some wizard put it there."

Kazul shrugged. "That's what makes it likely that it's the Key to the Castle. We caught one of the wizards coming out of the caves near the end of the battle, and he'd been inside the castle more than long enough to take the key. But if it will make you more comfortable, I can look at it."

I dug the key out of my pocket and held it out to Kazul. Kazul glanced at it and started to nod, then stopped suddenly and stared at the key very intently.

"It's the Key to the Castle, all right, but that wizard's *done* something to it." She sounded outraged.

"Wonderful," said Shiara disgustedly. "All we need is another wizard to get mixed up in this."

"He isn't *another* wizard," Kazul said. "He's the same one who stole the sword in the first place. And he's dead."

"You're sure he's not one of the wizards who didn't come out of the castle?" Shiara asked.

"I ate him myself."

"Oh." Shiara frowned. "Can you tell what he did?"

Kazul didn't answer. She stared at the key instead, and her eyes started glowing. The key began getting warmer and warmer in my hands. Just before it got too hot for me to hold, the key jerked in the direction of the castle outside. A second later, I dropped it. I stood shaking my fingers, while Kazul and Shiara stared down at the key, and Nightwitch walked over and sniffed at it.

"Nightwitch!" said Shiara. "Stop that. You'll get enchanted or something." She bent over and grabbed awkwardly for Nightwitch with her left hand. The kitten jumped away, and Shiara's fingers brushed the key. A look of surprise came over her face, and she picked the key up. "It feels like fire," she said.

"I know," I said. "It burned my fingers."

"No, I don't mean it's hot," Shiara said. "It just feels like fire."

"It shouldn't," Kazul said, sounding interested. "Bring it over here."

Shiara took the key to Kazul, who looked at it for a few minutes and handed it back. "I thought so. It's part of what that wizard did."

"But what's it for?" Shiara said.

"I don't know," Kazul admitted. "The fire spell is connected to something inside the castle, but I can't tell what with the barriers around the outside. He may have set a trap with it."

"May I have my key back, please?" I said. Kazul and Shiara both looked at me, and Shiara handed me the key. "Thank you," I said, and put it in my pocket. I wasn't quite sure why I wanted it; I only knew that keeping it felt right, somehow.

"Is there anything else we need to know?" I asked. "I mean, we've walked a long way today and we've been in a cave-in, and Shiara has a broken arm, and if we're going to do all these things tomorrow, I would sort of like to get some rest."

"Mrrrroww!" said Nightwitch emphatically.

Kazul chuckled. "It seems you aren't the only one who would like rest. Very well. Marchak!"

The middle-sized dragon who had brought us dinner appeared, and Kazul had him show us to our rooms. They turned out to be normal, human-sized rooms and quite comfortable. I was surprised until it occurred to me that the King of the Dragons would probably have occasional human visitors who would need a place to stay. Then I wondered how many human magicians kept special places for visiting dragons in their castles and towers and things, and right in the middle of wondering, I fell asleep.

A loud pounding noise woke me. Someone, probably a dragon, was knocking on the door of my room. "Just a minute, please," I called, and the pounding stopped.

I got out of the bed, which I couldn't remember having gotten into, and picked up my sword belt. I checked my pockets to make sure I had the key, started for the door, and stopped suddenly in the middle of the room. If the dragons expected me to do things with the Sword of the Sleeping King, I wasn't going to carry it under my arm like a bag of laundry. I put the sword belt on and opened the door.

"It's about time," said the little dragon in the hall. Shiara and Nightwitch were already there.

"I'm sorry," I said. "I didn't know you were in a hurry."

The dragon snorted and started off down the hall. We went after it. It didn't seem to be in a particularly good mood. Shiara explained that it wanted to come into the castle with us, but Kazul wouldn't let it. I couldn't see why it wanted to come. There weren't supposed to be any wizards inside the castle, and I thought the little dragon wanted to fight wizards. I didn't say anything, though. Arguing with a grouchy dragon isn't safe, even if it's only a small dragon.

The dragon brought us back to the cave where we'd talked to Kazul the previous night. Kazul wasn't there, but breakfast was, and we sat down right away. We were just finishing when Kazul arrived to take us out to the castle.

Kazul led us out of the caves and across the hard brown ground. All around us, dragons were polishing their teeth and sharpening their claws, and some of them were muttering spells under their breath. A couple of times, I saw elves hurrying through the crowd, and once I saw a group of intense-looking, red-haired people who had to be fire-witches. Everyone was very serious and grim.

None of us said anything until we got to the castle. Kazul led us around the outside of the shimmerings until we were at the front of the castle. If I concentrated on looking through the barriers, I could see a flat wooden bridge across the moat and a large door with steps leading up to it.

Kazul stopped and turned to the little dragon. "You'd better go find your place now," she said.

"But I want to–"

"Go!"

The little dragon went. Shiara and I looked at each other, and then at Kazul. Kazul smiled. "Are you ready?"

I nodded jerkily. Shiara bent and picked up Nightwitch. Kazul's smile widened. "When I say 'Now,' draw your sword and run for the castle. Don't look back, and don't stop for anything."

I nodded again because I didn't trust my voice just then. Kazul turned to the crowd of dragons, and suddenly everything was completely silent. A shiver ran down my back, and I put my hand on the hilt of the Sword of the Sleeping King.

I felt the bee-in-the-jar buzz that was Shiara's magic, and a strong humming from all the dragons, but the strongest feeling of all was the purring I'd felt from the first time the sword made my arm tingle. It came from the castle. Not from the shimmerings around the castle; they just got in the way. What I was feeling was the magic of the castle itself.

I took a tighter grip on the hilt of the sword. The tingling from the dragons got stronger and more positive, and abruptly Kazul turned and shouted, "Now!" As she spoke, the silver-and-green shimmering around the castle vanished.

I yanked the Sword of the Sleeping King out of its sheath and swung it at the golden glow that was still left between me and the castle. I felt an enormous shock as the sword hit, and then the shimmering vanished in an explosion of golden light.

I shook my head and heard Kazul shout, "Run!"

I took two steps and almost lost my balance. The ground wasn't hard and bare anymore; it was covered with slippery green fuzz. Shiara grabbed my arm just as I heard a series of explosions from behind us.

We ran. I could feel the jangling from the sword that meant there were wizards around somewhere, but I didn't stop to look for them. I was too busy trying to keep up with Shiara, hang on to the sword, and dig the key out of my pocket, all at the same time.

Shiara was standing in front of the door, panting, when I got up to it with the key. I didn't see a keyhole, but as soon as my foot touched the top step of the stairs, the door swung open.

"Daystar," Shiara said, "are you sure–"

Something hit the stone of the castle next to the door and exploded, showering us with little chips of rock. Shiara and I dove through the door and landed on the floor inside with Nightwitch on top of us. I sat up just as the door closed silently behind us.

"Hey!" Shiara said. "Watch what you're doing with that sword!"

"I'm sorry." I stood up, stuck the key in my pocket again, and held out a hand to help Shiara up. "Is your arm all right?"

"I think so," she said absently. "At least, it doesn't hurt any more than it did already. Now, which way do we go?"

"I don't know." The door shook as something hit it, and a moment later there was a muffled explosion. "I think we should get out of here, though."

"Aren't you going to put that stupid sword away first?"

"No," I said. "I'd rather have it in my hand, in case some of the wizards do get into the castle."

Shiara scowled, but she didn't object again, and we started hunting.

The castle was even more confusing on the inside than it was on the outside. Rooms opened into more rooms and then suddenly into a hallway or a flight of stairs. All of them were full of chairs and tables and books and suits of armor, and everything was dusty. The wizards' spell had kept spiderwebs and cobwebs out of the castle, but it hadn't done anything at all about the dust. Nightwitch didn't like it at all. She kept sneezing, until finally Shiara picked her up and carried her.

It took a lot longer to figure out where we were going than I'd expected. I could feel the sword pulling me toward the center of the castle, but it was very hard to just go in that direction. In spite of Kazul's instructions, Shiara and I kept getting into hallways that curved the wrong way and chains of rooms that ended with nowhere else to go. It was very discouraging.

Finally, we came to a pleasant room with a big window and a desk in one corner. "This doesn't look right, either," Shiara said. "Do you think–"

"Doesn't look right?" growled a voice up near the ceiling. "Of course it doesn't look right! It's been seventeen years since anybody has dusted in here. *And* I haven't had any visitors except the mice."

I looked up and saw a wooden gargoyle in one corner. It made a face at me and went on, "Who are you, and what are you doing in here?"

"I'm Daystar, and I'm looking for the King of the Enchanted Forest," I said.

"Oh yeah? What for?" the gargoyle demanded suspiciously.

"I think I'm supposed to return his sword."

"His–Oh, I see. Well, he isn't here. Hasn't been for seventeen years, and boy, am I going to give him an earful when *he* gets back."

"Come *on,* Daystar, we're wasting time," said Shiara.

"Try the great hall, down the corridor to your left," the gargoyle yelled after us as we left the room. "And send somebody to wipe the dust out of my ears! The things I put up with–"

Since nothing else had worked, we followed the gargoyle's directions and found ourselves in front of a large door at the end of a long hall. It was three times as wide as a normal door, and much taller, and it was made of gold with designs in relief. There was a staff lying on the floor in front of it, and I could tell from the jangling of the sword that it was a wizard's staff. When I stopped to look at it, the sword jerked impatiently toward the door.

"I think this is the place we've been looking for," I said.

Shiara tried the door. "It's locked. Where's the key?"

"Just a minute." I dug for it. As soon as I touched it, I felt the key pulling at me, the same way the sword was. "Hey!"

"What is it?" Shiara said. "Come on, hurry up!"

"It's this key," I said as I unlocked the door. "It feels almost like the sword, except–"

I stopped as the door swung open. The room inside was very large and very high, full of light and not dusty at all. In the center of the floor stood something like a shallow iron brazier, about three feet tall and nearly five feet across, full of glowing coals. On the other side of the brazier was a couch, and lying on the couch was a man.

He was dressed in expensive-looking clothes, but there were tears in them, as if he had been in a fight. He didn't look old, even though his beard was long and gray. His head was bare, and at his side was a jeweled scabbard, empty. He was asleep.

Shiara took a deep breath. "That must be him. Come on, Daystar, let's get this over with."

I stepped into the room and walked slowly toward the couch. *This is too easy,* I thought. As I came around the brazier, I saw that there was another wizard's staff lying beside the couch. Something felt wrong, and I slowed down even more. I stopped, standing next to the couch with the key in one hand and the sword in the other.

"Well, now that we're here, how do we break the spell?" Shiara asked, coming up on one side of me.

"Something's wrong," I said, and as I spoke I realized what it was. The key was still pulling at me, but as soon as I had stepped into the room, the pulling from the sword had stopped. All I could feel from the sword was the jangling of the magic in the wizards' staffs.

"Maybe if you lay the sword on him it'll work," Shiara said, ignoring me. "You have to try something or we'll be here all day."

"I wouldn't try anything at all, if I were you," said a voice behind us.

Shiara and I spun around. The doorway was full of wizards.

20

In Which Daystar Uses His Sword

I stared at the wizards for an instant, then turned and jumped for the couch, hoping I could break the spell before the wizards did anything. I didn't make it. As I brought the flat of the sword down, the sleeping man vanished. The sword clanged softly against the couch, and I spun back to face the wizards.

Something hit me as I turned, and suddenly I couldn't move my body at all. I could turn my head far enough to see Shiara, but that was all. Shiara looked as if she were concentrating on something, so I turned my head back to the wizards. They were standing around the sleeping man, who was now lying on the floor in front of the doorway.

"Well done," said one of the wizards to another.

"Thank you," the second wizard said. "It was a mere trifle."

There was a stir at the back of the group of wizards, and a moment later Antorell pushed forward to the front. He had a bandage around one arm, probably where the dragon had bitten him. "I want the boy!" he said. "Now!"

The wizard in front, who seemed to be the leader of the group, looked at Antorell coldly. "We permitted you to join us in order to give you an opportunity to repair some of the damage you did seventeen years ago. Not to further your private ambitions."

"But you said I could have the boy!"

"Antorell, you're a fool," the leader said. "You may have the boy, but *after* we have possession of the sword, not before."

"I'll give you the sword, then!" Antorell said angrily. He strode around the edge of the brazier and reached for the hilt of the sword, just above my hand. I wanted to jerk away, but I still couldn't move.

As Antorell touched the sword, there was a flash of blue-and-gold light that flung him backward onto the floor. If he'd fallen a few inches to the other side, he'd have gone into the brazier. I found myself wishing he had, then found myself staring at the brazier. Something about it nibbled at my mind, but I couldn't make it come clear. I didn't have time to think about it, because the wizards started talking again.

Antorell was picking himself up off the floor, and the leader of the wizards smiled at him nastily. "You see?"

"You knew this would happen!" Antorell said furiously.

"Of *course* I knew," the leader said. "Had you spent your time hunting that sword instead of trying to get some sort of ridiculous revenge on Cimorene, you, too, would know."

"Then demonstrate the proper method for me," Antorell said sarcastically. "If you know so much, you take the sword."

"I am not so foolish," the other wizard replied. "No one save the King of the Enchanted Forest can take that sword from a bearer who is not willing to give it up, especially not inside this castle."

"Then how do you expect to get it?" Antorell said even more sarcastically than before.

"We kill the King," the wizard said, gesturing at the sleeping figure on the floor in front of him. "When the line of the Kings of the Enchanted Forest is ended, one of us can take up the rule of the castle."

"What good will that do?" Antorell said. "The boy will still have the sword. And, as you have reminded me so many times in the past two days, he seems to be able to use it."

The leader shrugged. "If your tale is true, I shall admit to some surprise. I thought no one but the King could use the sword. Which is why one of us must become King."

"You accuse me of lying?"

"Why should I bother?"

Antorell scowled and started to raise his staff, then seemed to change his mind. "When the boy blows your own spells back at you, perhaps you will see what I mean."

"Nonsense!" the leader of the wizards replied. "You obviously know little of what you speak."

"No, of course not. I have only seen the boy in action," Antorell said with awful sarcasm.

The leader shrugged again. "What the boy has learned matters little.

The power of the sword passes to the ruler of the castle, and there is nothing he can do about it. He will be easy enough to take care of then."

Out of the corner of my eye, I saw a flicker of movement. Shiara was edging toward me. I had to force myself not to turn my head. The wizards seemed to have forgotten both of us, and I didn't want to remind them. I hoped they wouldn't remember until after Shiara had done whatever she was planning to do. I also hoped Shiara was planning to do something. I certainly couldn't, and I didn't think Nightwitch would be much help against all those wizards.

"Stop talking and let's get on with it," one of the wizards in the back said.

"An excellent suggestion. That is, if you are quite satisfied, Antorell?" said the leader.

Antorell glared and stalked over to the rest of the wizards. The leader looked around and nodded. "Begin."

Under other circumstances, the spell casting would have been very interesting to watch. The wizards spent quite a bit of time arguing about where each of them should stand, and exactly what the correct angle was for each staff, and in what order the spells should be said. The leader seemed particularly concerned that things be done right. Evidently there was something about the castle that would cause problems if everything wasn't perfect. Finally, they agreed on what they were going to do, and they got started.

As the wizards started chanting, something touched my arm. If I could have moved, I'd have jumped. It was Shiara. "Do something before they finish!" I whispered.

"I've been trying!" Shiara whispered back. "But it isn't working."

"Oh no." I was so upset that I spoke the words in a normal tone of voice. Fortunately, the wizards were too busy chanting to notice. "You haven't been polite to anyone since you apologized to Telemain, and you used that up on the last bunch of wizards."

Shiara looked stricken. "Daystar, I'm *sorry!*"

"There isn't anything we can do about it now," I said. "If you–"

I stopped because the wizards had stopped chanting. Shiara and I both looked at them, but the wizards didn't seem to be finished with what they were doing. They looked more like they'd been interrupted in the middle of things. The leader bent over the man on the floor, who was still sleeping. A moment later the wizard straightened with an exclamation and stretched his staff out over the man's body.

The figure dissolved into sparkles, leaving a little blob of mud on the floor, and the other wizards stirred in surprise. "A simulacrum!" said someone.

I let out my breath in relief. Simulacra are very hard to make. You have to mix earth, air, fire, and water in exactly the right proportions in order to get a good one, and that's fairly tricky. A really good magician can make a simulacrum that looks exactly like someone but doesn't have any connection to the actual person at all. As a result, a simulacrum can't be used against someone the way other types of magic can. What they're mainly good for is confusing people.

This one seemed to have done an excellent job. The wizards were glaring at each other accusingly. "If that was a simulacrum," one of them said finally, "where's the King? Who put it there, anyway?"

"Old Zemenar, probably," an older-looking wizard said. "The simulacrum looked like him, and setting up a decoy is just the sort of thing he would do."

"That doesn't make sense! He started this whole affair in the first place. Why would he put a false king in the castle to distract us?"

"Zemenar never trusted anybody. He probably wanted to do this himself, so he made it as hard as he could for anyone else to finish the job. Or maybe he was just being ornery." The older wizard shrugged. "Either way, I doubt that he expected to get eaten by a dragon."

"We have wasted enough time here," the leader of the wizards said with sudden decision. "Silvarex, take three others and begin searching for the King at once. We cannot allow him to escape again."

He went on giving instructions, but I stopped paying attention. He wasn't talking to me, and I had other things to worry about. I was still holding the key in my left hand, and as soon as the simulacrum disappeared, the key had stopped tugging me and started getting warm. My other arm, the one with the sword, was tingling under the jangling of the wizards, and my head felt very light. I had a sudden, strong feeling that there was something important I ought to remember, but the jangling of the wizards' magic kept distracting me before I could figure out what it was.

"Daystar!" Shiara hissed, practically in my ear.

I jumped a little and realized that the wizard's spell holding me was beginning to weaken.

I couldn't move very much or very fast, though, and if the wizards noticed, they'd just throw the spell at me again. I decided not to move at all until I was sure I could move the sword fast enough to block another spell, then whispered to Shiara, "Don't *do* that. They might notice."

Shiara snorted. "If you don't want them to notice, you'd better try to notice sooner. That was the third time I called you."

"I'm sorry," I said.

"So am I. What are we going to do?"

"If you could–Nightwitch!" I broke off in mid-sentence as a small black streak darted toward the group of wizards. One of them raised his staff; Shiara cried out and Nightwitch dodged. The spell hit the marble floor in a ball of light, and a moment later the kitten was among the wizards' feet. I couldn't see what was happening, but I could hear the wizards shouting.

"There it goes!"

"Stop it!"

"It got away."

"Find it," the leader of the wizards commanded. "You, Grineran, go after it. It may lead you to the one we seek."

One of the wizards nodded and left, and I blinked. There were only three wizards left now: a short, round one, the one who was giving orders, and Antorell.

Antorell was staring at Shiara and me. "What about them?" he said suddenly. "They may know something."

The leader of the wizards looked thoughtful. "For once, Antorell, you may have made a useful suggestion. Persuading them to explain what they know may be difficult, however."

Antorell grinned nastily. "I think I can manage it."

"Really." The leader sounded skeptical. "The girl is a fire-witch, and the boy has the sword, remember."

"Sword or no, he cannot be immune to spells or Silvarex would never have been able to bind him," Antorell said.

"What did you have in mind?"

"Something like this."

Antorell waved his staff casually in my direction as he spoke. Even if I'd been able to move, I wouldn't have been able to twist the sword into a position to block the spell before it hit me, especially since I didn't realize what he was doing until the pain struck. It felt as if I were fighting the fire-witch again, only this time the pain was all through my body instead of just in my arms. It was worse than anything I'd ever felt. I think I screamed, but I'm not sure.

Beside me, Shiara shouted, and a long ribbon of fire shot through the air in front of me, straight at Antorell. Antorell caught fire almost at once. As he slapped at his clothes and his staff, trying to put out the flames, the pain stopped abruptly and the key in my left hand got even hotter. Neither of the other wizards even tried to help Antorell. They just stood and stared at Shiara and me.

The ribbon of fire still hung in the air above the brazier, making a curtain of flames between us and the wizards. Slowly, reluctantly, it began to fade, and as it died, the heat from the key in my left hand faded along with it. *Fire,* I thought. Fire in the brazier, fire in the key; Kazul had said the key could open any door in the castle, and Shiara had said something about the key and fire . . .

I lifted my left hand, fighting the remnant of the wizard's spell, and threw the key forward into the brazier.

There was a *whoosh* of flame that leapt all the way to the ceiling, then died. I thought I saw something in it, but it vanished before I could be sure. The brazier began to glow, and the whole room was suddenly thick and heavy with magic, like the air just before a summer thunderstorm. I could feel the magic growing stronger, as if it was getting ready for something, but nothing else happened. I was sure there was something else I should do, but I couldn't think what.

"Stop them!" the leader of the wizards shouted.

"Move, Daystar!" Shiara cried, and ducked down behind the brazier.

I tried to follow her, but I couldn't move fast enough because of the remains of the binding spell and because I was worrying about what else I was supposed to do in order to finish the spell I'd started with the key. I saw Antorell and the other wizards bring their staffs up, and I tried desperately to move the sword far enough to block whatever they were throwing at me.

I made it, but only just.

The sword flashed as the wizards' spell hit it, and a tingle ran through me. The spell that had been binding me vanished. I could feel what was left of it flowing through the sword, along with the rest of the magic the wizards had thrown. It felt a lot like the jolt of power I'd gotten in the forest, when I'd used the sword on the spell the wizards had aimed at Shiara, except that this time I could tell where the power was going. It was flowing through me, into the magic of the Enchanted Forest itself. Back where it had come from in the first place, if Kazul was right about where wizards got most of their magic. Back to . . .

I felt my eyes widening and almost missed blocking the next spell. Then four more wizards appeared behind the three in the doorway. If I didn't do something soon, I wouldn't have time for anything except blocking spells. There was no way to find out whether I was right except to try.

I stepped up to the edge of the brazier, took a deep breath, and said loudly,

"Power of water, wind, and earth,
Turn the spell back to its birth.
Raise the fire to free the lord
By the power of wood and sword."

As I spoke the last word, I thrust the Sword of the Sleeping King into the middle of the coals in the brazier.

As the sword touched the coals, all the waiting magic around me surged forward, and suddenly I knew where it had come from. It was the magic of the castle and the Enchanted Forest itself, alive and growing, running like a net through the ground and the trees and the air. Fire shot up to the ceiling, the same way it had when I threw the key into the brazier, but this time the flames didn't fade. They got brighter and brighter until all I could see was fire. I heard a rumbling sound like the roof of the Caves of Chance falling in, and the floor shook under me.

A voice said loudly, "All hail the Waker of the Sword!" and voices all around me shouted, "Hail!"

Echoes from the shout rolled around the room, like thunder rolling back and forth across the sky. I couldn't see anything except fire, I couldn't hear anything except echoes, and I couldn't feel anything at all. Then something in my head seemed to snap into place, and the noise stopped abruptly.

I let go of the sword and stepped back a pace. The light in my eyes started to dwindle into flames again, but now I could see pictures in them, outlined in fire: dragons fighting wizards outside the castle, and dwarves fighting elves, and elves fighting wizards and other elves. I couldn't tell who was winning. Sometimes it seemed to be one set of fiery little shapes, and sometimes it seemed to be the other.

As I stared at the fire, I realized that I could feel the jangling from all the wizards' staffs and the deep rumbling of the magic of the Enchanted Forest and the purring of the castle itself, even though I wasn't holding the sword anymore. I could even feel the shape of the wizards' spells inside and outside the castle, including the one around and over the brazier. I could feel the magic of the sword, too, weaving a bright pattern through all the other types of magic. I followed the pattern until I saw how it worked, and then I reached out toward all the different kinds of magic and *twisted*.

The jangling of the wizards' staffs stopped abruptly as the power of the Enchanted Forest swallowed up the power of the staffs. Immediately, the flames in front of me swirled and pulled together, so that the pictures I'd been watching disappeared, and I found myself staring at a crowd of very angry ex-wizards through a shifting curtain of fire.

At least two of the wizards were wearing swords, and they were reaching for them. The leader started to point in my direction, and I ducked instinctively. Almost every wizard who's any good carries a spell or two outside his staff, just in case the staff gets stolen. The wizards at the castle didn't have any magic in their staffs anymore, but they could still make trouble with their spare spells.

I dove behind the brazier just in time to avoid something like a large lightning bolt. I swallowed, hoping these wizards didn't have very many more spells like that. I heard shouts, and I peered around the edge of the brazier, expecting to see the wizards with the swords coming after me.

Wizards were running in several directions, but none of them seemed to be heading for me. For a moment, I was puzzled, but then I saw Morwen, Telemain, and a couple of elves charging into the room from the hallway. I didn't stop to worry about how they had gotten there. I turned back to the brazier, to pull the Sword of the Sleeping King out of it so I could join the fight–and stopped.

The flames were still swirling in the air above the brazier, but they were denser somehow, and brighter. All I could see was a mass of white-and-yellow light, shot with power. Then something flashed so brightly that I had to cover my eyes. When I could see again, there was a door in the center of the brazier, right on top of the place where I had thrown the key, and facing the point of the sword. The door hung between two pillars that looked as if they were made of solid light, and I couldn't see anything around it except light and flames.

I stared at the door for a moment as it grew even more solid. I wasn't sure I wanted to find out what was on the other side. Doors like that are even worse than the one in Morwen's house; they can go *anywhere.* I reached for the Sword of the Sleeping King, but before my hand touched it, the door opened and a man stepped through.

He didn't look at all like the simulacrum. He was taller, with black hair and tired-looking gray eyes, and he didn't have a beard. He was dressed in plain clothes, but there was a feeling of strength about him, and power. Even without the thin gold circlet he wore I would have guessed who he was. I took a deep breath of relief as he stepped down from the brazier and onto the marble floor in front of me.

As he did, the doorway behind him melted back into leaping flames, which faded quickly until there was nothing there except the brazier and the glowing coals. The room was utterly silent. I looked up at the King of the Enchanted Forest for a moment, then turned to the brazier and reached for the hilt of the Sword of the Sleeping King.

The sword wasn't even warm from the fire, but the blade shone even more brightly than it had the day Mother brought it out of the Enchanted Forest and gave it to me. I looked at it for a minute, then turned back to the King and held it out.

"I've come to return your sword, Father," I said.

21

In Which the Battle Ends and Antorell Makes Trouble Again

For a long moment the King of the Enchanted Forest looked at me over the hilt of the sword. Then he reached out and took it. He held it up for a moment, then turned and brought it down hard on the edge of the brazier.

The brazier split and fell apart, scattering embers. As soon as it hit the floor, it started to melt and vanish, and in a few seconds there was nothing left of it except the key. The King bent and picked it up, then turned back to me and smiled. "Thank you."

"You're welcome," I said automatically. Then I noticed Shiara sitting on the floor, where she had dived when the wizards started throwing spells around. She was looking from me to the King and back, as if she couldn't believe what she was seeing. "Oh, I'm sorry," I said. "Shiara, this is the King of the Enchanted Forest. Father, this is my friend Shiara. She's a fire-witch."

Father bowed. Shiara looked at him and cleared her throat, then cleared it again and said, "Hey, um, are you really Daystar's father?"

The King smiled slightly and nodded. "Of course. Only the Kings of the Enchanted Forest can use the sword." He raised it so that the light flashing from the blade filled the room, then in one fluid motion he sheathed it in the empty scabbard at his side. He looked at me and smiled again.

Shiara blinked, then turned her head and glared at me. "Why didn't you tell me the King of the Enchanted Forest was your father?" she demanded.

"I'm sorry, but I didn't know it myself until just now," I said.

"Ha!" said Shiara. "Why–"

Before she could finish her sentence, Nightwitch pounced on her.

"Nightwitch!" Shiara sounded relieved. "Where did you come from?"

"I believe she came with them," Father said, nodding toward the doorway.

Shiara and I turned. A dozen wizards were sprawled on the floor in a tangled pile. Some of them were wrapped in vines, some of them seemed to be frozen, and some of them had elves and cats sitting on them. As soon as we turned to look at them, the elves all got up and bowed, then sat down again quickly before the wizards could get up and do anything. The cats just sat and blinked at us.

"I don't think you need to be quite so careful," the King said to the elves. "If you'll let them up one at a time, I'll decide what to do with them."

The elves nodded, and one of them stood up and bowed politely to the King. Father walked over to the wizard the elf had been sitting on and started asking him questions. The wizard didn't answer. Finally, Father shrugged and waved a hand. The wizard disappeared, and Father went on to the next one.

As soon as they got off the wizards, the elves started gathering up the staffs into a big bundle. Most of the cats just sat down and washed their paws. None of the wizards would say anything to Father, and he didn't waste much time on any of them. In a few minutes, there were only three wizards left. I was watching them when Shiara poked me.

"Daystar, where's Morwen?" she asked when I turned around. "Those are her cats; she has to be around somewhere."

"I don't know," I said. "I remember seeing her right before Father showed up, and Telemain was with her." I looked toward the door, where the last few wizards were, and blinked. "Shiara, where's Antorell?"

"Didn't he disappear already?"

"No, he didn't. I was watching," I said. Shiara and I looked at each other for an instant, then headed for the doorway.

No one tried to stop us. One of the elves gave us an odd look, but another elf grabbed his arm and whispered something to him, and he only bowed deeply as we passed. It made me feel almost as uncomfortable as I felt when the dwarves bowed to me.

Outside in the hallway we found Morwen kneeling on the floor beside Telemain and wrapping long strips of black cloth around his right shoulder. Pieces of odd-looking plants littered the floor, and a little way down the hall was a puddle of something dark and slimy. The puddle had a wizard's staff lying across it, and a wizard's robe was sort of crumpled up under the staff.

"Morwen!" Shiara said. "What happened? Can I help?"

"What happened was a battle," Morwen said. "I should think that would be obvious enough."

"But how did–" Shiara stopped because Telemain was stirring. A moment later he opened his eyes and looked up at all of us.

"What was that?" he asked rather hazily.

"That," said Morwen, "was a sword. They are long, pointed, and very sharp. You're lucky it didn't take your head off."

Telemain started to shake his head, then winced. "A plain sword. No wonder I couldn't block it. I thought it was a spell."

Morwen snorted. "You may be one of the greatest magical theoreticians in the world, but you don't have a particle of common sense," she said acidly. "Why, in heaven's name, didn't you duck?"

"I *did* duck!" Telemain said, looking startled and indignant. "He was aiming for my chest, not my shoulder. And if you think I'm going to put up with you and your–"

"You," Morwen said firmly, "are going to put up with me until that shoulder is healed. Which, may I remind you, means that I will have to put up with you for the same period of time. Fortunately, it shouldn't take very long–a few days, at most."

"A few days!" Telemain said. "Are you mad? It'll take at least a week!"

"Not if I change the herbs twice a day," Morwen said in an irritated tone. "I should know. It's my field."

"Well, it's *my* shoulder!"

"I'm so glad you noticed," Morwen said. "Stop fussing, or you'll make things worse and I *will* have to put up with you for a week."

"If I have to continue lying on this floor–which is cold, hard, and extremely uncomfortable–you'll have to put up with me a lot longer than that!"

Morwen got a peculiar look on her face. "I'll consider the idea carefully. Meanwhile"–she looked past Shiara and me–"Mendanbar, can you provide a room for this stubborn . . . magician?"

"Easily," said the King of the Enchanted Forest, from the doorway behind us. "Which room do you want?"

"The brown one," Morwen said before Telemain could answer. "He'll need a firm bed to support that shoulder."

Father laughed. "Of course." He started to lift his hand, and I cleared my throat.

"I would like to ask them something before they go," I said when Father turned toward me. He nodded, and I looked at Morwen. "Did you notice what happened to the wizard who was halfway around the brazier when you came in? I didn't see him afterward."

"You mean Antorell? Yes, I thought I saw him," Morwen said. "I'm afraid I don't recall. He wasn't the one I melted, if that's what you're asking."

"Could he have gotten away?" Shiara asked.

Morwen glanced at the King. "If you will allow me, I can find out fairly quickly." Father nodded, and Morwen made a chuckling sort of sound. Two of the cats poked their heads around the corner of the door frame.

"Daystar wants to know what's become of one of the wizards," Morwen said to the cats. "The one named Antorell."

The cats looked at each other, and one of them twitched its tail. The other one looked back at Morwen and said, "Rroowww!" and they both pulled their heads back out of sight.

"He got away," Morwen said, turning back to the King. "Scorn says he ducked down the hall while Telemain and I were busy with the rest of them."

Father frowned. "I'd better find him before he causes any more trouble." He looked back at Morwen. "The brown room, I think you said?"

Morwen nodded, and Father waved his hand. Morwen and Telemain disappeared. Father raised his hand to make another gesture, then paused and looked at Shiara and me. "I suppose you want to come, too?"

"Yes, we do. That is, if it isn't going to cause problems," I said.

I hadn't quite finished my sentence when the castle dissolved into mist around us. The mist cleared immediately, and we were standing on springy green moss with the trees of the Enchanted Forest all around us. At first I thought Father had taken us to a place a long way from the castle, but then I saw dragons and elves among the trees. I looked back over my shoulder, and there was the castle right behind us.

Shiara looked around. "Hey, where did all the trees come from?"

"They came from the wizards' magic," Father said. "When Daystar released the magic they had stored in their staffs, it went back into the forest, and things got back to normal in a hurry."

"When Daystar did *what?*"

"It was part of the sword and the fire and the brazier," I said hastily. "I think you were busy ducking."

"Oh," said Shiara.

By that time the dragons and elves had seen us, and everyone started cheering and bowing. In the middle of the cheering, one of the elves came over and bowed deeply. "It is good to see Your Majesty again," he said.

"It is good to be here again, Willin," the King replied. "How goes the battle?"

"I believe the dragons are the proper persons to provide that information," the elf said, sounding more and more pompous with every word. "If Your Majesty will wait here, I will arrange–"

"Mendanbar!" shouted one of the dragons. "So it worked!" As she made her way through the crowd toward us, the elf frowned ferociously.

"Your Majesty," he said in a low tone, "if you would prefer a more formal audience–"

"I haven't time for that, Willin," said the King. "Besides, I need you inside the castle, not out here. Someone has to look the place over, and arrange dinner for all these people, and see about getting some of the housekeeping staff back."

"Yes, yes, of course! At once, Your Majesty!" Willin bustled away, looking much happier now that he had a suitable job.

"How's the battle?" the King asked again as the dragon reached us.

"Quite finished," the dragon said. "There are a few still out herding prisoners together, but that's about all."

"Excellent!" the King said, but he was watching the trees out of the corners of his eyes, and there was a tiny crease between his eyebrows. "If King Kazul is about, I would like to speak with her."

The dragon smiled, and her eyes glittered as if she were enjoying a private joke. "Kazul will be here in a moment."

Father nodded, managing to look impatient and polite at the same time. Suddenly the cheering got much louder, and then the dragons drew apart and Kazul came through the trees toward us. She was smiling, and she looked very large and green and shining. She was so magnificent that none of us saw the figure with her until they were both quite close to us.

I was the first to notice that Kazul had someone with her. When I saw who it was, I blinked and swallowed hard. *"Mother?"*

"Cimorene!" shouted Father. He took three strides forward and took her in his arms. Kazul smiled and sat back, looking smug.

Mother was laughing and crying at the same time; I'd never seen her do that before. Not ever. I was still staring when Shiara poked me.

"Don't stare," she whispered when I turned. "It's not polite."

I looked at Shiara for a minute, and my face got hot. I couldn't really say anything, though, because she was right. I felt very peculiar, but fortunately Mother and the King stopped hugging each other just then and started paying attention to the rest of us.

Father went to talk to Kazul, and Mother came over to us. She gave me a quick hug and said, "Well done, Daystar."

"Thank you, Mother," I said. Shiara shifted uncomfortably, and I remembered that I still hadn't introduced her. "Oh, and this is my friend Shiara. She's a fire-witch."

"I can tell that by looking at her." Mother smiled at Shiara. "You'll stay with us for a few days, won't you?"

Shiara nodded.

"Good," Mother said. "Now, if you will excuse me, there are still a few things I have to attend to."

"Mother," I said, and she turned. "That wizard, Antorell. He was in the castle, but he got away. I thought you should know."

"He did not get away!" said a familiar voice behind me. "I caught him myself. Do you want him for anything, or can I eat him?"

We all turned. The little dragon was sitting on the other side of the bridge, holding on to one of Antorell's arms. Antorell's robe was dirty and he didn't have his staff anymore. He looked tattered and very unhappy, and the dragon looked extremely pleased with itself. "Well?" it said. "Can I eat him?"

I looked at Mother, and she shook her head.

"I don't think you should eat him," I said to the dragon. "The King talked to all the other wizards, and he'll probably want to talk to this one, too."

"Well, I want him back when the King gets finished with him," the little dragon said. "I caught him, and I'm going to eat him."

"He'll probably give you a stomachache," Shiara said.

I stopped listening to the conversation, because Antorell had straightened and was glaring past me, at Mother. He looked more powerful, somehow, but no one else seemed to have noticed anything unusual. I glanced uneasily over my shoulder and saw Father still talking to Kazul. I looked back, wondering whether I really had anything to worry about. Without his staff, all Antorell had were his extra spells, and he'd probably used them up in the battle. At least, I hoped he had.

Shiara and the dragon were still arguing. Suddenly, Antorell twisted and made a throwing motion with his left hand. The dragon shrieked in pain and let go of him, and he ran toward the bridge, waving his hands and shouting. I felt a sudden, intense surge of magic around him, and an instant later a demon appeared.

It materialized right in front of us, all purple scales and orange claws and silver-green teeth. Antorell shouted again, in a language I didn't understand, and pointed at Mother. The demon nodded, and one arm darted out.

I grabbed something I couldn't see out of the air in front of me and pulled. The demon vanished, and Antorell cried out in surprise. I yanked at the something again and sent Antorell along with the demon. After what he'd been trying to do, I didn't care whether the King wanted to talk to him or not. Then I saw that the little dragon was turning pink around the edges again. I let go of whatever it was, grabbed a different one, and twisted. The dragon gave a surprised-sounding squeak and turned green again, all at once.

I dropped the piece of nothing I'd been holding and turned. Mother was shaking her head. "That was a bit extreme, Daystar," she said, but her expression was proud.

"Daystar, what on earth did you . . . I mean, how did you . . ." Shiara gave up and just stared at me.

"I don't know," I said. I was at least as surprised as she was. "I'm not even sure what I did."

"What happened?" the little dragon asked. It looked around suspiciously. "Is that wizard dead?"

"No, but he probably wishes he were," Mother said. "Demons do not like surprise visitors."

"Oh, is *that* what Daystar did with him?" said Father's voice from behind me. "I wondered."

I jumped and turned around to see the King and Kazul standing there. The King was looking at Mother; Kazul was looking at the little dragon.

"Where have you been?" Kazul asked in a resigned voice.

"I've been catching wizards!" the little dragon said proudly. "Well, one of them, anyway. He threw dragonsbane at me again and called a demon and Daystar got rid of both of them. I didn't even get to eat him," the dragon finished sadly.

"I see," Kazul said, shaking her head. "I think you'd better spend the rest of the day with me. It may, just possibly, keep you out of trouble."

"I don't understand!" Shiara burst out. "How could Antorell do any magic without his staff? And how could Daystar do any magic at all? And what did Antorell have to do with the sword and everything?"

The King smiled at Mother, then looked at Shiara and me. "As long as things seem to be quiet out here, why don't we go inside? That way, we can be comfortable while I explain."

Shiara and I nodded. Father waved his hand, and the Enchanted Forest dissolved into mist around us.

22

Which Contains an Engagement, a Feast, and a Happy Ending

We appeared in one of the rooms inside the castle, a small, cozy-looking place with lots of bookshelves. It was just as dusty as all the other rooms Shiara and I had been through, but when Father waved, all the dust vanished. Mother muttered something about instant cleaning being no excuse for letting things get into such a state, and we all sat down. The King looked at us.

"I believe this should begin with you, Cimorene," he said. Mother looked thoughtful for a moment, then nodded and began.

Apparently, Mother really *was* a princess. She was the youngest daughter of the ruler of a very large kingdom on the other side of the Mountains of Morning, and she'd thought it was boring. So she ran away and became Kazul's princess.

Kazul wasn't King of the Dragons then. She and Mother got along very well, and after a while, Kazul started teaching her dragon magic. And then the wizards helped someone poison the old King of the Dragons, and all the dragons went to the Ford of Whispering Snakes to try and move Colin's Stone, and Kazul was the one who did.

Practically the first thing Kazul did after she became King was to kick the wizards out of the Mountains of Morning, which made the wizards plenty mad. So they decided to start a war by getting the dragons to attack the Enchanted Forest.

That was how Mother met my father. He came to see Kazul about some burned parts of the forest, and he found Mother instead. Then the two of them went searching for Kazul, who'd been kidnapped by the wizards, and by the time they got her free, they had decided to get married. Kazul was mother's matron-of-honor.

The wizards didn't make any more trouble for almost a year, but when they finally did, they made up for the wait. They stole Father's sword right out of the castle armory.

"They'd figured out that the sword was the main thing keeping them from absorbing magic in the Enchanted Forest," Father said, "and they thought that if they got rid of it, they could soak up the whole forest and use all that extra magic to wipe out the dragons. They didn't realize, at first, that even without the sword I could use the magic of the forest against them."

"Well, then what good was the stupid sword, anyway?" Shiara asked. "If you didn't need it to stop the wizards–"

"I *did* need it," Father said. "I can deal with one or two wizards at a time, but not the whole Society of Wizards at once. And I can't be everywhere. The sword is connected directly to the magic of the Enchanted Forest, so it protects the whole forest and not just the area where it happens to be. If you want the technical details, ask Telemain. He helpd me set it up."

With the sword gone, Father had to stay in the Enchanted Forest to keep the wizards out. Kazul and Morwen and Telemain all volunteered to go steal the sword back, but there was a problem. When the sword is outside the Enchanted Forest, only the King of the Enchanted Forest or a member of his family can stand to hold it for more than a few seconds. And Mother was the only other member of Father's family then.

Father wasn't too pleased about this, because Mother was going to have a baby–me–but they didn't really have any other choice. So Mother and the rest left to find the sword, and Father stayed in the Enchanted Forest to fight off the wizards. They didn't expect the whole Society of Wizards to attack the castle the day after they left, but that's what happened. Fortunately, Mother had a feeling something was wrong, and she sent Kazul back to check. When Kazul saw all the wizards attacking the castle, she flew back to the Mountains of Morning and ordered all the dragons to come help.

Meanwhile, Mother and the others found the sword, with Antorell guarding it. He was the son of Zemenar, the Head Wizard of the Society of Wizards, and Mother didn't like him much. So when he tried to keep them from taking the sword back, Mother melted him.

Unfortunately, by the time they got back to the castle, the battle was over and the wizards had put their shield up. Kazul sent some dragons out to look for wizards who had gotten away, and then she and Mother and Morwen and Telemain had a long talk about what to do next.

All of them were sure that the wizards had put a spell on the King, and they were just as sure that the sword could break the spell. Unfortunately, the sword could only be used by one of the Kings of the Enchanted Forest or his children, and then only when the earth, air, and water of the Enchanted Forest and the fire of the sword itself had recognized the person holding it as a rightful heir. And the only way to be recognized was to go out in the Enchanted Forest and hope you would do the right things at the right times.

So the dragons put their own shield up around the castle, to keep the wizards from sneaking inside, and after a while Mother had me. About that time Antorell found her. He blamed her for his father's death, because she'd taken the sword, and he tried to kill her. Mother had to melt him again.

After that, Mother decided that she'd better find somewhere to hide until I was old enough to use the sword. As long as it stayed inside the Enchanted Forest, the sword was invisible to wizards' magic. Mother, however, wasn't. If she stayed in the Enchanted Forest, one of the wizards' spells would find her. On the other hand, she couldn't take the sword out of the forest and still keep it hidden, any more than the wizards could.

So Mother hid the sword inside the forest, then left and never went back until the day she gave the sword to me. She put up some good spells to keep Antorell from finding us, then waited. She taught me all the right spells and manners and history and things, without ever telling me anything about the sword or the King of the Enchanted Forest or the war with the wizards. That way, I would have a chance of being recognized by the sword and reaching the castle without getting caught by one of the wizards' spells.

"I'm afraid it was rather hard on you, Daystar," she said. "But we couldn't think of anything else that had a chance of working."

"Well, *I* think we were lucky," Shiara said.

The King smiled at me. "Kings of the Enchanted Forest are supposed to be lucky."

Shiara blinked. "You weren't very lucky, were you? What did those wizards do to you, anyway?"

The King shook his head. "Zemenar and about ten others broke into the castle during the battle. I got a couple of them, but without the sword I was outnumbered a little too badly. They wanted to kill me, but they couldn't do it inside the castle without the sword, and they couldn't take me outside the castle because of the dragons. So Zemenar decided to put me in storage, in a manner of speaking, while he went back for the sword. The simulacrum was a decoy, in case someone managed to get into the castle while he was gone."

"But where were you for seventeen years?" Shiara said.

"There are . . . places that can be reached through the proper doors, places that can't be gotten into or out of except through such a door. Some of them are very large; some aren't. Zemenar found one that suited him and put me in it, then hid the door. Without the sword or the key, I couldn't get out until someone put the door back up." His smile was a little crooked. "I'm lucky that one doesn't need to eat in those places, or I wouldn't have lasted seventeen years."

"But I still don't understand about Antorell. He acted as if he wanted to do something to Daystar a lot more than he wanted the sword."

"Antorell never knew what the sword was," Mother said. "Zemenar, the Head Wizard, was the only one who knew the whole story, and after the way Antorell failed to guard the sword, the new Head Wizard wouldn't tell him anything."

"Ha!" said Shiara. "Served him right. But what did Daystar do to Antorell, anyway? And how? He never did anything like it before."

"He couldn't do it before," Father said. "The Kings of the Enchanted Forest can use the magic of the forest directly, but only after the sword has acknowledged them. Daystar wasn't acknowledged until he put the sword into the fire."

"Oh." Shiara sat back, looking thoughtful.

There was a moment's silence, then I thought of something else I wanted to ask about. "Mother, do you know anything about fire-witches' magic?"

"Yes, of course," she said. "Why do you want to know?"

"Could you teach Shiara how to do things?" I said. "That's why she came to the Enchanted Forest in the first place. She helped me a lot, and I think she ought to have some sort of reward."

"I didn't do very much," Shiara objected. "You kept me from staying a statue, and I think you saved my life when the roof of the Caves of Chance fell in. You're the one who deserves a reward."

"I think," Mother broke in before I could answer Shiara, "that it is time you told us what you have been doing these past few days. I have a general idea, but I would like a few more details, and Mendanbar hasn't heard anything about it yet."

I looked at Father, and he nodded, so Shiara and I went through our story again. I did most of the talking, with Shiara putting in a comment now and then when she thought I was leaving something out. I finished by explaining about Shiara's magic. Both Mother and the King looked rather startled, and then the King began to smile.

"A polite fire-witch," he said thoughtfully. "Very unusual."

"I don't want to have to be polite to people!" Shiara said angrily.

"Why not?" I asked. "You're getting much better at it."

"Especially not to *you!"* Shiara said.

"I can understand that," Father said. "It's his fault, after all."

"What?" Shiara and I said together.

"It's Daystar's fault that you have to be polite," Father repeated. "His and the sword's. One of the things the sword does besides control wizards is unlock people's talents, particularly magical talents. When you met Daystar, both of you touched the sword at the same time. You wanted to use your magic and Daystar wanted you to be more polite. I think the sword did the best it could, under the circumstances."

"I knew it!" Shiara glared at me. "I *said* it was that stupid sword's fault!"

"I'm sorry," I said. "I didn't know. But at least you can use your magic now, sometimes. Isn't that better than not being able to use it at all?"

"No!" said Shiara. "It's worse! I have to go home and be *nice* to people, and it probably won't work most of the time, because I have to mean it, and how can I mean it if I'm always thinking about being able to do magic? And it's *boring* at home, and people will still keep expecting me to do things I can't do. I don't even know anyone who could teach me about magic even if I could get it to work all the time. I'll never learn anything!"

Little flickers of flame started running down Shiara's cheeks. It took me a minute to realize that she was crying fire, and when I did, I didn't know what to do about it.

"That is *quite* enough of that," Mother said while I was still thinking.

Shiara looked up. "You don't know what it's like! It's horrible."

"On the contrary, I know quite well what it's like," Mother said. "And the solution is obvious. In fact, it's the same one I used."

"What?" Shiara blinked, and the flame tears stopped running down her face. "What do you mean?"

"You can become Kazul's princess," Mother said. "She doesn't have one at the moment. It would have a great many advantages on both sides. You will learn considerably more about magic, dragons, and the Enchanted Forest than you would anywhere else, and Kazul will get a princess who can't be accidentally roasted if one of the other dragons gets out of hand. And you'll be living nearby, which will give Daystar and Mendanbar a chance to figure out how to reverse that ridiculous politeness spell."

"But I'm not a princess!" Shiara said.

"If Kazul says you are a princess, then you are a princess," Mother said firmly. "No one is going to argue with the King of the Dragons. Besides, it will be excellent experience for you later."

I opened my mouth to ask what Mother meant by that, but Shiara asked, "But are you sure Kazul would be willing to do it?"

"Kazul will have no objection whatsoever to training the next Queen of the Enchanted Forest," Mother said calmly. "You don't need to worry about that."

I closed my mouth very quickly and looked at the floor, feeling my face getting hot. I heard Shiara say, "Oh," in a small voice, and then the King laughed.

"Cimorene, you're going a little fast," he said, still chuckling. "If Shiara wants to go live with Kazul, I'm sure we can make the arrangements, but there's no reason to hurry. She can stay here until she decides. There's plenty of room. Now, if you don't mind, I'd like to go back outside. Kazul was going to talk to Willin about a feast, and I haven't had a good meal in seventeen years. As a matter of fact, I haven't had *any* meals in seventeen years."

Mother didn't object, so the King moved us all to the feast with another wave. Everyone was there: dwarves and dragons and elves and cats, and even a few wizards who had been on the King's side. Morwen was there, too, but she spent quite a bit of time popping back to the castle to make sure Telemain wasn't doing anything she disapproved of.

Mother and the King sat at one end of a long table, and Kazul sat at the other. The elf Willin scurried up and down making sure everyone had enough to eat and plainly having a wonderful time. Shiara and I sat at the middle of the table, and the people sitting next to us kept changing. All of them wanted to hear about how Mother had stolen the sword back, and how Shiara and I had gotten into the castle and broken the spell.

"I'm getting tired of this," Shiara whispered to me while some of the people next to us were changing seats. "Let's go someplace else for a while, and let them tell each other about the stupid wizards."

"I'm tired of it, too, but I don't think we should leave," I said.

"You don't? No, of course you don't. How very irksome" said a squeaky voice from the ground by my left foot.

"Suz!" I said, looking down. "Where did you come from?"

"The forest, of course." The lizard ran up the leg of the table in a thin gold streak, then stopped and looked around nervously. "Is that–that *kitten* anywhere close by?"

"No, she's inside," said Shiara. "I don't think she likes the crowd. Why?"

The lizard looked at her. "If you'd ever been jumped on by something four times as big as you are, and been rolled around until you were dizzy, not to mention bruised, you wouldn't have to ask." He balanced on his tail and peered over the edge of a bowl of nuts.

"Would you like something to eat?" I said.

"I believe I would," Suz said. He made a very fast bouncing motion, and a moment later he was holding one of the nuts. "What are you going to do now that the wizards are gone?"

"They aren't all gone," I said. "I think a few of them were on our side, and some of the others actually got away."

"They did?" Suz considered for a moment. "I suppose they did. How very annoying. But what are you going to do?" He looked from me to Shiara and back.

"I'm going to be Kazul's princess," Shiara said before I could answer.

Suz fell over backward, just missing a silver bowl full of cranberry jelly. "Oh my gracious goodness my oh!" he squeaked. "However did that happen?"

"Mother suggested it," I said. I looked at Shiara. "But I thought you hadn't made up your mind yet."

"I just decided," Shiara said. "Home is boring, and this way I can learn things and maybe even stop having to be polite to get my magic to work."

I suspected Shiara was more interested in not having to be polite than she was in learning things, but I didn't say so. "I'm glad you're going to stay," I said instead.

"You are?" Suz said skeptically. He peered up at me. "Why, you really are! How amazing."

I didn't know what to say to that, but fortunately I didn't have time to think about it. Father and Mother and Kazul all stood up just then and everyone else got very quiet. Father looked around for a moment, smiled, and started speaking.

First he thanked everyone for coming to help with the wizards, and then he introduced Mother formally as "my wife, Cimorene." All the dragons and elves and other people shouted and applauded; the din was tremendous. Then he introduced me, and I had to stand up and be clapped at. After that, Kazul said that the dragons were pleased to be of assistance, and everyone sat down and started talking again. The whole thing didn't take very much time, which surprised me. I'd thought speeches at feasts were supposed to be longer.

Even with short speeches, the feast lasted longer than I expected. Shiara left after a while, to go find Nightwitch and talk to the little dragon. I stayed at the table. I didn't have much choice; every time I tried to get up, someone new would pounce on me and start asking questions. I got very tired of it, but I couldn't seem to get away. I was glad when it was finally over.

The next few days were a little hectic, but then the elves and dragons who'd been in the battle went home and things started to settle down. Morwen and Telemain were almost the last to leave, because of Telemain's shoulder.

Morwen had to stay to take care of it, and she wouldn't let Telemain go anywhere until he was well.

"It's simply ridiculous," Telemain grumbled at breakfast on the third morning after the battle. "I am quite capable of traveling with my arm in a sling."

"Yes, and the first time you ran across a slowstone or a pool of transformation water you'd take your arm out of the sling and start tinkering with it," Morwen said. "Which would *not* be good for that shoulder."

Telemain glared at her. "I disagree."

"Disagree all you like, but you're not leaving the castle for another two days," Morwen said. She picked up a basket of muffins, took one, and passed the rest to Mother.

"Two days!"

Mother raised an eyebrow. "Is our hospitality unwelcome?"

"No, of course not, but . . . Cimorene, I have a tremendous amount to do if I'm to be ready for the wedding in time."

I hadn't heard about any wedding being planned, but I was carefully not looking at Shiara anyway. Then Father looked up.

"Wedding?" he said.

Morwen smiled. "Telemain and I are getting married."

Shiara and Father and I all said, "What!?" at the same time, but we were nearly drowned out by a chorus of startled meows from Morwen's cats.

"Yes, married," Morwen said to one of them. "And it has nothing to do with you, so you may as well be quiet and accept it."

The cats made unhappy noises for another minute, until Morwen frowned at them. Then they all got up and went over to a corner of the room, where they sat muttering to each other with their tails twitching.

Morwen watched for a moment before she nodded and turned back to the table. "They'll get used to the idea."

"Um, congratulations to both of you," I said.

Father was looking at Mother. "Cimorene, did you know about this?"

"Not exactly," Mother said, and smiled.

"I see." Father shook his head. "Well, congratulations."

"Thank you," Telemain said. He started to reach for a plate of sausages with his bad arm, and Morwen stopped him.

Two days later, Morwen announced that Telemain's arm was well enough for him to travel. She promised to invite all of us to the wedding, even the dragons, and then she and Telemain left the castle, followed by a string of disapproving cats.

Shiara and Kazul were the last to leave. I was a little taken aback when

I heard. I knew that Kazul lived in the Mountains of Morning, but it hadn't occurred to me that if Shiara was going to be Kazul's princess, she would have to live there, too. I didn't say anything about it, though. I felt too silly for not having realized it before.

Father and Mother and I went out to see them off. Mother gave Shiara some advice about princessing, and Father told her that if she was going to glare at dragons, she'd have to learn to glare politely. Then they both went to talk to Kazul. Shiara looked at me.

"I'm beginning to wonder whether I really want to do this or not," she said. "Does he really expect me to practice glaring at people?"

"No, just at dragons," I said. "If he wanted you to glare at everyone, he would have said so."

"Well, I think it's–Nightwitch!" Shiara bent to retrieve the kitten, who had been investigating one of Shiara's bundles a little too vigorously.

"Where did you get all of this, anyway?" I asked as she straightened up. There were three bundles in the heap Nightwitch had been climbing, and I knew Shiara hadn't had any of them when we'd arrived at the castle.

"Morwen gave me that one, and Cimorene gave me the others," Shiara said. "She said I would need them if I was going to live with Kazul. I don't even know what's in all of them yet."

I couldn't think of anything to say because just then I realized how much I was going to miss having Shiara around. The Mountains of Morning weren't exactly close to the castle, and I didn't think Kazul would be interested in flying back and forth every day.

Shiara frowned. "What's the matter with you?"

"I was just wishing you were going to be living a little closer to the castle," I said.

"I don't see why. I'm going to have to come here a lot anyway, at least until you get that stupid politeness spell off of me so I can use my fire magic. So what difference does it make? *I'm* the one who has to do all the traveling back and forth." Shiara looked toward Kazul. "I think they're ready to go. Come on, Daystar."

She picked up one of the bundles and started walking. I didn't say anything, but I felt a lot happier than I had a few minutes earlier. Getting rid of that spell didn't sound easy, and until it was gone Shiara would have to spend quite a bit of time at the castle. I was sure that if I had enough time, I could think of some reason for her to keep visiting after the spell was gone, and even if I couldn't, Mother would be able to. Smiling, I picked up the other two bundles and followed happily after.